JERICHO

JERICHO

Anthony Costello

BANTAM BOOKS
Toronto · New York · London · Sydney

JERICHO
Bantam Book / April 1982

Library of Congress Cataloging in Publication Data
Costello, Anthony.
Jericho.
I. Title.
PS3553.07629J4   813'.54   81-15048
ISBN 0-553-05009-5   AACR2

Published simultaneously in the United States and Canada

PRINTED IN THE UNITED STATES OF AMERICA

0 9 8 7 6 5 4 3 2 1

To my parents, Dorcas and Philip
To Nana
To Russel Wendroff, who never faltered

In Memoriam, Francesca

JERICHO, MASS., 29.2 mi. N. of Boston (town, alt. 53, pop. 5,428, settled 1641, incorp. 1656).

Trans: Eastern Mass. St. Railway.

Airport: Jericho Airport (owned by city of Leveret), no sched. flights. Emergency landing, refueling only.

Accommodations: No hotels. One inn: Jericho Inn located in North Parish. Noted for baked-bean suppers.

Industries: Textiles; woolens.

Churches: Trinitarian Congregational, St. Paul's Episcopal, Unitarian, First Methodist, St. Mary's R.C.

Swimming: Lake Cochickawick (boating, fishing, swimming).

Information: Jericho Historical Society, North Parish Rd.

The area known as Jericho was originally called Cochickawick (Indian: "Land of the Great Cascade") and was purchased by Isaac Jericho Bodwell, minister and fur trapper, from Wenepoykin, Sachem of the Wampanoag, for twelve English pounds and a coat. It was later renamed Jericho in honor of its first settler.

A typical New England textile town, Jericho is rich with a historic past. From the *North Parish* where ancient elms cast their shadows over the broad lawns and stately residences, down to the bustle of the woolen mills in the district known as *Jerusalem* on the banks of the Merrimack River, Jericho displays the serenity and pride of one of the oldest towns in the United States.

Powder mills built during and after the Revolution were operated by Samuel Abbot.

Jericho sent seventy-three soldiers to fight in the Revolutionary War, most of them officers. A memorial to their valor rests on the Jericho Common in North Parish.

Originally a farming community, (Mulberry trees were planted to furnish food for silkworms in a futile attempt to provide silk), the manufacture of woolen cloth commenced in 1802 by Nehemiah Phelps, and Phelps Mills still operates today, manufacturing woolen goods for the women's and men's apparel trades. This is believed to be the oldest woolen mill in America to have been in continuous operation. The original mill building still stands at the corner of River St. and South Main.

The ethnic character of the town, originally totally settled by English and Scots, changed rapidly in the middle and late 1800s with the wave of Irish immigrants who came to work in the textile mills of *Leveret*, (known as the Woolen and Worsted Capital of America) across the Merrimack River and 4 miles N.W. of Jericho. Many of the Irish settled in Jericho. Later migration included French Canadian and Italian.

Principal Points of Interest: Lake Cochickawick; Phelps Mills, (Tours available); Parson Woodbridge House, Great Pond Rd.; Samuel Abbot House; North Parish; Academy Burying Ground.

Further information on tour of Historic Homes: Jericho Historical Society, North Parish Rd., North Parish.

 from *Massachusetts.*
American Guide Series,
published by Federal Writers Project, 1937

You're Harriet Hoskins and don't forget it.

Harriet Hoskins,
age 10

1 "They're here," whispered Harriet Hoskins who was fourteen years old. It was a Saturday in the spring of '31, and she and her mother Letty were making beds upstairs.

Letty looked out the window to the driveway below where Ed McGee, the police chief, and another man stood talking by the Buick. Letty's husband, Franklin, had borrowed against the car and hadn't been able to make the payments. A spasm of fear struck Letty but she gave no evidence of it. Calmly she went downstairs, took the car keys from her drawer under the china cabinet in the dining room, and went to the front door, opening the screen as the two men came up the steps.

"Hello, Letty."

"Hello, Ed."

"Hello, Harriet."

Harriet gave both men a sour look.

"Is Mr. Hoskins available?" asked the man from the loan company. "I need him to sign."

"He's not," replied Letty. "Will I do?"

"I'm sorry about this, Letty," McGee said uncomfortably as she signed one paper and then another.

"I know, Ed. It's not your doing." She handed the papers and pen back. There was an awkward pause.

"Uh . . . the keys, ma'm? Are they in the car?"

"Oh, how silly of me." Letty reached into her apron pocket and took them out. A rabbit's paw dangled. Franklin, Jr., had won it last year at the Topsfield Fair by covering a red circle with three discs so that not a trace of red showed. She removed the paw and handed over the keys.

Their faces glum, Cora and Alice, Harriet's older sisters, came out onto the porch from the parlor where they had been watching the scene.

"Oh, dear . . ." sighed Cora, setting her needlepoint down on the railing and looking toward the driveway.

Agrrrrrrrrr. The engine hummed. *Grrrrrrrrr* as it backed out. With a shifting of gears the Buick was gone and there was stillness again.

"It's a catastrophe," muttered Harriet.

1

"No it's not," replied Letty evenly. "It's just a car. Is there anything really important about a car? Not in the larger scheme of—"

"But it's *our* car," insisted Harriet, who wasn't in the mood for platitudes.

"*Was*," corrected Alice.

"All right, girls—" Letty returned briskly into the house. "Why don't we make some lemonade? Harriet, get the ice. Cora, let's fix sandwiches and we'll have lunch in the garden. How would that be?"

Chip. Chip. Chip. Little slivers flying. Harriet moodily hacked at the ice. In the pantry Letty found herself glancing at the hand-painted sign above the sink: *Riches are always restless; tis only to poverty the gods give content.* A smidgen more of "content" would certainly be useful on a day such as this. Once again the knot of fear tugged at her heart. The savings were gone. On Monday Franklin was going to see about getting the house refinanced. Determined not to give in to despair, Letty composed her features and set to spreading her homemade mayonnaise on the freshly baked bread. She turned to find Harriet behind her. "Don't sneak, Harriet, if you please."

"What are we going to do?"

"About what?"

"The car, Mother."

"We'll walk. Is there any place you have to go that your legs won't take you?"

"I guess not." There were. Millions of places. From the expression on Letty's face, she decided not to mention them.

"It's going to get *better*," stated Cora, who always looked on the bright side. Letty's oldest, she would graduate high school in three weeks.

"Better???" scoffed Alice. She and Harriet exchanged a glance and looked at Cora as if she'd gone batty.

Cora nodded. Cutting several stalks of celery into the tuna fish to make it go further, she began to hum.

"Where's Father?" asked Harriet.

"Down at Bartlett's Field with your brother," replied Letty. They were watching the Red Stockings' baseball practice. At least Franklin had been spared seeing the car go. She'd arranged it that way.

"Is he going to get another job or isn't he?" demanded Harriet, the sharpness disguising her anxiety over Franklin. Although the youngest of the three girls, she keenly sensed his shame.

"I'm sure he will."

"There aren't any jobs anymore. Don't be naive, Mother."

"That will do, Alice." Letty shot a glance at her middle daughter and counted to ten.

"There are close to fifteen *million* out of work," insisted Alice.

2

Letty concentrated on the sandwiches. Who would ever have thought it would come to this? Damn that Hoover!

One by one the textile mills of New England had closed and now even Franklin Hoskins couldn't get work. He'd been a salesman for the prestigious firm of Barton-Fuess of Boston, suppliers to the mills of items small as bobbins, large as giant carding machines. Letty would never forget the day a year back when she and Mary Boylan, the hired girl, were taking down the glass curtains in the dining room for spring cleaning and she saw the Buick come up the street at three in the afternoon. Why was Franklin back so early? she wondered, and suddenly she knew.

It was the beginning of what she was to call with characteristic Yankee understatement, "the bad time."

"Bobby Hinkle and I are going over to Leveret tonight to see Fred and Ginger," bubbled Cora as they all went down into Letty's rose garden to the picnic table under the peach tree.

"You have a date?" razzed Alice. "Thank goodness! Now we can all relax."

"La dee da," sang Cora, ignoring her sister. "Mother," she went on, "did I tell you the Perkins are on home relief?"

Letty frowned to herself. Mildred Perkins had no fiber at all.

"Why don't *we* get on?" asked Harriet, meaning to be provocative. "Then we could get the car back."

"There will be no dole on Mulberry Street," responded Letty tartly. "We will do for ourselves. There's many much worse off."

Alice nodded. "Especially in Leveret."

Leveret was the mill city where Jericho went to shop when Boston was too far. Yesterday Letty had been over there and been dismayed at the sense of despair that even a vibrant spring could not dispel. Four miles up the Merrimack River from Jericho, the once-proud woolen and worsted capital of the world was in trouble. During its heyday in the twenties, the city had boasted a population of over a hundred thousand; now the Boston and Maine coaches carried families fleeing. One quarter of the city's work force was unemployed. The mills that lined the Merrimack's banks were on half-shifts or shut down entirely.

But Jericho was calm. The bank hadn't closed. There were no bread lines. Jericho's five thousand souls wanted to believe they were safe. As if the tranquil beauty of their picture-postcard town nestled in the Merrimack Valley would protect them from the economic storms buffeting the rest of the country. Jericho had its mills, too, down by the river in the section known as Jerusalem. Norton Textiles had gone under right away in '29, but Woodbridge and Phelps were still operating. Disaster was in Leveret, that was for sure, and all over the rest of the country too. But it's not happening here, they told each other at the barber shop and Noonan's Drugs. Money was tight, ayea, but—

3

Later that day Harriet found herself staring moodily at the oil-stained spot of earth where the Buick had sat. Who would own the car now? The cherished Buick that had been their pride and joy, the good old Buick with the extra seats in the middle so they could all fit? What times they'd had! It had taken them to Ipswich for clam digging, on overnighters to the White Mountains, down to Maine in the summer. Two years ago she'd thrown up in it. They'd all thrown up in it at one time or another. A history of family picnics was written in mustard stains and ice cream drippings on its pearl-gray upholstery. The beloved Buick—washed and lovingly polished by Father and Frankie every Saturday—was no more.

Harriet scowled. They hadn't gone to their cottage at Moody Beach last summer and wouldn't be going this summer, either, so maybe Mother was right, maybe they didn't need a car. But what would they do on Memorial Day, only a week off? In the past they'd always decorated the Buick with tiny flags and followed the parade up to North Parish and then on to the cemetery for the services. Were they supposed to *walk* this year? How embarrassing.

She picked a hollyhock blossom from a clump by the barn doors, inhaled its sticky sweetness, then threw it down, irritated with the world. Overhead, the sky looked uncertain, with the hint of a shower. Wandering into the barn, where horses had been kept in the old days, she paused for a moment, watching Alice at work on a watercolor in her studio. Then she climbed the narrow stairs to her own area. Once, it had been an open space for the hay, but Letty had enclosed it and made a workroom for Harriet when she had remodeled and electrified the barn.

Eyes checking automatically to see if a certain pencil was still in the exact spot where she'd left it (it was; Cora hadn't been snooping), Harriet sat at her desk.

May 24, 1931. The Buick was repossessed today, she wrote in her journal, *and Father has now been out of work for over a year. . . .*

Pushing the journal aside, she turned to a large box under the table. It contained the "novel" she'd been working on for several years, chronicling the exploits of Madcap Cynthia Overstreet, nicknamed the Jazz Baby, and Devil-May-Care Bart Pettijohn, members of New York Society, both beautiful, both rich, both scandalous. She hoped the novel might ultimately be serialized in the *Saturday Evening Post*. In any event it would make her rather famous. That was the plan. Probably rich, too, but that wasn't important. Wasn't she an artist and above such grasping?

"How are we going to get to the tennis matches?" she called down to Alice.

"You would be concerned about that, wouldn't you?" was the tart reply.

Harriet made a face. Mother was right—Alice didn't know everything even if she thought she did. Alice didn't even have a boyfriend—didn't even seem to care. So naturally *she* wasn't concerned about parties and dances and going to the tennis matches at the club on Sunday wearing the shimmery lawn dresses that Mother had made. Harriet's was a pale mauve, almost silver, and she loved it dearly.

Franklin Hoskins had promised to take his daughters to the matches, and Harriet was looking forward to the day. He played golf at the club sometimes, but as a guest, not a member. Occasionally he played in a foursome with Abraham Phelps, which didn't impress Franklin one way or the other but had a profound effect upon Harriet, who'd always been impressed with the Phelps. Especially with Elliot Phelps, whose nickname in Jericho was 'the Prince.' She'd had a crush on him forever. Devil-May-Care Bart was really gorgeous Elliot Phelps.

But Alice wouldn't understand any of that, would she? Even if she and Alice were inseparably close (sometimes, however, like oil and water) Alice would never understand and would simply become sarcastic if Harriet were to admit to her that she longed to mingle with the snooty girls in Elliot's set, the girls who lived up at the lake. *My goodness, gracious me—Elliot Phelps! I haven't seen you since my return from the continent!* And he would smile and take her arm, offering a lemonade, no—champagne—and waltz her out onto the veranda under the envious eyes of all.

Harriet's daydream was interrupted by the sound of a lawnmower. She peered out one of the small windows into the Finnerans' back yard where Maurice Finneran, Jr., was mowing the lawn. The Finnerans had moved into the neighborhood ten years ago, much to Letty's displeasure. Even though the barn and the back of the Finneran garages separated the two families, the Finnerans were too close for Letty's comfort. "Why they've moved in—'a hop, skip and a *potato*' away from us!" she'd say, much to the amusement of her best friend and neighbor, Ada McQueston, who lived catty-corner across Mulberry Street.

Harriet wished she had something to throw down at Maurice, who'd tried to kiss her in the cloakroom last week. If she had a few small stones she could throw them silently down; then when the mower got to them, the blades would snap them up and get him in the eye. Her attention was diverted to Maurice's older brother Jerry, who was talking with a stranger who was wearing what looked like a long black dress.

"It's going to rain, Maurice," Harriet called out a moment later, emerging into the Finnerans' yard, the warning an excuse to satisfy her curiosity about the stranger in black.

"Don't you think I know that, dummy?" answered Maurice, pushing the mower, her following along.

"I wouldn't call me dummy if I were you, Maurice."

"Why not?"

5

"Just because," she replied, unable to think of a good reason he shouldn't at the moment. "Who's that?" she asked, looking over her shoulder.

"A friend of my brother's."

"Why's he dressed like that?" she whispered.

"He's a priest, dummy!" answered Maurice in a loud voice, causing the young man to turn and look at Harriet with the bluest eyes she had ever seen.

Acutely embarrassed, she lowered her glance and luckily found a crab apple, which she picked up and examined as if she'd never seen one before.

"Hi'ya, Harriet," said Jerry Finneran, who would be graduating from high school in the same class as Cora.

"Hello, Jerry." Harriet dared to look up for a moment, her eyes passing swiftly over the stranger, who seemed to be the same age as Jerry. She was fascinated to note that whatever he was wearing had a line of buttons that started at his throat and ended at the bottom above his shiny black shoes.

"This is Pat Flynn . . . Harriet Hoskins." Harriet felt slightly flustered. Should she offer her hand? Did one shake hands with a priest? Was he, in fact, a priest? This question was immediately answered by Jerry, who, speaking for his friend, said: "He's not a priest. He's gonna be."

Harriet nodded as if she understood. Patrick was looking up at the rapidly darkening sky. She stared at him, fascinated by his eyes, which were like brilliant blue shining stones. They seemed in fact to flash, and as he turned back, she thought she saw a streak of white in the air like car headlights on a dark night.

A clap of thunder caused them all to look up. "Better put it away, Maurice," called Jerry. Excusing himself, he left Harriet and Patrick and went to open the garage doors to put the car away before it rained.

They haven't been repossessed, thought Harriet. How degrading! The Finnerans still had a car and the Hoskins did not.

"It's going to rain," said Patrick.

"Are you from Jericho?" asked Harriet, feeling bolder now that she was alone with him.

He nodded. "Essex Street."

Why, it was only three blocks away. "Did you go to high school?" He shook his head. "When are you going to be a priest?"

"Not for a long time."

It all seemed terribly exotic. Harriet wished she had the courage to invite him over to the house. It would be keen to bring him in and casually introduce him to her mother as her new friend, the priest. What a lark!

She asked a few more questions. He was not very responsive. "Would you mind telling me what it's called you're wearing?"

6

"It's a cassock."

"Do you know what? I thought it was a dress."

"Cassock," he muttered, taken aback with her boldness. Harriet was aware of a vague feeling of pleasure at the sight of his white skin turning to a soft rose in three blotches, one on each cheek and another between his dark brows. She felt strangely calm and somewhat powerful.

Another crack of thunder directly over their heads startled both of them, causing Harriet to squeal, which made her very irritated with herself. The back yard became ominously dark, and she stole another glance at Patrick. The whites of his eyes were now electric, an eerie, luminous glow in them.

As the first few drops fell, she turned to go, calling goodbye as she ran. Patrick's eyes followed her, then he hurried up onto the Finneran porch.

"Who's she?" he asked Jerry, angry with himself for noticing the nicely turned, long legs on her as she dashed away and disappeared.

As the deluge erupted, Harriet plunged through the garden and up the incline to the steps of the back piazza. In the house Letty, Cora and Alice were going from room to room shutting windows.

"I just met a priest at 'Mick' Finneran's," called out Harriet, knowing that would get a rise out of Letty—and it did: "I've told you not to use that word, Harriet."

"You do."

"What I do and you do are two different things entirely. Am I understood?"

Subject to Letty's clear, brown-eyed gaze that rarely faltered, Harriet nodded.

" 'Never met a Catholic I didn't like,' " commented Alice, mimicking one of her mother's favorite expressions. Letty suppressed an impulse to snap at her. "Now, Mother . . ." cautioned Cora, who liked to think of herself as Letty's equal and friend. Letty smiled. "What's wrong with you all?" she asked, laughing as her daughters hooted. "You must all have spring fever."

"He's going back to his seminary tomorrow," continued Harriet. "It's called Villanova . . . near Philadelphia. He lives on Essex Street, and his name's Flynn. Do we know them?"

"No," replied Letty.

"Do priests ever marry?"

"You know they don't."

"Guess what he's wearing?"

"I haven't the faintest."

"See?" Harriet pointed from the window of the back bedroom to where a portion of the Finneran porch was visible, revealing the bottoms of two pairs of legs and the lower half of Patrick's cassock. "How will we get to church tomorrow without a car?" she asked suddenly, forgetting about Patrick.

"A hot air balloon," replied Letty. "I'm sure you girls can fill it."

"Aren't you witty, Mother." Harriet went downstairs and out onto the back piazza and sat on the glider while the rain pelted down. Suddenly she dashed down the steps and raced for the barn, climbing up into her workroom again.

Perhaps she could use him in the novel? A young priest with a solemn expression on his handsome face, a young priest with jet black hair and blue eyes who would fall for Cynthia, thereby making Bart jealous.

Inspired, she opened her notebooks and set to work, racing the pen across the page in the indecipherable scrawl she'd cultivated. The rain drummed on the roof above her head. Was he still on the porch? She craned her neck to see, but the angle wasn't right. A jag of lightning lit the sky, dancing above the roofs, followed by a giant crack of thunder, and she put the pen down as the queasy feeling that she'd had on and off all week returned to her insides. Was it the tuna fish? She frowned, unaware that tomorrow she would get what she longed for, what her best friends Libby and Marcia had got way last year—what *all* the girls in ninth grade had got—but she hadn't and had been worried about, thinking maybe there was something wrong with her, even though Mother had told her time and time again there was nothing to worry about and anyway girls who got their monthlies last lived longer than girls who got theirs first.

Franklin Hoskins married Letitia Winslowe in 1913. He was an orphan, his family unknown. Raised in foster homes, he would always be a loner. Letty was gregarious and, as her friends said, "ahead of her time." She and Franklin couldn't have been more different. They got along famously.

They'd met at a dance at the Trinitarian-Congregationalist Church, fallen in love in a rowboat on Lake Cochickawick, and courted in the dusky autumn evenings with the smell of leaves like fresh pencil shavings. "Letty Winslowe!" he'd call, riding up to her front yard in a buggy, dressed to the nines. Letty's snobbish mother, Sarah, complained, "Why did Franklin have to arrive like that? Couldn't he come quietly and knock like a gentleman?"

"Franklin's different," Letty told Sarah as she ran downstairs, heart palpitating, checking herself in the hall mirror, then checking her speed, too—opening the front door ever so slowly, emerging decorous and slightly aloof so that he wouldn't think her too easy.

Franklin was just getting started and had to borrow money for a honeymoon. There were two parts. His was a weekend in Boston, where he took her to three Red Sox games. Hers was two days at the lovely

Farragut-by-the-Sea at York Beach, Maine, where over lunch he told her she better not have another peach flambé because he didn't have a pot to pee in. But he *would*, he assured her. He had plans.

Letty wasn't worried. She had graduated, one of two women in a class of thirty, from the Normal Art School of Boston and already had a job of her own as a traveling art teacher to the smaller towns around Jericho. She was twenty-two, and Franklin was twenty-six, and they loved each other.

They returned from the Farragut and were given the honor of the sunny front bedroom in her father's house on Summer Street, where a week earlier they'd been married in a quiet ceremony in the parlor. The front bedroom was the room in which Letty and her three sisters, Iris, Georgiana, and Clara had been born, where, in fact, her father had first seen the light of day. It was the same room in which, twelve years later, her parents would die of smoke inhalation caused by a raging fire from an overturned kerosene lamp. John Ovando Winslowe was a simple man and had wanted no part of electricity.

Soon they had a pot. Then two pots. And two rented rooms of their own and a baby girl, Cora, named for Letty's great-great-great-grandmother on her father's side, who had come over with her husband, Nathaniel Winslowe, on the *Speedwell*, three months after the *Mayflower*.

Letty gave up her job as art teacher, for Franklin was prospering just as he'd said he would. He was a crackerjack salesman who could sell you anything—snow shovels in winter, then barrels of tar to fill the potholes come spring. Franklin could sell a sheep a wool sweater, admired Letty's father, John. He himself was a fine carpenter and cabinetmaker.

Alice was born, followed by Harriet, soon to be followed by Franklin, Jr. By then, Franklin had the best of his many jobs, selling for Barton-Fuess. "Franklin may not be a gentleman," Sarah said, "but he's certainly a comer." If she was somewhat impressed with the comfortable life that Franklin had provided for her daughter and grandchildren, Sarah wanted more. She saw her son-in-law's acumen as a potential means to enter the ranks of Jericho's rich. "Why doesn't Franklin settle down?" she asked. "Is it true Sam Norton offered him the manager's job at the mill? And he refused? I don't understand him, Letty. Or you, either. Why don't you talk to him?"

Letty shook her head. She knew Franklin didn't want to be tied down at Norton or any place. He cherished his independence; he loved life on the road, traveling his territory throughout the Northeast. Letty understood and never pushed him, accepted his need to get away, this complex man who was her husband. She saw his expression when he arrived back home, blinking his eyes uncomprehendingly, as if shocked to see four little ones looking up at him. No, she never pushed him, for she considered herself a fortunate woman. She had her children, a husband she loved, and an eight-room house, which she painted yellow with green trim. A wonderful big barn in back was given over to the children. Generations of pigs rooting in the soil had produced the richest loam in town for her garden and roses. A natural richness, she might have said. An appropriate richness of the earth. She was not interested in being wealthy. She didn't care that she wasn't a Phelps, a Woodbridge, a Saltonstall, or any of the town's monied aristocracy who lived up in Jericho's North Parish and around the lake. She was happy to be Letty Hoskins.

"Letty, you've always been a dreamer," said Sarah. "I suppose that's what comes of being an artist," she added disapprovingly, for Letty's "taint of Bohemianism" had always disturbed her. "Why don't you join the garden club?" she pleaded, unable to understand why her daughter had no desire to aim higher. "Or at least—come to D.A.R. with me. After all, *I* am a McCoy and *you* are a Winslowe. You mustn't forget that."

"I'm a Hoskins," corrected Letty.

"But, Letty, don't you know that Mrs. Abraham Phelps would give her eyeteeth to be in the D.A.R.? And do you know what I heard? I have it on the best of authority that Blanche Bowditch has hired some kind of so-called expert to find her an ancestor. What do you think of that? She thinks she can buy her way in. Just wait till we receive her application. Just wait!"

Charitably, Letty didn't point out that Sarah herself had managed to be accepted into the Daughters of the American Revolution only by the thinnest thread. Years of ransacking attic trunks for documents and records had finally produced a tenuous second cousin of an uncle whose father had fought in the Revolutionary War. But Letty, if she chose to join, had impeccable connections through her father, who was a direct descendent of Abner Winslowe, the famous "Acton drummer boy" written up in all the history books, the second fellow killed on Concord Bridge by the British.

It was all foolishness, decided Letty as she set up her easel in a field of spring wheat. What did she care about those silly, snobbish ladies who had nothing better to do with their time than trace their genealogy? Not a whit. The Daughters of the American Revolution were nothing but the daughters of laziness as far as she was concerned. And if there was one thing she could not abide, it was idleness.

"A day was made to be spent," she told Sarah. "Not to be wasted."

"Oh, Letty, don't you know that some people think you're odd?"

"Why?"

"Traipsing around town with the children in tow . . . Frankie strapped to your back. Why, Abigail Pearce said she saw you all hovering in a shed out by the lake in a pouring rain!"

"We were painting. We got caught in a shower," Letty replied, her Winslowe jaw set firm and implacable, allowing no truck with Sarah's nonsense.

Nevertheless, Letty eventually joined the D.A.R.—more for her daughters' sake than anything else. Or perhaps it was sheer stubbornness, giving Sarah in death what she wouldn't in life. Years later Letty would resign in protest when the D.A.R. refused to let Marian Anderson sing in Constitution Hall. A darkie might be a darkie, but no organization she was a part of was going to prevent that glorious voice from being heard. It just wasn't fair.

And Franklin prospered, but his feeling of aloneness grew stronger. A taciturn, gruff Yankee, he revealed himself rarely. Away for much of the time while they were growing up, he left the day to day rearing of his children to his wife, maintaining a certain aloofness from the frenzied activities of his gregarious family.

A popular figure on the road, he entertained in the best restaurants, stayed in the best hotels. He could be the life of the party when the salesmen gathered in Lewiston, Bangor and Manchester, Portsmouth, Concord and Springfield.

It was a side of him his family glimpsed rarely, for at home Franklin was an observer, rarely a participant, in the endless parade of block parties, art exhibits, musicales, and summer and winter carnivals that kept the house on Mulberry Street hopping. Warm and zesty, Letty kept her sorrows to herself and shared her joys, passing along her sensibilities to the children, watching proudly as the lessons learned bore fruit. It was she who held them all together, who soothed the hurts and mended the fingers, who dreamed their dreams, who comforted, joked, prodded and nurtured an atmosphere where self-expression was not only a right but a necessity.

But if Letty was the glue and the inspiration, Franklin had a mystique of his own. Sometimes, when he was home from the road, he would appear outside school, and they would find him. Strangers might have been surprised at seeing children run to his side, for this tall and immaculate, stern-faced man who stood by himself, perennial cigarette dangling from his lips, didn't seem like a father. When his children gathered around him respectfully, he said nothing, turning instead and starting off at a brisk clip while they hurried after. "Father's walks" was the way they would later describe these treks through town.

Sometimes he took his children out to the lake, where he would point out birds, having them give the names. Sometimes they would go down to the depot and count the cars on the freight trains passing through Jericho. No matter where they went the final destination was always Noonan's Drugs, where he bought them raspberry sodas or Moxies and a package of Necco wafers, which he would divide evenly among his four children, never giving Franklin, Jr., an extra, for he played no favorites.

"Where *were* you all?" Letty would ask when they finally returned to the yellow house on Mulberry Street. "I thought you were lost," she would

11

say, knowing full well where they had been—but the statement was the final part of the ritual.

They accepted his moodiness, came to live with it. He was change-able, could be one thing one day, another the next. If his silences awed them and held them rapt, the turning of those flinty eyes and the in-finitessimal clearing of his throat had the power to make a rebellious child think twice. The faint twinkle that might follow was like a sudden rush of sunlight in a hitherto darkened room.

Even when he was away, they sensed his presence—as if he had left his spirit to watch over them from his chair next to the radio.

He was their God. He was adored. He was Father. In '30, keeping it a secret from his wife and children, he began to drink.

One afternoon in March of '32, that cruelest winter of the Great Depression when the country was on its knees, Letty sat anxiously in the parlor, a room it was not her custom to find herself in at this time of day. Her fingers pressed in small, unconscious gropings at her wedding ring—as if she might remove it, which was impossible, for the flesh surrounding had swelled with the years. But had it been possible, she would have. And probably thrown it at Franklin, too. She was that angry.

An hour ago the manager of the Salem Hotel in Leveret had called to say that Franklin was there, had been there for three days, holed up in a room, drinking. Relief had flooded Letty, releasing her from days of racing for the phone, three days of lies to the children, making up stories that Franklin had been called out of town on a job-hunting foray. With the relief came a smidgen of contempt. She knew that Franklin knew someone would get in touch with her. It wasn't as if he'd run off to Boston or simply disappeared. No, he was just across the river in Leveret. Making sure she suffered. Paying her back for what she'd done. For what she'd *had* to do.

Letty shifted position on the window seat and glanced past the freshly ironed ruffled curtains and floral drapes, watching for Harriet. She'd called the principal and asked that her daughter be excused early. Snow was falling, but it gave Letty no pleasure. If ordinarily the change in a day's weather found an appreciative response in her artist's eye, today the pattern of lawns and hedges behind the slowly falling flakes seemed ominous and unsettling. Turning back, her gaze swept the parlor, which suddenly seemed overly chintzy and fussy. The tiny bluebells twining delicately up the salmon-colored wallpaper were the wrong shade. The loveseat was in the wrong place; the fabric lank. The Venus de Milo was not properly featured, and the two watercolors above the desk were the product of someone who *used* to paint, someone who hadn't got her brushes out in many a year. Would she ever again?

Rising, Letty glanced at her wedding portrait on the desk. As she

12

gazed at Franklin, a softening replaced the anger. How many mornings had she wakened these past two years to find him silhouetted in the rocker? "Woman . . ." he'd say, "woman—I don't know." It was a simple enough admission for anyone else, but not for a man who wore his pride like his cardigans, in all seasons no matter the weather. "What can I do?" he'd mutter, lips pursed, cranky to be in the house at midday, embarrassed, longing to be gone and nowhere to go. "It's not your fault," she had assured him. "It's happening to everyone. Everywhere."

Then one night, supper over, he came home late and beckoned her to the front hall where, with a courtly, swaying bow, he presented her with a box of raspberries, precious raspberries from S.S. Pierce, and a smell on his breath she'd never known because he'd always been a teetotaler.

Between the two of them they had managed to hide his drinking from the children. But Letty knew it was only a matter of time.

It wasn't just the sudden rages—any little thing seemed to have the power to make him fly off the handle—but he who had always been so fastidious about his appearance now went for a day without shaving, now did not seem even to notice if a soup stain appeared on his vest. When the ashes from his cigarette dribbled down his front, she noticed that often-times they stayed there. He no longer seemed to care.

There's a smell in the air, she wrote to her sister Iris that winter. But it wasn't the smell of the campfires burning in Leveret. Whiffs of despair now floated on Jericho, too. Fear on Main Street and on the peaceful Common. Something had broken down that wasn't supposed to. Broken down and couldn't seem to be fixed. Innocence gone and dreams smashed, and the loss like a bad smell in Letty's kitchen on Mulberry Street, in the great homes up at the lake, and the mill houses of Jerusalem down by the river. The country was breaking down and so was her husband, and she was powerless to stop it.

The eight-day clock chimed the half-hour as Harriet, out of breath and gasping, bounded up the steps and into the house.

"Harriet, you didn't have to—"

"Well? What is it? It's about Father, isn't it?"

"I have some milk on for cocoa. Come—"

"*Mother,* you didn't send for me to give me cocoa, did you?" Beads of perspiration glittered on her forehead. She pulled off her galoshes impatiently. "Where is he?" she demanded, as if Franklin were hers and not Letty's, as if her mother were suddenly not to be trusted.

"In Leveret."

"Leveret? What's he doing there? I thought you said—"

Harriet's energy threatened to undo Letty further. She retreated to the kitchen and stirred the milk down. "He's at the Salem Hotel, and I want you—"

13

"To go and get him."

Letty nodded.

"You didn't call the others?"

"No." Letty knew Franklin would never forgive her if she were to send Frankie. Cora would become hysterical, and Alice would only make him angry, as she usually did. But Harriet had always had a mysterious rapport with Franklin. It was unexplainable and somewhat baffling. Even Letty found herself envious that a fifteen-year-old girl with the temperament of a yo-yo, who fluctuated wildly between sullenness and flamboyance, should have the power to reach Franklin, whereas she, and so many others, had failed. It had nothing to do with flirtation or wrapping him around her finger. No woman on earth had that power. But Harriet was able to jolly him out of his moods and penetrate, if only rarely, the barrier of his reserve.

"I'd go myself," Letty said, "but . . ." The words trailed off. No, Franklin wouldn't want to see *her*. He'd made that perfectly clear in their brief conversation after the manager put her through—if conversation it could be called. A thing of fits and starts and mutterings and his final word—"woman"—which was a condemnation, not only of her but of generations of women, an entire sex. What a show he was putting on! Him and his wounded pride.

"No. You can't go. He won't want to see you. And I know why. It's because you borrowed money from Uncle George, isn't it? Father didn't want you to, but you did."

"There was nothing else I could do." Stung with the criticism, Letty flushed and turned back to the stove. "We were going to lose the house." Even if Harriet took Franklin's side, Letty knew what she'd done was right. "Your uncle made the offer, and I accepted it." If Franklin's pride had to be sacrificed, so be it. She wasn't about to have her family uprooted from their home, sent wandering like countless others. "I had no choice," she'd cried these last few days, repeating the plea to the sheets on the beds as she made them, to the dishes in the sink, to the colored strands she forced herself to braid. "No choice," she pleaded to these inanimate objects, as if they might respond, absolve, and comfort her.

"Father would have found a way. You went behind his back."

"I would do it again!" Angry at the accusation, Letty reached blindly for the saucepan and burned her fingers. "*Shit, shit, shit.*"

"Put butter—"

Letty waved Harriet aside, went into the pantry and placed her hand under cold water. "I don't blame your father. You know he hasn't been himself lately. I did what I had to do. It's water over the dam now, and I don't want to discuss it further." How had they gotten on to all *that*? She hadn't meant to. None of it. Shocked at her outburst, Letty accepted her stinging fingers gratefully. That's what you deserve.

14

"Don't you want a cup of cocoa to warm you?" she called, following as Harriet left the kitchen and returned to the front hall, where she quickly got into her coat.

"No," Harriet replied impatiently, wishing she'd bitten her tongue, for she could see that Letty was fighting weeping. Unnerved, Harriet hugged her. "Don't worry, Mother. Everything will be all right. I'll bring him home."

"Ayea." Letty rummaged in her pocket for a hankie as Harriet stared at her, large brown eyes intense. "I *will*, Mother. I'm the one to do it," she added with a vehemence that caused Letty to feel relieved and anxious simultaneously.

"Harriet . . ." *Tell her.* Guilty at what she was subjecting her daughter to, Letty reached out as if to prevent her from going, but she had no choice, and her arm fell aimlessly at her side. "Harriet . . ." she began again.

"What?" Impatiently Harriet flung her scarf around her neck.

"Father may be drinking."

Halfway out the door, Harriet paused. "Father doesn't drink."

"Ayea," nodded Letty softly. "Sometimes he does. Sometimes he does."

Anxious thoughts in a whirl and fears mushrooming, Harriet hurried urgently through town. As angry as Letty was with Franklin, so Harriet was with Letty, blaming her mother if her father was in trouble. If he drank, Letty was the cause, she was sure of that. What did it mean? At first she felt confused. She had had no experience with people who drank, except for what she'd seen in movies and read in books. There was a movie where Lionel Barrymore had fallen dead drunk in the gutter and his daughter, Norma Shearer, had found him. But Harriet was sure that Franklin couldn't be anything like that.

Then a chill swept her as bits and pieces of the last year assaulted her, causing her imagination to play dreadful tricks as she remembered how sad Franklin had been—a gray and angry ghost who lived among them. Sometimes last summer, when she was working on her novel in the barn, he would come up and sit behind her, and one day he brought *The Decline and Fall of the Roman Empire* with him, telling her he'd always wanted to read it and now that he had the time he would. But the next day he muttered, "The decline and fall of Franklin Hoskins . . ." and she felt her heart snap. Sometimes she sensed his eyes on her while she worked, but when she glanced back, he quickly looked out the window or stared at her as if he didn't know who she was. He rarely spoke, and after an hour or so he would leave, rising and stooping down to fit himself under the slant of the roof, disappearing, appearing a moment later as he came out below. Then he would wet a finger and raise it up, testing the wind direction, his

15

profile vivid against the green of the lawn, reminding her of the granite face of the Old Man of the Mountain glimpsed on high in the mountains of New Hampshire, her close-mouthed father whom she loved dearly.

Father may be drinking.

It was a crime, prohibited by law. Speakeasies were always being raided, their patrons thrown in jail, shamed. A moral outrage preached against in church, a despicable weakness that led to madness. A fresh wave of panic assaulted Harriet and she pretended she was still in the biology lab at school, where her only anxiety was whether she would have to dissect a frog or be saved by the bell. Another girl hurried through the falling snow as winter dusk settled on Jericho and the elms creaked ominously overhead. Another girl dashed past the sturdy Victorian homes, fear mounting and breathing labored. Another girl cut through back yards as lights winked on in warm kitchens where families gathered and fathers were where they were supposed to be!

Father was depressed. The country was in a depression, and she was going to save him, but her surety that she wouldn't fail was mocked by an equally forceful anxiety that something terrible was about to happen.

Calm yourself, ordered Harriet. *Why are you so scared?* Perhaps she was just letting her imagination run wild, for nobody was particularly upset by Rummy Johnny, who hung out at the depot, a gentle soul waving the trains through. But no matter how hard she tried, the gravity of her mission kept rising up to strike at her. If a part of her relished the drama, and she cast herself in the role of a heroine, unnamed fears mounted. Not even a fantasy that she was Greta Garbo rushing in the snow to save her lover helped, for Greta had slipped through a hole in the ice and drowned.

On South Main there was more activity, but Harriet didn't notice. Heading toward the mill district where she would catch the trolley to Leveret, she was startled as the four-thirty whistle from Phelps Mill shuddered through her and the mill itself appeared like a ship whose masts were its chimneys. Cars clogged the narrow streets. Bundled up against the cold, the workers streamed out of the mill. Some headed for the parking lot, others to the mill houses of Jerusalem down closer to the river, others to the waiting trolleys that would take them to Leveret.

Afraid she'd never get a seat, Harriet started to run, skirting the edge of the millpond, dodging bodies on the ash-strewn path. The first trolley departed, and she ran faster and began to lose her balance on a slippery spot. Hands reached out to right her as she plummeted down, nearly colliding with a black Dusenberg automobile parked at the gates of the mill.

"Let me be!" she cried, eyes riveted on the remaining trolley as a hand pulled her up and held her steady. It was Abraham Phelps himself, snowflakes glistening on his shoulders like diamonds. "Thanks," Harriet muttered, not at all politely. An uncontrollable anger boiled up in her, and

16

eyes blazing, she cried, "I don't need your help! My father does! Why don't you give him a job?"

Not waiting for an answer, she ran from Phelps, vaulted over a snow-bank and sank knee deep. "Make that trolley wait!" she yelled to the final passenger boarding. She pulled her legs out and darted across River Street. The wheels of a passing car flung slush on her as she banged on the trolley door. It opened, and she climbed aboard. With a shriek of wheels against steel and a shower of sparks from above, the trolley lumbered off.

Harriet found herself crushed in the mob with no place to sit and barely room to stand. She glanced at the rough faces, wearied into gentle-ness by the labors of the day; their bodies pressed close, holding her up, and she felt warm and almost cozy. The overpowering smell of wet wool in the car caused her a sudden lassitude and drowsiness overtook her. Resist-ing, then shutting her eyes, she allowed herself to sway with the others. Snatches of conversations drifted on the edges of her consciousness—Polish and Italian, a bit of French. "*Ont trouvés l'enfant?*" "*Non.*" It was the baby they were talking about, the Lindbergh baby, the kidnapped baby hadn't been found yet.

The tragedy of the baby momentarily took Harriet's mind away from her own worries about her father. Perhaps she would find the child and save the day, for the photos of the anguished mother filled her with grief. The false clues and cruel hoaxes perpetrated on the Lindberghs outraged her as they had the rest of the nation, which watched and waited and could talk of little else that winter. Yes, she would rescue the baby and be interviewed on the newsreels, the grateful parents hugging her while the world watched in wonder.

"Oh . . ." Five minutes later, she opened her eyes, momentarily disoriented, then remembering.

"Sit down, dear. You look dead on your feet, don't you now?" Harriet smiled gratefully at the Irish woman who made a place for her. Once again her eyes closed. She sneezed, then coughed. Was she catching a cold? The wrenching of wheels against steel jarred her awake again. Down went the trolley through clapboard houses, and the Merrimack River came into view. Although it was almost totally dark now, a few intrepid boys skated along the river's frozen edges. A mile upriver on the other side were the lights of Leveret. Ten minutes later the trolley clanged over River Bridge into the city. The giant falls, which roared in milder seasons, sending a fine spray up for blocks, were now reduced to several tamed streams forcing themselves through massive blockages of ice.

A chatter arose from the remaining passengers as the trolley reached the opposite bank in a dingy neighborhood and stopped as if at an invisible boundary to a foreign country, which was Leveret, city of the immigrants, brought over to work the mills in better times. Now, the streets echoed daily in the predawn darkness with the tramping sound of feet hurrying hopefully to the mills that lined the river's banks, the human tide lapping against the closed and guarded gates. *No work today.* The tide washed back into the red-bricked city, the men to stand dead-eyed on street corners, the women to hurry home, shame on all their faces.

"Not like the old days," commented the driver as Harriet moved to the front of the trolley and willed it to go faster. There were only a couple of people left in the car, and she was as grateful for the driver's company as he for hers.

"No," she agreed, eyes peering out into the darkness. The trolley's beam exposed snowflakes fluttering chaotically, and she gripped the rail. Only ten or fifteen minutes from the Salem Hotel, she tried to picture what she would find there and couldn't. "My father used to sell to the Ayer," she said, making conversation to keep calm, as the trolley groaned alongside the Ayer Mill, the flagship of American Woolen, which stretched for two miles along the river, guarded by immense watchtowers like an endless fort.

"I had a brother worked here. Got laid off. Your dad a salesman?"

She nodded, remembering the day long ago when Franklin had brought her with him. How frightened she'd been of the noise! Acres of whirring looms causing such a racket she could barely hear as Franklin shouted to her, explaining the process of making cloth. Her eyes had grown dizzy with the motions of the bobbins darting, spindles whirring, gossamer threads shining like spun sugar. "Those are yours, aren't they?" she'd asked him. "The bobbins are yours." "Mine?" he laughed, sitting her on his knee and introducing her to the other salesmen. "They're not mine. I sell them, that's all." She hadn't believed him. She was sure the bobbins were his; all those bobbins carrying the threads on each and every loom in the spinning room of the Ayer and the other mills all over New England. They were her father's, and if he chose to take them back, all the machines would stop, and no cloth would be made, and no clothes would be made, and everyone would be naked. That's how powerful he was; him and his bobbins.

The memory only made Harriet uneasy, for she sensed that Franklin had somehow lost his power. Everything was suddenly changed, including the Ayer. The trolley groaned on past the deserted mill, block after silent block. In the old days there would have been the chaos of shifts changing and clogged streets and from inside the roar of the looms where five thousand workers turned out woolen goods for the world. Now the gates were padlocked, the looms stilled, and the Ayer stood silent as a tomb in the falling snow.

"What's that?" she asked. Fires flickered in the distance.

"Hooverville."

"What?"

"They live there." The trolley passed a collection of makeshift shacks made from packing boxes and scrap iron. "They build 'em from what they can find at the dump."

"Who are they?" she asked, staring out the window, unable to believe it.

"Out of work folks. Sometimes whole families. Evicted. They sleep on automobile seats. You know—get'm from the auto graveyards. Terrible times," he added solemnly.

Astounded, Harriet nodded. She hadn't been over to Leveret for several months. She'd heard conditions were bad but nothing like this. A moment later the trolley approached a line of people outside the Arlington Mill and stopped. Policemen on horseback patrolled the line. "The Arlington must be giving out food," explained the driver. "What do they get?" she asked softly, barely able to comprehend what she was seeing as the trolley door opened and forlorn faces looked into the warmth, then turned away. Some of them had what looked like rags wrapped around their feet, rags instead of shoes.

"A tin of lard. Some canned goods."

She couldn't take her eyes off the feet. A woman clutching a box of food climbed aboard with her two children. They had blue, cold faces and dripping noses. The youngest had no mittens. He hit his hands together and began to weep.

"Here . . ." Impulsively Harriet removed her fur-lined gloves and thrust them at the boy, who seemed not to understand. "Here," she said again, putting them into his lap as his mother muttered something in Italian and the boy fumbled them on. "*Grazie*," she said to Harriet. "*Lei e molto gentile.*" She nudged her son. "*Grazie*," he whispered, gazing at Harriet, then at the too-large gloves, then back to Harriet as the trolley moved off again.

"Wait!" A sudden urgency gripped her, fear welled to such an extent that she had to bite her lip to keep from shouting. "Stop! Let me out here, will you? I'll take a shortcut."

By the time she saw the lights of the Salem across the Leveret Common, she was exhausted and in a state of panic. Premonitions of disaster swept her as she plunged onto the unshoveled paths of the Common, each foot a lead weight by the time she reached the hotel. The desk clerk looked up astonished as Harriet ran to him. Old men in cracked leather armchairs opened their eyes. Like the Salem, they'd seen better days.

"Mr. Hoskins," she gasped. "What room?"

In the mirror beside the elevators, a wild-eyed apparition looked back at her. It wiped its runny nose with the back of its hand, not caring if anyone should see. It turned away and dashed for the stairs.

By the time she reached the sixth floor, she had to stop. Heart pounding and chest burning, she leaned against the wall as clusters of gray grapes swam out of focus on a faded crimson carpet. Willing herself to move, she started down a dimly lit corridor, searching the numbers, finally arriving at 611, where an angry Negro maid was talking to a closed door.

"What yo wan', honey?" asked the maid, eyeing Harriet suspiciously.

"I want . . . to go . . . in there . . . ."

"Why yo's all outa breath, honey. What you wan' to go in theah foh? He's mean, that one. Won' lemme clean up," continued the maid, disgruntled. "I ain't supposed—"

"Is he all right?"

"Sure 'nuf. Why he—" The woman stopped as tears spilled out of Harriet's eyes.

"Father?" She knocked. "Father? It's me."

"Yo his daughter, honey? *Lordie*. I didn't know yo was his daughter! Here now. . . ." Harriet took the offered hankie. "Should be 'shamed of hisself." The maid reached into her uniform and brought out some keys. "We'll show him, jes' you wait, honey. . . ." The door opened, but only an inch or two. It held on the chain.

"Father?" There was no answer. "Thank you," said Harriet, turning to the maid. "Would you leave us now? I can manage."

"But I'm s'posed to get to that room. I'll catch it if—"

"You can do it soon. We'll be gone soon."

"Well, honey . . . yo do what yo can." The maid walked off shaking her head and muttering to herself.

"Father? Please?" Harriet pressed her face into the opening, then backed off at the stench of whiskey. Feeling sick to her stomach and fighting an impulse to run, she gulped some air and tried again: "Father? Please say something."

"Get the hell away from here, Harriet," muttered Franklin. "Go home," he ordered in a hoarse whisper she barely recognized, but his saying of her name gave her courage.

"I won't. Do you hear me? *I won't!* Open the door. I'm going to stay until you do. Do you hear? I'm not leaving." There was no response. "I love you, Father," she added, whispering into the opening and holding her breath at the same time. "Please come home with me. I'll wait till you're ready."

She backed off and sank down against the opposite wall. Soaked through with perspiration, she shivered, then sneezed. A moment later the manager appeared. "Having a little trouble?" he asked, then knocked loudly on the door. "All right, Frank. Open up. Your daughter's here." Other doors opened, and faces peered out as the manager knocked again.

"Let him alone!" Harriet pulled herself up. "Leave him alone! He's dressing. He'll be out in a minute."

"Hothead," muttered the manager, shrugging his shoulders and leaving. "*Father*," pleaded Harriet, "*please*." The chain slid in its track.

Frightened, she paused, then cautiously pushed the door open. She couldn't see him in the darkness. A glass smashing to the floor caused her to gasp, and she looked in the direction of the sound. Eyes becoming accustomed to the dark, she dimly saw Franklin sitting on the edge of the bed like a phantom. Hot and dizzy with fear, afraid she would vomit from the stench, she turned away.

"Go or stay but shut the goddamned door."

"I feel sick." She shut the door and snapped the wall switch, which bathed the room in a cold glare. She didn't want to turn around and see him.

"What do you want?" growled the phantom.

"Nothing."

"Sit down."

Head bowed, watching her feet on a disheveled scatter rug, Harriet took hesitant steps toward a chair by the bureau and sat. From under lowered lashes she could see Franklin's feet in black socks, but she didn't dare look higher, concentrating instead on the feet in a sea of butts with a smashed glass nearby and a bottle standing.

Franklin tried to clear his throat, and the grating, agonized effort of it caused Harriet to will herself to raise her head.

If a moment before she had been unable to look at him, now she could not take her eyes away. The image of him, her once elegant father, bent over the cuspidor in soiled undershirt and suspenders, his head jerking as if he had something caught in his throat, seared into her consciousness forever.

Body shaking with the effort, Franklin brought something up and spat, a dribble running down his whiskered chin. From a face gaunt and sickly sallow, his gaze seemed to pass over his daughter as if she were an object of no interest. Then his arm went down searching for the glass as if he hadn't noticed, or forgotten, that it lay broken. Staring at the pieces for a long moment, he rose, one hand on the bed for support, the other holding the bottle.

"Father—" Harriet cried, horrified as he stepped down on a piece of glass. An ooze of blood darkened the toe of his stocking. He looked down at it, body swaying, fascinated with the spreading blotch. She gasped, causing him to look at her in surprise as if he had forgotten her presence. Then he turned vaguely aside, shame sending him far away, deep into his past. A choked sound came from him as if he might cry, but Franklin hadn't cried since the day forty-two years ago when the matron at the orphanage told him that his mother had disappeared and would never come back.

Harriet couldn't move or speak as another wave of nausea hit her. It wasn't Rummy Johnny giggling to himself. She wasn't Norma Shearer, and he wasn't Lionel Barrymore. It wasn't "Father may be drinking," either. It was bloodshot eyes she didn't recognize, a terrible hacking in the throat and stooped shoulders, a filthy, unbearably hot room and stepping onto glass and not caring. It was a man she no longer knew—and the end of something.

"Sent you, did she?" Filled with sudden rage at Letty, Franklin took a defiant swig from the bottle. "Goddamn her. Goddamn all of you!"

Blindly, tears stinging her eyes, Harriet rose and lunged for the bottle. Franklin struggled with her, but five quarts of whiskey in three days had left him weak. Harriet pulled the bottle from his grasp and dropped it to the floor. A string of oaths erupted from him as he stared at her. Stirred by her face and something in her stance, a hallucination took him over, causing his face to crumple into vulnerability. Had she come back to get him? Was she here finally? Was she Marian?

"Father—what is it?"

The face was vague, filtered through years of rage and frustration at the fruitless search for the woman who had disappeared. Every city he'd ever been to in New England had found him in a phone book searching for her name. Hoskins—or her maiden name, Raymond. The orphanage had told him his mother's name was Marian. Once in Bangor, he found a Hoskins in the book and discovered a cousin of his father, who'd died of pneumonia before Franklin was born. But the cousin hadn't known Marian, and Franklin never found her. And if he had, he had any number of scenarios in mind, all of them violent.

"I . . . hate . . . you!"

"Father." Harriet flinched as Franklin raised his hand to strike, the arm suspended in shock as he met her terrified gaze. Mortified, he sank down, knees cracking hard on the fllor, then crawled to the bathroom and shut the door.

An eternity passed. Trembling, Harriet held herself, then clawed at the buttons of her coat and tore it off. She turned and threw open the window. A gust of wind brought snowflakes whooshing at her, and she swallowed great gulps of air, the nausea passing. *It isn't him*, she tried to tell herself as she turned back into the room. Disoriented, she repeated the phrase like a magic chant, over and over. From the bathroom the toilet flushed, but it seemed far away. It was all like a dream to her, and she would wake and find herself in bed. She had no idea what to do, and she stood, not moving, for what seemed a long time, until inspiration sent her to the phone on the bureau.

"Is there room service?" In her novel she'd written a scene where Cynthia had ordered coffee from room service for Bart, who'd had too much champagne. She did the same now, thinking to herself that this was a case of life imitating art, but the thought gave her no pleasure.

"Father?" she whispered, then louder, to the closed bathroom door. "*Father?*" There was no reply. Nervously she turned the knob and opened the door to find him sitting on the edge of the tub staring into space. He'd removed his undershirt, and the sight of his bare, hairless chest and pink nipples caused her to feel embarrassed and squeamish.

"I've ordered coffee," she said, averting her eyes from his nakedness. Even when he went swimming, he wore a top. "How's your foot?" Kneeling, she removed his sock as if from a child and wrapped some toilet paper around the cut toe. "I've ordered coffee," she said again, retreating from him.

"Shut the door," he mumbled, and she did as she was told and returned into the room more ill at ease than ever. Dazed, she wandered aimlessly about, thinking she should tidy up the room but didn't have the strength. Catching sight of herself in the mirror, she was disgusted with her appearance. She must let her hair grow, she must! Staring at herself in the mirror and hating her looks, she felt tears coming and fought them off as another thought struck her. She picked up the phone again and called the manager, apologized for her earlier rudeness, and asked if she could borrow a tube of shaving cream and a razor. Needing something to do, she forced herself to tidy the room, make the bed, and lay Franklin's clothes on it. Should she check on him? She found she didn't want to, so she simply sat and waited until the bellman knocked and delivered her order.

"Coffee's here," she called, and a moment later Franklin Hoskins opened the most difficult door of his life and emerged. Unable to look at his daughter, he sat in the chair next to the bureau and hung his head while she poured him a cup and brought it to his mouth.

"There's shaving cream, too," she said, pointing to it, hoping her thoughtfulness would please him. "You can tidy up and have some more coffee . . . and when you're ready we'll go home."

Franklin shook his head. "Not going back there."

"I know she shouldn't have borrowed the money, but she was only doing what she thought was right." He shook his head again, like a pouting child. "More coffee?" He took another sip. "Everything's going to be fine," she said. "You'll see. I have a feeling." Her words sounded foolish to her, but she kept talking, tried to be bright and chatty and normal, to breathe life into him, but he didn't respond.

"I ran into Mr. Phelps today. He might have something for you." She didn't dare tell him of her burst of anger at Phelps. How she would ever face him again she didn't know.

". . . all gone to hell."

"No, it hasn't. We'll find some money. Drink some more coffee."

"No."

"Yes."

"What do you know? . . . You're just a girl."

"What's that got to do with it? You always said I could accomplish anything I wanted to even if I was. Have you changed your mind?"

Franklin shook his head, then lapsed into silence, his eyes vacant like the windows in an abandoned house. "Go home, Harriet," he said after awhile. "Not without you," she replied, bringing the cup to his lips. "Bolsheviks . . ." he muttered. "Goddamn Bolsheviks . . . screwed it to hellandgone. I don't blame Sam Norton for taking his mill south . . . cheap labor . . . the darkies work for pennies. What's left for me?" An artery pounded in his temple, hinting at the mayhem within.

Harriet couldn't make sense of most of it as he went on in a nearly incoherent monologue about Reds and the country going down the drain and so was he. He mumbled on of unions and Jew agitators who were taking the bread away, of house and money, failure and shame. She tried to rebut his terrible, frightening pessimism, but he paid no attention, rambling on that he'd reached the end of his rope and damning Letty once again.

"That's unfair. You know it is. We can sell the house if you like and pay Uncle George the money back. We can take an apartment. This won't last forever. Father! Please, listen to me!"

It was money, or the lack of it, that had brought him so low. Money kept everything in order he used to say, but Letty said that *beauty* was order, and Harriet had made the pursuit of beauty her ideal, too. But if it was money that would ease Franklin's sadness, what wouldn't she do? Beg for it, steal it, connive for it—anything to ease his burden and make him whole again.

"I'll go away . . ."

"Where?" she asked, exhausted and suddenly angry at his obstinacy. "Where?" she demanded, feeling immediately guilty that she'd snapped at him. "Don't you think it's tough on all of us?" she asked gently, sinking to her knees in front of him, taking his cold hand in hers. "We have to be strong, Father. You know we do. There are people living in cardboard shacks by the river."

His head swayed back and forth as, unself-conscious, innocent, and young, she made an impassioned speech in behalf of life and living. Of going into Boston to ride the swanboats, of puppet shows and how he'd held her hand on the first day of kindergarten and told her she was the most special girl in the world. She reminded him she was going to be a famous writer and spoke of the days to come and did he want to miss them? For no matter what had happened, no matter what might happen in the future, it would be worth nothing to her if he were not with her.

Their eyes met briefly, then fled. "She doesn't understand," he muttered. "Who?" she asked, then realized it was Letty. "Of course she doesn't. She doesn't understand me, either. Let's run off. We'll join the circus. Didn't you say you always wanted to? We'll wire Uncle Harold and see if he can find us a job with Ringling Brothers." She began to laugh. Strength slipping from her, she could feel hysteria lurking around the edges, ready to pounce. Quickly she got up, clapping her hands together. "Fine," she said, "fine. You're not coming? I'll run off by myself."

"I can't . . . go home. Like this . . . I can't."

"Of course you can."

"No."

"Shave. See? There it is. And I have your clothes all laid out. Mother gave me fifty cents for a taxi so—"

"She controls it, does she?" He shook his head. "*No.*"

"Have some more coffee. And stop acting like a child!" Fearful at her own daring, she nonetheless couldn't stop—"I don't feel well myself. Do you want me to leave you? What shall I tell them? What? Shall I tell them they won't be seeing you again? Do you want me to tell Frankie that? Do you want me to tell him that you're a drunk and don't love him? Fine. That's what I'll tell him. Drink that coffee!! *Drink it . . .* you *bastard!*"

Shocked, they stared at each other. Mustering what remained of his dignity, Franklin got up, gathered the shaving equipment, entered the bathroom and shut the door. Harriet sat numbly in the chair and began to weep again. She wanted her father to come out and comfort her, but she knew he wouldn't. After a moment she couldn't stand it any longer. "Father?" she pleaded, knocking. "I'm sorry. Please forgive me."

His choked and muffled sobs from inside frightened her, but she opened the door and found him bent over the sink crying.

"Don't," she cried, throwing herself against him and wrapping her arms about his stomach. He turned and held her awkwardly. "Feisty, aren't you?" he murmured, stroking her hair as a sob shuddered through his body, passing into hers.

Men are ghosts, she couldn't help thinking. Frail and fragile. Like Mick Finneran, who had fainted today in biology. Like the man who held her now. Frail and fragile and—and dangerously not what they seemed.

A half-hour later, Harriet handed Franklin his hat and they went out into the corridor and she shut the door on her girlhood and they took the elevator down and she walked out of the Salem Hotel with her father on her arm. Would anything ever be the same again? She would wake, and none of it would have happened. She was bringing him home, just as she'd promised, but she had little sense of victory, only a feeling of loss.

2 Over a year later, toward evening on the Fourth of July in the summer of '33, four months after the inauguration of President Franklin Roosevelt, Abraham Phelps was to address an anxious town from Bartlett's Field just behind Main Street.

Jericho had been apprehensive since last winter, for Nate Wood-bridge's mill had gone under in March and Phelps had closed three of his mills in Massachusetts and one in Rhode Island. Jericho watched and waited, holding its collective breath. Would Phelps' workers, numbering eight hundred or so, be left jobless as had happened in Dracut and Brain-tree? Rumors of impending collapse swept the town. The stories multi-plied, sweeping up and down the tree-lined streets and into kitchens. Of Jericho's five thousand people, there were few whose livelihood did not depend either directly or indirectly on Abraham Phelps.

Gert Flynn and her husband Joe were among those anxious to hear what the town's boss had to say. Joe had worked for Phelps for over twenty years; for the last ten he had been a foreman in the dye room where the rough wool was washed and colored in great vats. Gert had worked in the mending room at the mill until she'd taken over the running of St. Mary's rectory a few years back.

As they left the yard of the house on Essex Street to walk the few blocks to the field, Gert sent a final, searching look at her son, Patrick, who was home for a few days, home from the seminary. *Don't get yourself into any trouble while I'm gone,* was the message.

Patrick returned into the house and sat at the kitchen table with a dish of Gert's coffee Jello. The house was quiet, and he heard a distant cheer from the field. He hadn't wanted to go and hear the speech, for he didn't like crowds. And since he hadn't been home for over a year, Gert was bound to want to show him off to her friends and cronies. "Are you a priest yet?" they'd ask or "Oh, you aren't a priest yet?" Or they'd call him "Father" and croon over him. Others, strangers, would stare—sometimes perplexed, sometimes hostile—and he would be sure to be made uncom-fortable, so why not stay home and avoid it all entirely?

Finishing the Jello, Patrick wandered out to the back yard. In the distance he could hear the high-school band playing a medley. There was to be a fireworks display, provided by Phelps, after his speech. Patrick debated cutting down some back streets and approaching the field from the west, thereby avoiding people. There was a woodsy section on an incline out behind right field where he could hide, a figure in black, invisible, and watch the fireworks.

Unsure, he sat in a yellow metal lawn chair and looked up at the sky.

Why had he sent Gert the letter revealing his doubts? It had brought her hotfooting down to Villanova only three days ago, but now the crisis was past. It was settled. He was staying on at the seminary. Was there any need for rash action? his counselor, Father Urban, had asked, while Gert nodded vehement approval in the background. Why not continue on? It was still two years until Solemn Vows. Why not continue his education, the best the Church had to offer? Patrick had accepted the offer, relieved there might be a way out further down the line, knowing at the same time he wouldn't have the courage to take it. *That* knowledge terrifying; bury it, hide it, deny it at all costs. Impossible to halt the inexorable progress toward God. Impossible to break the promise to Gert. One thing was sure: he'd never open his mouth again, never reveal his doubts again. Her hurt was too much to bear, the guilt too horrible even for him who bathed in it daily.

A day or two off, Urban suggested, then return refreshed. Gert had driven him home to Jericho. Tomorrow he would take the train back. On he would go, receiving the cowl and cincture, a devout boy among many, dreams of a career in professional baseball long gone. Was there another world outside? It seemed impossible at five in the morning, dark chapel mornings, shivering, chanting the Latin Office, their voices filling the empty spaces, driving away the cold and the world outside. Discipline and prayer and potato pancakes served by Sister Wilhelmina, who believed good priests were fat priests. Patristic Latin, Greek, and the History of the Church; Dogmatic and Moral Theology and the Truths of the Faith to protect him from temptation, banish the doubts and drive the devil away.

Poverty, Chastity and Obedience. It was the middle one that was the stickler—an endless battle to stay pure. Of the many misgivings that assailed him—that he was not worthy, that his was a weak vocation, that he would be unable to handle the rigors of the training and would crack under the regimentation and discipline—the struggle with his warm flesh was the worst.

Denial, his superiors told him, was the greatest gift a man had to offer God. How much stronger would be the one who denied himself the pleasures of the flesh, who offered his body chaste and pure, as Christ had done, for the salvation of mankind.

Patrick knew they all fought it. From the days back at St. Martin's

27

Prep. Purity in thought, word and deed. The icy eyes of the priest who taught Greek could spot a boy with impure thoughts; strong hands held a cane ready to whack a backside. The agony of his name called ("Getupta the board," snapped the priest, who was known as Father Gupper.) when he had a bulge under his cassock. Sure to be seen. Hiding it with a book. Backing sideways. The comparing in the lavatory at night (his the second largest), shocked into wildly beating hearts at the sound of Father Gupper's tread in the corridor.

He fasted, he prayed, he ran track. Had hairshirts been issued, he would have asked for two. "Is this a problem for you, my son?" the hushed voice whispered from behind the grille of the confessional. "Yes, Father," croaked the sinner, face in the shadows, compounding the sin by saying "three times," when the total was six, ten, or thirteen since his last confession. *Forgive me, Father, sin upon sin, impurity, world without end, Amen.*

And communion the next morning, when his hands would sweat and swell, the hands that grasped it daily. *Christ, have mercy, I've tried so desperately. . . .* Nights under sheets that caressed his flesh, blankets heavy—and he pulled a pillow to him, molding it to his body, the shape of someone unknown as he strained against the ticking, depositing his seed in pillows. *Christ, have mercy on me. In this cold Philadelphia winter, why am I so hot?*

"My friends, the survival of our beloved town, the survival of our very way of life is rooted in the traditions and faiths that . . ."

Even from Patrick's position on the wooded incline, Phelps' voice, amplified by loudspeakers, could be heard distinctly. Phelps was standing on a flatbed truck parked on home plate, the truck piled high with watermelons that would be hacked open and distributed during the fireworks. Patrick shut his ears to the speech, lost momentarily in reveries of childhood glories on this very field. There wasn't anyone in town who wouldn't agree that even at twelve he'd had the knack, the natural ability that with a little luck and the desire could propel him into the big leagues. Oh, he'd had the desire, hadn't he? A passion for baseball, a need to be on first base. A wave of bitterness boiled in his stomach. His hand went to the breviary in his pocket, touching its worn cover for comfort, a silent prayer on his lips. He couldn't see Gert among the thousand or so that filled the bleachers and spread over the field, but she might as well have been beside him. His attention was caught by a flash of blond hair as Elliot Phelps got up on the truck, late as usual, to stand behind his father. If only he were Elliot Phelps, thought Patrick, he wouldn't have a problem in the world.

"But those who preach doom in our land today will not win our allegiance, nor will they influence our decisions . . ."

28

Phelps' rasping voice penetrated through the anxious holiday crowd, which hung on his every word. Crying babies were jollied into silence, mothers fanned themselves nervously as dusk fell and the lights winked on over home plate, causing Phelps' bald head to shine. Beside him, a large American flag hung listlessly, for there was no breeze at all to stir it to life.

Harriet and Alice stood on the edges of the crowd, Harriet in a hot daze, Alice listening intently. "I know who you're looking at," she whispered as Harriet gazed at Elliot Phelps. Ignoring Alice's comment, Harriet shrugged desultorily and ran a hand through her hair. The day had started with the rat-tat-tatting of firecrackers. There'd been a parade, a baseball game (Jericho Red Stockings, eight; Andover Eagles, five) and a baked-bean supper at the Congregationalist Church. Frustrated with herself and the world, Harriet had participated in the activities with the enthusiasm of a snail.

"Look at those watermelons," scoffed Alice as Phelps paused to drink some water. "A pretty crude gesture if you ask me. Just as crude as him. Why doesn't he tell us all to eat cake?" People nearby glared at her and she glared back. "Let's see what he has to say about President Roosevelt," she whispered to Harriet. "Who cares?" was the reply. Alice gave her sister what had come to be known in the family as her severe look. "You know," she went on, "that Phelps hates Roosevelt as much as Father does." She nodded towards Franklin who stood by himself out in left field, his attention riveted on Abraham Phelps, as if the ruler of Jericho might save him.

There had been growing friction at home between Alice and Franklin. Alice had turned to Roosevelt as to the Messiah. She talked endlessly of his programs, devouring the Boston papers every day and mouthing his words. It was Harriet's opinion that much of her sister's fervor, initially anyway, had to do with getting their father to notice her. If she couldn't get his attention any other way, then she'd make him angry. "President Roosevelt . . ." Alice would begin. "Jew Roosevelt," Franklin would mutter. One day Alice shocked everyone, calling her father a "Republican, small-minded bigot." "Stop it, you two," barked Letty as Alice went on: "Isn't it ironic that Father and the President have the same name?" She was more than Franklin could bear.

"Why don't *you* go to him?" whispered Alice sarcastically as Harriet glanced toward Franklin. "*You* could help I'm sure."

Harriet's forehead creased in a slight frown. Why did he have to stand out there alone, calling attention to himself? She debated joining him, then changed her mind as an unsettling and gnawing anxiety crept up on her, a resentment deep down that she couldn't put her finger on, but it had something to do with him, and it frightened her. "I'll make it up to you," he'd whispered, asking her forgiveness after she'd brought him home from Leveret. All she'd wanted was for him to become Father again. She'd made him promise not to drink, but Franklin had failed to keep the promise, and all she'd been left with was a certainty that she didn't want or need him or anyone to make anything up to her at all. Ever.

Confused and guilty, Harriet knew she shouldn't feel that way because she still loved him, so she retreated into a fantasy of work and accomplishment. She had to make something of herself! She must write! Work harder. Bart and Cynthia and her novel of the rich on Long Island had long since been consigned to a box in the attic marked frivolous. She must start a new story! Salvation, Letty had always said, lay in work. Safety was in art. She would write! She would start using lipstick!

"What are you two doing?" Cora excused herself from a group of chums and joined her sisters. "What were you whispering about? Harriet, you look glum."

"She's daydreaming about Elliot," commented Alice wryly, "but she knows he's out of her league."

Harriet stifled an impulse to snap. She knew Alice was testy this summer because she wasn't going to be able to go to Wellesley College and take political science. Economic realities had squashed the dream. And Harriet would be in the same boat next year when she graduated. What was going to happen to her? Was she supposed to stay in Jericho and write sonnets in the barn? she demanded when Letty suggested she calm down. Calm? Calm she had never known.

"Isn't Elliot scrumptious?" gushed Cora. Stimulated, her eyes darted about anxiously, searching out potential swains. Two years out of high school, she'd never wanted to be anything but a homemaker. But where was he? Please, *where was he*? "I'll bet," chuckled Cora, "Harriet's wondering if Elliot will say hello to her, aren't you, Harriet? Guess what?" she continued, her high and fluty voice causing several disapproving glances from people nearby who were intent on listening to Phelps. "Isabel Hingham and I are going to Horticultural Hall on Tuesday to the flower show, and Isabel wants to ask Bobby Andrews to join us. Do you think a man would be interested in a flower show? I—"

"Now, 'Eleanor,' " interjected Harriet, amused at Cora's resemblance, when excited, to the President's wife, "there you go again."

"Oh, I hate that nickname, Harriet! You know I hate that nickname."

"I think you're really flattered."

"No, I'm not." It wasn't only Cora's voice, nor her fluttery good nature that reminded everyone of Eleanor Roosevelt. It was the teeth. All the girls, and Frankie, too, had what Letty called the Winslowe jaw. Inherited from her illustrious side of the family, it was slightly underslung and featured an ample mouth and lots of sparklers. But Cora always thought she got the worst of it.

"Where are you going?" she whispered as Harriet started off.

"Just going."

She moved through the crowd, their worried faces causing her to feel suddenly claustrophobic and angry. Was she to live forever in a world of injustice, a world where people waited for Abraham Phelps to tell them if they could eat next week? Where families in Leveret still lived in cardboard? What *was* going to become of her? A world of barely making do in her own family, an endless struggle to keep a hop, skip and a jump ahead of creditors because Father still hadn't been able to find work and had given up trying? A world of walking on eggs (was Father having a "good" or a "bad" day?), of Uncle George sending dribbles when he could, of Letty hocking her jewelry, selling dress material from a mail-order catalog, and baking cakes and nutbread that the girls sold door to door around town? "Being poor is nothing to be ashamed of," said Letty, who held them together with a gusto and courage drawn deep from her roots, "—builds character." Harriet decided rich was definitely nicer. When she rang the doorbells of certain snooty girls who lived up in North Parish and offered her cake, she forced herself to be bright and perky. It was chic to sell nutbread. Made one wise in the ways of the world. But it was a world where mothers struggled daily for survival and fathers would never be the same.

"Harriet, you have the face of a thundercloud," commented Letty as Harriet joined her mother, who was with her friend Ada McQueston in the bleachers. "Just hot," murmured Harriet, slumping down, head in hands, elbows on knees. ". . . *aim our sights realistically*," Phelps was saying, his words catching her attention. Yes, that's what they were telling you now. It *used* to be that teachers in school told you to aim high, but they weren't using that phrase anymore, were they? The assumption that lofty quests would produce results didn't hold a can of water anymore, wasn't worth, as her father would say, a snowball in hell. And it was worse if you were a girl.

"How do you think Elliot looks, Mother?" she asked, trying to push away her depression. "He's at Princeton, you know."

"A real problem to his father, I hear," murmured Ada McQueston.

"What kind of a problem?" asked Harriet.

"A wild boy. Very wild." Ada and Letty exchanged a glance.

"Sit with us," suggested Letty, but Harriet was off again, wending her way through a sea of bobbing heads that separated her from her childhood crush.

"How attractive Harriet's getting," commented Ada. "She looks like you."

"Just seventeen," replied Letty. "Ants in her pants," she added, but the lightness of it couldn't disguise the empathy she felt for the storms brewing in her daughter. Oh, how she remembered her own. But nowadays it was even more difficult for young people. They'd had the rug pulled right out from under them.

Harriet waved to her brother Frankie as the high school band re-

31

grouped behind the bleachers, their red uniforms vivid in the lights. Surrounded by girls, he'd played a trumpet solo at the spring prom and gained instant celebrity. A moment later she had worked her way to the front of the crowd and stood directly under Phelps, staring up at him. He could buy and sell everyone in this crowd. Yes, Alice was right about the watermelons. He *was* crude, and his attempt to put on aristocratic and benevolent airs was a sham. Did he think he was the Easter bunny with his large green watermelon eggs? This crowd would need more than watermelons if he were to close down. Anger rose in her again as he sawed the air, keeping the crowd in suspense. He had them at his mercy, he and other men like him who had reduced her father to a defeated shadow of his former self. By God she wasn't going to let them do it to her!

". . . *my great-great-grandfather started this business in 1803 with one loom. As you all know, we have the oldest continuously operating woolen business in this great country. And I have no intention of presiding over its demise one hundred and thirty years later. Phelps mills stay open!*"

A cheer rose from the crowd. Relief rippled in the hot evening air, but Harriet didn't join the almost hysterical clapping. It would take more, much much more to satisfy *her*. She watched as Elliot shook his father's hand, but she sensed the Prince was bored. How striking he was in his seersucker suit with his sandy blond hair and perfect features. Good enough to eat. Not that she had a prayer. She watched as he brushed a moth from his forehead, followed his eyes to the evening star twinkling in the darkening sky. Wild? She could handle him. *Wish I may . . . wish I might. . . .* She wished for Elliot.

A hush fell over the happy crowd, their confidence restored, Jericho restored, by Abraham Phelps. "*I love our town . . . and I love our country . . . and my family.*" Phelps turned to his wife, the famous Nancy Phelps, who was as beautiful as his son. Then, repeating the words, "my family," he turned back to the crowd and raised his arms, palms up, in a benevolent gesture whose meaning was clear to each and every one of them: *You* are my family. . . .

"Quite a performance, isn't it?" scoffed Alice, joining her sister. "Trying to make them think he's one of them. He isn't. He didn't tell them he intends to cut wages—but that's what he'll do. That's the 'sacrifice' he talked about. What's wrong? Didn't the Prince ask you to play tennis at the club?"

"Oh shut up for a change!"

"*Enjoy the fireworks, my friends!*" Phelps' last words echoed over the field. A bold young man jumped up on the truck to shake his hand as more cheers erupted. The watermelons were hacked open. Phelps was hoisted onto sturdy shoulders and carried like a potentate to his long black car as the band broke into "Jericho Forever!", segueing into "The Star-Spangled

Banner" as the first whistle of the rocket's red glare, the bombs bursting in air, shot overhead, exploding in a burst of red, white and blue streamers, drawing an "aaaaah" from the crowd.

There were those who said they saw tears in Abraham Phelps' eyes that night as he entered his car, which shortly afterward inched through the crowd of happy faces raised to the spectacle in the sky. The car headed out to South Main, Jericho's royal family hidden within, past the Hoskins family and a young woman who watched, who couldn't help the envy that now swelled in her at the mystery and power—the arrogance—of that man who had held the crowd in thrall, provided fireworks to entertain it—and not even needed to stay.

Harriet didn't either. She walked back through the empty streets, the explosions ringing in the sky only slightly less tumultuous than those in her head. She must get out! She must leave! She was different from the others, from all of them, from family and friends, from the whole town. She was a free soul with a special destiny, who would go it alone if she had to.

Do something! she ordered herself. *Do something! Do something! Do something!*

. . . And if we leave, must we not return to Jericho, home of our ancestors? And are we not pioneers, too, setting forth in these difficult times like those pioneers of old, who advanced stalwartly, braving the mighty Wampanoag, unflinching in their duty under God to bring civilization to the mysterious, heathen interior? Those pioneers who cast their eyes, who cast longing and wondering looks toward this unexplored region, a flash of silver—the majestic Cochickawick—under a pink sky of Tintoretto, where angels must surely burst forth with trumpets exploding; and beyond—a distant background of majestic hills, and still beyond, the isolated summits of grand old mountains. Beauty, majesty and mystery combined in the prospect. O Jericho!

So we, the pioneers of today, the graduates who leave these hallowed halls, must keep our eyes upon the hills, looking ever forward to our own mysterious interior where challenges await us, where uncertainties may lurk, but still we must—we will—keep the faith of our fathers, their courage in our hearts as a bright flame burning.

We are told that America is passing through a crucible, that we go forth in perilous times. Will we succumb to the naysayers? No! We will not falter. No! We shall go forth and slay the dragon, for we speak for courage and for faith.

And if we journey to the ends of the earth, must we not keep in

33

our hearts our Jericho, must we not return to replenish ourselves in the waters of Lake Cochickawick, must we ever forget out beloved, our eternal Jericho . . .

excerpt from the valedictory
address written and presented by
Harriet Hoskins, Jericho High
School, Class of '34

. . . *crack* . . . *crack* . . . *don't step on the crack*. . . . Two months after her eighteenth birthday, Harriet walked jauntily down South Main intent on her destiny, which would or would not be fulfilled depending on whether she stepped on a crack. Smiling to herself, she took large, then small, steps, enjoying the childish game that had, however, important and symbolic overtones. Each crack *not* stepped upon equaled ten dollars. By the time she reached Phelps Mill, she calculated she'd have five hundred—the sum she intended to try and borrow from Abraham Phelps.

"Lookin' spiffy, Harriet," called Mr. Beale, who sat in the sun in front of the fire station, lazy as Mahatma Gandhi's valet. Harriet smiled at the compliment and waved. Indeed, she did present a comely sight today. She'd chosen her outfit with particular care—a soft robin's egg blue sweater that bared her bosom as low as conscience would allow, a skirt that fit snugly over her hips and flared out below the knee. Only the world's smartest detective would guess it was bought for twenty-five cents in Filene's bargain basement in Boston and had major surgery performed upon it by Letty, who'd transformed the skirt into the stylish miracle it was. Completing the pretty picture was a knitted beret worn at an angle, slightly rakish, over one eyebrow.

Harriet paused by the millpond, suddenly beset with an attack of nerves. Suppose he wouldn't see her? Perhaps it was a cockeyed idea in the first place. No one at home knew what she was up to today. There would probably be hell to pay, whether she was successful or not. With nervous fingers she opened the old briefcase of her father's and checked the contents, which included several jars of jam and a portfolio of her writings. Included in it was her pièce de resistance—a short essay composed in a fit of giggling inspiration only last evening—an outrageous piece of flattery with the exalted title, *"ABRAHAM PHELPS, RENAISSANCE MAN,"* which sang the praises of the town's benefactor, extolling him as a "Patron of the Arts." If this description was as farfetched as it was ludicrous (she'd only had a few free band concerts and a new wing at the library to work with), no matter. She knew how to spin a phrase or two, didn't she? Even if Abraham Phelps was a notorious skinflint, she would woo and win him to her side with her little essay. She would make him become *her* patron, too.

34

Now in the cold light of day, so to speak, the whole project seemed absolutely preposterous.

Harriet turned to go, then turned back, glancing at the mill. Through the open windows came the clatter of the looms, mirroring her agitation.

Do you have a choice?

No.

March.

Checking her reflection in the water, she made sure her seams were straight, took a breath, plucked a black-eyed Susan from a clump, stuck it behind her ear and started for the main gate.

"Do you have an appointment with him?" asked Abraham Phelps' secretary, lips pursing in irritation when Harriet confessed she didn't.

"He's very busy. Are you looking for employment?"

"No, it's a personal matter."

"Does he know you?"

Harriet nodded. Intimidated by the interrogation, she felt her courage draining away. Perhaps she would just come back another day. Perhaps she would go out and jump into the millpond. "He knows me very well," she managed to say, coming up with what she hoped was a suitably arch look at the curmudgeon.

"I'll tell him you want to see him but—"

"Thank you so much. I'll wait, if you don't mind." She turned into the corridor and sat down, the mill thundering around her. Through the glass cubicle she could see the secretary talking on the phone.

"Good morning, Miss Hoskins." Startling her, Abraham Phelps seemed to have appeared from nowhere.

"Good morning, Mr. Phelps."

"Haven't seen you in some time, have I? I think I can give you a minute." His appraising eye took Harriet in, missing nothing. What was in the briefcase? Probably collecting for the Red Cross or some such thing. Why did they always come to him first? Phelps ushered Harriet into his large office.

"How is your family?"

"Fine, thank you."

"Your father? We don't get to see him anymore."

Still unemployed, she wanted to say but held her tongue, hoping he didn't remember her outburst at him a few years ago.

"And what can I do for you today?" Phelps' fingers tapped the polished desk. Harriet started to speak. The phone rang. He excused himself to take the call, eyes on her as he talked. Quickly she looked away. Broad tables were covered with catalogs and bolts of cloth. Startled, she caught the eyes in a portrait of Abraham Phelps, Sr., glaring sternly at her. There were also several framed photos, including one of Mr. and Mrs. Phelps and ex-President Hoover at a garden party up at Phelps Mansion.

Phelps picked up a paperweight and shook it, causing bubbles to froth madly.

"You know what I would have said, Charles—don't you?" Phelps swiveled away from her in his chair. Did he want privacy? Should she go back outside and wait in the hall? No, it had taken her a half hour to get in. Carefully she rose and moved away from the desk. At the end of the office was an open door leading to a sort of storeroom with bookcases and more catalogs. Pretending interest, Harriet picked up a book on sheep breeding.

A moment later Phelps set the receiver back in its cradle so carefully that, had Harriet been watching, she would not have been able to guess of the furies unleashed by the call.

"Son of a bitch," he murmured precisely, taking his time with each word. Then he spat into a spittoon beneath his desk.

The object of Phelps' wrath was luckily in Manchester, New Hampshire. Had Charlie Potter of Mohican Mills been in the office, he might have squirmed, slightly discomfited under the surveillance of those cool eyes, whose heavy lids would lower slightly, almost lazily, as an ironic smile played about the corners of the mouth. It was an expression that asked: How can you be so foolish as to consider crossing me? Are you sure you don't wish to reconsider?

Most did. Those who did not found themselves in the unenviable position of having been dismissed. Phelps rarely raised his voice however. His father had been the shouter. Abraham Phelps, Senior, had made men quake with his wrath, bellowing at them, growing purple in the face, finally succumbing to a stroke at the front gates of his mill as he roared his defiance of a mob come over from Leveret in 1912 when that city was in the grip of a strike that saw twenty-five-thousand operatives walk out of the mills.

The control of Phelps Mills passed to the son who had trained himself to be the opposite of his father, cultivating an iron will and self-discipline, which had allowed him to survive the old man's tyranny and achieve his aims with an even deadlier effectiveness. Those who had scoffed, considering him a lightweight, had done so at their own peril. In the twenty-two years since his father's death, Phelps had built an empire of thirteen mills throughout New England and lately in the South. Enemies had been confounded; competitors wiped out. His cunning was legendary. Once in the shadow of his father, the son now cast his own—longer, darker, and more dangerous for the country-parson charm in which he camouflaged himself.

"Son of a bitch. . . ." The curse was repeated. The hand shook the paperweight again. Charlie Potter had given in to the union.

Harriet watched as Phelps got up and walked slowly to a window opposite his desk. The floor trembled beneath her feet from the workings of the heavy machinery. She realized she was holding her breath.

36

"Does it make any sense to you, Miss Hoskins . . ." Involuntarily she gasped slightly as he spoke, for she was sure he'd forgotten about her completely. His voice was so low, she had to strain to hear. ". . . that I should be forced to give my mill away?"

"Why, no. It's yours, isn't it?"

"Yes, indeed. A correct answer. Logical. If only our 'beloved' President had your sense of logic, we could all breathe easier."

Phelps turned to her and smiled his Cheshire cat smile, which didn't make her less nervous. Gesturing for her to sit, he did likewise. "You see, Miss Hoskins . . . I am a man besieged." He pressed a button and his secretary appeared. "Get me Armistead. Five minutes."

Five minutes. Five minutes? Harriet wet her lips and tried to get started.

"Did you happen to see a blue eagle on my door?" Phelps asked, stopping her. She shook her head. "No," he growled. "And you never will." Once again, the bubbles frothed as he shook the paperweight. "There are those who would like me to knuckle under. There are those who think they know more about my business than I do. They'd like to tell me what I should pay my workers. And my workers would like to tell me that I don't have their best interests at heart. Who, I ask you, has kept this mill running during these difficult times? Has Roosevelt kept my mill running? Twenty-eight mills in New England have shut down in the last sixteen months. Have the unions kept my mill running? The unions are calling for strikes. No, I have kept my mill running and . . ."

Suddenly Harriet was struck with what he reminded her of! Not the bust of Cicero in Latin class, but an eagle! The Blue Eagle that he was so angry about, the one that had appeared on the windows of factories and shops all over the country this past year as the symbol of Roosevelt's National Industrial Recovery Act. Harriet couldn't wait to tell Alice of her discovery—Abraham Phelps had become the very thing he hated most!

". . . and I intend to keep it that way!"

"Is that why people call you the Henry Ford of Jericho?"

Phelps swiveled toward Harriet abruptly, staring at her with eyes like dark marbles, causing her heart to pound. What had she said? she wondered, fighting a sinking feeling.

"There are those who use that comparison to condemn me, Miss Hoskins, because Mr. Ford and I share the same views, but . . ."

"I—"

". . . I consider it a compliment!" Satisfied Harriet meant no harm, Phelps bestowed a small smile. "You seem a sensible girl. Very sensible, indeed. Guess what I read in the paper this morning? Would you like to hear?"

No, she didn't want to. Harriet glanced at the clock. Three minutes had passed. Two to go . . .

37

"They have a squad in Washington these days. They march up and down the avenues with balloons on very long strings. Now can you guess what they're for?" He didn't wait for an answer. "To scare away the pigeons that nest in the eaves of the office buildings. Are you understanding me? Roosevelt is using *my* money . . . the taxpayer's money . . . your father's money . . . to pay derelicts to frighten pigeons so they won't drop on his wife's head when she goes out to visit her communist friends!"

Phelps continued his condemnations. Harriet blanked out the words. She loved President Roosevelt, found him aristocratic, and appreciated his style. Not to mention that Alice had got work in the Civil Works Administration, which Roosevelt had created to provide jobs, and Frankie was out cutting trees in the state forest this summer on another of the President's relief projects. She decided this wasn't the time to mention it.

Phelps swiveled in his chair, his eyes meeting his father's in the portrait. "He is turning in his grave. Turning in his grave to see what that man is doing to the country. Giving it away. Mark my words. *He is giving it away. And if we don't stop him it will be gone before we know it!*"

Harriet shivered. The secretary's buzzer sounded. The five minutes were up. Phelps rose. "I've enjoyed our little chat. Drop by anytime. If you're looking for employment, unfortunately . . ."

"No. I'm not." She wanted to run. Instead, she picked up her briefcase and set it on her lap. Phelps eyed it warily. "I've just graduated from high school," began Harriet with the driest throat in the East, "and have been accepted at Syracuse University into the journalism school. It's a special one-year program that I . . ."

She barely got all the details out. "Good for you," said Phelps. "And then on to New York City, hmm? Well, you seem to have your future all mapped out. Your parents must be proud of you. I see you have gumption and I applaud it. Do you know my son Elliot?"

If Elliot had a quarter of this girl's get up and go, he might make something of himself. "A newspaper reporter, hmmmm? Unusual profession for a girl, isn't it?"

"I don't think so," she replied, irritated with the question. "There are many well-known women journalists. Last fall I met Dorothy Thompson and—"

"Who?" interrupted Phelps, frowning at the mention of the notoriously liberal columnist.

"Dorothy Thompson . . ." Flustered by his reaction, she hesitated. He was *supposed* to be impressed. "You see," she continued, hurrying on, "Miss Cooke, my English teacher, was a roommate of hers at Syracuse and we went in to hear her give a talk to the League of Women Voters in Boston, and afterward we had tea with her at the Parker House, and it changed my life. She did, I mean."

"Oh?"

"I'd always thought of being a writer, but after meeting Miss Thompson, I knew what it was I wanted to do. She was *so* stimulating. 'Is America a Paradise for Women?'—that was her topic and—"

"Is it, do you think?"

"Pardon? Oh. Well—no. Of course not. *I* don't think so. But it could be. That was Miss Thompson's point. If women would only realize the power we have. She told us we should seize our destinies. That's exactly what she said. I intend to seize mine."

"I thought it was . . ." Lost momentarily in the beauty of his wife Nancy's face in the photo, Phelps' expression softened. Certainly he had tried to make it a paradise for her. What had it got him? His son and his wife aligned against him.

"Well—" Phelps snapped back to attention. "This is all very interesting, I'm sure." He stood up. "What was it you wanted, Miss Hoskins?"

Harriet stood, too. Quickly she removed a jar of jam from the briefcase and set it down smartly with a small *whack* on the desk.

"What's this?"

"I'm selling jam."

Phelps cleared his throat.

"I'm selling jam to help pay my tuition to Syracuse. Would you like to try some?" Before giving him a chance to reply, she produced a spoon, unscrewed the jar, dipped the spoon in and offered it to Phelps, who was, uncharacteristically, nonplussed.

"I'm sure it's delightful, but—" Was ever an Adam tempted by a more persuasive Eve? Abraham Phelps didn't know it, but a spell was being woven about him, a spell of such enchantment that for a moment he felt dizzy. Cautiously he brought the spoon to his mouth. The combination of sweetness with a tart undertaste caused his thin lips to pucker. "Delicious. How much?" Color came into his usually sallow cheeks. He could feel the blood in his temples.

"Fifteen cents a jar."

"I'll take two."

"I also have elderberry, plum and raspberry."

"Make that six." Phelps extracted a magnanimous bill from his wallet, the feel of which returned him to reality. "I find you an extraordinary young woman, Miss Hoskins. You represent the best of the free enterprise system. But now I must regretfully—" He pulled his watch from his vest pocket. Harriet ignored it.

"I've also brought with me . . ." Before his eyes, which squinted then widened in astonishment, Harriet placed her portfolio.

"Well, well . . ." Phelps glanced at her, then back at the writings. Cursorily, his fingers flipped through the samples from the school newspaper, a story or two. Then his eye fell upon it.

Reaching behind her to the chair for support, Harriet's eyes focused

39

on the pattern in a nearby bolt of cloth. The clearing of Phelps' throat caused her to dare to look back. He was bent over, reading. The clock ticked loudly. The suspense was unbearable, and she was sure her heart had stopped.

"Renaissance Man?" Phelps' expression revealed nothing, the tone uninterpretable. He resumed reading. Finally he finished, shuffled the pages back together, and sat down. A slow smile flickered across his face. What an operator she thought she was!

"What do you want from me?"

"I . . . nothing . . . I . . ."

"When did you write this?"

Her stammered response and the violent blush which rose in her bosom confirmed his suspicion that she'd probably composed it very recently, very recently, indeed.

"Last week. I thought . . . it might be useful . . . when the new wing at the library is dedicated, but . . . I . . ."

"Is that what you thought?" Like a bird of prey toying effortlessly with its victim, he let her see none of the pleasure that her clumsy attempt at flattery had provoked.

"Please forgive me. I should never have presumed. . . ." All was lost. She knew all was lost. How could she ever have been so stupid as to have thought she could outwit him? How—

"On the contrary, Miss Hoskins." Phelps picked up a page again, unable to resist the rereading of a sentence that began, "Must not all of Jericho pay homage to him who has given so much?" and ended by comparing him to Lorenzo de' Medici. Operator, indeed! Still, he *had* always tried to do what he could. From under lowered lids (a reappraisal was obviously necessary) Phelps scrutinized Harriet with eyes used to quality. She was fresh and pretty with a pleasant scent that reminded him of his wife. In spite of the transparency of her trying to butter him up, he was charmed. "On the contrary," he repeated. "I think we shall have to take you seriously as a writer. Now, if you'll excuse me—"

"Do you think so?" Harriet gasped happily. The black-eyed Susan fell from her hair onto the desk. Solemnly Phelps returned it to her. "Do you really think so?" she asked again. His nod accelerated her joy. She took a breath:

"Because that's what I came to talk to you about. . . ."

"You did what?"

As Harriet expected, Alice was fit to be tied. Home from Leveret on her lunch hour, she was confronted on Main Street by a whirling dervish of a sister, whose beret-throwing, jig-dancing excitement—climaxed with a triumphant waving of a five-hundred-dollar personal check from Abraham

Phelps—caused her to regard Harriet with an expression not unlike that reserved for traitors.

Harriet's infectious joy had prevailed, however, and by the time the sisters had reached Noonan's Drugs, into whose coolness they ducked for celebratory sodas and lunch (Harriet splurging with jam money), Alice had come around to a wary appreciation of her sister's logic. "How else was I to go?" demanded Harriet, and Alice knew she was right.

"It's to be paid back in two years. That's the deal we made. At two percent interest. I insisted on that."

Reluctantly Alice found herself enjoying Harriet's description of her morning at the mill. It had taken, she had to admit, a certain amount of daring and imagination to approach Abraham Phelps. "Renaissance Man," however, drew a shocked and incredulous gasp.

"You *didn't* write that."

"I did."

"How could you? How could you characterize him as *giving*? How could you? I've told you what he's done. He's a tyrant. Who do you think drove the organizers out of town last summer? Don't you know Dorothy Thompson is concerned about those very kinds of issues?" Alice shook her head in wonder. She had applauded Harriet's choice of profession, although more than ever she feared her sister's approach was on a fantastical, glamour-struck level that ignored totally the possibilities in such a career for social and political action.

"Don't look at me like that, Alice. You climb the mountain your way, and I'll do it mine. In this case the ends justify the means. I know you don't agree, but you're Joan of Arc. Next to you, we're all sinners."

"You know why he lent you the money? To soothe his dirty conscience, that's why. He gives you five hundred dollars, and that's his good deed for the year. Now he can go back to hiring Pinkerton goons to spy on his workers if they talk union. And another thing—you mark my words— be careful. You're in his pocket now. Anything you have to do with such a man can lead to trouble."

"Cassandra!" Harriet laughed and tried to calm Alice down.

"Don't say I didn't warn you."

"I stand warned."

"What are you going to tell Father?"

Harriet frowned. "His pride will be hurt, but he'll understand. I'll make him understand—"

"I'm sure you will."

"—and I'll need your help," continued Harriet, avoiding Alice's jealous taunt.

"I wouldn't be of any use."

"Of course you will. Father loves you. You just don't believe it.

41

Mother is going to be shocked, so let's come up with an approach. First—"

"Look," interrupted Alice, pointing out the Flynn brothers, who'd just walked in. Instantly Harriet was up and tapping Patrick on the shoulder. "Hello. Do you remember me? Several summers ago in Maurice Finneran's back yard? I have the memory of an elephant."

"Oh," exclaimed Patrick, echoed by Dennis Flynn, the two of them liable to be knocked down like bowling pins by Harriet's energy. "Don't worry," she continued, "I don't remember your name, either. I'm Harriet Hoskins. Join us, won't you? Come meet my sister."

Had Roosevelt been in Noonan's, Harriet would probably have invited him, too, such was her need to share her glory with the world. A moment later (even though Dennis protested there wasn't really room) she had the Flynns squeezed in at the table.

"We're not having lunch," said Patrick, very taken aback when Harriet suggested that she would treat. For a girl to suggest such a thing didn't seem entirely proper. "We're just picking up some ice cream," he continued, not too sure he should be sitting here at all.

"So—do I call you Father Flynn?" asked Harriet.

"Not yet. A few more years."

"Really? But—"

"I know. We wear the collar, but we aren't priests yet."

"Well, I think your suit is very becoming. A definite improvement over what you were wearing the last time I saw you."

"My—? Oh. She means my cassock," Patrick explained to Dennis, who looked pinched. Not as good-looking as his younger brother, Dennis possessed a prissy mouth, once angelic, now inappropriate in a man of twenty-eight.

"I know you, don't I, Alice?" Dennis asked, trying to avoid Harriet, whom he found uncomfortably too full of life.

"I don't recall," she replied, looking at her lap, her relations with the opposite sex as passive as her political awareness was advanced.

"Where are you now? Still at the seminary?" Harriet asked.

Patrick caught her mischievous twinkle. Holding himself almost rigidly, he smiled warily back. Yes, he remembered her. A bratty kid. She didn't seem to have changed. As if from a distance, he could see she was very attractive, but he was pleased to note he wasn't at all affected. "I'm at Catholic University in Washington," he replied. "Graduate work." All doubts submerged, he might have added. He was set for life.

"I'm off to Syracuse University myself. In fact it just got settled today."

"Today? Congratulations."

"C'mon Patrick," grumbled Dennis, "the ice cream's ready."

"What about you, Dennis?" asked Harriet.

"He graduated Boston College," replied Patrick, answering for his brother, "and is at the tax assessor's office next door. He's going into politics."

"Politics? How interesting. Alice works for President Roosevelt, don't you, Alice? The Civil Works Administration over in Leveret."

"How'd you get that job?" asked Dennis, jealous. Alice shrugged.

"Alice began ringing doorbells for the President back in '31. She even sent him letters."

"Is your family Democratic?" asked Patrick. Alice and Harriet exchanged a smile. "Alice is a rebel," replied Harriet, "and the rest are Republicans."

Dennis got up and went back to the counter. "Do you think they look like brothers?" Harriet asked Alice. "I don't," she went on, answering her own question, "I don't at all. Dennis has sort of blond hair, doesn't he? And you're so dark, Patrick, I'll bet you're adopted."

He shook his head. "*Errare humanum est.*"

"What's that mean?"

"It means: I'm not."

"Well, think of that!"

Dennis returned, ice cream in hand. "Who's the oldest?" asked Harriet.

"He is," answered Patrick, "by five years."

"I never would have guessed," she replied with an exaggerated sweetness. "Do you think we look like sisters, Dennis?" He looked like an out-of-focus photograph.

Dennis rose up and down on the balls of his feet. "I've no idea."

"What do *you* think, Patrick?"

"Sort of," he said politely.

"C'mon Patrick." Dennis started for the door. "Nice to have met you," he called to Alice, deliberately not including Harriet.

"Well . . ." Patrick got up.

"Good luck."

"You, too. Bye, Alice."

The sisters watched from Noonan's window as the brothers crossed the street. "Don't they remind you of the scotch ad? Dennis in his white suit and Patrick— Look! He's waving."

"*Harriet.* You are making a spectacle of yourself," whispered Alice as Harriet blew Patrick a kiss, causing several nearby eyebrows to be raised.

"Oooo. I feel so *good!*"

"You were *flirting* with him."

"Was I? Do you think he's interested?"

"He's a priest!"

"Not yet . . . not yet . . ." She narrowed her eyes in a squinty, temptressy look. "He's keen looking. Don't you think?"

"I suppose."

43

"Oh, Alice, that's your trouble. Don't be so glum. Why didn't you chat with Dennis?"

"Who had a chance?"

"You were right, anyway. What a stuffy bore! Patrick isn't much better, is he? Quoting Latin like that—what a show-off! What do you think? I can't figure him out. He seems very . . . sure of himself, doesn't he? Sanctimonious. That's it. What a wonderful word. Why would anyone want to be a priest? Especially if they're good-looking. It's mysterious, isn't it? Let's celebrate," she exclaimed. "I think you need some fun. Kent and I are going dancing at the Canoe Club, and you're coming with us. I'll call him and see if he has a friend. I'll loan you my green crepe."

"I don't need you to be my social secretary. Anyway, I'm busy."

Harriet sighed. It was always the same. She'd suggest an outing—a movie or a dance—and was perfectly willing and ready to provide interesting dates for her sister, but Alice's answer was always a no. She was busy. Engrossed in her work, sometimes staying late in Leveret to attend political meetings and rallies of strikers and unemployed millworkers, she had no time at all for "frivolous" activities. When she was at home, she holed herself up in the barn, painting. And seemed to take no interest in her appearance whatsoever.

"But Alice, if only you'd—"

"You're going with Kent Appleton?" interrupted Alice, trying to change the subject. "What happened to Roger?"

"Long gone." Harriet pantomimed blowing a dandelion.

"You go through a dozen a month."

"Why not? Aren't they there for the plucking?"

"I thought Roger was crazy about you."

"Such a pity." He'd taken her up to the lake to neck, and when she wouldn't let him touch her in certain unmentionable spots, he got mad. Later it came back to her that he was spreading stories, calling her a tease. High-school boys! Small-town bimbos! *Oh, but she was leaving!* A sudden shiver of joy coursed through her as the morning's triumph rose up again. "Unfortunately," she continued, "I was not crazy for Roger. Nor do I intend to be for any man. No man shall know this fragile body. Do you think I'm too tall? Anyway, I may become a nun." Her eyes gazed across Main to the corner of Essex, where the Flynns had disappeared up the block.

"I'll bet you would."

"Him? A lost cause, don't you think? Gone to God. Oh, well. Alice, what is it? You look gloomy."

"Maybe I'm jealous." Of Harriet's way with men? No, she didn't want to admit to that. "Maybe I'd like to go to college, too. Get away."

"But why? You're already out in the world and doing what you want to do. Patrick said his brother was 'going' into politics. You already are!

44

You're helping to make decisions that affect people. You're putting people back to work. You're *out* there."

"I'm just a clerk."

"Not at all! You understand history. You have a . . . sweep about you. And you've never been afraid to fight for what you believe in. I'm proud of you."

Embarrassed, Alice turned away and shrugged, eyes misting. "I feel the same . . . about you. I think it's terrific you're going. I do. You've got more guts than I have."

"See? We're a mutual admiration society, aren't we?"

Implusively Harriet stood and pulled Alice up and hugged her. Dear Alice, the most sensitive of all of them. Rebellious Alice, who wore her heart on her sleeve and protected herself with a tart tongue. No matter the arguments, rivalries, and petty jealousies between them, the bond was palpable, solid as apples.

After lunch, Harriet walked Alice back down Main to the depot, where Alice would catch the trolley back to Leveret.

"You know," she said as they neared the mill, "I think I had Mr. Phelps so much in the palm of my hand I could've borrowed more if I needed it."

"What is it," demanded Alice sharply, "that you're after?"

"Why, Alice, oh, sister mine—I thought you knew!" A twinkle in her eye, Harriet turned a slow pirouette, her arms extended not only to the mill, but the town, the Merrimack Valley and the ships at sea (had there been some):

"I want it all."

3

Dear Mother,

I'm living in a bathroom. Yes, a bathroom. Pick yourself up and read on. Sorry to have been such a poor correspondent. These first weeks in the BIG CITY have my head swimming. Have a permanent crick in my neck from looking up. Local yokel, that's me. Even Boston doesn't prepare one for the magnificence of N.Y. I love it! This will have to be a short one, but I'll write you a longer later in the week with all of my exploits in vast detail.

Back to my nifty bathroom. As I wrote you, I was staying with my new friend, Virginia, but the room was impossibly crowded (and she's really rather messy), so one day last week Mrs. Mundy (the landlady) asked me to follow her down one floor, and there it was. It used to be the master bath of the house and is almost as large as V's room. Mrs. Mundy has provided me with a bed, hot plate, etc. I purchased some flowered chintz at Klein's in Union Square and with two boards over the enormous tub and a pillow or two—presto!—instant sofa. Sit-down dinners for six are out for the moment.

The bathroom is all tile (so very cool now) and I have a purple stained-glass window with a lily in the center over the sink. When I wash my face, I think I'm in church. (Yes, I'm going to church. On Fifth Ave. no less.)

Doesn't it sound like a lark? Only temporary, I can assure you. Only two dollars a week, too. I expect you to come down for a visit, and we'll do it up proud. (Enclosed is diagram—how I've arranged things.)

Several interesting Bohemian types in the house. Virginia, who's an actress, Mr. Mitchell, a painter (does miniatures), and a couple of actors and dancers. I'm the only writer. Did I tell you Greenwich Village is only two blocks away?

Am starting my first rounds of the papers this week. Have

already submitted a piece to *Colliers* and have a nifty idea for *Vanity Fair*. A satiric piece about living in a bathroom—something like "Where Is This Season's Career Girl Finding Accommodations?"—something like that. Perfect for V.*F*.—don't you think?

Harris and I went to see Orson Welles' production of *Macbeth* in Harlem (!) no less and then went dancing at the famous One O'Clock Club till dawn, as they say. (They are *not* "darkies," Mother.)

Harris trailed me around the city for a week, and then we had a fight. He asked me to marry him again. I told him no again. He's gone back to Syracuse now. *C'est la vie*, I say. I knew we didn't have a future, but he didn't. Anyway, I have too much to do.

My year at Syracuse has honed my skills, but Harris was very pessimistic about my chances. *I* know we're still in a Depression and jobs are scarce, but I *know* I'll find work on a paper. Or get into the mags. I am undaunted! Heard President Roosevelt's speech on the radio the other night about our "rendezvous with destiny." Exactly my sentiments. I feel on top of the world and ready for my own rendezvous. (Incidentally, Harris never bedded me, in case you're interested, but who knows what mysterious stranger I shall meet here?) (Joke! Don't panic.)

I miss you all terribly. I hated missing Memorial Day. Did you conduct your annual tour of the graves? Salmon and peas? Hope you didn't have to serve your creamed radishes. (Ugh—haven't been able to eat a radish since.)

Give my love to Cora, Alice and Frankie and a special hug for Father. Everyone who writes me gets a letter in return. Could you spare some stamps? I'm on such a tight budget.

Don't worry! The first to leave the nest shall return triumphant!

> Your loving daughter,
> Harriet

P.S. If you see Mr. Phelps give him a hug, too. (Another joke!) Seriously, though, I've written him to keep him informed of my progress.

The final argument with Harris Talbot had taken place along Fourteenth Street on a sweltering day. "Marry me," he pleaded for the umpteenth time. Harriet had met him at Syracuse and dated him for six months. She knew how Harris wanted her—exactly like the mannequins dressed up as June brides in the window of a bridal shop on the corner. Complacently smiling and orange-blossomed and Niagara Fallshoneymooned and living outside of Syracuse down the street from his parents in a white cottage with rambling roses. And a sweet little picket fence. There'd be a little-one-on-the-way and bridge on Saturday nights with the other young marrieds—and she'd slit her wrists within a year. She might as well have stayed in Jericho if *that* was to be the agenda.

Once again she'd tried to explain it all to Harris, who never listened and got hotter under the collar, accusing Harriet of using him to get a ride down to New York City where, he shouted, she would *not* be able to find work, so why didn't she give up this foolish idea and return to Syracuse with him?

"I'M A WRITER, HARRIS!" she hollered (the Third Avenue El was joining in the fray above their heads), and he hollered back: "HAVE YOU BEEN PAID FOR IT???"—and so it went.

Furious, Harris finally thrust the stuffed snake he'd won at Coney Island at her, sneered, "Have fun at El Morocco," and started away. Across the street he turned back and delivered the final thrust:

"AND GIVE MY LOVE TO DOROTHY THOMPSON!"

That very evening (had she now burned all her bridges behind her?) Harriet went up on the roof of Virginia's building to get a breath of air.

A pang of missing Harris assailed her. She regretted that it had ended badly and felt a desire to be held close, but she knew she had no choice.

A million lights twinkled through a haze of heat, and a great ringed moon promised another scorcher tomorrow. Alternately homesick (someone was playing a trumpet, reminding her of her brother Frankie) and mesmerized by the view, Harriet closed her eyes, opened her arms to the city and dreamed of fame.

Where *was* Dorothy? Out there somewhere. Dorothy, Dorothy. In the year and a half since she'd met her, the famous journalist was so much in Harriet's thoughts that she seemed to have become a close and trusted friend. And Dorothy Thompson was married to Sinclair Lewis, the most famous novelist in America, who'd written *Main Street* and knew all about small towns like Jericho.

Dorothy and Sinclair—what were they doing at this very moment? A late-night supper party after the theater? No, they were working. She was sure they were busy writing. He on a new novel and she on her column for the *Trib*. Somewhere out there in a book-lined study in an elegant townhouse in the Sixties or a huge apartment on Riverside Drive. Perhaps at matching desks, or in separate rooms with a connecting door left open so a word or two could be exchanged, a moment of inspiration shared. Dorothy would be working the harder as she had a deadline to meet. "More sherry, darling?" he would ask. "No thanks, sweetheart," she would reply, knowing a courier was waiting ("See that he's comfortable, Minnie") to whisk away the copy and rush it to the *Trib*, where it would be set into type. Tomorrow, millions would read what she had to say.

Later, as rejections and disappointments piled up, Harriet tried to get in touch with Dorothy Thompson. She sent her notes care of the *Trib* but received no reply. She became obsessed with finding her. Dorothy would help her. Dorothy would save her. Why, it was Dorothy who had started her on the journey!

Through a friendly elevator man at the *Trib*, she found out that Miss Thompson lived on Tenth Street west of Fifth Avenue. He didn't know the exact address, so Harriet rang doorbells until she hit paydirt. She left a cheery note with the German housekeeper and went home to wait for a reply. Nothing. She went back a few days later, and the housekeeper told her that Miss Thompson was due back from Europe on the *Normandie* at ten o'clock on Friday morning. It seemed a good omen, for she and Harris had watched the *Normandie* dock after its maiden voyage in June.

On Friday morning at nine-thirty, Harriet returned to Tenth Street and, book in hand, settled herself down on the stoop. "What are you waiting for?" asked the housekeeper suspiciously. "For Miss Thompson," replied Harriet briskly.

The day wore on. Had the boat been delayed? She began to feel foolish. Even so, she knew she couldn't retreat, knew she was going to wait. She had no intention of missing Dorothy. A plan made must be followed through.

At a quarter to three in the afternoon, two taxis turned the corner and pulled up. Out of the first came Sinclair Lewis. Out of the second came Dorothy Thompson.

"Miss Thompson . . . !" began Harriet, talking fast, stepping out of the way of the housekeeper and taxi driver, who were removing a mountain of luggage, not to mention two small dogs yipping. "My name is Harriet Hoskins, and I met you in Boston over a year and a half ago. . . . I know I'm catching you at a terrible time . . . was your crossing pleasant? It's just that I— Do you remember me by any chance? My English teacher, Miss Cooke and—"

"Annie Cooke? How is Annie? Excuse me . . ." Dorothy Thompson turned from Harriet back to the housekeeper. "Watch those, Lottie, they're breakables." Then back to Harriet: "I'm sorry, but we're just back from France."

"Excuse me," Lewis interrupted, reaching past Harriet to take a briefcase from the driver.

"What did you say your name was?" asked Miss Thompson.

"Harriet Hoskins."

"Miss Hoskins, this is my husband, Mr. Lewis."

Harriet shook his hand, momentarily riveted by his haunted eyes, which glanced briefly at her. He was the ugliest man she had ever seen. Oh, but what did it matter! What a writer he was! She could feel the bones in his hand. She tried to express how she felt, how she'd read *Main Street* when she was twelve and what it had meant to her. Lewis seemed barely able to pay attention and fled up the stairs. Harriet's eyes followed, transfixed by his talent. Pale sunlight caught his pockmarked face as he disappeared inside.

"Would you be free on Wednesday next?"

Harriet was so excited, she almost missed the invitation. Then she smiled. Tea on Wednesday with Dorothy Thompson? It had worked!

The following Wednesday after tea and vanilla wafers, she rushed home to tell Virginia all about it. "What a beautiful sitting room! Apricot damask wall hangings and tiny fluted tables with pots of mums. And guess what? Mr. Lewis stopped in while Miss Thompson and I were chatting, and he told me a writer should have something to fall back on and that I should run a gas station! He said he'd always wanted to own a little inn, himself, and Miss Thompson interrupted him, and you will not believe what she said: "'Balls!'"

"My, my—she sounds like somebody I'd like."

"You'd love her. I must admit I was slightly nonplussed. Oh, Virginia—I have been with the great and the talented! Miss Thompson said she's going to try and help me. I know it's all going to work out. I know it is."

But it came to nothing. Harriet had left several of her stories with Dorothy Thompson. Two weeks later they were returned in the mail by a secretary, who said that Miss Thompson had left for the Midwest on a lecture tour. In the packet was a short note. "Promising" and "full of life and color" were the compliments for her stories, and Harriet feasted on them until the following week when she went to meet Clyde Marks of the *Herald Tribune*. Dorothy had set it up.

"Let me level with you . . ." he began, and she felt cold all over. The gist of it was the same: Nothing. No jobs open for neophyte, dewy-eyed journalism grads—even if they were pretty, even if they "had a knack" as Dorothy Thompson had told him she had. Why, he could see fifty kids a day if he had the time.

Harriet bit her lip. "Would it make any difference if my name were Harry?" she asked gaily, trying to hide her disappointment. She'd noticed there wasn't a woman in sight when she walked through the city room. Alice, she knew, would have been proud of her for asking the question. "Please," she went on quickly, "I'm good. I *am*. I have ideas. Don't you understand? *I have ideas.* I'll sweep the floor if you'll let me. I've been in New York five months now, and all I do is wait in offices—"

"Go home." The best advice he could give her. Her eyes filled with tears. Go home. She thanked him, got up, and stood momentarily in the doorway of his little cubicle—one of those she'd pictured herself in countless times—while around her the city room buzzed like a narcotic she needed but couldn't seem to get.

"How'd it go today, kid?" asked Virginia, a week later. A hurricane of jet black hair, dark eyes, and red, red mouth, she clacked into Harriet's rented bathroom, mules tapping on the tile floor, to find her friend sitting dejectedly on the edge of the tub, soaking her weary feet.

"Same as yesterday. Same as the day before. I even left a resumé at the *Jewish Daily Forward*." She wiggled her toes in the water. "I've swelled to a size twelve."

"Walk all day?"

Harriet nodded. "I was going to take the subway home. Then I was so hungry I ate a hot dog and blew my transportation budget. I'm discouraged, V. I know I shouldn't be, but I am."

"Harriet," cautioned Virginia, "you're wearing yourself out. Pounding the pavement all day and scribbling all night? *Basta!* Ya need a little help, kid. Right? Till your break comes. Someone like my Benny."

Benny was a married man from Queens who wore alligator shoes and paid Virginia's rent, took her out to dinner, and bought her presents—in return for "favors." Harriet shook her head, smiled ruefully, and sighed. She still hadn't gotten used to Virginia's free-living style. "Maybe I'll just slip slowly into the water. . . . 'Girl Found in Large Tub.' "

"*Andiamo.*" Virginia gave Harriet's arm an affectionate squeeze. "C'mon. You need a pick-me-up."

A shaft of sunlight came through the stained-glass window, casting a purple reflection on the floor. Virginia crossed herself. "Never know whether to pee or pray in this place," she muttered, glad to see a small smile appear on her friend's face. She left, and Harriet trudged upstairs a while later. Virginia was bent naked, searching through the bottom of a clogged armoire for a slip.

Embarrassed by the voluptuous body that strolled about unconcerned, Harriet sat on the day bed. "What if I'd been Mr. Mitchell?" she asked.

Mr. Mitchell lived down the hall and liked to pop in unannounced to see what he could see. One night when Harriet had been up on the roof, he had waddled toward her in a robe that trailed threads, engaged her in conversation, pointed out the sights, lit her cigarette and opened his robe.

"You were in a state of shock for a month!" laughed Virginia, wiggling into her slip like a large pink salmon. "Anyway," she went on, "like I told ya—Mitchell's harmless. Most men are."

"I'm not so sure."

"I always let Mitchell take a peek. Once a week. Some give to the Red Cross. I let Mitchell take a peek."

"Virginia!"

"Just kidding." Virginia loved to tease Harriet, had spotted her right away as a bit of a prig. Perhaps a prig who didn't want to be, but a prig nonetheless. "Hey, wanna go to a party tonight?" Virginia found a couple of glasses and poured gin and ginger ales.

"Too pooped."

"C'mon. Do you good. Cheer you up. First we'll get ourselves in the right frame of mind. . . ."

Let hair down with V. *yesterday* wrote Harriet in her journal later, for as it always seemed to with Virginia, the subject turned to Sex.

"Stan, your favorite actor, will be there tonight," continued Virginia. "You like'm, kid, don'tcha? What's the latest? Hmmmm? Hmmm? Tell Momma."

Harriet shook her head. "Sorry to disappoint you."

She hadn't lacked for dates since her arrival in New York. At first she'd been considered an oddity—the girl with the Massachusetts twang and strange hairdo. But the braids she wore wrapped around her head like a close-fitting cap marked her as one who had no need to knuckle under to current fashion. She had a style of her own, and the men were drawn. Many of them were friends of Virginia's. None of them really absorbed her, but she usually managed to have a good time. She loved to dance, and sometimes they took her to the ballrooms around Times Square where she learned to do a new dance called the rumba. With the unemployed ones, she took the ferry to Staten Island and back, or went to Tompkin's Park and listened to their life stories. They all seemed to want to paw her.

"Stan is nothing but fresh," Harriet went on, sipping the drink, which was cool and tingly. "At least your friend Dave is polite, which is a welcome change."

"Oh, that one! Polite? I was wondering when you'd catch on. He and his roommate are—" Virginia flapped her arms as if flying.

"Angels?"

"*Gawd!*" Virginia practically did everything except jump out the window in glee. "*Limp wristed,* honey. Nice boys, but— I can see we have to educate you." Which she proceeded to do about that particular subject with a few pungent words that left Harriet numb.

"Stan told me you were a cocktease."

"I am not!"

"I know you're not, honey—you're just scared, right? Stan said you invited him up to the bathroom and—"

"He said he had a migraine, so I told him to come up and gave him an aspirin."

"Oh, yeah? I'll bet. Wait! Wait! I know why he got so hot and bothered. You live in a bathroom—right? So when he gets there, he just naturally wants to take his pants down!"

"Really, Virginia . . ."

"Really, Virginia . . ." mimicked the voluptuous one. "It's you cool

52

virgins always give'm the chills," she added, refilling the drinks. Harriet smiled to herself. She enjoyed the way Stan pleaded. She didn't like admitting that to herself and certainly couldn't to Virginia. It didn't seem entirely proper that she should enjoy the feeling of power, but she had to admit she liked having something he wanted, something she could hold back or grant, depending. Which she had no intention of doing. If she hadn't granted it to Harris, who had been the number one boyfriend of her life so far, she certainly wasn't going to with Stan. Judicious heavy-necking—that was as far as she'd chosen to go with Harris. Stan had got less.

"Men!" she spluttered, perplexed with the whole subject and wishing it would go away.

"Lemme at 'em!" cried Virginia. "The more the merrier. Get that chip off your shoulder. Let your guard down! Now listen, kid. . . ." Virginia plopped herself on the day bed and grasped Harriet's arm, all seriousness. "Level with me. Money's gone. Right? No jobs. Right? I don't mean just writing jobs. I mean any kind of jobs. Right?"

"I guess so."

"She guesses so. . . . Now *lissen!* Stan's stuck on ya—right? So if you were a little more friendly—a little less 'Jericho' my dear? Why then the rent would get paid, and the fridge would get stocked, *etcetera.* Ya see what I mean?"

"No to the former, yes to the latter. I mean, yes, I see what you mean. But no."

"Don't get all fancy on me—just 'cause you had a year at college!"

"I don't *love* Stan. And even if I did—I don't want to get married. I don't intend to be . . . infiltrated." She laughed, liking the ring of it.

"My, my. Infiltrated?"

"By men, marriage, and the conventional life."

"Is that *this* week's manifesto? *Jeezus.* I don't wanna get married, either. What's it get you? My mother's nothing but a servant."

"Exactly. Do you think, Miss Virginia Rocco, that it's possible to get married and still be an artist? It wasn't for my mother. She gave it all up. Had four children and no life of her own. And if you love someone, look at the demands they make. And if you're a woman you're expected to—"

"Gawd," moaned Virginia, "is this an *intellectual* discussion? What're you so hot under the collar for? I thought we were gonna get blotto and go to a party!"

"I asked Miss Thompson how she was able to do her work and still be Mr. Lewis's wife. Do you know what she said? 'My name is Dorothy Thompson.' I like that. I really do. *Why* hasn't she got in touch with me again? I wrote her two thank-you notes. I know she's busy and doesn't need her energy drained by little nobodies who— Virginia, what am I going to do?"

53

"You're gonna have another drink and relax, that's what you're gonna do." Concerned with the sudden freshet of anxiety that bubbled up in her friend, Virginia shoved off the bed like a large yacht and, despite Harriet's protest, slopped more gin into her glass. "Lisssen, honey. I'm no home run in the brains department. Not like you. And mosta the time I don't know what makes ya tick, but I know *this*—it's a man's world, and once ya accept that, ya can begin to operate. Woooooo!"

Virginia quivered like a Jello mold. Harriet felt lightheaded, giddy, and daring. "Sex is not for me," she announced from out of nowhere, and somehow that statement set Virginia off again, and the two of them couldn't stop laughing.

"It's 1935, for shit's sake! Aren't ya at least curious? You're nineteen! Now don't get all blushy on me—Mother isn't listening. Whatcha gonna do with it? Ya savin' it for Santa Claus?"

"I love Christmas," cooed Harriet, waxing nostalgic. "We used to leave cocoa out and a plate of plum pudding and—"

"Gawd, ya can take the girl outta Jericho, etcetera."

"Sex," said Harriet again, liking the saying of it. Sex. It was better in Jericho to pretend the subject didn't exist.

"Lemme have that glass. . . ." Virginia reached for it, and they had a tussle. "I don't want any more!" "Yes, ya do!" "No, I don't!" Virginia won, wrenching the glass away, sending liquid flying and the two of them into another cascade of laughter. She wobbled to the kitchen alcove and returned a moment later hugging bottle to breast, a magnificent leer on her face.

"I wanna know. Where'd ya first hear about the ole in 'n out?" She opened her eyes wide in amazement. "My God, maybe ya still don't *know*!"

"Really, Virginia," scoffed Harriet as she attempted to bring a match to her cigarette and missed. "Of course I *know*."

"Tell me!"

The room spun a bit. Harriet willed herself to right it. "Andrea Caswell told us. She came from a very fine family, but she used lipstick and was rumored to have done 'something' for the boys."

"Mercy!"

"She took Libby Stillings and Marcia Pratt and me under the bleachers after field hockey practice in the sixth grade and gave us a rundown on 'you know what.' But the worst part was . . . she said it was dangerous! She said you and a boy could get *stuck* together! And they'd have to throw cold water on you—like dogs!"

"Ooooh," moaned Virginia, holding her sides in laughter.

"I didn't believe any of it. I asked Andrea how come *she* hadn't got stuck but—"

"Ever on the side of logic."

"—I don't remember what she said. Her parting shot was that I should ask Elliot Phelps if he wanted to put his birdie in my nest. I think I knew what she meant, but I decided to test Mother."

"What'd she say?"

"Beat about the bush. It's only in the *Ladies' Home Journal* that mothers and daughters have those little 'talks.' She sent me to Dr. Alden for the facts. I got sick to my stomach . . . and that night . . . yes . . . it was finnan haddie we were having. . . . I hate finnan haddie. . . . Oooo, Virginia I feel so funny. . . ."

The room spun once again. The mood turned wistful. Harriet watched as Virginia rose fuzzily from the floor like a white melon. It was dusk, and she lit a lamp and poured the last of the gin, saying, "I was Wilkes-Barre High's Andrea whatsername."

"Oh."

"What happened to her?"

"Got pregnant in the eleventh grade and had to get married."

Virginia nodded. "But I didn't get married, kid. The old flush-eroo—got rid of it."

Shocked, Harriet didn't know what to say. She would have liked to get up and comfort her friend but was too embarrassed. Virginia shrugged, muttered something, and continued to stare out the window at her past. There was a long silence, which neither of them wanted.

"Yahooo!" Virginia suddenly erupted, turning and doing a shimmy. "You just wait for Santy Claus if you want, Miss Harriet Chastity—yer probably right. You leave him some cocoa and lay yourself down on Christmas Eve by the old fireplace . . . and hope he's got a big dong!"

"Virginia!"

"Bet ya can't say it." Virginia sat beside her again.

"Of course I can say it."

"Say it."

"No."

"You can't."

"*Dong!* There! Dong. Dong. Dong!"

"Ding dong dong," sang Virginia.

"Ding dong ding dong," chorused Harriet, caution thrown to the wind, mother having heart attack in Jericho.

"Who's?"

"What?"

"Who's???"

"Mr. Mitchell's!" blurted Harriet triumphantly.

"What an intro! . . . Aieee hee," shrieked Virginia, "that's not a dong! That's not even a ding! That's not even a fountain pen!"

"Not even a Fudgsicle stick!" shrieked Harriet back. Tears ran down Virginia's cheeks. Toppling off the day bed onto the floor, she rolled back and forth, collecting lint. The room turned upside down, and Harriet passed out.

She made two vows the next day. Not to ever drink gin and ginger ale again, and not to visit with Virginia, who brought out the worst in one and was a general bad influence. Both vows were broken almost immediately.

Two weeks later Harriet's money was all gone. But the Hoskins' luck was with her, and through a friend of Virginia's who knew somebody who was a friend of the manager of the Automat Restaurant on Fourteenth Street, she got a job and considered herself very lucky.

It was the same Automat she and Harris had discovered back in June. Five in the morning until two in the afternoon was her hitch. In the late afternoons she was free to haunt the papers once again, free to write her stories. She enjoyed the Automat the first week—didn't even mind rising at such an ungodly hour and crossing over Fourteenth Street with hardly a soul about in the gray dawn, the city sleeping like a numbed giant.

Across town she hurried in the darkness accompanied by milk trucks and newspaper trucks which passed her as they skidded around corners, barely slowing down as the bundles were thrown to the curb—bundles she was not a part of.

By the third week the fun of the Automat had become the drudgery of the Automat. "Look!" she had cried to Harris back then, delighted and clapping her hands when she first discovered the rows of little windows. You put your nickel in the slot and opened the door and got your darling little pot of beans or tempting cake, and the door shut and—presto—another appeared in the same place. "Elves are back there doing it," she said to Harris, "magical elves. . . ." But now *she* was the elf, and occasionally she caught glimpses of other girls as they put their nickels in. Sometimes she spotted an obviously hungry face staring with penniless eyes at a bran muffin, and she popped the door open herself, watching as the hand reached quickly for the free muffin. *It's me*, she whispered silently, *me back here performing the magic*—except it wasn't magic for her any more, whose dreams were not of pies and beans but of glory at *Vanity Fair*, *The New Yorker* and the *Herald Trib*.

One day she was caught and reprimanded by the manager, who threatened to fire her if she gave anything else away. She promised she wouldn't, but a week later she noticed a fastidious gentleman in a Chesterfield coat, who was sitting at one of the tables and staring at the food with a hunger as strong as his pride. Something about him reminded her of her father, and when she went out to wipe the tables, she furtively set a hot dog down, making up a fib that someone had left it, and it would only go to waste, so why didn't he just have it himself? No thank you, he replied politely. As luck would have it the manager's wife spotted her, reported her, and she was fired. "Go to hell," she told the manager, throwing her gingham cap into a sink full of water as out of the kitchen she walked. The gentleman had disappeared, but the hot dog was still there, so she picked it up and took it home and had it for supper.

A letter from Patrick Flynn to his brother, Dennis, Nov. 10, 1935.

Dear Dennis,

Was glad to get your letter with all the news. Are you really going to run for Board of Selectmen? Was it Ma's idea? Silly question.

Things are about the same here. Hard to believe my Diaconate is seven months away. I've already found out I'm to stay here in Washington afterward. I'll be assigned to assist in a parish somewhere in the city between Diaconate and my Ordination, which is scheduled for next October. It may seem a long way off to you but seems like next week to me. I break into a sweat every time I think about it. It seems to me that a big door is going to shut on me, that Almighty God has made some kind of mistake. I haven't felt as anxious since my days at Villanova. Needless to say—not a word of this to Ma. I wouldn't be writing to you about it, but today I feel down in the proverbial dumps. I ask myself—what do I want? What *I* want, as opposed to you know who. Does this shock you at this late date? Don't worry, I guess my doubts are natural. Next year at this time I'll be settled in. Father Patrick Flynn. O.S.A.—hard to believe.

The weather is cold and rainy. We're practicing "dry Masses" (that's what we call them), sacraments, etc.

Please keep this letter a secret (that's why it's addressed to you at the tax office and not home).

Write me a long letter. It gets lonely here.

> *Ad astra per aspera,*
> Love,
> Patrick

Nov. 18, 1935

Dear Harriet,

I've moved up—got a job working for the Works Progress Administration, which you probably know as the WPA. I'm in the Leveret office dealing with projects here in the city and Merrimack County. All my letters to Washington finally paid off.

Now listen to this—the WPA isn't just building bridges and the like. There's help for writers and artists, too—most specifically, a Writers' Project. I hope you understand how revolutionary this concept is. It's the first time the government has acknowledged that people in the arts need encouragement and employment, too.

You should apply to N.Y. office of WPA (address enclosed), and you may be able to qualify. You'll have to prove you've been a resident for longer than you actually have, but I'm sure with your larcenous nature you'll find a way. If accepted you'll get twenty dollars and change a week, and that should keep you in the style to which you haven't become accustomed.

Your difficulties in finding work just go to prove what I've said all along—unless we fight for our place and make men hear us—women will always be in a number-two position. You always thought the world was your oyster because you were so bright. It's not enough—is it? How I wish sometimes I were a man!

I went to a meeting of the Young Socialists Club in Leveret the other night. Their aims are similar in many ways to what the President is trying to do—they just want to do it faster. I find their ideas stimulating. There are several writers and painters and an actor or two in the club, so you see we're still alive here back home—even though you don't think life exists outside of your precious New York.

Everybody is fine. We're getting ready for Thanksgiving. Did Mother write you about Father's job? He's selling snow shovels! A lumber company in the city is turning them out, and Father's been going out to hardware stores. It won't last long—just a month or two—but he's already talking of getting a secondhand car, and he's *almost* his old self. Cora has gone to Fort Lauderdale for two weeks to take care of the Ragsdale children, so the house is quiet. Mother says it's the first time she's been by herself since all of us were born, and she threatens to get her paints out and do a watercolor or two.

Keep your chin up. Keep your letters coming. We are all looking forward to seeing you at Christmas. Cora, needless to say, has done most of her shopping and has her cards all ready to go. Have to quit now. I'm typing this on the federal government's time.

Love,
Alice

One night in early December Harriet went to a party in Greenwich Village where several musicians brought instruments and played some hot jazz, and she made a note to herself to write to Frankie and tell him all about it. A little cigarette was passed around, and it was very strange how light it made her feel and disembodied, too, which she didn't like at all. A boy she danced with turned out to be a girl, and the girl who did an impromptu strip on the kitchen table turned out to be a boy. So this was the Bohemian life. She wasn't at all sure it was for her. Good for you to know about all this, Virginia told her. Part of your education—and wasn't it all useful stuff for a writer? Harriet had to agree that perhaps it was. It was ultimately this very line of reasoning (among other things) that led to her decision to go all the way with Leonard Jacobs.

Leonard came late to the party because he worked as a "super" at the Metropolitan Opera, earning ten cents a performance for appearing in the crowd scenes. Passionate for opera, he was also working on his first novel and invited Harriet to come to his room in the late afternoon of the next day so he could read some of it to her.

She'd got a temporary Christmas job wrapping packages at Macy's and stopped off every afternoon after work and sipped sherry while he read. It seemed nicely romantic. One night he took her to the Met with him. Backstage found her wide-eyed. *Aida* was the opera that evening, and she was sent down into the bowels of the building to a large dressing room, which quickly became cramped and crowded as fifty women transformed themselves from shop girls, opera buffs and music students into dark-skinned, rag-wearing Ethiopian slaves. They were driven onstage by Leonard and the men who played Egyptian soldiers while the triumphal music swelled around them. (*Got whipped and fell to the floor writhing on the great stage of the Metropolitan last night*, she wrote home.) It was a grand, grand evening.

Leonard's novel was about a wealthy Jewish boy who forfeited his family's money to become a labor agitator in the coal mines of West Virginia. Politically progressive, he used words like oppressed, just like Alice. "The oppressed will have their day," Leonard said, and Harriet hoped that it might mean she would get out of Macy's, which *certainly* was oppressive.

"You and Leonard a hot item?" winked Virginia.

"I'm listening to his novel, that's all."

"Make sure he's got his Red Devils, or you'll be producing a short story of your own."

"I doubt it," she replied dryly.

Leonard was an intellectual. He was eight years older and Jewish, which made him seem exotic and somewhat forbidden. Also, he didn't push her, so she went a little further, allowing him to heavy-neck as she had Harris.

"But I don't feel anything," she complained to Virginia—which wasn't entirely true. She did. Like falling in an elevator when he kissed her. But too much feeling made her wary.

59

"You thinkin' of going over the falls with Shakespeare?"

"Be serious, V." Harriet paced the bathroom, determined that if there was to be a talk about it, it was not going to be like the last one. "I . . . you . . . you mentioned that I was a late bloomer, perhaps, and . . ."

Harriet confessed her fears haltingly. Was she repressed? She was sure she could take it or leave it. What was wrong with her? And if one gritted one's teeth and decided to try it—didn't it, well, hurt?

She felt like an idiot.

"I have a feeling Leonard's the kind of fella who knows what he's doing. Just let nature take its course. Easy as shellin' peas. But like I told you, make sure he's got his—"

"I'm in no mood for levity."

"Don't be so serious. It's supposed to be fun!"

At work she found herself debating. Should she encourage him to go further? If only he tried to force her, then she could tell him to go to hell and that would be that. But he was too well mannered. *It's up to you to let him know. Are you a young woman who allows herself to merely slip into situations, so to speak? No.* It had to be worked out, defined, analyzed—not wishy-washy and spilling over the saucer.

Do you love him? No. Then don't.

But she liked him. A fellow writer. And maybe Virginia was right. It *was* 1935. Didn't she want to be sophisticated? And how could she write about love if— No, it wasn't love. She mustn't kid herself. It was sex. An experiment. Just plain sex. "Just Plain Bill." Just plain Leonard.

A light snow was falling the day she walked down to the Federal Building on Houston Street to apply, along with hundreds of others, for a job on the Writers' Project. Snaking in a long line that transferred itself to folding chairs and then into another line, she was still dithering about Leonard. Cross with herself for her indecisiveness, she finally concluded she might as well do it and have done with it. With a logic that was purely Harriet, she decided it would be easier to get her questions answered with a man she didn't love. Safer, too.

Anyway, it was time.

She invited him for supper on Sunday night, three days away. "And we'll have the whole evening since you don't have to go to the Met and . . ." She wondered if he got the message.

In a whirlwind, she set about preparations, glad she only had a short time, knowing that a longer would make her falter. On Saturday after work, she dashed in and out of the markets on Second Avenue. Sunday evening at six Leonard arrived, irritating her with his promptness. "You look sensational," he said, and she accepted the chocolates. She served him a candlelit dinner next to the tub. "I never had dinner in a bathroom before," he laughed. She poured him some more Chianti and kept up a steady chatter as he ate. Leonard was smitten with the chops, enraptured by the cream sauce, gobbled the tiny rolls. "How did you do it?" he asked. "You don't even have a fridge. Papaya! What a treat!"

It was all nothing, she assured him. Nothing at all. Easy as pie. Why go into the details about the frenzy before his arrival? Why mention the tears when Virginia refused to call him to say the hostess was suddenly taken sick? Why remark on the cost of a papaya in December? Why reveal the fear and anxiety gnawing at her insides?

"I brought the rewrite of my third chapter. Would—?"

"I'd love to. Let me just clear . . ."

They settled down on pillows. As he read she found herself taking furtive peeks at him—each feature causing her added anxiety: the way his brows grew together and the hair on his wrists that crept out from under his shirt cuffs and—

"You seem distracted, Harriet."

"No, no," she replied. *Yes, yes.*

A minute or so later he laid the pages aside and kissed her. "Do I smell of chops?" he asked. She shook her head. She rose to pour more Chianti, but he didn't take any, reminding her that too much vino upset his stomach, so she poured a full tumbler for herself and realized she had to pee.

"Leonard? Would you excuse me for a moment?"

"Where are you going? Oh . . . sure. What a character you are. Only *you* would live in a bathroom."

He went out, and like a dervish she flew about, finding dance music on the radio she'd borrowed from Mrs. Mundy, lighting three small votive candles, and brushing her teeth. She patted at her hair, which was swept up and barretted in a cascade of curls. Her face glowed with the Chianti and the reflection of a fortuitous bunch of bright red paper poppies pinned to the V of her full-length organdy dressing gown. *You've made the decision*, she told herself as she checked the room. *So if he wants to . . . which of course he will . . . then you'll allow it, but it's your decision, so that's very fine, very fine indeedee.* "I love you, Leonard." She tried it on for size. Maybe it *was* true love. "Your turn," she called gaily, opening the door. Leonard grinned and went past her, and she put her hands over her ears so she wouldn't have to hear the toilet flushing.

"Pssst!"

She looked up to find Virginia hanging over the railing.

"Well???"

"Shhhhh!"

"Go to it!"

"Shut *up!*"

61

Virginia disappeared as Leonard opened the door and she went back inside and he took her hand and led her back to the bed and kissed her and put his tongue in her mouth.

Yes, he'd certainly got the message. He inserted his hand past the poppies and inside her top—which she'd let him do once before, but only for the barest minute.

His hand felt warm on her breast, and she didn't mind it too much, so she didn't stop him as she usually did.

Abruptly she sat up. "Leonard?"

"Hmm?"

"Let me have a minute, will you?"

Out he went to the hall again. She removed everything except her slip and panties, blew out the candles—then decided to relight one so he wouldn't stub his toe—and got between the covers. Outside the door Leonard was shadowboxing in the hallway, unable to believe his good fortune.

"Leonard," she called in a voice only ants could hear. "Leonard?" she tried again, a little louder. What if he'd gone? Relief coursed through her. Then the knob turned ever so slowly, and she shut her eyes. She heard clothes rustling, then his belt buckle clinked as it hit the tile, a portent of her doom.

Opening half an eye, she peeked. His naked backside presented itself, a small mat of fine hair above his buttocks, as he bent over fumbling with his wallet. He took out a rubber. Virginia had described the procedure. Then he mumbled something as four more fell out and dropped to the tile like Chiclets—little individually wrapped Chiclets—and she knew she wasn't in love with him.

Still she didn't stop it. The arguments buzzed in her head again as she felt him lie beside her. She talked to herself as he kissed her. This is a mistake, Leonard, is what she should have said, but couldn't bring herself to admit she'd made such a whopper. His hand was under her slip on her skin. "Ohh," she said as his finger went down *there*. She felt humiliated.

"First-time girl?" he whispered in her ear. Then his mouth was on her again and his weight, too. "Relax . . . relax . . ." he said, then his weight was lifted off, and she heard him rummaging around in the kitchen area and didn't dare look. Only a very small part of her was here, anyway, in the unfamiliar candlelight. Most of her had fled. Then she smelled it. Mazola oil. He brought the bottle to the bed and put some on his probing finger. *Am I a salad?* His finger prodded and pushed and entered and shortly was replaced by a more lethal weapon that felt like wood, it was so hard.

"No. . . !" She tried to push him away as the first wave of pain rocketed through her. She gasped and bit her lip and tasted blood. All her concentration went to willing the pain to stop. *Just deserts*, a part of her commented. There was blood now, too, between her legs, her own cold

62

blood, coldbloodedly sticky between her thighs, the blood of her cold-blooded experiment.

So this was what it was. This was what Mother had put up with and— Tears came to her eyes as he murmured sweetmeats in her ear. *Don't call me darling, you stinker*—hating it, hating him, and hating herself, hating being under him, powerless and tiny as he thrust slowly against her and she squeezed her eyes shut and willed herself far, far away, as trains passed through the depot back home and Leonard collapsed on top of her, gasping wildly, and she knew it was over and it wasn't even Christmas and he certainly wasn't Santa Claus.

A week later it *was* Christmas and to punish herself she denied herself the pleasure of her planned trip home.

"You're not going?" asked Virginia incredulously. "But you were looking forward— You haven't been home in a year—"

"I don't want to talk about it."

"Come home with me then. Wilkes-Barre's pretty zilchy, but—"

"No, thank you."

"Harriet. I feel crummy. You blame me, don't you? About Leonard, I mean. Egging you on and—won't you even talk about it? C'mon—"

"I'm on my lunch break. I have to get back."

The next day was the day before Christmas, and she knocked on Virginia's door. Virginia was packing a suitcase.

"I apologize," said Harriet, avoiding her friend's eyes. "It's not your fault. It's my own fault, and I've learned my lesson. I—"

"Oh, kid. I'm sorry." Virginia was stricken at the tears that Harriet fought and then gave in to. "There, kid, tell me . . . there. . . ." She took Harriet to her bosom and stroked her hair. There . . . there . . . kid. . . . Come on home with me, kid. . . ."

Harriet shook her head. She had decided on her punishment and would stick to it. A half hour later she waved goodbye to Virginia. Then she went up to the telegraph office on Fourteenth Street, pushing through the crowds of last-minute shoppers and carols playing and wrote out her message, which was that she had come down with the flu and had a temperature so she wasn't coming.

"Tough luck," said the clerk from behind his tinsel-decked window. "Let's see now, that's fourteen Mulberry Street, Jericho, Mass." Harriet nodded numbly. The preparations would be underway for open house, and the kitchen would smell of plum puddings.

Later she sat in the bathroom in the darkness, as six turned to seven, in growing despair. *What a fool I am. I should've gone.* No, what did she have to tell them anyway? She had no good news to bring them. There was no news at all. Nothing had worked out; the only Christmas present she had was her anger, and that she gave to herself.

63

She heard carols down the hall. "God rest ye merry gentlemen. . . ." And what were they all doing now? Frankie would be playing the piano, Mother, Cora and Alice gathered round, the guests with eggnog mustaches, the tree glittering in the parlor and a candle in every window of the beloved house, right up to the attic. She sat down at her typewriter and began a letter full of hope to Franklin, encouraging him and letting him know how proud she was of him and that she loved him. Then she decided it was all a lie and didn't finish it. *I'll write a short piece about a girl who's alone on Christmas Eve because she's a fool.* Peck . . . peck . . . peck. . . . One lonely finger on the Smith-Corona: *my name is harriet hoskins its christmas 1935 shit*

Determined to be bleak, she started to reread her pile of rejection letters, twenty-two in all.

Harris!

Grabbing her purse she started down the stairs to the phone. What a good idea! Why, if he started right now he could be here in four hours and— No, she couldn't give him the satisfaction of finding out he'd been right. It had turned out to be, as he had said it would, impossible. She had failed.

Sitting down on the landing next to the forlorn little tree that Mrs. Mundy had placed there, she noticed there was already a hint of brown needles. Should she go to a movie? On Christmas Eve?

Pulling her legs up and sinking her head down on her knees, she thought of that first day when Harris had driven her down from Syracuse and she'd seen the skyline from the George Washington Bridge.

New York!

It had been downhill ever since.

Tears plopped silently onto Mrs. Mundy's threadbare carpet. Harriet barely had the energy to get back upstairs. The next morning she could stand it no longer.

"Twenty-five cents, please."

Clang, clang, clang went the coins.

"Hello?"

"Alice!"

"*Harriet!* Why aren't you here? The flu shouldn't stop *you.*"

"Oh, Alice . . . Merry Christmas. . . . It's so good to hear your voice . . ."

"Wait . . . wait . . ."

She could hear Alice calling the others. "It's Harriet!" She heard carols on the Victrola; saw them all opening presents in the front parlor and—

"Alice? Oh, *Alice!*"

"I'm here."

"Alice? I'm so unhappy. Don't tell. I'm so unhappy. Promise me."

"Harriet."

"Promise me. I didn't mean it. I'm fine, really. I am. I don't know what came— *Promise* me."

"I promise. Here's Mother."

"Harriet."

"*Mother*. Mother. Merry Christmas."

"Harriet, what happened? How sick are you? We tried to call you after we got the telegram . . . we couldn't get through. Are you all right?"

"Is it snowing?"

"What happened?"

"I should've come . . ."

"You sound so far away."

"It's the connection, Mother. What are you doing?"

"We're opening presents."

"Oh! I knew you were. I want to be there. Oh, Mother, I miss you so . . . I miss you terribly."

"We miss you . . . wait . . ."

"Harriet? Merry Christmas!"

"Frankie!"

". . . not the same without you here. . . . Here's Cora."

"*Harriet*. I made you a set of yarn potholders for your kitchen area. They're yellow . . . very sturdy. I'll send them . . . Merry Christmas! Harriet—I have a steady!"

"Cora! How wonderful. Who is it?"

"Sam Cousins. He's from Salem. You don't know him. He's a baker. He works over in Leveret at Fazzi's Bakery. He doesn't do rolls or bread, just fancy cakes. I'm so excited. He—"

"SEND HER A LETTER, CORA," they called in unison in the background, and then it was Franklin's turn.

"Hello."

"Father . . ."

"We enjoy your letters."

"Do you? Do you, Father? I miss you."

"It's snowing here. . . ."

"That's what Mother said. It must be beautiful."

"Come home soon. Here's your mother again."

"Harriet?"

"—three minutes please."

"Wait, wait. Mother? Operator? Wait. . . ." Clang went another quarter. "Mother?"

"Ayea. I'm here."

"Oh, Mother . . ."

"Come home, Harriet."

"I can't."

65

"Why not?"

"I can't."

"You sound so far away. You sound so different."

"No, I'm not. I'm not. . . ." Could the Leonard Jacobs' taint be sensed—almost two hundred miles away?

"How do you do it? That job at Macy's sounds awful."

"It's not so bad . . . it's not. . . . It's over now, anyway."

"Come back, Harriet. Come back home."

"I can't, Mother. I can't."

"But why?"

"What would I do there? There's no work for me. At least here there's the possibility. It's tough, but . . . but I know things will get better, I know they will. And I . . ."

"Don't cry, dearest. . . ."

In the background she heard them all: "COME HOME, HARRIET!"

"I'm not sad, Mother. I'm not! I just miss you all. . . . Oh, I'm such a baby— Mother?"

"Ayea?"

"You'll see. One day you'll open the *Saturday Evening Post*, and you'll see me there yet. . . . You'll see. . . ."

"I know I will, I know I will. This is costing you—"

"It doesn't matter. Put everyone on again."

So they all came on, each of them to ask their sister again to come home, each to hear that she would stick it out, that it was all going to work for the best, that she loved New York and felt brave and looked forward to the New Year because it was going to be a grand one, yes it was, and finally she hung up and wept bitter tears and couldn't stop.

4 "Pat—you got my note."

Patrick's counselor, Father Morelli, had sent for him. Patrick found him in the rose garden behind the chapel, bent down between the rows. He should wear a hat, thought Patrick, noticing the pinkness of the ancient priest's bald head, like a large and vulnerable egg, white wisps of hair clinging to it, large, gentle ears drooping.

A smile spread on Father Morelli's frail parchment face as Patrick helped him up. "Not what we were," he said, addressing his legs. "Shall we sit over there?" He motioned to a shaded grotto where a statue of the Virgin looked serenely over the garden.

"Wait—my sprayer, Pat. Would you?" Patrick brought it to him, and with unexpected vigor the old man pumped the handle, producing a mist that enveloped the bush. "The Lord has seen fit to send me an unusually potent horde this spring. Rose bugs, I have to remind myself, must have a purpose, but then again, I wonder—is it possible He made a slight error when He created them?"

They made their way to the grotto and sat. Silent, Patrick stared at the tip of the Washington Monument rising above the campus buildings. Father Morelli casually asked Patrick how he was making out at St. Ambrose's. He had received reports of late-night vigils in the church, of a young man bowed in prayer who was obviously in deep trouble.

"Is Father MacIntire displeased?" asked Patrick.

"No, I shouldn't think so. In fact, he is impressed with your diligence." The old man's eyes laughed. "He has made mention of the honor he feels in having a future cardinal assisting him. . . ."

Patrick blushed at the memory. Gert Flynn had stayed over in Washington after the ceremony of the Diaconate to see him settled at St. Ambrose's, where he would assist until his Ordination. She'd made sure his superior knew he had a Prince of the Church helping him.

"A holy woman, your mother," continued Morelli. "Not unlike my own sainted mother, God rest her soul. Staunch in her faith. The Church has need of such women and their deeds"—a familiar type, all too familiar—"not the least of which is the fact that she produced *you*." The priest reached into the pocket of his cassock and took out a rumpled pack of

67

cigarettes. He lit one with a quavering hand, then held it between thumb and forefinger.

"How is your condition, Patrick? Any better?"

"A bit." Patrick became conscious of the pain. He shifted position knowing it wouldn't help. There it was again, up in his insides, the burning in his entrails that came and went with a life of its own these last weeks.

"You're going to the doctor?"

"Not since, Father. I can't. . . . It's too . . ." He shook his head.

"I understand, Pat. Not the most cheery undertaking, is it? But if it makes the condition better?"

"I'll go back then, Father. I'll try." On the first day, ashamed and embarrassed, he'd described the symptoms. Did he feel the need to urinate more often than usual, asked the doctor? Patrick nodded. Then the examination. Naked with only his dark stockings for protection.

Bend over, my son. A cold finger prodding. No colder however than the sweat that broke out over Patrick's terrified body as the burning worsened, the humiliation unbearable.

Unusual, mused the doctor after the examination. Unusual in one so young. An "occupational malady," so to speak, the doctor continued, trying to lighten the young man's burden. Common in older priests. The prostate gland acting up and—

Was it a bad joke? A part of Patrick wanted to laugh wildly. "Priest's prostate"—he'd heard the phrase bandied about. An enlargement of that gland, the doctor explained, had occurred, having to do with celibacy and the lack of use of his reproductive organs, causing the burning sensation; a burning, boggy prostate, which could be helped with massage and hot tubs, nothing to be overly concerned about, more of a nuisance than anything else, might clear up of its own accord, God was merciful. . . .

"Enjoying the baptisms?" asked Father Morelli. Patrick nodded. "I haven't dropped one," he said softly, eyes drawn to a hole in the toe of the sock of Father Morelli's sandaled foot. A bird called behind the two men. Morelli gazed at Patrick. He did not look well. The old man sighed and brushed ashes from his lap. The months between Diaconate and Ordination were ordinarily a time of intense joy. "Patrick . . . ?" Father Morelli patted him gently on the arm. "Let's talk, shall we?"

Patrick stared at the roses. "It's so unfair," he whispered. "It's so unfair."

The priest wasn't surprised. Patrick's struggle was as old as the Church itself. How many years had he gone through it himself? A certain day, and one realized it didn't matter any longer. The sexual urge was gone, only a memory.

"It's not simply a question of celibacy, Patrick. But of the life-force itself. It cannot be stilled, no matter how much we would wish it. Like an

68

underground river it runs, bursting forth one day with a fury, terrifying us with its power and urgency. It forces us to our knees and leaves us shaken. It is life, Patrick. It is life itself."

"Is this my reward?" asked Patrick bitterly. "All those years. . . ?" Patrick excused himself and walked forlornly away. How could he tell the old man what it was like now? That he was two people. That lust was in his heart and revenge in his thoughts, that he walked the streets before vespers deliberately looking at them, the girls, the women, smelling and tasting them on his lips, stiffening as their white skirts caught breezes—Catholic girls who lowered their lashes, murmuring respectful phrases; others who were more brazen, who caught something in his look and mocked him with their dresses rustling as they passed. Long-haired women with barrettes, short-haired; elbows and the flash of knees, ankles, eyes under hats, undressing them on trolleys.

"A good lookin' boy," his mother's cronies in the Ancient Order of Hibernians used to comment. "Beautiful man," murmured the middle-aged ladies on the steps after Mass in Washington. It wasn't just his good looks that inspired the admiring glances. It was his vocation. A beautiful man was a man who had given himself to God. "You're a temptation, Father," laughed a girl who stopped him on the street to ask directions to the Smithsonian. "I'm a deacon," he corrected her. "You're still a temptation," she replied and hurried off, leaving him blushing violently. It was *she* who was the temptation. No longer a beautiful man, he hurried back to his room in the rectory to give in, barely having to grasp himself before the explosion.

Then later, there was the other Patrick, who prayed in an agony of guilt in the quiet church, knowing he was an imposter, while the fever raged in him, sent by the devil, the fires of Hell, damning him for all eternity.

He stopped going to confession. He fell ill with the flu and was sent to the infirmary. His old roommate, Mike Swift, came to visit him one day. Large and amiable and possessed of a wondrous calm, Mike tried to cheer Patrick up.

"Pat, lad, tell your old uncle what's wrong."

"Just a cold."

"I've been assigned to St. Michael's up in Nyack. Ladies of the Sodality—here comes Mike."

"Congratulations."

"You'll be back at St. Ambrose's in a jiff."

Often he'd shared a laugh with Mike during the past year and a half. Now Patrick averted his eyes and was glad when Mike left. Father Morelli visited him, breaking the news that another deacon had been assigned to take over his duties at St. Ambrose's. He was too sick at heart to care. It was July, two months before his Ordination now, and he received a letter from

Gert with the plans for an enormous party in Jericho and the date set on the parish calendar for his first Mass at St. Mary's. He was released from the infirmary and assigned a room back in one of the dormitories. Every day he went to see Father Morelli, usually in the rose garden, unless it was raining.

"What does Thomas Aquinas teach us?" asked the old man. "Three things are necessary for the salvation of man: to know what he ought to believe, to know what he ought to desire, to know what he ought to do." And the next day he said, "It is not the devil who tempts you. It isn't the women, either. Perhaps *He* is tempting you, Patrick. Are you not willing to accept that in His infinite wisdom God may have another plan for you? Is it not possible that it is life that calls to you? And He is making it clear to you now? Do not attempt to fight Him, Patrick. Think about what I have suggested. Pray to Him. He will not fail you. God loves you, Patrick, no matter that you doubt it now. God loves you."

"I want to serve Him, Father. It's all I know. I love God." Guilt ambushed him at every turn, and there was no refuge. The Church had been his comfort, the Church with its calming certainties, while a storm called life brewed outside. But there had been no safety for him for years now, only growing anxiety that he'd tried to stifle. He hadn't been able to mold himself as the others had, had chafed under the unquestioning obedience, had grown unbearably lonely. God had always filled the void, but Patrick didn't know who He was any more and the loss devastated him.

"Are you so full of pride that you think you can serve God only by entering His service? Millions wake up every morning and thank Him and in that very act they serve Him well. And you—you who've been blessed with the years given to Him already—are you not one of the fortunates? You are already in His grace. Let's walk for a spell, shall we? You've done nothing to be ashamed of, Patrick. For you there is no defeat. I know you don't believe me. Ask Him, Patrick."

But he received no answer. Burdened with failure, Patrick spent his days mostly by himself. He didn't keep his appointments. He stopped seeing Father Morelli. He refused to return to the doctor. Time was running out and he knew it. One night he sat at his window reading his breviary and looked out across the campus and began to cry. He was surprised, for long ago he'd disciplined himself not to give in to such displays. Leaving the dorm, he began to walk. Long walks had always been a tonic. What was it he'd wanted? he asked himself, as he methodically reviewed his life. A dream of perfection with his Saviour, perfection within himself and the Church. And there had been years when he felt he'd achieved it, until reality knocked on his door. How he'd struggled! Refused to open it, resisted mightily, until the door burst open and he had no choice. Or was he using his sexual urgings as an easy excuse?

On he walked, the debate raging in his head, the questions and self-examination continuing. All the arrows pointed. If salvation was the issue, then he must leave and save himself. This life wasn't for him. He only vaguely understood why. The world outside was as terrifying as it was tantalizing, but if he didn't taste it he would wither on the vine and die.

A rage grew in him, propelling Patrick's feet, and he began to run, galloping past the gray government buildings, trampling his mother and all those who had forced him to live a life that wasn't his. Not true, not true, cautioned a voice. It was you who wanted it too, you bear the responsibility, you sorry suffering bastard, *run*!

That night he wrote his letter of resignation. Addressed to the Superior General of the Augustinian Order in Rome, he requested that Reverend Mr. Patrick Flynn be granted a dispensation from his solemn vows. At two A.M. he slipped the letter under the door of the provincial's office, and eight hours later Monsignor Flaharty called him in. Patrick's request was accepted with a cold face. His superiors had recognized for some time that here was a sheep who must be cut from the flock. The dispensation would be granted, the Monsignor informed Patrick. The formality of Rome's reply would take, however, three months or so. During that time, if he wished to be, he was still subject to his vows and to his breviary, one hour a day. He was free to go. Patrick knelt to kiss his superior's ring. Monsignor Flaharty withheld his hand and turned away.

Thus it ended. Three lines on a piece of paper and twelve years of his life came to an end. Patrick wasn't counting. Shame beat at him as he walked back across the campus avoiding friends whom he knew he couldn't tell. It was too shocking. He packed a few of his many books and left the rest along with two cassocks, two dark suits in the closet and five clean, starched collars in the bureau drawer. Wearing newly purchased Sears, Roebuck slacks and sport shirt, he left the dorm quickly and found Father Morelli dozing in the garden under the Virgin's outstretched arms. The old man's watery eyes blinked open as Patrick knelt beside him.

"May I have your blessing, Father?"

He felt the hand upon his head. They said a Hail Mary together. The frail arms enveloped him.

"It will be difficult, Patrick. Don't be afraid. You've shown great courage. I will pray for you daily. Write me. . . . You're a good lad. A very good lad."

Patrick walked out through the campus gates, past the high walls clinging with ivy slightly wilted in the noonday sun. He saw and heard nothing. He walked the blocks to the railroad station through crowds of summer-suited government workers filling the streets. No one paid much attention to the expressionless young man carrying a canvas bag. There was no thunder, no pelting rain to sting him, no icy blast. It was an ordinary hot, late August day in the city of Washington.

His pokey Saturday train pulled into the Jericho depot the next afternoon, and Patrick stepped down and glanced about furtively. Squinting in the sunlight, he shifted his balance and breathed. Hesitancy was inhaled, hesitancy was exhaled. Hesitancy emanated from him like waves of heat rising from hot tar. His blue eyes, which in milder light and on gray days gave off a brilliant incandescence that was sometimes startling, were now washed out and almost colorless as they swept involuntarily over the roofs of Jerusalem, drawn like a magnet to the steeple of St. Mary's. Ma would be in the rectory fixing dinner for Father Gahaghan. But she might not have gone over yet. She might still be at home, right across the street from the church. In either case she'd be unprepared for his arrival, unprepared for the blow he was about to strike her.

"Hey, Pat! Pat Flynn! *Hey!*" Patrick resisted an impulse to duck and run. "Over here!" It was his old friend Jerry Finneran, who slid out from under a truck at Morin's Garage.

"Son of a gun. . . !" The two friends met in the middle of the street. A big muscular fellow with an easy grin, Jerry wiped his hands on his overalls and shook Patrick's hand. "How long's it been, Pat? Son of a gun!"

Jerry talked a mile a minute. Patrick responded with nods and a word here and there. "Ya home to see your ma? I was up there only yesterday— deliverin' some ice. Saw your sister Rose, too. She's a looker, ain't she? Anyways, I see your ma at Mass all the time, ya know, and I ask about ya, so yesterday she invited me in and showed me your picture. Same one that was in the *Eagle* a while back—you in your robes 'n all."

"That was my Diaconate." Jerry looked perplexed. "I was made a deacon," explained Patrick, noticing Jerry glance at his civilian clothes.

"So when's the great day? Pretty soon, ain't it? Your ma—"

"Soon." Patrick cut him off. Everyone would know soon enough, and he had only a certain amount of strength today. It would have to be saved for her.

"Takes a long time, I guess, to become a priest. Boy, they don't let you guys out much, do they? Say, Pat, why don't I give ya a lift? Ya look tired. I'm takin' some tires up your way, so . . ."

A few minutes later, passing Phelps Mill, they started up Main Street. Patrick was grateful for the seclusion of the truck.

"Remember?" asked Jerry, cocking his head at the Winthrope Grammar School. "Remember the old Winthrope Nine? Sixth grade? You were a helluva hitter, Pat. D'ya get to play ball at the seminary?"

"I used to."

"Look the same to ya?"

"Sure."

"Sure. Nothin' changes in Jericho. Say, Pat, your ma mention my kids?"

"Congratulations." He couldn't remember.

"Yeah. Jerry, Jr., and Deirdre 'n another in the oven."

"How's Deedee?" Deirdre, Deirdre Moynihan. Pigtails and a note passed hand to hand in sixth grade under the desks: *I love you Patrick Flynn.*

Jerry shifted down, and Patrick saw they were at Essex Street. He looked up the incline and could see it, the fifth house up the block. Fear welled up in him again. He heard Jerry say something, but the words came from far away, muffled by the noise of the engine and the ragged beating of his heart. "Take me back," he said hastily, hoping Jerry wouldn't notice his panic, "—would you? I want to say hello to my Aunt Teresa."

Jerry nodded and put the truck into a U-turn and went back down the street for about a block. Patrick looked across to his aunt's beauty shop. Teresa would understand. No, he corrected himself—none of them would understand, but Teresa at least would be able to forgive him.

"I still live with my folks," Jerry was saying, "so stop by if you get a chance. Deedee'll be tickled to see ya."

They shook hands. To be like you, thought Patrick, to start over again, regular and uncomplicated. Hurriedly he crossed the street, looking neither left nor right. He could see ladies through the windows of his aunt's shop, so he ducked around to the rear and waited, hunched down in a shadowed place. A finger probed at a scabbed cold sore on his lower lip, causing a bright dot of red to appear. The lilt of Teresa's voice carried out to him. She was his mother's younger sister, and of his three aunts she had always been his favorite.

After a while he became aware of silence from within the shop, so he went around to the front, checking first, then entered.

"*Patrick!* What a surprise, dear. What—?" Teresa stared at his clothes.

"I've left."

"Left?"

"I'm through with it. I've left C.U. I've left Washington. I'm not going back."

Barely comprehending, Teresa raised a hand nervously to her face, toying with her glasses, then patting her hair. "Forgive me," she said after a moment and asked her nephew to repeat it. She blinked in dismay and locked the door and pulled down the blinds.

"Does she know?"

Patrick shook his head.

"Holy Mother of God. Saint Michael protect us. . . ." Teresa crossed herself and sank into a chair.

"I just got off the train. I came here first—"

"Give me a moment, dear. I'll compose myself and— It's just that it's such a shock. Patrick, are you in trouble? Is there—?"

73

"I'm in no trouble."

Teresa waited for more. Patrick offered nothing other than a muttered, "It wasn't for me, that's all." Teresa stared nervously at him. What had happened? Why would he leave now? After all those years, preparing. Why, now—less than two months before his Ordination? Why, he was practically a priest!

"What's on your lip, dear? You look so pale. Here, sit now." She swiveled one of the barber-type chairs. Terrible did not even begin to describe how he looked. "I have something for it," she said, and disappeared into the back, thoughts racing.

All those rites and ceremonies over the years and she'd been to all of them. He was her godson, after all. At his Diaconate only a few months back when all of them had gone down to Washington, nothing seemed out of the ordinary. He'd been as he always was. No sign of anything. It couldn't be true. Not sweet, darlin' Patrick, who'd never done anything to upset anyone, the soul of mildness and agreeability, who'd never rocked the boat. What had happened? Gert was going to have a fit! That was putting it mildly. Why, all of them were scheduled to be going back to the cathedral again to see Pat receive the fullness. All the relatives from both sides and—

Teresa took a breath and placed a hand on her ample bosom to check her heart, beating wildly now. His first Mass! "Blessed Saint Michael protect us," she muttered, barely able to contain her anxiety. It was already on the parish calendar! The glorious day he'd be saying his first Mass at St. Mary's, the invitations already being sent out, a celebration for two hundred afterward in the parish hall and— *It'll kill her!* Gert would have a heart attack.

"Coming dear," she called to Patrick as she found the tincture she was looking for. Her head swam. It would all have to be cancelled! The scandal!

"Here we are . . . and look what else I've found us. . . ." She set down a bottle of whiskey and then dabbed the tincture on his lip. "This'll sting. I remember you were always getting these on your lip, weren't you now? There, the worst of it's over."

"No, it's not," he mumbled.

"I see what you mean." She poured them a couple of shots. "Now what shall we do?"

"Turn on the juice," he replied with a wry grin, eyeing the permanent wave machine above him, a monstrous contraption with little electric wires hanging down.

"We'll come up with something."

"I better just go tell her."

"First of all and forgive my asking, but there isn't the chance—"

He shook his head. "No. It's done with."

"I'll come with you then."

"She'll lay the blame on you, too."

"Neveryoumind, dear. I can handle Gert. We'll get you cleaned up a bit. You do look a bit of a ruffian. I'll give you a shave. . . ." She downed her whiskey and caught his expression. "Ohhh," she laughed, high and tinkly, like fine china, "don't worry dear. I'm very expert. When Mr. Petrarca had his gallstones, some of his gentlemen came over to me, and I still have them as customers."

"I bet you do."

"Be gone with ya now." She blushed and turned on the taps until there was a good head of steam, and whipped up a lather.

"If you don't mind," he said, holding out his glass. Teresa nodded and poured him another. Already he was woozy from the first, for he wasn't at all used to drinking. "Thanks, Teresa," he said, not just for the whiskey.

"Give us a kiss." She offered her cheek, and he brought his lips there, feeling the coolness of her lovely skin, moist and clean like foggy mornings on Galway Bay. "You look good, Teresa."

"Do I, dear?" Pleased, she pulled her stomach in and moved to the sink on nimble feet. The wonder was those delicate ankles and pretty legs supporting her corpulent superstructure. Round hips and rear were tightly corseted, exploding above in the magnificent overhang of her bosom; she almost seemed to tilt. "The weight, you know," she tinkled. "Always a problem." Like a pro she laid the lather on his face.

"Is your hair redder?"

"We help it along, don't we now? We've even got your ma helping herself a bit with the color lately. Course she screamed and hollered when I was suggesting it. Now, she overdoes a wee. . . . You'll see."

"How's Uncle Matt?"

"Busy as ever, thank the Lord. He's partners with his brother now down at the body shop. I think I wrote you. . . ."

"Dennis isn't going to run for the board of selectmen?" Not that he was too interested in his brother's career at the moment. Playing for time and stalling was more like it. One ear listening to Teresa, who seemed to know what everyone was thinking before *they* did. There wasn't much in Jericho that escaped her.

"Wiser heads prevailed, I'm glad to say. There was an opening. Old man Hanigan passed on, and they usually give one spot to an Irishman, so naturally your ma wanted Denny to have a run for it. But he wouldn't have had a chance. Well, you know how your brother is. Now she's beating the beginning drums for Congress in two years. McGinty's retiring, and she's already got her eye on his seat for your brother, but. . . ."

75

"He's still with Tom at the tax office?"

"Oh, yes." Poor Dennis. Another who'd been browbeaten by Gert, the sad soul. "I suppose you know all about Rose and poor Timothy?"

" 'Poor' Timothy?"

"That's what I call him, dear. Timothy O'Brien. Your mother's in her usual tizzy. What with Timothy's father running for vice-president, she's got visions of Rose marrying in the White House, you know. Don't move now, there we are. . . . I know, I know—it's cockeyed, but you know how she dreams. Poor Timothy's not popped the question yet."

"How's Rose holding up?"

"Waiting like the rest." Teresa sighed. No love lost for the Beauty. "Yes, Rose is the same as when you last saw her. The men all look like they want her for their dinner. But she and your ma have their hearts set for Poor Timothy. No, Rose doesn't change, does she? Keeps right to her course. Never misses a penny, if there's one to find. She'll end up owning all of us. I suppose I'm being hard on her. No, Rose never changes . . . except for the worse." She gave him a wink and a wicked grin. "Settle back now . . . close your eyes and relax. We'll be finished in a jiffy."

Scrape, scrape, scrape went the razor. "Now we all know," continued Teresa, "that Timothy O'Brien's father hasn't much of a chance in the coming election. O'Brien's running with that Lemke fellow, and they're in cahoots with Father Coughlin, who we listen to every week on the radio . . . but I don't think Roosevelt, God bless'm, is worried about Michael O'Brien and the Union Party. Still, there's many who're listening. Gert'll be supporting O'Brien, don't you know. She'll be deserting the Democrats this election. Well, I can understand—what with O'Brien's son courting Rose . . . and the financial aspects, which I don't mind telling you would have anybody's mouth watering freely. What everybody's asking is: why's it taking Timothy so long to pop the question? The answer is: his father don't want his son marrying Rose."

Patrick had fallen asleep. A rush of tenderness welled in Teresa, and she touched her fingers gently to his cheek. What a hornets' nest he was walking into! God love him, she didn't want him hurt.

"Oh . . ." Patrick opened his eyes, forgetting, then remembering.

"Would you like to wash up, dear?"

He took off his shirt and undershirt, revealing a white and nicely proportioned torso, strong chest and arms, and broad shoulders, too—all of which came under Teresa's admiring eye. "A hundred percent better," she complimented, after he'd brushed his hair and splashed after-shave on.

"I better get going. . . ." His heart started to beat faster.

"I have a plan, dear. You'll telephone up to the house. Rose and your pa are there. Let them handle her first."

"That's being a coward."

"If you were a coward, dear, I don't think you'd be here today."

76

It wasn't true. He'd always been a coward. "What's the number? I forgot." He swallowed some more whiskey and picked up the receiver with sweating fingers. "Just break it easy," cautioned Teresa. "Say that you're home and have something important . . . but wanted to let her . . . and . . ."

Teresa's words of advice were blotted out by the immediacy of Gert's voice.

"Hello?"

"Ma?"

"Pat???"

Say it quickly or never be able to say it at all.

"I've quit."

Patrick and Teresa hurried out of the shop. Patrick had heard the phone clatter to the floor, then a thud, then silence.

"Don't worry," called Teresa, running after him. "She's fainted, that's all. You know she can produce a faint at the drop of a hat."

Patrick kept running. It's true she was a good fainter. Only one of the weapons in her arsenal. Still, what she'd just heard was probably the worst thing that happened to her since his brother Terrence's death, sixteen years ago.

"Patrick . . . !" Dennis Flynn came out of Noonan's Drugs with a container of ice cream in his hand. He couldn't believe his eyes. There was his brother, in civilian clothes, turning the corner of Essex and running up toward the house with Teresa struggling to catch up.

"Teresa . . . !"

Dennis ran across the street to his aunt. "Your brother's left the Church—" she began, trying to get her breath and fill him in. "He just called your mother—"

"Holy Mother of God!" Dennis went the same color as his tropical suit. "Holy Mother of God," he said again, then began running himself, calling after Patrick, who was now almost halfway up the block.

"Dennis, wait!" cried Teresa, starting up again herself, the three of them now running up the incline of Essex Street as Gert Flynn, daughter of the Houlihans, warriors to the Black Gradys, strode out upon her open front porch (trailed by supporting players, husband Joe and daughter Rose), her appearance causing the runners to stop dead in their tracks, speechless and indeed rapt.

So powerful was her presence, so full of a radiating energy, that those watching in fear and wonder at this moment would have to concur that what Gert had always hinted at might indeed be the truth—that she *was* privy to the machinations of the Almighty, that He (no God of love, but of terror and vengeance) had sent her down as His avenging angel, this piano-legged, large-boned woman of the rouged cheeks and frizzy hair, to

77

announce to a perverse mankind that Armageddon was come to Essex Street on a warmish Saturday afternoon at close to five.

"Hi, Ma. . . ." Who had croaked those two words? Patrick's knees were jelly; the liquor rushed at him, too. Gert's hands rose slowly to rest upon mighty hips. Piercing through rimless steel spectacles, cold gray eyes looked down at the prodigal returned, unloved. Patrick couldn't speak and wanted to run. But where? Not to the church behind him across the lawn, nor to the red brick rectory, either, where Father Gahaghan sat in his parlor, sipping a Manhattan cocktail and musing on a parochial school for the parish, little dreaming that the pride of St. Mary's was out there on the street in sportshirt and slacks.

Caught between Mother Church and Mother, Patrick hung his head. Teresa inched up to Dennis, and the two of them crept slowly closer to the arena. Maintaining the awful silence, Gert said nothing while Patrick picked at his lip and drew blood again.

"Hello, Pat . . ." It was Joe Flynn who spoke, assuring himself a place in heaven. Eyes never leaving Patrick, Gert turned her head slightly toward her husband, the threat made all the stronger by the smallness of the movement.

"Now, Gertie . . ." Joe cautioned in a placating tone.

"What'd he say?" whispered Teresa to Dennis. Stirred by Joe's courage and the five o'clock whistle from Phelps Mill, the two of them inched closer, partially concealed by a tree trunk. "Look at her!" muttered Teresa. "Giving him the third degree like that!"

Dennis pursed his lips at his aunt, not approving her comment. He removed his Panama hat, revealing a thinning hairline, and fanned his face.

"He's going to catch it." His eyes flicked nervously from his mother to his brother and back again. As always, he couldn't decide where advantage lay. Whatever admiration he might have for Patrick's courageous act of rebellion was tempered by the knowledge that *he* would never have such courage. Jealousy stabbed at his stomach, but he took pleasure in the knowledge that favorite Patrick, to whom he'd always been unfavorably compared, was going to get the shit kicked out of him. Was going to be subjected to what *he'd* put up with all these years.

"What's she think she's going to accomplish?" whispered Teresa.

"She's a saint," replied Dennis, moving closer so as not to miss the fireworks. How he hated her! How he worshipped her!

"Is your ulcer acting up, dear?" Teresa noticed his hand on his stomach. He ignored the question.

"Do you think I'd ever do such a thing to Ma?" he said loudly, hoping Gert would hear. "Would I? What are people going to think?"

Teresa held her tongue. But she couldn't help her satisfaction at the sight of a drop of chocolate ice cream that escaped the carton and dripped

78

upon her nephew's white suit, dribbling slowly down. *No*, she admonished herself, *be charitable.*

"The ice cream, Denny . . ."

"Oooooo." He dabbed hastily with his handkerchief, making it worse.

Had only minutes passed? Rose stepped forward on the porch, absolutely mortified. *"Do* something, Mother," she demanded, in that haughty and pouty way she had. She glanced her pretty head up and down the street hoping that Timothy O'Brien wouldn't arrive to witness this spectacle, hoping, too, that the neighbors weren't watching. Fat chance. The porches were filling up.

"Mother!" insisted Rose.

"Get inside," snapped the titan, finally breaking her silence. Rose disappeared in a huff, slamming the screen door.

"Now then, Gertie—"

"You, too." Followed by Joe.

"I brought ice cream, Ma," called Dennis, holding aloft the dripping carton like a rite of passage.

"Go back where ya come from."

"But, Ma—"

"Ya heard me."

"It's melting." Dennis retreated a few steps and hid behind another tree.

"All right now, Gert. . . ." Teresa stepped bravely forward to stand with her godson.

Gert's eyes narrowed. "You're on my property, Teresa Burke. You'll kindly get off it." The brogue thick, like stew.

"I hear you, Gert. You don't scare me a'tall."

"Had no children of your own," snapped Gert, striking a low blow, "so don't be interferin' with mine."

Wounded, Teresa held her ground. "Are you going to have the decency to say hello to your son and see what he has to say? Or shall I take him home with *me?"*

That did it. Pain, terrible pain, rose up in Gert, welled up, could not be held back. A tremor shook the sturdy legs, the strong jaw working, as the beginnings of a sound—primitive and dark from the ancient bogs—emerged, now rising, building to a terrible wail, a high, keening lament for a dream shattered.

"Ooooiaieeeee . . ."

"Saint Michael protect us," cried Teresa. She rushed up to give comfort, aided by Rose and Joe, who reappeared, joined by Dennis, who streaked from his hiding place, taking the front steps in a great hypocritical leap, to clasp his sobbing mother in his arms.

Almighty God have mercy on me. Head bowed, Patrick reached down for his bag and started off.

"Patrick!" Gert cried, as if to a love long gone. Knowing it wasn't finished, not by a long shot, Patrick turned to witness the final tableau, a frieze worthy of Michelangelo, as Gert finally succumbed, sinking, swooning into Joe's strong arms in the second dead faint of the day so far.

Twenty minutes later, Patrick sat alone in the gloomy living room of the house on Essex Street. He was not unaware of the irony of his surroundings. He had left the Augustinians, only to return to his mother's house—a squat, dark-brown box that parishioners had long since got into the habit of calling "the annex," meaning that it was an extension of St. Mary's Church and rectory across the street.

Gert liked the name, basked in it. Years back, when a crushed gravel pathway had been cut across the broad expanse of church lawn, she had hinted to the innocent that it had been installed especially for her. It hadn't been—but who could argue with Gert's logic when she told it the way she wanted to tell it? The pathway started directly opposite her front steps, didn't it? And led to the side door of the church, with a branch to the rectory, wasn't that so? And wasn't she the cook and housekeeper to Father Gahaghan (practically runnin' the parish, too, if you wanted to know the truth) and, therefore, wasn't it fittin' that an expensive chipped granite walkway, flanked by two circles of zinnias, no less, be created to facilitate her goin' and her comin', making life a wee easier for herself, who saw to the sainted Father's every need?

Patrick's listless eyes took in the front room, whose atmosphere now seemed to stifle and close in on him. It was all too familiar. Like any number of rectory parlors, all of them dark and shrouded, as if a priest's business needed somberness and shadow.

He didn't recognize the heavy-footed overstuffed sofa on which he sat, nor the matching chairs. Gert had had them recovered. No matter, the effect was the same—heavy and oppressive. Rectory chairs. Catholic rooms. Rectory rooms, reception rooms at the seminary, meeting rooms at the university—all the same, all known to him. Dark beige walls like babyshit and darker wainscoting, framed religious prints, the crucifix, the Pope, the coffee table with neat copies of the *Catholic Messenger*, *Missions of the Sacred Heart*, the diocesan newsletter, the statue of the Virgin in the corner, the fringed parchment shades and the doilies, always the doilies, protecting the upholstery from flesh. He had spent his life in such rooms.

A murmur of voices caused him to rise, and he went to the doorway and looked down the long, dark tunnel of the hall to the rear. Dennis had insisted the doctor be called to check Gert's blood pressure. Patrick turned back into the room, eyes traveling to the framed photographs displayed on the top of the radio console, placed to catch a visitor's eye.

There was his parents' wedding portrait, and one of his older brother Terrence, who'd choked to death at twelve. The three largest photos were of Dennis, Rose and himself—Gert's own holy trinity of Politics, Money and the Church. Dennis at a clambake shaking hands with old Congressman McGinty, whose seat Gert (standing alongside with corsage and big grin) wanted for her son. Rose on Timothy O'Brien's arm. The picture, snapped at a posh reception for the famous radio priest, Father Coughlin, the previous spring had appeared in the Catholic newspaper, the *Pilot*. It had been taken a week after Rose's graduation from Finchley.

Finchley was a two-year charm school in Boston that masqueraded as a junior college. Gert had sent Rose to have the edges of her sometimes waspish personality sanded down, to acquire breeding to go with the body she already had. ("Finchley failed," Teresa was wont to say, for all Rose got was a phony Boston society accent and her nose a little higher in the air.) Gorgeous Rose, smiling at the camera, exuding heat and ice at the same time, her special combination. Patrick looked closely at Timothy, who fit Teresa's description to a *T*. Raisin eyes peered out from the doughy face of the heir to a sizable chunk of the Massachusetts Street Railway Company.

Patrick resisted the impulse to turn his own photo face down. It was the largest of all of them, and in color. He picked up the fourteen-karat gold frame. There he was. Dressed in his white vestments on the day of his Diaconate, only a few months ago. Looking so peaceful you'd swear it was true. What was he doing here? Why not just go? Why not just—

"She wants to see you. . . ." Joe Flynn interrupted his son's panic. "After the doctor leaves," Joe added, hesitating in the archway that separated the dining from the living room.

"How is she?"

"What?" Joe cocked his head. "I didn't hear you, Pat." Patrick repeated the question louder. "She's all right," replied Joe. "You know your ma. You want company?"

"Sure, Pa. Sit down."

"What?"

"*Sit down!* Should you get a hearing aid, Pa?"

"Now what would I want it for?" Joe grinned, a twinkle in his eye. Teresa was right when she told a friend that Joe Flynn was going deaf so he wouldn't have to hear his wife and daughter.

A big man who'd grown quiet with the years, Joe sat cautiously—as if Gert might come in at any moment and tell him not to muss things. "We could light a lamp if you like," he said after a minute, but neither of them did. As always, Patrick was struck by his father's gentleness. "Why don't you trim those maples out front, Pa?" he asked loudly. "You'd have some sun in here."

"She wouldn't have it," was the reply, and Patrick had to look away as an impulse to shout and shake his father overtook him. Even if Joe was the only sane one in the family, his father had never taken a stand, never argued, never fought back with Gert.

81

"I guess she wouldn't," mumbled Patrick, guilty at his anger, admonishing himself for the sin he'd committed: lack of charity toward his father. Joe's big hands caught his attention. When he was little, he used to watch his father scrubbing those hands and arms in a tub outside the back door, never completely getting the color off, stained sepia to the elbows from his years in the dye room at the mill. On his clothes, too—undershirts and workpants splattered with color, the acrid smell of the wool clinging to him. In the back yard at four-thirty every day, Patrick watched and handed his father the Fels Naptha soap that smelled like cheese, so Joe'd be allowed in to supper and she wouldn't complain of the stink. "Let me see your hands, Pa," he'd ask, fascinated by the color etched in the lines, like ink drawings, like a road map. Then many years later he'd noticed the lines were gone, worn from his father's fingers, and palms too, worn smooth by twenty years of handling the rough wool. No lines left for the stain to seep into, gone, free of identification and markings, hands smooth as flat stones.

Had Ma done that? he'd asked himself. Was her power so great that she could remove the lines from his father's hands? He knew it was the wool, but still—

The memory caused a sudden tightening. You know how strong she is. She can make you go back. No, she can't. She can make you. *Sweet Jesus, give me the strength.*

"Red Stockings beat Dracut last week in the play-offs."

"Did they?" Patrick glanced at Joe, then shifted position. The burning was worse today. "What was the score?" he added, anxious to hear anything that would take his mind off his insides.

"Thirteen to eight."

"They must have a good team this year." He had to urinate again.

"What?"

"A good team . . . they have a good team?" He was almost shouting. The front door slammed.

"Father Gahaghan's been seen to." Teresa came bustling in from across the street, where she'd substituted for Gert at the rectory. "Has anyone seen to your supper? Why's it so dark in here? Did you notice the new venetians?" she asked her nephew, pointing to the blinds, which hung behind the lace curtains.

"What did you tell Father Gahaghan?"

"Nothing. He knows you're here. There's people saw you. He's coming over. I thought I'd best warn you so you're prepared."

Patrick nodded. "The word is spreading," he muttered glumly.

"Have you seen her yet?"

"The doctor's still there."

"What a performance! Fix us a wee one, Joe," she called loudly. "We'll all be needing it. I'll just go back and see what's doing."

"Not for me, Pa," said Patrick, who knew he'd need his wits about him. Joe sat back down and there was another silence. "So you've left?" he asked finally. Patrick nodded. "You're still Catholic?" Joe looked worried.

"Yes, Pa. I'm just not going to be a priest, that's all." He marveled at how easily he said it.

"A blow to your ma." Joe removed his handkerchief and gave his nose a mighty honk. Somewhere deep down there was a victory, but Joe wasn't able to experience it fully. It had to do with his wife not getting her way, had to do with his son springing himself from a trap and joining the human race. "All right then . . . you know what's best for you." Shyly he glanced at the stranger who was his son. "I'm glad you're back, Paddy. Maybe we'll hit a few balls like we used to."

Patrick felt a rush of love for his father; he would have liked to get up and hug him but was too self-conscious. "Thanks, Pa," he said, smiling gratefully. Joe smiled back.

"What will you do?"

Patrick shrugged.

"You've got your education."

"Yes."

"I could talk to them at the mill, if you like. See if there's somethin' for you."

"I don't know, Pa. I'll probably be off soon."

"Where would you go?"

Patrick shook his head. He had no idea. He had known he had to come home first; had never even contemplated the possibility of not returning. It had to be settled with his mother. He could never tell her the why of it, not totally. Certainly not the personal stuff about his insides. But some of it needed to be said and could be said, and he would try and do that when she summoned him to the rear of the house. She, who had started him on the journey, must be made to accept that it was over.

"Your ma tells me you're home for a surprise visit, Pat."

"A visit?" Patrick looked up at Dr. Durkin. Rose appeared behind the doctor, nodding and gesticulating, sending Patrick a clear message: Keep your mouth *shut*.

"What's wrong with your lip?" asked the doctor. What was going on in this house today? An undercurrent of hysteria from the moment he'd arrived. "Don't they take care of you fellows down in Washington?" Why was Pat dressed like that?

"They do all right. How's Ma?"

"Fit as a fiddle." Blood pressure a bit above normal. But this emergency call hadn't been required, not by a long shot. You couldn't tell Dennis that. Nor Gert, either. Her "blood pressure" was as well known as her cookouts for the Holy Name Society.

83

"When's the great day, Pat? What brings you home?"

"Dr. Durkin . . . ?" Diverting the doctor's attention, Rose's voluptuous body went into action. Like a hot-water tap, she turned on her sensuality, taking his arm and moving him toward the front hallway, where she switched to playing the helpless coquette, batting her lashes and uttering little sighs, as she diddled him out the front door and got rid of him.

Returning, she dropped into a chair like a piece of ripe fruit. Patrick got up, his bladder commanding his attention. "Wait," said Rose, picking up a movie magazine from the rack beside the sofa. She gazed at it, then threw it down.

"Timothy O'Brien is due. I don't want any trouble." Possessed of Patrick's vivid eyes and jet black hair, Rose was dressed for her date and looked stunning.

"I don't want to cause any trouble." Patrick noticed his father had shut his eyes and was napping peacefully.

"Timothy's father is practically a Knight of Malta, you know," continued Rose, importantly. "He is *very* pious." She glanced from her nails to her brother, whose scandalous return threatened her climb through the Catholic social hierarchy of greater Boston. "I just don't want anybody rocking the boat," she pouted, and the message was clear: Go back where you came from and be what you're supposed to be!

He was willing. *Run.* Run from this house where it began sixteen years ago as he watched the faces of his relatives, returned from his brother Terrence's funeral, and waited for an opportunity to tell Gert his secret, the secret he'd decided upon when Terrence's casket had disappeared into the ground to her terrible sobbing.

She had been busy with the food, so it wasn't until later that he managed to follow her into the bedroom. "What have you got for your ma?" she asked, eyes red with weeping, great body hunched in loss on the edge of the bed. He had something, and he whispered it in her ear: He would take Terrence's place, he would become the priest that Terrence was to have been.

Gert had clasped him to her and taken him back to the front room and stood him on a chair in front of them all, asking him to repeat for them what he had just told her. Thus, to a hosanna of cheers and weeping, it went on the record. Gert held him to her again, and his eyes met Dennis's and Rose's, their expressions confirming what he already knew—that, yes, he had indeed replaced the departed Terrence, that *he* was now the favorite and would go forth in the service of Holy Mother Church to fulfill his mother's dream. He was nine years old.

The promise made was quickly forgotten. But Gert never forgot. Patrick became the youngest altar boy in the history of the parish, and at thirteen he was sent off to St. Martin's Prep in Providence, Rhode Island. Four years later, he had graduated and found himself at Our Lady of Good

84

Council, the novitiate of the Augustinians on the Hudson River, found himself in white cassock making his first simple vows to God, prostrated at the feet of the archbishop while Gert watched with happy tears, causing the mascara to run.

Eight years later, only two months ago, he was admitted to the Church in the ceremony of the Diaconate.

A glorious day, a day of celebration and rejoicing. Was the rightness of his path not doubly confirmed by his mother's embrace? Strong arms grasped his shoulders, eyes filled with proud tears focused on his. "Father Pat . . ." she said, unconcerned that she was ahead of schedule, that he had not yet received the plentitude of the Church: *Thou Art a Priest According to the Order of Melchisedech.*

How could any of them have known he would never hear those words? Flowers perfumed the air, Dennis took his picture, Teresa kissed him, and the relatives pressed close. Once again, Gert took her son in her arms. Over her shoulder, his eyes met those of a girl who was part of another family group, somebody's sister probably, two pairs of eyes happening to lock for the barest fraction of a second on a beautiful day, the beginning of the end. "Hold it," said Dennis, and snapped another. Patrick forced a smile for the camera, but not all the smiles in the world, nor pictures taken, nor years upon years, could hide his terrifying awareness that he wanted the girl more than he wanted any of this.

A week later the burning started.

"She's ready to see you."

Patrick nodded to Teresa, who gave his arm a squeeze. "I'll be right here if you need me."

Halfway down the corridor, Dennis interrupted him. "She's called Washington," he whispered, trying to make up for his previous behavior. "I wanted to warn you."

Patrick continued down the hallway. *Here we go,* he said to himself, managing a wry smile—a woebegone shuffler with cold-sored lip and aching prostate. He ducked into the bathroom and waited over the bowl, bursting, but still it only dribbled out in difficult spurts. Eyes wandered, alighting on the shower curtain. Against a field of aquamarine and bubbles gamboled a covey of bare-breasted mermaids. He was disappointed they had no nipples.

"Where is he?" muttered Gert in the bedroom, sitting propped up by pillows on the bed, a shawl around her shoulders. The blinds were drawn, the room in semidarkness—an atmosphere calculated to inspire penance. Above her head, the rosy-cheeked cherub of the Infant of Prague smiled. Several palms from Palm Sunday were tucked behind the frame.

"Where is he?" demanded Gert once again, as Rose appeared in the doorway, secretly thrilled to see her mother disabled, even if it were partially an act. "In the bathroom," replied Rose disdainfully. "Do you want some fresh water, Mother?" she inquired in her English garden party voice. Of Gert's three children, she was the only one to call Gert Mother. She'd learned it at Finchley.

"Have you seen to supper?" snapped Gert, suddenly sick to death of her daughter and her insufferable airs.

"Let Teresa do it. I'm dressed and I don't want to muss myself. She's hanging around doing nothing."

"I want you to say *nothin'* to Timothy. Do ya understand?"

"What am I supposed to do? He'll see Patrick."

"I'll handle it."

"I told Patrick I don't want any trouble. Not when we're so close." Enemies in all else, mother and daughter were allies in the campaign to snare Timothy O'Brien.

"*Are* we close?" demanded Gert. " 'Cause lemme tell ya, I'm losin' my patience."

"Let me fluff that pillow, Mother," replied Rose, clucking piously, which was one of her talents.

"Stop now, you're givin' me a headache."

Rose flounced out, and Gert reached for her beads. *Now, Blessed Mother*, she began, as if she were having a chatty conversation over the back fence with a neighbor, *listen, Sweetheart, I need your help. . . .*

Announced by the dying of the flushing and a final thud of the pipes, Patrick appeared in the doorway. The very sight of him caused a wave of anger and betrayal to sweep over Gert.

"Come in and shut it."

Patrick did as he was told. Slowly his eyes became accustomed to the dimness of the room. Gert's spectacles seemed to shine in the dark. Across the bed his eyes were drawn to two narrow strips of sunlight at the bottom of the blinds. Trying to hypnotize himself, he stared as the breeze fluttered them.

"Do ya want to stab your ma in the heart?" Gert was never one to pussyfoot around. "Do ya want me never to be able to leave this room? Never to show my face? D'ya want to shame me in front of the world?" Patrick tried to think, tried to remember Father Morelli's words. "I haven't done anything to shame you, Ma."

"Tell *her*, then." Gert pointed to the statue of the Virgin on the bureau, lit by a candle flickering at her plaster base. "Tell Blessed Mother. Then the three of us'll solve whatever's troublin' ya. Haven't we always been able? You 'n me? Haven't we, Patty?" She sat forward suddenly, reaching for him, pulling him to sit beside her on the bed, cupping her hands about his jaw. "Look me in the eye. Are ya in trouble? What do I smell? You've become a boozer, have ya? Is that it?"

"Ma . . . my neck . . . I'm getting a crick . . ."

Letting out a huge sigh, Gert released her son, causing him to almost fall backward. For a moment the only sound was both their labored breathings.

"Patty, what is it? Are ya goin' to deny me what's kept me goin' all these years? My dream? *Our* dream?" A terrible depression settled on Gert; she felt tiny and vulnerable and totally at a loss. "Our dream," she murmured once again. Patrick shook his head. He had no idea whose dream it was any longer, he'd just lived it.

"All those years?" she continued, her voice full of sudden sweetness and loss. "Open your eyes, darlin'. Look at your ma. Tell me the joy I felt that day at St. Ambrose's isn't to be fulfilled. That day when you was first able to give Communion and it was to me that ya gave it first, wasn't it?"

Gert had made sure of that. The Church granted its deacons the power to administer three of the sacraments, Holy Communion among them, before Ordination, and both Gert and Teresa had been at St. Ambrose's on the red-letter day as Patrick turned, chalice in shaky hand, ready to bestow the wafers. Worried lest he begin with someone other than herself, Gert had elbowed her way into position at the rail, would've shoved aside the Pope himself to be first to receive Holy Communion from her son.

"When I looked up at ya that day," continued Gert, "I knew why He put me on this sweet earth. How many moments like that does a body have? Few and far between, lemme tell ya. Patty, are ya goin' to tell me ya only wanted to whet my appetite that day? And now you're goin' to deny me the meal? Don't, Patty . . . don't . . ."

Don't cry, Ma, he pleaded silently, as tears once again sullied her freshly rouged cheeks.

"I want to remind ya of who's listenin'." Gert blew her nose. "Almighty God is listenin' and His Blessed Mother and . . . your brother Terrence. . . !"

Holy Mary, murmured Teresa, outside the door, ready to help, *she's bringing in Terrence. . . .*

"Please, Ma . . ."

"Your brother Terrence, may his soul rest in peace." Gert crossed herself. "What can he be thinkin'—hearin' what's goin' on here today? Do ya remember your brother's face? Him tryin' to get his breath right out there in the very back yard? Chicken bone caught in his throat and—" She couldn't continue. Sobs wracked her again. *If I pull up that shade, I'll see him,* imagined Patrick. *Terrence's eyes rolling in his face; Pa beating him on the back trying to dislodge it; Ma screaming and Rose, too.*

Gert picked up her rosary beads. "Do ya think for one minute if Denny had come to me, poor Denny, that I'd have encouraged *him*? Never. But *you* come into the livin' room, didn't ya after the funeral and . . ."

"You brought me in."

". . . and the light of God was shinin' in your blue eyes and . . ."

"I was only nine, Ma."

"Don't nitpick with me, boyo! The light of God was upon ya, and I knew Terrence hadn't been taken from me in vain. What did ya promise me?" It was fairly thundered. It was Moses come down from the mountain, tablets in hand, only to discover a carnival in progress. Outside in the hall, Teresa crossed herself again.

The blinds billowed in a gust. Sunlight jabbed into the room. Patrick hung his head. "I tried to tell you once, Ma . . . at Villanova . . . you remember? But you wouldn't let me—"

"What are ya sayin'?" Gert's voice took on an edge. Eyes narrowed behind the spectacles. "Are ya sayin' *I'm* the cause of this? Many a boy has doubts along the way. If ya hadn't, I'da been worried. What are ya sayin' to me?"

"I can't go through with it, Ma. Try and understand. Please. I want to be in the world. I need—"

In a swift gesture, Gert snapped on the gooseneck lamp beside her, one not dissimilar to those used by detectives in the back rooms of station houses. Startled by the sudden jab of light, Patrick blinked as Gert thrust a small embossed card at him, a gilt cross on the front.

"Read it!"

"I know what it says."

"Read it! Out loud!"

" 'Mr. and Mrs. Joseph J. Flynn of Jericho, Massachusetts request the honor of your presence at . . .' " It was as if to a wedding, this invitation to his first Mass.

"Seventy-five of 'em gone out already," snapped Gert, "and the rest goin' out this week! What am I to do? Are ya tellin' me that blessed day is not to be? Tell me! Tell Almighty God and His Blessed Mother, too, that you're goin' to break your vows and disgrace us all. Patty, oh, Patty—*think!* Think what you're doin' to yourself!"

He felt he was going to be sick. Sweat broke out on his forehead and palms. Inside he felt hot stabs, reminding him, relentlessly reminding. "No . . . no . . ." he heard himself murmur.

"Now here's what we'll do," continued Gert, riding over his protests. "We'll have some supper. I've fixed potato salad and some cold cuts. I even made some of my date squares. I've talked to the Monsignor down in Washington and . . ." That wasn't true. She hadn't been able to reach anyone of importance, for the offices had been closed. But a lie in the service of God was no lie at all. ". . . we'll drive straight down there tomorrow. We'll straighten this out, whatever it is. If ya need time, there'll be time. Your ma only wants what's best for ya, Patty, only what's best. Please, Patty. *Please.*"

Her hand reached out and squeezed his arm. He could feel himself slipping, slipping slowly under the weight of her evidence. It was no use. She was right. Everything she said was right. He had made the promise. The promise to all of them. The promise to God. Everything she said was true. He was a shame and a disgrace, no matter what Father Morelli had said. He had disgraced her, disgraced himself and dishonored Him whose service he had sought to enter. He would never be able to live with himself. The Superior General might release him from his vows, the dispensation would be granted, but nothing, no, nothing, could release him from his guilt, from the shame of the loss of his vocation and the mess he'd made of his life.

Patrick fell forward and buried his head in the covers. Hope flickering in her wounded heart, Gert began a Hail Mary.

"Father Gahaghan's here," called Rose from the hall. "And Timothy, too."

Gert lay a tender hand on her son's head. It was unthinkable he should not be a priest! "Promise me you'll say nothin' till we get this cleared up. Please, Patty? There's a good boy . . . don't worry. Go and wash up now." As she got off the bed, her legs seemed unable to support her, so sapped was her strength. "Patty? Promise me? You'll say nothin'."

From the depths Patrick nodded. Gert leaned on the bureau for support, kissed her beads and left the room. Patrick got up. He had to go to the bathroom again.

Moments later he emerged and heard low murmurings from the front of the house. Warily, he crept down the hallway. The voices grew louder. The radio was on, tuned to the Rosary, and they were all kneeling, beads in hands, when he arrived in the doorway. Timothy O'Brien like a large lump, and Rose and Father Gahaghan and Joe, Dennis, Gert, Teresa, and her husband Matt, too—all on their knees, all working the beads, all looking up at him now.

"Here he is," beamed Gert, who would've interrupted the Sermon on the Mount in an emergency. "Home for a day or two to visit his ma." She cocked an eye at Timothy to see how he was taking it. Father Gahaghan (primed by Gert with the same story) nodded, but it was all he could do to keep the confusion off his face at the sight of his favorite altar boy dressed as he was.

"Hello, Pat . . ." he said, more a question than a greeting, his suspicions aroused as Patrick averted his eyes and mumbled a halting "Hello, Father." The gravelly voice of Bishop Cushing continued on the radio like a dirge.

"Join us, darlin'?" Gert's eyes pleaded with Patrick to remove himself from the doorway. Falteringly, he entered the room and picked up his bag. Gert's expression turned to fear. Other mouths fell open, prayers suspended, as Patrick started from the room, opening the front door, stumbling over the threshold. Stunned, Gert tried to rise and couldn't. "You're not my son," she gasped in an uncharacteristically tiny voice. "I don't want to see ya again," she added and began to weep.

An overpowering feeling of exhaustion dogged Patrick as he hurried down Essex Street. Numbness was upon his limbs and in his heart as he turned right on Main and trudged blindly on, away from the business district and the center of town, taking back roads with no plan, as the day gave way in a lemon yellow glow that Protestants call a Jesus light, and Catholics have no name for.

Out in the countryside a half hour later, he found himself in a grove of tall pines in the Old Burying Ground. He sank down upon an ancient stone, one of many, some tilted over with the years, nestled in ferns. *Here Lies the Body of Benjamin Lovett, Who Departed This Life July 10, A.D. 1762, in the 67th Year of His Age.*

Patrick's eyes fell upon other markers of early settlers, the Stearns and Bowditches, Ingalls, Winslowes, the Abbots, Kittredges, and Osgoods. Nathan, buried in 1732, slept peacefully to his right beneath a crooked stone. Sarah and Felicity, Patience and Susannah. Straighten our stones, they whispered to him. Are you the one come to right us?

A moment of peace filled him amongst the dead. Tranquility descended, then fled as Father Gahaghan's pained expression of shock and disbelief rose before him—as if the whole of Mother Church's reaction was contained in that glance of woe, and yes, distaste, for one who had come so far only to falter at the end.

A moment later he was on his way again, nearing North Parish. Jericho was divided into three parts—Jerusalem, the mill district down by the river, The Center with its business district and streets fanning out, where the majority lived, and four miles away, North Parish, which was the oldest and by far the loveliest part of town. The early settlers sank their roots in North Parish, and their descendants, Jericho's aristocracy, still lived in the stately mansions around the Common that Patrick now approached. Families on verandas sipped coolers and glanced at him, wondering who the stranger was. He hurried on past the gabled, green-lawned houses, on across the peaceful Common, whose broad expanse, protected by giant elms, allowed no shrieks or cries to mar its lovely stillness.

Past clumps of peach bell, spikes of lavender veronica he walked, stomach growling at the tinkle of glasses and cutlery from the inn. The bronze soldier guarding the entrance to the Common was at peace, his musket at the ready in case the need should arise again. Patrick hurried past the ancient general store, the hay scales and the Historical Society. Vesper bells tolled in the Unitarian Church and a screen door slammed, followed by a woman's laughter. There was a dance at the country club tonight. "I'll meet you at the dock. . . ."

The lake! Patrick turned down Great Pond Road headed for Lake Cochickawick, striding through sycamore and shady places, forced to the side of the road by a convertible sweeping by on a Saturday evening, laughter in its wake.

He jumped over a low stone wall and across an open meadow, which rose in a hill on whose summit were six evenly spaced, tall poplars. Climbing up, heart jumping, he began to run down the hill, sliding, crashing into the underbrush, into the darkening woods and onto the secret trail that he, Dennis and Terrence had blazed in younger days—three Indian scouts of the Wampanoag Tribe—splotched in dabs of paint.

Low branches snapped at him, blueberry bushes and raspberry brambles scratched. He fought his way through until he reached the lake's edge and a sheltered cove, now dark with the sun gone. His eyes searched the immediate shore for the rowboat abandoned the summer of Terrence's death. They had found it here, sealed its leaks with pitch, painted it blue with a yellow stripe, and, feathers in their hair, had launched it under Joe's watchful eye.

Disappointment welled up in him so keenly that he had to fight crying as he sat down with his bag. What a fool. Why should it still be here after all those years? Lostness whirred at him like the crickets chirping. Despair caused his head to rest upon his updrawn knees as he cradled himself while bullfrogs called and a swarm of insects fought a battle in the air.

Startled by a sound, he turned his head. A growl. A mongrel dog appeared twenty-five feet away, pink nose in the air sniffing. It barked. "Go away," said Patrick. The dog looked at him, sat and scratched, a sorry sight of a dog indeed, all tangles and burrs, the color of a sheep. "Go home," said Patrick. The dog regarded him solemnly, then dug into itself trying to pull out prickers. "All right—c'mere." The dog's head perked. It took a few steps toward Patrick, then sat. "C'mere!" A few more wary steps. "What shall I do?" asked Patrick. The dog cocked an ear. "Shall I catch a freight and go to California?" Thump, thump, thump went a rear paw, searching out fleas. "C'mere, fella." Another small move, then no further. A few feet away now, the dog watched Patrick through intelligent hazel eyes.

Patrick changed position slightly, making himself more comfortable, then took out his breviary and said his prayers. Above his head a bird called in a sky shimmering pink beyond the hills, pearl gray with flecks of silver and gold, promising angels, and he fell asleep.

Whoooooo, called an owl at close to two in the morning. The dog still watched from the shore as Patrick dipped the oars of a boat, not his but another, found in a tangle while exploring. Silently he glided out of the cove and onto the lake, the stiffness fleeing from his joints with the rhythmic stroking. Behind him, three miles across the lake, a car's headlights swept along the north shore. "Where are we, mama?" asked a sleepy child from the back seat. "We just passed the lake. We'll be home soon."

The strains of "Goodnight, Ladies," floated across the water as the dance ended at the country club. Young men and their girls walked whispering in each other's arms to cars, some down in gentle darkness to the shore.

In the middle of the lake, in total aloneness, Patrick pulled in the oars and let the boat drift. He reached down to touch the water, which wasn't too cold, so he splashed some on his face, then removed his undershirt and shirt and splashed with more abandon, dunking his head now over the side into the water, coming up, shaking his head like a puppy. A smallish laugh crept out of his mouth, unsure and tentative, a laugh not heard of late.

Across the water a girl whispered to her boyfriend, "I'm really tired." "Oh, come on," he replied, knowing what he wanted to do. Their canoe glided soundlessly away from the club dock.

In the middle of the lake, Patrick stood up, naked, stood without thinking. Stretching his arms above his head, he shivered—not from cold, but the discovery of his nakedness was a sudden shock. The water turned darker as clouds drifted over the moon. A warning clicked of temptation. He was already hard.

Stretching himself out on his back in the bottom of the boat, Patrick took himself in hand, conjuring females, unable not to. Suddenly terrified, he lifted his head slowly, eyes peering out over the edge of the boat in the direction of what seemed like a cry, but he could see nothing. A half mile away, the canoe drifted in darkness. Then he heard the cry again, unmistakable now in the silence of the night—the vivid sounds of lovemaking.

The girl's every murmur rocketed through Patrick. Unendurably excited, he scrunched low in the boat, this time on his stomach. All he had of her was her cries, growing now in urgency as he shut his eyes. Under him, his fist became her vagina and he plunged in, belly scraping heedlessly against the wet planking. Was she the girl on the train the day before yesterday who caused him a fifty-mile erection between Bristol and Trenton? She was all of them. To her whimpers he climaxed. Then, overcome with guilt and unmindful of discovery, he flung himself over the side and into the water.

"What was that?" the girl asked, frightened. "I thought I heard . . ."

Down stroked Patrick, powerful arms taking him far below the careening boat on the surface. Wildness was in his head. For wouldn't it be better to give in to this, too? To let his lungs fill with the lake and sink like a stone, atoning for chastity once again defiled, obedience long gone, and only poverty left, the poverty of his prospects?

In Washington Father Morelli waked and shuffled to the bathroom, trying to remember something. His mouth worked in silent prayer. On Lake Cochickawick, the surface was shattered once again as Patrick exploded from the water, a grin on his handsome mug, lungs bursting, alive.

5 Suitcase in hand, Harriet stepped down from the trolley. A homesick ache rose in her stomach as she glanced up the familiar vista of Main Street. Like a hungry child outside a bakery window, she feasted her eyes on Jericho, the white steeples glistening in the distance, the hundred-year-old elms silhouetted against a pale blue September sky. Apprehension gripped her, and she caught her breath and couldn't move.

Turned the color of ripe persimmons by the late afternoon sunlight, Phelps Mill caught her eye, its six o'clock whistle reminding her of a loan past due, reminding her of the less than a dollar in her purse, reminding her of that fabled day of success and hope over two years ago when Phelps had loaned her the money, freeing her to go forth into the world. And where was she now?

She was home.

The first to leave the nest wasn't returning to a brass band. Feathers ruffled and dragging was more like it—and feeling none too good about herself. "I'll be back," she'd vowed to Virginia at the bus terminal this morning—and the tears shed at that parting threatened once again as Harriet cut across Bartlett's Field in whose outfield two boys tossed a football. *No, not quite the stylish return you'd always imagined, is it?* There hadn't been an extra-cost swivel chair in the parlor car, no watermelon pickle, fresh linen and a club sandwich in the dining car. She'd taken a bus from New York to Leveret and the trolley from Leveret to Jericho, had barely been able to make the cost of the ticket. There'd been no one to greet her because, although she'd told her family she was coming, she wanted no hoopla, didn't know what time she'd get in, she'd see them when she saw them.

God but everything looked strange and familiar at the same time as she walked quickly through the tree-lined streets. The rhythm of the city still beat in her yet she could almost hear the stillness, broken by mothers who called their children in to supper. Memories stirred at every corner, but nothing compared to the rush of emotion that welled in her as she reached Mulberry Street. The Ingalls were bent down in their garden. Mr. Hibson had painted his house, and Mrs. Byrony was arguing with her cat;

all just as she remembered it, all known and loved. Her heart rose at the sight of the beloved, clumpy yellow house, gabled and sun-dappled halfway down the short block. "Oh," she sighed, and that was all and that was everything.

"Harriet—is that you?"

She froze, then waved gamely to Mrs. Ingalls, who called, "Are you home?"

"Just for a . . . visit," she called back, irritating herself with the fib, for they'd all know soon enough.

"Won't Letty be pleased. Tell her we'll be there in half an hour. My casserole isn't done yet."

Confused, Harriet nodded and started down the block. A car pulled up in front of the house, and she recognized Reverend Peabody and his wife. Concealing herself behind a tree, she watched Ada McQueston cross the street and enter Letty's garden with a covered dish in her hands. My God, was Mother throwing a party?

Anxiety overwhelmed her. Hastily she set her suitcase down, opened her compact, applied fresh lipstick, lit a nervous cigarette and fought an impulse to walk back up the street and disappear.

They all know I've failed.

Tears stung her eyes. The giant hydrangea by the corner of the house, its blossoms like pink powder puffs, swam out of focus and she heard her brother Frankie shout, "*Mother? Father? Cora, Alice—she's here!*"

Frankie bounded out the front door. "Think you can surprise us, huh? You wait right there, you ninny! Don't move. Do you hear me? Don't move."

Dazed, Harriet obeyed. Suddenly the stillness of the street was shattered by a joyous blast from Frankie's trumpet as he returned onto the front porch.

"*Welcome home!*" From an upstairs window a crepe paper streamer floated down, and she caught a glimpse of Alice grinning.

"Yoo-hoo-hoo . . ." called Cora from another window as the two sisters unfurled an old bedsheet with WELCOME HOME, HARRIET! painted on it. A moment later they came hurrying out the door and down the steps, calling out greetings as Cora tossed autumn daisies, the two of them laughing at their sister's stupefied expression.

"Cora . . . oh, Cora . . . oh, Alice. . . !" Crying, Harriet was passed from one to the other as Frankie gave another blast to topple the walls of Jericho and the neighbor children came running.

"Harriet!" Letty hurried across the side lawn from the garden and turned the corner of the house. Suddenly five years old and scared, Harriet ran to her, the two of them embracing while Letty's friend Ada wiped a tear.

"Harriet . . ." At a loss for words, Letty could only smile as she held

95

her daughter at arm's length, her eyes brimming with relief and love.

"I'm such a baby. . . . I didn't mean to cry . . . and there's company, too. . . . I . . . oh, Mother, it's so good to see you!"

Once again they hugged as well-wishers converged. Franklin stepped out on the front porch and announced himself with a clearing of the throat. Harriet turned, hesitated, then slowly walked up the steps to him. "Father," she said softly, searching his eyes for something she needed. A small smile quivered on Franklin's face and it was enough. "I'm back," she whispered, laying her head against his shoulder.

"What have you done to your hair?" asked Franklin, ill at ease. "What have you done to your eyebrows? Welcome home."

"Just like the old days, isn't it, Letty?"

"Ayea." Letty nodded to Ada, the two women looking out over the gathering on the genteel Protestant slope of the Hoskins' lawn and garden. Strung overhead, paper Japanese lanterns filtered a soft and magical glow upon the merry group of friends and neighbors who filled their plates from the dishes set out on the cloth-covered card tables that Franklin had placed under the red maple.

"And Harriet's back. Where is she? She disappeared."

"Freshening up. You know Harriet. She'll take her usual two hours."

"Won't she be tickled to see all her old friends! What a good idea you had. The timing's perfect, isn't it?"

Several mornings ago, over an iced tea on the back piazza, the two women had discussed the possibility of a get-together on Saturday evening. The previous day had seen the bulk of the canning completed. Franklin's vegetable garden had produced an abundant crop; in the coolness of the Hoskins' cellar the shelves held gleaming jars full of green and yellow beans, corn, succotash, tomatoes, pickle relish and carrots. Like squirrels, the Hoskins were ready for another winter. So why not take potluck together and have a party? Each of the neighbors would bring a dish.

Letty smiled to herself as her guests sampled the food and chatted. Stimulated, her heart filled. What better way to celebrate the waning of summer, the tangy start of a new season, the joy of living? Not to mention Cora about to be married and Franklin working again. Six weeks ago he'd been employed as a salesman by Whites' Sewing Machine Company, and Letty prayed the small measure of self-esteem he'd regained would blossom, putting an end to her husband's continuing bouts with liquor. And now there was added reason for celebration. Harriet's return was a good omen for Franklin, and the family was all together again. Yes, there was much to be thankful for. Not to mention survival.

"Isn't it a wonderful mix, Ada?" bubbled Cora, who loved a party. She bustled about, smiling happily, helping Letty as she always did, gossiping and laughing and enjoying everyone. There were Letty's friends from the Women's Union at church, along with Reverend Peabody and his wife and daughter; a sprinkle of Alice's set—mostly artists or "would-be's" (Franklin called them "advanced thinkers" when he wasn't calling them worse); and Cora's chums from high school, all of whom were married or about to be—and soon thank the Lord, she would be, too.

"Sam baked the pies, didn't you, Sam?"

Cora's fiancé, Sam Cousins, blushed and shyly smiled. His hair was cut very short and his big ears turned the color of cranberries as Cora went on to describe in loving detail his recipe for pie crust.

"What am I going to do with you?" he whispered. Cora giggled and squeezed his hand, her own blush echoing his.

The men talked Roosevelt, pro and con, and whether Alfred Landon, the Republican choice, had a chance against him in the upcoming election. The Literary Digest poll predicted the Careful Kansan would upset the President, but Gallup said the opposite. Maybe Roosevelt deserved it. The recovery was progressing, lots of new autos on the road, times were better, money looser. Not if you wanted to start a small business, though; the banks were still cautious. And what about that growing federal deficit?

How about the Olympics over in Berlin; did you see that Jesse Owens on the newsreels? Did you see how that tinhorn Hitler snubbed him? Owens showed him, didn't he! Those darkies sure can run, good for them. . . .

The women chatted fall fashion, food and whether the Baltimore divorcée, Wallis Warfield Simpson, would snare the King of England. H. L. Mencken said last week it was the greatest news story since the Resurrection. And did you see the Andersens' new house trailer? Just like the Andersens to be the first ones in on a new fad. . . .

"Is this your noodle casserole, Irene? Delicious."

"It has ginger in it—can you taste?"

"The beans are delicious, Letty."

"What would Saturday night be without beans?"

"What's keeping Harriet?"

Upstairs, the anxious one took another critical close look at herself in the bathroom mirror, added a hint more eye shadow, puffed on a cigarette and knew she was hiding out. "Where are you?" called Frankie, knocking. "You haven't greeted the guests. Everyone's asking for you."

"Are they?" What had she to tell them? she wondered apprehensively as she opened the door and admitted him. "You look different," he said, sitting on the edge of the tub and watching her as she continued putting on her makeup.

"Good different or bad different?"

"Good. You're smoking, huh? I don't think Mother approves."

"C'est la vie."

"You've cut your hair, too."

97

"Back to bangs." Two months ago she'd given in to a self-destructive impulse that had seen half of her hair land on the floor of the bathroom. "You like?" she asked, tilting her head from side to side. Cut an inch below her ear lobes, her fine, almost black hair swung forward then back. "A Dutch Boy cut," she added, scrutinizing herself. "Slightly out of fashion, I'll admit. Long hair is back and— Oh, well, when the rest of the world was wearing theirs short, I had braids, so maybe I'll confound them all again with my unmitigated individuality."

"Your eyebrows are—"

"Plucked. I'm a big-city girl now. Wicked and wild."

"You look good to me."

"You old smoothie," she laughed, ruffling his slicked-back hair while he protested vehemently. "Look at you! When I last saw you, you were a string bean with pimples. You've gone definitely handsome on me. Cora wrote me one of her long and wonderful letters all about you. She says all the Italian girls in Leveret are in a swoon. They line up outside the Classic every night."

"It's true," he replied, feigning boredom. "I'm a killer-diller." He was almost nineteen now. He'd graduated high school that spring and got a job playing trumpet with Jimmy Lanceford and His Lancers at the Classic Ballroom in Leveret.

"I gather Mother's none too pleased about you at the Classic."

He nodded. "I won't be there long, though. Guess what? I make twenty a week. That ain't hay. I give fifteen of it to Mother."

"I guess you're the success in the family."

"Alice helps, too. And now Father's working again so—"

"How is he?" she asked, noticing Frankie's face cloud.

"Fine," he replied quickly, almost insistently. "I don't think he likes Whites', though. He shouldn't be selling sewing machines. He should be back in the woolen business. But he's out on the road again. You know how he likes that. He's gone sometimes for two or three days. . . ." Once again, he frowned, and Harriet sensed his distress. "He's given us some . . . rough times, but he's better now, I know he is and . . . anyway, I'm getting out of here. Jericho, I mean. Headed for the big time as soon as I can and—"

"Rough times?"

"They're past. I hope. What made you decide to call it quits?" he asked quickly, changing the subject.

"I haven't. I'm going back. I'm here for a visit, that's all. A long visit, I'm afraid. Shall we say indefinite?"

"I'm going to try and get in with a New York band. Benny Goodman, that's my dream."

"Mr. Ambition. You sound like someone I used to know."

"It was good to see your name in print."

98

"You mean *Pegasus?* My one success in over a year in New York." *Pegasus* was a little Greenwich Village bimonthly, which had accepted a witty essay she'd written about the vagaries of New England speech, "New Englanders Speak New English." She'd been paid five dollars.

"Cora showed it to practically everyone in town. She was so proud and— What did I say?" Ill at ease, Frankie noticed she was weeping.

"Dammit, I've ruined my face. I'm too damned emotional for my own good. I guess it's coming home and . . . and not having . . . anything special to . . . not working and—"

"You'll have other chances. Why, you're the only one who had the guts to give it a try! Alice talks tough, but she's got as far as Leveret, that's all. And Cora won't ever leave Jericho. I'm gonna hit the high road, but that's expected. I'm a man. But you—look at all you've accomplished. You should be proud of yourself, you ninny."

Gratefully Harriet wiped her eyes and grinned at him. How solemnly he'd defended her! How wonderful to discover that a younger brother had overnight become an older.

"Oakie doke?" he asked, grinning back at her, giving her a quick, embarrassed hug as he left. "Oakie doke," she replied, applying fresh mascara, then stepping back to scrutinize herself once again. Yes, she was all intact. Certainly she'd be able to manage a gathering of people all of whom liked, loved, and admired her; hadn't she been through worse?

A final spray with the atomizer, a final pep talk ("You're Harriet Hoskins and don't forget it."), and she was on her way down the back stairs, the creak of the third one from the top producing a happy smile of recognition.

"Hello, hello, hello . . ." Out she stepped upon the back piazza, thrusting open the screen door, pausing on the top step, a tremulous smile upon her face.

"Harriet!" they called as she descended, apprehension temporarily banished in a buzz of warm welcome and admiring looks.

"Welcome home, Harriet!"

"Harriet, look who's here. . . ."

"*Marcia!*"

"*Harriet!*"

The two friends embraced as Letty beamed. "Harriet," exclaimed Marcia, wiping away a tear, "you look so different. You're so chic. So New York!" Always awed by Harriet, Marcia continued chirping like an excited bird. "Your mother called me and said you were back, and we immediately changed our plans and . . . doesn't she look wonderful, Libby?"

"*Libby!*"

Libby Stillings, the third member of that fabled, inseparable girlhood triumvirate, stepped forward with a wink and a wicked grin. "Is short hair coming back, Harriet? I thought—"

99

"As a matter of fact, I'm bringing it back. Single-handedly," she added, causing a ripple of laughter that did her heart good.

"I never can keep up," smiled the beautiful Libby, who was a junior at Radcliffe and trying very hard at the moment to out-sophisticate Harriet. "You do look smart," she added a trifle competitively as she pressed a cool cheek to her old rival's.

"Doesn't she?" interjected Marcia, ever loyal. "I think you look just stunning. So New York! I said that already, didn't I? Oh, Harriet! I've almost forgotten to introduce . . . Allan. My husband!" Marcia burst into self-conscious laughter as the young man, a lawyer who worked in Boston, stepped forward.

"I've heard a lot about you, needless to say."

"Have you? Oh, good!" Harriet smiled from Marcia to Allan, assessing him immediately as a bit of a stuffed shirt and therefore perfect for the conservative Marcia. "Who would have thunk it?" she added, kissing her old friend on the cheek.

"One down," giggled Marcia, "and two to go."

"Not me," replied Libby, "I'm playing the field forever."

"And *I* certainly won't be next," bandied Harriet, accepting a light from Allan. "Oh, it's so *good* to be home," she announced, mock-ivory bracelets clacking as she gestured sweepingly. After promising Marcia and Libby they'd all have lunch at the Puritan Tea Room on Monday and catch up, she moved on, greeting others who pressed around her.

"How long are you home for?" asked Reverend Peabody, presenting her with a cup of punch. "Just a visit," she responded gaily, wishing it had a bit of gin in it, but *that* was unlikely. "Can't say for sure," she added. The truth could wait. Yes, indeed, she went on, playing visiting celebrity, Gotham was a tough row to hoe. But it was the center of the universe, wasn't it? She was anxious to return. But she had some "prospects" in Boston that needed looking into and. . . . Yes, she'd really *rented* a bathroom; yes, she'd appeared at the Metropolitan and drunk champagne with Gigli; no, she hadn't been discouraged not to get work on a newspaper, not at all. Had they read her article in *Pegasus*? If not, she had copies. No, she hadn't met Brenda Frazier, but Sinclair Lewis and Dorothy Thompson were almost bosom buddies, etc., etc.

"What's this about a short visit?" Alice removed herself from her circle of friends, who were arguing as to how best to save the world.

"I feel so good!" exclaimed Harriet.

"Don't think I'm not wondering about the act you're putting on for us."

"How's the revolution coming, sweetheart?" teased Harriet in return. How good it was to see Alice! "Aren't you going to introduce me?" she continued. "Frankie tells me you have a steady. Which one is he? Let me guess."

"Which one is who?" Alice colored slightly behind her glasses as Wayne Thibeau came over and she introduced him.

"So this is the hotshot from the big city." Shorter than Alice by an inch or two and about the same age, Wayne grinned and thrust out his hand enthusiastically.

Harriet was struck by his looks—the face of an old man on a boy's body, with eyes that seemed to have seen it all. She liked him immediately. "Cigarette me, Wayne," she vamped, winking at Alice, who scowled slightly. "Do you work for the WPA, too?" He flipped a Lucky Strike out of his package. "I hear you're also a painter."

"I'm a bookkeeper at the Arlington Mill. The art gets done on the weekends."

"Save me!" interrupted Frankie, fleeing a group of adoring neighborhood girls and joining the threesome.

"Casanova," laughed Harriet. "Are they driving you batty?" she added, sprinkling her conversation with smart New York expressions as she turned again to Wayne. "I was telling Frankie that my worst disappointment in New York was not getting accepted onto the Writers' Project, but I'm afraid it was the same old story—they were taking authors who'd already been published." Wayne didn't look at all like an office type, not with the working man's look he affected—bushy mustache, cap tucked into his back pocket, and suspenders for all the world to see. "Now I ask you, Wayne—what's the sense of having a sister working for the WPA if she can't get her relatives jobs?"

"That's not the point of it, Harriet," interjected Alice.

"I thought at least you'd write another of your letters to the President and put in a word."

"She hasn't changed," grinned Frankie to Alice.

"I have!" Harriet exclaimed.

"I heard you mention that you knew Sinclair Lewis," said Wayne. "Have you read *It Can't Happen Here?*"

"Oh—that's his new best seller. I'm afraid I haven't. Is it good?"

"It's an important book. He raises the possibility of a fascist state in America."

"Harriet doesn't read books like that, Wayne. She just likes to drop the authors' names."

"Listen to you! I wouldn't mind dropping Dorothy Thompson's, let me tell you. She had a column in the June *Ladies' Home Journal*—dishing out advice to the girl grad. Do you know what her advice was? Quit. She said if a woman couldn't be a doer, she should become an *appreciator*. I found that hard to swallow—especially since a couple of years ago she was telling me to seize my destiny."

Wayne grinned to Alice. "You didn't tell me she was a firebrand. How's New York?" he asked Harriet.

"In a ferment. Writers writing, artists painting. I intend to go back and storm the ramparts again. Down but not defeated, that's me. Now I'd like to meet your other friends. . . ."

Alice led the way into her painting studio in the barn. "Here's my glamour-puss sister," she called to the close-knit group of Leveret's young Bohemians, who were examining her work.

"Are these your new things?" Harriet looked at the rough charcoal sketches of sad-eyed men in unemployment lines, poor families at empty tables. "What happened to the still lifes of red onions and cabbages? I'd say your subject matter's changed."

"So's the world," commented Wayne. "Art for art's sake isn't viable anymore. Artists must use their talent to educate. To upset, if necessary. To provoke."

Alice nodded. "Paintings should evoke a desire for solidarity. The viewer becomes a partner in the struggle."

"The struggle?"

"Against an oppressive social system, Harriet."

"Alice, where do you get such ideas?" asked Letty, coming in with a tray of punch. "Why is it necessary to remind people of unhappiness?"

"Really, Mother—do you want to paint fairies in the garden? Art must have a function."

"I thought its function was to uplift the spirit."

"I like these, Mother," Harriet said. "They're powerful. The trend in the arts *is* away from mere prettiness. I went to see *Tobacco Road* in New York, and nothing like it has been seen on Broadway *ever*. Who would have thought a play about down-and-out sharecroppers living in misery would find an audience? But it's an enormous hit. No, I agree with Wayne. We must use our talents to depict the world as it is, not the way we'd like it to be."

"Is there no place for fantasy?"

"Oh, I still have a few," laughed Harriet, then squeezed Alice's hand, whispered, "C'mon," and, propelled by memories, pulled her up the barn stairs and into her workroom. "Do you remember the old days? You'd be painting downstairs and I'd be up here writing my novel. Do you remember Bart and Cynthia?"

"You always were interested in 'society.'"

"Don't be so glib. You're always so sure you have the answer. I haven't been sitting cozily in an office getting a regular paycheck like you. I haven't known where my next meal was coming from these last months. Want my recipe for tomato soup? Ketchup and water. How dusty it is," she went on, sitting at her desk while Alice perched on the arm of the other chair. "What dreams we used to have!"

"What are you going to do?"

"Do?" From outside, the sounds of chatter drifted up, and Harriet peered out the tiny window tucked under the eaves. The moon rose higher. "I don't know," she confessed. "Keep writing. Keep trying. I can't stay too long. If I do, I'll sink here and never get out. Tell me about Wayne."

"Hands off."

Harriet laughed. "You didn't write me about *him*," she teased. How like Alice to have discovered romance and keep it a secret. "But I must say, it's done you good. You look wonderful. So pretty." Finally Alice seemed to be taking care of herself. "Do we lay it at Wayne's doorstep—this sudden transformation?" Alice shrugged. "I like him," continued Harriet. "He's very vital, isn't he? Seems plugged into a hidden current."

"He is. He's secretary-treasurer of the Young Socialists. Last winter he was the youngest one on the strike committee at the Arlington. Father calls him a bum."

"I knew he didn't seem like a mere bookkeeper."

"You're still a snob."

"I don't think so. Nine-hour days at the Automat took care of that. It seems," she went on, "that everyone has found *l'amour* while I've been gone." She caught sight of her father below in the garden. "His hair's gone totally white," she murmured. "I tried to get some information from Frankie, but—"

"I'm the only one who'll tell you what it's like living with a drunk."

"*Alice.*"

"You'll see. You got a taste of it before you left, but it got worse. Days when he wouldn't come home till after supper. Picking fights. Endless complaining. I don't know how Mother's managed."

"But Frankie said that lately—"

"Frankie wants to believe he's better. And Cora has never accepted the truth. She sees him through her usual rose-colored glasses. You'll forgive me if I say I'm not holding my breath anymore. I'm sick of him."

"You sound so angry."

"Wouldn't you be? Aren't you? But I'm sure that now you've returned, he'll be his old self again. Hah!"

"Yoo-hoo. What are you girls up to?" called Cora, appearing with Sam at the bottom of the stairs.

"Come on up."

"Only for a minute. We're in charge of the ice cream. Sam's been churning to beat the band, haven't you?"

"What flavor?" asked Harriet as they climbed up.

"Peach," replied Sam.

"Cora—he's so sweet!" Harriet gave a surprised Sam a quick peck on the cheek, and Cora trilled a laugh. Harriet had never seen her happier. What a perfect match they'd make. Sam was quiet, but Cora would take up the slack.

103

The sisters clasped hands and smiled at each other. "D'you know who you remind me of?" asked Wayne, poking his head up and joining them. "*Little Women*."

"We used to play we were," laughed Harriet. "Especially after we saw the movie."

"No trouble telling who you were," said Wayne. "Jo—right? You even look a little like Katharine Hepburn."

"Such a flatterer. I'm usually told I look like Norma Shearer."

"I was Meg," piped up Cora.

"And Alice," grinned Harriet, "was always Beth. That's because she's so good and sweet-tempered, aren't you?"

"Ha-ha."

Harriet sighed. "When I saw the Japanese lanterns in the garden, do you know what I thought of? The day they turned out the lights."

"Cora was *so* embarrassed," laughed Alice, "to be seen buying kerosene for the lamps. Kerosene—symbol of the poor. Do you remember?"

"Do I?" cried Cora, her laugh trilling an octave and a half.

"Now 'Eleanor,' " cautioned Harriet, winking. "Calm down, dearest. . . ."

"Oh, shush—" Blushing, Cora glanced at Sam.

"Did she tell you we nicknamed her Eleanor Roosevelt, Sam? It's meant very, very affectionately."

Cora giggled. "I came home that night, and they were all sitting around the dining room table with Ada, and I can't remember who else, and Mother laughed and said, 'We're having a "lights out" party,' and I just broke right down and wept."

"Do you remember what else Mother said?" asked Alice. "That we could always go visit Mrs. Brady—"

"She ran the poor farm," interjected Harriet, explaining to Sam and Wayne.

"Where they served roast chicken every Sunday," continued Alice, "and the 'beds are quite comfy.'"

"Do you remember when Mother gave driving lessons?"

"We were *so* broke."

"And Father started his vegetable garden that summer."

"Do you remember Mother's creamed radishes?"

"Oh, Harriet—don't remind us," sighed Cora, making a face that had them all laughing.

"Creamed radishes?"

"Doesn't it sound awful, Sam?"

"But the first summer, that was our most bountiful crop," continued Harriet. "Father would put on his gloves and straw hat and go out in the morning and count the radishes. The neighbors used to say, 'Look—

there's Franklin Hoskins in his vegetable garden. He looks like he has a million in the bank.' But believe you me, he didn't."

What fun it was! Hadn't they had some times! Bad times. But good times, too. Sam and Wayne exchanged a glance. Two more dissimilar people would be hard to find, but now they were linked, nodding at each other from time to time with expressions that asked: Do you think they'll let us join their magic circle? while the sisters chattered on, united in a tight knot of affection and reminiscence.

"Frankie! Come join us!"

"Looks pretty crowded." He grinned and came halfway up the stairs, crouching there, for there was no room left at the top.

"We were always having parties 'B.C.' "

" 'B.C.'???"

"Before the Crash—dumb bunny," explained Frankie to his oldest sister. "Don't you know that Harriet's very hep?"

"Look who's talking."

"Sometimes, Sam"—Cora paused, fussing and straightening his tie— "we'd have the whole block roped off and have a carnival. Mother was always throwing circuses and carnivals for church. We had art shows and musicales and poetry readings. . . . We haven't had a party in ages, have we?"

"I wonder why," murmured Alice as Franklin appeared below and looked up.

"Join us, Father," called Cora, shooting a disapproving look at Alice. "We'll make room."

Franklin shook his head, and Harriet didn't want to admit to the wariness in his eyes as he disappeared. "Father is having such a good time tonight," she heard Cora insist. Harriet found herself exchanging a glance with Wayne, whose expression was compassionate. "There have been many casualties of the Depression," he said softly, looking after Franklin.

"My father's still out of work. Mr. Hoskins is fortunate he's got a job again. Half the mills in Leveret never reopened."

"Ten million people are still out of work in the country," nodded Alice. "We're like a chronic invalid. The temperature's lower in the morning but shows no signs of returning quickly to normal."

"You're such a pessimist, Alice. Why not be positive? That's how Sam and I feel, don't we, Sam? What was it Mother always said. . . ?"

"When our ship comes in!"

"What are you all doing up there?" called Letty. "What ship?"

"Mother—you have a rose in your hair."

"Your father presented it to me."

"See?" cried Cora, feeling vindicated.

"The guests are neglected, girls. My, what a cozy group you all are."

"We're literally dripping with nostalgia, Mother." A moment later,

105

laughing and chattering again, they followed each other down the narrow barn stairs, and Frankie sat at the old piano that had been brought out to the barn for the summer and began to play.

"Why, that's our song, isn't it?" cried Harriet. "Frankie and I wrote the words and music!" As some of the guests gathered by the large open barn doors, the sisters linked arms and began to sing.

"*We are the girls from Mulberry Street you hear so much about—*"

"Mother, come on!"

A few more entreaties, a nudge from Ada, and Letty joined her daughters, catching the beat and kicking high.

"*. . . the people cheer and shout for us whenever we go out . . .*"

"Better than the Follies," called out Reverend Peabody as they all collapsed into each other's arms to enthusiastic applause.

"We'll have dancing now and the ice cream as soon as it's ready!" called Cora.

"Father?" Letty caught Franklin watching his daughters. Dabbing at herself with a hankie, she stepped over to him. "Here we all are again," she whispered, accepting the glass of punch he offered. Let it *be* the same again.

Franklin nodded. "What are you looking at?" he asked with a hint of belligerence.

"At how well you look," she replied quickly. "Dance, Father?" She curtsied as Frankie began a waltz. Franklin hesitated, then spun Letty to a round of applause. She caught glimpses of her children watching, and her heart filled as she looked up at her husband, who smiled carefully.

"Yoo-hoo, everyone—the ice cream's ready."

"Look!" cried Sam, pointing upward. "It's the *Hindenburg!*"

"So what?" demanded Alice, frowning, all things German being anathema. But she couldn't help staring, too, as the immense airship, its lights winking in the sky, moved slowly over Jericho. At the same moment a cream-colored La Salle convertible pulled up out front, and Elliot Phelps came down into the garden with a girl on his arm.

"What is *he* doing here?" Harriet ducked into the barn, pulling Alice with her.

"It's just Elliot Phelps slumming in the middle class."

"Didn't you know?" added Cora, passing through with dishes of ice cream. "He and Frankie are friends. They met over at the Classic Ballroom. Elliot's very interested in music."

"What? Frankie didn't tell me. Why didn't he tell me? Why didn't somebody tell me?" Harriet glared at Alice.

"Who's had a chance? Calm down. I know," added Alice with a wry grin, "that you used to have a crush on the Prince, but—"

"Oh, shut up!" Harriet took a peek outside. "He's the last person I would've expected, that's all. The last person . . ."

"Oh—the money."

"Well, of *course*, the money! What do you think I'm having a shit-fit for? My health? It's due. I wanted a little time. He'll tell his father I'm back and— Oh, *damn!*"

Whatever homecoming glow was left was thoroughly extinguished. Harriet began to pace back and forth in dismay. What came next was nothing she relished admitting to anyone, especially to Alice. "A couple of months after I quit the Automat, I wrote to Mr. Phelps . . . just a chatty note . . . I'd written him several. I—I asked if I could borrow some more money. He never replied. Right after I sent the letter, I knew I shouldn't have. I wanted to get it back. Do you think Elliot knows? I'm so embarrassed. He'll think I'm such a fool."

"You who conquered the father should have no trouble at all with the son."

"Alice—sometimes I cannot stand you!"

"Harriet—guess who's here?" cried Marcia breathlessly, hurrying into the barn, followed by a more leisurely Libby. "The Prince!"

"I know. Who's that with him?"

"Amy Bowditch. Very la-dee-da. She lives up at the lake. She's a senior at Wellesley. She and Elliot have been an item for some time."

"Poor Amy," commented Libby.

"Libby dated him a few times last year."

"Much to my regret. I don't think he's interested in nice girls, if you get my drift. He dates society types like Amy because of his father but—"

"And has a *reputation*," interjected Marcia, suddenly wide-eyed and sixteen. "Drinks like a fish and—"

"Girl talk?" Frankie ducked a head in.

"Why didn't you tell me?"

"Tell you what?"

"That you and Elliot Phelps were so chummy. *Traitor.*"

Frankie shrugged. "Slipped my mind, I guess." Puzzled, he regarded Harriet. The swells—Elliot Phelps and his crowd—had little repercussion for him. "What's the trouble? Elliot's keen. Here he is."

"Frankie?" called Elliot, appearing in the doorway with Amy. "Oh. Hi, everyone."

"Why, look who's here!" cried Harriet, voice slightly higher than usual, sounding a bit like Cora. "Frankie—why didn't you tell me Elliot Phelps was here? I'll bet he doesn't even remember me—does he?"

"He does," replied Elliot easily. "You're Harriet. You came to a birthday party at the Mansion when you were ten and refused to leave."

"Are there no secrets left?" Harriet laughed giddily. "Do you know my sister Alice?" she continued. "And my friends Marcia Pratt and—no, she's Andrews now—and Libby Stillings. I hear you do know Libby."

"Hi, Libby. Yes, we know each other."

"Hello, Elliot," said Libby rather coolly.

"Isn't this nice, though?" asked Harriet. "Isn't it, though?"

"And this is Amy Bowditch." Elliot introduced the willowy creature at his side.

"Hello," she said, glancing down her exquisite nose at them all.

"How wonderful of you to come." Harriet wished she had a cigarette. "Well, isn't this nice?" Gushing like a cut artery, she was saved from drowning in her own goo by Frankie.

"Yep," he grinned, "the country club set has discovered the Classic. They're tired of dull music—right, Elliot? They wanna swing!" Frankie snapped his fingers.

Elliot joined in. "Feed it to me!"

Libby and Marcia exchanged a glance. They'd both been curious as to why Elliot Phelps should be friends with Frankie Hoskins. The interest in jazz explained it.

"Here we are." Letty appeared behind the group with a tray of ice cream.

"Hello there, Mrs. Hoskins." Elliot nodded politely. "It's kind of you to have us. Frankie mentioned the peach ice cream, and we just couldn't resist. We were stuck at a very boring dinner, but it's nice to be here."

How sweet, thought Harriet. *He's practically one of the family.* She watched her mother, not ordinarily an easy conquest, warm to Elliot's honeyed charm. "Delicious," murmured Elliot, tasting, catching Harriet's eye.

"Excuse me, won't you?" she asked, wanting to disappear. "I'll take a dish to Father."

"Harriet, sit with me." Ten minutes or so later, Letty motioned for her daughter to join her on the glider on the piazza. "What's wrong? I haven't had a chance to have so much as a word with you. You've a bee in your bonnet, that's for sure." Harriet shrugged. "And what do you mean," continued Letty, "about being home only for a visit? Where are you going?"

"To Timbuktu, if I could. And right this minute." Her eyes found Amy and Elliot down in the lower garden with Frankie and several others. Frankie was teaching Elliot how to blow trumpet. "Did you know they were friends?"

"I don't think they're *friends*. Elliot's at least four years older than Frankie. Your brother mentioned he'd been to the Classic a few times but. . . ." Strange, thought Letty, it wasn't the sort of place she would have imagined appealing to the scion of the Phelps family. Nor could she see Abraham Phelps approving his only son's frequenting of a working-class dance hall with an unsavory reputation. She certainly didn't relish Frankie working there. But you couldn't say anything to young people nowadays. They seemed bent on going their own way, looking at you as if to say, well—you botched it up, didn't you? And with the state of the world these last few years, perhaps they were right. . . .

"Harriet, I can't get over how different you seem."

"How?" Her eyes never left Elliot. How beautiful he was. It was a strange way to describe a man. Angrily she rose and stubbed out her cigarette. "I wish I hadn't come home empty-handed, that's all."

"Harriet," cautioned Letty, distressed with her daughter's barely controlled fidgets, "are you under the impression that we love you only if you accomplish brilliant things? You're important to us—no matter what."

"Thanks," muttered Harriet, who suddenly felt totally out of step, a stranger with her mother and all of these people. What on earth was she doing here? "Dammit, I'm going to bed."

"Is your language the latest in New York, too? It doesn't impress me, my girl." Harriet had changed, there was no doubt of it. Letty couldn't quite put her finger on it, but this defensive young woman was certainly not the same eighteen-year-old who'd gone off two years back.

Mother and daughter were interrupted by Cora, who trooped by with several ladies, taking them into the house to show off the linens, towels and tea cozies in her hope chest.

"A fall wedding, Letty?" asked Irene Ingalls.

"Ayea. Late fall. November."

Down by the birdbath, Elliot raised the trumpet, producing a feeble *bleah* that had everyone laughing.

"I'm really tired, Mother, so—"

"May I use the facilities, Mrs. Hoskins?" Amy came up onto the piazza. Harriet managed a smile. Don't fall in.

"Harriet—c'mon down here!"

Pretending not to hear Frankie calling for her, she hid herself behind a trailing clematis.

Elliot's arrival had caused a stir, and he knew it. He enjoyed the glances that came from these people. A few of them worked for his father; none of those gathered tonight were of his class, but the discrepancy didn't bother Elliot. Attention was attention, and he relished it as he ran his hand through his hair in a characteristic gesture.

He was Elliot Phelps, son of Abraham Phelps; he was the Prince, heir to the Jericho mill and thirteen others—therefore regarded with respect, awe, fear and envy. No one in Jericho knew who'd coined Elliot's nickname. Some wag hanging around the depot, perhaps, who'd spotted Elliot stepping off the train from prep school, an aura of royal gold about him with his blond hair and camel coat as he handed his bags to the chauffeur and glanced at the mill and the town. It was all his; he couldn't have cared less.

He'd majored in classics and graduated Princeton in June. Not sure what he wanted to do (and with no money of his own), he had no choice but to return to Jericho and, at his father's insistence, enter the business. That scenario had been ordained the day he was born.

But Jericho found Elliot changed. In three short months he'd earned a reputation as a womanizer, a drinker, etcetera. Phelps was unhappy with him. Elliot had a shimmer of fast rumor about him now, an air of secrets and unpredictability that might be self-destructive, a tension and danger that made him irresistible to women.

"Listen to Elliot, Harriet," called Frankie as she reluctantly joined them. "I think he needs some inspiration." Elliot grasped the trumpet and made another attempt. Amusing the onlookers with his puffed-out cheeks and funny faces, he produced another wavery and feeble *bleaaaah*.

"Your turn, sport—I'll stick to listening." Aren't they chummy? thought Harriet as the two exchanged jive talk.

"I'm in the groove. . . ." Frankie did a quick bravura solo, making his trumpet almost croon.

"Bravo!" Elliot threw his arm around the younger man's shoulder. "Jericho doesn't know what it has in this cat. But soon the country will," he added, eyes meeting Harriet's. Quickly she looked away.

Flattered by the compliments, Frankie let go with another wail, then excused himself to get ready to go to work at the Classic. *The fates are not kind*, sighed Harriet, for within a moment or two the others had drifted off, and she was left alone with Elliot.

"I thought you were avoiding me."

"Me?" she asked, caught by his seductive eyes. "Why should I do that? Actually, it's just that I've returned home today. Just a short visit. And I'm rather tired, what with catching up."

"You have such an attractive family. You must be glad to be home. It's really amazing how you and Frankie look alike. I suppose you've been told that before."

Harriet nodded. Avoiding Elliot's bedroom eyes, which seemed to undress her, she swallowed some smoke and coughed so as to have time to get her bearings.

"He's a neat fellow, isn't he?" continued Elliot. "I wish I were part of a large family. It's so nice here. So calming."

Calming? Did the rich have need of calming, too? Harriet assumed they already had it. *Did* he know, she wondered, of her financial dealings with his father? He must. Then again, maybe—hopefully—not.

"Frankie's been spoiled rotten by four females," she bandied, continuing to talk of her brother, which seemed a safe-enough subject. Elliot smiled. "Such *attractive* females," he murmured, his eyes telling Harriet she was the most. She looked away, feeling slightly mesmerized. He was charming, she had to admit, even courtly. Breeding did tell. Fireflies darted in the murk behind him as she raised her eyes, astounded once again by his beauty. He was almost too perfect, this Arrow Collar man. Yet she couldn't read him and was wary. Above his head a lantern caused his sandy blond hair to shine, turning the shoulders of his light suit to pink. She wanted to get away.

"So nice to be here," he said again, and she thought she caught a hint of sadness in his voice.

"Yes." The heavy odor of the roses caused her to feel lightheaded. Conversation seemed to have run down. "Want a sip?" he asked, removing a silver pocket flask. She shook her head and watched him as he brought it to his lips. "Souvenir of my college days," he said, the silver surface glittering as he returned the flask to his breast pocket. "Why don't you come over to the Classic with us? I'm driving Frankie."

"Oh . . . no, thanks. . . . I'm really rather tired."

"Amy wouldn't mind. If that's what you're wondering."

"I wasn't," she replied, raising an eyebrow.

"Some other time . . ."

"Why not?" she replied, flicking her bangs and pleased with his pursuit, which she told herself was only justified (since he'd obviously recognized her as a special hotshot, not of mundane Jericho). Yet she didn't feel at all up to flirtatious banter, and Elliot's scrutiny made her nervous. " 'The Kiss of the Sun for Pardon . . .' " Having nothing more to say, she began to recite the poem hand-painted by Alice on a piece of wood attached low to the side of the barn behind the birdbath's cherub. " '. . . the Song of the Birds for Mirth. One is . . .' "

" 'Nearer God's Heart in a Garden,' " continued Elliot, " 'Than Anyplace Else on Earth.' Robert Louis Stevenson."

She nodded. He lit her cigarette. "Well," she began, trying to find a diplomatic way to make an exit.

"Tell me about New York. I envy you. I'd like to be there. Right now."

"Me, too."

"I imagine."

Each of them looked up toward the gathering, and their eyes met as if sharing a common bond that neither belonged here. Harriet was flattered that Elliot understood.

"Dad told me you had something published in New York."

Startled by the mention of his father, she managed a little laugh. "Just an arty nothing"—she had included a copy of *Pegasus* in the very letter in which she had asked to borrow more money—"with a circulation of about twenty." She stole a glance, wondering if there was hidden meaning in his comment. The low, incessant motor of the crickets mirrored her nervousness. There was something about his expression, something . . . amused. Was he playing with her?

111

"What are you doing these days?" she asked, trying to change the subject.

"Working for Dad at the mill. Sales." She sensed he didn't like it. She waited for more but it wasn't forthcoming.

"I'm just home for a visit," she said, forgetting she'd already made the point. He nodded. "How *is* your father?" she asked, wishing she hadn't.

"Do you really want to know?"

"Pardon?" Upset with the question, not to mention Elliot's slow smile, which reminded her of his father's, she had no chance to reply to his innuendo, for a babble of voices raised up at the house caught her attention. Grateful for the distraction, she looked to find Letty hurrying toward her.

"Excuse us, Elliot." Letty took Harriet's arm and led her over to Franklin and Wayne Thibeau, who were arguing loudly. "See what you can do," whispered Letty, distressed at the anger that had erupted in her husband's face.

"Communists!" Franklin jabbed a finger in the air at Wayne. "I'm surprised at you, young man. You're not bright. But if you want to go over to Spain and join up—that's your business. But don't try and tell me I should be supporting those Spaniards. They're Reds! Everybody knows it. So do you!" Heads nearby nodded approval.

"I don't mean to be disrespectful, sir, but the government of Spain was democratically elected, and they've only become dependent on the Soviet Union's help because—"

"Godless atheists!"

"—because we refuse to help them against Franco, that's why." Alice took up where Wayne left off. Behind her, their friends huddled, nodding. Franklin glared at his daughter, and she glared back, her face taut with intensity. "It's a *civil* war in Spain, Father. And it can be laid at our doorstep."

"The doorstep of all the imperialist countries," added Wayne. "It's our doing."

"Why does she have to provoke him?" whispered Letty. "Say something!"

"Father," interjected Harriet, trying to get his attention, "why don't we go and sit on the glider?" To her dismay she discovered that Elliot had followed and was listening to the argument. Would all of this get reported back to Phelps? She could imagine the expression on his face when Elliot told him of a garden party at the Hoskins' complete with radicals emerging from the bushes.

"We should join the Popular Front and fight fascism," continued Wayne. "The Soviets aren't our enemies. The Germans are. It's the Germans who are supplying Franco and the rebels. Why shouldn't we help the Loyalists?"

112

"Crap."

"Franklin . . ." called Letty.

"And who are you calling imperialist?" demanded Franklin, ignoring both his wife and daughter's attempts to lead him away. "I'm an American, you son of a bitch!"

"Father, this is silly. Now come and—"

"Don't give me that bull about Mussolini and Hitler, either," he went on. "Let them all fight it out among themselves. It's none of our business."

"Hear, hear . . ." If some of those gathered were shocked at Franklin's language, the sentiments he expressed found support. Once again, Harriet took her father's arm. "We haven't even had a chance to chat."

"I'm an American, too, sir," said Wayne, who couldn't let it alone, either.

"Enough, Wayne," retorted Letty firmly. "It's not the time."

"I'm not a communist, Mrs. Hoskins."

"Not yet," whispered one of Wayne's friends.

"Of course you're not. Now, weren't we going to have some songs? Cora? Marcia? Why don't we all—?"

"Don't come into my yard and try to get my neighbors on your side."

"He didn't, Father."

"Alice," warned Letty, "enough."

"Trash," muttered Franklin. "Bums. Now that you're back, talk some sense into your sister." He let Harriet lead him a few steps away, then turned. "Get out," he snapped at Alice. "You and your bums. Get out of my yard. You're not my daughter any more."

"Father—"

"Franklin—"

A buzz of dismay and embarrassed looks swept the gathering. "What are you staring at?" demanded Franklin. Suddenly they were all the enemy, and he didn't recognize his neighbors, whose faces seemed to mock him. "All of you—get out. This party's over."

"Father," pleaded Cora, tears stinging her eyes as the group fell into a shocked silence and Harriet led Franklin up the piazza steps and into the house. A moment later she had him settled in the rocker in the back bedroom.

"She makes me mad."

"I know . . . I know. . . . It's nothing to get so excited about, is it?"

"You're smoking like a chimney," he grumbled.

"And who did I get that from?" she chided gently, trying to get her bearings.

"It's all gone to hell . . . all of it . . . son of a bitch!" He banged his hand on the arm of the rocker. "Don't," he growled, rebuffing her as she tried to massage his neck. She stepped quickly away. Down below, the embarrassed gathering was breaking up.

113

"Have I spoiled it for you? I suppose you blame me." He wanted the feel of her hand soothing him, but guilt caused him to snap, "Disappointed you again? Haven't I! I haven't had a drink in a week," he pleaded, lying. "But nobody believes—"

"I do," she replied quickly. "Father—"

"I won't do it again," he promised, feeling suddenly furious with her gentleness toward him. "Are you staying in Jericho?" he asked, turning away, unable to face her. Especially her.

She nodded. On edge, she sat on the bed, then got up, the glow of her cigarette making nervous arcs in the dark room. "I'll get you some warm milk," she said, wanting to get away from him. The kitchen was deserted. In the pantry she surprised Letty, who was leaning on the edge of the sink in distress. "Why does he have to behave like that?" asked Letty. "How dare—" She bit her lip and turned away. "I'm glad you're back. Maybe— No, it's my responsibility."

Harriet hugged Letty soundlessly to her as Reverend Peabody poked a cautious head into the kitchen. "Mrs. Hoskins—are you there? We'll say good night."

Letty composed herself, and she and Harriet entered the kitchen. Harriet put the milk on. A pall had settled over the house. Behind her she heard her mother and the minister talking in hushed voices. She stirred the milk quickly to a boil that mirrored her own turbulence. Had her mother become an object of sympathy to her friends and neighbors?

"Elliot's leaving, Mother," Frankie called from the dining room. "He's taking me to work. He wants to say good night to you."

"You go, Harriet. I'll take Father the milk. Say good night for me."

"It's so nice to see you again, Harriet," said Mrs. Peabody. "Welcome home. Will we see you at church tomorrow?"

"Of course," she replied, taking her time as she went to the front of the house, for she had little desire to encounter Elliot again. Welcome home? What had she come home to? A mother who was valiant, visibly grown older and walking on eggs, at the mercy of a man who held her and his entire family in continued jeopardy? She felt like shouting, wanted to run, but instead she put on a bright smile and went out on the front porch.

"How's your father?" asked Elliot, separating himself from Amy and coming to meet her on the steps.

"Fine," she replied, embarrassed. "Overtired, I think."

"I thought you'd deserted me for good. Why not come up and see me at the Mansion sometime?" he whispered conspiratorially.

"Oh, thank you, but—" His invitation confused her. "I'm just here for a—"

"Visit?" Elliot finished her sentence with another of his slow smiles.

"Awfully nice to have met you," called Amy, barely looking. Frankie climbed into the rumble seat, Elliot into the front. Alice joined Harriet on the sidewalk and linked her arm with her sister's. "Those of us who know better," she began, pointedly looking from Elliot to Amy, "are boycotting silk because of Japan's militarism."

All eyes went to Amy's silk dress—yards of it, ruffles and flourishes, scallops and bows.

"Catch ya later, alligator!" Elliot smiled at Harriet and started the motor. He said something to Amy, and they both laughed. Not too sure what all these undercurrents were, Frankie grinned anyway.

"We *don't* know any better, Alice," called Elliot over the motor. He put the car into a U-turn, narrowly missing several others. Pulling up close to the sisters, he looked straight at Harriet.

"I'll tell Dad you're back, shall I?" He winked and waved. "I know he'll want to hear from you," he added as he drove off.

Later in the evening, after dancing with Amy and listening to the band, Elliot returned to Jericho and dropped Amy home. Restless, he went back to the Classic, watched Frankie and got drunk. Around midnight he left with another of his girls, Myrna, a regular in the low-life crowd at the ballroom, with a reputation that was worse than Elliot's. After making love to her and leaving just as quickly, he returned to Jericho again and drove slowly up Mulberry Street, staring at the Hoskins' darkened and sleeping house, eyes on Frankie's window and an ache in his chaotic heart.

6 "It's useless, Ma," yelled Dennis, trying to be heard over the rushing of the wind, for the top was down on the Ford. He'd been routed from the tax office to aid in the pursuit. A week after his return, Patrick had fled the coop. Following his night on the lake, he'd walked back to town on Sunday morning and spent the week in hiding at Teresa's. Several stormy sessions on the phone with Gert had led to a standstill of misunderstanding, animosity and violent recriminations on both sides. Patrick's decision to leave Jericho had been made this morning. He'd left a note for his aunt to say he was hitching to Boston, and she had come home for lunch and found it in time to alert Gert.

"Did you hear me, Ma? He's probably got a ride already. He's gone."

Gert's car skirted the edges of the state forest on Route 28, her eyes searching anxiously ahead, peering into cars as she whizzed by. The speedometer quivered to fifty, her hands a steely grip on the wheel. Ten minutes later in North Reading, a farmer going to market with a load of late corn looked into his mirror, wondered at the commotion of honking behind him, and pulled over.

Heart pounding, Gert stared at her son, who was sitting among the crates on the back of the truck. "Get down," she ordered. "What's this?" she added as something that looked like a sheep jumped down, sniffed at her and growled.

"It's called a dog." Patrick patted the head of the animal who'd followed him home from the lake.

"Don't give me any lip, boyo. I'd soon as sock ya as look at ya."

"Listen, folks . . ." interjected the farmer, wanting to be on his way. Gert gave the peasant a perfunctory smile. "Get along with ya now. He won't be needin' a ride."

"Ma," warned Patrick.

"Come home. I've somethin' important to show ya."

"She does," nodded Dennis, trying to help.

"What is it?" asked Patrick.

"You'll see." Cars sped past. The farmer left. Patrick sighed. What a fiasco! He'd made fifteen miles.

"Look, Ma, you'll have to understand—"

"C'mon. It's too hot to be standin' here!" Gert fanned her face nervously. The sight of her determined-jawed son caused her to wonder if she knew him at all. To just up and leave? How desperate was he? "Look," she went on, tone softening to almost a plea, "if you're not happy with what I've got to show ya, I'll drive ya myself to wherever ya want to go."

Patrick hesitated. Did he have a choice? He didn't know where he was going, had no real plan at all. "Things will have to be different."

"Anything ya like," nodded Gert with a tremulous sigh of relief as Patrick picked up his suitcase. "What's *it* doin'?" she demanded, as the dog followed Patrick to the car.

"He's mine," he replied, one foot poised on the running board, the other still planted rebelliously on the ground. The point was made. Gert raised her eyes to heaven asking help from various saints but managed, with a supreme effort, to hold her tongue. "All right," she sighed, "get in then—the two of youse."

She was in high spirits on the ride back. "Yes, I've somethin' to show ya." Her eyes sparkled. She turned to Dennis beside her. "He'll see, won't he, Denny? He'll see who's got his best interests at heart."

"WHAT???" hollered Patrick from the back seat, half unable and half pretending not to be able to hear her in the open car.

"HE'LL SEE—" Her eyes met his in the rear-view mirror.

Twenty minutes later Gert pulled up outside St. Mary's Parish Hall, a large, two-story structure with a couple of storefronts below and the hall above, on the corner of Main and Essex Streets, right down the block from the house.

"Hurry now." Out of the car she stepped smartly, pausing in front of the old shoe-repair shop that Father Gahaghan used to rent to Mr. Faenza till he passed on to his reward a month ago. In the window a three-foot, lifelike puppet of a cobbler wearing an apron stared intently at a small shoe, its hand with a hammer poised in midair.

"Phone's in, Mrs. Flynn," said a phone company man, emerging as Gert and her sons entered the vacant store.

"You're a poet," cracked Gert. At the rear a couple of painters were spreading dropcloths. "Didn't the sign painter show up?" she called, picking up a piece of cardboard that carried the instructions. She handed it to Patrick, trying hard to conceal her anticipation. "Read it. That's goin' on the window."

"What is it?"

"It's going to be a newspaper," answered Dennis as Patrick stared at the cardboard. "Ma's starting a newspaper."

"A what???"

117

Gert laughed at his expression and took the cardboard back, reading from it with a flourish: " 'Jericho Irish Spectator . . . Patrick Flynn, Editor-in-Chief.' "

"What???"

"What do ya think?" She took his arm and led him behind the counter. "The counter's stayin'. I wanted to get everythin' ready before ya saw it, but I didn't have time, did I? Certain people didn't give me time, did they? But far be it from me to mention—"

Gert's jaw dropped as Patrick turned to go. "What is it?" she cried.

"I'm not going to listen to—"

"Calm down, calm down. Ya know I get excited sometimes. Patty," she pleaded, "look what I've accomplished! This'll be your office. They're doin' it a nice beige. Aren't ya, boys?" she called expansively to the painters, while an anxious eye stole a glance at her son, hoping for a positive reaction. "There's two desks I got cheap comin'," she continued, "also a couple of typewriters. And filin' cabinets, too. There's another room to the rear for supplies and a toilet. A cot if ya need a nap—but ya won't have time. No heat in the place. We'll get you a stove when it's necessary. This all come about because . . ."

Father Gahaghan had planted the seed. Gert had known she was going to have to act fast if she was to keep Patrick with her. The parish newsletter needed a bright eye, suggested Gahaghan. Maybe Pat could see to it. Newsletter, indeed, thought Gert, catching the ball and running for a touchdown. Already she had circulation figures dancing in her head. Big plans from little acorns grew. "Well?" she demanded, hands on her hips. "Well?"

"But—"

"I won't be hearin' 'buts' now. I could use a nod or two."

"I don't know the first thing—"

"Tomorrow you've an appointment with Francis Dugan of the *Eagle* over in Leveret. He'll tell ya everythin' you'll need to know. Don't worry, you'll have help. Rose can do secretarial. Denny here wants to write a column, don't ya, Denny? I'm goin' to be available myself night and day. This is a family project."

Supremely satisfied with her plans, she paced the store, seeing it ready, swooning to the power of the press, ear vibrating to the sweet rumblings of a political machine, the first crank of the mighty gears—a dynasty aborning.

"Think of the possibilities, Pat—"

Gert nodded, interrupting Dennis. "That's right. We're a family on the move." And all nests feathered, she might have added, with Patrick at the helm and Denny running for Congress, the family paper behind him. Not to mention more pressing political necessities, such as convincing Timothy O'Brien's father that the Flynns were up and comers with a more

118

than eligible daughter for his fat-assed son. What better way to butter the toast than to have *The Jericho Irish Spectator* support Michael O'Brien's candidacy for vice-president in the coming election? Not to forget a praiseful endorsement for his good buddy, the sainted Father Coughlin on whose Union Party ticket O'Brien was running?

"But—" interjected Patrick, interrupting the fantasy.

"Don't nitpick with me, boyo."

"But Jericho doesn't need—"

"Nobody knows what they need till ya tell 'em. This won't just be a paper for Jericho. It'll be for the county, too. For all the Irish north of Boston right up into Maine. Why not, I say? Think *big*, else you'll stay small."

"But there was an Irish paper in Leveret that folded, so—"

"Stop arguin' with me. I won't have it! I thought you'd be pleased." Wounded, she turned to Dennis. "Listen to him! Arguin' with me after what I've—"

"Ma's even lined up some advertisers," said Dennis dutifully.

"That's right. You've already got Dillon's grocery, Teresa'll take an ad, needless to say, and the Leveret Gas Company. Now what do ya think of that? Father Gahaghan's givin' me a break on the rent, so's expenses'll be kept down. Your cousin Dinny Malone's gonna handle the printin'. I'm not goin' to have ya ruin your life runnin' off to an uncertain future. Jericho never had a paper. Now it does. It's fittin' ya should run it. You've had a brilliant education. *Who*, I'd like to know, is better qualified?" *Who* would now be staying home where he belonged and out of trouble? "What have ya to say to me?"

"I'd better get back to the office, Ma," said Dennis.

"Ya won't be there much longer," replied Gert, "pushin' pencils in a job that's beneath ya. You'll be in Congress two years from now, God willin', and Rose'll be Mrs. Timothy O'Brien, and I'll be able finally to rest easy. Now get on with ya." As Dennis departed, Gert said, loud enough for him to hear: "I don't know what I'd have done these last years without Denny. A mother couldn't ask for a son more loyal."

Why don't you let him alone? Patrick wanted to say but didn't.

The painters went out to the truck a moment later, leaving mother and son alone. With much sniffing and poking, the dog finished his exploration of the premises and seemed satisfied. "Where'd you find it?" asked Gert, unable to hide her distaste for the creature who was in need of a comb and a bath.

"Out walking."

"C'mere, doggy." At least she was trying. The dog seemed unimpressed.

"His name's Albatross."

"That's a queer name."

119

"It's a bird you can't get rid of."

"You're a bit of a queer bird yourself, aren't ya, Patty?"

"I don't think so. No."

"I suppose you'll be bringin' it home?" The question had to do with more than the dog. Both of them knew it and were mightily ill at ease.

"OK," said Patrick finally.

Gert nodded, found she needed to breathe, and started for the door. "Where were you goin'?"

"California," he replied vaguely, still stunned at what was being thrust upon him.

"To pick oranges like a common bum? Supper's at quarter to five. I've opened a small account for ya at the bank." She turned to go, but couldn't seem to. Against the bright sunlight outside, her silhouette filled the doorway as she turned halfway back to her son. "I was born one of eleven children in a stone house no bigger than this place. Stones from the earth. Stones everywhere. Fields of stones. And I knew I had to get out of there and come to America and make something of myself, which I have. I've searched my heart these last days. I've prayed to Almighty God to give me an answer. I don't understand what's come over ya. If it's all my fault, what's happened, if ya want me to shoulder the blame for it, I'll take it on. I'll never understand ya, but we'll make the best of it. Scoff if ya like, but all I ever wanted was the best for my children. Lemme tell ya, boyo—it's a thankless undertakin'."

◼

"Well, Pat," boomed Minnie Delaney, Gert's oldest sister and head of the Boston clan who were in the construction business, "you're not to be a priest—hah? I suppose you'll be gettin' married next. Handsome devil! Don't worry—your ma'll find her for ya!"

Behind the laughter, her eyes were Gert's, searching her nephew's face with a piercing glance. What was really going on? What was *really* behind this short-notice, early September extravaganza of a shindig that Gert had concocted to take the sting out of her son's defection from the priesthood? "Craziest thing I ever heard of!" Min had harumphed to her husband on the drive up from Jamaica Plain outside of Boston. "*He* quits the Church, and *she* throws a party. What's it all about? What's she coverin'? You think he knocked somebody up?"

If these and similar questions were on the minds of all the relatives, friends, local politicians and hangers-on who had been invited to "welcome my Pat home" and celebrate—unbeknownst to them—the birth of Jericho's new weekly; if a buzz of curiosity lay just beneath the surface of the jolly crowd that filled the back yard on Essex Street—Gert would provide the answers before the day was out.

Patrick's return to town over a week ago had rocketed along the family grapevine like a thunderclap. But the formation of the newspaper had been guarded like the secrets of the confessional. Teresa had been threatened into silence. No one but the immediate family and Father Gahaghan knew of the week's furious activity behind the tarpaulin hanging across the window of the former shoe-repair shop under the parish hall.

As for the very reluctant honoree, Patrick was on his second highball. Today's celebration was definitely a cross he'd rather not bear. He grinned blankly at his Aunt Min, concentrating on the blossoms of her voluminous dress as she continued to question him. Since the guests had started filling the back yard a few hours ago, he'd run a gauntlet of barely concealed looks of grief from his various aunts, overly hearty handshakes and backslapping from some of the men, pious disapproval from others, and outright stares from a passel of cousins. If most of the gathering now stuffing themselves and imbibing freely had been more circumspect with their questions and suspicions, it was Aunt Minnie who came right out now and asked: "What's up, Pat? Why'd you quit?"

Patrick hoped she'd choke on the large piece of ham now disappearing into her mouth. "We're glad to see you, of course, precious," offered his spinster Aunt Moira, who wore black and exuded sanctity mixed with cologne, "but we thought we'd be seeing you under different circumstances. We were looking forward to your first Mass. . . ." Minnie nodded emphatically.

"Don't be botherin' my Pat with a lot of questions now." Running interference, Gert hove into the group and grasped Minnie's fleshy upper arm in a tight squeeze. "It's to be a surprise. You'll hear all about it in good time. You'll be just as glad as I was when you hear the happy news of why he's come back. Have ya had enough to eat?"

"You can't fool me, Gert," scoffed Minnie. "What's this so-called *surprise*? Why're we here?"

"For a party! What's it look like?" Gert linked her arm solidly with her son's, while her expert caterer's eye swept the groaning picnic tables where latecomers were busy ladling the goodies onto paper plates. "More comin'," she hollered, the precariousness of her position revealed in a brogue thicker than usual on this momentous Pull-The-Wool-Over-Their-Eyes Day.

If Min was all the more suspicious at her sister's high spirits, she consoled herself with the feast provided. Two kegs of beer and a flowing bar presided over by Dennis had put the group of just over forty in a mellow mood, ready to accept anything that Gert might have to offer. Not to mention the well-satisfied good fellowship that a turkey, two baked hams, three kinds of salad, baked beans, hot dogs, hamburgers, and Gert's famous date squares had induced.

"How does she afford it?" whispered the crones.

"Doesn't she know there's still a Depression on?"

121

"You know Gert. Gets it all cut-rate. Orders for the rectory, don't you know."

"Has investments, too."

"Thick as thieves with Monsignor O'Malley, who's secretary to His Eminence, Cushing himself. You know how her and Rose is always at those functions. Noses in the air. Butter wouldn't melt. She gets her tips right at the chancery."

The Church hadn't gone broke during hard times, and neither, as the gossips were noting, had Gert.

"I was just telling Pat that now he's not to be a priest, you probably have a girl picked out for him," continued Minnie, still sniffing for clues.

Gert roared. "As if he'd need my help! Aren't I right, you Hennessey girls? He's a proper catch, isn't he now?" The Hennessey twins, Mary and Lucy—both likely candidates—blushed prettily. Gert made the introductions, letting it be known that the two damsels had been educated by the Sisters of Mercy and were now in their senior year at Marymount, ". . . well-bred Catholic girls and a credit to their mother!" Patrick chafed in his new light suit. "Well," demanded Gert, "isn't he a sight for sore eyes, my Patrick?"

Mary, by far the lovelier of the two, with a skin of Easter lilies and tangerine blossoms, nodded approvingly. Beneath her decorous convent brown, her eyes met Patrick's in a provocative twinkle. "Look!" she exclaimed, "there's the evening star."

"Make a wish," ordered Gert. "Everybody, make a wish."

Patrick wished he were someplace else.

"I wish for better times . . . success and prosperity for everyone," said Mary as if reciting for the nuns.

"Oh, you're not supposed to *say*," admonished her sister. "It won't come true."

"It'll come true, dearie—don't be worryin'," replied Gert, halting further conjecture.

Several others nearby raised their glasses in hopeful agreement. Gert's eyes sparkled, then darkened a moment later as she got Patrick to herself. "You've had enough," she said, indicating his glass. He muttered to Albatross, who looked up at Gert and growled. "And would it be too much to ask for a smile? Ya look like you're at a funeral!"

"I didn't want any of this . . . saving face. . . ."

"I haven't broken my back to get this together to have ya look like you've a poker up your rear!"

Startled, Patrick erupted simultaneously in his usual three blotches of scarlet. "Everybody looking at me. . . ." he stammered.

"When they *stop* lookin' at ya, you're dead. So be grateful. Ya brought it on yourself, didn't ya, boyo?"

"All a lie," he taunted in return, glowering. Even if he *had* agreed to

122

her throwing this party, even if he'd also agreed (under duress) that she could concoct a story of how he'd come home to start a newspaper, he couldn't resist a perverse pleasure in making it as difficult for her as he could.

"And what would *you* have me tell 'em?" demanded Gert, bristling at his accusation. "He's suddenly quiet, isn't he, now?" she asked Dennis who joined them.

"Suddenly quiet," echoed Dennis.

"Now listen to me! If ya think I'm goin' to hide under a bushel basket for the rest of my days, you've another think comin'. I had another party planned, didn't I? On October twenty-third, after your Mass. Have ya forgotten that date already? Have—"

"Ma—"

"Don't 'Ma' me. It's too late for that—far too late. *I* haven't forgotten. And nobody else has, either. But I'm not to have *that* celebration—so we're havin' *this* one! Why won't ya help me out? Where's Rose?" she added. "She and Timothy should've been here by now." Worried, Gert checked her watch.

"They're driving all the way from Long Island," reminded Dennis soothingly. "They'll get here."

"And what about Gahaghan? Did ya check the rectory?"

"You know he's at old man Finnerty's wake."

"There'll be a wake here," she muttered, eyeing Patrick, "if people don't do as they're told. Has the band arrived? How many'd they bring?"

"'Bout fifteen," replied Dennis. "They're up the street like you told them."

"Good. When I give the signal— Everything in order at the office?"

"The 'office,' " ridiculed Patrick. "You make it sound so important, don't you?"

"You saw it yourself, Ma. It hasn't changed."

Gert's glare transferred itself from Patrick to Dennis. "I'll not be havin' any of *your* lip, neither. Don't think I haven't noticed ya lookin' at every pair of legs."

"I'm *thirty*, Ma. I'm five years older than Patrick, and you treat me like I'm ten years younger." Made brave by his brother's rebelliousness and his own intake of whiskey, Dennis took a breath and went on. "And while we're at it, I'm thinking of getting a place of my own."

Gert's eyes became flint. Dennis blanched and massaged his hands. "I'm tellin' the two of ya," warned Gert, "you'll see me to an early grave. Pour me a small one, Denny." She turned on Patrick again. "The whole world doesn't need to know ya got cold feet. Get 'em well fed and soused, they'll believe *anythin'*. When the others get here, we'll go down and cut the ribbon, and I'll make my speech. I'll handle it. I told ya I would. . . ." She grasped his arm in a fierce grip that made him wince. "Aw, darlin', once we're past this day, it's clear sailin' ahead. Do it for me, won't ya? And couldn't ya put a smile on your sweet puss for your ma?"

Patrick gave it a try.

"Relax, Ma," soothed Dennis, anxious to get back in her good graces, "it's working. Everyone's having a good time."

"More than a penny it's costin' me, too. You'll all be eatin' fried bread for months. Go on, Denny, pour him a short one—a *short* one—and tell him a joke." She checked her watch again. "Now remember—when I give the signal . . ." She turned to go, then turned back to Patrick. "*Mingle*," was her final instruction. "You, too," she added, poking Dennis. "There's votes here."

"He's not running for anything," replied Patrick, knowing it would provoke her. Gert buried him with a look and shoved off like a tugboat, the crowd eddying about her.

"You could be more grateful. She's—"

"Do you know you're getting bald, Denny?" Patrick was immediately remorseful as a stricken Dennis raised a nervous hand to his lank hair, two fingers smoothing and arranging the hapless strands. "Know any jokes?" Patrick added quickly, pouring himself a large dollop. "*I* do. I'll get my violin and Rose'll be on the piano and you can recite. Remember the old days? You think my violin's still around? Sure it is—she probably bronzed it. Sorry what I said—about your hair. . . ."

He didn't want to end up like Denny, a passive fool who danced to Gert's every tune. Patrick took another swallow, noticing the first lines of bitterness at the corners of his brother's mouth and eyes, warnings of future corruption and a lesson, he realized, for himself and those like Denny, who believe they also serve who only stand and wait.

Giving himself a lash for his own passivity, Patrick wandered off, thoughts in a windstorm. Why had he capitulated so quickly to her crazy idea of a newspaper? And the larger fear was: Had he belonged to the Church only to exchange its subjugation for the not so gentle tyranny of his mother?

"Say, Pat—" Patrick turned to find Jerry Finneran with his wife Deedee and couldn't help staring at her as she smiled pertly up at him.

"Doesn't an old girlfriend rate a kiss? Welcome home, Pat."

He touched his lips to her cheek.

"Thick as thieves," said Jerry, grinning. "I remember ya two. She's taken now, Pat. Ya had your chance."

"Jerry tells me you have a couple of children. Congratulations."

"Almost a third." She patted her large belly. "He's raising the devil today. I think he wants to join the festivities."

A moment later Patrick took refuge at the far end of the lawn, the party behind him. Hidden in shadow and falling dusk, he leaned woozily

124

on the gate that led to a vacant lot and toolshed. At his feet a hose dribbled into his father's peony bed. Raising his glass, he found his hand trembling. They could've been his, those kids and the one to come.

A longing ache inside him, he took a sip of his drink. "Havin' a good time, Albatrossum?" he asked the dog, who joined him and lay down, stuffed with hamburger. "You lonely?"

"I hope I'm not interrupting. . . ."

He turned to find Mary Hennessey, blond hair shining in the semi-darkness. "No . . ."

"What a nice party."

They made idle chatter for a moment. Suddenly conscious of the soft curve of her shoulder, Patrick looked quickly away and waved to Deedee.

"Who's she?"

"Old friend." His tongue felt thick.

"Girlfriend?" inquired Mary sweetly. Deliberately she bent over and plucked a peony, allowing him a glimpse of cleavage. He bit into an ice cube until his teeth stung. He nodded. "She was the . . . first girl . . . I ever kissed. Told me I had chapped lips." Why had he said that? Mary pealed a delicate yet throaty laugh.

"Where was I. . . ?" he mumbled. "Where are you?" she flirted, lazily pulling petals, enjoying his naiveté and the flustered expression of him. "Don't you know you're not supposed to mention old girlfriends?"

"Drunk . . . not used to it . . ."

"Why did you decide not to be a priest?" asked Mary in a silky, cool voice as she placed a petal in her palm and blew it at Patrick.

"Huh? Oh? I—" He tried to remember, shook his head and blinked as Mary inhaled and wafted another petal his way.

"Why would you want to be in the first place? You don't seem like the right . . . type."

"Years of being an altar boy . . . incense gets to your brain. Get you a drink," he mumbled huskily, throat parched and temples pounding at the look he'd caught in her eye that had nothing to do with the convent girl she was supposed to have been.

"Ginger ale for me," she smiled as he lurched off.

"Be right back," he called. Who had uttered those fatal words?

"PADDY!" Great arms crushed him in a bear hug. Another of his father's brothers, Uncle Jack Flynn, a big, rough Irishman with blood vessels bursting in his face, pummeled Patrick affectionately. A beery leer on his face, his eyes traveled from his nephew to Mary at the fence, three-quarters of a hot orange moon now rising behind her.

"Son of a bitch, Pat—yer all right!" Jack turned and bellowed to his brother at the grill: "He's your son, Joe—that he is!"

Min looked at Moira. All of the Houlihans cast disapproving looks.

125

"He use ta come over to his granny's and sit on her two-seater," confided Jack to those nearby, " 'n I caught him at it once, didn't I, bucko?"

Scarlet, Patrick tried to extricate himself from his uncle's grasp but failed.

"He tried ta bribe me with a quarter so's I wouldn't tell his ma. Helluva hitter, even when he was a tyke—good man with his *stick!*"

Jack roared at his joke and was joined in hesitant laughter by several others, who were nonetheless sympathetic to Patrick's plight. Jack gripped his nephew by the shoulders. "What's all this, Pat? Yer ma's got somethin' to tell us, has she? Wouldn't miss Gertie's waggin' tongue fer—"

"Wouldn't you now?" Jack turned to find her behind him, hands on hips, ready for battle. "You'll kindly take your hands off my son, Jack Flynn. You're nothin' but a drunken slob!" The day's anxieties causing her to momentarily lose control, Gert's eyes swept other Flynns, their wives and children. "You and all of ya! If ya can't behave yourselves—"

"Ma," protested Patrick as the Flynn families bridled as one. "Now, Gert—" called Joe. "Hoity-toity bitch," muttered Fay Flynn, Jack's wife, luckily too low for Gert to hear.

"Here's Rose and Timothy arrived," called Teresa, saving the day, as the two of them made their entrance at the side of the house to a chorus of approval from the Houlihan clan. A smile broke over Gert's face, her anger gone as quickly as it started. She poked a finger into her brother-in-law's gut, which bent him double, then offered her cheek, which he bussed roundly to scattered applause.

"You're turned off, d'ya hear me?" Gert yanked the glass out of Patrick's hand as she propelled him toward Timothy O'Brien and Rose.

"I'm supposed to be bringing Mary a ginger—"

"She'll get it herself. D'ya hafta be spendin' all your time with the likes of her?"

"I thought you said she was 'a well-bred Catholic girl'?"

Too nerve-racked to rise to the bait, Gert whispered harried instructions, "You'll be nice to Timothy, d'ya hear? Maybe ya can make him forget his first impression of ya. It wouldn't hurt ya at all to get on his good side, would it? For the sake of the paper, if nothin' else. Ya know the clout his father has. Watch yourself now."

With Patrick in tow, Gert invaded the circle that surrounded her daughter and Timothy. "Well, Timothy!" she cackled, giving the brainless, shilly-shallying fathead a kiss. "The son of the next vice-president of the United States!"

"Bullshit," whispered Teresa to Min.

"And here's my Pat who's been so lookin' forward to greetin' you," beamed Gert in honeyed tones, hoping to erase any memory the sanctimonious prig might have of her son's rush from the house the previous Saturday during the saying of the rosary.

With a face like a jug whose features seemed an afterthought, Timothy regarded Patrick with blinking, beady eyes and took his hand in a lukewarm grip, as if fearful of contamination.

"Hello, there."

"Hullo, there."

"Sorry we're late, Mother, dear." Rose inserted herself into the pause, adjusting her draped jacket of baby lamb in a diversionary tactic. If it was a fairly ludicrous choice for a warm fall evening, she wore it well. "But we just couldn't tear ourselves away from the dear Duchess Carney, could we, Timmy?" A low buzz followed the dropping of the name. Agnes Meeghan of Poughkeepsie, New York, had married Ignatius Carney (a million or two), given mightily to the Church (a million or two) and been dutifully rewarded by the Pope, who made her a Dame of Malta. Thus, she became the "Duchess" Carney and had the money to enforce the title with style.

"And guess who else was at the reception?" continued Rose, her voice supremely arch. "Cardinal Pacelli. *Everyone* knows he's to be the next Pope." Those who didn't murmured anyway. Gert preened.

"Isn't that so, Timmy?" Suddenly cute, Rose brushed an imaginary speck from his front, the gesture saying: Mine, All Mine.

"She'll be burpin' him next," Teresa whispered to Min.

"Nauseating," agreed Moira, unmarried and refined.

"Yes, Rose," nodded Timothy, who was as stupid as she but not as canny. Perspiration on his forehead, he looked at her worshipfully, salivating. Patrick felt a hot dislike.

"What were *you* doin' there, Rose?" called one of the Flynns not altogether kindly, as conversation resumed about the reception at the Duchess Carney's estate at Southampton.

"To be with Father Coughlin, of course," she replied haughtily. "The Duchess is one of his greatest admirers."

"I hear she gave him half a million," whispered Teresa to Moira.

The mention of the famous radio priest produced the largest buzz of all.

"And when we told Father Coughlin," Timothy interjected, finding his high-pitched voice, "that we were coming up to a gathering in Massachusetts, he asked us to bring ya his greetings and thank ya for all your support in our great crusade for the Union Party's victory in November. And Congressman Lemke and my father send the same." Timothy had run out of breath and turned red.

"We're all Democrats here, O'Brien," called Jack Flynn to a round of applause—and a dark look from Gert. "So was I," replied Timothy, "and so was my father and Father Coughlin and Roosevelt—*once*. The corpses

127

of the Democratic and Republican parties are stinkin' in our nostrils. We're gonna drive the money-changers out of the temples. And the international Red bankers, too. . . ."

Parroting Coughlin's well-known slogans, Timothy found himself in a heated argument. Linked to Gert's arm, Patrick stole a glance to the rear of the yard where Mary still waited.

"Coughlin's a demagogue."

"Who says so?" snapped Rose, not knowing what the word meant but she sure didn't like the sound of it.

"*I* did," called Jack Flynn, "and I'll say also that the Union Party's got about as much chance as a snowball in hell."

"Is that so?" demanded Gert, and the debate was on.

"Roosevelt's sending us all to the poorhouse," argued Timothy, raisin eyes peering out to find supporters.

"That's right—he's mortgaged three generations to pay for his schemes."

"Coughlin says he wants to give us all a guaranteed wage."

"And who d'ya think's gonna pay for that?"

". . . wants to lower the taxes, too, doesn't he. . . ?"

"He called the President a liar on his broadcast . . ."

". . .'anti-God,' too. Any man does that should be ashamed—no matter if he *is* a priest."

"Cardinal O'Connell himself says Coughlin shouldn't be meddlin' in politics. It's not a priest's business. . . ."

"What d'ya think, Pat?"

"Pat'll know."

All eyes focused on him, and he recognized the expectant look on the faces of his relatives, who had always turned to him as a final authority, a settler of arguments, on matters of morality and the faith.

"Pardon?" he asked, wanting to say: I'm Patrick Flynn. One of you now. Not what I was. Will you ever let me forget?

"Father Coughlin's a saint!" interjected Gert in a mighty tone. If the group was torn between its natural allegiance to Roosevelt and the seductive panaceas offered weekly on the radio by Father Coughlin, she wasn't. "Now let's not be botherin' Timothy," she added, halting the talk and whisking him away toward the food. "Don't be upset, darlin'," she whispered in his ear, stomach recoiling at the large blackhead she found there. "I'm sure we're all goin' to be on your pa's side come election day. White meat or dark, darlin'?" She heaped a plate for him. "And wait'll ya see what my Pat's accomplished. Oh, you'll be pleased. And," she added pointedly, "your father'll be, too!"

"Say, Pat," whispered Jerry as Patrick once again tried to get to the bar and back to Mary, "what *do* ya think of Father Coughlin? My ma sends him a dollar a week. There's many that does."

"I know." *The Spectator* would be supporting Coughlin because that was the way Gert wanted it. But were his mother and sister so greedy for money and power, so willing to forsake their principles that they couldn't see that Timothy was a tub of lard and an idiot to boot? Patrick was disapproving and saddened at the same time. *And who are you to condemn principles forsaken, morality trampled?* asked a devil.

"You like her, don't you?" Dennis fixed his brother a highball. "Don't you? She likes you, too. I can tell. Look—she knows we're talking about her. Why isn't there someone for me?"

Patrick downed half his drink, collected the ginger ale, and hurried off under the gaze of his aunts, who were talking of his mother.

"Dollar signs in her eyes," snorted Min, eyes darting from Gert, fawning over Timothy, to Patrick, who was now back with Mary—as if unsure which potential scandal demanded her full attention.

"And won't you be dancin' for joy at Rose's weddin' if Gert pulls it off?" countered Teresa. "I never saw you turn up your nose at the gravy, Min, dear."

"Well, if Timothy's going to ask her, why doesn't he?" sniffed Moira. "And look at *him*, would you? Right back to her!"

"Aw, stuff it now, Min," added Teresa, as her two sisters glared at Patrick. "He's a young man, she's a pretty girl—and don't you both wish you were forty years younger yourselves!"

"He's *supposed* to be a *priest!*"

"Not liquored up and carousing with women under a moon."

"The Almighty works in mysterious ways. . . ." Like the cat that swallowed the canary, Teresa winked at her sisters, relishing the surprise that would soon be sprung on all of them. "Look," she cried, "here's Father Gahaghan."

The arrival of the priest prompted Gert to give the signal to Dennis, who left the yard at the rear, passing by the cozy twosome, who paid him no attention as he disappeared behind the toolshed to alert the Knights of St. Patrick Marching Band waiting hidden on the next block.

"I feel like the prize bull at the Topsfield Fair," Patrick confided to Mary, stares burning into his back, "—the prize bull who's suddenly discovered to have hoof and mouth disease."

Her laughter, like tinkling prisms, buoyed him higher. He joined in, surprised at his long dormant wit, now loosened by the liquor.

"I thought you'd gone for good," she whispered.

"Never," bandied the gallant, as he stole a glance (helpless not to) at her twin globes glowing in the light of the moon.

"And what *are* your politics?" she asked, a hint of sexual innuendo in the question.

"Dunno," he mumbled, reeling. Had his feet brought him back of their own accord? Should he ask her for a date? "*Salus populi suprema*

129

lex," he said, retreating into the safety of Latin as Mary moved subtly closer. "Ohh!" she exclaimed, an open-toed foot sinking into the soaked lawn.

"I'll turn it off," he said, glad to have an excuse to flee, lest she catch sight of the growing bulge that distended his light slacks. Finding the nozzle a few feet away, he was unsuccessful in stopping the flow.

"It's stuck," he called, turning sideways away from her to conceal himself. "I'll fix it." Quickly he went through the gate and into the tool-shed to look for pliers.

"All right, everybody." Gert's voice rose above the crowd. She grabbed for Teresa. "Where is he?" Teresa looked to the back of the yard.

"He was just—" Where two bodies had been only a moment ago, now there were none.

"So you were almost a priest. . . ." Mary allowed the door of the shed to shut behind her.

"I'm lookin' for—" Blindly Patrick's hands rummaged through garden tools. A rake clattered to the cement floor. He tried to catch his breath and couldn't, for the overpowering smell of manure filled the airless confines of the shed.

"Did you know your eyes glow in the dark?"

"I can't find—"

"I don't think you even know how attractive you are."

He barely heard his mother calling to him above the rushing in his ears. Outside, moonlight glinting on the brass, the band advanced silently and stealthily into the vacant lot like Indians about to attack a peaceful settlers' clambake. Gert started for the shed.

"Don't you want to kiss me?" Her eyelids quivered in a shaft of light let in by a tiny window. He wanted to lap them.

"No . . . I can't. . . . Still under my vow of chastity . . . can't . . ." Feverish, he forced his eyes to the tiny gold cross at her throat.

"Really? Chastity?" As she moved closer, he saw her eyes glance lower to that which could no longer be camouflaged. "I'll kiss *you* then," she whispered, "and it won't be of your doing—will it?"

Dumbfounded by her brazenness, excited beyond endurance by her seeming indifference to his damnation, Patrick made one last feeble plea as Mary came close. Easy prey, his back wedged against a potting table, he reached behind him for support, one hand sinking into a flat of peat moss, the other gripping the handle of a shovel as she pressed herself against him, her mouth on his.

". . . sweet Jesus . . . No . . . oh, sweet Jesus . . . Holy Mother . . ." Thrusting himself against her, he ejaculated in his shorts.

"Ohhhhh . . ." The spasm caused him to lift, then drop the shovel, which clanged against a watering can. The sound echoed in a clash of cymbals that shook the shed as the band outside broke into "When Irish Eyes Are Smiling."

"What have you done?" Mary cried, backing away from Patrick's still shuddering body, eluding the arms that now reached out to embrace her. "You naughty priest . . ."

Frightened by the music, Albatross barked loudly, pawing the shed door in search of his master. Mary slipped triumphantly out, running into Gert and receiving a look that could only be described as indescribable. The band marched through the gate and around them toward the open-mouthed crowd.

"You'll pay for this!" Gert spat at her son, who was turned away from her, frantically pretending to search through tools. "Don't think you won't!" she hollered over the music. "Now get yourself out here!"

"Patrick, dear," called Aunt Moira. "Patrick . . ."

"Oh, sweet Jesus, what have I done . . . ?" Shocked into sobriety, Patrick's eyes widened in horror at the sight of the large and viscous stain that had wet through the light material of his slacks. A week's prayerful and determined abstinence from the use of his trusty right hand had produced what the more sacrilegious boys at St. Martin's used to call "a cupful in the service of the Lord." Halfway to his knee, the wetness glistened, hideously blotching the fabric in a telltale stigma, the final sacrilege.

Porch lights winked on. Those neighbors already out on their porches rose in stupefaction from creaking gliders at the sight, not to mention the sound, of the band emerging from behind Gert's house, followed by the rowdy crew of forty, drinks in hand. Blocks away, people looked at each other. Was there a parade scheduled? An army of children hopped on bikes, heading for the trumpets.

"Where the hell we goin'?" and similar questions were bandied back and forth. Startled by the onslaught of the band into the back yard, herded dazed into formation behind the musicians, and told they were going on a "short journey," the group was now in a high-keyed state of gleeful hysteria as it made its way down Essex Street.

At the head of the procession, the band's flag fluttering green above her, marched Gert, like the Pied Piper of Hamelin leading the rats to the river's edge. She'd been in more parades than she could remember; if this three hundred yarder to the parish hall was the shortest distance covered, the emotional toil of the past week, climaxed by what had just occurred, made it seem the longest by far.

"Get him up front," she whispered angrily to Teresa, who fell back in the ranks. The nerve! Every eye on him and where is he? In the toolshed with that Hennessey hussy! The very idea that he should allow such a compromising situation to take place was outrageous. Had he no sense at all? For his own good he'd obviously have to be watched like a hawk.

Bile in her throat, Gert managed a bright smile. *Help me to get through this day, Sweetheart,* she prayed to the Virgin. "Look at that stunnin' car of Timothy O'Brien's," she called as the procession passed the large black Packard festooned with American flags. "Don't it lend luster to the neighborhood?" she added, eyes peering longingly past Rose to Timothy. If only there could be *two* announcements this evening! Why couldn't the fathead get off the pot and convince his father? Well, maybe after today. *Please, Sweetheart, let it happen. . . .*

"Aren't ya hot in that fur, Rosie?" called one of the unemployed Flynns.

"Shanty mick," muttered Rose. Gert suppressed an impulse to trip her daughter, thus allowing those behind to trample her.

"Isn't it a grand evenin'!" Teresa worked her way back, finally arriving at Patrick and Moira.

"What's wrong, dear?"

"Nothing," he grinned hastily. He'd had no time! No time for anything! No time to change his pants. Nothing. And in that panicked state— the music crashing in his ears, everybody hollering, his aunt calling to him—who would've had the sense to even consider possible solutions? Short of impaling himself on a pair of garden shears, there was nothing he could do. He'd been swept up and into the throng, Moira holding onto his arm. His other, bent against his stomach as if in a sling, was draped with his suitcoat, which hid the wetness. He would move it for nothing. Rigor mortis would find the arm locked so rigidly, bones would have to be broken. *O my God I am heartily sorry for having offended Thee . . .*

"She wants you up front," whispered Teresa. Patrick's heart began to hammer. Relatively safe in the darkened street with his coat against him to hide his shame, he could only quail at the prospect of what would happen when he reached the office. He could feel the fabric clammy against his leg. Would it have dried? And what would it *look* like dried? As he moved forward with Teresa, his eyes met Mary's for half an immortal second, the cause of his downfall smiling like an angel.

The band reached Main Street, turned the corner, and came to a halt in front of the tarpaulin-covered storefront. "What're we stoppin' for?" cried those in a festive mood who wanted to go further. Traffic slowed to gawk. Now swelled by an assortment of passersby and children, the crowd milled about noisily on the sidewalk and street. "It's the parish hall . . . the old shoe-repair place . . ." A buzz of curiosity swept through them as they eyed the tarp. What was Gert up to? What was behind there?

"All right now . . . hush up all of youse!" Suddenly illuminated, Gert stood on an apple box as Dennis worked the spotlight, which lit the crèche on the church lawn at Christmas. Tinted hair flaming, spectacles glittering, she waved the crowd into a hush of anticipation:

"Now some of youse used to bring your shoes in here, but those days are long gone. From now on, my Pat wants ya to be bringin' your feet!"

Proudly, and with a "have at it, boyo," Gert gestured to Patrick to remove the tarp. To the accompaniment of a drum roll, he stood on tiptoe, his free arm reaching up to where the canvas was hung on nails passing through eyelets. Forced to use both hands, he transferred his coat to his shoulder as he strained to get the tarp free of the nails. The coat slipped and was caught by Gert, who folded it over her arm. Ominously now, the drums continued as he finally got the tarp free, bunching it against himself as it fell.

Simultaneously, Gert reached in the doorway and flipped the switch. The crowd stared open-mouthed as the new fluorescent tubes in the ceiling sputtered to life—front, middle, and rear—each producing an *ahhh*, until the whole spanking-new, crepe-paper-streamered, balloon-laden office popped to bright life.

Triumphantly Gert pointed to the golden letters on the window. "*The Jericho Irish Spectator!* Patrick Flynn, Editor In Chief!" she called, in case there was anybody unable to read.

Jaws dropped. As the band struck up, Teresa, loyal partisan that she was, gave a cheer. Others joined in hesitantly. Patrick's eyes went blind with the exploding flash cameras from two of Leveret's papers, invited by Gert and promised a good story. "Ex-Seminarian Starts Paper in Jericho" would be the headline two days hence, with a photo underneath of the new editor, eyes shut and a large something clutched to his middle, which was the tarp.

Surging forward in a babble of questions, the flummoxed crowd fell into respectful silence as Father Gahaghan sprinkled Holy Water in the doorway and began his blessing, which, appropriately enough, was the blessing of St. Patrick.

". . . of God upon you all, men of Erin, sons, women, and daughters. Prince-blessing, meal-blessing, blessing of long life, health-blessing, blessing of excellence, eternal-blessing, heaven-blessing, cloud-blessing, sea-blessing . . ." Continuing, the priest ducked under the ribbon in the doorway and went inside.

The weight of all those blessings sank Patrick lower. As Father Gahaghan sprinkled water in the interior, he reached a furtive hand down behind the tarp to feel his pants. *Still wet.*

". . . blessing of dexterity, blessing of glory, blessing of deeds . . ." intoned the priest, bestowing drops on the typewriters and desks, finally returning to the doorway. ". . . of happiness be upon you all, laics, clerics, while I command the blessing of the men of heaven, a Perpetual Blessing upon *The Jericho Irish Spectator* and Patrick Flynn!"

Whether for the sentiments expressed or the fact that it was finally over, applause greeted the end of the blessing. Eyes filled with happy tears,

133

Gert removed scissors from purse with a flourish that caused those pressed close to flinch. Handing them to Timothy, who was as nonplussed as the rest, she gave him the honor of cutting the ribbon, and the throng surged inside as Joe Flynn poured paper cups of champagne to toast the new paper and its pertrified editor.

"Ooooo . . . watch it!"

"Look what he's done!"

Having grabbed for the first cup of champagne and deliberately pretended to bobble it (thus spilling it over crotch and legs) Patrick dabbed mock-anxiously at the now larger wetness, which—to his enormous relief—obliterated the smaller.

"Poor lad's excited. . . ."

"And well he should be," added Gert, making the best of her son's unseemly display, "—such a grand night!"

"A drop of champagne spilled is good luck," called Teresa.

As "good luck!" echoed around him, Patrick—returned to the living—raised his freshly filled cup, a great grin spreading on his face, ready for anything.

It went on to the wee hours. The band played for dancing upstairs in the hall. At one o'clock Police Chief McGee stopped by to caution the racket. Gert poured him champagne. The party continued.

If there were those who found it all hard to believe, if doubters sniffed that it wasn't of whole cloth, so to speak, if Minnie on the drive home insisted that she for one found it fishy that Patrick should suddenly develop a passion for journalism a month before his Ordination, her husband's comment that there was no way to prove otherwise found him speaking for the majority.

"But would you believe her carryin' on like that!" insisted Min.

Gert's speech had touched all the bases. Properly primed, stuffed, and lulled into an almost narcotic state by the cramped space, heat, cigar smoke and fresh paint, the gathering had sat rapt as Gert ran a gamut from her early beginnings in the old country (applause), to the Great Famine, Ellis Island, and those first dark mornings in Leveret, when at fourteen she'd trudged with thousands of others along the Merrimack's banks to take up her needle ("Paid the wages of niggers, we was.") in the mending room of the Ayer Mill.

"The blarney!" continued Min. "Famine, indeed! None of us was even *born* then! And Ellis Island? Why, none of the Houlihans came over that way."

"She tells a good tale," chuckled her husband.

Tears had been induced in the gathering as the ghost of Gert's first-born Terrence was summoned to her side; then, applause for the living, as she introduced her children—Dennis, about to enter "the political arena," and Rose, "a lovin' daughter." Then the tears had run afresh as Gert spoke of the plans, hopes, and dreams that she, and many of them, had had for Patrick.

"The brass of her!" Min shook her head. Moira agreed with a "tsk, tsk" from the back seat of the car. "And did you see him squirm when she cried out how she wanted him to be a priest? And how he called her from Washington to say he had 'other plans'? I still say it's a crock!"

"Such a shame," sighed Moira.

"You can bet who's goin' to be running the ridiculous thing," added Min. "Did you hear her tellin' Timothy the paper was goin' to support Mr. O'Brien? *She'll* be holdin' the reins, don't be doubtin' it for a minute."

"What's Pat say about that?"

"Pat? She's always had him under her thumb."

Moira nodded. "He did seem a bit dazed, the poor lamb."

"Dazed by that blond, that's what." Min turned to her husband. "I suppose Gert got you to take an ad?"

"Sure enough," he replied, burping. "I like Gert. Even if she did give me heartburn."

The Houlihan sisters notwithstanding, the day 'Pat Flynn came home to Jericho to start his paper and his ma threw a blowout of a blast' became, in time, an unalterable legend, told and retold, embellished and passed on by those who had been there. The absolute bravura with which Gert had brought it all off silenced most of the whisperers.

As for Patrick, he sat there, listened to Gert mangle the truth, and wondered if it was all a bad dream. As the lie he'd agreed to filled the office like the smoke that had risen and hung, a cloud over their heads, he vowed to cease being guilty.

He wasn't a coward. Anyone who could survive today couldn't be classified as such. Nor had he a leg to stand on if he criticized his mother for blaspheming the true facts, for he had let her. He, who sat with wadded, crusty tendrils of pubic hair itching, had let her, and who was he to judge which of them had committed the greater sin? The God that his mother quoted so freely would hopefully have mercy on both of them.

If his own sin was mortal, he had a strange satisfaction that at least it was a sin committed in the real world where he wanted to be. No, he would not allow himself to be buffeted by guilt for having left the seminary. He had done what he had to. If turbulence was ever ready to shake him, the rightness of his decision seemed solid. He had opted for life.

In the moments after Gert finished her speech, the office ringing to cheers, he rose shakily, allowed himself a wry smile, and was propelled toward her amid backslapping cries of congratulation. Aghast at her gall, yet not unawed at what she had accomplished, he found himself wrapped in her arms in a tear-stained embrace, the prodigal returned, and peace— momentarily—between them.

135

With face saved, scandal averted, rumors laid somewhat to rest and a newspaper born, Gert's victory was all the sweeter for having her son against her bosom once again.

Chafing, crushed in those strong arms, the smell of Gert's Seabreeze in his nostrils, Patrick had a thought:

Perhaps Father Morelli had counseled him wisely. There were other paths, other ways to serve God, and Gert, by her outrageous concoction, had allowed him to stay in Jericho and given him an opportunity. Dreams of California and the open road notwithstanding, Patrick knew in his secret heart he could make something of it. He was where he belonged.

7 Elliot watched his father rake Jack Tyler and another foreman over the coals. Tyler was an old-timer who'd been at the mill forever, but Phelps wasn't in a mood for mellow sentimentality.

"The son of a bitch's own fault," he snapped, ending a discussion of an employee who'd had a hand caught in a carding machine. Tyler's lined face remained implacably calm, but his eyes revealed a veiled contempt as he regarded his cap and switched it from one hand to the other.

"That's not why you're here," Phelps continued. If safety matters needed to be discussed, if his employees' grievances needed airing, this wasn't the day for it. "Those goddamned women aren't up to quota. You get them there," he added, pointing a finger at the other man, who nodded and knew what was coming next. "Or I'll find someone who can." Phelps shook his paperweight and swiveled in his chair, glancing at Elliot, whose disinterested stance infuriated him.

Jack Tyler and the other man exchanged a look as Phelps moved on to a discussion of troublemakers. The latter, he warned, would find themselves blinking in the sunlight outside the gates.

Lately there'd been vague rumblings of discontent, which had been reported to Phelps by his Pinkerton-led network of spies. Throughout the three acres of the plant, tiny cracks had appeared in the ranks. Talk of union was growing again. Whispers of inequities were exchanged over lunch pails. A raise in pay. Safety precautions.

A year ago Phelps had formed a union for his employees—a sham organization whose purpose was to make them think they had a say. Derided behind his back, Phelps' 'union' was seen for what it was—a sop, a cracker thrown, a diversionary gesture to forestall his employees from entertaining any hope of joining the burgeoning rebellion of American labor that was poisoning the country and destroying the American way. Phelps was his usual rabid self on that particular subject, and as he warned Tyler to report any subversive talk to him, Elliot watched the two men turn to stone. Tyler, he knew, wasn't a snitch. The old man's nods were necessary if he wanted to keep his job. If screws were going to be tightened, surveillance increased, Tyler wouldn't be a party to it.

137

"Some of the men feel—"

"Have them take it through proper channels." Phelps cut Tyler off. "I've bent over backward to be fair! You'll all be out of work if this kind of crap continues!"

Elliot lit a cigarette and knew his father's purpose in having him witness the reprimanding. His father was grooming him, demonstrating a lesson in authority and the wielding of power. But Elliot felt only distaste for the barely concealed cruelty which threatened him even more than it did the two hapless foremen. The lesson went unlearned.

He watched his father shift gears and put on his paternal disguise as he asked after Tyler's wife. Feeling suddenly trapped, Elliot wished he could be dismissed with the two men, but Phelps beckoned him, directing him to the chair opposite the desk. Fearful as he always was when alone with his father, Elliot lounged casually in self-defense while the looms rumbled through the floor and into his nervous system.

"So then . . ." Not knowing how to begin, Phelps spat at his spittoon, the vulgarity his defense against a threatening sense of powerlessness as he regarded his son. Transferring his gaze to a safer photograph, where a younger Elliot looked on the world with innocent eyes, sudden feelings of tenderness arose. To the degree that it was possible for him, Phelps loved Elliot, but his son was a painful mystery.

"McGee says he's going to have to throw you in jail the next time. Teach you a lesson. I've half a mind to let him." For the third time in as many weeks, Elliot had been stopped for drunk driving. "Did you think I didn't know? McGee said you asked him not to tell me but—"

"But naturally he did. Do you have the chief on the payroll, too?" But the glib bravado that worked so well for Elliot in the outside world was bogus and impotent in the face of his father, who glared at his son with eyes that said: What you are displeases me. Elliot shrank.

"Are you prepared for your meeting with McManus this afternoon?" Phelps asked, turning to the safer subject of business. On the wall behind, his own father glared down at him from the portrait, bullying even in death, watching for softness.

Elliot shrugged. Phelps' sallow cheeks flushed with the insolence. "What is it?" he barked, losing control and angered with the loss. "Elliot . . ."

The hint of a plea in his father's voice caused Elliot to sense he might have an opening—if only for a moment. "Dad," he began, the word causing an answering echo in Phelps. As if it might be possible for them to ford the dangerous and swollen river that ran between them, father and son stared at each other, then the eyes scattered.

"I've heard the Pawtucket plant is experimenting with some new Belgian dyes," Elliot continued tentatively. Wary, Phelps nodded. "I'd like to go down and see what it's all about."

"Why?"

"Why? I've told you. It interests me. You said yourself we have to keep up with the new colors. Keep in step. I thought I—"

"Your future is here in Jericho. At the main plant. The sales department is the best place to learn the ins and outs."

Phelps believed absolutely in the latter statement. His father had started *him* in sales. Yet when Elliot accused Phelps of wanting to keep him tied to a short leash, Phelps knew it was true. Justifiably true. Elliot must be kept in Jericho, where Phelps could keep an eye on him. If he allowed his son to go to one of his other mills, Phelps was sure he'd never see him again. "You know what our plans are," he continued placatingly. "If later on you want to experiment with—"

"*Your* plans." Frustrated and knowing what he'd suggested was futile, Elliot got up. "That's all you care about. What you've built up. It's not for me. It's not—"

"You'll make your mark. I don't have any doubt. Once you buckle down and pay attention. Built up? Who the hell have I built it for?"

Hurt that Elliot didn't understand, Phelps looked away to the photographs of his empire of mills that lined the walls. What would it all have been worth if it couldn't be passed on to his son? But the sudden vulnerability was masked as he turned his hard gaze once again on Elliot, who retreated behind another shrug that camouflaged his sadness that he couldn't be the son his father wanted.

Elliot remembered how Phelps had paraded him in his sailor suit, his father's pride instilling courage and safety. The closeness stopped at an early age. Nancy Phelps had filled the void, explaining to Elliot that her husband was married to his mills and father to his workers. Elliot was left in her care while Phelps checked in occasionally to keep an eye on his son's progress. Escapades and pranks that saw him kicked out of a couple of prep schools briefly forced the father to get involved. Elliot promised to do better; Phelps was secretly pleased with his son's rebelliousness. All boys who were really boys had a streak of contempt for authority when they were young. But time and distance took their toll, and father and son grew further apart. Before Elliot was even eighteen, Phelps realized his son was different. A boy who preferred college and hated the mill, whose temperament was nervous like his mother's. With nothing in common, it was too late for either of them to catch up; the damage was done. But somewhere, deeply hidden, sometimes painfully conscious, Elliot longed to have his father love him again, wanted to erase the disappointment, be held on high once more, hoisted up on his father's shoulders, secure.

The gulf between them had become unbreachable two summers earlier. Phelps had been sitting at the same desk when a call came that stopped his heart and filled him with a terrifying sense of his own failure. The caller had suggested that a certain sum be deposited in the Bay State Bank of Leveret or a certain irate father would bring charges of sodomy against Elliot. The boy was fourteen and Polish. The blackmail had been paid.

The incident had never been mentioned again, but it was always between father and son, and sometimes Phelps woke with it, praying it was gone, this evil sickness that must at all cost be kept from the world, kept from the boy's mother and from his own consciousness, too, if possible. Phelps had only to observe his son's restless and moody behavior since graduation to wonder fearfully. He'd had Elliot followed to Boston. The reports came back that Elliot frequented bars on the waterfront. What he did there, Phelps refused to imagine. But if the degenerate and loathsome sickness had returned, Phelps intended to abolish it.

"By the way," he said with a forced casualness, "I've invited the Hoskins girl to dinner on Sunday."

On his way to the door, Elliot froze. Face flushed and frightened, he managed to laugh. "Fixing me up? Want to pick out my suits, too?"

"You told me yourself you liked her."

"Not any more," muttered Elliot, too low for his father to hear.

"Certainly she's a cut above your usual companions. Why not get to know her?" Throat dry, he shifted papers on his desk to no purpose.

"You don't approve of Amy?" Elliot focused on the door, his back to Phelps because he didn't dare turn.

"A nice girl . . ." Of no backbone. A society twit without a thought in her head. "She's not who I was referring to." Phelps frowned and swiveled his chair. "I don't like that crowd you hang around with at the Classic." Whores were necessary at a certain time and place in a young man's life but—

"I thought you'd be pleased." Elliot turned on his father. "Why don't you say what you mean?" he added in retaliation, taking a perverse pleasure in his shame, which he saw mirrored in his father's eyes. "Why don't you?" he went on, louder. He had a wild thought to grab the shears on a nearby table and cut out the hated queer part of himself; his father would nod approval and smile on him again. "I thought you were always one to call a spade a spade. *Why don't you?*"

Both fearful at what was now in the office with them, father and son couldn't look at each other. Unable to disguise his distaste at Elliot's question, which had hit home, Phelps hid behind his heavy lids. Trembling and near tears, Elliot left the office. The Prince was queer, and his father knew it. For Elliot, the latter was the most horrid part of all.

"I gather it was Abraham's idea . . . inviting this Hoskins girl?"

"Uh-huh." Elliot glanced at his mother's reflection in her dressing table mirror, watching as she applied lipstick to the exquisite mouth. If he were to shock her with something—and there was much he could shock her with—the lipstick might tremble in her hand and smear, creating a gash across her cheek.

"Do you like her?"

"I don't really know her," he replied, disturbed with the fantasy, which he didn't understand, for his mother was his best pal and confidante.

"I don't know why he feels it necessary to have her to the house. But then, I never have comprehended your father, have I?" Catching something in her son's expression, Nancy Phelps turned. "How handsome you look, my prince. What is it?"

"Nothing."

"You seem . . . so wrought up lately." Nancy crossed to Elliot and lay her hands on his shoulders, her eyes questioning. "Why don't you take Monday off, and we'll go into Boston and have lunch?"

"I don't think Mondays off is quite what he has in mind when he says I'm supposed to 'toe the mark.' "

"I'll take care of it. What's bothering you, darling?" Nancy went on, sensing Elliot's agitation and rebellious mood. He shook his head. "I wish I'd never come home."

"Oooo," she replied flirtatiously, "what a thing to say. If you hadn't, we wouldn't have had all the fun we've had this summer. Haven't we?" Elliot nodded and shrugged. "What is it?" Nancy asked. "The mill? Of course it is. You shouldn't be there."

"Do I have a choice?"

"I'm going to think of something. You have such ooomph, darling." Cupping his face, she bent down and kissed the top of his head, blond like hers. Thank goodness he had nothing, absolutely nothing, of his father in him. "You have a brilliant mind and the soul of a poet." Elliot blushed. "Hang on for a while and I'll work on him." It had been Nancy's idea that Elliot might pursue something along the line of textile design, for he had an appreciative eye for color and her own perfect taste.

"What about you?" Elliot asked as Nancy turned away and sighed. "You out of sorts, too?"

"You sense it, don't you? You always do." Long ago the bond had been sealed, the seduction completed. Nancy confessed to Elliot when he was eight or nine that no one, especially his father, understood and appreciated her as he did. The flattery had filled Elliot with pride, the secret disclosure impossible to resist. They'd been co-conspirators ever since, yet Nancy knew nothing of Elliot's sexual turmoil, which he hid from the world and certainly from her. Terrified on the one hand she might find out, Elliot lately had longings to tell his mother everything, confess to the shameful urges that tore him apart. Of the sailors in Boston whom he couldn't resist. Of Frankie Hoskins, whom he'd fallen in love with this summer.

"Bored, darling. That's what I am." Regarding herself in the full-length mirror while Elliot lay back on her bed and stared at the ceiling, Nancy scrutinized her face. "And Palm Beach four months off. I am *counting* the days."

"She's a candidate. When do I get my trust?"

Nancy didn't know which to respond to first. "When you're twenty-five. You know that." Would he leave her when he came into his money?

"Three years to go. I won't last."

"Of course you will. The Hoskins girl?"

Revealing none of the rage that swelled in him at the thought of Harriet's arrival in an hour, Elliot nodded.

"A 'town' girl we don't even know? What's gotten into him? Don't worry, darling. We'll amuse ourselves. And the Larkins are coming."

"Nifty," replied Elliot sarcastically.

"Now, now . . ." Nancy wagged a finger. "It won't be so bad. I need a smile now."

Sprawled on the bed, Elliot leaned on his elbow and complied.

"That's better. How do I look?" she added, voice husky. Perfect complexion lit from the reflected glow of her peach silk dressing gown, Nancy touched her cheek, then swept up her hair. "Which would you prefer? Up or down?"

"Up."

"Up it shall be."

Nancy returned to her dressing table and began to do her nails. Elliot excused himself and went to his father's bathroom and locked the door. Agitated, he watched himself remove his clothes in the three-way mirror. Three naked Elliots presented themselves as he masturbated quickly, washed his hands, and dressed again. No calmer, he returned a moment or two later to his mother's room.

"Darling?" Nancy turned to him and held up her hands. "Do you want to blow them dry?" she asked with a delightful twinkle. "Like you did when you were little?"

"Sure." Blushing, Elliot sat at her feet. Would his father be sad, he wondered, if he were to enter his bedroom and find his son hanging from the light fixture in the ceiling?

Three yellow-bricked stories up, past turrets and towers, the slate roof blazed with the sun's last efforts as Harriet rang the bell at Phelps Mansion. Frankie had brought her, and as the car went back down the hill, a flock of birds rose angrily, chirping out of the woods beyond the circular driveway.

"Good evening, miss."

"Oh . . . !"

Three Irish setters and two Dalmations burst into the hallway and bore down on her.

"Don't worry, miss," assured the maid, "they're friendly."

"Worry" didn't do justice to Harriet's anxiety. She'd run into Phelps on Main Street earlier in the week. He had been cordial and glad to see her. Having no success story to dangle, Harriet was ill at ease and embarrassed, but the money she owed him hadn't been mentioned, and the conversation was brief. Two days later, his chauffeur had hand-delivered an invitation to dinner, and she hadn't known what to think. She had no idea whether Phelps or Elliot was behind the invitation. The latter's enigmatic behavior on the night of her homecoming didn't make her anxious to see him again, and she'd tried to think up an excuse not to go. Letty had prevailed, however. Good manners must be attended to; Harriet had made her bed with Abraham Phelps, and now she'd have to lie in it. Wasn't it ironic, Alice had remarked, that at any other time Harriet would've given her eyeteeth for an invitation to dine with the tyrant and his family, and now it had come and she didn't want to go!

"I'm Harriet Hoskins." The dogs milled about, barking. "I believe I'm expected."

"Right this way, miss."

Feelings of social inferiority arose in a hot flash as she stepped into the imposing entryway. *Why,* she asked herself as she was led down a corridor wide enough for two cars, *do the rich always have so many dogs?*

Because they can afford the dog food.

But she had no time to appreciate her witticism, for doors swung open, revealing a vast parlor, and she heard her name announced.

Time suspended, and her breathing likewise, her eyes were drawn to Abraham Phelps, whose face appeared from behind a high-backed armchair, his bald head struck by a beam of light.

"Hello," she heard herself call in a voice she barely recognized. Fingers snapped and unsnapped the clasp of her purse as Phelps came toward her.

"Harriet," he said warmly, undoing her with this first-time use of her first name, "I'm glad you could come." Regarding her intently, he took her arm, found it trembling slightly, and steered her toward four faces that looked up curiously from low divans before the marble fireplace.

"This is Harriet Hoskins . . ."

Fifteen minutes later, she was in an even more nervous state. A brave smile on her face, she took a sip of her martini and tried to stay afloat. The warmth of her benefactor's greeting, far from relaxing her, had produced the opposite effect. And Elliot's behavior was a mystery. "I didn't think you'd come," he'd whispered shortly after her arrival and since then had said nothing much, regarding her with an unreadable smile or ignoring her completely. She had the distinctly unnerving feeling he was waiting for her to make a fool of herself.

Did she dare smoke? Had she already made a faux pas with her

143

request for a martini? It was only later she realized the women were drinking sherry. *Say something,* she ordered herself, *something witty so they'll like you.* Focusing on the hors d'oeuvres, she felt a kinship with the jellied mound of caviar. Even if protected by smaller mounds of chopped yolks and onions, buttressed by wafer-thin pieces of rye toast, it nonetheless threatened at any moment to slip from its moorings and slide precipitously, *plop,* onto the plush carpet.

"Why should *we* tighten our belts?" pouted Mrs. Samuel Larkin of Boston. A tall, flat-chested woman in her middle forties, her unfashionable dress and sensible pumps evidenced a life of golf and the raising of children. "*We* are the ones who are being bled dry by that man's taxes, and now he has the audacity to suggest we tighten our belts! Nobody in Boston is having any of it. The stores are full and people are shopping. Expensive things, too. I'm all for it. Remind me to tell you, Nancy, what Cissy and I found at Peck and Peck. She's so excited about Wellesley. But getting a daughter ready for college *is* exhausting. Do you remember our first week?"

"Of course," Nancy replied in a voice redolent of small lunches at the Harvard Club. As innately elegant as her friend was plain, she took a sip of her sherry while her fingers toyed with a single strand of pearls that Harriet calculated would pay off the mortgage on Mulberry Street many times over.

"You went to college, didn't you, Miss Hoskins?" Nancy turned to Harriet with a serene smile, her eyes subtly putting her in her place.

You know I did, Nancy dearest. "Syracuse University. But only for a year," Harriet added, irritated with herself for seeming to apologize. Optimistic pep talks that saw her confounding them all with her New York chic, impressing them with her woman of the world persona, fled in the face of Nancy Phelps' coolness. If she intimidates you, Alice had suggested, imagine her on the toilet—always a good equalizer. Impossible. There was no way to imagine Nancy Phelps in such a position. She probably had one of her maids do it for her.

Courage instilled at her own joke, Harriet decided: What the hell? and took out a cigarette. Phelps lit it. "But Dad—" Elliot piped up in pretend astonishment. "I thought you didn't approve of young ladies smoking."

"I approve of Harriet," replied Phelps, ignoring Elliot and smiling at her.

Elliot exchanged a glance with his mother. Phelps continued to chat with Harriet, whom he sensed was nervous. The more he paid attention to her, the more irritated Elliot became. "Any other vices?" he asked, interrupting their conversation, hoping to get her goat and his father's as well.

" 'Fraid so," Harriet bandied back, wondering why he seemed to mock her. And why did she have the uncanny feeling that Mr. Phelps was watching her, even when he wasn't? Obviously Mother was right—money and past-due loans weren't going to be mentioned on such an occasion. She wasn't going to be dragged down to the cellar and tortured by the maids. Yet, she felt on the spot—as if she were being graded. If so, she'd get an F. She didn't belong here, didn't want to be here, didn't—

Harriet's self-recriminations were interrupted by the discovery that Mr. Larkin was looking at her legs. Solaced by this small victory, she was once again engaged in conversation by Phelps, while the rest of them talked dogs, horses, the final tennis matches at the club.

"Well, we *are*," said Mrs. Larkin, "going ahead with Madge's debut." Somewhat defiantly, she glanced at her husband, who appeared indifferent. "Sam doesn't approve. . . . I think he agrees with Abe about such things. . . ."

Samuel Larkin roused himself from his lethargy. "Madge didn't seem enthusiastic about a debut, and I took my cue from her." Suitably attired in a banker's pinstripe, his voice was a carbon copy of the two women's—a low Boston drawl. Generations of breeding and old money had produced in them an unruffled, assured and quiet sense of their superiority.

"She was just saying that." Mrs. Larkin nodded as one of the maids refilled her sherry. "You know how young people are these days. They hear all this radical talk. Madge—"

"How's your sister?"

Startled, Harriet looked up to find Elliot grinning at her.

"Fine," she replied hastily, realizing he was baiting her about Alice.

Unsure what the interruption was about, Mrs. Larkin paused, glanced from one to the other and then went on: "Anyway, Madge got it into her head she shouldn't have a debut because a friend took her into the South End. My heart goes out to those people, but *really*, I think it's all exaggerated. All this continued talk of the 'emergency.' Those people aren't as badly off as they pretend to be." The others nodded. "That's why I'm so pleased with the activity in Boston. People are definitely looking on the bright side. Why, we had to push Madge's date way back to December. The Copley's completely booked with parties. I think it's a good sign. No question."

"I'm so glad you got Madge to see the light, Louise. A young girl's debut is one of the most memorable events in her life. I treasure the memory of mine."

"Were you a deb, Miss Hodgekins?"

"Pardon?" Not sure at this point *what* her name was, Harriet laughed apologetically.

"*Hoskins*," corrected Phelps, making it clear to Louise Larkin he was displeased.

"I do beg your pardon. I thought I heard—"

"No . . . but . . . I mean, that's quite all right. No, I'm not. I mean, I wasn't." Would't she love to squeeze one of her lemon wedges and send a seed straight to the chipmunk eye of Louise Larkin! "Those" people? Could one "pretend" to be hungry? Obviously the woman lived in an ivory tower. Knowing she'd only get herself in hot water, Harriet suppressed an impulse to say something, but the general let-them-eat-cake philosophy of the group grated.

"Not a *deb*?" Elliot's shocked tone caused laughter from the ladies.

"You *are* a cutup, Elliot," tittered Mrs. Larkin, glancing at Harriet and dismissing her as a rather uninteresting, not to mention wordless, creature.

"Mummy—she's not a deb!" Elliot rolled his eyes and fell backward.

"Don't be naughty, darling," reproached Nancy, administering a pretend slap on the wrist.

"*Elliot*—" Phelps' black marble eyes went brutal.

"She knows Elliot was just being playful," interjected Nancy, sending a look to her husband that warned him not to go further.

"Don't mind my son . . ." Phelps managed a smile to a shaken Harriet. "He's full of pranks. I'm told it's part of his charm."

"Is that what you heard—Dad?" replied Elliot mockingly.

"Are those new drapes?" asked Louise quickly, dying to know what was going on.

"Do you like them?" asked Nancy as the unsettling moment passed. Elliot took a breath, shrugged his eyebrows and knew he wanted another drink. But Phelps had counted the two he'd already had, and he didn't dare. "I've had the room painted, too," Nancy went on, rising with a languorous yet athletic grace. Kissing the top of Elliot's head, she directed the maids in the lighting of lamps.

"I had to promise Abe I wouldn't do another room this year. You know how he is about change." With an inward shudder, Nancy Phelps recalled the day she'd first come to this gloomy house, so unlike any other in Jericho in its hideous triumph of eclectic vulgarity. Her father-in-law, determined to outdo William Wood of American Woolen (whose own Romanesque monstrosity dominated a neighboring town), had sent his minions to ransack the minor palaces of Europe. Lavish bad taste was the result; the only unifying theme the money it had all cost.

"Now, my dear, I'm all for change, if it doesn't—"

"Cost an arm and a leg," interrupted Nancy, cutting him off. Frustrated with her life, there was little in the world she found favor with, including her husband. Twenty years younger than he, their marriage had been arranged by her ailing father. Nancy brought three mills to the marriage and told herself she loved Phelps, whose ardent wooing ceased shortly after the ceremony. She was left, a blond ornament, to fend for herself. Her son had been her salvation; in her secret heart, she didn't care what Elliot did, so long as he was happy—and near her.

"I don't believe in throwing money down the drain." Phelps reached a hand toward his wife. "Except for you, my dear."

"We'd never have guessed," replied the most prized of his many possessions, whose unseeing cold eyes wounded him as she condescendingly patted his hand. As Phelps watched jealously, his wife turned to Elliot and touched his arm, her coolness vanished. Then she gestured around the parlor. "Do you like the color scheme, Louise? Elliot is my final authority on design, aren't you, darling? I tell Abe he should take advantage of his son's talents," she added pointedly.

"I think I do," replied Phelps with a forced gusto that hid a sudden dangerous fantasy of shouting at his wife that her adored son was a fairy.

"I don't," replied Nancy, giving a light smile that hid the years of arguments over Elliot.

"When's dinner?"

"You know cook doesn't like to be rushed."

Harried, Phelps lit a cigar and smiled at Harriet, whose fresh good looks revived him. Noticing Elliot glaring at his father, she smiled quickly in return and wondered what on earth was going on with this family. The strange undercurrents diverting her from her own self-absorption, she glanced around the parlor and had to admit she liked the understated, yet opulent charm of the room—inviting, comfy, and moderne at the same time. Once again she sensed Elliot watching her, but when she raised her eyes, his fled. The Larkins were debating the purchase of a new automobile, and Harriet felt Phelps' energy level accelerate as he interrupted:

"I don't agree with that kind of reckless spending, Louise." Phelps couldn't abide the Larkins and their airs; he put up with the couple for the sake of his wife. That they were envious of his money while at the same time looked down upon him as a member of the mercantile class only earned them his contempt. "I'd say there was a lack of confidence in the country. At least among the people I know. I wouldn't invest in a new plant at the moment. Nor expand, either. Why should I take a chance with my capital when I live under the thumb of an administration that spends money recklessly, follows unsound principles of public finance, and listens to the advice of commie braintrusters who don't know their ass from their elbow!"

Louise didn't like the reprimand, but she nodded and exchanged a glance with Nancy that asked: How do you put up with him?

"Well, Abe, the election's less than two months off," remarked Larkin.

"I think we should shoot him!"

147

Jolted, Harriet's eyes widened in shock at Mrs. Larkin's comment.

"I wish for your sake, Abe, that someone would. I suppose it's an awful thing to say, but he's a traitor to his class."

"I declare a moratorium on Roosevelt," interjected Nancy. "One can't go anywhere these days without—"

"I don't think shooting him is the solution, Louise," Phelps replied with a hearty laugh, "—though it is tempting."

"Well, maybe Nancy's right. Maybe if we all stop talking about him, he'll go away."

"I doubt it," he replied drily.

"And that wife of his! She makes such a fool of herself. Pretending to be everyone's mother. She should look after her own! The oldest son is a known drunkard."

"I've heard she entertains Negroes . . ."

"*Sam,*" tittered Mrs. Larkin.

". . . in her bedroom!"

The others laughed. How she hated them. Frazzled with anger, Harriet bobbled her glass while setting it down. Infinitesimal spillage occurred, immediately wiped up by a maid.

"I happen to admire Mrs. Roosevelt." Blushing and slightly hoarse, Harriet looked at Larkin.

"Sorry," he shrugged, embarrassed. "Just a joke. I can see you're a fan."

"That's not the point," replied Harriet, further inflamed as he chuckled. Throats were cleared in the quick and chilly silence. Harriet's upset putting them on the defensive, the women glanced at each other, and Larkin clinked the cubes in his glass. "That Roosevelt woman," commented Nancy, a slight edge in her voice, "has no business meddling in politics."

"I agree," added Louise. "She should be ashamed of herself." Nancy nodded.

Furious, Harriet bit her lip and concentrated on counting the spots on the Dalmation asleep at Elliot's feet. What would Nancy look like with a hat of caviar? she wondered, fighting an impulse to get up and walk out.

"What are the New York papers saying about Roosevelt, Miss Hoskins?" asked Larkin, trying to mollify her.

"They're all against him."

"It seems New York has *some* sense after all."

Larkin nodded to his wife. "But I'm afraid he's going to be reelected."

"I hate to agree with Sam, but the tide has turned against us. The little people have been taken in—"

"Little people? Who exactly do you mean?" The words popped out before Harriet could stop them. Louise Larkin was nonplussed. "Are the men in Leveret who can't find work because the mills haven't reopened 'little'? Is it *their* fault, as you seem to imply?"

"Aha!" crowed Elliot, "—a Democrat in sheep's clothing! See, Dad? I warned you."

Harriet realized Phelps was watching her intently and she shut up, but Louise was miffed.

"I *meant*," she insisted, "that the majority have been taken in by his bread and circuses. And that's why he'll win."

Elliot was disappointed that his father didn't jump on Harriet for her views. Instead, Phelps turned on Louise.

"I didn't think you and Sam were quitters."

"Don't misunderstand us."

"It's just that the opposition's so splintered. Landon is ineffectual, and Coughlin, for instance—"

"Coughlin is a fool who wants it all for himself."

"What's the feeling in the League, Abe?" asked Larkin, referring to the group of millionaire businessmen determined to overthrow the President. "Can you stop him? I wonder."

Phelps' eyes dilated in anger. Hands grasped the armrests of his lion-pawed chair. "We will. We must."

"A moratorium?" reminded Nancy.

"How's Jericho, Abe?" asked Larkin. "Any unrest?"

"Jericho," replied Phelps, as if describing a favorite spinster aunt whom he supported, "is fine."

"So is Boston," affirmed Louise. "Boston has *always* been fine." Nancy nodded and shut her ears as her husband and Larkin began talking of the mill. "Tell me about the benefit, Louise."

"Oh, yes. Abe? Did I tell you that Lev Saltonstall's chairing our men's committee?" Disinterested, Phelps barely nodded. "We'll have a round of golf in the afternoon and then dinner and dancing. Some of our D.A.R. ladies will have booths set up to sell cakes and raffle tickets."

"D.A.R.?" Pricking up her ears, Harriet couldn't resist the temptation to make social points. "Mother's·in the D.A.R.," she went on, and could almost see Letty's tart face. Trumpeting her membership in the snotty Daughters of the American Revolution wasn't something her mother would approve of.

"Your mother? How interesting. I believe I met her once at Garden Club. . . ." Dismissing Harriet's illustrious, if threadbare, genealogy, Nancy resumed her conversation with Louise, leaving Harriet with Elliot's ironic eyebrow and a hot-flash dislike of herself for her obvious attempt to win the women's approval.

"Hear you may have some trouble at the mill?"

"Trouble?" Phelps shot a look at Larkin. "There won't be trouble. My

149

people know which side their bread's buttered on. If they try and have the union in, I'll shut down. I'll shut down quicker than they can say John L. Lewis!" Muttering a curse at the head of the CIO, a man he detested as much as he did Roosevelt, Phelps crossed to the liquor cabinet and poured himself a whiskey.

"Now as for the dance . . . I'll be there. But you know Abe. He won't leave the mill. However, Elliot has consented to be my escort."

"How charming," cooed Mrs. Larkin.

"I don't think he's too pleased." Nancy Phelps touched her son's knee. "Darling? You won't be ashamed to be seen on the dance floor with your old mummy, will you?" Elliot shrugged shyly. "Don't worry," she continued, "I won't monopolize you. You'll have plenty of time for your other amours."

"Ashamed!" tittered Mrs. Larkin, "won't he be dancing with the belle of the ball? It reminds me of what happened at Pops last season. . . ."

"Not that old chestnut, Louise."

"Now, Nancy, you know you love me to tell it." She turned to Harriet. "Nancy and Elliot were at a Pops concert and . . ." The story of how Arthur Fiedler had thought Elliot must be Nancy's husband produced amused chuckles once again. "Now what do you think, my dear—don't you think they make a lovely couple?"

"What can she say, Louise?" smiled Nancy. "Don't put Miss Hoskins on the spot like that."

"It's true, Harriet . . ." Thoroughly sick of the story that contained an implication that he was something other than virile and in his prime, Phelps nevertheless came to Harriet's rescue. "I married a beautiful woman who remains ever young. If Elliot was once mistaken for her husband, there are people who think I'm her father."

Having turned the joke on himself, Phelps was pleased when Harriet rebutted him. "Mr. Phelps, I don't see how. You're a dynamo."

"Is that martini to your liking?" he asked, flattered. "Why don't I fix you another?"

Abruptly Elliot left the parlor and went to the pantry, where he made himself a double scotch and soda. A moment later the guests were startled by the boom of an organ that rumbled through the walls. The dogs perked up as the music became a high wail, then playfully wild, followed by a final chaotic chord that gripped the first floor, its echo lingering as Elliot appeared in the doorway and bowed. "Thought I'd serenade you," he remarked casually, rejoining them. "One of my own compositions. A short one."

"What do you call it?" asked Louise.

"Oh . . ." Elliot paused and grinned. "Ode To A Dynamo."

Phelps was not amused.

Louise tittered. *"Elliot,"* laughed Nancy, "you *are* being naughty today. What will our guests think?" she added, concerned for his suddenly flushed face and bright eyes. Feeling his forehead to see if he might have a temperature, she turned to Phelps, her eyes amused. "Now Abe," she cautioned, "don't be touchy. I rather liked it myself. It had a . . . feeling. Very modern. Quite powerful."

Elliot nodded, picking up on the game. "Exactly. That's what I wanted to express. Dad's . . . strength. What do you think, Harriet?"

Though he revealed nothing, Harriet could sense Phelps' contained anger. She found herself sympathetic and completely on his side. "I didn't think it was much of anything," she replied, meeting Elliot's glance and holding. "It made no sense at all."

"I guess you don't understand music, either," he sighed with mock sadness.

"I guess I don't," she replied coolly. She didn't understand what was going on, but she sure as hell wasn't going to sink into the carpet any longer and retreat from this spoiled brat, his bitch of a mother and her insufferable friends. Ignoring Elliot, Harriet turned her body deliberately sideways and faced Phelps. "Tell me about your activities," he asked her, grateful for her obvious empathy and pleased that she'd come to life.

"I wish I had something concrete to report. Especially to you," she added, lowering her voice conspiratorially, thrilled with Phelps' answering nod, which confirmed a deep and long-standing relationship which none of the others were privy to.

Curiosity aroused by the sudden closeness between Phelps and Harriet, Louise interjected herself in a pause: "Abe told us you sold jam to pay your way to college?"

"Yes, I did." Harriet and Phelps exchanged a smile.

"Good for you," commented Larkin.

"Jam?" Elliot sprang up, startling them all with his sudden movement. "What kind?"

"Strawberry, raspberry, and plum," Harriet replied, mowing him down with the clipped phrasing.

"Abe tells us you're a writer, Miss Hoskins?"

"A journalist, yes," she replied to Larkin.

"Might I have read—?"

"Take a look at this, Sam." Phelps crossed briskly to a cabinet, took out the copy of *Pegasus* that Harriet had sent him, and handed it to Larkin. "As you can see, Harriet's been published. I think she has a lively style. I may not know my modern music, but I recognize a writer when I see one. Perhaps you'll autograph it for me after the others have looked it over," he added to a lightheaded Harriet, who nodded quickly and began to enjoy herself.

"'New Englanders Speak New English'—what does it mean?" asked Mr. Larkin.

"It's a comment on our style of expressing ourselves. Like saying that we're going 'down' to Maine when we really mean 'up.' Things like that."

"How quaint," offered Mrs. Larkin, curious as to why Phelps was championing the outspoken creature.

"Exactly."

"Pardon?"

"That's the point. Quaint."

"I see."

"Do you write for a paper, too?" Larkin asked.

"That's my aim."

"Odd profession for a girl, isn't it?" asked Elliot, leaning against the mantel.

"Why? I don't think there's much a man can do that a woman couldn't—if she were given the chance."

Phelps smiled to himself.

"*I* do."

"*Elliot*," laughed Nancy.

"For instance? Do you mean sexual intercourse? No, we can't do that," Harriet went on, as a hush fell. "Obviously we can't do that. I obviously didn't mean that."

The ladies exchanged distasteful glances, but Elliot's grin was his first true one of the cocktail hour. Larkin joined him, and Phelps laughed heartily. "Hoisted on your own petard, Elliot." Phelps winked at Harriet, who was tensed, adrenalin stirred, ready for anything. Nodding warmly at her, he lit her cigarette and couldn't have been more pleased. Her bluntness struck a responsive chord; his memory of her two years back when she'd infiltrated his office and nicely manipulated him into loaning her money was now fired anew with her spunk. As one of the maids announced dinner in ten, he went to the bar and poured himself another whiskey. He couldn't help the fantasy that saw Harriet married to Elliot. She was just what he needed.

"What exactly *do* you mean, Miss Hoskins?" inquired Nancy, who might have read her husband's thoughts. If that were not disturbing enough, she noticed that Elliot was regarding Harriet with a sudden certain interest. "I don't understand," Nancy added, forced to take a new look at her adversary.

"Pardon?" feigned Harriet, sensing the upper hand.

"About women," prompted Larkin, likewise energized.

"Women? We control the country. We do the shopping, don't we?" Harriet sipped her martini with elaborate casualness. "Therefore, we run the economy. Why shouldn't we have a right to make the laws and influence opinion? Perhaps, Mrs. Phelps, you don't shop that often yourself"— Harriet glanced at the maids, then continued with an exquisite politeness that couldn't be faulted—"so you aren't aware of your influence."

Nancy Phelps' eyes narrowed imperceptibly, but she deigned not to accept the inherent challenge of Harriet's remarks, choosing instead to regard her with an amused and slightly ironic expression that Harriet recognized as a carbon of Elliot's.

"Influence?" scoffed Mrs. Larkin. "I have influence where it counts. With my husband."

"Exactly," nodded Harriet. "I understand completely."

"You do?"

"We've always had influence with men. Why shouldn't we have it on our own? Look at Mrs. Roosevelt. She's a doer, compassionate, and has achieved enormous good. Yet, if she weren't the wife of the President, would she have a fraction of the influence? A chance at all? Would anyone listen? Think if she *herself* were elected and had *real* power."

"You must be joking," exclaimed Mrs. Larkin incredulously, regarding Harriet as if she'd arrived from an unknown and dangerous planet.

"I think we have to be given the opportunity. I can only speak of my own experience as a journalist. The attitude seems to be that women aren't wanted. There are exceptions, but generally, we're regarded suspiciously, even with hostility. As if we'd trespassed and should go back to the kitchen where we belong."

"You sound like a crusader, Miss Hoskins." Nancy's expression indicated how unattractive that was.

"Young people are these days." Mrs. Larkin sighed. "Thank goodness Madge has got over it already."

"Perhaps your daughter's letting you *think* she's got over it. Maybe she's no longer telling you *how* she really feels," Harriet went on, returning the jab with a subtlety not lost on Phelps, who was relishing the exchange. "Many young people today can't talk to their parents. From what *you* say about your daughter, she and I think alike. I'd like to meet her."

Stung with the implication that she and her daughter were no longer in perfect communication, Louise Larkin's pinched face flushed. "Alike?" she asked coldly. "I don't think so. Do you, Sam?"

"They'd probably get along," nodded her husband, who didn't mind seeing his wife put on the defensive.

"My daughter and I are very close, aren't we, Nancy?"

"Of course you are."

"Dinner in five minutes, ma'am," whispered a maid.

"*How* do you think you're alike?" demanded Mrs. Larkin. "Madge isn't a radical."

"Neither am I," retorted Harriet, color rising. "Your daughter feels guilty about having a debut because she's seen there are many people still in trouble. I agree. My own father only found work again two months ago. I'll bet Madge and I would ask the same question: Should my father and millions like him be tossed on the scrap heap, accused of being loafers and given no help while others throw parties? I'm sure you don't mean to be, Mrs. Larkin, but I think you're out of touch with reality."

"Do you?" Mrs. Larkin coughed lightly and hoped the cavalry was coming, but Harriet continued on, her outward calm hiding a fervor that revealed itself in a sudden shortness of breath. "The President is going to be reelected—because he *cares*. And everyone in the country knows it. I'm sure Madge does. *I only wish I were eight months older so I could vote for him myself!*"

"Bravo!" cried Elliot.

"Did you hear that, Abe?" Hoping that Harriet had gone too far and that Phelps would put her in her place, Louise was astonished to find him unperturbed.

"What can I say, Louise?" he asked, rising. "Radical or not, I like a young woman who speaks her mind. Ill-advised though she may be," he added to Harriet, his admiring glance belying the sharpness of his comment. "Let's go into dinner."

In the flurry of rising, Elliot managed to get Harriet aside.

"You were sensational," he whispered. "And you're a spoiled brat," she snapped back.

"Me? I did it on purpose. It was a test. You passed. You're Cinderella. The slipper fits . . ."

"Harriet?" Phelps extended his arm, and the procession started off, Phelps and Harriet leading, Nancy and Elliot in the middle, followed by the Larkins, trailed by the dogs.

"I guess you think you're the Queen of Sheba."

"As a matter of fact—I am." Harriet fairly floated out onto the broad veranda behind the mansion and joined Elliot, who was waiting, the dogs milling about him.

Phelps and Harriet had dominated dinner conversation, and Elliot, wanting to get away, had complained of a stomach ache and said he was going for a walk. Phelps had suggested Harriet might want to join him. Perhaps they should go for a ride in the speedboat? Put on the spot, Elliot had agreed, but he was in a nasty mood again.

"Suuu . . . *perb*." Cheeks lit with a flame struck by Phelps, exhilaration shone in Harriet's eyes. "Harriet is not an ordinary young woman," he'd assured them all as she left the table. Her tales of life in New York had found a receptive audience in the men, while the women were reduced to mummies, swathed in silence. Phelps' appreciative laughter still sounded in her ears. Why, he'd actually seemed to be courting her! She felt more confident than she had in months.

"What a view!" she murmured as she and Elliot stepped down past stone lions. "I think your grandfather picked the best spot in the whole valley. . . ." Past swimming pool and tennis court, an opening in the thick

154

woods below revealed the lake, rolling dark hills beyond, and a silver bend of the Merrimack, which reflected the lights of Leveret.

The dogs raced in excited circles as Harriet and Elliot started across a broad lawn. "Do you really have 'fish to fry' in Boston?" he asked after a while. "I think that's what you said. *Do* you have a job there?"

"I'm going to look into a few things, yes."

"You made it sound as if you had something definite. Were you trying to impress my father?"

"Was I?"

"I guess you thought he wanted a progress report on his investment."

"That's none of your business. It's between your father and me."

"And aren't you both cozy!"

"Perhaps." Not about to let him faze her, Harriet laughed, delighted with herself. "All right," she teased. "I want you to tell me why you were such a stinker, and if you don't I'll tell your mother you were a bad boy, and she won't take you dancing with her."

"Ha-hah." Her ebullience grated. Wouldn't he love to burst her bubble, put her in her place and drive her away. Elliot took a swallow from his flask and offered it to Harriet, who accepted. Pausing by the tennis court, he snapped on the lights, then snapped them off again. "Are you going to teach me to play?" Harriet asked, attempting to infiltrate his moodiness. "Would your mother approve?" She began to imitate Louise Larkin: "Elliot and Nancy took the cup last year, and then we ate sautéed 'little people' for dinner at the Saltonstalls'. . . ."

Elliot smiled distantly. "She is dreary. What about my mother? Do you have a couple of smart cracks?"

"I wouldn't dream."

"Do you think she's beautiful?"

"Not as beautiful as you," Harriet replied and caught his mocking eye, which she matched with a raised brow of her own. That she was still attracted to him was a mystery. "You be sure and tell your mother not to worry," she added, winking. "I wouldn't think of stealing you away."

"Did you sleep with anyone in New York?"

"That's for me to know."

"I don't intend to find out."

"Your loss."

"You have virgin written all over you."

"Where does it show?"

Enjoying the banter, Harriet sat on a low bench on the edge of Nancy's rose garden. Elliot squatted beside her. Impatient to move on, the dogs barked as he took another swallow and glanced at Harriet, then quickly away. "What?" she asked as a sudden shiver coursed through him. "Are you chilly?" He shook his head, and Harriet sensed he was unhappy. "Tell me."

155

"What shall I tell you?" That he liked her well enough but liked her brother better? That ever since the day Dobie Pratt stepped naked out of a shower in his lower-middle year at Exeter, he'd known he liked their brothers better?

In the half darkness Harriet's resemblance to Frankie was startling. Abruptly Elliot stood up and started off.

"Wait . . ." Could she interpret his bizarre behavior as that of a swain reluctantly smitten, but smitten just the same? She hoped so. "Who invited me tonight?" she asked, catching up with him.

"Me."

"Then why did you try so hard to embarrass me?"

"Sometimes I can't control myself."

"What's that supposed to mean?"

"Whatever you like."

Stymied, she shook her head. "Hmmm . . ." she murmured, buying time and trying to read him.

"I lied. Why should I invite you? You're not exactly my type."

"What's your type? A snob and a bore like yourself?" Amazed at how quickly he'd got her on the defensive, Harriet was further upset by Elliot's low laughter. "I think there's less to you than meets the eye," she snapped, trying to regain her position. "In any event, I'm tired. I think I'll go home."

"C'mon. My father said I should take you for a boat ride. What my father wants, he gets. I'll be good."

"Don't bother. Are you afraid of your father?" she added, hoping to prick him in a vulnerable spot and pay him back.

"Are *you*?"

"Far from it."

"You're pals, right? Hah-hah."

"I think my brother must be blind. He said you were fun."

"What else did he say?"

"Nothing."

Once again, Elliot walked away. Heading down toward the water and talking to the dogs, he thought of Frankie, whom he'd met on his first night home from Princeton in June. Restless, Elliot had gone to the Classic Ballroom, and there stood this astounding young trumpet player, whose talent Elliot appreciated, whose body he craved. Frankie had looks and an innocence that, combined with a sexy abandon when he played, caused Elliot to want him. That he was probably unapproachable made him all the more desirable.

"C'mon!" Elliot beckoned to Harriet, who was gazing at the stars and taking her own sweet time. "Let me give you a piece of advice," he said as she joined him.

"You?"

"You're guilty of an error. It'll only make you unhappy. You believe it's important. Don't you? Life. It's not."

"My, my. Such a cynic. I've got your number, Buster Brown."

"I doubt it." Elliot turned on her with sudden energy. Furious and not sure why, he asked Harriet if she wasn't pleased at the way everything was working out.

"What do you mean?"

"Never mind. Didn't I tell you sometimes I say things? Don't pay any attention. Don't let it get you down. Don't you feel fine? I know how nervous you were about seeing my father. I know everything. There wasn't anything to be worried about, was there? I doubt very much you'll even have to pay him back the money you owe him. That is—if you play your cards right. I'm sure you will."

Angered at his insinuations, Harriet tried to get a word in. Elliot silenced her with a raised hand. "As I said, you did beautifully tonight. Passed with flying colors. A few rocky minutes at the beginning, but then you were terrific. Your views contradict everything my father believes, but you still won the prize. And the stuff about your ancestors I particularly liked. What was his name—that illustrious uncle killed by the British? And, oh, yes, your great, great uncle whatsisname who lived in Concord next to Thoreau? Very impressive credentials. You touched all the bases, didn't you? You really know how to sell yourself. I wish I had the knack."

"Are you drunk or crazy? Perhaps both. I don't like what you've implied, I'll tell you that."

Stimulated by her anger and smiling as if he'd won something, Elliot wondered how far he dared go. "I haven't finished," he said, while Harriet glared at him. "My father doesn't care about your genealogy. He's pragmatic. My mother, yes, but in this case, she doesn't count. You're the *real* snob, aren't you, my little Daughter of the American Revolution? Don't you think Dad knows all about you, anyway? And everything about your family, too? You wouldn't have been invited if you weren't . . . suitable. Somewhat suitable, at least. Now the question remains: Do *I* find you suitable? Time . . ."

"What on earth are you talking about?"

". . . will tell. Don't let me mess up your big opportunity for you. You don't think so at this moment, but—I like you. I really do. Rich little poor girl. Jam? I was almost in tears. . . ." Elliot walked away onto the dock. "Wait," he called as Harriet turned briskly and started off in the opposite direction. Elliot shouted to her again. Because she didn't want him to have the victory of upsetting her, she pretended to catch her heel in the lawn, turned halfway back to him and called: "I don't find *you*—"

"What?"

"Suitable."

"Of course I'm not. At least we've got *that* settled. C'mon! Don't be a spoilsport. I was testing you." He knelt down and stuck a hand into the water. "It's warm—want to go for a swim?" Harriet shook her head. "Oh, c'mon, I'm harmless. Don't disappoint me. I thought you were made of sterner stuff. That's why you're here tonight."

Having had enough, Harriet turned away again. "I like you," Elliot shouted. "I *do*."

She couldn't resist glancing over her shoulder, watching, strangely fascinated, as Elliot disappeared into the boathouse. A moment later she heard the muffled roar of the motor and the door rose and he came out piloting a speedboat, which he maneuvered to the side of the dock.

"I want you all to sit right there," he ordered the dogs, who raced up and down the planks. "No going in the water. No. You OK?" he called cockily to Harriet over the idling of the motor.

"Of course I'm OK," she shot back. "I don't like to be toyed with, Elliot," she added, returning to the dock.

"Sure." He helped her into the boat.

"It's extremely disconcerting to have a conversation with someone when you don't know if they're being serious or . . ."

"Pulling your leg." They said it together. Motioning her not to speak, Elliot linked his little finger with hers:

"What color's the grass?"

"Green."

"What goes up the chimney?"

"Smoke."

"May your wish and my wish never be broke."

Elliot wished he were normal, and Harriet wished lightning would strike and she'd be offered a job in Boston next week. Even Leveret would do.

"Did you wish for me?" asked Elliot.

"What an egotist you are." She didn't remember that once at Bartlett's Field, she had. "For no apparent reason," she added.

Elliot let go the steering wheel and kissed her and she tasted the brandy on him. The boat slapped against the dock as he kissed her again and she tried to avert her face. "You'll have to learn to kiss better than that," he laughed, letting go of her and grabbing for the wheel.

"You stink. I'm getting off."

"Don't wanna go for a ride with the Prince? Rather screw instead? There's a cot in the boathouse. No? Here we go!"

He jerked the boat into gear with a whine, then a roar. The dogs barked excitedly, pacing back and forth. Harriet caught his expression—a grinning clown, the dock lights reflected in his eyes as one hand tousled chaotically through his gleaming hair. "Hang on!" he cried as the boat shot away.

Three-quarters of an hour later, Elliot swung his car in lazy curves from one side of the road to the other as he drove Harriet back to town. By the time they reached Main Street, she'd reached her limit and then some.

"Let me out. I'll walk the rest of the way."

He pulled over by Longbottom's Market and Harriet got out, slamming the door. Briskly she crossed the deserted street and hurried along past the dark storefronts. Out of the corner of an eye, she saw the La Salle continue in the opposite direction and disappear round a corner. More furious with herself than Elliot, she shuddered inwardly at the memory, all too recent, of the crazed ride across the lake where, for one terrifying moment, she was sure he'd meant to kill the both of them.

Behind her in the distance, the quiet of the night was shattered by shifting gears as a car accelerated. Was he coming back? Harriet increased her pace, heading for a beacon of light that splashed onto the pavement from the only brightly lit window on the street.

Suddenly, she heard the energetic clack of a typewriter. Pausing, she glanced in the window and saw Patrick bent over his desk at work.

"Hello?" she called, stepping into the open doorway. Albatross barked and approached, sniffing. "Is he friendly?" Patrick looked up.

"Don't I know you?" she asked, trying to place him.

"Patrick Flynn."

"*You.* We were just talking about you at dinner!"

"Favorably, I hope," he said, finding his tongue. "Who's 'we'?"

"At the Mansion. But I didn't recognize your name at first and— Do you remember me? I'm Harriet Hoskins. You were going to be a priest!" she exclaimed, Patrick's vivid blue eyes jogging her memory.

"My plans changed."

Harriet might have been curious to know more, but at the moment Elliot pulled up out front.

"Here you are," he grinned, entering the office. "Hi, there," he called to Patrick. "I'm Elliot Phelps. You're Joe Flynn's son. I know Joe. We have the same boss. Know your mother, too. We were just discussing you at dinner. Not your mother. She wasn't there." Elliot laughed. "Have you two met?"

"We know each other," Harriet replied coolly, giving Patrick a quick smile, thus aligning herself with him.

"How nice," replied Elliot sarcastically. "Burning the midnight oil?" he asked, striding behind the counter as if he owned the territory. He glanced at Patrick's desk, then at Patrick, and the animosity between the two men was instantaneous. Threatened by Patrick's virility, Elliot needed to put him in his place. "Well," he remarked fliply, looking about with an amused smile, "an up-to-date newspaper office. Just what we need here in Jericho. Hmmm," he added, raising an eyebrow at the crucifix on the wall. "Got a john?" he asked, moving to the rear and opening the door. "You *do*. What a surprise!"

Elliot disappeared to use the bathroom. Embarrassed, Harriet exchanged a glance with Patrick. "I apologize. He's had one too many."

"That's OK," he replied, calming the desire to shove his fist in Elliot's face. Harriet sighed, and Patrick asked if he could get her something. "Some water?" Harriet shook her head but smiled gratefully. "Just tired," she added, suddenly aware of his intense scrutiny, which caused her to lower her eyes and fiddle with her purse. "As I said . . . I didn't place your name, but Mr. Phelps mentioned your paper this evening. He said he'd taken an ad."

"My mother used to work at the mill."

"Are you running this yourself?" The very idea of an Irish Catholic newspaper starting up in Jericho had produced a good deal of merriment at the dinner table.

"It's a family effort. The first issue'll be out in a week."

"I see. When did you . . . get back to Jericho?"

"A few weeks ago."

"Me, too."

In the silence that followed, she sensed him watching her again. "Your plans changed, you say?" she asked after a moment, needing to regain her composure and get on top of things.

He nodded. "And you?" he asked, feeling his face hot.

"Just got back from the big city and—"

"And she's looking for work," called Elliot, reappearing. "Did you know she's a writer, Pat? Have you got something for her?"

"Don't be an ass, Elliot."

Abruptly Harriet walked out the door and headed for home. A few minutes later Elliot pulled up beside her. "I was just trying to help."

Harriet ignored him, but he continued to drive slowly along beside her. "I apologize," he called as she turned the corner of Mulberry. "I saw how he looked at you. Do you like him? There was a spark, wasn't there?" Why, Elliot wondered, should he be jealous? As Harriet reached the house, he stopped the car and got out.

"Let me give you a piece of advice," she heard him say as she let herself in. "Go back to New York. There's nothing for you here."

"Go to hell, why don't you?"

Letty, Cora and Alice were at the dining room table. Letty was cutting the patterns for the bridesmaids' dresses. "How was it?" asked Alice. "I've conquered the Phelps," replied Harriet wryly. Returning to the front hall to hang up her coat, she glanced out the window and was surprised to find Elliot still standing beside his car, gazing forlornly at the house.

8

Dear Virginia,

God, I feel down. Am sitting here at a table in the playground of my old grammar school. Why am I here, you ask? This kid wonders, too.

I know I'm at some kind of turning point, and I'm afraid I won't recognize the right road. Or worse yet, I'll take the wrong one. All the old questions don't seem to have the same answers anymore, and the old answers don't fit the new questions. What am I going to do with the rest of my life? I was so sure I had the answer to that one. Yet here I am feeling dazed, a fifth wheel rolling nowhere, reduced to bumming cigs from my father, who keeps asking me what my plans are. My mother has taken to waking me up in the mornings with cheery greetings, such as "Idle hands are the devil's," etc. Daily, she tries to tempt me with a project or two. Do I want to help with the plans for my sister Cora's wedding? Do I want to go to Boston to look at china patterns? Do I want to use my free time to help out at church?

I don't.

I've "been to Paris," as they say, and life back on the farm ain't what it was and never can be again—

"Say . . ."

Startled, Harriet looked up to find Elliot leaning against the seesaw on the other side of the jungle gym.

"It says here," he called, nodding to the *Boston Herald* in his hands, "that Mrs. Simpson has fled to the French Riviera to avoid the King's advisors. You aren't avoiding the Prince, are you?"

"What are *you* doing here?"

"I could ask you the same. Do you think Mrs. Simpson and the King will marry?" he added, coming closer across the playground.

"I hope so." The whole world was wondering whether the English government would allow Edward VIII to marry the American divorcée, Wallis Warfield Simpson of Baltimore.

"Me, too. But then, *I'm* a romantic."

"I am, too," Harriet retorted, dismayed at how easily he'd got her on the defensive.

"I think you're pragmatic."

Harriet sighed brusquely. Above her head perfect clouds like exploding cotton sailed across a vivid September sky. She wasn't looking.

"Well?" asked Elliot.

"Well, what?"

"*Have* you been avoiding me?"

"Yes."

"I want to talk to you."

"So you snuck up on me?"

"I didn't. I was on my way to Noonan's for lunch, and who should I see but— Wait," he pleaded as she got up to go. "What do you think of *The Jericho Irish Spectator?* I see you bought one of the inaugural editions. Not much to it, is there?"

"No." Harriet glanced distastefully at the paper, her irritation with *it* overcoming her desire not to speak to Elliot at all. "I feel sorry for him . . . Patrick Flynn . . . editor in chief. It's ludicrous. I don't mean to sound superior, but it's worse than could be expected."

"Is that your professional opinion?"

"It's not so much that it's limited in content," she continued, ignoring his comment, "—news of Hibernian socials and Saint Mary's and the like. But what there is is so lacking in any kind of style. The writing, I mean. Turgid doesn't begin to describe it. There's no attempt at an attractive layout. No photos. Oh, never mind."

"You sound angry."

"I am. Amateurs shouldn't dabble. And, yes, in answer to your question—I *do* consider myself a professional. And it makes my blood boil to see—"

"You're awfully pretty when you get excited."

"Please, I'm not interested." In no mood to spar with him, she collected her purse.

"How about lunch?"

"No, thanks."

"But I called you, and you didn't call me back. Don't I get an A for effort? Don'tcha know people call *me*—not vice versa? How did you like the lighter I sent? What about the message I had engraved?"

"There's nothing to 'forgive,' and I've already 'forgot' all about it."

"I was a shit . . . I guess."

"Yes, you were a shit."

Elliot grinned, kicked an acorn, glanced quickly at Harriet, just as quickly away. He wasn't sure why he'd called her, let alone sent a gift. Filled with conflicting feelings, he'd done everything he could to drive her away, yet here he was.

"Seen Patrick again?" he asked.

Harriet caught Elliot's glance, lumped him as a childish dream that proved to have feet of clay. When would she learn? Behind them from the open windows of the school came the singsong chant of children reciting. The noon whistle blew from the mill, and traffic picked up on Main Street.

"No."

Suddenly he swung himself up on the jungle gym and scrambled to the top. Balancing himself with arms extended, he started slowly across the topmost bar.

"I'm Flash Gordon . . ." he called.

"Be careful . . ." She shielded her eyes from the sun and looked up at him. Framed by roiling clouds, he continued across like a tightrope walker.

"Would you be sad if I fell?"

"Stop showing off. I'm going—"

Quickly he swung down, lithe body curving through the bars. "What's wrong? I was just trying to amuse you. You *are* in the dumps. Let's go eat."

"I'm busy."

"Aw, c'mon, kiddo. Don't be a wet blanket."

"I don't like 'kiddo,' either."

"Sorry." He extended his hand. "Truce?"

"I didn't know there was a war." His burst of appreciative laughter caused Harriet to smile in spite of herself, and she shook his hand. Still, all in all, she was very doubtful whether she wanted to have anything further to do with him.

"Noonan's?" he asked.

"Some other time."

"OK. Suits me. I tried. Have a good life." He walked away, surprising her by giving up so quickly. Had she made too hasty a decision? No, he was trouble. She had only to pick up the phone, and a dozen old boy-friends would come running. *Get moving*, she ordered herself. Head in hands, she discovered a headache had crept up.

"Mrs. Simpson . . . ! Hey, there—MRS. SIMPSON!"

Out on the sidewalk Elliot waved to Harriet and jumped up and down, the Arrow Collar Man gone berserk.

"WALLIS??? IS THAT YOU? WALLIS WARFIELD SIMPSON???

LONG TIME NO SEE! GOT TIME FOR A CUPPA COFFEE AT
THE PALACE?"

Passersby stared. Harriet tried not to, but couldn't help laughing.

"WALLIS???" he pleaded.

"Edward???" she called as he came toward her. "Is it *you?* Who
would've thunk it?"

"We got a problem here, Denny," whispered Billy Meeghan conspiratorially to Dennis Flynn the same day. The two friends sat at Dennis's
corner table in Noonan's window as they usually did at lunchtime. "This
paper here," continued the pasty-faced crony and confidante, "has got a
problem or two, and I would be doin' you a disservice if I didn't make
mention—"

Dennis waved his flunky silent. His eyes swept from the passing
parade on the street to the interior of the drugstore where a clatter of
silverware and conversation arose from counter and tables. The heady
aroma of freshly ground coffee mingled with perfume and soap, sizzling
hamburgers and Tommy Noonan's famous cheese dreams, the odors
fraternizing as did the crowd, for Noonan's was the hub of Jericho.

Talk, as it was all over town today, was of the first issue of *The Jericho
Irish Spectator.* Dennis's nose sniffed the air of public opinion. As usual,
he misread it.

"A success," he intoned, "—a definite success. If talk is divided—
that's all to the good. Divide and conquer. How many people do you think
are, right at this moment, reading my column?" With a great rustle that
demanded attention from nearby eaters, Dennis shook open a copy of *The
Spectator,* only one of a collection of regional newspapers that he brought
to Noonan's to peruse in public. But like the books in his library, the
newspapers were a prop and went largely unread.

"This is going to be my springboard," he went on. "I already have my
base of operations at the tax office, right? Now I have my column to let
voters know how I feel. Two years from now, Billy, we'll be headed for
Washington and—"

"Hey, Dennis—your ma's deserted Roosevelt, has she?" called one of
Noonan's regulars from the counter, holding up *The Spectator.*

"Ya could go blind reading the print. . . ."

"How come there's no funnies?"

"Buy a comic book," huffed Dennis.

"That's what I been tryin' to tell you," whispered Billy urgently. "We
got a potential hornet's nest here. You could be associated with a losin'
venture that's gonna hurt—"

"What are you talking about? Everybody's reading it, aren't they?
Over in the city, too."

"People're curious. It's the first issue. But I been catchin' a whiff. It ain't favorable. My pa didn't like it. Not at all. There's other Democrats feel the same. Now, sure, there's lots of folks like Father Coughlin, but they don't like Lemke and O'Brien and the Union Party. That's a lotta bull-tweed. I mean, just because Rose is datin' Timothy is no—"

"That's all Ma's doing." Abruptly Dennis changed the subject to what was closest to his heart—the ending of his tormenting thirty-year-old virginity: "Have you lined up somebody for tonight?" It was Billy who was the procurer. It was Billy who had the collection of pornography hidden in shoe boxes behind the furnace in his father's cellar.

"I can make a few calls."

Dennis leaned closer, his voice hoarse. "I want to see *Ecstasy*. You know what the ad says? *'The picture all Leveret's whispering about.'* Know why?"

"Sure. Ya can see Hedy Lamarr's tits. Except you can't. It's a lotta baloney. I saw it last night."

"You saw it? *Without me?* Who's she?" he added, frowning as Harriet entered the drugstore with Elliot. Envious at the sight of two winners, he slouched and hailed a waitress.

"Bicarb, Helen," he muttered, jealous eyes on the twosome who sat down a few tables over. "I may take the rest of the day off, huh, Billy? What do you think?"

A moment later, trailed by Rose, Gert entered Noonan's with an extra flourish on this first day of *The Spectator*. Rouged and ready for compliments, her eyes scanned the place as greetings were called to her. She beckoned to Dennis. "Where's your brother? He's not over at the office. His lunch'll be gettin' cold. I see you're wastin' your time with Billy Meeghan again . . . an unemployed loafer who'll never make a nickel of himself. . . ."

Gert set the covered lunch basket down on the counter. Once again her eye swept the interior of the drugstore, alighting finally on the stack of *Spectators* on the cigar counter. Calculating by the height of the pile the number sold, she broke into a grin.

"How're they sellin', Tommy?" she called to the proprietor. Lovingly, her hands straightened the stack.

"Like hotcakes, Gert."

The grin went broader. "That's right," she called back, "—and how the notoriety becomes ya, Tommy." She held up a *Spectator*. On the front page was an article titled "Jericho's Prominent Irishman of the Week," featuring Tommy Noonan.

"Doubled my business," he bandied back.

"Isn't it so?" Gert paused to accept congratulations from a couple of lady partisans. "And we sold over fifty after mornin' Mass; I'm told they're

165

grabbin' it up over in the city. Now it's just the first issue," she continued, working the counter, chatting with friends, giving necks a squeeze. Heads turned all over the drugstore at the loudness of her voice. "What do ya think, boys? What's your opinion? A collector's item, hah?"

"Sure enough, Gert. . . ." Nobody was about to tell her any different.

"Would you believe her?" asked a shopper to her companion, neither of them of the Faith. If the reaction of the Irish was mixed, the Protestant majority in town couldn't help be either confused or amused. The Irish, they worked the mills, they cleaned—if you kept after them. Did they really think they needed a newspaper? Who even suspected they read?

"Who on earth is that?" asked Harriet as Gert continued her quest for compliments and reassurance.

"That," replied Elliot, "is the mother of the editor. Shall I call her over? I know you want to offer your congratulations."

"Don't you dare."

"Well now, look who's here. . . ." Gert made a beeline for Elliot and beamed at the sight of *The Spectator* on the table. "Aren't ya a good lad, Elliot! What's your feelin' about it? An educated lad like yourself, I'd value your opinion."

"I think it's super, Mrs. Flynn." Elliot's foot nudged Harriet under the table. "Do you know Miss Harriet Hoskins?"

Introductions were made. Gert beckoned Rose and Dennis to the table and did likewise.

"I remember you, Dennis," smiled Harriet, "right here at Noonan's with your brother."

"You know my Pat?" Gert gave Harriet a fast onceover, then returned to more important matters. "Did ya happen to notice my Denny's column, Elliot? And Rose here made her debut in print with her society jottin's."

"Oh, Mutha . . ." cooed Rose, putting on her snooty voice. Trying to catch Elliot's attention, she uttered a sigh.

"Just terrific, Rose," commented Elliot, giving Harriet another nudge. "Don't you agree, Harriet?"

"I do." Fascinated, she watched Rose flirting with him. So this was Patrick's sister. She recognized the eyes.

"You must be proud, Mrs. Flynn."

"That I am, Elliot. Sure enough, I had little to do with it myself, but I'll tell my Pat of your compliments and I'm sure he'll appreciate it. Poor fella's been workin' his tail off. There's been scoffers, lemme tell ya. Well, they'll be laughin' out of the other side when we get rollin'. Excuse me, dearie—" Gert reached past Harriet and picked up the paper and shook it open. "Here's your father's ad, Elliot—right in a prominent place. I hope he's pleased. Thank him again for me, will ya? And tell him I'll drop in for old times' sake one of these days when I get a blessed minute."

166

"I'll do that, Mrs. Flynn. By the way, Miss Hoskins is a journalist with quite a bit of experience . . . just back from New York, in fact, where she worked on the *Times,* so you might want to get her comments before she accepts a tempting offer with the *Boston Herald.*"

Harriet could have killed him. Three pairs of Flynn eyes focused on her. "Is that so?" demanded Gert, pulling body up as squint bore down.

"I think it's . . . wonderful. Such an effort and—"

"Here's the editor himself," called Gert, interrupting Harriet as Patrick entered the drugstore. "Where was ya? I have your lunch. Here's Elliot Phelps and . . . his friend. They love the paper."

"Thanks." Patrick barely acknowledged Elliot, whose superior expression inflamed him. Had they made up? he wondered, smiling at Harriet. He felt strangely deflated. "I was down to the depot," he went on, hiding his feelings and turning to Gert. "They sold out already."

Gert's beam would've lit a stadium. Patrick grinned, too. Harriet was annoyed. How pleased they all were with themselves!

"What a grand day it is." With a flurry of words, Gert concluded the interview ("Back to work, all of youse"), and the Flynns departed, heading across the street to *The Spectator* office.

Elliot exploded in laughter.

"You're awful! Putting me on the spot like that!"

"But you enjoyed yourself, didn't you? That's my mission today— drive away your blues." He began to hum.

"It's catchy."

"Cole Porter, didn't you know? I write a song or two myself—when Dad isn't looking." He snapped his fingers and drummed on the table. "Aren't I a tonic? Hmmmmm? Aren't I better than a bath in Poland Springs water? 'Oooo, Elliot, what a good lad ya are. . . .' " His imitation of Gert's brogue made Harriet laugh. Feeling spun like a top with his clowning, she returned to her chicken salad sandwich and had to admit she felt better. "Calm down," she whispered, noticing other diners looking at the two of them, amused at Elliot's antics.

"Whatsamatta?" he retorted. "Don't we hold the mortgage on this place? Tommy, who holds the mortgage on this place?"

"You do, Elliot," called the proprietor, winking.

"See? We own it. You and me. The best-looking couple in the joint. Right? Right. Guess what?—'I drink milk from contented cows.' 'Isn't it easier from a glass?' Hah-hah. Forget it. What are we doing tonight?"

"Oh, no. No, you don't."

"You don't find me irresistible?"

"Nope."

"You're not scared of me, I hope. I told you—I'm really harmless. I'll give you an affidavit from my father."

"I never know when to believe you."

167

"You're lucky." Elliot regarded Harriet over the rim of his cup and wondered if he could fall in love with her. He felt he should. Not just because his father admired her. That was enough reason *not* to. But he was desperate to put an end to his agony, and he felt drawn to Harriet's vitality and confidence. Or was the attraction because she reminded him so of Frankie? He didn't know. One of those days, he said to himself, determined to get a grip. One of those days he didn't know *who* the hell he was.

Harriet watched a depression settle on him. Confused, she finished her sandwich and got out a cigarette. "Where's my lighter?" he wanted to know. "Gave it away," she replied, trying to make him smile. "After all, why should I keep a present from a man I had no intention of seeing again?" Winking, she brought it out of her purse.

"Awwww. Good. You know, I've been pining away for you. Brokenhearted baby, that's me."

"Put it in a song. Anyway, that's not what *I* heard. I'm told your heartache hasn't kept you from the Classic this past week. Frankie tells me you have quite an entourage."

Elliot shrugged, confused that he could make it with tarts but not with "nice" girls. He'd tried to, unsuccessfully, with Amy in the boathouse one night. He had his pick of cheap shopgirls who hung out in Leveret, but not all the conquests he'd notched on his gun could blot out the intensity he felt at the sight of a good-looking man.

"Has your brother been spreading gossip? Wait'll I get my hands on him," he added, laughing to himself at the danger. Would he ever dare? Especially now that he knew Harriet? Every time he was with Frankie lately, he was fearful he'd give himself away. Frustrations were relieved in Boston, where he struggled, told himself not to, gave in, and followed sailors into alleys, the risk terrifying and exciting him, guilt and revulsion demolishing him when it was over. Maybe he should tell her about himself? Elliot rejected the possibility.

"I have to go!" Harriet exclaimed, glancing at the clock. "I don't like to admit that I've fallen so low," she replied when Elliot asked her why, "but Alice found out about an opening at Sutherland's over in the city, and I'm going to apply. Can you see me in hosiery? Can't wait to sell gloves. If you hear of a body floating in the river . . ."

"I don't see you as a salesgirl."

Harriet smiled gratefully. "Join the club."

"Nothing's happened?"

"I've presented my resumé to the *Herald*, also the *American*."

"Aha! What about those hot prospects you told us about at the Mansion? I'm glad to see I'm not the only fibber in town. Maybe you and I are alike. Charming liars." Elliot wondered: Would it be devious of him if he continued to see her? "A matter of survival, isn't it?"

Harriet watched Elliot's mood plunge again, like a cloud hiding the sun. He lapsed into silence and stared out the window. "I'm a lie," he mumbled after a while, "a charming, goddamned lie."

"Why are you so hard on yourself?" She noticed his fingers shredding his paper napkin. "I know," she went on, "that you're not happy with your work at the mill. What would you really like to do?"

"No idea. Absolutely none. Leave town. Wanna come?"

"At least you can. You can do whatever you like because you're a man. You don't have to play by the rules that I'm supposed to."

"Are you kidding? Rules? My father makes the rules."

"Don't let him. If you want to design fabrics, then do it. Show him what you can do. Work in your spare time. Why don't we write some songs together? You and Frankie and me? We'll send them in to a song publisher. Who knows, maybe Frankie could even get the band at the Classic to play them. Don't let *anybody* tell you what to do or put you in a niche."

"You don't understand. I'm 'the Prince.' Heir to a dynasty of thirteen mills. Ain't it grand?"

Harriet found herself noticing a wisp of hair that curled behind his ear, a vulnerable wisp that seemed at the moment the very essence of him. "You love him and hate him at the same time, don't you?" she asked. "I guess we all . . . I guess I feel the same about my father."

"I never had a father."

"I did," she replied, dismayed to realize she'd used the past tense. "And as for my mother, I love her dearly, I empathize with her, but I don't want to be anything like her. Coming back after a couple of years, I see her so clearly."

"He's always watching me."

"I know what you mean." Elliot's vulnerability loosening her own, she continued, "Do you think I just talk a good line? With my positive thinking and all that? The other night you told me I knew how to sell myself. But I've always been good at that. A perky smile and everyone thinks I'm wonderful. It didn't help in New York. I want to *succeed*. Glory, too, I'll admit. But where am I? Talk about niches! My family always encouraged me, but now I get the definite feeling Mother thinks I should settle down and not rock the boat. *I* feel like I should have a mission but haven't found my voice yet. Sometimes, I think I'm just a superficial ninny. I need to keep writing, but I'm not sure what about. People, politics, social issues? Certainly I can speak for my generation, maybe for women, no, for all of us. Look what happened—we were promised the moon, and now we don't have carfare. Everything's changed. Talk about aborted dreams! Loss of confidence! Older people seem dazed to me. We *mustn't* let them tell us what to do. How do *they* know? We have to be tough. We're going to need to be if Alice is right about the precarious state of the world."

"I don't think I've met anyone quite like you."

169

Pleased with his smile and the acknowledgment, Harriet's mouth crinkled into a laugh. "Were you really brokenhearted that I didn't return your call?"

"Sure."

"Good," she said, feeling nicely relaxed and flirty. "And since I've bared my soul, I want to ask you something. Why did you insinuate the other night that your father—"

"Fixed us up? He did. Why not? He recognizes a good thing when it comes along. Aren't you the Queen of Sheba?"

"Hmmm."

"So. We can't disappoint Dad. Shall we go out tonight?" Without waiting for an answer, he rose swiftly and went to the counter, where he paid the check, chatting and waving to other customers.

Who was he? Harriet wondered, as she fixed her lipstick. A set of Chinese boxes. You opened one, only to find another. Stimulated, yet wary, she wasn't sure she should see him again. She wouldn't feel safe until she knew the layout of the board, understood the moves, and got control of the game.

Outside, they could see the Flynns through *The Spectator* window across the street.

"Busy as bees," commented Elliot.

"A little 'loving hands at home' rag," Harriet scoffed.

"C'mon . . ." He took her arm and attempted to steer her across the street. "Why not?" he asked when she protested. "Why not try? It's better than Sutherland's, isn't it? *Make* them hire you. You seem to have some ideas. You know what's lacking, so let's go over and talk to the micks."

"Are you kidding? They aren't looking for anyone. Did you see that overpainted washerwoman's face when you told her I was a writer? She doesn't want any fingers in *her* pie. No, thank you very much. It wouldn't be *my* cup of tea, either. Anyway, I give it two weeks."

They continued down Main Street and parted at the mill, he to return to work, she to take the trolley to Leveret.

"I'll call you tomorrow?" he asked, his ambivalence conquered for the moment. Yet he didn't want to lead her on.

"All right," she replied, surprised she hadn't hesitated. "Don't be blue," she added. "Takes too much energy. Listen to me!—I should fill my own prescription."

"Bye, Wallis . . ."

"Bye, Edward . . ."

Two days later, Sutherland's called her. She had the job. Twenty-two dollars a week. She would start on Tuesday. On Monday, appalled at the very idea of a fate worse than death behind the notions counter, Harriet took Elliot's suggestion.

Immersed in a biography of Saint John of the Cross, a Catholic mystic whose breadth of vision he wished he could make his own, Patrick didn't notice Harriet watching through the window. "Hello," she called, causing him to jerk upright as she appeared in the doorway, a vibrant, yellow-slickered apparition on a rainy afternoon.

"Cats and dogs as they say! Are you alone? I don't want to interrupt if you're busy." Glancing about, satisfied the coast was clear of other Flynns (especially Gert), she got out of her slicker and shook it. Tiny droplets flew through the air. Patrick blinked. Albatross sniffed, wagged his tail and curled up again with a sigh.

"I hope you don't mind my dropping in. I was running errands, and I thought I'd see how you were doing, although, to tell you the truth, I don't know why I'm out on a day like this. My, it's dark in here," she added, noting that the fluorescent tubes were unlit. "How can you see to read? You'll ruin your eyes."

"I keep another pair in the drawer," Patrick replied and switched on the lights, but the brightness did nothing for his black mood, and Harriet's perkiness irritated him. With no desire for company, he eyed her warily as she lit a cigarette. Saving them both from an awkward silence, the phone rang.

He looked tired, Harriet decided. "How's the newspaper game?" she asked when he'd finished and came around the counter to stand at the rain-lashed window, looking out. "It can't be that bad."

"It's OK," he replied, face a mask revealing none of his troubles. Another ad canceled. Four in the last two days. The second issue was already late for the printers. He didn't have enough copy. How had he got himself into this mess? At the rear of the office, the tea kettle whistled, forcing him into a politeness he didn't feel. "Cup of tea?" he asked, hoping she'd refuse.

"What a nice idea."

How to begin? wondered Harriet a moment later as they took their first careful sips. "Well, it's ironic, isn't it? Here we are again, paths crossing. But I don't count the night Elliot and I barged in. I want to apologize for our rudeness. Especially mine. I left without saying good night, didn't I?"

"There's no need."

"You know how these lovers' quarrels are."

"I don't," he replied, and Harriet was unable to get her bearings, for Patrick's directness prohibited idle chatter. Ill at ease, she crossed her legs and found she provoked no reaction. "I was surprised to see you that night," she went on, recalling how intensely he'd looked at her—almost as if he were memorizing her features. If she hoped his interest would prove useful to her today, she was mistaken, for Patrick was too immersed in despondency. Whatever fantasies he'd had about Harriet mocked him. She was Elliot's girl, Protestant, and out of his league. He wanted to get rid of her.

"Almost like fate, isn't it?" Harriet continued, feeling like an idiot and not knowing how to proceed. "Is that your Bible?"

"A breviary. A book of prayers."

"Religion fascinates me," she said, trying to take up the slack. Was it a proper subject to pursue? His expression indicated otherwise. Still, it wouldn't hurt to let him know that even if Catholics were beyond the pale at home, she, for one, didn't consider religion an obstacle that would prevent his hiring her. *That* prospect seemed at the moment, however, a veritable pipe dream. "My best friend in New York is Catholic and—"

Patrick shuffled papers and cleared his throat. "What an undertaking this must be," exclaimed Harriet, sensing dismissal and shifting gears. "I was the editor of *Jericho Jottings*—the high-school paper—and there was never enough time. But what an opportunity! A paper of your own! Why there're people who'd give their souls to be in your shoes. Did you get it? Shoes? The old repair shop?" Was he always like this?

Exasperated, Patrick removed a piece of paper from the typewriter with a snap. "Since you're dropping hints . . . I don't have any jobs available here. There've been several people looking, but I don't."

"Job?" she replied, angered by his abruptness but hiding it. "Did I say I was? I'm not. As a matter of fact, I'm waiting on several offers. Do I look that desperate?" She grinned. "I am."

"Didn't mean to be rude. Sorry." Once again he went to the window, hands plunged in his pockets. The rain drummed down on the empty street. Noonan's new neon sign winked on, for even though it was only the middle of the afternoon, darkness seemed to be settling over the world, dragging him with it.

"I'll bet you've been laughing up your sleeve. You wouldn't be the only one."

"Why should I laugh? You're to be congratulated. It's always rocky at the beginning."

"I've been working my tail off . . . haven't we, Albie?" he added, kneeling down as the dog came over to him. He rubbed its neck, an unguarded and gentle affection in his eyes, which stirred Harriet tenderly. "Maybe I could help you," she said.

"I can't give you a job."

"If you can't, you can't. I could still help. Make a suggestion or two."

"Thanks. Maybe some other time. Today isn't—"

"I understand completely. It's your paper. I certainly wouldn't take it kindly if some stranger—"

"No, it's not that. I'd like to hear. It's just—"

"Although I think I could put my finger on the problem. I'm sure I can. I've had some experience. But if you don't—"

"What exactly do you see as the problem?"

"Let me just start by making a brief remark about your readership— your potential readership, that is. Why is it an Irish Catholic newspaper?"

"Because it is," he retorted defensively, retreating past the protective barrier of the counter to his desk. "It's called *The Jericho Irish Spectator*, and that's what it is."

"You don't have to bite my head off."

"Sorry," he mumbled, blushing. Others had asked him the same question. Patrick didn't want to admit to Harriet that it was a Catholic paper because Gert wanted it that way.

"*Regular* newspapers have been struggling to survive these past few years, so how can a paper that limits itself to one particular group possibly hope to succeed? Economically it's just not feasible. New York still has a few of those foreign papers, I grant you—but in Jericho? No one will be more tickled than I if you pull it off, but—"

"What about a Catholic paper that deals seriously with issues? A paper that reconciles Catholic thinking with . . . with larger issues in a Protestant country? I know what I have so far doesn't begin to—"

"Isn't that too intellectual? This is Jericho. I admire that you're think-ing expansively, but the paper's for sale at Noonan's and down at the depot. You have to get people to buy it, don't you? Doesn't it have to pay its way? If you're subsidized, you can print what you like and damn the costs, but otherwise you have to produce a product that makes people want to buy it."

Subsidized? Gert had figured a budget of thirty dollars a week to get *The Spectator* on its feet. She was dreaming, realized Patrick.

"May I?" asked Harriet, coming around the counter. On the alert, Patrick stood, intimidated by her closeness. "Could we clear a space?" she asked, spreading open a nearby copy of the *Boston Herald*. "Let's compare layouts. We'll get back to content later. See how the eye wants to look at the page here in the *Herald*? The vitality? The photos? Incidentally, we call them art. See how they enliven the space? Look at the variety of type. Now look at *The Spectator*."

"You're not telling me anything I don't know. The printer's been doing the layout for me. In fact, I've got to go over to Leveret in a few minutes. And I can't afford 'art.' I'm on a tight budget. Look, I just got started."

"I'm not being critical. Your printer may know how to set type, but he's obviously unqualified for a newspaper. Layout is *your* responsibility. Not some hack's, who's better left doing wedding announcements. In-cidentally, is he selling you your newsstock, too? I thought so. You should have a semigloss medium weight. If it costs a few extra pennies, it's more than worth it. It lets the reader know he's picking up something with a little class, as opposed to something to wrap fish in. Who *is* your printer, anyway? What's he charging you? I'll bet he's taking you for a ride."

"He's my cousin, Dinny Malone, that's who."

"Walked right into that one, didn't I? Patrick, don't be so serious! Anyway, nepotism aside, Dinny Malone knows nothing about newspapers. There're half a dozen printers in Leveret better qualified that I could introduce you to."

So sure of herself, wasn't she? Making statements like the Pope making Canon Law. Exaggeratedly, Patrick waved his hand to clear the air of smoke, a defensive maneuver if ever there was one. He wasn't used to a woman— The thought collided in his head as Harriet took a determined stance, hands on hips, reminding him of Gert.

"Now—content. What do you have here? A story of your sister's visit to Duchess Carney, whoever *she* is. Very nice. Did your sister *write* it, too? I'm sure she's a lovely person, but. . . . And your brother's column . . . not bad, but. . . . And something by Father Gahaghan . . . and here's a story about Father Coughlin. It's all so . . . what can I say? Insular, that's it. Insular."

"You mean Catholic."

"Not necessarily. Listen, now. What I'm about to say sums it up. A weekly can't compete with the dailies. You must offer the reader something else. More personal. The human touch. For example, this 'Prominent Irishman of the Week' feature—good idea. You need more of this. Human interest. But need it always be an Irishman? Couldn't it be a woman? A little less Irish, a little less Catholic? Just for variety? I know, I know—it's an *Irish* paper, but—"

"You don't give up, do you?" Click, click went Harriet's lighter as she lit another cigarette. Her perfume infiltrated his nostrils.

"I'm not one to beat around the bush, if that's what you mean. What I'm getting at is: Only twenty-five percent of Jericho is Irish Catholic. Enough said. Now, to get back to reader appeal. Why aren't you covering local sports?"

"I can't do—"

"And what about all the other activities in town? Aren't there Irish in the Grange? What about scouts, Reading Circle, Fish and Game, American Legion? Then there's the garden club, Historical Society, Eclectic Club and the D.A.R. Well, I guess there's no Irish there, but still— As I said, what about the Irish *woman*? Surely she must be interested in what's going on locally. Aside from news of St. Mary's and the Hibernians, I mean. Or is she at home burning peat? A little joke there. Why not sponsor a cooking contest? And get in *names*. You need *names*. People want to read about themselves and their neighbors in a local paper. The more names you get in, the more readers you'll have. Are you with me? Now—the cardinal rule of journalism is: Don't be boring. If someone hasn't baked their daughter in the oven, make it up. I'm exaggerating, of course, but you get my drift. . . ."

The short and floppy scalloped sleeves of Harriet's dress seemed to eddy and float at Patrick as she bent to illustrate a point. Responding to her question as to why he wasn't answering a distant fire whistle, he growled, "How am I supposed to be covering it when I'm sitting here?"

"I didn't mean it literally. There might be a mad arsonist at work. Maybe it's one of your relatives. Joke, joke," she added hastily, growing irritated. "Do you always glower when someone tries to help you? I don't like to be made to feel like a dose of salts."

"You have some good ideas, but . . ." That much of what she said made sense only put him further on the defensive. ". . . nothing that I didn't know already."

"Really? Then obviously I've wasted your time."

What had he done to provoke her? Patrick wondered, unaware that he hadn't played his role of unsuspecting apple falling easily into her lap. "I don't understand you," she said hotly, leaving him and picking up her slicker. "Your attitude astounds me."

"*Mine?*" he retorted, torn between appeasement and mayhem. "*Mine?* You just 'happen,' so you say, to stop by. You try to impress me . . ."

"I am not trying to impress you."

". . . with your 'expertise,' making me feel stupid. Laughing at my expense with your so-called jokes, criticizing my paper and . . . making cracks about my religion. I wasn't born yesterday." His prostate throbbed as it always did when he was agitated.

"Are you paranoid, too? Is that a Catholic trait? You're *not* cut out for the newspaper business. You should've stayed in the seminary. I don't care what kind of a paper you run. Do what you like. Print essays in Latin if it pleases you. It'll fold anyway. I'll leave you where I found you—in the Dark Ages!"

Turning, Harriet switched out the lights and went out the door.

A pencil snapped in Patrick's hand, as he stood in place trembling. Like an automaton, he walked to the window, pulled the shade down, then slammed the door she'd left open. Its shade stuck. A cascade of oaths erupted as he yanked, pulling the shade clear off the roller, which spun crazily. He flung the shade to the floor.

Violence begat violence. Careening behind the counter, he crumpled up several *Spectators* and threw them. The phone rang. It was Gert.

"I can't talk. I'm busy." He crashed the receiver into the cradle. A

175

moment later it rang again. He ignored it. Picking up the ashtray full of lipstick-stained butts, he dashed it into the wastebasket with such ferocity a cloud of ashes rose to smite him. Coughing, he returned to the door, flung it open and fanned the air. The phone continued to ring.

"Get out of the way!"

Albatross retreated under a chair. Patrick returned to his desk, picked up his breviary, opened it, and paced, lips moving. Shame for his uncharacteristic outburst overtook him, and he sat down. Close it this very afternoon. And go. His eye caught Harriet's cup; lipstick on the rim. Grimacing, he picked it up. Unable not to, he brought it slowly to his mouth and placed his lips where hers had been, tasting. Heedless of the rain, he walked out the door, then turned the corner and saw her halfway up Essex.

"Harriet!" he called, starting to run after her, slowing down as he got opposite his house, wondering if Gert was at the window. "Wait!"

Harriet turned as he approached. "I can't hire you," he said, "but—"

"I don't want to work for you."

"You don't?"

"Why can't you hire me?"

"Can't afford . . ." he mumbled, hair plastered down on his forehead, face dripping. Harriet extended her umbrella. "I'll work cheap."

"It's not that." She saw him glance to the brown house across the street. "I live there," he explained.

"Oh," she replied, understanding. "Your mother. . . ?"

"No," he insisted quickly. O sweet Jesus, there'd be hell to pay.

"Because I'm a woman?" she asked, shocking him that she seemed to be able to read his mind, forcing him to admit that it didn't seem entirely proper. And not just any woman, but the sudden and urgent focus of his doomed longings.

"Have you heard?" Harriet went on. "We got the vote. We have brains, too. We may not be able to absolve sins, but we can save *The Jericho Irish Spectator*."

Unable not to be shocked at her irreverence, Patrick hesitated, muttered a prayer to himself and took a final stand. "I know, from what you said, that you know a lot. But this is a special situation. It's a Catholic paper and—"

"I'll convert."

The gleam in her eye proved irresistible. "C'mon," he said. "C'mon back and we'll talk about it."

As they started down the street, Patrick had a sense of more than his mother watching. With a scholar's appreciation of history and the events that shaped it, he saw destiny peering at him, destiny hung on a simple "c'mon." A look into his future, too, and the possible momentousness of it—fearful, yet exciting. And the sense that his journey had taken another turn, a forward step, with that sweet nothing of a "c'mon." *Nothing*, he was certain, could ever be the same again.

9 "The paper will be on the street the day after tomorrow," Harriet announced to Elliot when she and Patrick returned from the printers. It had taken them over a week to put another issue of *The Spectator* together. Exhilarated, Harriet was in fine fettle. "Did you notice our greenery?" she asked Elliot, who was waiting to take her to lunch at Noonan's, which had become a daily ritual. She gestured to the begonias and African violets, borrowed from Letty, that decorated the front window. "O, I just love to have a bit 'o the green, don't I now, Patrick?"

Never himself when his rival was around, Patrick managed a grin at Harriet's attempt at a brogue. "I'll be back in a jiff," she assured him.

"V*ade in pace*," he muttered to himself as the twosome left the office. Go in peace—with Elliot? No, that wasn't what he wished for her at all.

Grappling with his mother, Harriet, *The Spectator*, mounting debts, and his own expectations of himself, he felt snowed under.

Gert had been furious that Patrick had hired Harriet. "How dare ya make a decision like that without consultin' me?" she'd snapped. "This is a family undertakin'! She's not of the faith!"

Patrick had stood his ground, but the animosity between mother and son continued. His days started with Mass. Then, from the frying pan of Gert's kitchen ("What's she up to now? I'm not puttin' up with much more," etc.), he encountered the fire that was Harriet. No matter how early he got to the office, the clack of her typewriter and the smell of coffee greeted him. Late September sunlight through the windows and there she was, under a cloud of smoke, denouncing him gaily as a sleepyhead, ready with the day's schedule, brimming with ideas and projects, which she bounced off him like Ping-Pong balls as the phone began to ring. The office would fill up with people dropping by to chat and have a cup of coffee, for she seemed to know everyone in town. Why shouldn't they have the welcome mat out? she asked him. The office should be a forum where people could feel comfortable and air their views.

And on those mornings when Harriet wasn't there, when she was already off and running, Patrick would find himself so disappointed that he had to fight the impulse to leave. Then he would find the note she'd left him on his now very organized desk. Sometimes it was typed, sometimes scrawled. He would read the list of appointments and chores, contenting himself with it until her return when, most of the time, he wasn't able to even look her in the eye. On went his mask—his only defense against his passion. Then Elliot would come to take her to lunch.

"But you're with her alone all day, ain't ya!" asked Jerry, whom Patrick asked for advice. "What an opportunity for ya! Ask her out to a movie or somethin'."

"She doesn't even see me. I'm the invisible man. She's dating Elliot." That he was jealous of the twerp inflamed Patrick even more.

"Make yer move."

Patrick shook his head. "I'm a man of conscience," he replied, mockingly. "A celibate fool."

"You're a thinker, Pat. You'll figure it out."

"Haven't you heard, Jer? Thinking's a sin. I think; I am. *Cogito ergo sum.* But I wonder *what* I am."

Who was she that she had the power to haunt him? Belligerently Patrick made a list of reasons that, added up, would cause him to see the light and forget about Harriet. It wasn't like him to have acted so impulsively; maybe Ma was right, she'd create turmoil for him. He wanted his brain unfried, thoughts pure, intellect unmuddied so he could concentrate his energies on the paper. Life was rocky enough in this period of transition into the world. Harriet would take him over and run his life like Gert. She was Protestant. She wasn't interested. Yes, he admitted that he hadn't felt as alive in years as when he was with her—but the aliveness was terrifying.

Added up, the conclusion was obvious.

He had to have her.

Up the street at Noonan's, Elliot grumbled. "Do you always flirt with him like that?"

"Was I?"

"How'd you get the job in the first place? Didja show'm your tits? I'll bet you did, and you're not telling."

Harriet pretended to be shocked.

"I don't like it," Elliot announced, playing the role of jealous lover, which was entirely new to him.

"Poor 'Edward.' " The continuing attention of Jericho's most eligible bachelor accelerated her joy. She told herself she had no time for romance, yet—

"I never get to see you anymore."

"What do you mean? We've been together three evenings the past week." Elliot had taken Harriet to the opening night of Symphony in Boston, to the theater, wined her and dined her. "That doesn't even count our lunches. That's more than I've seen my own family practically, what with my schedule."

Wasn't it wonderful to have a schedule! Destiny seemed assured, beating its wings in a delicious buzz as each glorious twelve-hour day sent her to sleep in happy exhaustion, only to rise refreshed, ready for anything. She was having the time of her life.

"Mother thinks I'm batty," she went on. "He can only pay me seventeen a week, which is peanuts, of course. But I don't care. The plans I have! Mother and Father are not known for their warmth and generosity toward the 'unfortunate Irish.' Alice is upset because the paper supports this Father Coughlin. So already I'm embroiled in controversy. What a week it's been!"

Harriet took a fast bite of her sandwich, caught her breath and rushed on. "Like walking through a mine field! The gorgon looking over my shoulder all the time. And Patrick's writ the book on stubbornness. I've done most of the copy. I've managed to make a few changes. I intend to drag them both out of the bogs and into the light—mother and son. Kicking and screaming. At least we lost Rose, who was a terrible typist and spent most of her time doing her nails, reading movie magazines, and flirting with every pair of pants who happened by. When you see the paper, I want you to pull no punches in your critique—although the next issue will be my *real* debut. That is, if I can get Patrick to agree—"

"He's fallen for you."

Harriet nodded, secretly pleased that Elliot knew, flattered also that Patrick had. Yet she knew she had to be careful with the latter's feelings. Not only was he her boss, but his mother watched her like a hawk. "I don't believe in mixing business with pleasure," she said, hoping she matched Elliot's sultry expression. "Do I hear the green-eyed monster breathing heavily?"

"Mebbe yes . . . mebbe no." Elliot snorted like a bull. "I'm being jealous. Isn't that what you want me to be? See? I'm two steps ahead of you. Remember that and we'll have a long and happy life making whoopee."

Enjoying the byplay, Harriet laughed. "There you go again—the enigmatic prince."

"He's handsome."

"Who? Patrick? I suppose. He and I see the world through entirely different lenses, I'm afraid. Anyway," she added, trying to read Elliot, "I've always had an affinity for blonds myself."

"I guess you'll be staying in Jericho?"

"Naturally. For the time being." Nervous, she didn't understand his question. "Aren't you glad?" she asked, hopping out on a limb despite herself.

"I'll let you know." Elliot grinned. "Sure. I like ya, kid."

"My day is made."

Elliot laughed, but he was troubled as his eyes darted round Noonan's, then back to Harriet. He'd been with Myrna last night. He rarely kissed her. Stuck it in and departed quickly, feeling like he was OK, like other men—until he hit the street and saw one. And she bored the shit out of him. He was never bored with Harriet, but the decision he'd made to try and fall in love with her and drive away his demons only made Elliot feel all the more agitated. If she evoked uncustomary feeling in him, it was nothing compared to the intensity he felt for Frankie. *Give yourself time*, he told himself, but it didn't help.

"Love 'em and leave 'em," he said to Harriet, as if sending her a warning. "That's my story," he added, winking to take the sting out.

"Is that to be my fate?" she moaned, dabbing at her eye with her napkin.

Elliot laughed. "I like ya, kid."

"You said that already."

"Twice is better." Elliot made a face. Lately none of them satisfied him. Neither Myrna nor the sailors. Only Frankie, who was untouchable. "At least you're . . . excited about something."

Unable to follow Elliot's train of thought, Harriet asked what he meant.

"A job you like. Dreams. Plans. Must make life easier. Enough about the Prince. What do *you* think of the Prince?"

When Elliot walked Harriet back across the street to *The Spectator* and saw the way Patrick looked at her, he felt miserable. *That* was the way he was supposed to be, feel, live his life. He hated Patrick. He wasn't going to let Patrick get her, he told himself as he started back for the mill, and mocked himself once again for his jealous lover pose. He thought of Dobie Pratt, whom he'd fallen in love with at Exeter seven years ago. He had a photo of him tucked away that he took out occasionally—Dobie, himself, and someone else whose name he couldn't remember, snapped at a football game. Somewhere around that fall, the shower door had opened and Dobie stepped out and Elliot's life changed. He ran back to his own room that day and knelt down in front of a mirror and sobbed. *It was wrong.* What would his father say? He wasn't supposed to feel that way toward a boy, a feeling that wasn't even hot, but one of warmth and tenderness, a rush of love and a desire to take care of Dobie.

He was one of *them*.

One of those he'd heard about, like the two men dragged past the freak show at a summer carnival. Queers, who'd been caught and arrested, shoved by the police through a crowd of New Hampshire rowdies, who spat disgustedly and hollered names, while Elliot watched, terrified.

Dobie never knew. Elliot bought him lunches and followed him around and threw snowballs at him in a rage he didn't understand. It would go away, Elliot told himself. A year later he let a man suck him in the woods. He vowed it would never happen again. Two years later, coming home from Princeton on the train for a weekend, a man, maybe thirty, he couldn't tell, sat next to Elliot in a practically empty car and, under cover of a newspaper, touched his leg. Neither of them spoke, but when the train reached Leveret, Elliot followed the man off the train and went to the Richwood Hotel, where he got laid for the first time. When it was over, he was relieved because he hadn't liked it, which meant he wasn't queer. And it hurt. Nevertheless, he was curious as to why the man had sat beside him in the first place. "How did you know?" he asked, and the stranger replied, "The back of your neck," and Elliot believed it and knew he was marked.

"It's not so bad," the man said gently as he hailed a cab for the boy who couldn't look at him. "You're not alone. There are others. Don't be afraid."

If there was a promise of something hopeful, Elliot hadn't believed it and still didn't.

"Elliot is mad for me," Harriet announced to the family.

Was he? she wondered, getting ready for bed. Who could tell? Did she want him to be? Did the stars come out at night? But she was also confused. "You know," she confessed to Alice, "I sometimes can't figure him out at all. He's Dr. Jekyll and Mr. Hyde. Gay and charming one moment and—" And withdrawn, moody, and cutting her with his sarcasm the next. But Harriet was more than willing to solve the enigma that was Elliot Phelps.

"You sound like you think you're in love," scoffed Alice.

"I think he'll be my smart affair for fall." She smiled to herself. Who could resist? She could—if she had to. But it would be difficult. Who could resist the glamour, not to mention the gossip from her friend Marcia, who'd called yesterday to say the whole town was talking?

"Oh? Is it the old fantasy reborn? Money and power and the house on the hill? Don't be a fool."

Harriet knew Alice was agitated because her boyfriend, Wayne Thibeau, was leaving in a day or so for Spain to join up with the Loyalists.

"Are those reasons to reject him? I guess for you they are." Yes, she was aware of Elliot's name, money and position, but he fulfilled deeper fantasies. He was the unconventional knight of her girlhood dreams, the prince who complimented her own sense of herself as royal, who appreciated that she was different and special. His mercurial nature was hers, they thought alike, were two of a kind, his savoir-faire was what she needed. With Elliot, every day was an adventure and the sky the limit.

"Don't say I didn't warn you."

"You don't like him," Harriet replied, "because of his father. But he's nothing like his father. He hates the mill. He doesn't set wages or have anything to do with those things. He's very sensitive."

"He's his father's son," insisted Alice, who found Harriet's dreamy-eyed expression disgusting. Harriet shook her head. Her growing intimacy with Phelps had likewise stimulated her, but she knew she couldn't tell Alice. She and Phelps had had several discussions regarding *The Spectator* and its possible benefit to Jericho. That he was openly encouraging her relationship with Elliot was added icing on the cake of Harriet's well-being. More important, Phelps validated her person. Despite opposing political views, he continued to champion her work, character and independence.

"You barely know Elliot," contended Alice. "You—"

"I feel as if I've known him all my life."

"Crap."

"Alice, what is it?"

"What's what? What would you know about love?" added Alice with such vehemence that Harriet was forced to retort: "What would you? Wayne's the first boyfriend you ever—"

"Because I'm pregnant. That's how."

Two days later, Harriet asked for the morning off to accompany Wayne and Alice to Boston. Wayne was leaving on a train to New York, where he would join fifty others on a freighter bound for the Loyalist-held port of Cadiz. Patrick asked Harriet if she'd mind if he joined in seeing Wayne off. She didn't know why he'd want to; he was sure to be offended by Wayne and Alice's progressive views. Then again it might be good for him.

"I wish you'd come to the party last night," Alice said to Patrick, as the foursome boarded the train for the forty-five-minute ride into Boston. "I'd rather Harriet had brought you than Elliot Phelps."

"I didn't think Patrick would be interested," Harriet said diplomatically. "We can't use the story for the paper. Can you imagine your mother's reaction if we did? Let's see: 'Last evening at the Canoe Club in Leveret, fifty of Wayne Thibeau's friends gathered to see him off for Spain. Joined in the gathering were many of Leveret's prominent citizens, including members of the Young Communist League, the Socialist Club, and other sundry shakers of the status quo. . . .'"

Wayne laughed. Nervous today and trying not to show it, he grasped

Alice's hand. "Don't forget my coworkers from the Arlington, Harriet. At least *they're* respectable."

"Oh, yes. . . . And several of Mr. Thibeau's former friends from the offices of the Arlington Mill, most of whom looked a little dazed. At the bar your reporter overheard the following comment: 'Wayne must be nuts to quit a steady job in times like this to go off to Europe to fight in somebody else's war.' "

Wayne nodded. "My parents didn't come last night. They feel the same."

"How was your mother this morning?" asked Alice.

"She cried. I didn't get to say goodbye to Pop. I guess that's the way he wants it. He was out of the house already." Jittery, he tugged at his cap and glanced out the window. "There it is," he exclaimed. "Goodbye, Arlington."

They all glanced out the window as the train passed by the mill and out of Leveret, heading south. Wayne continued to crane his neck until the familiar sights were gone. He wondered if he'd ever see them again.

"I heard that comment of Elliot's last night, Harriet."

"Which?"

"That all the 'best' people are turning to Russia. How shallow can anyone be? Him, I guess."

"I thought it was a rather witty remark myself," replied Harriet, irritated to note that Patrick had nodded in agreement at Alice's assessment of Elliot.

"You would."

"Well, you know Elliot." Harriet smiled to herself. Elliot had very much enjoyed last night's party. He'd met the Reds and would, he told her, tell his father all about it. She wasn't too keen on that idea.

"Yes, I know Elliot." Alice held tight to Wayne's hand as if she'd never let go. Harriet forgave her sister her waspishness and marveled at her outward calm. She herself was still unnerved that Alice had got herself pregnant, and her sister's decision to let Wayne go off without telling him filled Harriet with apprehension.

Alice had explained that she didn't want to force Wayne to make a choice between staying with her and going to Spain. The latter commitment was too important. But as they got closer to Boston, she was scared. Her fervent belief in the rightness of her decision didn't help the anxiety that crept up on her, and she tried to focus on what Harriet was saying to Patrick.

"Don't you think we should put an item in the paper about Wayne's going? He's from Jericho and the only one from these parts who's volunteering. He's even Catholic." She winked clandestinely at Alice. "It wouldn't get us into hot water with your mother, would it?"

Down in the dumps with the talk of Elliot, who seemed to be around even when he wasn't, Patrick shrugged. Feeling the outsider, he hadn't said much.

"Tell Patrick about that speech your friend gave last night," Harriet suggested to Wayne.

"Steve Bobeck?"

She nodded. "I was intrigued myself. I wish we *could* put it in the paper. It would certainly shake people up."

"Steve said that all Roosevelt is doing is providing aspirin for the country's problems, whereas communism promises heroic surgery."

Patrick shook his head. "I don't understand," he said quietly. "Aren't things better now? Why do we need something so drastic?"

"Because millions are still unemployed. A*nd* badly housed, underfed, undereducated. But the rich are still getting richer. There's no real equality in this country even though 'all men are created equal.' We've never achieved the promise of the Bill of Rights."

"And in the Soviet Union? They don't even have a bill of rights."

"But the principle of equality isn't just a principle over there. It's a daily fact of existence. It works for the people. Capitalism is for the rich. There aren't any rich in Russia. There may be abuses, but there always are in the first years of a revolution. Russia will change the world for the better. Sure, Roosevelt has taken tremendous steps, but like Steve said last night— it's only a partial remedy. The Communist Party could make a clean sweep of everything that's hateful in our lives. There I go," he added, exchanging a smile with Alice. "Ask me a question and you get a speech."

"But the right one," nodded Alice, and Harriet wondered how—since they were so busy proselytizing—they'd found time to make love. Was the making of babies without being married OK? Not considered an example of capitalistic excess? Harriet found herself viewing Wayne with mixed feelings. She'd asked Alice why Wayne hadn't taken precautions, but Alice had only shook her head. Harriet wondered: Was Wayne so wrapped up in his beliefs that he didn't know passion led to diapers? If he couldn't be faulted for not responding to what Alice refused to tell him, it would nevertheless be Alice who would pay the price for his naiveté.

"I don't agree."

"That's OK—it's a free country."

"Not if *you* get your way, it won't be."

An argument had erupted between Wayne and Patrick, whose face was flushed.

"Do you think I'm the bogeyman?" Wayne grinned like an imp, and the tension was diffused.

"Don't know what to think." Patrick grinned back. "All new territory to me," he added. "Never took the train to Boston with a Red before. Definitely heretical. Are you really a Catholic?" he asked, for it was difficult to reconcile Wayne's beliefs with the teachings of the Church.

185

"I am. There are priests in Spain who feel the same as I do."

Patrick shook his head, disbelieving, feeling suddenly inadequate. Even if he couldn't accept Wayne's radicalism, he was impressed with the intensity of the man's belief. Whereas he—what did *he* believe in? Where had he been all his life except cloistered from any and all viewpoints that didn't fit the rigid dogma of the Church? He felt like a victim of his past, and the thought unsettled him further.

"Why are you going over there?"

"To fight. Are you going to give me the Church's position? The Church supports Franco. The bishops over there are threatening the Loyalists with excommunication. Is that how *you* feel?"

"Don't know. Don't have all the facts."

"Get them," Alice said. "Ignorance isn't an excuse. At least," she added, giving Patrick a smile that hid the turbulence that Wayne's talk of fighting had produced, "you're willing to listen. That's a start." Once again she gripped Wayne's hand and stared out the window at passing towns that seemed unreal.

"Why are you supporting Coughlin and the Union Party, Pat?" asked Wayne. "I thought for sure you'd be a Democrat."

"I am." Patrick blushed. "At this point I'm not sure."

"We're supporting Coughlin because of Michael O'Brien," interjected Harriet. "Because of Patrick's sister. She dates O'Brien's son, and that's the reason. Patrick's mother is behind it. And she's bankrolling the paper so—"

"Not entirely." Patrick didn't like the easy familiarity with which Harriet bandied his family's business in front of strangers.

"The Union Party's a farce."

"That's what I told him, Wayne."

Patrick wished the subject hadn't come up. "A lot of people believe in Father Coughlin," he replied defensively, "and I'm running a Catholic paper. Look at the money he's raised to help the poor."

"He's a fascist."

"He's a *priest*."

"So were you—almost. But you left, didn't you?"

"I didn't leave the Church. I still believe."

"I still believe in the tooth fairy," interjected Alice, "but I wouldn't stake my life on his coming down the chimney on Christmas Eve."

"That's a *slightly* mixed metaphor, Alice," laughed Harriet, glad to see her sister smile. "Now if I could convince Patrick *The Spectator* shouldn't be an Irish Catholic paper—"

"But it is."

"I think we should come out for Roosevelt."

"I know you do."

"Although I don't care who we're for as long as we sell. I'm the

186

pragmatic one. Patrick's the dreamer. He'd like it to be a serious Catholic weekly but—"

"I want the paper to serve a useful purpose. Look, maybe it can't be an Irish paper. You're right. But my hands are tied. My mother started the paper. If you're going to be pragmatic then understand she's making up the deficit. I can't just . . ." He trailed off, not wanting to say that, having rocked Gert mightily this fall, he couldn't just up and go his own way now. At the same time, he was embarrassed to be doing her bidding. "Give me a break, OK?"

"Don't let Harriet browbeat you, Patrick. She has tendencies."

"Don't I know," he managed to reply to Alice. Were they all against him? Found him a fool? Patrick retreated, lapsed into silence. But Wayne's earlier denunciation of Coughlin rankled. "Why do you call him a fascist?"

"He wants power for himself. Sure, he's done some good. And there are millions who listen to him. Pop does. Fascists always start off by doing good deeds and promising better. But their object is to subjugate the people, not free them. Their objective is tyranny, a dictatorship for their own use and power."

"I don't believe he wants that. He couldn't. The Church would've spoken out against him, and it hasn't."

"Cardinal McConnell has."

"But the *Church* hasn't."

Impatient, Wayne tugged at his mustache and zeroed in on Patrick. "Look at the facts. Coughlin's in the Hearst camp. What do you think Hearst wants? He'd buy the presidency if we'd let him. And probably set up Coughlin as his secretary of state. Coughlin and Hearst are both antilabor. They're not on the side of the workers—even though they say they are. Coughlin told his people not to join any unions. He said they were run by the communists. If only we did! Coughlin's full of praise for Mussolini and Hitler, and what are they? Dictators. Both fascists. Who do you think's giving money and arms to Franco, *another* fascist. Mussolini and Hitler, that's who. Don't you know that?"

"I guess I didn't."

"Take a look at this month's *Atlantic*. They call Coughlin a danger to American democracy."

"And you're not?"

"Touché," laughed Harriet.

"How can a priest be dangerous?" insisted Patrick.

"You'll have to find that out for yourself, Pat. Why do you think I'm heading over there? Fascism comes in many disguises, including a Roman collar. I'm a communist because the Soviets are the only government to recognize the threat of Hitler. Roosevelt's scared to face up to it. This country's so afraid to get involved in Europe again, we've got our heads stuck in the sand. Spain is the battleground *now*. But if we don't stop Franco and his gang, it's going to spread."

The foursome arrived in Boston's North Station, took the subway over to South Station, and had an hour to kill before Wayne's train left for New York. At his suggestion they ducked into a bar in the station and ordered a round of drinks.

Wrapped up in each other and no longer contributing to the conversation, Wayne and Alice were far away. The discussion on the train still reverberating, Patrick smiled at Harriet, who seemed incredibly beautiful, her skin shimmering in the dim light, eyes flashing under her broad-brimmed hat. "I have a confession," he laughed, trying to break through her correct and arm's-length impersonality. "I was never in a bar before with a girl. At high noon, no less. I feel like a real sinner."

"You'll get used to it," she replied. Two steps ahead of Patrick, she sensed he wanted to get personal and changed the subject. Frustrated, Patrick took a sip of his drink and was forced to acknowledge that his plans to win Harriet from Elliot had gotten nowhere. He'd asked her to a movie; she'd politely refused. Lunch? She had a date with Elliot.

"Are you bringing sketch pads?" Harriet asked Wayne. "Will you have a chance to paint over there?"

Wayne nodded. "I want to get to Toledo, too. See if El Greco did it justice. That is, if Franco doesn't get there first."

In the ladies room, Harriet found Alice weeping, the sadness all the more telling, for Alice disliked letting anything show.

"What will . . . I do . . . without him? Suppose something . . . happens?"

"Alice, dearest. Tell him."

"No."

"Alice, please . . ."

"No."

"This is misplaced heroism. It *is*. You just said it—"

"I know. Don't you know I know? Unmarried and pregnant in Jericho? And if he doesn't come back— Do you think I look forward—?" Alice gasped and caught her breath. "I want the baby. If anything happens to Wayne, I'll have the baby. I love him so, Harriet."

Moved, Harriet took Alice in her arms. She seemed not much older than a baby herself, Harriet thought to herself. Never had she seen Alice as vulnerable. "We're the same person, Harriet. I never thought I'd meet . . ."

"So if you tell him, what would happen?"

"He won't go. He might blame me."

"Blame *you?*" Harriet wanted to remind Alice that it was Wayne who had got her pregnant, but she held her tongue. She knew Alice well enough to know that once she got something in her head, nothing would change it. All Harriet could do was hug her. Alice sobbed and swore at herself. "I don't want him to see me like this." A moment later as she dried her eyes, she asked, "Don't you understand? I know what this means to him. Let me alone for a bit. I'll be fine."

Impulsively, Wayne ducked into the Catholic Chapel at the far end of the station, which served travelers seeking solace before their journeys. The others followed. The shadowed and quiet place where a transient or two sat nodding seemed another world from the busy station. Patrick and Wayne dipped fingers into the font, crossed themselves, and knelt. "May I light a candle for you?" whispered Patrick, and the other nodded, pleased. They went together to the altar, leaving the sisters in a pew.

So this was where Patrick had spent his life. Harriet watched him, his bowed head evoking curiosity. All those years spent hidden away in the mystery that was the Catholic Church. A mystery that extended even to this tiny chapel with its musty incense smell and candles flickering. What must the cost have been? Perhaps she'd been too impatient with him; he was obviously finding his way.

Beside her, Alice prayed and thought of the future, then banished it, for she had no answers.

Thoughts drifting, Harriet was struck by Alice's comment that Wayne and she were the same person. Harriet felt the same about Elliot, who came into her thoughts, and she wondered if her growing feeling for him compared to the depth of Alice's love for Wayne. If she wasn't sure, a great deal of her doubts about him had vanished last evening. Elliot had wept in her arms and told her he loved her. If his agitation mystified her, his vulnerability and need tugged her heart.

Wayne rose and checked his watch, and he and Patrick returned to the sisters. "Hey," Wayne whispered to Alice, who was crying again, "—none of that." Alice tried to smile, but her anxieties got the better of her again. Jauntily Wayne slung his knapsack over his shoulder as if he were going on an overnighter with the scouts. With his free arm he hugged Alice to him, and the foursome left the chapel, returning to the tumult of the station, with its train announcements and bustling crowds.

They wandered, suddenly aimless, toward a gate where travelers hurried through. Above their heads steam rose from the electrified crock advertising Brick Oven Baked Beans.

"Look after her for me. . . ." Wayne turned to Harriet, who wondered: If he knew he was going to be a father, would he stay? Perhaps Alice didn't want to know the answer. But when Harriet saw how Wayne looked at Alice, she was moved. Impulsively she embraced him. "Alice has always wanted to save the world," she whispered in his ear. "I'm glad it was you she found to help her. Keep safe. *Come back*," she couldn't help adding.

"I intend to." Shorter than Harriet, Wayne's dark eyes seemed older than ever as he darted a look over her shoulder. "If it's going to be saved, we'll need you, too," he replied to Harriet, voice catching as his eyes met Alice. "You too, Patrick. Good luck with *The Spectator*. You'll find your way."

"Good luck to you, too. You've given me some things to think about. I'll pray for you."

"Will you? That's nice. Ordinarily I might not believe that, but coming from you, I do."

Alice suddenly walked away, hurrying to a concessionaire hawking balloons and panda bears. She returned with a small American flag on a stick, which she handed to Wayne, then wrapped him, hiding him in her arms. "Don't forget your sandwiches . . . you know you forget to eat sometimes. I know . . . I'm supposed to be strong and resolute, aren't I? You're not helping," she scolded affectionately as her love's eyes filled with tears.

"I'm a softie after all," he whispered. "Be brave. Don't cry, honey . . . no . . . don't . . ."

United in the grip of this tender farewell, Harriet and Patrick stood back and exchanged a look. Tears in her eyes, Harriet relished the drama; her reporter's instinct knew it was a great story. Unfortunately, it couldn't be told.

Feeling lonelier than ever, Patrick watched the couple. Wayne had a cause and a woman he loved, who loved him in return. What else could any man desire? He barely knew him yet felt a strong pull. What was in store for the cocky and brave little fellow? It seemed unreal to be seeing someone off to a war that, while it was on the front pages, seemed to have little to do with America. None of this generation, reflected Patrick, had had any immediate experience with battle, had been too young to know the shocks, the partings, deaths and tragedies of the Great War. Patrick remembered only a delight at what seemed like festive crowds, who burned an effigy of the Kaiser on Bartlett's Field when he was five. It would never happen again, Joe said, that trauma that had shaken the world out of its naiveté. Yet here was a son of Jericho who warned that it would, who talked of it with a chilling immediacy, who prophesied an era of political, racial and intellectual intolerance unless America woke up to its responsibilities. And he had the guts to be in the front ranks and take his stand. Patrick was envious.

Alice's shoulders trembled with weeping. Wayne stepped away and, with the last of the passengers, was nodded through by the gateman into a shaft of brilliant sunshine where he turned, raised his cap in a salute, waved his flag and disappeared.

Alice looked after him for a long time, not moving. Finally she got herself in hand, blew her nose briskly, and returned to Patrick and Harriet. "Did you notice the name of the train? *The Patriot*. He is, you know. That's what he is, and I'll never see him again."

It began to rain the next day, washing Jericho clean, preparing the town for a sensual Indian summer. Once again, Patrick asked Harriet out; once again, she turned him down. From the sidelines, he watched the romance blooming between her and Elliot, and grew more frustrated. All day long he had her by his side, at six o'clock she was gone. He took to running laps with Albatross around Bartlett's Field at lunchtime, leaving the office early so he wouldn't encounter Elliot, returning late so as to miss him again. One morning when Harriet arrived for work, she found Patrick glaring at her. "Do you like me at all?" he demanded. Embarrassing them both, he went back to running.

With Patrick's feelings out in the open, sexual tension invaded the office like the uncommon weather outside. Lovesickness made Patrick oafish. *Patrick is becoming impossible,* Harriet wrote in her diary. She felt stalked. The sheer physicality of him made her uneasy. Often he seemed to make sure he was in her way when she returned to her desk. Her neck burned with his looks. When she turned, she found him turning away. He took to making cracks about Elliot, which angered her.

Despite Elliot's mercurial temperament, she felt so much safer with him than she did with Patrick. Elliot's lack of lechery had puzzled her at first, but his gentlemanly conduct was more than agreeable. He loved her mind and her pizazz, didn't paw, whereas Patrick stared at her sometimes with a primitive hunger she found disconcerting. Elliot was ambrosia; Patrick was meat and potatoes. Elliot smelled of Brooks Brothers' cologne and English soap; Patrick of sweat. She wanted a strictly professional relationship with him, nothing else. He wasn't her cup of tea at all. From a distance she was aware he was very attractive, but she wasn't in the market. A stick in the mud and a mother's boy, his Celtic gloom reminded her of Franklin; his silences, too. He was wrapped up with his family, in constant struggle with Gert. The Flynns seemed from another world of repression and superstition, the mysterious Irish, and Harriet wanted no part of them. And although she knew it wasn't a particularly attractive thought, she had to confess to herself she felt Patrick Flynn was beneath her.

Finally she was forced to say something, practiced it ahead of time, wanted to be firm but gentle. "You're making me uncomfortable."

"Oh?" he challenged, blood rushing in embarrassment.

191

"You know I'm dating Elliot."

"That's your bad luck."

"Patrick, that's rude." Harriet paused. "You and I have a good give and take, a working business relationship. I think we should keep it that way. For the sake of the paper. Don't you?"

"No."

"I'm flattered. I really am, but—"

"Don't bother." Patrick sulked. The next morning he apologized. "Sure," he said, putting on a brave front that hid his crushed heart. "You're right. The paper's what's important." He ached all over and caught a cold. It didn't help.

Patrick arranged a meeting with Gert, Harriet, and himself to discuss the paper. On the morning of the historic get-together, Gert stopped in at Teresa's to have her roots retinted. For the past week she'd been busy with three different teas in the county, beating the drum for Michael O'Brien's candidacy. If her campaigning would bring a nod from the old fart in Rose's direction, it would all have been worth it, but the activity had kept her away from *The Spectator* office.

"What's she up to?" demanded Gert of her sister, for Teresa, whose shop was only down the block, had become a regular dropper-inner at the paper.

"I think you're lucky to have her," retorted Teresa. "She's a breath of air, she is. And Pat's got a confidence about him, too—which is all to the good. Do you know she's asked me to try a hand at writing down some of the tidbits I come across? How could I? I asked her. I've no ability in that direction. A sort of a gossip column is what she wanted. Oh, there's much I could tell, isn't there? But I don't think I'd ever be able. Nobody'd tell me anything again, would they now?"

"I'm to hear some of her 'ideas' today," muttered Gert, irritated that her sister had been won over so completely. "I'll give her an idea or two myself. Give her enough rope, she'll hang herself. She's full of brass."

"Not unlike yourself, Gert dearest," winked Teresa. Gert leveled her with a look. "I don't mind tellin' ya—I'm suspicious of her motives."

"Don't be worrying—she's very cozy with Elliot Phelps, so you've no cause for alarm about her and Pat—"

"What are ya talkin' about?" interrupted Gert, bristling. "Let'r *try*," she went on, scowling. "She'll be out in the street so fast. . . ! Are ya darin' to imply my Pat's a fool? She's an employee, that's what she is and not his kind!"

Up the street she marched to *The Spectator*. Strained pleasantries consumed barely a minute. "You see, Ma," Patrick began, as Gert settled herself into a chair with a cup of tea that Harriet had ready, "Harriet feels that—"

"Does she now?" interrupted Gert, bestowing a thin-lipped smile upon the girl, finding her skirt too tight over her hips, her manner too good to be true, etcetera—only a part of a catalog of criticisms that would be delivered later to Patrick in private.

"It's so good of you to drop in, Mrs. Flynn. Is that tea strong enough for you? I know you like it strong." Harriet smiled sweetly, determined to ruffle no feathers. *She looks like a Christmas tree*, she found herself thinking, for Gert's usual rouge, hair, not to mention the red, cut-glass beads and pimento-and-green-checked fall suit brought to mind the holiday season, and here it wasn't even Halloween!

No missteps, Harriet warned herself, and exchanged a glance with Patrick, who was thinking the same. Co-conspirators, the game plan they'd decided upon would include an inordinate attention paid to whatever Gert wanted, a bowing and scraping if necessary.

"How did you like this issue?" Harriet asked. "Now it's only the beginning, Ma," added Patrick. Gert glanced with a semi-sour look at the paper in her hands. "But it's an improvement, don't you think?" nudged Harriet.

Interspersed with the Irish news and St. Mary's activities were the beginnings of a women's page, a classified section (three items), several breezy news stories and "The Spectator Kitchen," featuring Letty's Souffled Spoon Cake, Ada McQueston's Shredded Wheat Bread, and Gert's Date Nut Bars Supreme.

Gert nodded perfunctorily. "Your sister's doin's in Leveret are not the business of *The Spectator*," she announced, referring to a story on page one, "Local Girl Rides Dump Truck," which told of Alice Hoskins and a group of friends, who had picketed a city relief project on the Leveret Common that refused to hire women.

With punch and vitality the story described the camaraderie of the pickets with their hand-painted signs ("We Can Rake Too!"), of the crowd of gawkers on the Leveret Common, and the good-natured ribbing that took place. It was a "gentle protest," wrote Harriet, but a success, for the next day three sturdy girls, one Polish and two Italian, were hired, and Alice was accorded the symbolic honor of riding in the cab of a city truck onto the work site to the cheers of fifty or so women.

"I liked that story, Ma. I think Harriet's right. We have to start including human interest—"

"Your mother was involved in this, too?" asked Gert, interrupting Patrick. Harriet nodded. "And my older sister. We all feel the same way. Why shouldn't a one-hundred-and-fifty-pound woman be able to pick up bricks as well as a man?"

193

Loonies, thought Gert to herself, *they must all be loonies, these Hoskinses.* "The Sodality tea with Monsignor O'Malley's hidden on page four," she went on, picky, hoping to catch Harriet.

"It won't happen again." Wouldn't she love to jab her with a hatpin.

"Where's the story of Father Gahaghan openin' the drive for the parochial school?"

"It wasn't an oversight, Mrs. Flynn. We're going to make Father Gahaghan our 'Prominent Citizen of the Week' next issue." Had Gert noticed that "Irishman" had been changed to "Citizen"? Harriet hurried quickly on. "I'm interviewing him on Wednesday. I thought it would give the campaign a classier send-off. We'll be able to use a photo of the Father, plus one of the proposed building site. That is if we . . ." Glancing at Patrick, Harriet paused, hesitant with dropping the bomb.

". . . if we switch to a printer who can handle photos, Ma."

Eyes narrowing (less for what Harriet and Patrick were suggesting, than the awareness they were finishing each other's sentences!), Gert demanded: "Switch?"

Quickly Harriet thrust a sheet of facts and figures into Gert's hands. Gert eyed them suspiciously. Harriet talked fast. "We'd like you to consider Smith and Houchins. They do quality work. I had experience with them when I was the editor of the high-school paper. They'll give us a larger paper, dimension-wise, that is. And it won't be smudged or out of focus, hard to read . . ."

Gert's head swam. She had to admit—the paper looked a mess. "What's it goin' to cost me?"

"The initial outlay will be higher, Ma, but it will more than—"

"Higher? How much higher?"

"*But,*" Harriet quickly went on, "it will more than pay off in terms of a better look. Better stock, art—that's photos—and in turn, we'll see an increase in advertising revenues because people will know we mean business."

"And what are they thinkin' now?—if you don't mind my askin'.'"

"I think potential advertisers are waiting, Ma."

Harriet nodded. "But did you notice that Mr. Phelps took another ad? He's assured me personally that he'll continue to. He'd like to see the paper succeed. He believes it's good for Jericho. I think he also feels that we should broaden our coverage."

"That's what my son says," responded Gert grimly, noticing another conspiratorial glance between the two of them.

"I'd like your permission," Harriet went on, "to cover more non-Irish activities. Did you notice the Red Cross display in the window? The drive begins next week, and we want the town to know *The Spectator*'s involved. In *all* areas. Not limited to—"

"It's *The Jericho Irish Spectator.*"

"*Roma locuta est, causa finita est.*"

"What's that?" asked Gert, always impressed when Patrick spoke Latin.

"It had something to do with Papal infallibility, Ma—except you're not the Pope. Look," Patrick went on quickly, "what do you want for the paper?" To get Rose married? Was that it's only purpose? he wanted to ask. Ready to blow, he caught Harriet's glance and calmed himself. With her backing him up, he marshalled his arguments: "We sold five hundred or so the first issue and two hundred the second. This issue we went up to three hundred, and I think that's partly due to Harriet's adding what she has. Unless we sell a thousand, we won't even pay the expenses. You'll go broke. Not enough people care about the paper if it's Irish. We have to make some changes."

"Changes?" Gert shifted buttocks. "I'd say there's been enough changes already."

"Ma—are you listening or aren't you!"

"Our potential advertisers are waiting for us to increase circulation," Harriet interjected, as Patrick threw up his hands in frustration. "And our readers—our potential readers—are waiting for us to come up with a paper they'd enjoy reading."

"That's a lot o' potentials, dearie." Gert glanced from her son to Harriet and back again. What was she after? Tryin' to insert herself and take over?

"Indeed it is, Mrs. Flynn." Harriet stifled an angry look. "But potential is all we have here at the moment. I admire your foresight in starting the paper. *I* think Jericho needs a paper, too. We're growing. Let's grow together."

Another diversionary cup of tea was poured, the negotiations suspended for the moment as a plate of chocolate chip cookies was produced. "My mother made them," said Harriet as Gert bit warily into one. "Patrick tells me that you're a wonderful cook, Mrs. Flynn, didn't you, Patrick?"

"Did I?" Patrick winked at Albatross.

"You know you did—ohh, you're pulling my leg, aren't you?"

"He's a comedian, he is," commented Gert, growing weary. Had she gotten in over her head with this newspaper? It had become a bone of contention between her and her son and looked to become, she had to admit, a drain on her pocketbook. Worse was the infiltration of the know-it-all Hoskins girl and her obvious solidarity with Patrick.

"How're you and Elliot Phelps gettin' along?" asked Gert, needing to set her mind at rest, needing to squash the unpleasant gnat buzzing that hinted of possible involvement between Patrick and Harriet. "Datin' him, are ya?"

195

"Yes, I am," replied Harriet, caught off guard.

"What's that got to do with what we're talking about?" asked Patrick sharply, knowing exactly what Gert was up to.

"I'm not allowed to ask a question?" demanded Gert, smiling at Harriet. "A wonderful boy, Elliot is," she went on. "Known the family for years," she added, not liking the sudden squall on Patrick's face. "Admire my 'foresight,' do ya, Harriet?" Quite an operator, wasn't she? "I'm two steps ahead of—"

"Ma," warned Patrick.

Gert knew she couldn't go too far. Innocent eyes were turned on Patrick. "Never ya mind," she said, waving aside his protest. "Perhaps I'll consider what you're sayin'. Perhaps I will. About that new printer, I might." Behind the spectacles, Gert gave Harriet another thrice-over. Her own grin notwithstanding, here, Gert realized, was an opponent she hadn't expected. An adversary with a way about her, whose dogged determination was recognizable. No glow of kindred spirit was fired, however. No grudging respect. Rather an added wariness at the prowess of the enemy.

"I certainly hope you will. . . ." smiled Harriet, not bothered a whit to be under Gert's now flinty gaze. Should she genuflect? Insufferable, pious old battle-ax! For two cents she'd spit in her eye. ".I really appreciate—"

Gert sighed, heaved herself up, and walked behind the counter as if she were the chief inspector. Her diligent stroll took her to the rear door, which led to the storeroom and toilet, then back again as if claiming the territory, as if reminding everyone, and especially you-know-who, whose paper this *really* was.

"I'd like, if ya don't mind, a word with my son. . . ."

Harriet excused herself and went across to Noonan's, where she vowed to get even with the Hibernian colossus named Gert Flynn. Gert watched her go. Sure enough the creature made a certain amount of sense, not that Gert was going to admit it publicly. What was the smartypants *really* after? Her son?

"Changes? Changes, is it? Because of her? Ya know," she went on, not liking the blush of him, "that I had my heart set on a Catholic paper. Have ya forgotten? And ya know why we're supportin' Father Coughlin and O'Brien. Rose's future. D'ya want to turn your back on us all? After the election, we'll see where we stand. I could close it down right now, boyo, if you're not satisfied. How would ya like that? Then you and Miss Harriet Butter-Wouldn't-Melt would hafta find somethin' else to do."

"I'm sure we could," he returned sarcastically, but he knew it had been easier for him to stand up to Gert when Harriet was with him.

"What's come over ya? She's not interested in *you*, lemme tell ya! She's usin' ya to make her *own* way. Don't be a patsy. Stick to your own kind and don't break my heart. I started the paper for ya. Seems all ya want to do is hurt my feelin's."

Gert felt cheated and thoroughly out of sorts as Patrick glared back at her and held his tongue, his brain full of mayhem. "So," she went on, after a pause, "I'd like ya to think of what *I* want for a change. Don't I deserve it? After what I've been through?" After what you've put me through, was the not so hidden message.

"Well?" Patrick demanded, face flushed as Gert got up to leave.

"Well?"

"What about what I want to do? What about what we've been discussing?"

"I'll think about it."

"That's not good enough," he heard himself say. "I'm not going to be kept on a short leash anymore—not as far as the paper's concerned. It's too important to me."

"Oh?" Gert's eagle eye bore into a resolute Patrick, who was determined to stand his ground. "Oh?" she demanded, forced to take note of him and uneasy. "There's possibility for compromise, isn't there?" she asked, softening her tone and tousling Patrick's head. "We'll do business with this Smith and Houchins outfit, if that's what ya want. And let her add some of her stuff. Why not? I'm not the one to stand in the way of progress." Snap her like a twig if she got outta line. "Alright, boyo?" Still, Gert couldn't let it alone. The gnat continued to buzz. "You're not interested in her, I hope. You're a babe-in-the-woods patsy if ya are. She'll chew ya up and spit ya out before ya can say uncle. Course yer not."

"Course I'm not," Patrick mimicked, trying not to hate her.

In Noonan's Harriet glanced across the street and wondered what was going on. Thinking of Patrick and his mother, she realized that Patrick was drawn to women and afraid of them at the same time, and the cause of his conflict and uncertainties was obviously Gert, who ran his life with the determination of Attila the Hun. A moment later he burst into Noonan's and with an exhilaration Harriet hadn't seen before, bounced himself up on the stool beside her as if he were straddling a horse.

"What? *What?* Tell me!"

Enjoying keeping her in suspense, Patrick grinned, swiveled his stool, and saw Gert heading up Essex. "She's OK," he murmured, very aware that he was here, she was there, and the earth hadn't opened and swallowed him up.

"Well?" asked Harriet again as Patrick raised his coffee cup to her in a toast. "To us," he said. "We have a new printer. We won!"

Harriet gasped in delight. "Patrick!" She raised her cup in acknowledgment of a bond between them she couldn't deny.

"A new lease on life!" He laughed.

197

"A fighting chance."

"Can I take you to the movies? How about *Tomorrow We Live* with Joan Crawford?"

Harriet hesitated.

Unfazed, Patrick grinned. "You have a date with the Prince? OK. Lost your chance. I might not give you another."

They both knew he would.

10 *It was,* Harriet later recorded in her journal, *one of those days. . . .*
It started with sleeping late and being awakened by *Il Trovatore,* the Saturday broadcast from the Metropolitan Opera, which Letty had turned on while she fitted Cora in her wedding gown of ivory slipper satin. Franklin and Frankie put up storm windows, and shortly afterward an argument started between Letty and Franklin about the costs of Cora's wedding.

"Do you think it grows on trees? You've invited half the goddamned town."

"Calm down, Father," replied Letty, pins in her mouth and determined not to rise to the bait.

"Hats? Bags? Gloves?" growled Franklin, waving the bills. "Who do you think we are? The Rockefellers? I'm getting tired of being on the edge of bankruptcy."

"Tell that to the horses," interjected Alice, contributing a characteristically acerbic comment that zeroed in on Franklin's steady attendance at Rockingham Park, following the ponies.

Cora wept, and the house was soon in an uproar. Harriet snapped at Franklin, and Letty defended him, whereupon Harriet turned on Letty. "Why are you suffering in silence? You're nothing but a pin cushion!"

The fights between Letty and Franklin over money and his drinking had escalated, and Harriet usually found herself caught in the middle, unsure whose side she should be on. Furious with her father and angry with her mother for putting up with him, the holy state of matrimony seemed more than ever a cruel and unrewarding hoax.

"And you're a hothead," responded Letty, who added fuel by comparing her daughter to her Gramma Sarah, who had silly ambitions to join the upper classes. Stung, Harriet replied she had no such desire, and her relationship with Elliot was her own damned business!

Neither Letty nor Franklin approved of Harriet's closeness with Elliot, and the quarrel escalated. "And what about that loan?" Franklin demanded. It didn't sit well with him that Harriet's debt to Phelps had neither been mentioned, nor any attempt made to repay it. "That's between him and me," was Harriet's reply. Her rationale was that if Phelps wasn't in a hurry, she wasn't either.

All the bases got touched. Letty asked Harriet why she didn't settle down. (But not with Elliot.) Why was she so constantly dissatisfied with herself and the world? Harriet retorted that Letty had obviously lost touch with her own dreams and turned into a pastel of her former self. Old resentments bubbled as the bridesmaids' dresses were fitted on Harriet and Alice, who was in a moody and anxious state waiting for a letter from Wayne. The Anvil Chorus seemed to be beating in everyone's head, and Harriet finally stormed from the house and went to the office to be alone but found Patrick.

"I thought we were taking the day off?" she asked him, and he could tell she was upset about something. "I thought I'd come down and check the street and see how we were selling," he replied. "What's wrong?" he added. "Men," she replied flippantly, not wanting to talk.

"Elliot?"

"No, not Elliot," she snapped, darting an irritated look at him. "My mother," she went on, "just accused me of being unforgiving. 'An unforgiving spirit is the trademark of a graceless heart.' Do you think I'm graceless?" Why *should* she forgive Franklin? She doubted he even *liked* her any longer. Harriet shook her head as Patrick asked again if he could be of help. She wasn't going to allow his concern to penetrate; instead, she got to business. "Well—what have you heard? How are we doing?"

The Jericho Irish Spectator (set in a more imposing type), VOLUME I, NUMBER IV, Oct. 15, 1936, had appeared the day before and been given a second look by the town.

Eight pages long (increase of four), on glossy, medium-weight paper, printed by the firm of Smith and Houchins, the paper featured Harriet's editorial on page one, guaranteed to make Main Street merchants sit up and take notice.

Quoting statistics from Washington that showed Jericho's retail trade averaged under eighty-one dollars per person per year, Harriet nudged the town's shoppers, chiding them for not supporting local merchants. Her salvo concluded with a call for aggressiveness and punch in boosting Jericho.

Interspersed with the morning's battles, Harriet had made phone calls, seeking reactions to the newly revamped *Spectator*, which both she and Patrick hoped would attract attention and increase circulation. Did so-and-so like her review of *Hamlet*, just come to Boston? *(The Melancholy Dane, played by Leslie Howard, is in our midst again. . . .)* And how about "CINEMATICA," the new movie column? *(Like the seasoned actor he is, Frederick March does his noble best in his portrayal of Anthony Adverse, but the script defeats him . . .)* There was also a column contributed by Cora: "WHAT ABOUT YARNS AND NEEDLES?", and local non-Catholic activities were covered. The paper had a homey, cheery readability that prompted favorable talk and increased sales at Noonan's, Longbottom's Market and the depot, where *The Spectator* was sold.

Still, Harriet wasn't satisfied. "What is this paper really?" she asked Patrick, picking up a copy, her critical eye fighting with her sense of accomplishment, the critic winning. "Still not much," she went on, "even if it does look better. It actually looks like a newspaper for the first time, doesn't it? But it's neither . . ."

"Fish nor fowl."

"Exactly."

"I think we should be proud of ourselves."

"But there are weeklies in New England that have an influence far beyond the towns they actually serve."

"I'd be content to get in the black. We may sell six hundred the way things are going."

"We should be selling three times that much! And we still don't have enough advertisers. Do you realize the money we could make in political ads in these next weeks before the election? Do you know how many people—Catholics included—aren't supporting us because of Coughlin and O'Brien?"

Patrick had read the article in the *Atlantic Monthly* that Wayne had suggested, had also written to Father Morelli in Washington asking for his mentor's advice and guidance. Father Morelli had not yet replied, and Patrick was left with his own ambivalence about Father Coughlin. He wasn't ready to challenge a priest; who was he, anyway, to take such a stand when the Church hadn't? He wasn't a revolutionary, he'd explained to Harriet. He'd barely got his feet wet. "And my hands are tied. She's allowed us some things. We just have to put up with the rest for now."

Harriet hadn't much respect for Patrick's kowtowing to Gert. As far as she was concerned, if Gert's financial backing was the reason for Patrick's timidity, why not just give her the heave-ho and seek it elsewhere? Abraham Phelps, for example. "He called me to tell me he liked my editorial. And he's going to continue to advertise. Why aren't the others joining us? There are over twenty-five businesses on Main Street and only six are with us. Maybe the editorial will help. I suppose you think I'm impatient? I am. And we should be supporting Roosevelt, too. Although in a Republican town that would probably make us as many enemies as our being for Coughlin."

"What's with you today? You're racing."

"That's the way I am. If you don't like—" Harriet sighed and slumped. "Sorry. Bad morning."

"Tell me," he urged, hoping she'd let her guard down.

201

She shook her head. "Tell me about the rally."

"Coughlin's? If it upsets you, I'll do the interview with him myself next week."

"Not on your life. The most controversial figure in the country? I don't have to like him to interview him. How many are expected?"

"Ma said Timothy told her they expect to fill the Leveret Stadium—about ten thousand. They had three times that at a Union Party rally in Pawtucket last weekend. Lemke and O'Brien also spoke, but the crowds are there to hear Coughlin. It was Timothy that arranged for us to do the interview. And with O'Brien too. Look, I know the Union Party's a farce. But the election'll be over in three weeks, and we won't have the problem any more."

"Fine. We'll switch our support to Mussolini. I'm sure your mother has some Italians she wants to butter up."

"Hah-hah. What are you after?"

"Power. We're a newspaper. Not a lonely hearts service for your beautiful sister. Do you know what my mother also accused me of this morning? Of being impressed with the Phelps! Why shouldn't I be? He runs the town, and we need his support. I'd like to have that kind of influence and power any day in the week."

"Power?" Patrick was torn between a grudging respect and the feeling that Harriet's aggressive stance wasn't quite the proper behavior for a woman. He knew her well enough to know he'd better not mention the latter.

"To *right* things. Don't *you* want to? If we're doing recipes and chit-chat and reporting bake sales for the Grange, it has to have a purpose—so we can make ourselves heard, let people know what we think on important issues, educate, lead. We should be taking stands on issues. Instead, we're treading water and supporting a reactionary priest. I'm sorry, but it makes me mad. What did your mother say about the issue?" she went on, sensing Patrick's belligerence growing. "I suppose she's her usual nasty self? Or is she pleased?"

"Pleased. When sales go up, she's happy. Look, I told you—"

"Yes, your hands are tied. And you—are you pleased? What do you think of my column?" Entitled "A Woman Who Sees (Things as They Are)," the column was full of everything that was on Harriet's mind, a personal comment on current events that asked: Why couldn't a woman have a family and children and still participate in the world? Did one have to be sacrificed to the other? "Of course," she explained to Patrick, "having a family is not my own desire. I'm different from most of the women I know."

What she chose not to explain or tell him was the troubles on Mulberry Street and her growing frustration with Letty and Franklin. This morning's bickering was becoming standard. Franklin might be, as Wayne had suggested, a casualty of the Depression and, therefore, more than worthy of compassion, but Harriet was caught between her love for him and Franklin's refusal to let her in. The malady had worsened, his desolation scared her. It bothered her terribly that every day her father's detachment from her grew worse. But she couldn't talk to Patrick about it, even if she might have wanted to. He might be understanding, but he was a man, part of the opposition, so—as she'd always done—Harriet put her sorrow and hurt into her work. It was Letty she was writing about (and her fears for her own future) when she asked in her column:

> Under what circumstances may romantic love be valuable without being disastrous for the woman who would be artist and fall madly in love? Perhaps under conditions in which she is centered in her own work, with a faith in her own powers, free to follow her own impulses. . . . Perhaps then she can experience the ecstatic self as only One Part of her Whole Being. For unless her expectations are worldly and diversified, she has no reason to believe that from romantic love comes salvation.

"Interesting," commented Patrick, his vagueness irritating Harriet, "but I'm not sure what it is you mean. Methinks you doth protest too much."

"Oh?" she challenged. "What it means is that a woman shouldn't put all her peas in one pot, especially a man's pot. Is that simple enough for you? I know your background doesn't permit subtlety."

"No?" he retorted, growing hot. "You're certainly not subtle. If you had your way, the human race would come to a halt."

"How archaic can you be?"

" 'No reason to believe that from romantic love comes salvation'? What's that supposed to mean? It's been the salvation of billions of women before *you* came along. I don't think they regret it."

"How would you know? The only woman *you* know is your mother. And she's *full* of regrets. Come to think of it, she and I might be alike in some ways. Forget I said that."

"You're not at all alike," Patrick replied quickly. "What about Elliot?" he went on. "Is your column about Elliot? You'll get no 'salvation' from him."

"Why not?"

"Self-involved, superficial. Anyone can see—"

"Is that so? Well, I don't imagine you'd bend over backwards to notice his good points. In any event, it's not about Elliot. It's about being trapped. Elliot understands who I am," she continued defensively, not caring to share that the night before last he'd gotten drunk, lashed out at her for no reason at all, and left her in an all-night diner in Leveret, just walked out.

"Does Elliot want to trap you?"

"Most men do . . . to women, I mean. They don't call it that, of course. They call it marriage."

"You don't want to get married?"

"Why should I? Why would I want to? For romance? Conversation? Satisfying sex? I can have all those without marriage."

She enjoyed shocking Patrick. Her way of keeping him at arm's length. And it was good for him to have his conservative point of view jolted. "Besides," she continued with a grin, "marriage isn't a word. It's a sentence." She gathered her purse. "Say, Elliot and some friends and I are going dancing at the Classic tonight. And to hear my brother. Why don't you join us?"

"Thanks, but Jerry's wife's gone to the hospital an hour ago." *Satisfying sex? Had she with Elliot?* His insides clenched. "The baby's expected tonight, and I promised to wait with him."

"How many does she have?"

"It'll be the third."

"Must tie her down. Well, to each her own. Come afterward then."

"No, thanks."

"Why not? You might meet someone."

Like a baby fresh from its bath, Patrick's skin blotched rose, and Harriet felt guilty.

"That was glib of me, wasn't it? I apologize."

"Cruel," he nodded, playing the fool for her with his hand on his breast, managing a smile, too.

"But I'm taken."

"So you say."

"If you knew him, you'd—"

"Don't care to. Too rich for my watery Papist blood."

Harriet laughed. "You don't give up."

"I'm Irish."

Flattered in spite of herself, Harriet laughed again and started for the door.

"I would've been ordained tomorrow," Patrick said, knowing that would keep her.

"Oh? You don't ever talk about it. How do you feel?"

"It's strange. Sometimes I feel as if I'm still half in that life and half here. A part of me'll be there with them tomorrow. Ma will be there, too. A mild fall day in Washington, and one hundred and fifty men will have achieved their dream and hopefully aren't as terrified as I was. And one hundred and fifty happy families watching with tears in their eyes. That's the way it was supposed to be for me."

"You have too much life in you to be a priest."

"Do you think so?"

"It's odd, isn't it? How two people can work as closely together as we have and not really know each other."

"What are those you're wearing?" Patrick asked as an overwhelming impulse to take her in his arms shook him. Yet he didn't want to risk offending her.

"Culottes—a fancy name for trousers. Well, I should be—"

"Harriet?" He reached for her hand and held it. Flustered to be under his ardent gaze, Harriet laughed clumsily and averted her eyes. "What?" she asked, very aware of his breathing and the warmth of his hand.

"Just wanted to say thanks for everything. Couldn't have done it without you."

"We did it together."

"Sure," he said and shut his eyes and brought her to him and kissed her.

The day continued in its chaotic course when Harriet returned to the house.

"Alice is in a state. The letter came after you left—"

"Wayne? Is he all right?"

"I think so. She didn't say much. You know your sister."

Unfinished business lurked in the pantry. "Where's Father?" asked Harriet, aware of the edge in her voice.

"I expect him for supper," replied Letty, moving into the kitchen to check the beans.

"Mother—" Letty and Harriet eyed each other warily and exchanged a gingerly hug. "I'm sorry about this morning," Harriet said. "I am, too," replied Letty.

Upstairs, Harriet found Alice lying in disarray on the bed, the shades drawn.

"He's all right, isn't he?"

"He's on the outskirts of Madrid. He doesn't think the city can hold out. It's practically surrounded . . ." Wayne's letter was clutched in her hand. Alice smoothed it on the bed, then turned to Harriet. "And *you!* You don't give a damn, do you? You and Elliot Phelps!"

"What on earth are you talking about?"

"Naive! . . . Don't you know what's happening? Here—read it! The rebels took over a sanitarium . . . killed the doctors . . . and shot the patients right in their beds. . . . It happened the day he got there."

"But what does that have to do—?"

"Because it's all the same—don't you see? You live in a fantasy—playing girl reporter—fussing with your newspaper. Who cares who took a ride on the Burlington Zephyr?"

"That's unfair. You know what I'm trying to do with the paper."

205

"I've told you. Wayne told you. Coughlin's a fascist! Do you understand? The election next month is crucial—absolutely crucial. What are you doing about it? Nothing . . . nothing . . ."

"Alice, you know there's nothing I can do. I've talked to Patrick. Just today—"

"Then quit."

"Quit? You're crazy, Alice. I know you're upset but—quit? You bandy all these words about—fascist this and fascist that. You're worse than Father. He sees communists behind every bush and you see fascists."

"It's time you woke up."

"I'm just trying to keep the paper going. I don't care about Coughlin. If you say he's evil, then I believe you. But I don't intend to quit. What's come over you?"

"You're interested only in yourself. You always have been. What about you and Phelps? I told you then . . . when you borrowed that money. You knew how I felt. I still can't get over it. How can you have anything to do with such a family? Ignore the facts if they get in the way of your ambition. I think you stink!"

"That's not true," replied Harriet, shocked. "I know you're worried about Wayne but—"

"What am I going to do? What am I going to do?"

Elliot kissed Harriet in greeting, held the car door for her, and tried to hide his agitation about his mother's coolness and the quarrel that had erupted between them over his continued dating of Harriet.

Silent herself, Harriet shook her head as if she could shake off her uneasiness, but her thoughts kept returning to Alice. Wayne was in Madrid and Alice was on Mulberry Street and over two months pregnant; baked beans were bubbling in their Saturday night crock, and she was headed to Leveret with Elliot to go dancing. It all seemed unreal.

"Pardon?"

"I said you looked especially sexy tonight, Wallis."

"Oh. Thanks, Edward . . ." Her heart wasn't in the game. "Elliot!" she exclaimed as he took a curve too fast. From out of nowhere a squall erupted when Harriet began to talk about *The Spectator.*

"Save me from small-town girls with big pretensions. Who cares about the goddamned paper? Nobody but you."

Hurt, Harriet snapped back: "*You* don't care about *anything!* That's your trouble. How many have you had already?"

"Don't worry, I'm not after your 'tweety.' "

"Why do you say things like that? I won't put up with it."

"Hah!"

Their eyes met, the friendship teetering for an instant. "I'm sorry," Elliot said, his tone so helpless that Harriet's anger fled. "What's the trouble?" she asked, wondering if the whole world had gone crazy today.

"She doesn't understand . . ." muttered Elliot to himself. Confused, he felt he'd explode.

"Who? Me?"

He shook his head.

"Your mother?"

He shook his head again. Harriet touched his arm. "Calm down, darling. We're going to have a wonderful time tonight. Did you and Frankie accomplish anything?"

"Listen to this. See what you think. The lead-in goes like this. . . ." Elliot began to hum the beginning of a song that he and Frankie had composed over the piano in the barn this afternoon. " 'I won't give my heart to anyone, because anyone will break it in two, scubba doo, doo, doo. . . .' My lyric," he added.

"Catchy. I hope it doesn't refer to yours truly."

" 'I won't give my heart to anyone. . .' " he sang again, then broke off, thinking of Frankie.

". . . except my mother," sang Harriet, finishing the phrase wryly. "You and Patrick! You—"

"Patrick?" Elliot bristled.

"Two of a kind. I know the saying is that a boy's best friend is his mother but— Or is it his dog?"

Elliot laughed, and Harriet was pleased. "Do you love me?" he asked suddenly.

"You know I do."

Elliot reached behind him and placed a copy of *Fortune* magazine on Harriet's lap. "Page seventy-six. Where it's underlined. Read it."

"Aren't you smart," she laughed, scanning the article, which was a survey of morals in a mythical American town. "Is this a hint?" she added, reading aloud: " '. . . a confidential checkup of one group of more than two dozen young business-class persons in their twenties showed seven out of every ten—evenly balanced as to sex—to have had sexual relations prior to marriage.' "

"Well, I know how you love statistics. So I thought—"

"Did you now?"

"And you *are* a 'young business-class person.' "

"Uh-huh. And in my twenties, too. Do you always keep this in the car for your victims to read? If they hesitate, you quote them statistics. My, it is a bit dog-eared, isn't it? From so much use?"

"Only you, kiddo," he bantered back, thinking of Frankie again and the incredible closeness he'd felt working with him. The exhilaration of collaboration felt like lovemaking. But it wasn't. "How else do you know if you're going to get a lemon or not," Elliot went on, "unless you experiment?"

"I think 'experimenting' gets people into trouble. More than ever I'm *very* sure of that."

Elliot pulled in Caringi's parking lot and nuzzled Harriet. "We are going to, aren't we? I want to."

"Elliot . . . you'll muss me . . ."

"I wanna muss ya."

"I'm sure you'll find me a lemon," she replied, returning his kiss with a fervor that surprised her.

"Maybe you'll find me one, too."

Harriet drank half a bottle of wine with dinner, and it helped to temporarily banish her worry about Alice. And Elliot was on perfect behavior, easy and charming and just the way he was supposed to be. They held hands under the table, and she claimed him with a kiss, claimed him in front of Marcia and Allan and Libby and Libby's boyfriend Graham, claimed him for all the world to see.

Stuffed with pasta, fresh clams and spumoni, the six of them left the restaurant feeling high on wine and good conversation. Arms linked, the future bright and unclouded, they walked up Leveret's Broadway, mingling with the Saturday night crowds, which were thick in a mill city. Everybody was going to the movies, and there were six theaters in a row and two across the street. "That's Marcia," called out Harriet, pointing to the movie poster of Jane Withers in *Gentle Julia*.

The game was on. "I'm William Gargan," said Marcia's husband Allan. And Libby insisted that she was *Nobody's Fool* at the Strand. Marcia and Harriet heartily agreed. The game continued as they crossed to the other side. *Love Before Breakfast* with Carole Lombard at the Colonial caused Elliot to agree. "I always do," he said. "And *then* I eat my Wheaties."

"We haven't found anyone for you to be, Elliot," called Marcia.

"Why not Narcissus?" said Libby under her breath.

"Jealous?" whispered Harriet, overhearing. Territorially, she linked her arm with Elliot's.

Passing by the Club Rendezvous, their noses in the air (schmaltzy music for the old folks), they headed further up the street toward the Classic (considered slummy and, therefore, fun) where Jimmy Lanceford and His Lancers held forth and Frankie Hoskins was featured on trumpet and you could really let your hair down and *swing!*

The waiting line snaked out into the street and the place was mobbed. "I'm Frankie's sister," Harriet announced, pointing to the glossy photo of her brother in the display case. "You and a hundred others, 'sister,' " replied the beefy bouncer, who was letting in nobody at the moment.

"At least he's popular," Harriet commented to the others. Elliot, meanwhile, not used to waiting in lines, was greasing the palm of a seedy-looking assistant manager in a seedier tuxedo. The money and the fact that he was a regular patron did the trick, and in they went, the six of them, squeezing past the "lower classes" (Libby whispered it to Marcia), whose eyes betrayed hostility as the handsome trio of couples passed them by.

"Saturday night hotbloods," cried Elliot enthusiastically, "with their tomatoes. Are you all hepcats? Squirts and polecats?"

"Hi, there, scrumptious!" the more forward girls called back.

Heavy-lidded Italian and Polish eyes undressed Marcia, Libby and Harriet. Stray German and Canuck hands were everywhere. Up the packed stairs, the progress slow, the frenzy increasing as they finally reached the top, three flights up, eardrums deafened by the exploding brass.

"I've been molested thrice!" Harriet shouted to Elliot, but he couldn't hear her. She locked her arm with his, and they emerged onto a spacious balcony that ran around all four sides of the enormous room and hung over the dance floor. A wildly surging crowd jammed the aisles; tables on the descending tiers were squeezed with couples.

"It's a madhouse!" shouted Allan.

"I'll see about a table," Elliot shouted back, leaving Harriet with the rest of them. With difficulty, they worked their way to the railing on the edge of the balcony and looked down.

"*What is it?*" cried Marcia. They couldn't hear her, but her expression of amazement asked the question.

"It's called 'swing,' " shouted Harriet. The din was impossible. Two hundred couples packed the dance floor below as the trumpet section rose wailing, whipping them to a greater frenzy. The bodies flickered in slivers of colored light from the mirrored glitter ball above their heads, a stained-glass window exploding.

"There's Frankie!" mouthed Harriet, pointing and waving. He couldn't possibly see her. Her body at the mercy of the hard-driving beat of the drums, she began to move. She shut her eyes, then opened them fast, grasping the railing as the rhythms built and swelled, demanding a letting-go that filled her with conflict.

The first trouble was over the table. Having greased another palm or two, Elliot managed to have a table cleared of its occupants, a group of hard-eyed laborers and their girls, who weren't thrilled. Amid angry mutterings, Elliot and his group were seated.

"We could've waited," Harriet whispered.

"Why should we?" he replied. Allan and Graham exchanged a glance, the girls busied themselves with their compacts, the unpleasant moment passed and they ordered drinks.

A few minutes later, they were joined by Frankie, who was on a break. With him was the provocative Jeannie Lo Bianco, who caused the whole table to sit up and take notice.

"This is the canary with the band," announced Frankie, playing man about town with such earnestness it was charming.

"How do you do, Miss Lo Bianco?" said Elliot as if he'd never met her before. He rose and bowed. "The best warbler in the biz."

"Such a cutup," smiled Jeannie knowingly. Frankie grinned. A chair was produced and Jeannie sat down. Conscious of their eyes, she yawned—remembering in time to cover her mouth. She always yawned when she was nervous.

"So, you're his sister." Jeannie blew smoke. Harriet nodded. "I'd never have guessed." Jeannie laughed and turned to Frankie. "You didn't tell me you had a twin."

"That's what everyone says, Miss Lo Bianco."

Jeannie rolled her eyes at Harriet's formality.

"Call her Jeannie," said Frankie. "Everybody calls her Jeannie."

"Jeannie." Trying to conceal her amazement (not at all sure she approved), Harriet watched as Frankie squeezed the bare arm of the sexy singer, whose pencil-thin eyebrows and scarlet mouth were those of an unmistakable femme fatale. "What an interesting job you have—singing with a band—it must be so exciting, don't you think so, Marcia?" Harriet was amused to find her friend was agoggle, glancing furtively from Allan to Jeannie and back again, quite intimidated. Libby, of course, found Jeannie common.

"It's no bed of roses on a hot night, believe me."

"Boobedee do do dee," sang Frankie. Slightly envious, Harriet realized she had never seen her brother behave in quite so expansive a manner. His hand caressed Jeannie's flank, and Jeannie playfully slapped it away. Of the people at the table, only Elliot knew that Jeannie Lo Bianco slept around, and one of the people she did it with was Frankie Hoskins. He envied her.

"Well, this place really 'sends' me," announced Harriet, trying on some of the talk she'd learned at parties in New York. "Roseland is bigger, of course, but for Leveret, the Classic seems to be 'with it!' " Everyone laughed. Frankie gazed at Jeannie. So what if she was five years older? Only last month she'd let him. It was the first time for him, and he was still in awe.

"This's my Jeannie," he said, enjoying showing off before his sister and her friends. Jeannie accepted his attentions with a kind of lazy conde-

210

scension. She wasn't sure what she was doing with this kid. Wet behind the ears, out of her league, but, baby, could he play! Not just on the bandstand, either.

"It's really jazz, isn't it?" asked Libby's date, Graham, as they got into a discussion of the new kind of music. Graham was a senior at Harvard and almost as stuffy as Libby.

Frankie nodded. "It's the latest. It's a craze—sweeping the country. Started last year. Benny Goodman—you've all heard of *him*, I hope? Well, he got tired of playing syrupy dance music, and one night he said to the boys: 'OK—let's *swing!*' And they kicked out, and that's how it started. Out in Los Angeles. Jeannie told me all about it. She's been to Hollywood, you know."

"My!"

"Well," offered Marcia, hesitantly, eyeing Jeannie again, deciding that under the proper circumstances she might be fun, "—it's so . . . what do I want to say . . . ?"

"Sexual," offered Elliot. Nervous as always when he was with Frankie and Harriet, he did a mock leer.

"Yes. I guess that's it." Allan and Marcia exchanged a glance.

"Isn't it?" agreed Harriet. "Terribly primitive."

Elliot and Frankie burst out laughing. "It's not anthropology," said Elliot. "You're supposed to *dance* to it!"

"We're going to," replied Harriet, noticing that he'd already ordered another round of drinks. "We're going to get in the groove and cut a few rugs. How's that?"

"Who's the chick?" Elliot winked at Frankie. He shifted position and his leg bumped Frankie's under the table. For as long as he dared, he let the contact continue.

"A real alligator," Frankie nodded back, smiling at Elliot, oblivious. "Elliot knows as much about it as I do. He's got a great collection of records. You know," he went on enthusiastically, "we're doing some songs together. We've lost our lyricist but—"

"I *have* been busy," interjected Harriet, pleased that her brother admired Elliot.

"Do you play slow numbers, too?" asked Libby.

"Sure. And wait'll you hear Jeannie! We'll do some foxtrots and waltzes, too. It's only Leveret, after all. You have to go into the clubs in Boston for some of the really hot stuff."

"Boston?"

"Or New York, I guess."

Harriet nodded.

"Chicago," said Jeannie, "is where the action is."

"You must be the youngest professional trumpet player around, Frankie," Allan said.

"Maybe so."

"In the *world*," Elliot said. "You're all going to say, 'I heard him when. . . .' "

"And Jeannie'll be with me, won't you?"

"Sure, pal." Jeannie patted Frankie's head. "If you'll excuse me all," she said, putting on her manners, "I'll just be going."

Frankie rose quickly and pulled back her chair. "Me, too. Back to work. Time to entertain you ickies."

"Ickies?" asked Harriet when the couple had left.

"Squares," explained Elliot. "C'mon, who's for some jive?"

"In a minute. I want to get my bearings."

A moment later, the band kicked off and the Classic shook. Elliot excused himself to push through the crowd on the balcony, greeting some people who waved to him.

"Look at him," whispered Marcia a moment later to Harriet, calling her attention to Elliot carrying on, his arms around a threesome of two flashy girls and an older man.

Libby caught Harriet's glance and felt sorry for her. Didn't she know that Elliot sometimes paid for those kinds of girls and was known for the little presents he gave? "He's not even pretending *not* to know them," she commented distastefully to Graham. "Really," she went on, this time to Harriet, "—he loves being different, doesn't he? But I guess you're used to that by now."

"Yes, I am," Harriet replied. "And I like that he is." Even so, when Elliot returned a moment later and led her down the wide stairs to the packed ballroom, she couldn't help asking him who they were.

"Friends," he replied, eyes dancing, his color high. "C'mon, kiddo, we hafta get you loosened up. . . ."

Elliot knew everyone at the Classic. He gave the regulars his dazzling smile, a word or two, a wave, a hug. They weren't types he'd invited to dinner at the Mansion. It wouldn't occur to him that the expression on his mother's face, if she were to see these cheap girls, would give him a guilty pleasure. As he took Harriet in his arms, she noticed his eyes close, a strange calm on his face hiding the turbulence. He seemed, she reflected, more in his element in this vaguely shady place of glitter and noise than anywhere she'd ever been with him.

"Relax, kiddo . . . relax . . ." Expertly he led her, weaving about the crowded floor, pushing her away, twirling her, and pulling her back. The lights changed, and Frankie got a nod from Jimmy Lanceford. Harriet watched as he rose in a spotlight. A hush fell over the crowd; they were mesmerized by Frankie's wild and passionate call. To shrieks and applause, he finished, leaving the dancers spent—ready for Jeannie to croon softly into the microphone the slow and lazy wonder of a "Moon Over Miami."

"He's *wonderful!* I never realized how good he was. Good doesn't begin to describe him. . . ." Harriet was very excited. At home, Frankie had always been the nicely mannered, slightly spoiled younger brother. But here—in this place of music and dancing, sweating bodies, with his jive talk, squealing fans, and Jeannie Lo Bianco—here he seemed transformed, a young Bacchus bent on pleasure.

"I told you," nodded Elliot, waving to Frankie, who stood to the side of the band, toweling his face as his followers gazed raptly up at him.

"She's good, too, isn't she?" added Harriet, responding to Jeannie's soothing yet sultry tones. Feeling the need to be held and protected, she nestled closer to Elliot, laying her cheek against his shoulder. His aftershave smelled sweet. As his arm tightened about her waist, she could feel herself melting, needing to put the topsy-turvyness of the day behind her. Above their heads the ball revolved, the colors changing, bathing them now in a magical silver.

"They're an item, you know," Elliot whispered in her ear, his comment jolting her back to reality. "I guess you didn't. She's a cradle robber."

"You mean . . . ?"

"Sure thing."

Harriet sensed Elliot didn't like Jeannie. Glancing at Frankie again, she tried to sort her feelings. She knew she should be shocked; but somehow she wasn't. Once again, she snuggled close to Elliot.

"Look who's here," he exclaimed, "—a covey of micks! Including your boss." She followed his eyes. Why—Patrick had come! She found herself glad to see him. "I wish you wouldn't call him that."

"Why's he here?"

"I invited him."

"Why?"

"Oh, stop worrying," she flirted. "Let's dance over that way."

Patrick was with Dennis, Billy Meeghan and Jerry Finneran. Harriet waved as she and Elliot danced near by. "Hello, there," she called. "I'd like to dance with him," she whispered to Elliot.

"Only one . . ."

"Yes, Master." She nestled closer. The current moved them on, past Patrick and his group. "Later," she pantomimed to him.

"Why didn't she come over?" asked Dennis. Nervously he wiped his sweating palms, then dabbed primly at his forehead. Famished eyes roamed about, feasting on tidbits of female flesh.

"Lotta lookers, huh, Denny?" asked Billy Meeghan, who winked and danced in place, a cigar clamped in his teeth. Deedee Finneran had given birth only a couple of hours earlier, and Jerry had passed out the cigars.

"I don't know," muttered Dennis, mouth dry. "Lots of tramps," he added, rising and falling on the balls of his feet.

213

"Quitcha kiddin'," remonstrated Billy. "Lookit the knockers on that one, will ya? Like to ring her doorbell any old time! Hey—I know her! Hey, Joycie! C'mere!"

Joyce Gillespie and her sister Elaine both turned. Joyce waved.

"Don't like the look of this crowd," muttered Dennis.

"Sure ya do. *Girls*," called Billy to the sisters, "come on over here!"

"Ya think it's proper, Pat," whispered Jerry, "for me to be in this place when Deedee's just—had a *boy*!?" He let out a whoop. "C'mon, fellas, the drinks'r on me! C'mon, Pat." Jerry followed his friend's gaze to Harriet in Elliot's arms. "Ya can't fight City Hall, Pat," he said sympathetically, throwing an affectionate arm over his shoulder. "Only leads to sufferin'. C'mon, now. Ya can have your pick."

Patrick said nothing. He craned his neck, bobbed his head, following Harriet with his eyes, never losing sight.

"Now, how I'm gonna *pay* for that baby is another story. . . ."

Patrick concentrated, willing Harriet to leave Elliot and come to him. Across the floor, through the dancers, she would come. And as she did, the ball would come loose from the ceiling high above and crash down upon that hated blond head, smashing it into a million blood-drenched fragments.

"Here—drink up." Jerry thrust a glass at Patrick, who unclenched his fist and took it. *I wish I'd never met her.* He drained the glass. "Easy does it, Pat."

"Hey, Denny, Pat . . . meet Joyce Gillespie and her sister Elaine." Billy made the intros. Dennis smoothed his hair. Joyce was plumpish with a twinkle in her eye. Elaine hadn't wanted to come and was ill at ease.

"I've heard of you," Joyce said, looking up at Patrick. "You have that paper over in Jericho. I've seen it."

"Have you?" he asked, then felt a tap on his shoulder and turned around, and the rest of them ceased to exist.

"Hello," said Harriet. "May I have this dance?" She caught a glimpse of the plump one's disappointment that she was stealing Patrick away.

"I'll have to check my card," he replied evenly, staring at her, mesmerized by her disheveled bangs and the tiny pearls that dangled from her ears, quivering under the bowl of her dark hair, which glimmered and shone in the lights. "Yes, I think I'm free," he said and took her in his arms.

"It's nice to see you," Harriet smiled, both of them awkward because of this afternoon's kiss, which Harriet had liked and not liked, and didn't want to encourage. The number ended, and Elliot quickly came to get her. "I owe you one," she called to Patrick as Elliot took her arm and escorted her back upstairs.

"What's the rush?" she asked. "I'm jealous," he replied, feeling intimidated as he always did when Patrick was around.

"So that was Patrick," whispered Marcia. "How do you do it, Harriet?" A moment or two later, Marcia nudged her and she turned and there he was, those very recognizable blue eyes flashing in the half-light of the balcony.

"I came to collect." Amazed at his own daring, Patrick felt ill at ease in front of them all.

"This is Patrick Flynn . . . my boss." Harriet made the introductions.

"Hello, there."

"Congratulations on your paper."

"Won't you join us?"

Unequipped for small talk, Patrick sat down, smiling gamely, while Elliot chatted incessantly, clowning for the table. Harriet could tell Patrick was nervous; he looked pale, solemn and, she decided, very endearing. She tried to put him at ease as the conversation swept giddily over current movies and the like. A moment later, she finished her gin and stood and they went down to the dance floor, leaving Elliot with a pout on his face.

"What happened at the hospital?"

"Jerry had a boy." Jostled from behind and brushing against her, Patrick wished he'd be jostled again.

"Don't you mean his wife?"

"Yes. I have something for you." He rummaged in his suit-coat pocket and brought out a small box. Through the cellophane window Harriet could see a gardenia. "A woman was selling them outside the hospital," he explained, the sudden antic charm of him surprising Harriet as Patrick smiled like some pure shepherd boy out of a nineteenth-century novelette, rosebuds in his cheeks. Harriet removed the flower and brought it to her nose, shivering with the voluptuous odor. "How did—?" she asked, and Patrick replied that once he'd heard her mention that gardenias were her favorite flower. Pleased, Harriet placed the blossom over her ear and met his eyes. Flustered, she was all too aware of a sudden closeness, a liking him, that she hadn't experienced quite as strongly before. Had she made a mistake in her original assessment of him—consigning him to the cubbyhole of the earthbound?

A momentary pang hit her as she thought of Alice again. She wished she had someone to share her worry with. Elliot would only make a quip. Patrick, she felt, would be sympathetic. "You're a very good dancer," she said, deciding it would be a betrayal of Alice's confidence to reveal anything. "You really are," she added, surprised. Above her on the balcony, she caught a flash of blond hair and knew Elliot was watching.

"Ma sent us over here . . . to Leveret . . . to a dancing school when we were little."

"I like these slower numbers better, don't you?" she asked. He nodded and felt dumbstruck. Jeannie was singing "Pennies From Heaven." Patrick's insides clenched and unclenched to the soft beat of the music.

215

Resting lightly in his, Harriet's hand felt indescribable. A foot of unbreach-able air separated his body from hers. He prayed he might clasp her tighter; this would be his last dance; he would be executed in the morning.

"Pardon?" he asked, flustered at not paying attention.

"I asked what you thought of Frankie. Isn't he something?" Patrick nodded enthusiastically and moved subtly closer. She felt him against her and had a fantasy of him naked. Startled, she was immediately businesslike. "I enjoyed our chat this afternoon." "Why do you pretend I'm not here when I am?" he asked, and she had no reply. She saw Elliot coming down the stairs, headed for the main bar, and hoped he wouldn't get too high. "Do I have a chance?" asked Patrick, following her glance.

"Patrick . . . please . . ." She was relieved as the music picked up, the noise making conversation difficult. After the number was over, they were both tongue-tied and she wished Elliot would come and rescue her. She glimpsed him and he blew her a kiss. Deliciousness flooded her. Yes, they'd all fallen, hadn't they? Including this so serious man who'd held her like a piece of fragile china. Trying to make conversation with him, she was nervous at the way he stared at her, as if he were waiting for some-thing.

"I want us to be good friends," she said. "OK?" she added, not wanting to hurt him. But there was no other way than to tell the truth.

"Could a good friend have another dance?" Patrick managed to ask as a hot pain stabbed him.

"Of course."

Harriet felt a twinge of guilt for thinking of Elliot while dancing with Patrick. Slightly tipsy, she closed her eyes and recalled the former's earlier hinting. The rush of excitement in the pit of her stomach—did it mean she was ready? What a strange night. And the moon wasn't even full.

The bar was packed. Elliot blinked at his reflection in the neon-lined mirror and found himself hazy. "Hey, Max!" he called to the owner of the Classic who was pitching in, making drinks on a busy night. "Scotch and soda . . . snap it up there."

"Spoiled bastard," muttered Max.

A voice inside warned Elliot he'd had enough, but he paid no atten-tion and took a long sip of the drink, scowling slightly at the sight of Patrick and Harriet dancing again.

"Been avoiding me, sweetheart?"

Elliot smiled, recognizing the voice. "Hello," he said before turning, then nonchalantly gave his profile to Myrna, who smelled of perspiration and twenty-cent toilet water. "What's your name?" he asked, her seductive expression grating on him.

"Myrna," she replied in a husky voice that matched her dark brows and eyes, which were too heavily made up and deeper than a well.

"Ralph's my name . . . pussy's my game," he whispered in her ear.

"Oh? I wouldn't have thought so. Doesn't an old love get a nod?"

He drew a finger along her arm. "Old? I wouldn't say last Wednesday was very 'old.' It *was* Wednesday, wasn't it?"

"And you're tight again, too, aren't you? Such a bad baby."

"Spank me . . ."

Myrna laughed. "Who is she?" she asked, following Elliot's eyes to Harriet.

"No one you know."

"I guess not. One of your high-toned friends?"

"Frankie's sister."

"Do I get to meet her?"

"Sure."

"You would, wouldn't you? Am I going to see you later?"

"I don't know." Elliot called for another scotch, anxious to get away. "Have to bring a friend a drink," he explained.

"Love me and leave me? Is that tonight's game?"

A moment later, Elliot cut in on Patrick. "Sorry," he said in that superior way he had. Patrick plunged his hands into the safety of his pockets. "What can I do," asked Harriet, trying to lighten the moment, "when royalty calls? We'll have another," she assured Patrick, "before the evening's over."

"What was that all about?"

"Wouldn't you like to know?"

"You and he were awfully chummy."

"So were you. Who is she?"

"No one who counts."

"Exactly."

"Where'd you get that?" he asked, noticing the gardenia.

"Patrick—"

"Take it off."

"Don't order me like that. I don't like it. How silly you are," she added, kissing his nose.

"I can't lose you," Elliot whispered, lips brushing Harriet's ear. "Need ya, kiddo. Know I haven't been such good company the last week but . . . I love you, Harriet Hoskins." He felt like an imposter and shut his eyes, which were glassy from scotch. "Cross my heart," he added, blond lashes fluttering open, his vulnerability arousing Harriet's heart as it always did. An ache of tenderness rose, exhilarated happiness rushed at her, causing her to feel lightheaded. Snuggling closer to him, she wanted the dance to go on forever. What a merry chase he'd led her this past month—twists and turns through the labyrinth of his personality, culminating in the magic that was now. Yes, she would make love with him, yes.

"I love you, too," Harriet whispered back, loving the sound of it.

217

Jeannie was crooning that it was " 'a sin to tell a lie.' " And she hadn't. And the band played on. Harriet was floating. A dreamy moment or two later, Elliot held her apart from him in the middle of the floor.

"It's all yours . . . ours. For you and I," he continued, "are not of this planet, but live instead"—he pointed to the ball revolving slowly above their heads—"up there. In *silver*."

"Where's Elliot?" asked Frankie a few moments later, the band on a break. The dance floor milled with people, eyes discreetly and not so discreetly searching. "You shouldn't be by yourself."

"I lost him. Gone to the men's, I think. And I'm a big girl."

A momentary soberness took Harriet over, then she hugged Frankie to her and couldn't help giggling.

"Look who's tipsy," he grinned, then frowned. "Be careful."

"Me? Not me. Not little Miss Muffet. So, Franklin Hoskins, Junior, I hear you and Miss Jeannie Lo—"

"Bianco."

"Gotcha . . . that you and Miss Lo Bianco are an item."

"Who says?" he asked, blushing.

"Who says??? You've done everything but announce it from the bandstand. You old possum." She tweaked his nose. "Does Mother know?"

"Sure. I keep her informed of every detail." They laughed, delighted with each other. "I guess," she said, "you're no longer my baby brother." Wiping away the beads of perspiration, Harriet ran a finger across his forehead. "You played better than I ever heard you tonight."

"You were here."

"Was that it?" He nodded. "Do you remember your prediction," she asked, "—about Elliot?"

Frankie thought for a moment, then grinned broadly. "Has he asked you?"

"He will."

Giggling to herself, Harriet moved off as a thought struck her: she must find Marcia, who had a lady gynecologist in Boston. Properly prepared and in charge of her own body, Alice's fate would not be hers.

It was too painful. He would have to get rid of her. Why did he have to be so grateful for the few drops she'd sprinkled on him? Why did he have to be such a sorry bastard? . . . She was with the people she wanted to be with, wasn't she? . . . And he'd never be comfortable with them . . . but then, who was he comfortable with?

She was with Elliot.

Blackness swept over Patrick, and he gripped the railing of the fire escape. A mist had come up from the river, and he was chilly. Closing his eyes, a panicked thought: He would never dance with her again.

"Excuse us . . ."

He moved to accommodate a couple who squeezed by and climbed up further, joining others, perched like so many cooing starlings on the stairs of the fire escape. A siren sounded somewhere. Patrick looked up at the sky and wondered what had happened to the old dream? Where was the Lone Eagle? Up there corraling the stars, taming time and space—yet he, too, had had his wings clipped and was stuck, moribund on the earth.

Was this what You wanted for me? If this is the way of the world, Father, I want no part of it.

He glanced at the crowd on the fire escape, eyeing the girls. Burn them all with his stiff, virgin prick, that's what he'd do! And the fire would cause such a smoke, it would drift to Mulberry Street and blacken her yellow house, filling her nostrils, causing a violent seizure of coughing.

"Hey, Frankie—wait!"

Trying to camouflage his drunkenness, Elliot caught hold of Frankie and followed him through a door marked No Admittance.

"Can I use yours?" he asked, for there had been an interminable line at the men's room. Carrying himself carefully so his friend wouldn't notice his condition, Elliot trailed behind Frankie and into the locker room where the band members changed and were now on a break, finishing up their cigarettes. Elliot called out greetings to those he knew and followed Frankie into the bathroom.

" 'Bout to burst," said Elliot cheerfully, placing his drink on the sink.

"Where's Harriet?" asked Frankie, standing at one of the urinals.

"With the others," lied Elliot, assuming she must be. "Say, I hear Artie Shaw's due in Boston next week. We oughta go hear him." Taking his place next to Frankie, whose steady stream splattered the porcelain noisily, he had trouble with the buttons on his fly. He glanced sideways. *Don't,* he ordered himself but was helpless to obey his own warning as his eyes skittered down lower and he saw what he wanted to see.

"Can't piss for nothin'," he muttered, terrified that Frankie might have noticed, but Frankie's stream continued blissfully.

"Lots of good lookers here tonight, huh, Frankie?" stammered Elliot, his nonchalance fled.

Frankie shook himself dry, and once again Elliot's eyes went there as Frankie stuffed it back in, unaware of anything.

On the way to the sink, Frankie gave Elliot a playful shove, washed his hands, and with a "catch you later, Prince," left.

Alone, Elliot's eyes widened in fright at the close call. Another member of the band came in to take a quick piss, and moments later the music started again, the beat rumbling distantly through the walls.

His heart hammered. Finally able to pee, he finished and turned to the mirror above the sink. Sweat bathed his temples. Graffiti scrawled on the slimy wall looked like worms crawling. He downed half his drink and looked at himself again, the ironic smile shattering as tears filled his eyes.

Unable to locate Marcia, Harriet's attention was diverted by Patrick, who was twirling Joyce Gillespie on the far side of the floor.

"Boyfriend deserted ya?"

Surprised by the voice in her ear, she was even more surprised to find herself propelled onto the floor.

"No, thank you," she said, trying to extricate herself from the whiskey-smelling Neanderthal. She hoped it was a joke. "You are hurting my arm." The band was playing a fast number. "*Please*," she cried, eyes searching for help, but her protests were meaningless in the din as she was hurled about, ricocheting against other bodies, till the stranger pulled her into a packed and tight corner and pressed himself against her. Her eyes widened in surprise; an unreasoning panic took hold of her.

A young Italian janitor entered the now empty locker room, glanced at Elliot, who was sitting on a bench with his head in his hands, and continued on into the bathroom. Elliot followed. The boy spoke little English, but he understood when Elliot went into a stall and held the door open. Fighting a battle with himself, Elliot knelt. A moment later the Italian stared down at Elliot's bobbing head, lips sliding on his cock. The boy gasped, pulled back, and stepped out of the cramped stall. Buttoning his fly and adjusting his apron, he disappeared.

Elliot put his head over the toilet bowl. Recoiling from the stench, he tried to vomit and couldn't. He hoisted himself up and almost passed out. Recovering, he crashed from the stall, gulped the remains of his drink, then fled from the bathroom, through the empty locker room, back down the passageway and out onto the dance floor.

"Elliot—look! Help her!"

The blast of the music staggered him; vaguely he recognized Marcia, but couldn't make any sense of what she was saying. He tried to focus, his eyes following where she pointed. Through the bodies he seemed to see Harriet struggling with someone. Then Patrick blocked his view and someone got hit. The three of them went down, disappearing, as a few girls shrieked, were drowned out by the music, and a circle closed around the mayhem.

"Pat . . . !" Jerry Finneran and Billy Meeghan tried to pull Patrick off the man who was under him. Straddling the outlaw, he smashed his fist clumsily into the man's pasty face, producing a yowl of pain. A chorus of boos greeted Jerry's attempt to end it, for what was Saturday night at the Classic without a good brawl? The bouncers arrived to more boos and broke it up. Patrick threw an arm off him, glaring at any who tried to touch

him, then led a dazed Harriet from the floor as the dancers started up
again, only slightly appeased by the blood oozing from the nose of the
defeated one, who was picked up and carried away.

"We saw it . . . we were coming . . ."

". . . thought it was someone you knew, but . . ."

"Where's Elliot?"

Libby and Graham, Marcia and Frankie all converged.

"He's there." Marcia pointed to where Elliot stood frozen in the same
spot across the floor. The nightmare in his head reflected on his face, his
eyes glinted in fear like a trapped animal's as the gels changed, washing
him in color, from silver to ghastly yellow, to blue and guilty red.

"I'm coming . . . !"

Elliot forced his legs to move. His hands grasped at bodies to keep
from falling. People were laughing.

"Where were you?" Harriet made no attempt to hide her displeasure
at Elliot's terrible state.

"What happened . . . ? Was getting you a drink . . . and . . ."

Reluctantly Patrick released the precious body that had leaned against
him for support. It wasn't, he realized, the stranger whom he'd wanted to
pound into oblivion only moments ago, but this drunken fool who stood
swaying in front of him now.

"You make me sick." Harriet avoided Elliot's hand, which reached
out to her.

"Sorry," he mumbled. They were all looking at him and from one to
the other. "Sorry . . ." he said again, falling to his knees, then to the floor,
pretending to pass out.

"Aren't we gonna go have chop suey with the others?" he asked an
hour later.

"You know we aren't." Harriet was driving because Elliot couldn't.

"Why not?" His tone was plaintive.

"Oh, shut up."

Her sharpness caused Elliot to retreat. The car passed over River
Bridge, reverberating on the metal grillwork, jangling his nerves as the
evening's events flickered relentlessly like the images in a magic lantern.
The dark mills on the river's banks seemed to loom and close in, and he
shut his eyes. "Where *are* we going?"

"I'm taking you home."

"Pull over," he said a moment later. He opened the door and vom-
ited. Patrick, who'd been following, pulled up behind in Gert's Ford.

"Everything all right?" he asked, coming up to the driver's side,
surprising Harriet.

"Do you know how to get the windshield wipers to work?" she asked,
glad he was here. A few drops of rain had begun to fall.

221

"There's our hero," sneered Elliot, lying back against the seat, his face pale in the beams of cars.

"Don't pay any attention to him. He's still drunk."

"Go way . . . Micky Flynn," ordered Elliot as Patrick reached in to the strange dashboard, searching for the correct knob. "This's *my* car. . . ." Elliot stumbled out the door and came around, fists in the air, challenging Patrick.

Harriet got out, too. "Get back in the car, Elliot."

"Go fuck yourself."

Shocked at this profanity, Patrick grabbed for him.

"Don't, Patrick, please," cried Harriet. "He's drunk."

"You should be ashamed of yourself." Coldly Patrick released Elliot, who almost fell.

"Make him go, Harriet," pleaded Elliot, beginning to babble. The rain became steadier. Patrick removed his coat and held it over Harriet's head. "I think you'd better go," she whispered. "I can handle him. Please." She squeezed his arm in thanks.

"Get the hell away!" bellowed Elliot.

"Are you sure?"

"Yes." Harriet turned to Elliot again and told him to get in the car.

"Not till *he* leaves. And don't follow us, either!"

Reluctantly Patrick returned to the Ford. Tires whined on the wet pavement as he pulled out and passed Harriet. A moment later, she and Elliot were off, too.

"I stink," he mumbled.

"Do you mean your smell or your character?" she asked coldly.

"Who gives a shit?"

Angry, Harriet concentrated on driving.

"Let's go away . . . ." Elliot pleaded. "We could be in New York in the morning. We'll stay at the Plaza and get married and—"

"*Shut up.*"

"I hate Jericho. We'll never come back."

"Surely you don't want to marry a middle-class Miss Puritan like me? I wouldn't think of it."

"Is Patrick your new hero? That turd? You know what they say about priests, don't you? Didya ever see one without his altar boy?"

"If you think that's clever, it isn't. You're ridiculous. I don't understand—"

"I told you . . . you never would."

"*Please!* You pride yourself on being an enigma. You're not so complex. You've had a fine education and every opportunity. Life is *not* so difficult."

"One sets a goal and works toward it—is that it?"

"Yes," she retorted, his sarcasm making her angrier. "Exactly. What's

222

wrong with that? You call me an opportunist. Of course I am—and proud of it. You could use a little yourself. What's wrong with you, anyway? How can a man of twenty-two say he has no hope? If you don't want to stay at the mill—then quit. Roll up that window. You'll catch a chill."

"Yes, Mummy."

"Don't think you can joke me out of it, either. You look at me sometimes as if you blamed me for something terrible. Dammit, I felt so close to you tonight! But you managed to spoil it, didn't you? What am I doing here? You warned me, didn't you? It's my own damn fault I didn't listen. I—"

Elliot tried to say something. Harriet cut him off. "*I'm* talking. And I *haven't* finished. Is that what you think of me? Just a poor little nobody who's supposed to be sooo grateful because the 'town catch' swept her up?" She was exhausted and near tears. "Yes—since you asked—Patrick is a gentleman. You're certainly not."

Elliot's face was in his hands. A trolley lumbered toward them from the opposite direction, its beam lighting the interior of the car.

"Do you think Frankie's angry at me? You think he still likes me? Who cares?" he added a moment later. "I want a cigarette." He searched through his pockets. "I want a cigarette!"

"I hate that tone of voice. They're in my purse."

Elliot couldn't work the clasp and got himself into a fury, telling her to pull over, grabbing the wheel when she didn't. The car swerved on the slick pavement. Narrowly missing a parked truck, it came to a lurching, stalled stop in the driveway of the Delight Drive-In Diner. Horns blared at the intruding car blocking the access. "Move it!" Elliot screamed. "Get out! *I'll* drive."

Harriet did as she was told, grabbing her purse and exiting the car, slamming the door. Furious, she walked through the circle of cars parked around the restaurant like Conestoga wagons and went in. Inside, the carhops peered out, wondering if the rain would stop.

" '. . . Don't be snooty . . . find yourself a sweet patootie,' " blared the jukebox as Harriet sat at the counter. Trembling with rage, she managed to order a cup of coffee and light a cigarette.

A few minutes later, Elliot came in and sat—smiling as if nothing had happened—on the opposite side of the U-shaped counter. She saw people stare and whisper, for he looked a total mess. He tried to get her attention, and she lowered her head in embarrassment as the looks and talk were now directed at her, too. Once she had reveled with Marcia about the gossip that linked her with Elliot, but it wasn't fun any more. Knowing he had it in him to cause a scene, she got up and went into the ladies' room and stayed there for fifteen minutes. When she came out, he was gone.

It was close to one A.M. and the last trolley had gone by. The rain had turned to a light drizzle. She had no choice but to walk home, a little over

223

a mile and a half, but the walk would do her good, clear her head and get her thoughts in order. But no matter how she tried to ward it off, a depression sank her down. Elliot's behavior only seemed to confirm her generally low opinion of men as selfish and egotistical creatures, who, if you loved them, would only drain you of your energies and break your heart. Well, she wouldn't capitulate—neither to Elliot, *nor* Patrick. How could she have forgotten her maxim that she wasn't going to allow a man to get to her? Hadn't she learned it long ago, hadn't Franklin taught her that lesson on a snowy day in the Salem Hotel? They were needy cases, all of them, these men who vied for her attention. Let them all take a flying leap into oblivion.

Angry, Harriet kicked at wet leaves as she walked. Her coat was still in Elliot's car, and she shivered slightly, but a brisk pace soon warmed her. Determined to make the best of things, she told herself that tomorrow was another day; she had her work on the paper. If Patrick continued to press her, she would quit and find a way to return to New York. She would start afresh.

Ten minutes later she saw the La Salle pulled over to the side of the road. Her first impulse was to cross the street and avoid it, but something warned her to check on Elliot.

Snoring, he lay in a cramped position on the front seat like a rumpled, open-mouthed angel of Giotto's in Letty's book of Old Masters. Harriet didn't know what to do. Sadness overtook her, for it was finished between them. She would share her spirit and joy with him no longer; she would give up trying to make a dent in that bitter armor in which he clothed himself. It was over, and he had seen to it.

Miserable and shivering again, she tried to reach in the window and retrieve her coat. Elliot's eyes opened. Neither of them spoke; he got out of the car.

"I told him . . ." she heard him say, talking of his father, "when I graduated from Princeton, that I didn't want to . . . to come back here. But he insisted, so I— Oh, God! Oh, God, I wish I hadn't come back. I wish to God I never had!"

Abruptly he walked away, crossing over the road and disappearing down a banking on the other side.

"Elliot . . . !" she called and went over. She couldn't see him. Calling his name again, she started down the dirt roadway of a sand and gravel company, past mountains of sand rising on either side of her, through parked dump trucks and under a conveyor belt that led to a great crane with a light or two on its top. Close by, she could see the river moving blackly.

"*Elliot . . . !*"

"Last one in's a rotten egg!" Naked, he dashed out from behind a truck and ran into the water, then out again. "It's freezing!" He went in again, splashing water over himself. "I needed a bath, didn't I?" he hol-

224

lered. "Shit! It's colder than a witch's tit!" He ran out of the water toward her. "Ever seen one?" he grinned, teeth chattering. "Give me your coat. Quick." She did, and he flung it over his shoulders, trying to wrap it around himself. "Hold me, for God's sake, hold me! I'm catching pneumonia." He put his arms around her and his whole body was shuddering. "C'mon," he said, trying to kiss her. "I've found a cozy spot."

"Put your clothes on."

"I will. I will. Over there . . ."

He led her back behind a truck. Her shoes sank into the wet sand. Quickly he wrapped his arms around her again as his mouth sought hers.

"Please," he pleaded. "I'm freezing."

"Then get dressed." Elliot's hands were on her, his body shaking. "Don't," she said as he tried to undo the buttons on her back.

"Let me . . . let me . . ." One of his hands had pulled her dress and slip up and was trying to pull down her panties, while the other arm held her firmly against him. Their eyes met for an instant. "*Please*," he cried. It was Frankie he seemed to see. He closed his eyes and tried to kiss him.

Harriet struggled to break away as Elliot pulled her down with him. "I'll marry you!" he pleaded. Her hands slipped on his wet flesh as she tried to get away from him.

"I will! Don't worry . . . I'll make sure . . . I love you . . . I'll marry you, kiddo—"

Outrage gave her the strength to shove him away and she scrambled up, pulling her coat from him as she did.

"You bastard!"

"*Cunt!* I said I'd marry you! Why didn't you listen? Isn't that what you're holding out for?"

His body began to shake uncontrollably and he started to cry. "*Harriet!*" he screamed as she ran from him.

11 They didn't look like fascists. But then again, what did fascists look like?

Harriet hurried along with the mob headed for the Coughlin rally at Leveret Stadium. October 22, a Saturday, and cars choked the roads. Two weeks before the national election, and the faithful came from as far west as Albany. On the Hartford Pike from Connecticut, too, from Worcester and Springfield under gray morning skies that cleared to bright and clear blue as the hour approached.

From north and south, from Manchester, Lowell, from Haverhill and Boston, the cars snaked along Route 28 through hills of glorious fall foliage, bypassing Jericho, heading on down into the Merrimack Valley, filling the parking lots of the stadium.

They arrived on trains, in trolleys, on buses and on foot. The families were dressed in their Sunday best, the children scrubbed and eager. They clutched American flags and wore Union Party buttons pinned to their coats.

Blue collar and starched, too, Catholic and non-Catholic, former Republicans and Democrats, laborers and displaced intellectuals, the worried and the frightened, the frustrated, the discontent, and the belligerent, the poor—seeking answers and a cure and a slice of the pie. For they'd had enough, had lived through seven years of grinding depression and were sick of hard times.

Under the bunting they thronged past the peanut vendors and balloon sellers and hawkers selling Coughlin's newspaper: "Get your *Social Justice* here! Make a pledge to the Father!"

They'd come to see *him*. They'd come to hear him in person—the voice on the radio, the mellifluous voice they'd heard these past years, the spellbinding orator they and thirty million others had tuned in to on Sundays, forsaking Jack Benny, mesmerized as they sat by their radios. On Mondays they'd gone to the post office and sent him their quarters. Dollars, if they could afford to, but there wasn't a risk, was there? Hadn't he promised them they'd have their contribution back a hundred fold? A decent living annual wage, that's what he'd told them they'd have. Promised them that, he had.

"We're the people—that's who we are!" They clapped and nodded at the impromptu speakers, who climbed on boxes and shoulders to greet them as they filed into the stadium.

Yessir. Howdee. Well now . . . !

They tipped their hats and waved and smiled at one another, for they knew who they were. And Father Charles E. Coughlin, God bless'm, was their leader. He'd given them their candidates and formed their Union Party. Together, they would defeat the dictator Roosevelt, the liar Roosevelt, who had failed and betrayed them. They would defeat him and elect "Liberty Bill" Lemke and Michael C. O'Brien. They would deliver the nine million votes needed, but failing that—they'd elect so many congressmen that Franklin Double-Crossing Roosevelt would be powerless. Justice would triumph. The country would belong to them again. They'd take it back from the Jew bankers and the Bolsheviks and the bankers' servants, the politicians. The Kingdom of Heaven would be restored right here in America just as the Father said it would be. They'd be reborn.

Reborn.

Hadn't they toiled by the sweat of their brows to make America the great nation it was? Only to have Hoover destroy it? And the Great Betrayer promise to give it back? Well, they'd show that son of a bitch! Last week the Father had said that bullets might be necessary. If so—they'd have the courage to stand up and be counted!

Yessir!

Through the crowd Harriet caught a glimpse of Alice and her friends, who were picketing against Coughlin. What with the throngs of people, she was late. She searched for Patrick as a cheer arose from inside the stadium. Then her attention was caught by a skywriting plane:

WELCOME, FATHER COUGH—

Another cheer rose up. Had the priest already got here? she asked one of the many policemen and was told he hadn't. She looked about for Patrick again, then headed for Alice.

"What a mob!" She had to shout to make herself heard.

"It's not a picnic, Harriet," replied Alice, marching in a circle with the YCL and Young Socialist Club of Leveret, placards and signs on high. Harriet took out her notebook and began to ask questions of the marchers. Many of them she recognized from the night of Wayne's going-away party.

"Can the Union Party really defeat the President?" she asked Steve Bobeck, who'd delivered the fiery speech that night.

"They can get enough votes to throw it to the Republicans and Landon."

"Coughlin's got candidates running in every congressional district, too."

"Reds!" screamed a scarlet-faced angry man, one of several who were baiting the demonstrators.

"Fascists!" several of the group yelled back. Bobeck told them to keep quiet. "We're not here to shout," he reminded them. "Or provoke anything, either."

A dozen policemen on horseback interjected themselves between the pickets and the immediate crowd, which was muttering and calling out more names.

"Alice, come with me. I don't like the look of this." Harriet saw something in the eyes of the crowd that sent shivers through her—a deadness behind the fevered happiness, a desperation that made her anxious. Sirens sounded in the distance. Band music could be heard from inside the stadium, followed by another roar, which deafened the brilliant afternoon.

"I have to find Patrick. Alice, please come!"

Harriet was propelled away from her sister as the crowd surged toward the stadium entrances and the sirens grew louder. She found herself herded aside by other police, their arms locked together, keeping everyone out of the way of the approaching motorcade. The Leveret police were ready for trouble. As the bitter and dirty campaign neared its final reckoning, there had been incidents, growing in intensity and violence, at several recent Coughlin rallies. Two bomb threats had been called in this morning.

Already inside the stadium, the Flynns were ensconced in the O'Brien box on the fifty-yard line. Michael O'Brien would be arriving with Coughlin, but Timothy was seated with Rose, along with Joe, Dennis and Teresa's husband, Matt.

Hawkers worked the aisles, pitching popcorn, Crackerjacks and copies of Father Coughlin's newspaper. Gert preened and greeted friends while Patrick scanned the aisles for Harriet.

"*Mother.*" Rose nudged Gert, her attention diverted from unwrapping a hard candy for Timothy by the arrival in an adjacent box of Monsignor O'Malley and entourage.

"Monsignor . . ." beamed Gert, rising and greeting him. "Isn't it a grand turnout?" she added, sweeping her hand toward the crowd as if she'd had a hand in the ten thousand herself.

Outside, the sirens wailed at a fever pitch as the priest's motorcade came into view and cheers rang out from the latecomers.

Prevented from moving, Harriet stood on tiptoe, trying to see over heads. Past the backs of policemen, she caught the snatch of white of a clerical collar and a flash of sun glinting off spectacles. So this was the famous Father Coughlin. Short and rather unprepossessing was her immediate verdict—the size of him determined by contrast with the large and burly police. Michael O'Brien, she gathered, was the silver-haired, lumpish man who waved to the crowd along with Congressman Lemke, whom she recognized from the newsreels.

Around her, the crowd, packed closely by the vigilant police (all of whom, she noted, were cheering the priest), broke into a frenzy of applause and "God bless you, Father's." She cringed as her head was knocked from behind, hat sent askew, by a child using her for support as he climbed upon his father's shoulders to get a better look.

Down further, the chanting of the demonstrators rang out as Coughlin raised a hand. Then he disappeared, hidden in a phalanx of blue coats, moving slowly through the packed and jostling crowd toward the entrance.

At first, Harriet thought it was a stone that traced an arc through the air—then it splattered against a cop. Another egg followed. Then a tomato. The missiles rained down upon the priest and his armada. Who was doing the throwing? Harriet craned her neck. Alice's group was still marching in a circle, looking confused themselves. As rotten fruit and eggs catapulted down, a gasp of outrage shook the crowd. Later, Harriet recalled a hush that fell, an eerie stillness like the eye of a hurricane.

"Get the Reds . . . they did it!" Like a beast awakening, the crowd grew angry, surging against the policemen's backs to get at the demonstrators. Jostled into fear, Harriet was pushed forward by those behind her.

"Bastards!"

"Stone 'em back!"

"Stone the Russkies!"

More eggs fell into the crowd. A woman beside Harriet screamed as one exploded on her shoulder, splattering Harriet, too. The scream was drowned out by a tumultuous roar of ten thousand as Coughlin entered the stadium.

The dam of blue that held back the furious crowd burst, only to be repulsed by the mounted police on the other side. Harriet saw a friend of Alice's caught in a fight with someone. Clubs raised by the policemen fell indiscriminately now upon pro and anti-Coughlinites, as the crowd, like crazed ants in a smashed anthill, turned upon itself.

"It's not us—it's them!" shouted someone as the people near Harriet were herded into line again by the re-forming police. An angry outcry of agreement arose. Harriet saw Alice and tried to head in her direction as the mounted police, goaded on by the crowd, turned on the demonstrators with raised nightsticks.

"Alice . . . !" she screamed, terrified, as the crowd in uncontrollable fury rushed to join the police, who were chasing the demonstrators past the hot dog vendors, whose carts were overturned. A pot of mustard careened through the air, its contents staining the sky in a mad yellow streak as Harriet screamed again and was knocked down from behind.

• • •

229

Coughlin gripped the microphone. His other hand, clenched in a fist, made circles in the air.

". . . IF YOU APPROVE OF WHAT I'M SAYING, I WANT TO HEAR IT!" The response was wild. "IF YOU AGREE, STAND UP!" Ten thousand did as they were told.

Coughlin played them like an organ. He stoked and lashed and flattered and scared and comforted. He rose on his toes. In the sky the plane wrote his name again.

No one noticed Alice, the disheveled young woman with a lens missing from the frame of her glasses as she searched the boxes looking for Patrick, who stared mesmerized and in shock as the priest ripped off his black coat, then tore his Roman collar from his neck in a fury:

"AS I WAS INSTRUMENTAL IN REMOVING HERBERT HOOVER FROM THE WHITE HOUSE, SO HELP ME GOD, I WILL BE INSTRUMENTAL NOW IN . . ."

"Who's that?" Rose noticed Alice arguing with a policeman, gesticulating, pointing toward the box. Timothy brushed popcorn from his lap.

". . . IN TAKING A COMMUNIST FROM THE CHAIR ONCE OCCUPIED BY GEORGE WASHINGTON . . . !" The crowd was on its feet again. Reporters from the wire services dashed to the phones. Never had the priest gone this far.

"Patrick . . . !" Alice ducked past the policeman and came running down the steps. She called Patrick's name again, causing all the Flynns to look up. Gert gave Alice a hard-eyed stare. Alice's breath came in gasps. "I got . . . away . . . but . . ."

"I can't hear you," shouted Patrick.

"*Harriet . . . they arrested Harriet!*"

Harriet tried to tuck the ripped shoulder of her dress under her bra strap. Her knees were skinned, her elbow caked with dried blood. She had a gash on her cheekbone, which was slowly turning to reddish blue. "I'm a *reporter*," she insisted for the umpteenth time, but no one would listen.

"You and your kind oughta be locked up for good—assaultin' the Father like that," was only one of the responses she got. Behind her in the cell at the Leveret police station, the moans of the wounded rose. As another group of demonstrators was shoved into the cell, she tried again. "*Jericho Irish Spectator*," she insisted, frustration building into anger. "*Irish!!!*" she repeated but was ignored. "My purse was lost so I can't prove who I am. Don't I have a constitutional right to make a phone call?" Nor would they give her any information about Alice. Harriet had no idea if her sister had been arrested or was hurt.

Others were worse off, and she turned her attention to them. A friend of Alice's named Danny was sitting next to her on the floor of the crowded cell. Fresh blood seaped through the undershirt wrapped around his head.

She could tell he was in shock. "We need a doctor," she called as another cop passed by, keys rattling. "Did you hear me?" she demanded, reaching through the bars to try and grab him. He stared at her contemptuously. "Shoulda thought of that, sister, before you . . ."

By the time Harriet was taken to the front of the police station two hours later, her anger had built to a cold-eyed fury.

"Alice!" she called to her sister, who was waiting with Patrick in the teeming anteroom. "Are you all right?"

"I'm fine, considering. Is Steve here? How is he? You don't look so hot yourself."

"It's a madhouse back there. I didn't see him."

"That's a nasty bruise on your cheek."

Stunned by Harriet's condition, Patrick could only stare dumbfounded at her. Grim-faced, he turned to the desk sergeant, confirming her identity in a level and controlled voice that camouflaged a raging desire to grab the fat-ass by the throat. Turning back to Harriet, he removed his jacket and attempted to put it around her naked shoulder.

"No," she said, rebuffing him coolly—as if somehow it was all his fault. She knew it wasn't, but at the moment, it seemed it was.

Patrick wet his handkerchief at the bubbler and attempted to use it on her skinned elbow. She waved him aside and turned, eyes blazing, to the sergeant. "Sign this," he said.

"I'll sign it when I'm good and ready. I told you I was a reporter. I told them in there, too. No one paid any attention. I asked for a doctor and *still* no one's come."

"C'mon," said Patrick, wanting to get out of the place.

"I haven't finished." Harriet turned again to the sergeant, who'd had a bad afternoon himself. "Don't think I'm not going to report all this!"

"Sorry, miss. Mistakes get made."

"Oh? It's 'miss' now. But it wasn't 'miss' an hour back."

"Let's go."

"Go yourself—if you're in such a hurry," she snapped at Patrick. Alice, meanwhile, was trying to get word about her friends back in the cells. "Coughlin's shock troops," she muttered as several policemen passed by.

"And," continued Harriet to the sergeant, "don't think I'm not going to report about what happened out at the stadium. I saw it. You people were on horses and had nightsticks. Do you call that fair? I saw what happened. And I'm not leaving," she added, "until I make sure a doctor's coming. There are people bleeding back there."

"OK, miss. We've got someone on the way."

"I'll wait," she replied, still not satisfied. "And I'd like a list of the prisoners. Why weren't we allowed to make a call? They have friends and relatives who'll need to be notified."

231

"We're getting to it, miss. We'll see to it."

A half hour later, an ambulance pulled up out front, and several doctors passed through to the cells. Shortly afterward, Danny was brought out on a stretcher. His glazed eyes sought Harriet's, and he gave her a thumbs-up sign of victory. There wasn't much else she could do. Holding the torn part of her dress against her shoulder, she left the station as late sunlight filtered through the cranberry-colored maples and rusty oaks on the Leveret Common. It seemed unreal.

"Well?" Harriet demanded, turning to Patrick. She was a wave of energy that could have toppled the eagle on the top of the courthouse. "Have you seen enough? Do you see what we've been trying to tell you?"

"*Seig Heil,*" muttered Alice, turning and giving the fascist salute to the station.

The three of them took the trolley. Traffic on River Bridge was impossible. Upstream, Leveret Bridge over the falls was jammed bumper to bumper with cars from the rally, headed north. They'd sung "God Bless America." Now they were headed home.

Harriet and Alice sat together, attracting stares and whispers because of their bedraggled state. The bruises, broken glasses, dried blood and ripped clothing were badges of their courage, talismans of the battlefield, which they wore proudly like two heroines. Harriet, being Harriet, indulged in this fantasy more than Alice. For now that it was over, the horror past, and she was safely on her way home, she couldn't help her excitement which boiled even higher. She saw herself as a survivor—an important figure who'd been caught up in the maelstrom—a veteran with a story to tell. Incandescent, she talked nonstop, reliving the afternoon, comparing atrocities with Alice.

"Here's what we have to do," she exclaimed, interrupting herself and turning to Patrick. "We'll come out against that priest of yours and his flunkies. We'll expose him for what he is, and I'll tell what *really* happened outside the stadium . . . and in the jail, too—an eyewitness account. What a story! I tell you—it's gold! A bang-up exposé of the whole kit and caboodle—Coughlin, O'Brien and Lemke *and* the Leveret Police Department. And we'll do what we should have done all along. We'll come out for Roosevelt. You know we have to. We *must*." She looked to Alice for approval, then turned to Patrick again. "Are you listening?"

Wishing he weren't, Patrick nodded. Dazed by the afternoon's events, his feelings and thoughts in a whirlwind, he stared out the window, then at his lap, finally to the floor, which was littered with dried tangerine peels. Out of the corner of an eye he saw Harriet wince in pain as the trolley jolted her elbow. He felt it more than she did. "You know I can't do what you're asking," he said. "I know that you're upset," he added hastily, not looking at her. "And you've a right, but . . . you know I can't do that."

"*What?*"

"Calm down, Harriet," he pleaded.

"Did you hear him?" She turned from Patrick to Alice and back again. "Then what *are* we going to do—if you don't mind my asking?"

Heads turned toward the threesome. Patrick felt eyes upon him. What had he done, they asked, for the girl with the bruises to be so incensed at him? "I *am* doing something. I'm not at the reception, am I? We were supposed to interview them. We're not there, are we?"

"You call that doing something?"

"Let him finish," said Alice.

"You know why I can't come out for Roosevelt or the rest of it, either."

"Fine," snapped Harriet. "If you can't, there's others who can. I'll give the story to the *Eagle*. Don't think they won't have the guts to print it, because they will!" Frustrated tears glistened in her eyes.

Alice took Harriet's hand. "We've all had a rough day."

"Tell him he doesn't have a leg to stand on, Alice. Tell him."

"He knows he doesn't." Alice loaned Harriet a hankie. Patrick put his head in his hands. If only *he'd* been there instead of her! If only the cops had knocked him down, trampled and bloodied him instead of her. He'd have gotten his licks in. Pounded the bastards, maimed the bastards.

"Calling the President a communist," muttered Harriet. "Coughlin's a lunatic. Do *you* think Roosevelt's a communist?" she asked Patrick.

"You know I don't." Only a few days ago he'd gone with the sisters into Boston to hear the President. Half a million were spread out on the Common, and the roar from the crowd had been louder but very different from this afternoon, as Roosevelt said, "You look better than you did four years ago. . . ." People had wept when he left, turning to wave, steadying himself on his braces, and Patrick had been one of them.

"Can we all agree on one thing?" asked Alice. "Coughlin is a menace. Can we?"

"No," Harriet interjected. "He won't. Wayne told him. You have, and I have, too. Today he's seen for himself, and all he wants to do is bury his head in the sand. You watch, he'll tell us it'll all be over in a couple of weeks, so we should sit tight and—"

"I'd like to hear Patrick."

The trolley let out a shriek as steel ground against steel on a curve. The sound seemed amplified in Patrick's head, mixed with the roar from the stadium. Seen? Yes, he had seen. Now it rose before his eyes again as the trolley jolted and jarred him—the image of the priest, the image seared into Patrick's soul—Coughlin tearing his collar from himself in a frenzy, face purple with venom. A priest! Ten thousand of them screaming. Had

233

the Church screamed, too, in that moment of tearing—the Church torn apart, as he had been? Yes, he had seen.

He stared at Harriet. Chasms seemed to open on all sides. "I admit," he began, "that I went along with Coughlin because he didn't seem— I never thought the Union Party had a chance. But I didn't have much choice, as you know. Rose is practically engaged to Timothy, and my mother—"

"His mother!" snapped Harriet. "His mother sets civilization back a hundred years every time she opens her mouth!"

"Harriet, be still."

"But he's pussyfooting around. He's—"

"No. I'm not. Do you want to hear what I have to say? Or are you satisfied to indict me? It's easy to condemn."

"Go on."

"A few days ago I got a letter from my adviser in Washington, Father Morelli. I've been sending him the paper. He asked me why I was supporting Coughlin and"—he looked at Alice—"he said some of the same things that Wayne told me—that Coughlin was a danger to the country. But also that he was dangerous to the Church."

"Why didn't you tell me that?" demanded Harriet.

"Because I didn't want to admit it. I didn't want to have to face it, maybe. For all the reasons I've just mentioned. I was wrong."

"So . . . ?"

"But that doesn't mean I can go off half-cocked and do what you want. I have to take my family into consideration and—"

"His precious family," muttered Harriet. "This is a *moral* issue we're faced with here and—"

"A little less righteousness would be helpful," suggested Alice. "You wouldn't recognize a moral issue if it fell on you."

"That's unfair! Those fat cats," Harried continued, "—why should they be allowed to get away with it? I saw O'Brien. Vulgarians. Every last one of them. It makes me sick. The Catholic Church is beginning to make me sick, too."

Patrick contained his anger. "I need time to see what I can do."

"Check it out with your mother by all means."

"Harriet," said Alice, "a little less name calling would be helpful. 'Fat cats' indeed! You've had your eyes on the fat cats ever since you opened them."

"*Oh?*"

"You're the protégé of a fat cat—remember? Your patron?"

"What has that got to do with what we're discussing?"

"Let me put it this way. If Phelps had been speaking today—would you be in such a big rush to expose *him?*"

"But what does Mr. Phelps—?"

"Because they're the same. Coughlin *and* Phelps. Cut from the same cloth. And what about Father? Your own father?"

"He's your father, too!"

"I didn't say he wasn't. All I'm saying is—if you're going to get so high and mighty, I'd think twice. You can't be selective about the enemy."

"That's ridiculous."

"Is it? I see little difference between you cozying up to Abraham Phelps. Not to mention Elliot . . ."

Fresh tears welled in Harriet's eyes at the mention of his name. Only a few minutes ago, the trolley had passed the sand and gravel pit beside the river, and last Saturday night came rushing painfully back. She turned angrily to Alice. "You're jealous of my relationship with the Phelps, aren't you? And with Father, too! Admit it!"

Immediately ashamed, she wished she could apologize, but couldn't seem to. "And how," she continued, "can you defend Patrick, when it was you and Wayne who warned us about Coughlin in the first place? Explain *that* to me!" That Alice—who'd always accused her of being frivolous— didn't understand her now, was more than Harriet could bear. "And furthermore, since you seem so interested, I haven't seen Elliot for a week! I've broken it off. Are you satisfied?"

Patrick felt a surge of joy that was tempered by a glance from Harriet, whose expression read: *You* won't be taking his place.

There was a strained silence among the three of them. Alice looked at Patrick and felt a kinship. Even if *The Spectator* had taken a position she couldn't stomach, she knew he was caring and decent. His evident struggle with his conscience was worthy of her respect. "He's in a spot," she volunteered. Patrick looked at her gratefully, and Harriet shook her head.

"I don't think I'm going to be able to work for you any longer unless we tell the truth."

"I'm sorry you feel that way."

"I'm afraid I do."

"Oh, Harriet . . ." cautioned Alice, "don't throw the baby out with the bath water." Didn't she know that Patrick was worth ten of Elliot Phelps any day of the week? "Isn't there some kind of compromise possible?" But no one had any answers.

The trolley jarred to a halt in Jerusalem and half emptied out. A few young men kicked at piles of yellow and tangerine leaves with a glee that made Alice suddenly sad, for the boys' innocence was something she'd lost and would never find again. Removing her glasses, a spasm of fear caught her as she realized she might have miscarried today. Wouldn't it have been a merciful and silent way out of her predicament? she asked herself and was immediately plagued with guilt at her cowardice. She wanted the baby. Last week, unable to keep it to herself any longer, she'd written to Wayne and told him she was pregnant. Ashamed she was so soft, and disliking

235

herself for having retreated from her earlier decision, she'd assured him she didn't expect him to return. It was a lie. She wanted him out of danger. She needed him home.

"Awww, Rosie . . . please talk to me." Timothy O'Brien's pudgy hands gripped the steering wheel as he drove Rose home from the gala reception held after the rally for the bigwigs in the Knights of Columbus Hall in Leveret.

Rose crossed her legs with a whisper of satin and silk which was audible beneath the hum of the motor. Thrusting out her lower lip in a sultry pout, brilliant eyes flashing, she tossed her head and shifted her body so that all the parts moved in tandem like a beautifully oiled and perfect machine. This bit of voluptuousness completed, she folded her hands piously in her lap. Should she bring out her rosary beads? She was furious with him!

Thoroughly unsuited for such an action, Timothy tried to go on the offensive. "How do you think it made me look?" he asked petulantly, voice in its familiar whine. "I'm the one arranged for Patrick to interview them. Why didn't he show up? Couldn't have taken that long to get Harriet out of jail. It's nine o'clock."

"Don't try and change the subject, Timothy."

"Rosie . . ." Timothy sweated and pleaded. "Aren't you goin' to forgive your Timmy who loves ya so?"

"You're not my 'Timmy' any more," Rose responded in a throaty voice that made him squirm. "No," she continued, adding a sigh, "—not any more. Not after what happened."

"I said I was sorry. What d'ya want me to do? To make it better . . . Rosie?"

They both knew what he was supposed to do. For months now.

"I thought those patty shells at dinner were a little dry, didn't you? You'd think they would have had fresh patty shells, wouldn't you?" Rose was using her elocution voice now.

"Awwww, Rosie . . . please. Does your ankle still hurt?"

As always, Rose had been a great success at the reception. Laity and clergy alike had been forced to halt in mid-sentence when she made her appearance (late—she always managed to be a little late) in the receiving line. Male eyes filmed slightly with desire as she took her place next to Timothy with Bishop Murphy of Lowell on her left, Father Coughlin two places down, and Michael O'Brien on the other side of his son. Groins tingled. Rose even managed to make one or two appropriate comments and was lucky enough to avoid those subjects that might reveal her stupider side. But even if revealed, it wouldn't have mattered.

After the creamed chicken and peas dinner at which she'd sat at the table next to the head table, she got up to go to the ladies' room. As her black satin body rose like a heavy hot moon over the littered terrain of the table, she caught her heel and faltered, slightly twisting her ankle.

"Ohhhh . . ." she cried like a wounded bird. Soon there was a tightly packed circle about her. Her leg was lifted by any number of willing hands, her ankle examined by not one but two willing doctors. No damage done was the consensus.

Rose fluttered her lashes, cooed bitty words, blushed, winced when the ankle was touched and uttered small cries. In actuality, she felt little pain. But how could she resist pretending to worse when a bishop, a congressman, and Father Coughlin himself were in various states of concern, kneeling and supplication?

Later, Timothy had knelt, too. After holding on to his arm and hobbling the full distance of the hall (her hat of shimmering upswept fronds making her seem a foot taller than he), she went to the ladies' room, fixed her face, and then allowed Timothy to ease her into a soft sofa in the cloakroom to rest before making the journey back through the twenty-five tables for dessert.

"Darlin' . . ." Timothy had got down on his knees with a certain amount of effort, huffing and puffing. "Let me see."

"It's all right, Timmy," she said, her voice a dying fall. He picked up the precious foot, undid the ankle strap and massaged the ankle. Perspiring badly, he kissed it, leaving a bit of wetness on her silk stocking. Little fingers moved up the underside of her calf.

"Timothy!" she warned, for she had no intention of letting him play 'doctor.'

"Just fer the circulation, Rosie," he stammered, bending lower, belly nearly brushing the carpet—a precarious state of balance as one hand held her slightly uplifted leg and the other massaged her calf with burning fingers.

Then, like a squirrel darting for its nest, Timothy's hand shot up under her dress in a surprisingly fast movement for one so usually slow. A finger managed to probe through her panties to the sacred spot for the barest hairbreadth of a split second. Then it was caught in a vise as Rose tightened her thighs, raised her other leg, and—with a shove—sent him sprawling.

The Packard turned right on Main and went up Essex.

"Mother's already here," said Rose, noticing the porch light. Once again, Timothy pleaded forgiveness, but Rose continued the silent treatment. After the offense committed against her dignity, womanhood and the Virgin Mary, she'd been so upset as to almost tell Timothy she wouldn't be seeing him again. Instinct had prevailed, however, and she realized she had a trump card. An actual game of bridge would have had

237

her hopelessly confused from the deal on, but engendering Suffering and Guilt, that was another story. Having trained at Gert's knee, she was adept at both. Not only would she heap those coals upon Timothy, she would threaten him with the loss of her. She knew what he was after. But the piper, he'd *have* to learn, would *have* to be paid. Mightn't this course of action be just the ticket to tip the scales and bring him to the all-important moment? Mightn't it be the ploy to force him to overcome his own trepidation, not to mention his father's objections and *ask*? "Oh, Timmy," she would coo after a moment's demure hesitation, "it's taken me so by surprise, but . . . yes . . . *oh, yes* . . . *dearest!*" Or a hundred other variations she'd learned at the movies. Then a tear or two. A tear of joy that her apple-honeyed-moneyed-dumpling darling was finally *hers*!

"What would you say if someone did such a thing to one of your sisters?"

"I know," he groaned, "I'm awful. I know I'm awful, Rosie."

"I don't think I want you to call me Rosie any more, either."

Timothy's beady eyes glimmered helplessly in the light from the street lamp. He took out his handkerchief and mopped every inch of face and neck. His tiny balls ached. "Ya know how crazy I am about ya, darlin'. You're driven me dizzy. Ya know how much I love ya, and it breaks my heart when you're cross with me."

"I don't call that love." She took out a hankie and dabbed at her eyes. "I think I'll retire. Yes. I'm rather fatigued."

Rose waited as Timothy lumbered miserably out of his side and came around to hers.

What are they standin' there for? wondered Gert, spying through a slit in the venetians.

"Am I still invited fer dinner tomorrow?" Timothy whined.

"I don't think so."

"Rosie . . . I mean, Rose . . ."

"Good night," she said, the way her idol, Carole Lombard, said it. Sort of airy.

"Don't I get a kiss?"

Rose sighed, wiggled a bit, and adjusted her fur about her shoulders.

"I swear," said Timothy, lapsing into a slight stutter, "—on m-m-m-my sainted m-m-m-mother's grave"—he crossed himself—"that it'll n-n-never happen again."

"No. It won't."

Rose walked away from him with the slightest hint of a limp. Continents moved beneath the fabric, hips shifted as she dangled it before Timothy's mesmerized and famished eyes. Unconsciously he put the finger that had earlier hit the spot into his mouth. He thought he could taste it. Like lilies.

"*Rosie.*"

She turned on the first step, regarding him exasperatedly through lowered lashes. The street lamp made her hair shine like wet ink. Timothy moved to her, helpless not to stare at her tits, which were on the same level as his eyes.

"Ya . . . know . . . what I . . . want . . . Rosie?"

"What?" she asked sharply.

"Not . . . what . . . I didn't mean . . . what I meant . . ."

Gert tried to hear. Why in hell hadn't she left the front door open a crack? She could see the fathead wringing his hands, a silly-assed smile on his moon face. Gert had to pee, but she had no intention of leaving and stood riveted, nose pressing so tightly against the metal of the blinds, she was getting a crease in the flesh.

". . . was . . . you and . . . me . . . Rosie . . . awww." Still, Timothy couldn't bring himself. He did the next best thing, however. "I thought," he stammered, "if . . . if I'm still invited . . . tomorrow . . . that I might bring . . . Dad . . . to dinner. Wouldn't ya . . . like that?"

Time stopped. Rose looked deep into Timothy's eyes. Even Gert, who couldn't hear, sensed something momentous happening out on the front stoop.

"Why would you want to do that, Timmy?" cooed Rose in a girlish yet throaty whisper. Inwardly she trembled. Bringing his father! A shiver passed through her, starting in her toes and spreading upward. But could he manage it? She reached out and straightened his tie. "He's never been here, has he?"

Timothy sensed the reproach. "Not that I haven't . . . wanted to bring him, Rosie. You know how he is."

Tears glistened. "He doesn't think . . . I'm good enough for you, Timmy."

"Nawwww, Rosie . . ."

"Yes, it's true. Mother asked him to dinner, and he said he was busy. You know she's asked him before, too."

"I'll see to it, Rose. Don't cry, darlin'."

"Well . . . if you can . . . wouldn't it be nice. . . ?" She laid a hand on his shoulder. With the other, she diddled the buttons on his vested paunch. It was time she put him on a diet. "But if you can't . . . I'll understand . . . but maybe I'll have to be alone for a while because—"

"I'll bring him."

"I know you'll try." Timothy nodded eagerly. Rose took his face in her hands and kissed him full on the lips, a kiss that promised everything, *if*— Then she brought his head tenderly to her bosom like Jean Harlow did to Clark Gable.

Bladder pressing, Gert grabbed onto the radio console for support, shocked by this intimacy occurring in full view out front. Yet at the same time, what if it meant—? Gert crossed herself.

239

Timothy's arms jerked spasmodically at his sides, hands clenched like a baby's fists. Opening and closing them, the fingers waggling.

"Two o'clock," said Rose, releasing him. He nearly fell. "Don't be late."

12 "Where is he?" demanded Gert to Teresa the next day. The O'Briens had arrived promptly at two and were in the living room drinking sweet Manhattan cocktails and munching cheese-filled celery stalks. Patrick was nowhere to be seen.

"He'll be here, don't worry," soothed Teresa, wondering herself at Patrick's absence. The two women scurried about the hot kitchen. Agitated *in extremis*, Gert shot a look at the clock once again. "He'd better," she muttered, banging the oven door shut after checking the standing rib roast that Teresa, thanks be to God, had in her icebox and loaned for this special occasion. It had been too late for Gert to do any shopping last night.

"Now what can I do next. . . ?" Teresa knew what a difficult day this was for her sister. Not only was Michael O'Brien finally come to dinner, but it was October 23—a day engraved in all their hearts and especially in Gert's—a day engraved in gilt letters fading now on the Mass cards consigned to a shoe box; *that* day, that special October 23 when the Reverend Patrick Flynn was to have celebrated his inaugural Mass across the street at St. Mary's, with three hundred in attendance.

"Timmy hungry," cooed Rose in the living room where she sat between the O'Briens, alternately feeding Timothy tidbits of celery as if he were a pet, while turning the pages of her scrapbook for his father. Possessed of a calm that surpassethed all understanding, Rose noticed that Timothy was more nervous than usual. Perspiring freely, his hands reached out to grab assorted hors d'oeuvres from the coffee table. She patted his knee.

"And here," she continued, wiggling slightly at a fantasy itch that caused a thigh to brush against the elder O'Brien, "—here I am with Governor Curley and Mother."

"The Governor's an old pal of mine," said O'Brien, feeling woozy with the scent of her.

"Really?" Rose batted her lashes and inhaled.

"Heh-heh," chortled O'Brien. What a ripe piece of ass she was! Vain as a fat old peacock, he sucked in his gut. Beneath his expensive clothes, the corset he always wore did its awesome duty. With a fleshy hand, he patted his silver hair. Face like a baked apple, he was the perfect picture of the "old pol." O'Brien had inherited a streetcar company from his father and parlayed that into his position as head of the Metropolitan Transit Authority of Boston. It wasn't by chance that the largest supplier of subway cars happened to be his own company.

A year ago, his old friend "Charlie" Coughlin had given him a ring, and O'Brien had jumped at the chance to play politics. Added to the Union ticket because of his money and connections, he'd lately been lambasted in the liberal press as a buffoon who was in over his head. It didn't bother him a bit. Six months of a grueling campaign hadn't diminished his zeal or his gusto.

"And here's the dear Duchess Carney," continued Rose.

"You don't say?"

"Is that so?" said Father Gahaghan, feeling left out. Invited to lend the occasion the proper religious patina, he was anxious to buttonhole O'Brien himself. The building fund needed all the help it could get. "Nice weather we're having, Mr. O'Brien," he called, trying to get his attention, slightly awed—as they all were—to have a celebrity in the house.

"Very nice, Father. Yes, indeed."

"What?" asked Joe Flynn, cupping a hand behind his ear. Dressed in Sunday best, he stuck a finger between his neck and his stiff starched collar.

"I was tellin' Mr. O'Brien what nice weather we were havin'," hollered Father Gahaghan.

"Yes, sir," said Teresa's Matt, likewise in his Sunday best, likewise uncomfortable.

Joe Flynn nodded.

"Should get him a hearin' aid," offered Timothy, cheeks full.

"We've tried," said Rose, "but Father won't hear of it."

"Hah-hah," laughed Father Gahaghan, doing his part.

Rose looked prettily blank.

"Ya made a joke, Rosie," explained Matt. Managing to conceal her irritation at his use of Rosie, Rose smiled and tried to think what it was.

"A sense of humor just like her mother," offered Gahaghan.

"Heh-heh . . ." laughed O'Brien warily.

"What???"

"We were saying," shouted Dennis, "that Rose has a good sense of humor, Pa."

"Rose?" Joe winked at Matt. Luckily, Rose didn't catch it. "Rosie's a good girl," he added, as Gert entered the room with a warning look for Joe and a plate of hot canapés for the O'Briens.

"Hmmm-hmmm," salivated O'Brien. "Such good smells, Mrs. Flynn."

"Couldn't have done any of it without Rose," replied Gert, a nervous smile plastered on her face. "Poor thing was up to the wee hours last night with the bakin' and then up at dawn this mornin' to help with the cookin'—but that's the way she is."

Those who knew better nodded and regarded their laps. Rose blushed prettily, crossed and uncrossed her legs, sending ripples through the two O'Briens who flanked her. The reality of the day had been five hours to get herself ready with an hour out for Mass. The first hour was given to a hot tub, the second at Teresa's shop for the hair, the third on clothes and makeup, and the remaining time spent with the society page and the funnies (as far as she usually got), sitting demurely so as not to muss the work that had gone before. Needless to say, she looked stunning.

"Where's your other son?" asked O'Brien, to Gert's consternation. "I keep missin' him, it seems."

"Down to the office," stalled Gert. "Poor fella's had his nose to the grindstone. He'll be here soon, I'm sure. And he's anxious to meet ya. Why, he's one of your biggest supporters, as I told ya yesterday." Gert had had to smooth things as best she could. "I don't mind tellin' ya," she went on, patting doilies, plumping cushions, "runnin' *The Irish Spectator*'s been a joy to all of us. It's just a small family enterprise. Rose's been workin' on it herself—aside from her charities—and Denny, too. There's times we feel bent low with the labor of it, but if it's for a good cause—who's complainin'?"

"I'm appreciative of your efforts," bandied back O'Brien, enjoying all the bowing and scraping. "Every bit helps," he added, his voice taking on a self-important resonance as if he were speaking for the ages. "Every bit helps in our great crusade, which'll sweep us to victory next week and oust the traitor from the seat of government!"

"Amen!" agreed Gert as O'Brien basked in scattered applause from Father Gahaghan, Matt and Dennis.

"Well, now," said O'Brien, deigning to drop a crumb, "I've a little somethin' for the lad—if I get to see him." He smiled benevolently. Gert stopped in her tracks.

"For my Pat? And what would that be—if ya don't mind my askin'?"

"Ooo . . . a little surprise."

"Denny," directed Gert, "why don't ya try down to the office again?" She turned to O'Brien: "Has my Denny been tellin' ya of his plans for Congress when McGinty goes? Just think—your Timothy'll be runnin' in his district . . . and my Denny up here, God willin'. And now, if you'll excuse me, I'll go see to things."

"I hope," said O'Brien, "that I've not put you to too much trouble with this short-notice acceptance of your kind invitation."

"Short-notice's the best notice," bandied back Gert. "And not a drop am I exaggeratin' when I tell ya how honored we all are to have ya with us today."

"Amen," intoned Father Gahaghan.

243

"Many's the time I've asked him," continued Gert, "haven't I, Timothy, darlin'?—ta bring ya ta dinner. So we're all just tickled ya could make it today."

"Heh-heh," muttered O'Brien, catching the *"and it's about time ya made it"* behind Gert's blarney. The two war horses smiled at each other warily. It wouldn't have occurred to them (and neither would have relished the comparison), but they had much in common.

"May I help, Mother?" asked Rose as Gert started to leave.

"You've done enough, darlin'," cackled Gert. "Stay and entertain the men."

Pushy broad. Not missing a trick, O'Brien smiled heartily as Gert left the room.

"The fathead," she muttered to Teresa, sweeping through the swinging door, plastered smile replaced by grim-lipped fidgets as she collapsed into a chair in the sanctuary of the steamy kitchen. "Lemme tell ya—the Flynns were kings in Ireland when the O'Briens were cleanin' pigsties."

"How's it going?" asked Teresa, who'd overheard it all anyway. "I've put the rolls in and—"

"*Fathead!* Like father, like son." Gert glanced at the clock. "Where is he??? I'm ready to serve in ten minutes. O'Brien said he had somethin' for him. What could it be? A fat check, I hope, for all the trouble it's cost me. If the Blessed Mother sees fit to see me through this fall . . ." Gert heaved herself up and accosted the oven once again, poking at the roast. She slammed the door. "I told him I wanted him here! How dare he? I want the family together, I told him. How's it look? Especially after his not showin' up at the reception yesterday!" Pans rattled.

"Shhh, dear."

"D'ya know what he had the nerve to say ta me this mornin'? D'ya know???" Outraged at the memory of the painful scene that had occurred between herself and Patrick at six A.M., Gert slurped the drippings as she stirred them for gravy, splattering the stove. "Had the nerve to tell me he'd been troubled by what happened yesterday at the stadium. Would ya believe it? Said his conscience was troublin' him over supportin' Father Coughlin and O'Brien!"

"I know he was upset. Check those rolls."

"They're fine. What d'ya mean, ya know?"

"He stopped by the shop yesterday after the rally. I know he was upset over what happened to Harriet and—"

"I don't wanta hear that one's name!"

"What about the greens, dear? Shall—?"

"Comes ta *you!*" muttered Gert. "Comes ta *you* first!"

"Maybe if you were a little easier on him. How many of these greens. . . ?"

"All of 'em. The way those two eat! I told him he'd keep his mouth shut! That's what I told him! A week before the election and he tells me his conscience is troublin' him??? I ask ya, Teresa—"

"Timmy needs more celery," announced Rose, entering the kitchen.

"There ain't any more," snapped Gert. "Let the fathead suck his thumb."

"I won't have you calling Timothy that, Mother." Rose gave Gert a sharp look. From now on, she would claw to the death anyone (including her mother and fellow conspirator) who dared to deprecate her darling.

"Slip o' the tongue, dearest," apologized Gert, patting Rose on the shoulder. "Don't she look grand?" Surveying her daughter, her hands reached out to pat a curl in place. Teresa fussed, too—the two women like nurses ministering to the favorite wife of the king, who'd just learned she was pregnant, would produce an heir and save the monarchy.

"How's it goin' in there?" asked Teresa.

"Father Gahaghan's talking to Mr. O'Brien about the parochial school."

"Get him off *that*," directed Gert. "Ya know how pushy the Father gets, God love'm."

Rose departed. Gert returned to the subject of Patrick. "His conscience! I asked him—was his conscience troublin' him when he come slunkin' home a coupla months back, takin' ten years off my life? Ya can bet he had no smart answer for that! He knows what this means, havin' O'Brien here. And not just for Rose, neither. For all of us. O'Brien can be helpful to Denny, too. God knows, and the Virgin, too, that Denny needs a boost. And what about *The Spectator?* Holy angels, give me the strength! Ya know what he said to me this mornin'? Said he was sick of hearin' about the O'Briens. Tells me the paper got *started* for the O'Briens! Accused me of makin' him support Father Coughlin *because* of the O'Briens! He *dares* accuse me! He knows well enough why the paper was started! So's he could hold his head up, that's why. Would ya rather be diggin' ditches? I asked him. With everyone laughin' at ya? 'Cause if so—I'll arrange it! That's what I told him. The ungrateful—! *And today of all days!*" Gert paused in her frenzied stirring. "I tell ya, Teresa, he's drivin' me to distraction! What's come over him so sudden? Taste this gravy for me. Maybe it's better he doesn't come . . . maybe it's better. . . ."

"Any more cherries?" asked Dennis, entering the kitchen.

"There was half a jar. . . ."

"Mr. O'Brien likes three in his cocktail."

"Three??? He'd be better off havin' none, what with the size of him." She directed Dennis to a cupboard. "And tell yer father I want him to carve in five minutes."

"There's green cherries here," called Dennis.

245

"Giv'm green! Am I supposed ta be up ta my ears in cherries on a day like this? Give your brother another try at the office."

"Do you want me to bring Mr. O'Brien the cherries or—?"

Gert glared at Dennis, who exited hastily. "I wonder about him sometimes," she confided to Teresa. It was only in the dark hours of the early morning that Gert sometimes opened her eyes and admitted to herself that Denny was a weakling who didn't have the stuff. "He's my own, but I wonder about him sometimes."

"No answer," said Dennis, poking his head in.

"We'll start without him. Take this butter in. And tell yer father I'm needin' him. Go on. And do yer duty. Smile! Smile! I'm proud of ya."

Thoroughly harried, Gert batted about the kitchen. "Should I cut the Yorkshire puddin' at the table? No. Yes, else it'll fall. Today of all days he gives me trouble!" She slammed plates on the table. "*I told him! I told him that, even if Coughlin and O'Brien were the devil himself, Rose is goin' to marry Timothy!* I want no rockin' of any boats! This family's got no agitators in it! Or workin' for it, neither! And ya know who I mean!"

"But Harriet had nothin'—"

"Get them bread baskets down." Gert opened the oven door, and the roast emerged gloriously to "ooo's" from Teresa. Joe came in. Gert wrapped an apron around his middle, and he set to carving while she poked at the broccoli and whipped the potatoes like a dervish. "Jesus, Mary, and Joseph—the cream sauce!" Overlooked, it had curdled. "Ruined!" she cried, close to tears. "I've had all I can take."

"I'll fix lemon butter, don't worry." The sheer exhaustion on her sister's face had Teresa concerned. "Compose yourself, dear. All's well. It's goin' beautifully. . . ." O'Brien's bombastic laughter filtered in from the living room. "See?"

"Today of all days!" Gert plopped mashed potatoes on the plates. Wisps of damp hair clung at her forehead, her spectacles were fogged. Emotion choked her voice. "I tried to prepare myself for today. And for last Sunday, too, when he . . . was supposed to be . . . ordained." A tear slipped out and rolled down her smooth, rouged cheek.

"Gertie . . ." said Joe softly, concerned.

"Get on with ya! We're waitin' on ya!" Gert blew her nose. "But at Mass this mornin', I couldn't help . . . seein' him up there and I . . . I tried to tell myself it's for the best but . . ."

"There now. . . . Why don't you freshen up and let me serve?"

"No, I'll do the broccoli. He wouldn't go across to Mass this mornin', ya know. Said everybody'd be lookin' at him. Rememberin' he was supposed to be saying the Mass. So he went over to the city."

Teresa nodded. "It's a difficult day for him, too. He probably needed to be by himself. You know how sensitive he is sometimes. No broccoli for

246

Matt, dear. It repeats on him. Stir this butter for me, will you? I'll see to the rolls."

"That'll be O'Brien's," sighed Gert, still sniffling, as Joe eased a magnificent slab onto one of the plates.

"It looks lovely, dear. Dennis? Come fetch. . . . We want everything piping hot, don't we?"

Gert suddenly took hold of her sister's arm. "It'll work out for Rose, won't it?"

"The butter, dear. Keep stirring or—"

"*Won't it?*"

"Course it will."

"It's her last chance."

"Don't be silly."

"Pray that he gives his blessin'."

"I am, dear."

Gert clasped a hand to her breast. "It hurts—will it ever stop hurtin'? Oh, my God—the salad dressin'!"

"I'll see to it."

"It's better he doesn't come, feelin' the way he does."

"My, doesn't that smell good."

"The relishes. . . !"

"I've got them."

"*Holy Mary, help me, sweetheart . . .*"

At the dinner table, Michael O'Brien allowed his gaze to drift past Rose's profile to his son next to her. Timothy's napkin was tucked in at his neck. Methodically he shoveled in food; his expression demonstrated no guile, nor was his breath as effortful as usual. He looked almost like a good boy who'd just received a glowing report card from the Sisters and was now having his reward. Except Timothy'd never got a good card from the Sisters. A wave of sadness and regret overtook O'Brien as it struck him once again: his only son was sure enough a loser.

With as little illusion about Timothy as Gert had about Rose, O'Brien sighed. Hard to believe his son was now thirty-six. He'd put him to work at the streetcar works, gave him some responsibility, and what happened? Six of 'em came back with the wheels on backward. Useless, that's what he was. Spending more time at the races in the company of tarts than he did on his duties. Thirty-six! Sweet Jesus!

O'Brien's poached-egg eyes surveyed the table. Sure enough, there were other families he'd rather be sitting down with than this one. Other matches he'd rather make. Like the Cudahy daughter. Or one of Joe Kennedy's girls. Fat chance. None of them sweeties was goin' to pay any attention to Timothy. O'Brien's gaze took in Dennis. Jesus! He had as much chance of makin' Congress as . . . Timothy. Heartburn attacking, O'Brien sighed, looked up and caught Gert looking at him hungrily. Holy Mary! She and her crony the priest; thick as thieves the two of 'em; butterin' him up like a hot cross bun.

"No, Timmy."

"Awww . . . Rosie."

"No, no, no!"

O'Brien's attention was diverted as Rose gaily slapped at Timothy's hand, which was crawling for a fifth roll.

"Naughty Timmy!"

"Awwww . . ."

Our Lady of Fatima protect us! Slightly nauseated by this byplay, O'Brien groaned inwardly. "Will you put me on a diet, too, Rosie?" he guffawed, accepting another slab of roast from Gert ("Inspirational, Mrs. Flynn") at the same time.

"Not *you*, Mr. O'Brien," giggled Rose, red lips slippery.

"Diet," scoffed Gert as if the word were a mortal sin. "An extra roll won't hurt Timothy, and here's a bit of Yorkshire pudding to go with it." Gert attempted to serve. Rose, already playing the role of wife, stood her ground.

"What can I do, darlin'?" Gert asked Timothy, who looked peevish. "When she makes up her mind, she's unbendable." Timothy shivered.

O'Brien's thoughts returned to last night. "Have ya knocked her up?" he'd inquired after Timothy had rushed upstairs to the library, huffing and puffing and pleading. He hadn't seen his son that energetic in a month of Sundays. No, Rose'd be too smart for that. A regular operator.

"I love Rose," Timothy had replied indignantly.

"Ya sure it's not the tits, lad?"

"I want to marry Rose!" Timothy's face had gone red with frustration like a baby past its feeding time. "Ya know what you're lettin' yourself in for, lad," he'd told his son. The mother was a tiger. The daughter was dumb like a fox. "If you don't give me permission . . ." Timothy had threatened. What an asshole! But it wasn't the lad's fault. He missed his mother, God rest her soul. . . .

O'Brien belched and was whacked on the back by Rose playing nurse. *Jesus*. What a difficult decision. And if he didn't agree, who'd be next? A chorus cutie who'd take Timothy for all he was worth? Not that this looker beside him wasn't interested in the bucks herself. Nor the mother. But they weren't criminals. Maybe he could keep an eye on 'em; a known evil was better than an unknown and—

O'Brien glanced at the two lovers; a coupla misfits if ever there were. Still, she'd look good on Timothy's arm. Whip him into shape. She wasn't a tart. Nice Catholic girl with a pussy he wouldn't mind havin' a go at himself. But what a family! Maybe the battle-ax would disappear into the woodwork. Fat chance. *Shit*. Well, why not?

Resigning himself, O'Brien belched. Not that he couldn't still have a little fun with Gert, he told himself, reviving at the prospect. Make her sweat. "Can't tell ya, Mrs. Flynn," he beamed broadly, "what it means to come into a good Catholic home to Sunday dinner with your charmin' family. God bless ya for invitin' a tired old campaigner."

"Old, indeed! Why, you're a man in his prime." The others nodded agreement.

"What a satisfyin' meal," continued O'Brien, about to dangle a goodie. "How I've longed to break bread with the family of the girl my son's so fond of." He patted Rose's hand.

"And aren't we just as fond of Timothy?" Gert bandied back, wondering what the old fart was up to. "Sure we are. And I hope this'll be the first of many happy occasions."

"Well—" O'Brien hesitated. Gert's heart plummeted like an elevator come loose. Toying with them all, O'Brien paused again, chewed, mumbled inaudibly as if distressed, picked his teeth, wiped his lips, took a sip of water, and looked up and around the table at those who were on the edges of their seats and said:

"I'm sure it will be. The first of many."

He winked at Rose.

She giggled. Timothy grinned. Teresa nudged Matt's knee, and Gert, in a state of barely controlled hysteria, found herself buttering a piece of meat.

Everyone began talking at once as the bird of hope rose flapping, winging high. O'Brien settled back with a benevolent smile. Gert and Teresa hurried to the kitchen to get more food, the two of them clasping each other with happy, hushed cries of enormous relief and joyous tears, which were interrupted by Dennis who popped his head in to announce:

"Saint Patrick's here. I think he's had a few."

"It looks good for Rose," whispered Teresa urgently, intercepting Patrick in the darkness of the hallway. His heart sank. He saw Gert bearing down. Avoiding her, he entered the dining room, was introduced to O'Brien, and took his place at the table. Behind him on the sideboard, the clock ticked, the sound magnified, ticking in his head like a time bomb.

"Sorry we missed ya yesterday," O'Brien said a few minutes later. "But we're glad to have ya on our side."

Patrick clenched a fist under the table, unclenched it, then felt Teresa pat his knee reassuringly. Six Carling Red Caps, drunk at Jerry Finneran's, gurgled in his stomach. What would O'Brien look like, he wondered, if he were to nail him with what he'd found out this morning over in Leveret?

249

After Mass, he'd walked to the police station to do some checking of his own and talked to his second cousin, Sean Ahearne, who told him in confidence that the scuttlebutt around the station had it that yesterday's riot had been instigated by some paid thugs, financed by the Union Party itself. Furthermore, Sean had implied that it wouldn't be going too far to lay the smelly fish on the plate of the mountain of blubber who sat opposite Patrick now.

The wrath he'd unload on O'Brien, if only he could! If only he could also tell O'Brien that *The Jericho Irish Spectator* wouldn't be supporting him *or* Coughlin any more. That it would be coming out for Roosevelt on Wednesday. One more nail in Coughlin's coffin, and O'Brien's, too. *If only.* The road to hell was paved with "if onlys," reflected Patrick, lashing himself for his impotent fantasy. Because he wasn't going to tell O'Brien anything. And he wasn't going to do any of the other on Wednesday, either. Because he couldn't sacrifice Rose and his mother for the sake of his newly discovered and shaky conscience, that was why. And he hated himself for the fact that he couldn't.

"That picture in the *Herald* this mornin' didn't do you a bit of justice, Mr. O'Brien," blarneyed Teresa, hoping to steer the conversation to safe shores, but the subject that bubbled up was yesterday's rally.

"Thank you kindly, Mrs. Burke, although I'm not partial to the *Boston Herald.*"

"Coughlin Brands Roosevelt A Red" had been the headline this morning. "Callin' it a 'riot,' " fumed O'Brien, cheeks flushed. "Can you imagine them suggestin' our boys acted unduly? What were they to do? Let the Father be dragged down by a bunch of Bolsheviks? Doin' their duty, God bless'm—that's what. If a few heads got cracked, they deserved to."

"Amen," agreed Father Gahaghan.

"A disgrace," muttered Gert, not daring to look at Patrick as she served him his plate.

"One of the blessed things about Charlie," continued O'Brien, growing misty-eyed, "is the man's Christian charity. We've been gettin' hecklers right along. But Charlie forgives 'em. I'll wager he even includes them in his prayers. Misguided fools that they are. What d'ya say, lad?" Not very talkative, that one. O'Brien turned calculating eyes on Patrick, trying to read him.

"What's that?" cried Gert, seizing upon a strange thumping sound under the table to divert attention. "Look who's here," she added with a forced smile as Albatross emerged from under the lace where he'd hidden. "C'mere, doggy," she called in a voice similar to that used to lure Hansel and Gretel into the gingerbread cottage. Albatross ignored her, scratched, and produced an offering of hair that was deposited on the swirled maroon carpet.

"A present for ya, Gert," laughed Matt. Gert smiled thinly, all the more nervous at Patrick's rebellious act of bringing the dog into the dining room.

"*Sede, Albatrossum.*" At Patrick's command, the dog lay down beside him.

"Understands Latin, does he?" chortled O'Brien between mouthfuls.

Patrick nodded and burped. "We're thinking of auditioning for Major Bowes' Amateur Hour."

"Heh-heh . . ." O'Brien's three chins quivered. Sensing Patrick's hostility, his eyes narrowed. "Ha-ha," laughed Matt, the others joining in a little too loudly, all uncomfortable with the sudden undercurrents between the two men.

"Patrick never goes anywhere without his dog," cooed Rose, anxious at her brother's strained appearance. "Isn't that sweet?" she added, popping a ripe olive into Timothy's mouth.

"Are you fond of animals yourself, Rosie?" asked O'Brien.

"Oh, yes. Once we had a parakeet, didn't we, Mother?"

As conversation continued of feathered friends, pets and beasts, Patrick stole a furtive glance from Timothy to Rose and back again. It wasn't his business, he reminded himself, to pass judgment on the man Rose wanted even if he was an asshole. That wasn't the issue he'd wrestled with this past twenty-four hours, but one of conscience and morality. And as Jerry had agreed only an hour ago—it was a no-win situation. Could he screw up his mother's hopes, having screwed up so much of them already? Not today. Especially not today—this hallowed day of his never-to-be-said first Mass when he already carried enough guilt.

Even so, he'd got up this morning and tried to explain his feelings to Gert. It had been stupid to even try. So why had he come today to this goddamned dinner? To hear O'Brien mouth lies and say nothing? Was there a kind of perverse pleasure he took in suffering? But wasn't he at least curious, Jerry had asked, to meet O'Brien and get a sense of him? So here he was, playing the game for the family's sake. Wasn't 'discipline' his middle name?

"More Yorkshire puddin', darlin'?" The condemned man eating hearty, Patrick nodded to Gert. I'll be a good boy was the message he sent her. Haven't you given me Holy Orders? Patrick almost relished the spasm of pain that hit his prostate.

"Was it the Paulists you were with, lad?" O'Brien's question caught him off balance. The fat shit, why was he bringing that up?

"Augustinians."

"Any regrets?" Once again, Patrick's eyes encountered Gert's. He'd half expected to find black crepe hanging in the bathroom this morning.

"I'm running a newspaper now."

251

"So ya are. And as I said before, we're pleased to have ya behind us."

"Are you?"

"Now for dessert, Mr. O'Brien." Stomach doing handstands, Gert rose swiftly. "Guess what Rose has made for ya?"

"Mother, it was supposed to be a surprise!"

"Speakin' of surprises," chortled O'Brien benevolently, "when does your paper go to press?"

"Wednesday," answered Patrick, on guard.

"Good. Since you couldn't make it yesterday, I've arranged for ya to have a private interview with Father Coughlin at the Parker House tomorrow. Two o'clock sharp. Plenty of time for ya to get it in your paper. By the way, what happened to your friend got put in the pokey yesterday?"

Patrick's toes curled in his shoes. Roast beef blood in his mouth, he stared at O'Brien. "Not a friend," interjected Gert quickly. "And she had nothin' at all to do with them people."

"Nothing," assured Teresa.

"She works for us—that's all," continued Gert, boiling at having to defend the creature. "But she's nobody—"

"Ma," warned Patrick.

"Ya know what they say—" O'Brien's eyes became squinty as steel. "Tarred by the same brush."

Patrick wanted to tip the table over on him. "She had nothing to do with what happened." Perspiration broke out on his forehead. *But you did, didn't you?* He bit his tongue.

"Oh-ho!" guffawed O'Brien. "You're testy, lad. Isn't he testy, Timothy?"

"Testy," echoed his son. O'Brien winked at Rose, then looked across at Patrick again, noting the flush on his face. "Would I be jumpin' to conclusions, lad, if I was to guess you had a romance brewin'?"

Faces went white. Teresa found herself looking at Dennis, for certainly she couldn't look at Gert. To her surprise she found Dennis knew it, too. Rose discovered it by the expression on Teresa's face. And so it went.

"*Her?*" cried Gert with a mighty laugh. "Aww, you're a kidder, Mr. O'Brien, God love ya."

"She works for me, that's all," mumbled Patrick.

"Just pullin' your leg, lad." Obviously enjoying the tempest stirred by his remarks, O'Brien thought he'd have a bit more fun. "Now I asked Timmy, didn't I?—why do they have a Protestant workin' on a Catholic paper?"

"She's qualified, that's why." Abruptly Patrick stood. "I won't be able to make that interview," he heard himself say.

"What's your favorite pie, Timmy?" asked Rose quickly, sensing from her brother's expression that the lid was about to blow the pot.

Timothy pondered. "Mince?"

"Think again."

"Why not, lad?" asked O'Brien, staring up at Patrick. Gert was in shock.

"Apple?"

"No, silly! Chocolate—"

"—cream pie!" finished Timothy triumphantly.

"Because—"

"Good for you," cried Rose nervously, trying to ride over her brother. "But in honor of your father, I've renamed it: *Brookline* cream pie!"

Appreciative, strained laughter and a flurry of plate clearing couldn't divert what had to be concluded.

"Because I'm coming out for Roosevelt."

Silence shook the table, a sudden hush followed by chatter, the young zealot and the old campaigner locked in a stare of mutual animosity.

"Are ya now?" O'Brien flushed in anger. Gert gasped. "How dare ya!" she cried, rising like a fury, the lace on the table quivering. Albatross barked. Unable to face O'Brien, who was being placated by Rose, Gert fled to the kitchen, followed by Teresa.

"*She's* behind this! She's finished! I'm gettin' rid of her, d'ya hear? *Finished.*" She slashed a knife into one of the two pies. "Yesterday was the last straw. How dare he? How—"

"But that wasn't her fault," answered Teresa. "You said yourself—"

"I knew she'd be trouble right from the start! She was the cause of his gettin' into that ruckus over at the Classic last week, wasn't she? Oh, I know you'll be defendin' her just as you always— What's he doin'?" she asked as Dennis hurried into the kitchen.

"Timothy's pleading with him to stay."

"Quick, take these in. He won't be able to resist." Gert directed Dennis with the plates. "She's *out!*" she roared as Patrick appeared in the doorway.

"No, she's not."

"*You!*" hissed Gert, hand clenched to her breast. "Ya dare to do this to me today!" Mother and son stared mesmerized at each other, neither aware that something was almost finishing—a final, long overdue, slicing, tearing, fraying of the cord, a few tenacious fibers still holding, but barely.

"I love her."

Gert's strangled cry was echoed by a similar sound from the dining room. Followed by Patrick, she and Teresa rushed back in through the swinging door.

"What is it?"

"*Water,*" gasped Joe, who'd taken the first bite of pie. His face was an odd blue. In a spasm he reached for his water glass, knocking it over.

253

Bending almost as low as his plate, the mouthful of pie shot out in a whoosh.

"What???" cried Rose as her father's action was instantly duplicated by Timothy, who'd taken an enormous bite.

"Aaaaagh. . . !"

"What is it? What?" cried Gert.

"*Salt!*" gasped Timothy.

"*Salt!*" echoed O'Brien, rising in his seat and nearly toppling. Veins bulged in his temples. Flecks of chocolate dribbled from his mouth. He downed a glass of water, spilling some of it over himself, then reached out blindly for another.

"More water. . . !"

"*Maaaaa,*" cried Rose (breeding fled), "*what did you do?*"

"Holy Mary. . . !" Glued to the spot, unable to offer aid, Gert's face was a study. Images of identical canisters careened in her head; hands flying while she made the pies last night; three sheets to the wind in excitement and triumph at O'Brien's impending visit; not noticing as two and one half cups of—

"*Salt. . . salt . . .*" jabbered O'Brien, as goblets were thrust at him.

Gallantly Patrick offered his. "Take mine, Mr. O'Brien."

Had he ever felt such joy? Life was beginning to be worth living.

13

THE SPECTATOR CHANGES ITS MIND

Anyone who tells us that the choice between President Roosevelt, the Democratic nominee, and Alfred Landon, the Republican, is a choice between carbolic acid and rat poison indulges in dangerous demagoguery. Father Charles Coughlin gave us that choice at Leveret Stadium on Saturday afternoon.

The Spectator wishes to repudiate and apologize for its support of Father Coughlin and the Union Party, its nominees William Lemke and Michael O'Brien, its congressional candidates in the County and the State.

The Spectator's conscience has been stirred, its eyes opened by the events of last Saturday when Father Coughlin denounced President Roosevelt as a traitor. Right-thinking men and women can only be appalled at such inflammatory and demagogic slander. A careful perusal of the Union Party platform elicits foreboding. Coughlin offers no chance to influence the country except negatively. His program is pie in the sky.

Sic Semper Tyrannis! Thus always to tyrants! May they sink in their own darkness and be repudiated.

The Spectator feels that Father Coughlin is misguided; we would humbly ask him to reacquaint himself with the principles of his Faith.

As for Landon and the Republicans, they denounce the New Deal and accuse the President of bankrupting the country. Behind their conservative rhetoric lurks a thinly disguised disdain for "reliefers," the poor and the hopeless. What do the Republicans offer that is positive? Like Father Coughlin—little.

In answer to his critics who accuse him of reckless spending, Roosevelt replied last week that to have balanced the federal budget in the last few years would have been a crime against the American people. "Americans were suffering," the President said, "and we refused to pass by on the other side. Humanity came first."

The Spectator agrees. A few hard economic facts come easily to mind. From 1931 through 1933, there were over 6,000 bank failures in the country; from 1934 through 1936, there have been 166. The stock market is climbing, industrial production is 65% higher than in 1931. These statistics filter down to men and women working, providing for their families, educating their children . . . and the cycle of rejuvenation continues.

To be sure there are weak spots. Across the river, Leveret has not recovered. The textile and woolen industry is still moribund. Millions across the country are still unemployed. Jericho has lost two of its mills in the last six years but is fortunate that Phelps Mill operates at capacity.

The presence at the gates of the mill of union organizers in the last few days causes *The Spectator* to hope that reasonable and equitable solutions will be found between management and labor.

The Spectator wishes to humbly acknowledge President Roosevelt. We believe he is blessed. The jaunty warmth of his smile indicates a man of character, who exhibits a humanness and caring that puts to shame the other candidates. Here is a man who has freed himself from the shackles of his privileged and sheltered past, who has overcome a physical infirmity and gone on to provide leadership, inspiration and hope to a nation that, four years ago, was sodden with defeat.

The Recovery continues. The Issues are clear. *The Spectator* gratefully and heartily endorses the reelection of Franklin Delano Roosevelt as President of the United States.

editorial reprinted from
The Jericho Spectator,
Oct. 25, 1936

"Slightly purple in the prose—but wonderful!" Harriet found it necessary to be slightly blasé on the surface, for Patrick's editorial moved and excited her and forced her to take yet another look at him. "Wonderful!" she exclaimed after she'd read his first draft, made a few suggestions, edited a word or two—but there was little she could see to change. "You're in there," she said to him. "Your own 'humanness.'" The "recovery," she realized, was his. "I think you're the one throwing off the shackles," she laughed, "although I'm sure your mother's at the foundry ordering another set."

Patrick grinned. Where had it all come from? The words he'd written

256

had a clarity, had spilled out of him with a directness that had surprised him. Surprising, too, was the enormous pleasure he felt. "The editorial's as much yours as it is mine," he told her. "Yours . . . and Alice's. Wayne's, too. My mentors." An education had been thrust on him since he'd left Washington, and Patrick felt his horizons broadened, concerns deepened. Daily contact with people had awakened him. The sap was rising, and he felt fit. "I may continue to write editorials," he announced with a bravado that astounded Harriet. "Perhaps I'll become the H. L. Mencken of Jericho. I know, I know—don't say it. My style's still turgid. I'll learn!"

There was a tiny part of Harriet, one she'd rather not acknowledge, that felt uneasy at Patrick's having seized the day. Would she be left behind? "You're the one who set me on the path of righteousness," Patrick insisted, wrapping her in a feeling of such well-being that her pettiness fled. "You were right to goad me on. What would I do without you? You keep me honest. I asked myself what did it matter what *The Spectator* printed? Sure, I wanted to stall. But I couldn't stomach O'Brien . . . his insinuations about you. . . . I couldn't have lived with myself. My whole life's been spent stalling . . . doing what Ma wanted, what the Church demanded. I didn't go as far as you wanted me to—no real mention of O'Brien. Or his hand in the riot. I can't prove it. I'm not a crusader. I'll leave that to you. When O'Brien reads this—I hope it'll be OK for Rose. . . ."

"But you said the ring's on her finger."

"I know. But to see this in print . . ."

The Spectator was on the street. It was Wednesday, three days after the O'Brien dinner. O'Brien had been upset, not enough, however, to pull his son out of the Rose Flynn sweepstakes. His reasons for allowing the match to proceed outweighed his future daughter-in-law's turncoat brother, but Patrick was worried that his editorial might undo things.

In those awful moments following the en masse regurgitation of Gert's pie, O'Brien turned watery eyes on Patrick, ready to give him a lashing. Gert hadn't been able to speak ("Turned, no doubt," quipped Harriet, when Patrick told her the story, "to a pillar of salt."), but Teresa had begun to laugh, her laughter escalating and rescuing the moment, volunteering that a pinch of salt was good luck. O'Brien had managed a wary smile, and the cat was soon out of the bag as to who had made the pie, and everyone trooped into the kitchen to examine the canisters. Denny had been sent to Noonan's for two quarts of vanilla and the next day Rose and Timothy had gone into Boston together to purchase the ring. The announcement of the engagement had appeared in yesterday's *Boston Herald* and the *Leveret Eagle*. Gert had seen to that. Before O'Brien's Packard had turned the corner, she was on the phone giving out the story.

• • •

257

"You're fired, dearie." A few moments later that Wednesday morning, Gert descended (Rose in tow) on the office. Did "dearie" begin to cloak the vengeance Gert hoped to wreak on Harriet, whom she blamed for everything? It was easier to attempt an annihilation of Harriet than face up to the truth that Patrick was out of control.

"Good morning, Mrs. Flynn." Disregarding Gert's announcement, Harriet continued with a call. People had been dropping in, the office was in a flurry. Temporarily denied the kill, the two women stewed at the counter. Patrick had gone out to check the street's reaction; Harriet hoped he'd hurry back.

"Thank you . . . thank you for your comments. Yes, it is a madhouse here. . . ." Harriet glanced up at Gert, then back to the phone. "Yes, I think it's a real beginning for us, too."

As she set the phone down, it rang again. Gert picked up a copy of *The Spectator* from the counter and waved it at Harriet:

"It's all your doin'—this! Don't think I don't know—"

"Good morning Gert . . . Rose . . ." Mrs. Longbottom from the market hurried in, stymieing Gert further. Since the paper was now for Roosevelt, Mr. Longbottom would resume his advertising. "My husband sent me over . . . he wants to say congratulations and will drop by later. Here's our list of next week's specials for the ad. Oh, and Rose, best wishes to you, too."

Rose nodded archly. The engagement ring sparkled. When O'Brien read the editorial, would she have to give it back? Her brilliant eyes darted to her photograph, which Patrick (hoping to take the sting out of the rest) had featured prominently on page one, along with the announcement of her engagement.

"I have to run—" As Mrs. Longbottom left, police chief McGee came in to ask for Patrick and offer his congratulations.

"All your doin'," continued Gert, a moment later, interrupted by more droppers-in, more calls. She was boiling.

"But Mrs. Flynn," soothed Harriet, "haven't you noticed the reaction? It's so *positive*."

Gert's eyes glazed as she picked up a copy of the paper. Patrick's editorial was bad, traitorous enough, but there was something much worse, a symbolic and devastating rupture with her son—the evidence in the paper's masthead:

Three words instead of four. *The Jericho Spectator. Irish?* Disappeared.

Harriet had impulsively hugged Patrick when he'd surprised her, taking the first sheet off the press last night and ceremoniously bowing as he handed it to her, but Gert wasn't here for embracing.

"Mrs. Flynn, I know you're upset, but doesn't it make sense? Did you read page three?" There was a paragraph ("The Spectator Changes Its

Name") in which Patrick explained that in the interests of broader appeal, and also to fulfill the real needs of Jericho, *The Spectator* had undergone a change of name as well as policy.

"You're a cheeky one, aren't ya?" exploded Gert. "Who d'ya think's been payin' your salary? *I'm* payin' it. But no more!"

"I think that's unfair."

"She's not worth bothering with, Mother." On edge with the close calls of the last week, Rose was not at her best. "You're an employee! How dare you meddle in our—"

"Where's my son?"

"I think you should be proud of Patrick, Mrs. Flynn. He's taken a courageous stand."

Patrick's very name on Harriet's lips only made Gert more furious. "Whether he's here or whether he isn't," she announced, turning to leave, "I don't want to see *you* when I get back. I never met a person with more brass. Right from the start ya wanted to take over, haven't ya?"

"That's not it at all," replied Harriet, dander up and stunned at the naked animosity of the woman. "It's got nothing to do with the paper. It's because you know how he feels about me!" Gert's jaw loosed. Blatant truth wasn't bearable today. "Don't worry," continued Harriet hotly, not intending to allow herself to be indicted by this harridan, "—we have a professional relationship. That's all."

"Slap her face, Mother," offered Rose.

"She's fired," snapped Gert as Patrick came breathlessly in the door. "And I'm closin' it."

"No, she isn't. Calm down."

"Ya heard me."

Mother and son's eyes locked. Patrick's stomach fell, and he was suddenly two or three and there she was, that Godlike creature who dispensed life and comfort, who could take it away just as quickly and leave him frightened and bereft.

"Do ya like givin' me a kick in the teeth? Nobody does that to me, boyo. Not you!"

"I did what I had to, Ma." Embarrassed at the scene, Patrick's eyes sought Harriet's. It hadn't been merely concern for his mother and sister that had caused him the million doubts on Monday night when he'd written his piece. He'd been fearful of making a break with his past. Even if his legs had walked away, a part of his soul was still subject to those twelve years. If he'd concluded that Coughlin was no longer of the Church and not worthy of his respect, what about himself? He was still of the Church and always would be. He couldn't deny it, nor burn all his bridges. Even if he continued counting the days until the final letter from Rome released him officially, it wasn't a release from service that he desired.

"You'll be responsible if—"

"If what?" interrupted Harriet. They had no shame, these people. Heads rolling and bloodletting in public, oblivious to good manners. She felt acutely uncomfortable but couldn't help rising to Patrick's defense.

"Stay out of this."

"No," Harriet insisted, giving back to Gert as well as she got. "Don't be so theatrical, Mrs. Flynn. My opinion is that Patrick's bent over backwards to be conciliatory in his editorial. He hasn't attacked anyone." Deeply felt and at the same time conservative—so like Patrick himself. She knew the cost to him of these last few days. "And I don't think," she continued, "that what he's said can fail to impress anyone who reads it. His sincerity shines. As I said—I think you should be proud of him and stop threatening."

Uncharacteristically speechless, Gert stared at her rival.

"Land, you're all here, aren't you now?" Possible mayhem was averted by the arrival of Teresa. "The whole street's talking," she beamed, giving Harriet a quick peck, leaving no doubt as to whose side *she* was on.

"I know," agreed Harriet. "We can't keep ahead of ourselves here, either." Once again the phone rang. She answered and gave it to Patrick. "The *Boston Herald*. . . ."

All of them watched as his expression went from frown to bemusement as he set the phone down.

"How would they have heard of us?"

"What. What?"

"They want to send someone up to interview me. They're curious as to why six days before the election we—"

"We're on the map!" cried Harriet, taking Patrick's hand and shaking it as he broke into a grin, while Gert took it all in with sinking heart.

"You'll talk to no one!" Torn between pride in the Boston paper having noticed her son and her fear of Harriet, Gert wagged a finger at Patrick. "D'ya hear me?"

"Ma!" Exuberantly he vaulted the counter and bussed her. "C'mon, Ma—you know Roosevelt's going to win. We're all on the winning side now, aren't we?" Gert wasn't buying. Patrick took Rose's hand. "Rose? You're not mad at me, are you? Don't worry. We'll all be dancing at your wedding, won't we, Teresa?"

"Sure, enough. O'Brien's no fool."

"I'm closin' it," muttered Gert, desperation causing foolishness.

"Not now, Mrs. Flynn. You can't."

"Gert," frowned Teresa, "I'm surprised at you."

"It's my paper, Ma."

"*Your* paper?" challenged Rose.

Gert's eyes focused on the empty spot on the wall to the side of Patrick's desk. "The crucifix is down, I see. The Sacred Heart, too. What's come over ya?"

"We aren't a Catholic paper anymore, Ma," he replied gently.

"Is it Protestant ya are now?" Gert looked from Patrick to Harriet and back again. "You'll see me in hell first," she said and walked out.

"Good morning, Mr. Phelps."

"Harriet. Patrick." A few moments after Gert's departure, Abraham Phelps appeared. "Have you come to scold us?" Harriet asked, giving him a quick smile that hid her nervous wondering as to his purpose. Phelps asked if he could have a word in private, and they stepped outside. "No," he replied, with a smile of his own that camouflaged distress, "the paper isn't why I'm here. Naturally I'm disappointed. But not surprised. I came to ask you to lunch." He saw her hesitate. "It's important."

When he left the mill to eat, Elliot saw his father and Harriet drive by. He ducked. Needing a drink, he decided to go over to Leveret. Driving out the gates, he waved at the union organizers who'd appeared there on Tuesday following a fruitless and angry confrontation with Phelps the previous week. Representatives of the A.F. of L. had attempted to negotiate with him. Phelps had had them ejected from the mill, and the union had decided to make a stand. Of Phelps' thirteen mills, the flagship in Jericho had been chosen. The objective was to put pressure on Phelps and force him to allow his eight hundred employees to take a vote and decide for themselves.

Elliot doubted there'd be a strike. The union had tried before and failed. He hoped there would be; he'd like nothing better than to see his father locked in his red-bricked fortress while the town marched outside. But Phelps had most of his long-time employees under his thumb; they knew if they struck, he had the power and the capital to hold out and force them back.

What was he telling her now? wondered Elliot, his thoughts turning to his father's luncheon with Harriet, imagining the two of them together in a booth at the Red Tavern. It would all be handled with his father's usual impeccable attention to detail. Elliot glanced at himself in the rearview mirror. *Caved in, didn't you, kiddo?*

An hour or so earlier, Phelps had asked his son if he'd invited Harriet to the Assembly at the country club next Saturday.

"No."

"Why not?"

"We're not seeing each other any more."

"I'm sure you'll be able to fix things with her. If you need my help—"

"I tried to screw her. Why don't you do that for me, too!"

Phelps contained his rage, his face went chalk white.

"I'm not going along with it any more. She was your idea right from the start."

261

"I don't know what you're talking about."

"Liar."

Phelps' hand reached out for his paperweight. "If you mean," he began, "that I've championed Harriet, I have. I like her. She's a girl of spirit and intelligence. You're lucky to have her."

"I don't want her."

"It's time to think of your future. If you won't, I will."

"It's all business with you, isn't it? For the sake of your goddamned business! I swear I'll tell her everything."

"Tell who what?"

"Nothing."

Phelps swiveled his chair to the side and missed the anguish in his son's face. "Dad?" Phelps chose not to turn. Desperate, Elliot wanted to explain that he couldn't stand himself any longer. He didn't want to see Harriet again. He was too ashamed. He was skating on thin ice, and the proof was what had happened at the Classic the Saturday before last when he'd followed the beloved tuxedoed boy through the door marked No Admittance and almost revealed himself.

Dad? he pleaded, this time silently. Phelps swiveled back, an unintentional flicker of disgust in his black eyes, causing Elliot to shrink. "Do you know her brother, Frankie?" Elliot asked, forced into slyness and retaliation.

Phelps froze and pretended he hadn't heard. "Think of your mother," he said, holding himself rigid lest he give in to an impulse to destroy his son. "She's worried about you."

"Leave her out of this." Trembling, Elliot stood up. Sensing his son's vulnerability, Phelps pressed on. "I know you don't give a damn what I think, but your mother would be—" He paused, choosing his words carefully. "Since, as you say, you want to 'tell' someone something, shall we 'tell' your mother?"

At the sight of his suddenly miserable son, Phelps softened but revealed nothing. Elliot would thank him in the end; it was for his own good; what purpose had he other than to insure his son's happiness and future?

"Harriet is a bright, sensible young woman. Don't worry—I'll take care of it."

"I don't love her."

"Learn to."

Elliot knew he'd lost. *Buy her and sell her, you fucker.* He'd kill himself first.

Phelps set out to make Harriet comfortable. He ordered her a martini and wrapped her in a smile. Although her curiosity was piqued as to the purpose of this luncheon (Phelps' urgency having caused a host of speculation), Harriet was still upset at the scene Patrick had pulled as she'd fixed her face in the bathroom at the office. Was Elliot going to be at lunch? he'd asked sarcastically.

Returning Phelps' smile, she realized she was disappointed he wasn't. Conflicting feelings rose, including a strong pang of missing him, the latter almost canceling her hating him. Let him suffer with his guilt! Let Patrick suffer, too. Patrick, who insisted she not go to lunch with Phelps, who told her not to bother to return to work if she did. Everyone in that family thought they could push her around! If she knew Patrick was bluffing, Harriet was of half a mind to take him at his word and let him stew. No matter how proud she was of him, she had no intention of putting up with his jealous antics. He could take a flying leap! Elliot as well.

Armoring herself lest further feeling for Elliot undo her, Harriet acknowledged Phelps' toast and glanced at the menu.

"Broiled scrod, I think."

"Good choice. Steak, rare."

The waitress departed. As he always did, Phelps complimented Harriet on her appearance. She sensed her patron was agitated; he knew she was curious, but he bided his time.

He'd chosen the Red Tavern with particular care. Jericho's smartest, perched on a rise overlooking the north shore of the lake, the tavern was a noontime custom for many of the Merrimack Valley bigwigs, who ducked into its darkened interior to sip a cocktail and talk shop. Harriet's presence here with Phelps was a subtle indication that he included her in the ranks of the movers and shakers.

"Joined the Democrats, Abe?" asked Dave Furber of Furber Machine Works.

Phelps smiled. "Miss Hoskins is trying to convert me," he replied, giving Harriet a wink. As Furber and Harriet exchanged a few words about *The Spectator* (Furber complimentary), Phelps noticed that Harriet seemed visibly to glow, her energies and sense of herself stimulated by Furber's comments.

"I thought you'd be raking us over the coals!" Harriet exclaimed to Phelps a moment later. Earlier he'd toasted the paper.

"I'm not happy. But to try and influence the younger generation is a losing proposition. They find out for themselves in due time. Are the changes in *The Spectator* Patrick's doing? Or yours? Yours, I'm sure. If I know you," he added intimately.

"I'm sure I had an influence," she replied, warmed. "But he did it. As you and I've discussed, I've been telling him right along that we couldn't survive as an Irish Catholic paper. But I had no idea he'd be able to make such a complete turnaround. There were family considerations and— I'm excited, I have to admit. I think our new policy gives us a fighting chance. He took a gamble, though—supporting Roosevelt in a Republican town. I hope we don't lose any of our advertisers."

263

"Patrick seems to have the town's welfare at heart. You seem impressed with him. A romantic interest?"

"No. Not at all," Harriet replied, confused with the question.

Satisfied with her answer and knowing he'd made her nervous, Phelps quickly patted her hand. "Didn't mean to pry. I want what's best for you. Do you believe that?"

"Yes," she replied shyly. Did he know about her and Elliot, or didn't he? More in the dark than ever, she took a bite of her fish. Phelps smiled. A fast chewing of meat, washed down with a gulp of scalding coffee, and he let her hang for a moment. Confusing the opposition was always a good ploy. Not that Phelps felt himself in an adversary role with Harriet, whom he genuinely liked and admired. Elliot's angry thought that his father would try and buy her was likewise not the case. Phelps knew better than to try, knew he had to be subtle. She had her pride, was quick, yet he understood her vulnerabilities. The rapport between them, which he'd assiduously cultivated since she'd been to dinner at the Mansion, would prove useful as well.

Ill at ease with the silence between them and with no idea of the wheels turning across the table, Harriet decided to make conversation. "What's going to happen at the mill?"

"Happen? Nothing." Phelps dismissed the agitators with a hearty laugh. "I noticed Patrick mentioned he hoped 'reasonable solutions' could be found. Those people, however, aren't reasonable. You send Patrick down, and I'll give him the facts. No, I'd better keep my mouth shut. Or you and I'll be crossing swords. Have to admit, you're a worthy opponent. Roosevelt-lover or not, I'll continue to advertise."

"I wondered if, after today, you would."

"Why not? I'm not vindictive. We both know Jericho needs a paper. I know how much the paper means to you, know how important your work is."

"Mr. Phelps, I—"

"I thought we agreed . . . ?"

"Oh," she replied, having forgotten his request of over a week ago that they dispense with formality. "Abraham," she added, flattered anew.

"What about Furber? Has he taken an ad? No? I'll speak to him."

"We need all the advertising we can get. We're stone broke."

"I'll help."

"I wasn't fishing," she replied quickly, and they both thought of the money she owed him, which neither had ever mentioned—Harriet because she was too embarrassed and Phelps because he never minded having anyone in his debt. The time, he reflected, was propitious to bring it up. "Speaking of business matters, I knew you hadn't forgotten our own. I'm sure your salary at the paper won't permit— In any event, the debt is canceled."

"I couldn't accept that, Mr. Phelps—Abraham," she corrected as he cocked an eyebrow. "I fully intended—intend—to repay you. It was my responsibility to mention it—"

"Subject closed. I'll be hurt if you argue. It's small potatoes for the happiness you bring my son."

"I—"

"Closed."

"I'm very grateful." Harriet found herself pushing a piece of scrod into her peas and out again. "I have to . . . tell you something." Unable to accept his generosity under false pretenses, she revealed she wasn't seeing Elliot.

Appreciative of her character, though he'd long lost touch with his own, Phelps pretended ignorance and heaved an abrupt sigh.

"I'm sorry," was all Harriet could say, his distress upsetting her.

"I know you're not."

"Pardon?"

"I know you've broken up with him. Haven't been entirely truthful. I guess I didn't want to accept it. I've failed," he added, laying down his fork. A pretense of weakness and impotence had always been one of Phelps' most efficacious stratagems. Yet his distress wasn't totally a sham. "I don't understand him. Never have, I'm ashamed to say," he went on, scrutinizing Harriet carefully from behind veiled eyes. "Moody. Keeps bad company. Drinks too much. I'm not telling you anything you don't know." How much, if anything, did she know of Elliot's problem? "At the end of my rope," he added, feigning another sigh, yet speaking the truth.

"I can see how worried you are," Harriet replied, her sympathetic instincts aroused as Phelps calculated they would be. Touched by his helplessness, she reached across the table and took his cold hand in hers.

"It was only this morning . . . that I learned from Elliot . . . that you and he had a . . . misunderstanding."

Misunderstanding? "Is that . . . what he said?" Lingering outrage assaulted her, battling with her curiosity.

"I can't tell you how unhappy the news made me. I have an ulterior motive," he added. "You're the first person who's had a steadying influence on him. I know how exasperating he can be."

"He is a lot to handle," was all Harriet could think of to say as tenderness for Elliot rose in spite of herself.

"Where've I gone wrong?"

"You haven't. Elliot's wonderfully intelligent. He's creative and kind. He hasn't found himself yet. But he's young." She felt wonderfully mature herself.

"Time is money. He has responsibilities. Others to think of. The town. When I go, he's got to be ready."

"Elliot—" Harriet paused and gathered her thoughts. Even if she

265

never saw Elliot again (which seemed impossible), even if she couldn't forgive him, nor allow him back into her heart (despite everything, was he still there?), she wanted to be of service.

"I understand . . ." she began again, "that he's your only son. And you want what you think is best for him. Which, of course, is the mill. But that isn't what Elliot wants. He—"

"He doesn't know what he wants," interjected Phelps brusquely. "What would you suggest?" he added, not letting Harriet see his irritation. "I need your help," he added, softening his stance and regarding her imploringly.

"Well," she replied, unable not to be flattered by his latter request, "I feel I know him. As I say, he's very creative. Why not give him a year or two? Away from the mill. Let him explore. He might surprise you. I know it's a cliché, but you can lead a horse to water . . ."

Explore? Phelps found Harriet's suggestion ridiculous, but he nodded and didn't let on.

"You see," she continued, "Elliot doesn't feel confident. He doesn't have your . . . sense of purpose."

"You have. You understand purpose. You're one of a kind. Bright. I'll think about what you're saying."

"How is he?" she couldn't help asking.

"As unhappy as I am," Phelps replied, seizing the opportunity she gave him. Whatever distaste he felt at the charade he was perpetrating was banished with the frightening memory of Elliot's behavior this morning. His son was clearly on the brink of disaster. The horrendous implications of Elliot's homosexuality were beyond comprehension; having no experience with the evil thing, nor able to admit to its dark and unknown attraction for his son, Phelps had no solution, no choice but to use—and quickly—the innocent young woman who sat across the table. She would marry Elliot. Marriage would banish the nightmare. If Elliot was sick, Harriet Hoskins would be the cure.

"Would I be out of line if I asked you if you loved my son?"

Her blush gave him hope.

"I—I'm not sure how Elliot feels about me," she stammered.

"I am. He asked me if I'd do what I could to patch things up."

"He did?" Harriet couldn't disguise the flicker of doubt that appeared on her face. She knew Elliot and his father didn't have the kind of rapport that would lead the former to make such an extraordinary request.

"This morning," Phelps replied quickly, seeing her hesitation. "If he hadn't asked, I would've let the matter drop and not interfered. I'm embarrassed myself," he added, giving a forced chuckle, eyes meeting hers to reassure her. "Not my style exactly. Fixing quarrels for my son. But you and I are friends. I thought I'd see what I could do."

"He really sent you?" Excitement she couldn't help mushroomed,

266

and Phelps saw it. He nodded. "I don't know what happened between you, but whatever it was, I can assure you it came from Elliot's deep feeling for you." Greased by need, the lies came easily, and of necessity were compounded. "Elliot loves you. He told me so himself only an hour ago."

Phelps hailed the waitress, leaving a slightly stunned Harriet to let what he'd said sink in.

"I've upset you. Didn't mean to. Thought I could help."

"No . . . I . . . ." Ignited by his revelations, she fumbled in her purse for a hankie. Elliot appeared before her, his face causing a tremulous ache. How desperate he must have been to have sent his father. If a moment ago that possibility had seemed unbelievable, now, in the grip of her accelerating feeling, Harriet found herself thinking how adroit and imaginative Elliot was. Knowing how angry she'd be, he'd asked his father for help. For if there was anyone who might be able to achieve a rapprochement, it would be her patron and champion, who gazed across the table at her now with such concern that she hastened to reassure him.

"You haven't upset me. . . . I just don't know what to say."

Once again she grasped his hand. "You've been playing Cupid!" she exclaimed, laughing now.

"Have I succeeded?" he asked, knowing he had. There was nothing he couldn't accomplish.

Once again, Harriet couldn't speak, could only nod. "Thank you," she murmured a moment later. "Thank you, Abraham."

"Clicquot? Good. Twenty-eight—an excellent year." Elliot nodded to the wine steward, who poured a dollop. Putting on a show for an appreciative Harriet, he held the glass up, perused the liquid with judicious eyes, swirled it, sniffed, tasted, put on a weighty brow of possible ambivalence, tasted again, paused, set the glass down and pronounced: "Not bad."

Harriet broke up in infectious giggles, and Elliot nodded to the steward. The lovers toasted each other, raising champagne glasses across the table in Boston's elegant Hampshire House restaurant.

"To my darling Wallis."

"To my dearest Edward."

"And to dear old Dad. We mustn't forget him."

"To Cupid himself."

"You're not going to tell me what he said?"

"He said enough," Harriet bantered. "I'm here."

"You're so beautiful. I'm so glad you're here."

"So are you. I am, too. What's past is past."

Elliot's apology had been heartfelt; Harriet's acceptance was equally impassioned.

267

"I'll drink to that."

"You'd drink to a sore throat."

"To us." Elliot raised his glass and fought for calm. His toast to his father had lacked the usual sarcasm, for he needed the opportunity Phelps had provided and was as relieved to be with Harriet as she with him. From a terrifying morning and a depression he could no longer remember (who was the person who'd insisted he didn't love her?) he'd accelerated to a state of manic exuberance. If the latter had determination in its underpinnings, Elliot didn't want to second-guess himself.

"Here we are. We belong together," he added, wrapping himself in romantic fantasies that would keep him from falling off the tightrope. "Who'd of thunk it? Tell me what he said."

"I got your message, that's all. Sly one," she added flirtatiously.

"Sly?" He was curious to know more. "Did he offer you the moon?"

"He offered me . . . you."

"Me?" Elliot felt he would cry. "Me," he said flatly, as if he were unknown to himself, a foreign body flung off from the universe, endlessly circling, desperate to return.

Once again they raised glasses, linking their arms, and sipped. Harriet read in Elliot's eyes the truth of what Phelps had told her at lunch. The final Chinese box was opened. It was love.

Like magnets pulled together by an irresistible force, they talked non-stop, catching up—as if the week and a half they'd been apart were a year and there would never be enough time. The waiter served the lobster thermidor, the aroma rising in whiffs of sherried steam, wooing their appetites as they wooed each other. Ecstasy was the first bite of the lobster, melting in their mouths. The future was theirs, the past a bad dream, banished in the face of their intimacy, which gave them power and a sense they could do no wrong. The latter feeling was specially strong for Harriet.

"Since your father was our peacemaker, I intend to reciprocate," she announced gaily. "I shall bring you and your father together. I did some spadework for you today. Told him that you and the mill are oil and water."

"That was risky. Did he raise the roof?"

"No. He listens to me. We spent a good deal of our lunch talking about you, in fact. Were your ears burning?"

"Sizzling. Well?"

"Between the two of us, we're going to make you happy."

"Ahhh. Go on. What's my fate?" Elliot gave into a daydream that Harriet could get him out of the mill.

"I suggested he give you a year off."

"With him paying for it?"

"We didn't get into details, but—"

"I don't think he'll let go of the leash. But maybe you *are* a miracle worker. What am I to do with my year? Polish my tennis game?"

"You're to be productive. Travel, perhaps. Compose . . ."

"Without you?" Frankie appeared in his thoughts, unsettling him. He would get rid of those feelings, exorcise them from his heart and love Harriet. Will would prevail and conquer indulgence. Immediately he felt better.

"I'm not going anywhere. Let's see, what else? Find yourself. That's what I told him. That's your objective. I think he agreed."

"It's a conspiracy! You and he have it all worked out I see. How can I go wrong?"

"You can't. And less of that," she added as Elliot ordered an after-dinner cognac.

"How," he wanted to know, "am I going to become this paragon of virtue, seeker of truth and follower of the straight and narrow if you're not by my side?"

"But I told you. I'm not going anywhere. You're my project for winter."

"Let's get married."

"To this local yokel? I'll have to think."

Beneath the delicious camaraderie rose a sudden awareness in both that he was serious. "You're not serious," Harriet laughed, buying time in the face of an overwhelming excitement. Hot brandied cherry juices melted the ice cream in her parfait; she wasn't on top of the world—she was orbiting.

Carried away himself, Elliot uncharacteristically blushed and was likewise tongue-tied. Gazing was enough for the moment as they held hands and didn't dare breathe. Neither remembered how the check got paid or how they floated out of the restaurant. A light rain had fallen; now the city smelled fresh as they walked into the Public Gardens and strolled, arm in arm, on the wet-slicked paths which reflected the lights. They stopped and kissed, then walked on under the dripping trees, past the lagoon with its swanboats docked for the night. Up on the hill the golden dome of the State House shimmered like their hearts.

"Let's run away. Tonight! Elope. *Let's!*"

"Darling, we can't do that." Once again, they kissed.

"Why? Don'tcha want to hitch your wagon to my star? No, you're right. What would we live on? I get my trust in three years. We'll have to stay in creepy Jericho till then."

Down the street, three blocks over, was the YMCA, its red neon sign calling him. No, he would never go there again to watch the naked men in the pool, nor loiter in the toilets with fantasies of getting caught and arrested. The bars and alleys of the waterfront would be out of bounds, the

269

tight-panted sailors forsaken. He would let Harriet end his torment and the double life that had driven him crazy. He would satisfy his father. Normal like the others. Oh, how he longed to be!

"Could we manage Jericho till then? If we're together, we could. We'll be married. I'll even buckle down—just the way he wants. Then when I get my money, we'll kick the applecart over on him and run for our lives." *She would save him.*

"But he's on our side. We don't have to—"

"*No*, he's not. *He's not.* Don't let him fool you. Don't—"

Harriet stopped Elliot's agitation with an embrace. "There," she murmured, sitting him down on a bench and smoothing his brow with her kisses. He was trembling. "Oh, please," he whispered. "*Harriet.*"

"Dearest . . ."

"Marry me. I want you to. Oh, please."

Calmer than she had ever been in her life, Harriet laid her head against Elliot's shoulder. She loved him, needed that special exhilaration that only he could provide, had lost her heart to this troubled and charming boy whose need of mending caused Harriet to want to be the glue. Did she want to marry him? Their lips met again and she looked into his eyes.

"I'm scared," he admitted.

"Don't be," she whispered, as the answer to her question rose up in an intoxicating rush. Exquisitely the answer floated at her like the perfume of freshly washed grass.

Yes.

14 Halloween was three days away, but goblins were already loose in Jericho.

Patrick moved out of the house and went to stay at Teresa's. He'd had it with his mother, he told his aunt. Gert withdrew her financial support, and *The Spectator* was on its own.

Harried with the estrangement, Gert was further bombarded when she received a furious call from Michael O'Brien, who'd read the interview with Patrick in the *Boston Herald* ("Ex-Seminarian Turns On Coughlin In Jericho Paper"). O'Brien threatened to break the engagement; Gert threatened back and vowed she's slap O'Brien with a breach of promise suit *and* give the story to the Boston papers. How would that look a few days before the election?

And so it went.

Two days after she'd accepted Elliot's proposal, Harriet and Marcia hurried down Main Street at the crack to catch an early train. "That's Meyer Shapiro," she told Marcia, pointing out the labor organizer, who was already at his post outside the gates of the mill. Passing out leaflets to Phelps' operatives, who streamed into work, Shapiro doffed his battered fedora to Harriet.

"I want to interview you," she told him, and made a date to meet him at Noonan's the next day.

"My pleasure," responded Shapiro, whose grandfatherly manner and rumpled suit disguised his shrewdness. "Join the union!" he called to the hurrying workers. Most ignored him, for Phelps had threatened reprisals to anyone who so much as talked to Shapiro, let alone read his poisonous literature.

A few moments later, Harriet and Marcia were on their way to Boston and an appointment with the latter's gynecologist, who would outfit Harriet with a contraceptive device.

If she was slightly unnerved at the prospect, her continuing state of exhilaration buoyed her. The seed planted by Abraham Phelps had germinated. Fertilized by Elliot, blossoms had sprouted. And nestled on a silky branch, wrapped in a cocoon of romance, Harriet was a butterfly

271

aborning. Soon she would emerge, brilliant and fluttering, into the sunshine with her love Elliot by her side, the dream come true.

"Pessary. Odd word, isn't it? Sounds medieval."

Marcia nodded. "Did you read the pamphlet I gave you?"

"Yes."

"You'll have to say you're married."

A shiver of delight coursed through her. "I'll just say I'm Mrs. Elliot Phelps."

"Did you know it was illegal in Massachusetts up until last year? For a woman to—"

"Illegal? Who would make a law like that? Some man. Don't we have a right to decide for ourselves? Did you sleep with Allan before you were married?"

"Of course not. But obviously, you're going to."

"With Allan? Not my type."

Conspiratorial schoolgirls, who once (at Harriet's urging) had gone to the library to look up Sex, Procreation, and Reproduction, the two friends giggled.

"Is that why we're going today?"

Smiling to herself, Harriet nodded. "I want to be ready. And I'm not of a mind to have little ones scampering for my attention. Not just yet." She was sure Elliot would be knowledgeable about such matters, but Alice's predicament caused her to want to make sure no chances were taken. Properly prepared would lead to relaxation and pleasure. Even in her euphoric state, there was a place for practicality and realism.

"I think . . . tomorrow night." Delicious anticipation hit her in the gut as she imagined him undressing her.

"The Assembly?" Marcia was wide-eyed in enthusiasm.

"After. Maybe we could take a room at the inn. It's such a romantic spot."

"You're so sophisticated. I've never seen you so . . ."

"Happy. I'm so happy, I can't stand myself. I've loved Elliot from the first day I met him. Do you remember? When I went to his birthday party at the Mansion?"

Marcia nodded. "It's destiny. Does Patrick know?"

His name produced a tightening in Harriet's stomach. She shook her head. "I don't dare." It was going to be very difficult to tell him; she didn't want to hurt his feelings; she knew it would be worse than that. "Alice told me I can't see Patrick for the glare of Elliot. She couldn't be more mistaken. Patrick's never been a contender. And I see Elliot very clearly. Alice has suddenly become Patrick's champion. She was flabbergasted when I told her."

"And you haven't told your parents?"

"Not yet. Elliot's going to come by in the next day or so and do it up properly. I insisted on that. Mother will have to be won over, I'm afraid. Father . . ." Harriet hesitated, for she had no idea how Franklin would respond. Lately, she could never tell.

Patrick came into her thoughts again. Yes, she respected him; yes, her admiration had mushroomed. However, since her luncheon with Phelps, he'd been alternately distant or pumping her as to whether she was seeing Elliot again.

"Is this going . . . to hurt?"

Marcia shook her head. It was nice, for once, to know more than Harriet.

"Dr. Abrams is very kind. You'll like her. At least she's not a man."

"Does she put your legs up in those . . . what are they called?"

"Stirrups." Marcia blushed.

"*God.*" Her stomach felt upset. "I've decided against that dress I showed you," she went on. "You were right. It wouldn't do for the Assembly."

"I love it, you understand but . . . it's just too provocative—bare-shouldered and so slinky. I can't believe you found it for ten dollars. You look wonderfully sexy in it but— So what have you decided on?"

"Cora's ice blue. Hopefully, no one will remember it from her graduation. Mother's taking it in for me. Do you like it?"

"The dress?"

"No—sex."

Two ladies nearby aborted their conversation as they heard what they thought they'd heard.

"Am I supposed to?"

"I hope so." Poor Marcia. "I can't wait," Harriet whispered. Deliciousness rose in her again, the latter imbued as well with a kind of awe. She saw Elliot's face and tasted his kisses, read the response in his eyes when she would present him with the exquisite gift of herself.

"How is Mrs. Phelps taking all this?"

"Nancy? To tell you the truth, I haven't seen her. We're all having dinner at the Inn tomorrow night before the dance, so we'll cross swords then. That is, if she didn't swallow her golf clubs when she heard the news. Abraham will handle her, I'm sure."

The conductor passed through the car, and something about his eyes reminded her of Patrick. "A part of me loves him. Like a brother. Even if he *has* made life difficult. He acts as if he owns me sometimes. But . . . what's most important to him right now? He may think *I* am, but I'm not. He eats, sleeps, and dreams *The Spectator* lately. Did I tell you he got a check from Mr. Phelps for six weeks' advertising? In advance. One hundred and twenty dollars! Patrick wanted to send it back, but then he realized he couldn't. My God, that money will temporarily save our life. Mrs. Flynn, needless to say, is no longer making up a penny of our deficit.

The vindictive bitch! We increased our circulation by ten percent this week, everyone is suddenly aware of the paper, and she's jumped ship! Even if people are upset that we came out for Roosevelt, at least we've created some controversy that may lead to something. Does she care? If it can't be done her way, she abandons us. I'm glad Patrick's out from under her thumb. I imagine she'll be singing and dancing when she hears I'm marrying Elliot. Anyway, because of Mr. Phelps—I mean, Abraham—Patrick won't lose his paper. That's my prime concern."

"I never thought you'd be married so quickly. You always said—"

"I know, I know. Talked a good line, didn't I? I certainly never intended this would happen. I wasn't going to get married till the cows come home but—" Harriet shook her head and lapsed into a daydream about Elliot. The train rocked her, and she felt almost sleepy. "We understand each other so," she murmured a moment later. "We're going to have a very modern marriage. I'll still have my independence. We discussed it last night. No children until we're both ready. Elliot understands who I am. I'll continue to work." Would Patrick fire her? The unsettling thought upset her equanimity. She hoped he wouldn't be that foolish. No, she decided, once over the shock, he'd realize that *The Spectator* was bigger than both of them, more important than his hurt.

"I won't be just a wife," she went on, "stuck in a house thinking up menus and knitting booties. We're going to make our own rules. That's the way we are."

"Good evening, Miss Hoskins."

"Good evening, John." Harriet smiled at the Phelps' chauffeur and got into the back seat of the black Cadillac limousine, careful not to crinkle her gown. A bouquet of blood red roses lay waiting on the broad seat. Phelps had called an hour ago. Would she mind if the car picked her up and brought her to the Mansion? A surprise awaited her.

When she was let in the front door, she had the strangest sense that something unusual was about to happen. *Good evening, moose,* she whispered, passing under the stuffed head. Ushered into the organ room, she found Elliot standing silhouetted before a low fire. Pale and striking in his formal evening wear, she had never seen him handsomer.

Silently they kissed.

Caught by the flickering flames of the fire, the moisture glistening on the silver champagne cooler seemed to dance, its sparkle no competition for the three-karat diamond set in platinum that Elliot removed from a small velvet box. The ring had been a rush order, hand-delivered to the Mansion from Phelps' jeweler in Boston only an hour ago.

Dazed, Harriet let Elliot take her hand. The ring went on so effortlessly, she had no sensation of it and had to take it off and look at it later in the chintz-curtained ladies' powder room at the country club, to believe that it was real.

Once again the lovers embraced, then separated at a knock on the door. Elegant in tails, Phelps entered the room. The sight of the ring on Harriet's finger revived him from the unpleasant scene he'd concluded with his wife upstairs. She would thank him in the end.

"Forgive an old sentimentalist for intruding on what should be a private moment between two people I'm very fond of. Harriet," Phelps added with a hearty stride toward her, "I couldn't be happier. How lovely you look."

"Abraham . . ." She curtsied and kissed him on the cheek. Phelps shook hands with his son and poured champagne. Harriet sensed Elliot was nervous that Phelps had joined them, but she found his presence appropriate and fitting. He was her ally, the benefactor who had returned Elliot to her.

"We are honored, Harriet." Phelps raised his glass. "Mrs. Phelps will be down shortly."

Above their heads, Nancy Phelps paced her apricot-colored bedroom, furious with betrayal.

Phelps took hold of Harriet's shoulders and kissed her on both cheeks. What he was keeping from her caused a certain amount of guilt, but the emotion was distant, dismissed with the necessity of this marriage. There would be benefits for Harriet, too, Phelps hastened to assure himself as he released her to Elliot. She was a practical girl. As he watched the two of them, Phelps felt relief and anxiety course through him simultaneously. He looked to the future, willed it the way he wanted it, and banished his apprehension. Yet an unaccustomed prayer rose in his heart as his son raised his glass to Harriet.

"Wallis . . ."

"Edward . . ."

"What's that?"

"Just a joke, Dad," replied Elliot. He was terrified.

Long ago, Harriet had a fantasy. Elliot would waltz her out the French doors at the club onto the wisteria-draped veranda under the envious eyes of all.

Aside from the wisteria, which had succumbed to the change of season, it had all come true.

"I think we've shocked everyone," she whispered in Elliot's ear, floating on romance, drama and champagne. Hidden in a far corner of the glassed-in porch overlooking the dark fairways stretching to the lake, the two of them were alone for the first time in the evening. "Did you see their faces? I don't think they've had such a tidbit to chew on in ages! When I danced with Senator Saltonstall, he was trying very hard to place me.

Hadn't he met me at a cotillion in Boston last month? I assured him he hadn't. Then he asked where you and I had met. I told him in a bar."

"You didn't." He wanted to run; he lightly kissed her instead.

"I didn't." Harriet's eyes twinkled mischievously as she straightened Elliot's bow tie. "We are the evening's main attraction, aren't we?"

An hour ago, Phelps had silenced the band, made his happy announcement, and Harriet had heard him introduce her to the hushed room. It seemed as if she were in a dream, the unreality momentarily unsettling her, and she held tight to Elliot's hand, accepting the applause with a slightly bemused smile. Moments later, the band had segued into "Oh, Susannah," Alf Landon's theme song. The election was Tuesday, and as the Republican gathering applauded heartily, Harriet's eyes met Phelps' in an amused glance. No politicking tonight, Harriet? Agreed, Abraham.

"I always did want to invade the ranks of the bluebloods." She ran a playful finger down Elliot's starched front.

"Bunch of bores."

Harriet wouldn't have guessed that the old families of North Parish considered her patron a parvenu, whose money and power forced them to a grudging acceptance. Wearing her Gramma Sarah's pearls, which Letty had loaned for the occasion, she couldn't help laughing at the irony, for Sarah Winslowe would've bartered her soul to be in her granddaughter's shoes this evening. Harriet, too, had endowed Jericho's elite with a mystique they didn't deserve. The five yearly Assemblies at the country club had evoked longings, as well as insecurities, but tonight she wasn't at all intimidated as she'd thought she'd be.

"Your father has made me feel so at home."

Under the umbrella of Phelps' warmth and position, and with her love by her side, she had moved about the room accepting best wishes. Sitting under the black and orange crepe-paper streamers at the pumpkined tables with candles glowing (the women's committee had chosen a Halloween motif), Jericho's gentry had watched with varying degrees of surprise and curiosity. Returning the well-mannered greetings with as cool an eye as was possible under the circumstances, Harriet was the picture of equanimity. If the powder room was buzzing about the 'town' girl who worked for that newspaper, if the ladies wondered why Nancy Phelps wasn't here tonight, the conjecture only stimulated Harriet. Dancing with Phelps, she couldn't help her sudden and exhilarating sense of arrival. It might be a smallish mountain on whose peak she stood, but it was definitely the top.

"Were you surprised?" Elliot smiled wistfully at her. The music drifted to their hideaway spot, and he tried to let it calm him. The earlier terror was replaced with a dazed and odd stillness, the panic muted by liquor. Elliot knew he mustn't get drunk tonight; he didn't know how he'd be able not to.

"Surprised? Bowled over." The ring glittered as she held it up. "It's so beautiful. I think I had a premonition," she added. "I told mother about us as I left the house." She laughed. "You haven't even asked my father for my hand yet. You wonderfully impulsive ninny!"

"I'll come by tomorrow."

"You're warm," she murmured, laying the back of her hand against his cheek. "I hope you're not coming down with something."

"Just all the excitement."

"Are you worried about your mother?" she asked, sensing he was troubled. Nancy Phelps had been taken with a severe headache, Phelps had explained earlier, and had not accompanied them.

Elliot shook his head. So be it, Nancy had remarked coldly when he told her he loved Harriet. So be it. Thus, the only person in Elliot's life to have showered him with love had withheld it. The young woman who gazed up at him now with expectation in her eyes only made him nervous. He didn't trust her enough to take a chance and allow her to make up for his loss.

"She'll be OK." Dismissing his agitation as normal jitters, Elliot clung to Harriet's hand, the contact anchoring him.

"Of course she will," replied Harriet soothingly, matching Elliot's disquiet with her powerful surety. "She wants you to be happy. She loves you, too."

"C'mon . . . let's go back in."

"Darling?"

"I love you so." *Faker.*

Elliot took her arm, and they returned via the bar, where he caught Harriet's expression of watchfulness. Was she going to start counting his drinks as his father did? he wondered angrily. Guilt hit him, for he knew she was only looking out for his welfare. Laughing loudly at a story someone was telling, the familiar faces of college chums he'd never paid attention to were hazy with a depression he strove to conquer. The girls he'd dated, and the ones he hadn't, drifted past, offering kisses or veiled looks of disappointment. "Was Amy brokenhearted?" Harriet whispered as his old girlfriend departed. "I suppose she's one of many here tonight who set their cap for you. . . ." Around them the easy chatter of the college crowd, home for the weekend from Harvard and Yale, Radcliffe and Wellesley, rose and fell with a breezy nonchalance. "But I won, didn't I?" she added, unable to help the swell of triumph over these snoots, who'd never given her the time of day.

Elliot nodded, nuzzling Harriet's ear with his nose. Confused, as if her victory would mean his defeat (he couldn't put his finger on why), he spun her around the floor in a fox trot.

"I think you're bored. I have an idea," she added, as they finished. "Let's call it a night to this group. Let's go celebrate! We'll go to the Classic. I can't wait to tell Frankie. Did you know he predicted us all along?"

"He did?" Even the irony was distant. Elliot hesitated. The last person in the world he wanted to see tonight was Frankie.

"And then . . ." Once again the sexual anticipation that had gripped her the last few days caught her up, but she decided it wasn't the appropriate moment to let him know she wanted to make love tonight. They would both be more relaxed at the Classic. "C'mon," she insisted, "you need some real music. Let's go swing!"

She had a final dance with Phelps before she and Elliot left. She told him that, although she appreciated the generosity of his suggested wedding gift, a four-month world tour would take her away too long from the paper. Phelps nodded as if he understood. There was time. *The Spectator* was sure to fold, which was fine with him. He didn't want Harriet working. Marriage to Elliot would be a full-time job. "You're good for him," Phelps said as he led her back toward the table where Elliot waited, looking more sixteen than twenty-two. "Yes," Harriet replied simply. "He's a challenge," remarked Phelps, whose three bourbons caused him to be heartily effusive. "But you were born to rise to it."

Aware that he was laying it on just a bit, Harriet was nonetheless thrilled. Never had she felt wiser, nor more sure of herself. Elliot was her darling, but Phelps and she were equals, recognized each other and had, she was certain, from the day they'd met.

Arm in arm, she and Elliot walked the half mile past the deserted fairways to the Mansion. Elliot looked up at the darkness of his mother's bedroom, then got his car out and they drove to Leveret.

At close to ten Gert got a call from Maisie Harrigan, who worked in the kitchen of the country club, telling her that Abraham Phelps had just announced the engagement of Harriet and Elliot. Time seemed to stop as Gert set the phone down and sat in her robe at the kitchen table. The same relief felt by Phelps coursed through her, and immediately she drove to Teresa's, waking that house up with an insistent ringing of the bell. "She's marryin' Elliot Phelps." Gert delivered the news to a groggy Teresa before she'd barely got through the front door.

Patrick heard the words as he started down from upstairs. A chill froze him. Trembling, he pulled his uncle's borrowed bathrobe around him and sat down in the stairwell. "Where is he?" he heard Gert ask Teresa. "I'll tell him myself. It's best that it comes from me."

"Saint Michael, protect him. . . ." Teresa crossed herself.

"I've no heart for tellin' him, lemme tell ya." Gert frowned at the look

278

her sister gave her. "I've not," she insisted. "But it's for the best. He'll see. But I'd have accepted her if it came to that. If she was what he wanted, I'd have put aside my worries and tried to—"

"Bullshit, Gert." Teresa shook her head sadly at her sister's hypocrisy. Gert glared. "Enough talk. Wake him up. I want him home with me. I'll make it up to him," she added. "You'll see."

"Patrick . . . !" Teresa suppressed an anxious gasp as her nephew appeared on the stairs. Then she couldn't look at him any longer and had to turn away, digging in the pocket of her robe for a handkerchief.

"How will you make it up to me?"

"So ya heard." Patrick's blood-drained face and violent eyes caused Gert to be scared. "Sit down, Patty?" she asked, uncommonly gentle. "It's for the best. She's where she belongs. I know ya think your heart'll never mend, but it will. I'll see to it. Come on home."

Patrick turned and went back upstairs, got into his clothes and returned in five minutes. Ignoring Gert, he walked out the door and kept walking. A half hour later, he was standing at the packed Saturday night bar of Grogan's Bar and Grille in Leveret, while a hot lava stream ran in his head. Harriet had betrayed him. He took the blame on himself. He'd never been worthy of her, now she was lost. O lost. A whiskey neat, downed quickly. Another. *Naive*, he cursed himself, prostate throbbing. He'd let her walk over him, given her a job when she needed it, now she'd abandoned him. Grievances ran amok. Like a martyr seeking pain, he'd walked past her house on the way over to Leveret, knowing she wasn't there, knowing where she was, seeing them together in her moment of triumph. No more! He would exorcise her from his heart. He would fire her on Monday.

Patrick's revenge turned to lust as he glanced into the grille and focused on a pair of breasts that seemed to grow larger as a young woman stretched, and he recognized Joyce Gillespie, whom he'd met and danced with at the Classic. She was having a friendly drink with Billy Meeghan, the two of them in a booth in the grille, for ladies weren't allowed in the bar.

"Hello, there. Remember me by any chance? Hi, Billy."

"Oh . . ." responded Joyce, looking up as Patrick towered over her, staring at her with such unabashed fervor that she was forced to lower her eyes. Still, he was a handsome devil.

Invited to sit, Patrick did—next to Joyce, who was animated and chatty. When Billy excused himself a moment later to go to the men's room, Joyce made sure Patrick understood she wasn't *with* Billy, who was a twerp.

"Let's ditch him," Patrick suggested, stimulated by Joyce's warm reception. The liquor made him bolder, determination and fantasy led to daring shortcuts, and he put an arm around her waist and drew her to him,

279

causing her hat to go askew. Like the good sport she was, Joyce laughed and let Patrick know she wouldn't mind getting to know him better, yes, indeed.

Hard under the table, a burning flame, Patrick's single-mindedness produced a confidence and ease he never dreamed he had. "Where would you like to go?" he asked with a simple directness that produced stomach spasms in both of them. A hotel, he wondered? Sin was the agenda. Let her lead him through the rites of passage. Did he want to come up to the house for a nightcap? Joyce suggested, a twinkle in her eye promising more. Oh, yes, and then some.

Arm in arm, they left Grogan's quickly and began walking. Her sister Elaine and father, Joyce explained, were in Fall River for the weekend, seeing to an ailing aunt. Her father was a plumber, she kept his books. "Plumbing"—she gave the word a sexy cast. She didn't tell him she was thirty-three and lonely.

Patrick wondered: Were all the women in the world as bold and fun as this dimpled baked apple who barely came up to his shoulder? Why hadn't he been out finding her months ago? Plums for the picking. Harriet came into his thoughts, but Patrick willed her to be gone. A moment later, she was back. Like a tormenting river she ran in him, allowing him no peace. He walked faster, almost pulling Joyce with him up the steep incline of Tower Hill where she lived in a modest house that seemed to hang over the city. He could see Jericho.

They went down into the cellar, called the playroom. Joyce's father had paneled it and built the mahogany bar. She made them highballs and challenged him to a game of Ping-Pong. He had a semi–stiff erection that couldn't be ignored any longer. *Clop, clop, clop* went the ball, back and forth. Patrick deliberately missed, put his paddle down and went to her. "Ohhh," he moaned, wrapping his arms around her with such clumsy force, she grunted in surprise.

"There now—no rush, is there?"

Embarrassed, he stepped back, but Joyce grinned.

What a custard she was! He might marry her. She picked up her paddle again. "You like my melons, don't you?" she asked, her boldness astounding him. Harriet hovered, blowing him down, raising a dust devil of hurt, humiliation, and anger. Roughly, he pulled Joyce to him again, a hand pawing uncontrolled at her breasts as a stifled cry came out of him.

"Stop now!"

"I apologize."

"You're a bull in a china shop, aren't you?"

"Sorry."

"A little gentleness," she murmured, up on her dignity. How, Patrick wondered, could gentleness be achieved when all he wanted was to smother and be smothered in return? "All right then," Joyce said, helpless not to soften at the sight of him, mouth open, breath ragged, face blotched deep raspberry.

'You're hungry," she whispered.

"I was in the seminary," he replied, playing chaste, hoping the admission would buy him back her interest. Joyce looked at him, disbelieving. Patrick spun a few quick phrases in Latin and blessed her with a charming grin she found hard to resist. She took his hand and led him upstairs into the darkened house, but they didn't make it to a bedroom. Pausing in the parlor, Patrick put his arms around her again, then sank to his knees, burying his head against her stomach. "I love you," he cried, but it wasn't to her.

Wedged against the back of a sofa, Joyce protested, but Patrick was unstoppable. Hands wildly tugging at her belt, fingers all thumbs on her buttocks, he gave up and chose the path of least resistance, moaning and crooning to himself as he bunched her dress up around her hips and feverishly pulled her panties down, gasping in surprise at the strong smell of her like seaweed which rose to his nostrils, almost precipitating an explosion in his pants as his fingers foraged in that crinkly place he'd dreamed of but never touched till now.

Gasping herself, Joyce felt herself picked up, her rump half on the sofa's back, half off, as Patrick supported her and struggled to get his own buckle undone, his buttons too, trying to shake his pants to his knees where they caught, then fell around his ankles.

With a cry neither of them had ever heard before, Patrick closed his eyes and gave it to the substitute without mercy.

🔳

"Hey, Frankie . . . ! We're engaged!"

Stunning in their evening wear, both enjoying the attention they received, Harriet and Elliot made an entrance down the stairs from the balcony to the packed dance floor of the Classic Ballroom at a little after eleven. The trumpet section was their willing accomplice as it rose with a blast, heralding the perfect twosome's progress through the dancers to Frankie, who cupped his ear, questioningly, then grinned and nodded happily as Elliot raised Harriet's hand, demonstrating the ring.

With the band on a break a moment later, Frankie and Jeannie joined the exuberant couple, and kisses and congratulations were bestowed. Heartache welled in Elliot as Frankie shook his hand and clapped him on the back. The passion he wanted banished, threatened; short of breath, he wished he hadn't come. A moment later, he pulled Harriet out onto the dance floor. Watching Frankie over the bobbing heads, Elliot willed his feelings away. "Oh, you'll see . . ." he sang, snapping his fingers to the beat and concentrating on Harriet, "how happy we'll be. Yessireeee. . . !"

"To my friends and my real engagement party!" he announced a while later, raising his glass to his usual hangers-on, who clustered around his table offering best wishes.

"How'd you get him lassoed, Harriet?" winked Myrna, who was introduced as "an old friend." Exhilarated and beginning to enjoy himself, Elliot clowned. "She's got my number," he sang, drumming fingers on the table, jumping up and down to greet well-wishers. Harriet joined in the good-natured ribbing that took place. "Now you sit on him if he misbehaves," giggled a girl known only as Miss Dimples. "Oh, I certainly will," she replied, nodding when Myrna asked if she and the others could now consider themselves jilted. "But you're all invited to the wedding, aren't they, Harriet?" asked Elliot, anchoring himself to her arm again. Harriet smiled her agreement, knowing they wouldn't be.

"Lookit that rock, will ya!" The girls and their boyfriends joined in a toast to the couple. Harriet had no idea why this crowd of riffraff should stimulate Elliot; she was having too good a time to dwell on the possibilities. These people were a part of his former life; he wouldn't need them from now on. The realization struck her that Elliot, no matter the camaraderie he professed toward this crowd, was as much an outsider here as he had been with his peers at the club.

"That's my favorite! C'mon, honeybunny." Needing to dance and keep moving, Elliot almost scooped Harriet out of her chair. Down they went again, clinging together while Jeannie crooned and the Classic was momentarily hushed in bittersweet. The up-tempo number that followed had Elliot jumping up to join bandleader Jimmy Lanceford, who glanced with a "here he is again," expression.

Carried away with the beat, tails flapping like a penguin as he rocked back and forth, Elliot did an impromptu shimmy, which had the nearby dancers laughing. "Take it off, Prince," someone yelled. Elliot undid his bow tie to further urgings; the drummer responded with an interpolated bump and grind rasp on his drum while Frankie did a fast run and Elliot waved him on.

"I'm engaged!" he announced, pointing to Harriet, who swayed to the music below him. "There she is!" Elliot cried, and as the spotlight swung onto her, Harriet squealed in delighted shock. Around her the dancers kept the beat, clapping best wishes to both of them.

"There's my girl . . . !" A goofy innocence about him now, he shut his eyes, let the music have his body and dreamed of them all, wanted the crowd to love him forever. Intoxicated with a fantasy stronger than scotch, he jumped off the bandstand and into Harriet's arms. The euphoria fled as he looked in her eyes. Suppose she let him down? Quickly he clasped her to him as an unreasoning panic flooded him. *But she was the one who would make it better!* Determined to outrace his fear, he pulled her out into the mass of bodies, hiding in the center while the glitter ball darted fragments on his perspiring face.

Walking down from Tower Hill and cutting through the city to catch a trolley back to Jericho, Patrick was in a foul and despairing mood again. What happened a while ago was what he'd dreamed and waited for these many years, but the pleasure was fleeting, and he felt empty and more dissatisfied than ever. As he wended his way through the Saturday night crowds emptying out of the movie theaters on Broadway, a rage grew, for the loss of his virginity had left him lonelier than ever. Blaming it all on Harriet, he muttered conversations full of revenge and walked right past Elliot's car. Turning back, his heart hammered as he looked up at the Classic's winking neon. Suddenly obsessed to see Harriet, he pushed through the doors. *Martyr!* Grappling with the desire, which he knew would only make him suffer, he found himself urgently tossing two bits at the window.

"We're almost closing. Why bother?" The ticket taker raised her eyes from buffing her nails. "You've got it bad, honey," she murmured, pushing a ticket at Patrick, whose expression gave him away. "Good luck," she called after him as he took the stairs three at a time.

"Why didn't we think of it!" laughed Harriet as she and Elliot caught their breath and burst out a door onto the fire escape. "In mapping your future, we neglected the obvious! You have the looks and you *love* carrying on. You're an actor! I want to leave for Hollywood immediately!"

Kisses interrupted their laughter. High on booze, dancing, and the magic between them, their bodies pressed together as Elliot's tongue slipped between Harriet's lips and met her own. Breathing ragged, they separated, then kissed again with greater urgency.

"It's going to be fine. Isn't it?" he asked.

"It's going to be fine."

"Fine."

"Fine."

"Let's elope! *C'mon*. We could be in New York by morning." Long engagements, Phelps had suggested over dinner, were old-fashioned. Elliot couldn't agree more. He wanted it done. Married and settled, the legal reality would be a dam to contain his chaos. "Eggs Benedict at the Plaza," he continued. "I used to stop off sometimes from Princeton. Let's . . . oh, let's. There must be a willing justice of the peace. It's easier in New York. C'mon."

Enjoying the potential drama of a midnight flight that would see the sun rise over the skyline of Manhattan, Harriet was tempted but told him no.

283

"I want to go *some* place," he whispered passionately as another necking couple brushed past. "To Hollywood or New York?" she whispered back, the banter stilled with an embrace that left them both breathless.

"You know what I mean. Do you want to wait? Don't pull Miss Puritan on me," he pleaded. "Aren't we a couple of iconoclasts?"

"My husband to be . . ." she murmured. Shyly, lightheaded and with a sexual tightening in her stomach, she imagined what it would be like. A surge of passion swept her against him again, her body answering his request. "I think you're reading my mind," she whispered in his ear as a siren sounded on a nearby street, for Elliot's sudden feverish kisses vindicated her foresight in preparing herself. The foreign body inside her was a passport to intimacy, and she went almost limp in his arms.

"Hmmmm . . ." What was he going to do with her the rest of his life? Sex would drive away the doubts, Elliot told himself as he clasped her tightly. "Let's check into the Salem." Suddenly he drew back with a mock warning:

"I'm not what I seem. I'm really a virgin."

"You imp."

"I think I'd rather wait till my wedding night."

"Not me."

The byplay calmed their nervousness. "We'll have a nightcap," he suggested.

"You're cut off."

"Awww. Mommy. It's my engagement! I'll get us a bottle of bubbly to bring with us. How about that?"

Once again they embraced, then returned, arm in arm, back into the thumping blast of the Classic and saw Patrick.

"Does he know?" Elliot asked, exchanging a glance with Harriet, who, even from a distance, could read the tension in Patrick's rigid stance. Halfway down the stairway that led from the balcony, he was a dark pillar, eyes searching, as couples climbed past him, rising to the tables above. Harriet shook her head and wanted to avoid him, but he spotted them.

"C'mon," Elliot suggested. "It has to be done." Excited by the possible confrontation, which took his mind off himself, he led Harriet through the dancers and up the stairs to where Patrick stood, unmoving and miserable. The tailspin escalated as Harriet got to his side.

"I know," he said, before she had a chance to say anything. "News travels fast."

If anyone expected Patrick to play the role of bereft but gracious loser, they were mistaken. "Congratulations," he said coldly, ignoring Elliot, who held out his hand.

Patrick's nakedly pained eyes met Harriet's, who didn't know what to say and had to look away. Below them the dancers whooped as the band dived into its final set, but the threesome on the stairs were oblivious to the music. Patrick turned his stare on Elliot, who shrugged off the missing handshake with contempt of his own. As relentless as the beat, the animosity between the two men caused Harriet to press close to Elliot, who put his arm around her waist and smiled at Patrick with subtle victory in his eyes. Inflamed, Patrick locked his hands behind his back.

"So . . ." he managed to say, looking again at Harriet with such defenseless anguish that, despite his rudeness, her heart ached for him. "Patrick . . ." she said, hoping to calm him, but his name on her lips only made it worse, and tears threatened him.

Insecure at the depth of his vanquished rival's passion, Elliot felt like an imposter again as he tightened his arm around Harriet's waist.

"Do you want to keep working for me?" Patrick asked curtly, breaking the tense silence.

"Of course I do. Do you want me to quit?"

"Quit? Why? Why should I want you to quit?" Too far gone to care that he was making a fool of himself, Patrick went on: "Don't *you* want to?" he asked, raising his voice to be heard above the din from the floor below.

"Why should I?" She had no reason to feel guilty, she told herself as Patrick's condemning eyes bore into her. Anger welled at his boorishness.

"You won't need your salary any more."

"Do we have to discuss this right now?" Elliot asked. "C'mon. Let's get going," he added and whispered in Harriet's ear that the bar was going to close and he wanted to get their bottle of champagne. Telling her he'd be right back, he glanced a final, contemptuous look at Patrick. "You're a sore loser," he said, deliberately kissing Harriet on the cheek, eyes meeting the mick's again as excitement filled him at the possibility of Patrick's taking a swing.

"Hurry . . ." Quickly Harriet sent Elliot off. Frightened at the violence in Patrick, she'd had more than enough. "Why?" she asked simply, but she knew; knew she should leave as well and tried to, but he restrained her, his fingers gripping her arm.

"What happened to your famous principles? I thought marriage was supposed to be a trap? What a phony you are."

"You're behaving like an ass."

"Nothing's changed, I guess."

"Are you satisfied? You're a boor."

Rapid-fire, the taunts continued back and forth, a mutual wounding that neither desired and neither could help.

"You deserve each other. That weakling—"

"You stink."

"I don't want you to work—"

"That's fine with me."

Simultaneously they broke away from each other. *"Wait,"* Patrick pleaded, jostling through bodies as he followed her down the stairs. Shame impelled him to take her arm again and apologize. "Why don't you make yourself scarce?" she replied, throwing his hand off.

"You really gonna do it, Prince?" Myrna asked in the bar as Elliot gulped a drink and ordered a bottle of champagne to go.

Ignoring her, he closed his eyes and let Jeannie's ballad wash over him. A final fanfare and the band wound it up, rising to applause as the glitter ball wound slowly down.

"Elliot!" called Frankie, joining him. "Is he gone?" Elliot asked Harriet, who appeared a second later. Still shaken, she nodded. "C'mon," he cried, "I'm not gonna let him spoil my good time. Frankie wants to know whether we want to go with him. A bunch of them are going over to the Delight for chop suey. Shall we? I'm starved. Aren't you?" he added, squeezing Harriet to him while his eyes told her that the Delight would be only a stopover on their amorous destination. She nodded, and he left her with Jeannie in the bar while he trooped back to the locker room with Frankie and the band.

Full of chatter and stimulated by the musicians, who were high on five hours of music, Elliot felt on top of things again as he locker-hopped, bestowing compliments, talking jive, and accepting congratulations. The sight of the young Italian passing through with mop and pail gave him a momentary shock. He pretended not to know him, and the boy did likewise.

"Did I tell you I got the new Bix Beiderbecke?" he called to Frankie, who was in the second row of lockers. Coming around the corner, he found Frankie turned away, half undressed in undershirt and shorts with one foot up on the bench as he unbuttoned his black garters. Elliot stared at the fabric, taut over Frankie's buttocks.

Stomach in knots, nodding to several others who were likewise getting out of their tuxedos, Elliot examined a pin–up on the inside of an adjacent locker door. There was a mirror, too, but his looks, which ordinarily reassured him, didn't.

"Are you pleased, kiddo?" he asked softly.

Nodding, Frankie hung up his pants, while an overwhelming impulse to kiss him on the nape of his neck gripped Elliot. Scared, he began to chatter. "I'm gonna take good care of her, Frankie. You'll see. I know how close you and she are. Yessiree. Say, we're almost brothers now, aren't we?"

Frankie grinned and mopped his brow with a towel. Elliot wished he could do it for him.

"I love her."

"I know you do, sport. I'm happy for you. She's the best."

Tears filled Elliot's eyes. Embarrassed, he sat down on the bench.

"I'm keyed up, I guess," he muttered, wanting Frankie to understand, wanting to confess his love, take him in his arms and end this terrifying charade. He blew his nose as fresh tears welled.

"Is this what happens when you get engaged, Prince?" grinned Frankie, throwing a sympathetic and comradely arm round Elliot's shoulders.

"Guess so . . ." Frankie's arm burned against his neck. "I better go check on the girls," he murmured, knowing he had to get away fast. But a dangerous excitement raced in him, and he couldn't move. "You smell good," he whispered hoarsely, shutting his eyes.

"I do? Mostly sweat."

"Frankie—"

"What?"

"Nothing." Feeling crazier than he ever had in his life, Elliot jumped up. "You alligator," he cried as he ruffled Frankie's hair. *He was pulling the wool over her eyes.* Filled with self-loathing, he threw a couple of mock punches at the boy he wanted, who fended them off laughing.

"I don't mind the bumps in life, babeeee . . . long as I've got you . . ."
"Can't you shut him up?" Jeannie asked, rolling her eyes at Harriet. The foursome were wedged into a booth at the Delight, and Elliot continued to hum. Chatter from the busy restaurant rose around him, and he heard the crowd at the Classic applauding him again. It would never be enough.

"You were with it tonight!" he called to the drummer, who arrived late with his girl on his arm and joined some of the other musicians in an adjacent booth. Elliot needed a drink, but liquor wasn't served. His suggestion that they drive down to a roadhouse on the county line had been vetoed by Frankie, who was worn out and wanted to wind down. Snapping his fingers to the beat from the jukebox, Elliot continued to chatter.

"When's the date?" interrupted Jeannie, Elliot's manic energy wearing thin.

"Soon," he answered. "Soon as we can. Right, kiddo?"

Why wasn't he safe in bed with Harriet in a room at the Salem? Was he putting it off? It wouldn't be as easy as it was with Myrna, who expected nothing and got less. Or with Amy, either. He remembered the decapitating failure when his reputation as a lover had failed him with Amy in the boathouse a few months ago. But it would be wonderful with Harriet, he told himself; Harriet, who loved him, who was as Frankie said, the best of the lot and then some.

"I wanted to elope," he continued. " 'Nope,' she said. 'Nope, no elope.' I'm a poet." He would fuck her gently and take his time. "Got to have a church wedding and be respectable!"

The sexy fantasy was replaced with turbulence as he caught Harriet's

287

amused glance. Consumed with sudden hatred for her, he involuntarily gasped, then clowned. "How come you didn't tell me you wanted respectability?" he asked quickly, glowering at her with mock sternness. "I might not have asked if I'd known."

"Oh?" she bantered back. "You can always change your mind, Buster Brown." She knew he was higher than a kite but allowed it, for this was a special night and she was woozy herself. Giggling as Elliot suddenly nuzzled her, Harriet wondered if he'd forgotten their tryst. "Let me get a bite and we're off," he whispered, reading her thoughts as the food appeared. Elliot ate ravenously.

"So finish telling me about Patrick. . . ." Frankie said, wanting the story to be completed.

"I hate him."

"Awwwww," cried Elliot. "No, you don't."

"I do. I don't know how he knew we'd be there, but he deliberately tried to spoil things. Elliot, you'll get indigestion!"

Upset with the confrontation with Patrick, Harriet wasn't about to let him dampen her spirits. "I have no doubt he'll be trying to get in touch and ask me back, but—"

"Awwww, he loves you . . . ! *I won't give my heart to anyone, cause anyone'll break it in two* . . ." he sang, winking at Frankie, who took up the rhythm of the song they'd composed together.

"Love? I don't call that love. Do you?" Harriet turned to Elliot, who was talking to Frankie about the latter's plan to cut an audition record and send it around in New York City. Flushed with the memory of having almost given himself away in the locker room, Elliot was aware of Harriet trying to get his attention, but he concentrated on Frankie. Who was he anyway? A smart aleck kid with a swelled head.

"Hmm, honeybunny . . ." he murmured, turning to Harriet for reassurance, but he couldn't see her clearly and blinked, surprised at his loss of focus. "Going bananas for you, honeybunny. Can't see street . . . I mean straight," he added, wagging his tongue. Even a couple bottles of champagne and three times as many drinks of the hard stuff hadn't got him as drunk as he wished he were. "I don't want you workin' for the mick anyway," he announced with a brogue. "That's my decision."

"Oh-ho," laughed Jeannie. "I see trouble ahead."

"*Your* decision, is it?" replied Harriet, putting on the gloves. "I think we'll have to have a talk."

"Jesus, but that's a beautiful ring," commented Jeannie as the diamond caught the light.

"Nothin' but the best for the little woman. . . ." The ring was on her finger. Elliot felt it around his neck. "Right, kid?" he added, trying to rouse Frankie, who'd let his head rest against Jeannie's shoulder in sudden tiredness. Danger flickered again, and Elliot wondered what would happen if he leaned across the table and kissed him on the lips. Serve her right.

"Right, Prince," nodded Frankie, wondering if Jeannie was going to let him come up tonight. Sleepy-eyed, his lips met hers, and Elliot's mood plummeted. Angry with himself, he wished Harriet would let go of his hand.

"We'll be off in a bit," he whispered, the ring's glitter mocking him. Everything denied seemed suddenly undeniable. Who was he, anyway, but an empty, superficial queer, whose attempt to straighten himself out would surely fail? A lifetime of pretending? Was that what his future was? Even if he snuffed Frankie out of his heart, what about the next, and the one after? *But you won't,* admonished a voice. But Elliot wasn't listening.

"You're not so hot, you know," he said suddenly, staring at Frankie, surprising the booth with his from-out-of-nowhere belligerence. "You think Benny's gonna listen to a hick from the sticks? You may be a big fish in Leveret, but— A joke," he added quickly, aware of the awkward silence around him. "I'm your biggest fan. You know that," he went on, miserable and confused at his attempt to hurt Frankie. "You know that," he added urgently. "Don't know what came over me. Too much booze. Tonight's my last spree. We still friends?"

Confused himself, Frankie nodded.

"Need some air, I guess."

"Shall I come—?"

Elliot shook his head and kissed Harriet on the cheek. "Be back in a jiff. Need to fill the lungs."

"He's overexcited," Harriet said to her brother by way of explanation. "You know how he is." Slightly nervous, she glanced toward the entrance, where Elliot chatted with someone, then went out. As used to Elliot's mercurial shifts as his sister, Frankie shrugged off what had happened.

"You gotcha work cut out for ya with that one, honey," commented Jeannie as Elliot tapped at the window and made faces at them all.

"She's exactly what he needs."

Harriet smiled at her brother and realized she was tired. Looking after Elliot, who disappeared past the parked cars full of eaters, she wondered if they were ever going to get to the Salem Hotel. That possibility seemed distant, and she found herself disappointed, but the night had caught up with her, and she was more than willing to go home and hoped Elliot would understand. On her way back from the ladies' room a moment later, she ran into him as he burst back through the door.

"I'm sorry about what happened. I don't know what— He's not angry with me, is he? God, what's wrong with me? I'm delirious, I guess."

A third of a bottle of the champagne he had in his car had fueled Elliot's agitation.

289

"Of course he's not," she replied, suggesting it was time to call it a night.

"*Please*, Harriet. I just need to calm down. We need to be by ourselves for a while. Sweetie, *c'mon*. You're not mad at me, are you?" he added, sensing her hesitation. "You're not—"

"Darling, of course I'm not. I'm just . . . suddenly exhausted."

The drummer in the band interrupted. He had a flat and needed a tire iron. Elliot said he had one and would be there in a minute. "I guess I just don't want the night to end," he continued urgently to Harriet, pulling her out of the way of the carhops, who brushed past carrying loaded trays. "OK, I know you're pooped. I love you so. We'll go home."

"You're not—"

"Furious," he leered. "You better give me a rain check. Tomorrow!"

"You have a rain check for the rest of my life," Harriet replied, kissing him on the nose.

"I'll help Artie, and then we'll be off. Love ya, honeybunny."

"I loathe honeybunny."

"Awwww."

"He OK?" asked Frankie when she returned. Harriet nodded. "It's been quite a night for both of us. Artie has a flat, and he's helping him. Then we're going."

"C'mon, toots, I'm pooped myself. We don't want to miss the last trolley back." Jeannie yawned.

"We'll drive you," suggested Harriet. "If you don't mind the rumble seat again." She sat back and closed her eyes, dreaming, shutting out the jukebox and the Delight's chatter. A few moments later, Frankie touched her shoulder, waking her.

"Can't find him. Artie doesn't know where he is, either."

Groggy, Harriet suggested the men's, and Frankie went to check while she went outside the restaurant and looked about. Only five cars or so were pulled up at the front for service. Elliot, she figured, must have run into someone he knew and was visiting. Starting around the circular building whose neon star winked on and off on its roof, she glanced in car windows but didn't see him. Apprehensive suddenly, she waved goodbye to Artie and his girl, who drove off. Had Elliot simply wandered away for a walk? If such behavior might be extraordinary, it was also very Elliot. Frankie had probably found him, she told herself, taking gulps of cool air to clear her head.

About to return inside, she noticed Elliot's car, which was parked off to the side of the lot. Had Frankie checked it? Smiling to herself, she reasoned Elliot had probably got in and fallen asleep, the poor baby. She hurried across the parking lot and pulled open the door.

Illuminated by the dashboard lights, she saw a startled stranger, in whose lap Elliot's head thrashed as he sucked his prick.

"Elliot . . ." she gasped involuntarily as he bolted upright.

"Elliot." Stunned, she couldn't move nor speak, had no sense of the stranger's echoing footsteps across the lot, saw only the madness in Elliot's glittering eyes as they met hers.

"I'm—" He stopped himself. Was it 'Sorry' he wanted to say? He had no idea. Remaining silent he stared at Harriet as she turned and ran. Relief he didn't understand flooded him.

15 Mill whistles blew all over the Merrimack Valley on election night. As if from a great distance, Harriet heard them as she drove to the Mansion to talk with the state police whom Phelps had called in to investigate Elliot's disappearance.

Dreading the confrontation, her imagination playing terrible tricks on her, she was ushered into the organ room, where Phelps and a trooper were in urgent conversation.

"Have you heard anything?" Phelps asked, more haggard than she'd ever seen him. If she was surprised with the question (Phelps and she had spoken only an hour ago), Harriet knew it sprang from desperation. Shaking her head and grasping his hand to comfort him, she felt suddenly faint and had to sit.

The last few days since Saturday night were a haze from which she hadn't fully emerged. Sunday morning, still in shock and feverish, she hadn't got out of bed. Phelps had called, but Harriet couldn't talk to him. Later, he called again, telling Letty that it was urgent he speak with Harriet, who reluctantly went downstairs and took the receiver in dead fingers and learned that Elliot had not returned home. Did Harriet know where he was? What had happened? Harriet wasn't able to tell Phelps anything. She had no idea where Elliot was, and to reveal what had happened was an impossibility.

"Pardon?" Disoriented, she focused on the trooper and asked him to repeat the question.

"You were the last person to see him, miss?"

"I don't know. I guess. I . . ." She fumbled in her purse for a cigarette and had to get up. Agitated that her memory was being jostled, an image of Elliot appeared. It was shiny with slime. It was unthinkable.

"Was there a quarrel?"

She shook her head, paced to the organ. "No," she whispered.

"Who else was at the Delight that night?"

As best she could, Harriet reconstructed the evening. Yes, Elliot had been drinking. Yes, he was keyed up. No, her brother was in the dark as well, hadn't seen Elliot again.

"Lovers' quarrel, miss?" the trooper asked once more, sensing that the obviously distraught young lady was withholding information. "You got engaged that night, didn't you?"

Tears stung Harriet's eyes, but it was some other girl who was weeping. She nodded. "I told you. He went to help someone fix a tire. He didn't come back."

"Just like that? Without giving any indication? What did you do?"

"I left." She had no memory of her blind flight from Elliot's car and out to the street, where she hailed the last trolley of the evening.

"And your brother?"

"I told you. He didn't see Elliot again, either. He was looking for him, but he never found him."

Letting Harriet compose herself, the trooper turned to Phelps, whose hands moved in and out of his pockets. "He's been gone before, you say? Without telling you?"

"A day or two, yes," admitted Phelps.

"You've told us everything you know, miss? Try and think back."

Harriet didn't want to. The last thing in the world she wanted was to relive any of it. All she wanted was to return to the dumb and faraway place of the last few days, hiding under the covers and hoping she'd get sick. Seated on the bench before the organ, her eyes asked Phelps to release her.

"Give us a moment," he said to the trooper, who nodded and left the room.

"What happened?"

Harriet shook her head.

"I need to know."

"Abraham . . ." she pleaded.

"*Was* there a fight?" he asked. Knowing he needed some kind of explanation, Harriet nodded. Once again she saw Elliot's mad eyes.

"What about?"

"Just . . . a fight . . ." She tried to think, come up with something that would satisfy him. "That's probably why . . . he's gone. He'll be back. I'm sure he'll—"

"What was the fight about? You're not telling me everything." Apprehension caused Phelps to bear down. "Start at the beginning."

"I told you." Someone had left a duster on the keys. "He went outside to help Artie and—"

"Artie?" The sudden clutching at the name caused her to look up at Phelps, whose eyes bore into her. "Who's Artie?"

"The drummer in the band," she replied, not understanding his agitation.

"And?"

293

"And Frankie went out to help, too, but he came back and said Elliot . . . was gone."

"When was the fight? If he was gone, when was the fight? Where was Artie?"

Confused with the barrage, Harriet tried to get her bearings. "Artie and his girlfriend left and I . . . found Elliot outside and we . . . quarreled."

"You're lying."

"Abraham," she gasped. "I'm not. It was because . . . he was drunk. And I was mad because—"

"He's been drunk before. Why all of a sudden should you—"

"It was my engagement night!" Once again she wept, but her tears had no effect on Phelps, who knew she wasn't telling the truth. A premonition gnawed at him as he watched Harriet's bowed head and trembling shoulders. Imagination seeing the worst, his guess that Elliot had done something unconscionable was confirmed when he heard Harriet whisper through muffled sobs that she was breaking the engagement.

"Why?" he barked, but she shook her head.

Distant voices interrupted her growing panic. Nancy Phelps, sedated earlier, but now a crackling wire, strode into the room.

"Where is he?" she demanded of Harriet.

"I don't know."

Nancy whirled on her husband, who reached out to her. Slapping away his hand and fighting for control, she spat at him: "You're the cause of this. You haven't let him have a moment's peace."

Stiffly she turned, her cold eyes passing over Harriet as if she were an object. "Leave my house."

Phelps took his wife's arm and led her out of the room. Stunned, Harriet didn't move. After what seemed forever but was only five minutes, Phelps returned, his coldness frightening her as he shut the door behind him.

"Who else knows about this?"

"About what?" she asked dumbly.

"I don't want it discussed. Whatever it was."

"I don't understand."

"I never have either," he replied curtly and left her.

A moment or two later, she was standing under the portico, blinking as if confused to find herself outside so quickly. Automatically she checked to see that she had purse and gloves, car keys in the purse and—

The light in the portico went out, and she got into the car and sat very still. Too numb to cry any more, she stared at the dark woods. More than ever, it was a dream and she'd wake and be terrified, but only for a moment, until she realized it was something while sleeping, a close call, a day dropped out of the calendar vaguely remembered, but nothing had really changed and there was Alice's pastel of tiger lilies above the oak dresser to prove it, and she would have her talk with Mother about wedding arrangements and lists to be made—the joy of lists—and in a month she'd marry her lover, and it would all be the way it was supposed to be.

Placing her hands on the steering wheel, Harriet was surprised to find her engagement ring missing—as if someone else had left it quietly on the lacquered table in the organ room, the room in which it had been slipped magically on her finger four nights ago.

"A landslide for President Roosevelt," announced Joe, pleased. "Landon's just conceded, he has." As if in answer, the mills in Leveret erupted in a sustained hooting that echoed over Republican Jericho, which was quiet in defeat.

Joe stole a quick glance at Gert, wondering if he should confess that in the sanctity of the booth he'd ignored the Union Party and stayed true to the Democrats. Gert beat him to it.

"A fine man, President Roosevelt," she beamed. "Voted for him myself." She winked.

"You did what?"

Patrick's expression caused Gert a merry laugh. "Look at ya! Did ya really think I thought O'Brien had a chance? Been a Democrat all my life. Will ya tell me I committed a sin 'cause I wanted to insure your sister's happiness?"

"You put me through all that and then you. . . ?" Patrick found it so outrageous he almost had to laugh. His insides knotted in anger, and he wondered why he'd come here tonight. Gert had invited Teresa and Matt for dinner and to listen to the returns on the radio. Hoping to repair the rift between mother and son, Teresa had convinced her nephew to join them.

"Fix him another, Denny. . . ." Gert was more than pleased to see Patrick. Magnanimous with her own victories (Harriet out of the romantic picture; Rose's wedding set for February), she was willing, she told him, to let bygones be bygones, was having his room repainted for his return. Over the baked ham and scalloped potatoes, Patrick had declined. Gert wasn't fazed.

"You going to call down to Brookline, Ma?" Dennis asked. "Talk to O'Brien?" Rose was the only one not present in the living room as the returns crackled in. She was offering consolation to Timothy and his father.

"That I am. Give my condolences to the old fart and tell him to go back to makin' streetcars, which is where he belongs. Hah!" Satisfied with the state of the world, Gert clinked the cubes in her glass and crossed to Joe, bussing him on the head. "Right, Pa?" she hollered. Joe grinned, hoping the kiss was a signal for later on.

"Listen!" exclaimed Dennis. "They're talking about Father Coughlin! Lemke and O'Brien aren't expected to get even a million votes."

"Eight million less than promised," commented Patrick, exchanging a look with his mother. "I guess Rose won't be married in the White House, Ma," he said, wishing to sting her.

"No thanks to you," she shot back, then tousled his head affectionately. "Ya done the right thing, boyo," she continued, enjoying the consternation her words provoked. "Your editorial was a corker. I was proud of ya."

"You forgot to mention it."

"I had other things to consider, didn't I? Well, it's all worked out for the best. And we've got a newspaper that's on its way with an editor gets interviewed by the *Boston Herald*. Everythin's dandy. Taking Irish outta the title might not have been a bad idea, either," she went on. "Talk's been favorable, horizons broadened. Now that I've some time, I've a few ideas of my own—that is, if anyone's interested. Consolidate our gains."

Patrick wasn't interested in talking about the paper. Nor did he tell Gert that he wouldn't accept her financial help. There were too many strings attached, and he'd decided to make it on his own or else.

"So . . ." Gert straightened a doily. In an uncharacteristic letting-go for the parlor, she sat on the sofa, removed her shoe and blissfully massaged a corn. ". . . did ya hear me, Patty? Now that the election's over, I'll have more time. . . ."

She didn't press. Didn't even have to ask if Harriet was out of the picture. She knew Harriet hadn't been at the office yesterday or today. It was enough. "Did ya hear me?"

Not if I have anything to say about it, Patrick said to himself and followed his aunt into the kitchen. Knowing how miserable he was, she squeezed his arm. "It's bad for you, isn't it, Patty?"

Quickly he shook his head as a wave of self-inflicted hatred hit him. "Let's go out and celebrate, Denny!" he urged, returning to the living room. "C'mon." Not even Roosevelt's victory could assuage the continuing pain in his heart, but he was determined to try.

Dennis looked unsure. Gert arched her back so as to see the clock in the dining room. "Almost eleven," she frowned. "Is Denny under a curfew now?" demanded Patrick. "Let's *go*, Denny. All right—I'll go myself. Can I have the car, Pa? *Pa?*"

"Sure ya can," offered Gert with an easy smile. "Blow off a little steam, boys. Be my guest. See?" she added, her eyes meeting Patrick's. "I'm not the big bad wolf certain people think I am. Certain people should maybe be thankin' me for havin' their best interests at heart, but—"

"Where're the keys?" asked Patrick, starting out of the room.

"Certain people," continued Gert, louder as he disappeared, "should be thankin' their lucky stars and their Saviour, too, that they've been prevented from making a mistake that—"

"Since you're talking about Harriet—" Face blotched in anger, Patrick returned swiftly. "Since that's who you're talking about, I never had a chance with her anyway, so you don't need to waste your breath about anything being 'prevented,' because—"

"Who's talking about *her?*" asked Gert, all innocence. "But since *you* are, I'll say it again: She's where she belongs. So're you."

Furious, Patrick went to the hall closet to get his coat. He overheard his father say that he liked Harriet. "Don't I myself?" Gert replied, stealing a glance at the Virgin, who didn't blink. "Get that look off your puss," she called to her son, who stood glowering in the doorway, wanting to kill her. "You've your whole life ahead of ya!"

"Ready, Denny?" asked Patrick impatiently.

"How I long for the day," Gert was saying to Teresa, "when my boys'll find some nice Catholic girls who'll support 'em in their careers." Opening her purse, she extracted a five-dollar bill from her change purse and tucked it in Dennis' breast pocket.

"When'll that day be, Ma?" asked Dennis.

"There's no rush," replied Gert. "Buy your brother an ice cream cone," she added. "He needs a bit o' sweetness in him," she laughed as Harriet rang the doorbell.

"I want to get tight," she told him as she drove a surprised Patrick over to Leveret. Car-tooting caravans of revelers cruised the streets as if it were New Year's Eve.

"God bless you, President Roosevelt!" cried the crowds as impromptu parades clogged the intersections, the cry echoing in the joyous hoots from the mills, whose owners were wrathful in the suburbs.

Arm linked to Patrick's, offering no answers and saying little, Harriet tried to lose herself in the revelry. She pulled Patrick in and out of a couple of packed bars, where the noise mercifully allowed no conversation. Claustrophobia got the better of her, and she had to get out of the city. At close to midnight, they ended up back in Jericho at the Red Tavern, which was almost closing. Two fast gin fizzes later, she'd accomplished her objective. The turmoil was dulled somewhat but not enough.

"I've become de-engaged," she announced suddenly, waving her hand at him. "Shortest engagement on record. I want to get in touch with Ripley."

"You broke it off?"

"Footloose and fancy free, that's me. Isn't it the funniest thing you ever heard?" Eyes brilliant with a hysteria that threatened to overtake her, she laughed and shook her head. Concerned, Patrick attempted to calm her, but she recoiled, startled, as he placed his hand on her arm. "Don't want to talk," she said quickly when he tried to find out what had happened.

"So, do you want me back? Or am I still fired?"

"Look, I'm sorry about— I *was* an ass. I—"

"Ancient history," she interrupted, not wanting to be reminded about Saturday night.

"Of course I want you back. It wouldn't be much of a paper if—"

"Oh, you'd do fine. Anyway, I'm not available. I'm taking off. New York. Elliot was right. I don't belong—" The saying of his name shocked her, and she shut up. "I'm a fiancée without a fiancé," she laughed a moment later. "Poor little me. Don't you want to take up the slack? How much do you love me? Prove it. Just kidding. You probably can't stand me . . . wouldn't blame you . . ."

Waving him silent when he protested, Harriet got up quickly, and the restaurant spun. "C'mon, I hate this place," she said, eyes focusing on the booth where she'd had lunch with Phelps a week ago. The memory of his assurances of Elliot's love caused a hot rage to burn in her. She glanced at Patrick and decided to seduce him.

Driving him down a rutted lovers' lane on the north shore, Harriet took a perverse satisfaction in the spot she'd picked, for on the opposite side of the lake the lights of the Mansion blazed like a birthday cake. Perhaps Elliot had returned. Perhaps he was dead. She hoped so.

Anger and betrayal beat at her as she led Patrick to a deserted icehouse on the water's edge. The woods were full of creatures laughing as she kissed him. Questions swooped like tormenting crows. No matter how she tried to blot them out with Patrick's kisses, pieces of the puzzle fell into place. Didn't Elliot's drinking point to a soul in torment? Hadn't he always warned her he wasn't what he seemed? But worse was a mushrooming horror at the memory of Phelps' brutality this evening and a growing feeling that what she'd tried to keep from him to spare him was something he already knew.

"Oh, goddamnit," she murmured, breaking away from Patrick and running to the water's edge. "Do you want it signed, sealed and delivered?" she asked, turning back to him with a forced flirtatiousness and kissing him with sudden passion.

"Who knows?" she added. "Maybe I've loved you all along and just didn't recognize it." She knew it wasn't true and hated herself for the calculation behind it, but her words produced the desired response.

Wary, but unable to debate with himself, Patrick took her in his arms. Beggars couldn't be choosers, and Harriet had uttered the magical words he so desperately wanted to believe, her body was pressed against him, her face lifted to his, and that was all he knew.

Harriet shut her eyes as Patrick kissed her. That other girl returned a kiss when she could, responding automatically as her eyes opened again and flickered, obsessed, to the glittering palace where the Prince lived.

Stars trembled in the sky, and she might have remembered a hot evening long ago at Bartlett's Field when she'd made a wish on the evening star, wishing for Elliot, forgetting that you had to be judicious about what you wished for because you might just get it. And how confident that girl had been! So sure she understood him and would be good for him. Only to find he'd never wanted her at all.

Why was she doing this to Patrick? she wondered, as she broke away again and retreated into the darkest corner of the icehouse with a desire to fuck in the cold night air, to ease the panic, the desire only half-conscious to punish herself for something she must be guilty of, a fault or lapse in character, a terrible failure—but what it was she wasn't sure.

"Do you love me?" she whispered—as if to give the act an aura of respectability. "You know I do," was the reply, but she didn't really hear. It was Elliot she loved.

Why was she doing this to Patrick? she asked herself again as she lay down on his topcoat. She had no grudge against him; her hatred was across the lake, directed at her never-to-be lover who was gone, directed at his father whom she'd thought was her trusted friend and champion. Her violence was for him, her vengeance his, all for him as he paced, frightened for his son, guilt-ridden, she hoped, and suffering with the knowledge that he must bear the responsibility if Elliot had gone off and shot himself or something else typically Elliot. Let him suffer and wait, him and his hysterical wife, let them pace (let them wait forever!) through that house of many rooms, rooms to become engaged in, parlors for lies and sitting rooms for tears, traps of rooms for girls like me . . .

She wanted to die.

"Don't," she said coldly, clenching herself tight as Patrick's prick penetrated. "You're hurting me," she cried, trying to push him away. "No. *I don't want to.*"

She opened her eyes, frightened at the sudden fury in his, and gave in, a fury rising in her, too, directed at Patrick now, hating him and hating Elliot, hating mankind, each and every one of them and most of all herself.

Seventy-two hours later, they were married.

16 "My God . . . *my Gawd*! What the hell are *you* doing here?" Virginia stepped out of a cab and found Harriet, Patrick and Albatross sitting on her stoop at seven in the morning.

"We've been waiting for you! Oh, Virginia!" Harriet ran down the steps, hugged Virginia as if her life depended on it, and promptly burst into tears.

"Kid, what—?"

"I'm married!" Recovering, she blew her nose. "This is Patrick. We were married last night."

"Married?" Virginia stared at Patrick. *Patrick?* Only a couple of days ago she'd received a letter from Harriet announcing her engagement to Elliot Phelps. Confused, Virginia shook her head and her hangover answered back.

"And this is Albatross—Patrick's dog."

"Congratulations." Then it hit her. "Patrick? *You're Patrick!*"

"I think so," he grinned. "But I'm not sure."

"We've barely had any sleep in the last few days," explained Harriet.

"Forgive me, honey—I'm in no condition, either." Virginia squinted from Harriet to Patrick and back again. "He's the one you work for on the paper? The priest!"

"Not quite—" interjected Patrick.

"Bless me, Father," winked Virginia, "for I have sinned. It's been fourteen years since my last confession." She roared at her own joke, then winced with her headache.

"I'm afraid I can't help," he replied stiffly, and Harriet sensed he didn't know what to make of the irrepressible Virginia. "Don't mind her," she cautioned, laughing and wiping tears. "She loves to shock. Especially men. She's super."

"Well, let's not stand here collecting flies." Virginia led the way. "No dogs," announced Mrs. Mundy, the landlady, peering out of her room on the first floor. "Oh, Harriet—it's you. Welcome back. I see you found Miss Rocco." Irritated at the early morning commotion, Mrs. Mundy smiled thinly and was slightly nonplussed when Harriet embraced her like a long-lost bosom buddy.

"May I show Patrick my old bathroom? Oh, I haven't introduced— This is my husband, Patrick Flynn. We just got married." Who had said those words? *My husband, Patrick Flynn.* Who was *he?* Harriet began to chatter like a magpie. "Is Mr. Mitchell still here? Oh, I want Patrick to meet everyone. It's so exciting being back in New York. I can't tell you—"

Virginia groaned. "It's too early for me. Much too early."

A moment later (Harriet conducting a running commentary on the history of the old brownstone), the three of them trooped up to the third floor.

"Still as messy as ever." She couldn't stop talking. "Where have you been? We've been trying to get you for two days! Can you put us up for the night? Can you put us up forever? Our plans are in a . . . what shall I say? . . . a state of flux. Do you have any coffee? Why don't I make us some coffee?"

"I should go see about the car," Patrick said. "I can't leave it there."

"You have a car? You came in style."

"The 'bribemobile,' " laughed Harriet. "His mother gave it to him— for getting rid of me. But he didn't get rid of me. Did you, darling?" Feeling more anxious than she ever had in her life, Harriet kissed Patrick on the cheek.

"Just a secondhand Hudson," he explained to Virginia, a wacky grin on his face. He didn't know whether to keep standing or sit, but hadn't much choice since all available surfaces were deep in magazines and intimate female garments.

"I'd love to have seen your mother's face when she found out we used her little gift to elope!"

Patrick nodded. The hectic events of the last days (and lack of sleep) had him dazed and as high-keyed as Harriet. He didn't want to think about Gert, nor anything that would puncture his euphoria. If he'd been a coward last night and called Teresa to ask her to tell his mother that he was married to Harriet, he forgave himself.

"*God,* where do I start to tell?" Harriet giggled, didn't know why, and continued on as Virginia rolled her eyes and washed down a couple of aspirin with a Coke. "The car is at the entrance to the Holland Tunnel. The muffler fell off just as we got through. . . . We were driving down from Nyack—that's where we were married last night—so we just left it. At midnight. We couldn't take Albie on the subway, so we walked over to Union Square. Not enough money to check into a hotel, so we went to the Automat where I used to work, but that closed shop at two, so we crossed the street to that all-night Hayes Bickford to wait for you to get in. And we got some of the next issue written—"

301

"*Harriet*," moaned Virginia hoarsely, "start at the beginning! My head is spinning. Mama mia! Can't you slow her down?" she asked Patrick, who shrugged charmingly. "Wouldn't try," he said, adoring eyes following Harriet, enjoying her recapitulation.

"V—where's the coffee? Oh, here it is." Harriet smiled brightly over her shoulder at Patrick and set about the preparations. "Now where was I?" she asked, agitatedly rinsing cups in the tiny, dirty-dish-laden sink. "I've lost my train of thought."

"Sure you had one?" asked Virginia, beginning to wonder what was behind her friend's bouncing off the walls. "Patrick—take a load off your feet," she added, shoving aside clothes on the daybed.

"We're both exhausted," Harriet said, setting the coffeepot on the hot plate.

"He looks bright-eyed and bushy-tailed to me. The beginning?" reminded Virginia.

"The beginning?" Harriet's mind flashed backward. Was the beginning a week ago today when she'd ecstatically jumped out of bed and immediately tried on her gown for the Assembly? Catching sight of Patrick gazing at her (which made her nervous), Harriet wished he'd leave so she could collapse and tell everything to Virginia. If she didn't talk to someone—and soon—

"We got to New York on Thursday. Where were you?"

"What's today? I've lost track."

"*Saturday*."

"I was home. Wilkes-Barre. My yearly visit to the coal mines. Got back last night and stopped at Freddie's to get blotto and *l'amour*. Necessary after a visit home."

"Don't you love her?" Harriet asked Patrick. "She rebelled against the nuns. You have a lot in common. Hands off, V. Don't you dare bat your eyes at him. He's taken." Feeling like a fraud, Harriet embraced Virginia. "She was my best friend in New York . . . my salvation. . . ."

"Kid . . ." Touched, Virginia hugged her.

"I do love a good cry. . . ." Wiping her eyes and ordering herself to get a grip, Harriet cleared a chair of two dresses and a slip, hung them in the clogged armoire, retrieved a bra from the floor and stuffed it in the bottom, patted Albatross and sat.

"Don't mind me," she exclaimed to the world in general. "I'm overexcited, I guess. That's what comes of going without sleep for forty-eight hours. Oh, I told you that already. All right—the beginning. Where was I?" Unable to sit still, she jumped up and crossed to the window. "God, I love New York! My blood is racing already. The city just picks you up and forces you to dance, doesn't it? I feel like I never left. How long—? Less than three months ago. I told you I'd be back, V, didn't I? And here I am.

302

Let's stay, Patrick. Let's never go back to Jericho. How's Freddie, V? Is he working? Freddie's a dancer—he's her steady."

"No, no," interjected Virginia. "Now there's Ralph, too."

"Ralph? How about Benny?"

"Benny's still in the picture. Like the little fellas?" Virginia picked up her latest present, a trio of stone martens, and draped it around her shoulders. "Look at those beady eyes. They're biting each other on the *tail!* What a life!"

"Elegant."

"You think so? They give me the creeps. I'll take a silver fox any day. But Benny saves that for the little woman in Queens. Say, keen-looking," she went on, noticing Patrick's solemn expression, "—don't mind me. My bark's worse than my bite. It's all an act."

Troubled by Virginia's looseness, he smiled gamely.

"A *wonderful* act," exclaimed Harriet. *Let him be shocked, the stick in the mud.* Her bubble of anger confused her, and she felt like a traitor. "Of course he doesn't mind," she said quickly. She sat down beside him on the cluttered daybed and took his hand.

"Well, you two lovebirds, I guess I'm not going to get the story. No, Harriet—sit! I'll take care of the coffee."

Suddenly Harriet was lost. "You start," she said to Patrick. Unable to obey Virginia's instructions, she got up again and watched the pot.

"Go on, Patrick . . . do you prefer Pat or Patrick?"

"He likes Patrick."

"I asked *him*, Miss Mouth Running Faster Than Usual. Go on, Patrick. *Andiamo*. You'll make more sense of it than she has so far."

He cleared his throat. "We were married last night up in Nyack— that's up the Hudson River—by my old roommate from—"

"Hudson!" interjected Harriet. "He has a Hudson, and we drove up the Hudson River last night. Well, perhaps it's a good omen. After all—"

"*Basta*," cried Virginia. "You are hurting my head."

"I'll be good." Harriet forced herself to sit. An uncontrollable hand darted out to stroke Albatross.

". . . by my old roommate at Catholic University who . . ."

"Looks just like Friar Tuck."

"I give up." Patrick grinned.

"I'm sorry. Go on. No, don't go on. You're starting at the end. Virginia wants to hear it from the beginning. All right. Let me. . . ."

Harriet continued on, and Patrick felt his thoughts drift back. Like Harriet, he wasn't sure where the beginning was. When she'd dared to appear at the office on Wednesday morning to apologize for the night before at the lake, he'd wanted to kill her. He wasn't going to be her patsy any more, he'd roared, adding that she might as well clear out her desk and

303

get out for good. Later, surprising him, she'd returned, telling him she had no place to go and sobbing like he'd never heard anyone sob. He was willing putty once again.

". . . on Thursday morning, we were on our way into Boston. Supposedly to check out an ad agency that might get us a national account for the paper. But we never made it to Boston, did we? Because—he proposed in a gas station, and I accepted!"

"Just the way I always dreamed it should be," guffawed Virginia. "To hell with front porches in the moonlight. In Wilkes-Barre they're covered in coal dust. Go on, go on."

I accepted. Why had she accepted? "So, we started for Washington, because Patrick wanted to be married by his old teacher, Father Morelli. Naturally, he wanted to be married in the Church. What was it you said, Patrick?"

"What?"

"In Latin. Started with *extra.*"

"*Extra ecclesiam nulla salvatio.*"

"Which means—"

"You forget, kid—I speak the lingo. Salvation—right?"

"Exactly." Harriet nodded. "Outside the Church there *is* none. Thank goodness I learned in time! Where are you going?"

"I should see to the car. And I want to see if Western Union has anything." He'd wired Teresa for a loan. "And *you* need a nap."

"You're right. Virginia and I will gab all day if you let us. A long soak in the tub and a nap—it sounds heavenly. Don't go yet."

Harriet didn't know why she said it, and Patrick couldn't resist the plea. "I'll have a cup of coffee, I guess," he replied and sat back down beside her. She wished he'd gone.

"It's almost ready," piped up Virginia, glancing at Harriet. What the hell was going on? She sensed troubled waters and couldn't put her finger on it.

"Anyway, Father Morelli was ill with the flu and in the infirmary, and we weren't even able to reach him on the phone. We didn't know what to do. We stopped at a church in Connecticut, and Patrick spoke to a priest there who told us to go home."

Home. Harriet shuddered inwardly at what would await them. She wondered if Patrick was thinking the same. "So we decided we'd continue on to New York. We got here the day before yesterday at five, and Patrick pulled up somewhere and there was a cop directing traffic . . . Irish, of course . . . I think they all have a sixth sense about each other . . . and Patrick waved him over and said, 'We want to get married. Where can we go?' The cop suggested we drive to a town named Armonk where there was a justice of the peace, but Patrick explained about wanting a priest, so the cop suggested we drive downtown to the Chancery on Fifth Avenue, which we did, getting there just before they closed. And we spent that night walking the street, window shopping and dozing in the car."

"Wait a minute. Where does Nyack fit in? You were married at the Chancery? Blow that one past me again. Coffee's ready. Say, are you kids hungry? It's not every day I find orphans on my doorstep. I'm unprepared, however."

"I'm not hungry," Harriet said.

"I'm not hungry," echoed Patrick.

Harriet lit her fourth cigarette of the past fifteen minutes and continued. "We didn't get married at the Chancery. We had to get the dispensation there. For a Catholic to marry a non-Catholic. We're renegades, don't you know?"

More than ever she felt someone else was living her life. She knew she mustn't think too much about Patrick's fantastic proposal or her equally fantastic acceptance or what had happened since it all began. No debating with herself or questions asked, better, in fact, not to think at all. Better to suspend belief entirely and busy oneself with the impossible logistics, as they both had yesterday at the Chancery of the Archdiocese of New York. Better to laugh, be gay, and crack jokes today. Better to keep the blinkers on and try and ward off her hysteria.

"You see," she continued, "Patrick had hoped—didn't you?—that Father Morelli would be able to cut through some of the red tape and the regulations, but, as I told you, he was sick. So Patrick asked at the Chancery, hoping to find someone he might have known at the seminary. And there was! At least there was an uncle, a Father Loughlin, who turned out to be Patrick's old roommate's uncle, and he was the one we talked to first. Then we called Mike Swift, Patrick's old roommate, who has a parish up in Nyack. That's where we headed at six o'clock last night and he married us. And he does look like Friar Tuck. He couldn't have been sweeter. The three priests we talked to at the Chancery couldn't have been colder if they'd been sitting on ice. It took us all day before they'd consent and grant the dispensation. That's a story in itself."

"They were only following orders."

"Are you defending them? They made you mad, you know they did. Treating us like lepers! They gave you the third degree."

"I wouldn't say that."

"You know they did. Mike," she went on to Virginia, "explained why last night. The Church doesn't exactly make it inviting for those who 'tempt fate by conjoining with the unanointed.' *Mixed* marriages should be performed quickly, preferably in an alley."

"But we weren't married in an alley, were we?"

"No, but I didn't think they were going to let us at all. 'I'm a Congre-

305

gationalist,' I told them. I gathered that was close to carrying the plague. Mike told me Baptist would have been worse. They asked me if I wanted to convert. I said I didn't. I was handed several pamphlets in case I wanted to change my mind. Then we were ushered out to wait for another priest. Patrick went down to city hall to get the license. And I sat there waiting."

Gold-framed portraits of stern-eyed cardinals and overfed archbishops looked down upon her, their expressions asking: What are you doing here? It was a question she didn't dare answer.

"I thought a trapdoor was going to open and I'd be fed to the alligators."

Harriet laughed, and Virginia joined in, but Patrick was growing nervous with his wife's chatter. Glancing at her, he was possessed of a sudden disturbing thought: Who was this person who seemed intent on talking herself to death? Quickly he put an arm around her to reassure himself.

"By the time," Harriet continued, "we finally got in to see a Father Brenner, I was ready to throw in the towel. We'd already been interviewed twice. 'I'll sign anything!' I cried. I hope he didn't think I was a nut. 'Waive this' and 'waive that,' and was I aware of such and such? I'm still not exactly sure what I signed. Children will have to be brought up Catholic . . . and I'm not supposed to prevent Patrick from practicing his religion— which I'd never do anyway. It's blackmail, of course, about the children. But I'd have signed anything at that point. Wait'll my mother hears! I finally had to threaten them that we'd live in sin. That did it. So, after getting dispensations from Jesus Christ, Holy Mary and the Marx Brothers, we headed for Nyack and were married last night."

"Ahhh, the Catholic Church," nodded Virginia. "I remember it well. I'm glad it's only a memory."

Patrick's expression made Virginia wish she'd kept her mouth shut. "You don't practice?" he asked, unable to hide his discomfort.

"Not me, honey," she replied, trying to crack a joke to relax him. "I'm a bad girl, a lost sheep, headed for you know where and enjoying every minute of it."

"Is there any place I could shave?" he asked abruptly, face flushed. He'd better get out and breathe some fresh air, he told himself. Maybe lack of sleep was making him touchy. "You wouldn't have a razor, would you?"

"You kids came *prepared*."

"We have only the clothes on our backs and five dollars or so," responded Harriet. "And a broken-down auto sitting at the entrance to the Holland Tunnel. I don't even have a ring. We used his school ring from Villanova. Isn't it a lark?"

"Ahh, these shotgun weddings," laughed Virginia. "They're the best," she added, handing Patrick a tub of shaving cream and directing him

306

across the hall. "Shotgun?" murmured Harriet. "That's what it'll be when we get home. Wait," she cried, as Patrick opened the door. Quickly she kissed him, then turned and with a trembling hand poured herself another cup of coffee as the abyss loomed.

"I'll make it up to him. I will." Ten minutes later, Harriet watched from the window as Patrick left the building. Albatross whined. "He'll be back," she soothed, rubbing his neck. "I have an awful headache."

"I shouldn't wonder—with the act you've been putting on."

"Do you think he guesses?" Relieved she was alone with Virginia, Harriet lapsed into silence, then blurted, "Look what I've done to him! I can't let him see how I feel. All I want to do is tell him it was a mistake. Last night . . . sitting in the cafeteria . . . it was all I could do to keep from telling him that I wanted out. A few hours after marrying him . . . and I wanted out. I worked on the paper instead."

"What the hell is happening? My teeth nearly dropped! I hope I didn't appear too hornswoggled, honey, but I got your letter—look, there it is—about you and Prince Charming, and this morning I find you on my doorstep with Father Flanagan of Boy's Town—tall, dark, and handsome, and just my type, incidentally—and you're *married to him*??? What in Jesus H. Christ happened back there behind the walls of Jericho?"

"Would you like to know why I got in that car three days ago, intending to go into Boston on business and see a play, and then decided to keep going and get married? Would you like to know why I did that? Now why did I? I really don't have the foggiest." She laughed almost hysterically. "Even as we drove into the driveway up in Nyack, I was panicked. He knew I was having second thoughts. Second? More like two hundredth. He told me we didn't have to. I shook my head. Oh, wasn't I a game little fool! And then, later, walking in the dark to the church, I said to myself: Tell him you need more time. Excuse yourself and— But it was too late."

She would wake, and it wouldn't have happened. For the umpteenth time in the last seventy-two hours, Harriet was possessed of a feeling of sleepwalking. There was someone else here in New York City standing like an exposed nerve in a window, eyes a little too bright, a cold cup of coffee in her hand, and a cigarette mouth.

"What have I done? What have I done? Why did I jump? I always jump, don't I? *What is wrong with me*? Talk about rebounds! This sets a record."

"But—"

"All right . . . you asked about Elliot." His name caused an ache. "I'll tell you . . ." Slowly and painfully it came out. When she finished, Harriet felt numb again and couldn't even cry.

307

"Kid . . ." murmured Virginia in sympathy and tried to hug Harriet, who broke away, for any physical contact was more than she could bear.

"That bastard," growled Virginia, concerned for the vacant stare on her friend's face.

"It's over and done with . . . I don't even want to think about it any more." She shook her head. "Oh, Elliot . . ." she whispered. "I can't believe it. How did it happen? I loved him." Involuntarily she gasped as she opened the car door again and saw him. "See what happens when you fall in love?" She put her face in her hands. "I haven't seen him since that night. He disappeared."

"He should've. Forever."

"No. He's back. He called the morning Patrick and I left Jericho. I was eating breakfast, and Alice answered the phone. I couldn't talk to him. An hour later, I said yes to Patrick. Alice always warned me never to have anything to do with that family. I pooh-poohed her."

"Phelps tried to palm a fairy off on you, honey."

"That's what Alice said. I still don't want to believe that, but—"

"You got the royal shaft, kid. Moneybags and the Prince gave you the old shafteroo. *Jeezus*! Look, it's past now. You got burned, but you've got yourself a *real* man now, who'd obviously knock himself out for you—"

"He must be naive. Doesn't he know?"

"He's in love. C'mon—look at the silver lining here. Where's your old positive thinking? I know you can't see it yet, but Patrick—"

"Who? Oh." Vaguely Harriet brushed her bangs from her brow. "Patrick. Yes. Patrick. There he was. Everytime I looked—there he was. I'll say one thing for him—he's tenacious."

"Does he know? About Elliot?"

Harriet shook her head.

"Don't tell him."

"No. How can I? I led him on that night at the lake. Now look what I've done. I'm a horror." Someone else was a horror; it couldn't be her. Someone else had been betrayed and turned to Patrick; it wasn't her. Someone else was drenched in guilt.

"Bull. He's not a baby. He knew what he wanted. And you may have married him on the rebound, kid, but if I know you, you knew what you were doing. You wouldn't have married him if you didn't love him."

"Love? I don't even know the meaning of the word. I told myself I did. I even told him I did, but—"

"C'mon. He's right. You need a nap. I'll draw you a tub. You kids haven't even had a proper wedding night. I'll go bunk with Freddie and—"

"He practically raped me at the lake. Nothing I didn't deserve. I'm not looking forward to the next round. Oh, Virginia. . . !"

"It'll all look better when you're rested."

"I called my mother last night, and she wept on the phone. I haven't heard my mother cry since I was ten. I didn't dare talk to Father. They were barely over the shock of my engagement to Elliot. They hardly know Patrick. The other night after I left him up at the lake, he followed me home on foot and began yelling at me from the street. They were fit to be tied. . . ." The monotone continued, her voice disembodied. "He woke up the whole block. He didn't dare tell his mother . . . called his aunt last night instead. How can I go home. . . ?"

"That's not important now. Cross that bridge—"

"I don't want to. I don't love him."

"Harriet—"

"I don't love him."

"Kid."

"I don't love him."

Oldsters looked up from dozes under the fluted columns as Patrick, Harriet and Albatross entered the cavernous lobby of the Ocean Breeze Hotel in Atlantic City, New Jersey. Atlantic City was Patrick's idea. Virginia's room wasn't quite what he had in mind; even if it were only for a day or so (Teresa had wired twenty-five dollars), he wanted a proper honeymoon. Normal couples had honeymoons. Nothing about his marriage so far was normal, but this would do the trick.

Virginia had treated them to dinner and given them a proper sendoff with a can tied to the fender and a handful of confetti, which stuck to the wet car as they drove off through a light mist. Patrick was buoyant, Harriet very subdued, letting the fragrance of her gardenia corsage lull her into an almost hypnotized state as they drove down the Jersey shore. Despite a four-hour nap, she was still exhausted.

Off-season, the grand dowager of a hotel was only twenty percent occupied, and the clerk, an old hand at Depression honeymoons, gave Patrick a cheap rate. Harriet wandered back across the lobby and stared out the windows. Stragglers hurried along the boardwalk and the waves thumped the shore. A raucous bridge game in the card room continued as she returned aimlessly to the desk where Patrick registered them. The scratches of ink that spelled her new name were no more unreal than anything else, but Harriet smiled. "I think it was . . . such a good idea . . . coming here," she whispered. Time, Virginia had counseled, she needed time. She'd suffered a blow; it would heal. "Isn't this fun, Albie?" she asked as they went up in the elevator.

It was the largest bed either one of them had ever seen. Deluxe honeymoon suite, volunteered the bellman, winking at Patrick who tipped him a munificent quarter. The combination bedroom and sitting room reminded them both of a bordello in the movies—all red velvet and stuffed chairs and chipped gilt with a mirror opposite the bed.

Patrick ordered a bottle of champagne from room service. "Always wanted to do that," he admitted, laughing like a happy kid, all of whose dreams were coming true. "Me, too," Harriet nodded, and couldn't think of anything else to say.

"To my wife . . ." he toasted, the light in his eyes causing Harriet to feel like a fraud again. Managing a smile, she did the best she could and returned the toast. Patrick sensed how nervous she was, but he wasn't fazed. He would banish her tension with his love and make her laugh again.

"Well, here we are. . . ."

"Here we are. I can't believe it. I'm still so tired."

"We'll go for a long walk on the beach tomorrow. Would you like that? I hope it's sunny. Might even go in for a dip."

"It would be freezing."

Both caught each other glancing at the bed which couldn't be avoided. Both thought of what was to come. Both remembered four nights ago at the lake. Both pretended it never had happened.

"I don't know how long we should stay. I want to get back. I called home."

"You did? What did she say?"

"She wouldn't come to the phone. Pa was fine. A little shocked, I guess, but he sends you his best wishes. She'll come around," he added. Gert's outrage was the last thing on his mind at the moment.

"I hope so."

A bit more polite conversation. "Why do you want to get back?" Harriet asked.

"Pa said there's going to be trouble at the mill. The union sent over some more pickets from Leveret. Phelps is getting upset. I want to stay on top of the situation."

Patrick wished he hadn't mentioned Phelps; he saw Harriet look away and wondered if she was thinking about Elliot. Immediately he buried the unpleasant thought, for he wanted no uncertainties to mar his jubilation. Yes, he knew they were strangers to each other again, but that, he told himself, would pass.

"Can't believe it, either," he whispered, crossing over to her chair and sitting on the arm. "I'm the luckiest fellow I know."

Harriet responded with a nervous smile as she felt his hand lightly stroke her hair. He bent down and kissed her, and she shut her eyes. A moment later, she excused herself to go into the huge bathroom, while Patrick tested the bed, had another glass of champagne, and roughhoused with Albatross. He had little knowledge of what he'd got himself into, wouldn't have guessed that Virginia's impulsive embrace as they left New York had underpinnings of concern that Patrick had his hands full.

If he'd entered the marriage with eyes open, they were nonetheless veiled with passion and a powerful wanting to believe.

There were unmistakable uncertainties that might have the power to infiltrate, but Patrick gave them no weight (even as he cataloged them). As he gazed out the window at the sea, he still didn't believe Harriet had accepted his proposal, knew it had all happened too fast, recognized the rebound.

None of it mattered. The extraordinary circumstances of his marriage were reduced with a simplicity of purpose; nothing was allowed that might disturb his determination and joy. Even the violence and fury of their recent clashes were seen as perhaps necessary forms of foreplay between two wildly divergent temperaments.

He prayed. He had faith. He had her. She was his.

That was all he knew, and that was more than enough and then some.

Her reflection startled her in the mirror. Like an automaton, Harriet washed her face, redid her lipstick, sprayed herself with cologne, and put on one of Virginia's nightgowns that made her look like she was wearing a silk parachute.

"You're so beautiful," Patrick murmured when she returned. He'd lowered the lights, and the bedcovers were folded neatly back. "Am I?" she asked, surprised, as she accepted the glass of champagne he offered. She knew she wasn't.

In the bathroom Patrick washed, shaved again, and struggled into a borrowed pair of Freddie's pajamas, which were too small for him. Excited, his head felt light in anticipation; his stomach did flip-flops, and he grinned at himself in the mirror, then quickly made a sign of the cross.

Standing at the circle of a window under the turret, Harriet gazed with unseeing eyes at the sea. She had little sense of what she was doing here. Aimlessly, she reached down and patted the dog.

A smell of burnt toast drifted in through the transom; in the distance a radio was playing. The shimmer of the moon on the water jolted a memory of something Elliot had once said, but she couldn't remember. From far away she heard the rushing of the taps. At least someone wanted her; no, that wasn't what she should be feeling. She was feeling nothing. Even the pain was gone.

"Oh," she murmured, startled, as Patrick put his arms around her and kissed her on the neck. "It's me," he whispered, but when Harriet turned to him, she wasn't able to recognize who he was.

He led her to the bed, and they slipped under the covers. He turned out the lights. Gently he put his arms around her, and the feel of her body inflamed him. There was no response. Unable to face anything, not even frightened, Harriet was a million miles away, the distance unbreachable.

"I'm just so tired," she heard herself say. "I'm sorry," she added, unable to pretend anything. Eyes squeezed shut, she felt his kisses pause, then stop. "I can't," she whispered in the tiniest of voices and heard the intake of his breath, as if he'd been startled. Not daring to breathe, she felt the mattress give as he moved away. "I love you," she heard him say a moment later as he reached for her lifeless hand. She pretended not to hear. How long it was, she wasn't sure, but soon afterward she fell mercifully asleep.

17

Alice opened the door in robe and slippers and peered, glasses-less, at the tentative couple who were out of focus.

"Why is the house dark?" whispered Harriet. "Is everyone asleep? It's only ten-thirty."

"I told you," muttered Patrick. Albatross barked. "Shhh!" Patrick wanted to go straight back out the door. He'd rather have spent the night in the car than take a chance on waking anyone. They'd canceled their second day at the Ocean Breeze this morning. Strangers in the unreality of an empty hotel, the impulsive recklessness of their marriage caused them to retreat into separate worlds, and Patrick decided they might as well come home and face the music.

"Oh, God, Alice—" Harriet hugged her sister. "I didn't think you'd all be asleep!" What's the lay of the land here? her eyes asked.

"It's Sunday night. Father's going off early to Providence in the morning. Beside, we were all exhausted talking about you two. *Patrick!* Congratulations. I couldn't be happier." Beaming, Alice shook his hand and kissed him.

"Why, Harriet—" Waked up, Letty appeared at the jog in the stairwell, followed by Frankie.

"Mother—" Harriet and Letty exchanged a pregnant look, but there was no chance for anything further as Cora appeared and everyone began talking at once.

"Why are we whispering? We're all awake."

"Hello, Mrs. Hoskins. . . ." Monumentally ill at ease, aware that Letty was trying hard not to stare at him, Patrick smiled shyly at her.

"Patrick. Come in. Why are we all standing in the hallway?" Flustered, then recovering, Letty held out her hand in a sudden silence, hoping Patrick wouldn't see her discomfort. Why, he was practically a total stranger. Her only clear picture of him was a hothead yelling for Harriet in the early hours of the morning. No matter how much she'd gone round with it the past few days and tried to prepare herself, the reality of her new son-in-law in the flesh was too startling to be believed.

313

"Sorry to wake everyone," Patrick said, uncomfortably the center of attention, dazed at the questions behind their eyes and the chatter that erupted around him.

"*Sam!*" The spotlight shifted, Cora's peal of giggles causing everyone to look at her fiancé, who appeared in a borrowed robe from the dining room, where he'd been sleeping on a cot. "Look at Sam!" cried Cora, who'd never seen him in nightclothes before. He had been given Monday off from the bakery so that he and Cora could apartment hunt, and he'd stayed over so they could get an early start.

"You two haven't met?" Alice asked, introducing Patrick to Sam, who was blushing at Cora, tickled himself at the sight of his bride-to-be in her nightgown and slippers a week before the wedding.

"Where's Father?" Harriet was answered with a clearing of the throat, and all eyes shifted as Franklin appeared in the stairwell, lips pursed, his flinty gaze taking them all in, finally resting on Patrick.

"Father," cried Harriet a trifle loudly, "you know Patrick. This is Patrick."

"I know." Franklin accepted her kiss on the cheek, but his eyes never left the intruder.

"Hello, sir. I'm sorry we disturbed your sleep."

"I am, too." The three words lay there like a halibut gone bad. Franklin exchanged a look with Letty. He knew Patrick less than she. All *he* knew was that his favorite daughter had run off and married an Irish mick; he would have preferred Elliot any day in the week. "Do you have a license?"

Patrick flushed. "Yes."

"Why'd you bother?" Franklin went back to bed.

"He's leaving for Providence early in the morning," Letty said quickly, trying to paper over Franklin's hostility. Once again everyone began to chatter, the hallway filled to capacity with robed figures trying to act natural as Letty tried to get traffic moving and Albatross added to the commotion by bounding through the parlor into the dining room and back again.

"Let me just light a lamp—"

"Albie! Come here! *Sit.* I'll put him out."

"Not at all. What a nice dog."

"You had the dog with you all the time?"

"He was our chaperone." Wanting only to be given a bed to crawl into and wake up in China, Harriet laughed nervously.

"Now, how will we work this? Sam has the cot, but maybe Frankie could move, and—"

"I'll bunk with Frankie," Alice offered.

"Why don't I make coffee?" suggested Cora, linking her arm with Sam, whose eyes were closing.

"Not now, Cora," Letty replied hastily. "Let's all go back to bed. We'll visit in the morning."

"We still have some crumb cake. . . ." Cora was ready to make a party. Curiosity insatiably aroused by the strange new twosome, she couldn't possibly get back to sleep. "Where were you married? We—"

"All right, girls," insisted Letty. She shooed everyone back upstairs. "Goddamn," murmured Franklin when she got into bed with him. Fifteen minutes later, the house was quiet again, and Harriet and Patrick were in the bedroom she usually shared with Alice, each in a twin bed—wide, oh so wide, awake.

"Why on earth would she do a thing like that?" Cora asked the next morning. At seven-thirty everyone except Harriet and Patrick were downstairs. Franklin had left even earlier. "Run off that way without telling—?"

"It's called 'elopement,' Cora," replied Alice tartly. "Surely you know the meaning of the word? The whole point is *not* telling."

"Land sakes," clucked Cora in astonishment, "you're awfully calm about it. You're the only one, I'm sure. What are people going to think? Sam will have poached eggs, won't you, Sam? I'll fix them, Mother. I know just how he likes them."

"You do?" asked Alice, a glint in her eyes. "Did you hear that, Mother? They're not even married, and she knows how he likes his eggs in the morning. Sounds fishy."

"Oh, Alice, you do love to be provocative." Cora and Sam exchanged their usual blush. Questions about Harriet and Patrick, as they had the last three days, abounded and continued as the family sat to breakfast, which Letty decided should be in the dining room since there were too many bodies to fit at the kitchen table unless they ate in shifts.

"But so sudden!" continued Cora. "I didn't even know she'd broken up with Elliot."

"Nobody did," replied Letty. Completely in the dark and needing answers herself, she hadn't been able to get a word out of Alice, who she suspected knew something. "Pass those doughnuts to Sam, Frankie. They're not as good as yours," she added and couldn't help thinking that Sam was an open book. Certainly he would never unsettle her; he was known, easy and understandable—unlike the mysterious stranger asleep upstairs in the middle bedroom.

"Did they have a fight?" asked Cora. "They must have. Maybe it was because he disappeared like that." She turned to Frankie. "Have you talked to Elliot? He's *your* friend. What on earth happened?"

"Dunno. Haven't seen him." Frankie recalled Elliot's drunkenness and all-round crazed behavior on the night of his engagement. If he hadn't understood any of it, he knew that as far as he was concerned, he was glad his sister was out of it.

315

"She made the right choice."

"Why do you say that, Alice?" asked Cora. "I think you know more than you're telling."

"I think that's enough questions," said Letty. "I'm sure Harriet will fill us in if she's a mind to. Until then, I think we should keep our curiosity to ourselves."

"Mother—I can see you're fit to be tied." Cora couldn't stop conjecturing. "Why, she only got engaged last week and—"

"Upstaged by Harriet, 'Eleanor'?"

"Oh, shush, Alice. You know how I hate that nickname."

"Stop bubbling like a teapot."

"What must the Phelps be thinking?" Cora went on, ignoring Alice. "People are going to be very curious. Have you talked to the Phelps, Mother?"

"Why should I?" She hadn't been consulted about the engagement, why should she be concerned about the breakup? She hadn't been consulted about anything, neither Elliot, nor Patrick. If Letty was pleased that the former was out of the picture, it didn't mitigate her anger at Harriet, who'd gone off and outdone herself with this stunning rebound of a marriage.

"Poor Father. . . !"

Letty frowned to herself at Cora's comment. Franklin was as confused and furious as she was herself. A terse: "Find out what happened," as he left the house this morning. A terser goodbye.

"We don't really *know* Patrick," continued Cora. "I like him—at least I think I do. But Harriet never so much as indicated she felt in any way, well, *that* way about him. He's—"

"Catholic," interjected Alice.

"That's not what I meant. He's a stranger to us—that's what I meant."

"*Irish Catholic*," said Alice, opening her eyes wide like the bogeyman.

"Ooooo!" cried Cora, dashing up from the table to the kitchen, where Sam's eggs were like rocks in the poacher. Her expression had them all · laughing.

"You may as well know, Sam," explained Alice, "that Mother has a pet peeve—"

"I'll redo these in a minute, Sam—"

"She's not," Alice continued, "a snob about anything else, but as regards our Irish brethren—"

"That will do, Alice. I'm sure Sam isn't interested." Letty went back to the stove to see to more coffee.

"He's going to be a member of the family. He needs to know." An amused gleam in her eye, Alice turned to an embarrassed Sam, who knew he was caught in the middle. "It all started when Grampa took Mother for a walk when she was very young along the river above the dam in Leveret and showed her Micktown and scared the pants off her with a few stories."

"What kind of stories?" Sam asked politely. He never knew what to make of Alice; she seemed as if she didn't even belong in this family.

"Of incest and peat, of murder and rape and things that go bump in the night."

"Really, Alice. We're having breakfast." Cora came to the doorway, then went back to watch Sam's eggs. "Don't listen to her, Sam. Or you either, Mother." Cora patted Letty's arm.

"And once," continued Alice, "when Mother was teaching, there was a poor little Irish ragamuffin in the fourth grade who smelled so bad, she investigated. He'd been *sewn* into his clothes for the winter!"

Ayea, thought Letty. That's the way they were. Darkies you could feel sorry for; it wasn't their fault. But micks had no one to blame but themselves. Agitated, she touched the metal of the coffeepot and burned two fingers. "Shit, shit, *shit!*" Chagrined, she fled to the pantry and thrust them under cold water. What must Sam think of her?

"See what you've accomplished, Alice?" Cora served Sam's eggs and hovered with jam and fresh coffee. "My own fault, " Letty said as she returned to the table and sat, sending a sharp look at Alice.

"Do you think we should meet the Flynns, Mother?" asked Cora.

"I suppose. Not just yet." Letty had never met Gert, had only heard of her through Harriet and might have seen her once at Women's Club, but she couldn't remember. She had talked to her, however; at least Gert had talked. An hour after Letty had received Harriet's call from Nyack, the phone had shrilled again: "*If you'd brought your daughter up properly, this wouldn't have happened!*" And Gert had slammed down the receiver. No, Letty was in no rush to encounter Gertrude Flynn, who obviously was a hysteric with the manners of a scrubwoman.

"What must the Flynns be thinking of this? They must be as flabbergasted as we are. Perhaps we should invite them for—"

Cora stopped herself as Harriet, Patrick and Albatross entered the dining room.

"Good morning . . . good morning." The headache that had been with her on and off for the last days was with her again. Harriet tried to be chipper, but the sight of her family filled her with unreasoning dread.

"Good morning, Patrick. You sit right there next to Alice."

"Good morning, Mrs. Hoskins. No, thank you, I won't sit. I should get right to the office."

"At least have some juice and a cup of coffee."

"Just like Sunday, isn't it?" Harriet darted a look, relieved that Franklin wasn't about. "Everyone at the dining room table. Isn't it festive?"

317

Letty's instructions to make the couple welcome produced a sudden overzealous burst of chit-chat, a pretending that all was normal and well. As fast as it bubbled up, conversation ceased.

"We really must dash," Harriet said, jumping into the silence. "We're four days behind." The dining room looked different, everything was unfamiliar, and when Letty suggested she not smoke until she put something in her stomach, Harriet looked at her so strangely that Letty was momentarily at a loss for words. "Cream and sugar, Patrick?" she asked, recovering.

"Black," he replied, smiling gamely.

"Well, you two . . ." Cora began. "What a surprise! We were—"

"When's the wedding rehearsal?" interrupted Harriet.

"Friday, of course, but—"

"She beat you to it, Cora," interjected Alice. "You thought you'd be first."

"Where were you?" Sam asked Patrick.

"Atlantic City."

"Niagara Falls for us."

"Wasn't it cold?" Cora slathered jam on Sam's toast.

"I'm sure it'll be cold up there, too," Harried replied. "What do newlyweds do? Look at the falls, I suppose, but—"

"Oh, they'll find something to occupy themselves." Frankie laughed. Cora giggled at Sam, who examined his eggs, ears turning cranberry.

"C'mon, Albie . . ." Needing to flee the gauntlet of barely concealed glances and strained naturalness, Patrick excused himself. "I'm coming, too," Harriet said, rising, not wanting to be left alone.

"I'll stop in at home for a few minutes."

They exchanged a quick glance, both aware everyone was looking at them. "Shall I come? No," she went on hastily, "I'll go straight to the office and open up. I think I'll walk. It'll do me good."

Patrick left, a large buzz erupting at the table as he went out the front door.

"Harriet," cried Cora, voice up an octave in anticipation, "fill us in! We're all dying—"

"Cora," warned Letty.

"Have to dash." Harriet snuffed out her cigarette, flung arms into her coat, grabbed for her purse and fled, leaving Cora unsatisfied and Letty troubled.

"Well, I never. . . !" Cora exclaimed. "What was that all about?"

"They're in a rush." Alice rose, took her hat and coat from the hallway closet, and caught up with Harriet halfway up the block.

"Slow down. Don't mind Cora."

"I couldn't care less about Cora."

"They'll get used to it. Even Father. You can win him back. He gave us the usual bad time the night before last. Missed supper. Came home stewed. Lashed out at Mother."

"About me?"

"Who knows? I suppose. Who cares any more?"

"You do. Why pretend?"

"You're wrong there. Anyway . . . you certainly took them all by surprise. Me, too. I'm glad."

"Are you?"

Alice sensed turbulence.

"Have you heard from Wayne?" Harriet asked, changing the subject.

Alice shook her head. "Why did I tell him? I wish I hadn't. Because I was scared, that's why. I hate being scared. Maybe when he got the letter he joined the French Foreign Legion. Maybe he doesn't want to be a father. *You* told me I should write him."

"Because I could see you wanted to. You had no choice."

Harriet tried to hear what Alice was saying, but her concentration was scattered. Faster and faster she walked, as if she could outdistance her anxiety. Everything would be fine, she told herself, when she got to the office and threw herself into work.

". . . can't expect regular mail delivery during a civil war, but I'm worried. Why haven't I heard from him? Mrs. Thibeau hasn't had a letter, either. If you want to know—I see you don't—I'm going bananas."

"Sorry." Harriet paused abruptly and grasped her sister's hand. "You'll hear from him. I know you will. You have such courage. I . . . seem to have run out." Involuntary tears stung her eyes and she bit her lip, but when Alice asked what was wrong, Harriet shook her head and started off again.

Sheets whipped on the line. Patrick hesitated in the back yard. The sky looked like snow. He went in the door to an empty kitchen.

"Ma—?"

Rose sashayed through the swinging door, looking pinched and harried. "You've nearly killed her this time."

"Have I?" he asked, the question's mildness cloaking a sudden impulse to slap Rose across her pouty face.

"You've caused nothing but trouble since—"

"Where is she?"

"She won't see you."

"I asked where she was."

"Don't talk to me like that."

Patrick brushed past her to the hallway. "Ma?"

There was no answer from behind the closed bedroom door. He returned to the kitchen as Joe came in from outside and sat dumbly at the kitchen table, his lunch pail in his lap.

"What is it, Pa? Why're you home?"

Joe shook his head, trying to clear it. "He shut us out. Locked us out, he did."

"Phelps?"

Joe nodded, frowning. "He can't do that. Can he, Patty? He can't do it. He did it. Forgive me, Patty," Joe added, a beam of a smile replacing the troubled frown as he offered his son his congratulations. Had he brought Harriet with him? Patrick explained he thought he'd better see Gert himself first, so Joe went into the bedroom. Returning a moment later, he shook his head. But his ma would come around, Joe assured Patrick and poured his son a cup of tea, and they sat at the kitchen table.

"What happened, Pa?" Joe explained as well as he could the events that had led Phelps to shut down the mill this morning. The union had sent over more pickets from Leveret, and there'd been fights between them and some of Phelps' employees. "Shouted at us we were scabs," Joe said, indignant. "I've been workin' for Mr. Phelps for twenty years. What call did they have? Accused us of being company men. Some of the boys didn't take to that kind of insult and you had your punches thrown and Ed McGee's been havin' his hands full keepin' order. Every mornin' it happened and also at closin'."

But there were younger ones, Joe went on, men as well as some women, who joined in clandestine gatherings at the Depot Tavern to talk with Meyer Shapiro and his organizers. Phelps had his spies everywhere and some of those attending the meetings found themselves dismissed for "inefficiency" the next day, and things mushroomed. Within twenty-four hours a petition with over a hundred names, requesting an open union election, was presented to Phelps. The leader of the delegation, Paul Marienetti, worked in the dye room with Joe. Phelps refused to see any member of the committee personally. They were all fired, and this morning the mill's gates didn't open at seven, the whistle didn't blow and there was a force of Pinkerton guards blocking the way.

"Eight hundred of us, Patty. Locked out." Joe shook his head, dazed as the town itself. Standing around down there, they were, in tight and angry knots. Even if Phelps was bluffing and trying to teach them all a lesson, Joe went on, his action had earned him a wave of distrust and fury. Threw out the good and the bad, and the result was that even those who'd been thoroughly loyal and satisfied like himself were now picketing in front of the mill. Joe would be on the line himself this afternoon.

"He shouldn't be allowed to get away with it, Pa." Who was Phelps, Patrick wondered, growing angry, that he should vent his spleen on a whole town? About to say more, he saw Joe look up, and he turned to find Gert standing in the kitchen doorway.

"Ma—" he began, rising, halting in place at the look of her. Guiltily, he had to avert his eyes from her face, drained with no makeup, hair disheveled and fingers fussing with the cord of her robe.

"You're not my son."

"Ma—"

"Gertie . . ."

"Don't ever be bringin' her here."

"Ma—"

"You're not my son."

How many times had she said it? Sometimes in jest, sometimes not. On the day when he'd returned from Washington, but never so telling as now. Her words chilled Patrick, stopping his vulnerable heart. Worse was what came next:

"What a fool ya are! The talk is he threw her over. There ya was, wasn't ya! Acceptin' his cast–off. . . !"

"I'm out of work, Gertie," Patrick heard his father say as he blindly left the house.

"It's the talk of the town!" Teresa beamed as the newlyweds arrived for dinner three days later. "People need something to take their minds off their troubles. What with the mill closed and all. Don't worry—it'll die down. Don't you both look tired."

"We're exhausted."

"Sorry we're late."

"You got the paper in?"

"We just came from there," replied Patrick. "We'll be a day or so late, and it's only four pages, but we made it."

"And it may be one of the last issues," continued Harriet, scowling.

"No, it won't," Patrick replied, tossing down nuts with a forced bravado.

"Holy angels!—the paper's just getting on its feet. What's happened?"

"Smith and Houchins want to be paid. I don't want to talk about it now. I want to relax."

Teresa and Matt exchanged a glance. Matt shook the cocktail shaker and poured the Manhattans. Teresa raised her glass to Harriet. "Welcome to the family, dear. How I've prayed that you two sweet people—I'm speechless."

"For a change," grinned Matt.

"There're other families I'd sooner wish on you, Harriet," continued Teresa, "but it's all we've got, so we'll make the best of it. Gert'll see the light. Don't you worry. God love ya, the both of ya. When you called me the other night, I set the phone down and bawled—didn't I, Matt? Just bawled. I don't care what anyone else is saying—*I couldn't be happier.* I nearly forgot—" Teresa picked up a copy of *The Leveret Eagle* from the coffee table. "Did you see this afternoon's paper? It's all about you two. 'The Romance Of Journalism'—right there as large as you please."

"What. . . ?" Harriet took the paper. On the front page next to stories about the war in Spain, further debate over whether Edward would abdicate, and the lockout in Jericho, was an article about Patrick and her, plus their photos—hers from graduation, hair pulled in a bun, and his Diaconate portrait in white vestments.

"But how—" stuttered Harriet. "Listen to this: 'Friends of the young editor and his assistant'—*assistant?*—'were surprised at the suddenness of the elopement, as no one suspected there was a romance blooming. . . .' But how did Joe McCall get this?"

"I told him."

"You?" She turned to Patrick. "You did?"

"Sure. I ran into him yesterday in the city. What's wrong? Is it supposed to be a secret?"

"Of course not," she replied quickly, smiling for Teresa and Matt's sake. She knew she hadn't been exactly in a rush to make an announcement. She knew Patrick knew she hadn't. Not that everyone didn't seem to have found out anyway. There had been a steady stream of dropper-inners, phone calls, and starers in the window since they'd returned. It got so bad on their first day at the office that Patrick had finally pulled the shades, locked the door and taken the phone off the hook so they could work in peace.

"Now tell us everything. How was Atlantic City?"

"I had a good time." Patrick scanned the article, the irony of it producing a stab. 'Romance'? There'd been none. Merely a repeat of what had happened the first night. If he was patient then, the litany of excuses since ("I'm tired," or "nervous with the family so close," etc.) had him on edge. How had it happened? He'd loved, lusted, prayed and wished for her, and now she was his—but she wasn't. She kept him more at a distance than she had in the days when she was dating Elliot. Terrible doubts had commenced their gnawing. Confused and disheartened, Patrick didn't know what to do.

"Sure enough," soothed Teresa, who sensed they were in a pickle with each other, "you've got a lot of pressure on you, don't you now?"

"That's the truth." Harriet sighed. "We're an item. A notorious item, it seems."

"Who says?" asked Patrick, roused. But the barely concealed looks of disapproval, amazement and general dumbfoundedness were easier to stomach than the offers of congratulations that mocked him.

"You know we are." Harriet turned to Teresa. "Mrs. Harrigan from the card shop *happened* to call this afternoon to tell us she wouldn't be needing any more advertising in the paper. Now what do you think the real reason was?"

"She's a good friend of Gert's," nodded Teresa. "Sure," she went on, "everyone's in a dither. Well, I say, let'm talk."

"And Father Gahaghan," continued Harriet, "—he wasn't exactly friendly. What if Mrs. Flynn asks him to evict us?"

"Gert'd never—"

"I'll handle that," Patrick responded, irritated. If there was going to be criticism of his mother, he'd do it himself. Surer than hell he wasn't going to allow his wife to. Wife? Hah. And who cared what people were saying? Did she have to make a song and dance out of everything?

"A refill, darlin'?" asked Teresa quickly, concerned for the undertow. "Guess what I'm thinking?" she went on, hoping to get a laugh out of them. "Why, your getting married like that—so dramatic and thrilling—it might increase circulation!"

Matt laughed.

"Now I've had a couple of my ladies," Teresa continued, turning serious to make a point, "who've asked, I'll admit, a few questions. About the religious difference, don't you know? I tell 'em, if God wanted the world to be only Catholic, He wouldn't have made any Protestants! The two of you were meant for each other, and don't let anyone tell you different!"

Teresa tapped the coffee table for emphasis, and Patrick's and Harriet's eyes met, hung fragilely, then fled.

Helping Teresa in the kitchen a moment later, Harriet apologized. "I *am* in a slight state, I admit. It just seems suddenly we have an avalanche to contend with and—" She stopped herself, lowering her voice. "What are they really saying, Teresa? There's gossip, isn't there? About . . . you know . . . how quickly it happened and—" It wasn't even necessary to mention Elliot's name.

"I tell whoever's rude enough to ask," said Teresa, grasping Harriet's hand understandingly, "that it's a woman's prerogative to change her mind."

"I've seen the faces. Mrs. Russom looked at me yesterday like I was insane. They're either branding me as some kind of fickle wanton, or they're—"

"Calm yourself, dear. You've the jitters, I know. And so does he. He's moody this evening. Don't I know how he gets low sometimes. The Irish are like that. The Irish and the Jews. The world ends in a second. But the joy returns just as quickly. You know how he worships you."

Harriet nodded, but Patrick's worship didn't help. Somehow, it only made her feel all the more guilty.

"And his mother—"

"What about my mother?" Patrick appeared in the kitchen doorway.

"Now, now, we all know Gert."

Harriet raised an eyebrow. As far as she was concerned, Gert could jump on a sinking barge. Nevertheless, she tried to send Patrick a conciliatory look, but his head was stuck in the Frigidaire, while he picked cucumbers from the salad. That he had every right to be angry with her only increased her defensive touchiness.

"My mother feels the same as yours, but she would never put you through the third degree."

"I don't exactly sense I'm as welcome as the first crocus."

"Oh?"

"There now, doesn't that look nice?" interjected Teresa hastily, removing the roast lamb from the oven. "I'm sure," she added, "that everyone needs time to adjust. Gert'll be fine. Your ma needs to take to her bed every month or so. Calms her down. Course it's hell on the rest of us. I bet she'll have you both over to dinner before you know it. Thanksgiving Day, maybe. And it'll be mended."

"Now what's this about the paper?" Teresa asked during dinner.

"Smith and Houchins won't carry us forever. At the most, they'll print two more issues." Patrick felt harassed and ate too fast. "Ma isn't going to be making any more 'contributions.' I wouldn't take them anyway."

"She'll be happy if the paper goes under," Harriet said. "I imagine she'll feel vindicated."

Patrick snapped: "Without my mother, there wouldn't be a paper. And we aren't," he continued quickly to his aunt, "going to be getting any support from Phelps, either." For obvious reasons, he might have added, exchanging a quick look with Harriet. "After he reads this week's issue, he's definitely not going to be wanting to help us."

"What did you say?" asked Teresa.

"I'm going after him."

Harriet felt a rushing in her ears at the mention of Phelps; in the distance Patrick and Teresa were talking, but she couldn't concentrate nor understand the vague resentment she felt—as if Phelps were *her* property and she reserved the right to handle her own affairs. She didn't want Patrick seizing something that was hers—even her rage.

"It's shocking . . ." Teresa was saying. "Business is off at the shop. People don't know what's going to happen. There's an ugly temper brewing, dear. You be careful."

"I agree," nodded Harriet.

"Why?" Patrick asked. "You'd challenge the time of day if we'd let you. Now you want to back off?" He found himself suspicious and didn't know why. "Look what he's done."

"I know what he's done," Harriet replied, testy. "I just think we ought to be judicious and not bite off more than we can chew. He's not going to sit still if you provoke him."

"Provoke him? He's done the provoking. It's an outrageous act of contempt. I've been down there to see for myself," he went on to Teresa and Matt. "It's so strange to be on South Main and not hear the mill. It's like Sunday. I've talked to them. There were five hundred standing around today. Some of them are still as dazed as Pa was. They think Phelps'll open up and everything'll go back to normal. But it won't. Of course I'm going after him! I may not have a voice for more than a week or two, but I'll do what I can."

"How much do you owe?" asked Teresa. "Perhaps, Matt and me—"

"No," Patrick replied firmly, "you've done enough. It'd be a drop in the bucket, anyway. We owe everyone. Don't worry, I'll come up with something. I'm going to look for a job."

"A job?" Harriet was open-mouthed. "That's the first I've heard of that. They aren't hanging on trees. What kind of job?"

"Tutoring work, maybe. I'm not sure. I could always teach."

"We should concentrate on getting ourselves out of the corner. Not go off on tangents."

"Look," he retorted, "I'm trying to keep my paper going. I'll do what I have to."

"What do you think *I* want?" she replied, hurt at his use of the first person singular.

"There now," comforted Teresa, exchanging a worried glance with Matt, "I'm sure you're both wanting the same."

"Also," continued Patrick, "I'm wondering: What's *The Spectator's* real function? Obviously I haven't found it because if I had, there'd be more circulation and advertising support. It was all very well to have that flurry of excitement when the *Boston Herald* ran that interview with me, but it didn't bring us in so much as a red cent in revenue. So—"

Feeling left out, Harriet interrupted. "It seems to me *I* was the one who brought up some of those very questions quite some time ago."

"Oh, I'm not denying that you taught me everything I know. Without you, I'd be shoveling coal. Or digging ditches. Remember, Teresa? That's what Ma always said. Without her, I'd be digging ditches. Well, maybe I will." Why was he being sarcastic with her? He didn't want to be. But everything about her irritated the piss out of him. How dare she behave like this in front of *his* relatives. He'd kept his mouth shut with *hers*.

"I could get a job. Christmas is coming and Sutherland's would take me on."

"I don't want you working," he replied, jaw set. It seemed like a personal defeat. "I'll take care of it."

"That's such an old-fashioned attitude. Don't you agree, Teresa? You're a working woman."

"Here we go . . ." muttered Patrick.

"That I am," Teresa replied quickly, unsure where to jump, for hot coals were underfoot no matter.

"Don't you and Matt pull together as equals?"

"I'm sure we do, dear." Teresa gazed fondly at her husband. She made twice as much money as he did, but she had the grace to let him think he was in charge. So much easier.

"And Matt's not upset that Teresa has a job of her own. Are you, Matt?"

Never having thought too much about it, Matt glanced at Teresa for a clue as to a possible answer. "You know what they say," he grinned. "The man's the head of the household and the woman's the heart."

Patrick nodded. Harriet made a face. "I hate to step on your emancipated toes—" Patrick responded, then paused. He knew he risked a bonfire but couldn't help throwing the match. "But it's a lot of crap. Men and women aren't equal and never have been."

"Oh?" Harriet challenged in return. "Certainly not in *your* house. I know exactly what you mean," she went on caustically. "The exact opposite of what Matt said, isn't it? Your mother's the 'head' and as for the 'heart'—it belongs to your father. I doubt *she* even has one."

"How dare you?" Patrick muttered. Grim-faced, he started the car. "Embarrassing me like that? Ma warned me about you. Stop trying . . ."

"You're beginning to sound like her."

". . . to run everything. Including me. She tried it and it didn't work. Who the hell do you think you are?"

"You give as good as you get," Harriet shot back. "You picked at me all night and—"

"I don't want to talk about it."

"I thought there were two of us."

"You could've fooled me."

"What's that supposed to mean?"

"What's wrong with you? I haven't done anything to you. I'm not your enemy."

"I wonder."

"Do you want to be my wife or don't you?"

"What's that supposed—?"

Both knew what he meant, but they skirted it. Harriet rolled down her window and breathed deeply, fanning smoke and sexual tension out into the air.

326

"Mrs. Patrick Flynn. Love, honor and obey—remember? It's very simple."

I'm Harriet Hoskins, she yelled inwardly, guilt forcing her on the offensive. "Is it? Obey? If that means keeping my mouth shut and walking five paces behind, find some other docile cow. That's not me."

"You shouldn't have married me," he said, praying she'd rebut him. His prostate throbbed and his insides clenched. "Why did you?" he asked, desperate with her silence.

"Because you asked me."

"I should've left you with Elliot." Once again, he needed her to deny it, but she didn't, and Patrick blew. "Why'd you break up with him? Did he throw you over or vice versa? I got the impression it was over between you. I got the impression you at least liked me. I didn't think I was a dose of salts. You married me, didn't you?"

"Stop shouting at me. Stop it!"

"And another thing," he added, as they pulled up on Mulberry, "I want us out of here." It was easier to become inflamed with tangibles than face the gnawing in his gut, where no answers came and if they did, were unacceptable and frightening. "Your family's trying so hard, it makes me nervous."

The car jolted to a halt, jouncing them both.

"Now it's my family's fault? They've been superb!"

"Your father?"

"He needs time. Why are you so impatient with . . . everything?" Harriet began to cry. Her tears wrecked Patrick and he tried to put an arm around her, but she rebuffed him. Scared, they stared at each other.

"Do you love me or don't you?" Patrick couldn't help the demand. Fear escalated in him as Harriet continued to cry, but she was feeling too much pain, had once again retreated. In an uncomprehending rage, Patrick got out of the car, walked around to the back of the house, got Albatross and went for a walk. Should he go to the office and sleep? Or to Jerry's? And tell him what? That six days after his marriage he wanted to be unmarried? He had a piece of paper that said he was married, but he didn't know what to do with his wife.

He spent an hour out, hoping no one would be up when he returned. The only person in the house he had any rapport with was Alice. He went in the cellar door, climbed up to the kitchen and poured himself a tentative glass of water in the pantry. What was he doing here? *Mea culpa, mea culpa, mea maxima culpa. My fault, my mistake, my grievous mistake.* What a misbegotten fool he was. Ma was right.

Leaving Albatross by the woodbox, he tiptoed up the back stairs. He had to make peace.

Shaken herself, Harriet heard him and set down the novel she'd been trying to read. Catching sight of herself in the mirror opposite the bed, she

327

swung her bangs defiantly. What had she done that was so terrible? she asked herself, knowing full well.

"Hi." Patrick hung on the doorknob. "I'm sorry," he whispered.

"Me, too."

Ships in the night, sending signals, but no boarding parties forthcoming. Too much fog. Way too much fog.

Patrick took his robe and pajamas and tiptoed to the bathroom. When he returned, the room was dark. Unsure, he sat on the edge of Harriet's bed and tried not to breathe. The radiator clanked, then there was silence again. Apprehensive of rejection, he took her roughly in his arms, a move that was more of a challenge than loving. "Oh," she murmured, frightened.

"I won't bite."

"But—"

"Never mind." Smacking a fist into his palm, Patrick turned away and sat on his bed, then got up again.

"Patrick—" she pleaded.

"Why don't we get it annulled?"

"Is that what you want?"

Once again he smashed his fist into his palm. "You weren't even a virgin. That night at the lake. You weren't—"

Shocked at his insensitivity, she turned her face away, but the bludgeoning continued.

"Did Elliot get there first?"

"I hate you," she gasped, crying now.

"Why shouldn't you? You married me on the rebound. I'd hate me, too!"

"Patrick . . . please . . . don't."

"Do you still think you 'might have been in love with me all along'? Isn't that what you told me? Only a sucker would've believed that, but *I* did, didn't I?"

"*Patrick*," she pleaded, "*they'll hear.*"

"Good! They don't like me anyway. Do you think I'm interested in a plate of Elliot's cold leftovers? I fell into the trap, didn't I? I don't know if you used me to get over Elliot, or even with him, but you're not going to break my heart, I'll tell you that."

18 🌿

You've kept the lid on too long, Mr. Phelps.

The Spectator has canvassed your employees. They wait for justice outside the guarded gates of your fortress. You locked them out; now you have a strike on your hands. Even if you reopened tomorrow, the majority of your employees would refuse to return to work. The majority, welded into a force by your obvious disregard and contempt for their well-being, are now more determined than ever. They insist on a vote, insist they have a say in their future, insist there be an open election to decide for themselves whether they wish to join the ranks of the A. F. of L.

Congress has granted them that right. The recently passed Wagner Act sanctions collective bargaining and guarantees labor the right to organize.

The Spectator calls for negotiation and compliance with the law of the land.

The Spectator supports the working men and women of Jericho.

They have a right to security and relief from the peevish whims and destructive actions of management. They have a right to be free from spies, free from toadies, free from dismissal without cause. They have a right to equitable wages and safer working conditions.

They have a right to be heard.

Progress will not be thwarted by a handful of economic royalists.

Labor's cry is heard throughout America and rings out clear on Main St.

Freedom is the issue.

Can you in good conscience abandon eight hundred of your employees and their families?

329

Thanksgiving is coming, Mr. Phelps. Will you eat your turkey and let the men and women, the sons and daughters of Jericho, go hungry?

Jericho is waiting for your answer.

Editorial reprinted from
The Jericho Spectator,
Nov. 11, 1936

19

"*O Promise Me That One Day You and I . . .*" Jeannie Lo Bianco's pure soprano floated high from the loft of the Congregationalist Church as Letty wiped a tear and Franklin stood stoic, giving away his eldest daughter Cora to Samuel Cousins of Salem.

Pale November sunlight streamed through the tall windows, turning Cora's wedding gown translucent, the ivory slipper satin shining like the light in her eyes.

Standing with the bridal party, Harriet felt as vulnerable as the tiara of tiny flowers in her hair, more fragile than the delicate fingertip veil that brushed the bridge of her nose.

"I now pronounce you man and wife," intoned Reverend Peabody, and Harriet had a sense of déjà vu. In the nine days since she'd heard those words herself, her marriage had assumed the proportions of a terrifying and tragic charade. There'd been no loveliness like today, no family and friends gathered to share what was supposed to be one of life's supreme moments. Two strangers had been joined with two strangers as witnesses, a stranger officiating in a dark and alien church at close to midnight, with her clutching, dazed, to a bouquet of hastily assembled chrysanthemums, while Albatross barked and barked at a squirrel on the roof.

That she had no one to blame but herself only made the situation more agonizing.

Sam lifted Cora's veil, and they kissed; her wedding ring caught the light, the diamond sent sparkles piercing Harriet's heart as Elliot came drifting into her thoughts. Like an illusion he continued to haunt her. She would have married him in this very church with the same Reverend Peabody performing the ceremony. She would be standing where Cora was, wearing white instead of hyacinth blue; many of the same people would be gathered, and she'd be Mrs. Elliot Phelps.

But if there was nostalgia for a love lost, it was quickly supplanted with pain. Elliot's betrayal was as potent as the perfume of the flower-bedecked altar. Shaken, Harriet stole a glance to the filled-to-capacity church and found Patrick in the fifth pew with his head bowed. His vulnerability caused an ache, and she wondered if he was wishing the same thing she

331

was. If they'd had a wedding like this, would it all have been different between them? Their eyes met and Harriet had to avert hers. Like a tight-fitting corset she couldn't get off, her guilt at what she'd perpetrated caused a panic that allowed for no amends she might make him, no matter how much she wanted to.

Bathing the gathering in the magic between them, Cora and Sam turned as the organ soared. Love was in the air, shimmering like the motes dancing in the sunlight's beams. From a surprising place, tears welled in Harriet's eyes as she caught sight of Cora's expression.

Envious of Cora? Yes, right now, at this moment, she was.

"Wasn't it lovely?"
"Nicest wedding I've been to in years!"
"Hello, so glad you could come!"
"The church looked beautiful!"
"Cora and Sam did the decorating."
"The flowers! Like spring."

Harriet stood in line with the other bridesmaids as the guests inched past. Exchanging kisses and greetings, they moved up the line—past best man and maid of honor, on to the two sets of beaming parents and Reverend Peabody, until they reached the climax of Cora and Sam.

"Harriet, don't you look lovely."

"Miss Bradshaw—hello." Harriet greeted the town librarian, who was an old friend.

"I know this is Cora's day, but I haven't had a chance to give you my best wishes. Nor Patrick, either." Miss Bradshaw smiled toward Patrick, who was several people behind her. "I liked very much what he had to say in the paper. Mr. Phelps has been generous to the library, but what he's done is unconscionable. Alice, you're blooming!" she went on. "We don't get to see you anymore. I remember the three of you when you were no higher than weeds. Time flies, doesn't it?"

"When you're having fun," responded Alice under her breath as Miss Bradshaw continued on her way. "You're being scrutinized."

"Uh-huh. Hello, nice to see you." Harriet had on a vivacious smile, but this was her first appearance in public with her new husband, and eyes were on her. Let them talk, let them rot. But her fighting stance was shaky. She felt like a foreigner—as if she'd wandered into some happy family other than her own.

"Jeannie . . . you sounded super." Harriet and Jeannie exchanged a cheek. "Are you going to sing for us later?"

"Gee, I don't know." Feeling as out of place as Harriet, Jeannie swallowed one of her nervous yawns and looked up at Frankie. "The kid brought his trumpet but . . . with this crowd. . . . ?" Jeannie tossed a quick look in the direction of Aunt Iris, who was giving her the once-over.

332

"Rattle their pans. Do 'em good," offered Alice, as Jeannie and Frankie moved on. "Jeezus," Jeannie muttered to him soto voce, "lemme outta here!" "You're doing fine," he whispered back, holding defiantly to her arm.

Out of the corner of her eye, Harriet saw that Patrick was almost to her. The nasty fight a few nights ago had shocked them both; they'd been overly polite and distant since.

"Hello." Lapsing into the safety of a fantasy, Harriet peeked at him over her bouquet of pink rosebuds and sweet fern. Who was the handsome stranger? "Don't I know you?"

"What?" Patrick replied, unsure. Grinning tentatively, he exchanged a glance with Alice. "Pat Flynn."

"The renowned editor of *The Spectator*?"

Not sure what Harriet was up to, Patrick grinned again. Should he kiss her? Bravely he did.

"That won't work," whispered Alice, winking as Patrick moved up the line. "You can't pretend you don't know him because . . ."

"Where's your sense of fun? *Hello*, Ada. I love your gown. Mauve is such a good color for you."

". . . he's too real for that."

"Real? Who's real?"

"Aunt Iris! *You* are. Don't you love weddings? Don't they cast a spell?"

"You look peak-ed, Harriet," replied Letty's oldest sister.

"Are you getting your sleep?" inquired Clara, the middle one of the three Winslowe girls. Alice suppressed a laugh. "I'm on top of the world," replied Harriet gaily. "Wasn't it a beautiful ceremony?"

"We missed yours," Iris replied pointedly. "Didn't we, George?" Her husband nodded. So did Clara and Arthur. They all glanced up the line toward the pagan who'd invaded the ranks and carried off one of *theirs*. Patrick sensed the attention behind him as he shook hands with Letty and saw Franklin look through him. This morning as the relatives gathered at the house, he'd overheard Iris say, "Sudden, wasn't it?" And Clara had whispered, "But who *is* he?" He guessed many here today were asking the same; his marriage was viewed with an almost superstitious fear of the unknown.

"My—?" Pretending innocence, Harriet smiled brightly at Iris and added what she hoped was a suitably bemused batting of lashes, as if to say, 'Ain't life grand and inexplicable?'

"*Wedding*," replied Iris. "*Your* wedding."

"I would have loved for you all to be there but . . ."

"Weddings," interjected Alice, coming to the rescue. "I think they're impractical. Cost too much and give everyone the impression life's worth living."

Clara and Arthur, who lived in another century in West Andover, exchanged a look and regarded their niece as if she'd arrived from Mars. But Iris wasn't perturbed.

"That cynic routine of yours is wearing thin, Alice. I saw tears in your eyes during the ceremony."

"Move it along, dear . . . we're bunching up."

"We'll be dancing at yours next, Alice, I dare say," continued Iris, who never paid any attention to George.

"I doubt it," replied Alice, exchanging a glance with Harriet, which the latter couldn't decipher. *What?* her eyes asked. Alice put mouth to ear. "I have news," she whispered provocatively, then shook her head, grinned and said nothing more.

"I'll say this," continued Iris looking from one to the other. "Of all of you—and I include your brother—Cora's the only one of you who turned out normal."

"Normal?"

"Normal?" echoed Alice. "Cora? She'd label a piece of lint if she had the chance."

"And pack it away," added Harriet.

"And label the box!" they said in unison, breaking out in infectious giggles.

"You girls," tskked Iris.

"My girls," boomed Uncle Harold Winslowe, Letty's older brother, who'd come all the way from Chicago where the circus was in winter quarters. "Was at a wedding last week," he announced, winking at Harriet and Alice. He was only a ticket taker for Ringling Brothers but "show biz" was stamped all over him. "Sheena, the Jungle Queen, got hitched to one of the Alonzo midgets. Damnedest couple you ever saw! I want to dance with both of you," he added, roundly bussing his nieces on the cheek. "If only I wasn't your uncle," he sighed, then moved away in search of pretty women.

"Hello, nice to see you. *Tell me,*" Harriet whispered to Alice in between greetings. "You heard from him?" Alice nodded. "*Alice.*"

"*Later,*" whispered Alice—the cat with the canary—relishing the excitement on her sister's face.

And so it moved, the line, eddying upward to the summit of Cora. Undercurrents wiggled, turbulence diddled many of the participants, but Cora remained serene. Accepting kisses and bestowing more, she was a monument of tranquility and sudden power; even her usual pealing tones were modulated as she received the cornucopia of best wishes. "Jeannie," she cooed, as the brunette bandsinger and Frankie reached her. "What would we have done without you?"

"Ayea," nodded Letty, fingering Sarah's pearls and eyeing Jeannie with what she hoped was a gracious smile. Did she have to pencil her eyebrows like that? "What *would* we have?" she added, echoing Cora. Ada's eldest, scheduled to sing, had come down with the hives, and Frankie had suggested Jeannie. Letty had met her only once at the Classic. The sight of her at Friday's wedding rehearsal—sashaying down the aisle in a red dress—had filled Letty with tart disapproval.

"You have such a sweet soprano," Letty went on, straightening her son's bow tie in a proprietary gesture that had more to do with Jeannie than the tie's need of aligning.

"Gee thanks, Mrs. Hoskins. It's a pleasure, I'm sure, Mrs. Hoskins. You look awfully swell today," Jeannie added, fussing with her handbag.

"And so do you," responded Letty, as she accepted a kiss from her son. Even if Frankie loudly proclaimed his independence, he was still a baby as far as Letty was concerned. She hoped, whatever it was, it was a passing infatuation. She didn't need any more upsets; no, indeed. Letty glanced back down the line at Harriet and embraced Iris.

"Well, Letitia, it was a beautiful ceremony. I bet you never dreamed you'd have two of them gone so quickly."

"George."

"Franklin."

"No, I didn't," replied Letty, keeping an eye on her husband and brother-in-law, who were making strained small talk beside her. Ever since Letty had borrowed the money from George to save the house in '32, the two men had been at odds.

"It *was* a surprise," added Clara. Like Letty, her sisters were full of good sense and strong virtue. They were of the same mind, however, that their younger sister had brought up her children much too freely. Alice was as incomprehensible as ever; look at Frankie with that flashy *Eye*talian. But the proof of the pudding was Harriet, whose unconventional and startling elopement with an Irish Catholic had rocketed along the family grapevine like a thunderclap. She might have married a darkie, as far as Iris was concerned. "We thought that Phelps boy was a catch." Letty nodded vaguely and tried to ignore her insufferable oldest sister who she was glad lived in Bayonne, New Jersey.

"Cora!" Iris beamed on Cora, who was understandable and therefore admired and loved unabashedly. "Cora, you are the prettiest bride I ever saw. You have a pearl here," she added to Sam, who nodded happily.

"He knows that," replied Franklin, who smiled quickly to let them know he wasn't being contentious. "Don't you look handsome yourself, Franklin," offered Iris guardedly. What Letty had put up with! Franklin nodded and chose not to bestow a compliment in return. Erect, dapper in a cutaway—white carnation matching his hair—he raised a hand to signal for a glass of champagne. Moving off, George cast a glance that Franklin pretended not to see. But he was in an expansive mood, and when one of Letty's church committee members, who had volunteered to help serve, offered him her tray, he raised his glass to his in-laws and downed it with a bad-boy bravado.

"I'm thirsty, Mother," he protested, smiling to himself as Iris and George sent a final disapproving glance and disappeared into the throng. "Remember ours?" he whispered, giving Letty an uncharacteristic public kiss on the cheek. Surprised and delighted, she nodded, the memories stirring. It was all going well, she told herself, greeting the next in line. So far, she had to add, then told herself not to worry. Franklin was fine today; she knew the signs, pro and con. How many years, she couldn't help thinking, had she lived with "so fars"? But today wasn't a day for dwelling on the past. Yet, she felt ancient—and like a new bride at the same time. That's what weddings evoked, she reflected, smoothing her pale rose taffeta as her thoughts went back there—that late summer afternoon in the front parlor of her father's house. And she'd taken Franklin's hand and found it trembling in hers. Her mother had looked on, pinched at the new son-in-law who was an orphan and a nobody, but what had it mattered? Letty loved him then and loved him still. Despite the upheavals, she would go on loving him forever—never more so than today as they sent their first-born out into a rambunctious world.

"Father," she murmured, and returned his kiss.

"Weddings—what a farce. C'mere." Alice pulled her sister away as the receiving line broke up. "I want some champagne."

"Me, too. Tell me. What did he say?"

"To weddings!" Alice took a large sip, eyes widening as it went down. "I needed that, as they say. Whew."

"*Tell me.*"

"The letter came yesterday. I slept on it last night. He's been working with the ambulance corps. He had diarrhea. He's going to hitch a freighter back and—*we're going to be married!*"

"*Alice!*" Harriet hugged her sister, whose face lit with the first true smile of many a month.

"No hoopla like this for us, though. Out of town I think would be best. Under the circumstances. He seemed pleased about becoming a father. I feel like dancing. Maybe I will." She waved to the musical trio—Frankie on piano and two friends on base and violin—who played sedately in a corner. Alice twirled, then grasped Harriet's arm, dizzy.

"Impending motherhood must be doing me in," she quipped. "I hate this gown. Puke pink. Thank God it's Empire style, so I don't show. I don't, do I? I'll be almost in my fourth month by the time he gets here. I'm surprised Mother hasn't sensed something. I spend so much time in the bathroom in the morning. But she's been busy. This crowd'll have a field day, won't they?"

She nodded to the festive gathering, who were now at the buffet sampling the chicken salad, savoring the ambrosia and gossiping animatedly. "Why don't I *really* give 'em something to chew on?" Alice grinned like the imp she rarely revealed.

"What a good idea! One scandal after another. I have the perfect time for you. Make sure you catch the bouquet, sniff it, cry, then announce you're pregnant."

"Ha-ha. You're as funny as a crutch."

"If you need my help with Mother, you know I told you you could count on me."

Alice shook her head. "Not yet. I don't dare. And Father—" She shuddered inwardly at Franklin's reaction. Harriet nodded in sympathy. "No," Alice went on, "I've decided to wait till he gets back. It'll be easier. Naturally it's not going to be at *all* easy but— Oooo, I feel funny. . . ."

"My half-a-glass sister."

"He's looking at you."

"Father?"

"Your husband. What's with you two?"

"Oh, you know—one little 'I do,' and it's rigor mortis for both of us." Once again the uneasiness rose in Harriet as she stole a glance and tried to laugh it away.

"For corpses you're both pretty lively. We've heard the shouting."

"Not any more you won't. He's changed," she added in an unconscious attempt to marshall a grievance against him that might take herself off the hook. But it didn't help, the responsibility was hers. She had no reason to blame him, she told herself, let alone feel anger. That she did only confused her as she gazed at Patrick, who she could see clearly and not clearly, too bewildered to recognize that he had become a symbol of all men and their power to hurt.

"How? He's terrific. Don't you admire him? Look at the leaps he's taken."

"That's not the issue. We were partners on the paper. Now there seem to be new rules. And he doesn't want me to get some parttime work. And—"

"Look at his editorial."

"I know. He's liberal in print and conservative with me. Who would've thunk it?"

"Red herrings," Alice scoffed. "So he's conservative. Look at his background. What did you expect? C'mon, now—*that's* not the issue. Listen—he talked to me."

"He did?" Harriet was very dismayed.

"He doesn't know what's wrong. Can't figure you. Why're you shutting him out?"

"I—"

"So what if you married him on the rebound? He knows that. But

337

you're not making it easy. He's on the rebound, too. From the Virgin Mary." Alice raised her glass, finished the contents, and got the hiccups.

"Alice, be careful . . ." warned Harriet as tears of laughter ran down her sister's cheeks. "What a . . . combo . . . you two are," continued Alice, getting a grip. "You've got such a wall around you, you can't even see him. I know Elliot burned you. He's not Elliot."

Harriet flushed; the scar on her heart shifted slightly.

"It's not his fault. Stop being a nervous tick. He loves you, for God's sake! What does it take to claim you?"

"Don't know."

"Slit his wrists and present you with a cupful?"

Harriet smiled wistfully. Not wanting to discuss it further, she hid behind her bouquet, for Alice's probing opened too many questions that couldn't be answered.

"Weddings . . ." she sighed. "Somehow . . . everything seems possible." If only it were so. If only she could make it so.

"Steal him away," grinned Alice, "and go home. No one's there. You can have a nice private roll in the hay."

"Hmmmm," Harriet murmured and told herself to get a hold. "You're right," she exclaimed. "I'm going to snap out of it. Watch me snap. Your news has given me such a lift! And it's Cora's wedding. She's about to leave the nest for eternal happiness. I want some, too! Let's have some more champagne. I want to be giddy!"

The sisters clinked glasses and burst out laughing. Harriet willed herself to be swept up and carried away by the infectious spirits that flowed around her. Love, music and romance would bear her triumphant. "I'm determined to be happy," she announced, winking at Sam's best man and blowing kisses to Uncle Harold. Chatting with the Cousins clan and nibbling at the buffet, she occasionally found her eyes wandering to Patrick, who was deep in talk with several men. Conversations ran with him in her head. "Hello, hello," she murmured, greeting friends and sundry with an outward effervescence, while she watched Patrick and tried to sort her feelings. In those Indian summer days when she was sure he wasn't a contender, there must have been *something*. Why else would she have turned to him? Hadn't she found him, despite the clash of their personalities, attractive? Where had it gone?

She caught his eye and raised a tentative hand in greeting. Through the protection of her veil, she continued to glance at him. No, he wasn't Elliot, a knight in shining armor who turned out to be wearing tin and broke her heart.

Hello, she smiled, as she inched to the edges of the circle that had Patrick at its center. Talk was intense of events at the mill.

Everyone seemed to know who he was, she realized, glad of the

338

tender feeling of pride that surprised her. Their eyes met, two pairs of eyes on a tightrope with no nets.

She *wanted* to be his wife, she *did*; wanted it to be wonderful, knew she should make love with him—it seemed, on the one hand, a terrible flaw in her that she hadn't, added cherries of guilt—but how could she when he was so impatient with her, bullying her as he had. And she didn't feel anything, not the way she should, not the way she wanted to, not the way she had with Elliot when he kissed her and . . .

Once again the pain was there, fragmenting her. And the continued cropping up of the name Phelps as she listened to the conversation was added impetus for moving on. Lightly she touched Patrick on the arm and went to Letty and Franklin. She kissed her mother and Franklin, too, but his eyes focused close to his face and not on Harriet, and she found herself falling in an empty space. "Oh," she giggled, relieved, when Uncle Harold came up behind her and spun her around jovially. "We mustn't dance yet," she admonished, "not till Cora and Sam . . ." The room continued to spin even after Harold righted her, but her laughter camouflaged a sudden hallucination as Franklin stared at her, followed by Patrick, then a flash of blond that was Elliot. With his father behind him. And round again, the men glaring at her, racing faster now, one after the other, interchangeable, all frightening.

"Oh, my," she murmured, leaning against Harold's shoulder. "It must be the champagne," she said, sighing, so glad when his arm anchored her.

"Where's Patrick?" she heard him ask as she dared open her eyes. "Talking about the mill," she replied, noticing that Franklin was smiling at Cora, and Patrick wasn't looking at her either and the blond belonged to Dorcas Abbot's husband. "He's caused a stir," her uncle was saying, and she nodded and accepted a light with tremulous fingers.

"Bunch of lintheads," scoffed Franklin. "They never had it so good. I hope Phelps makes 'em crawl. . . ."

"Now, Father," soothed Cora, smoothing his starched front while Franklin preened. "How's my chickadee?" he asked, calling her by a long ago pet name as memories flooded him of a time when he was almost happy. A raining May morning at Leveret General and, if he was initially disappointed she was a girl (who cried, it seemed, for a solid six months after), he'd grown to love his little fussbudget.

Harriet watched her father and Cora bask in each other. She felt no envy, only hurt at his continued coolness. She didn't know the reasons for the change in him that had escalated since her return from New York; his stress might be caused by the drink, but he never confided in her as he used to. Her marriage to Patrick had been the final straw, or so it seemed, but whatever the reasons, he was lost to her—never to Cora, but he was to her.

"Pardon?" Disoriented again, she focused on Iris, who was saying she hadn't had a chance to talk with Patrick, and why didn't Harriet march right over there and get him and bring him back?

"Why I wouldn't dream of interrupting my husband when he's talking business," she managed saucily. "I don't think it's a woman's place to, do you?"

"Harriet's just an old-fashioned girl," added Alice, joining them while Letty lowered her nose into her corsage and cast a wry eye on her two slightly tipsy daughters.

"Who says I'm not?" Harriet put on a mock-feisty pose.

"Of course you're not, Harriet," chided Cora with merry eyes, her sparkling teeth sending off glimmers. "You're the least old-fashioned girl we know."

"Now *here*'s an old-fashioned bride," fussed Iris. "Isn't she beautiful?" added Harriet, hugging Cora, whose mounds of hair behind each ear looked like cinnamon buns. "How does it feel?" she whispered, trying to banish the running stream in her head.

"Oh," sighed Cora, the exhalation brimming with a wealth of contentment and joy, which Harriet prayed would rub off on her. O why couldn't she feel for Patrick what Cora did for Sam?

"We'll have dancing in just a minute and then we'll cut the cake. . . ." Leaving the relatives lit in her reflected glow, Cora moved away and into a knot of adoring high-school chums.

"Isn't she the wonderful little organizer?" Iris smiled fondly. "Always was, wasn't she, Letty?"

"Not a nervous bone in her body," nodded Clara, one eye on Harriet.

"Why should she have?" laughed Alice. "She's been planning it for two years. Probably has her funeral arrangements worked out, too."

The aunts looked askance; Harold roared. Franklin cleared his throat. A moment later, Frankie played a fanfare on the piano, and Sam swept Cora out onto the floor for the first waltz. Applause rose, ebbed, then swelled again as Franklin cut in and took Cora in his arms and Sam bowed to Letty.

Harriet and Patrick found each other across the room, each of them questioning, as if waiting for the other to make a move.

The floor began to fill with dancing couples. A *tisket, a tasket, I've lost my yellow basket*. But she hadn't. Lost her basket, nor her heart, her numbed and unresponding heart. Could he be trusted with that fragile organ that beat feebly? she might have asked, but her usual clarity about herself had long since disappeared. O let it beat faster!

Why couldn't she be simple and uncomplicated like Cora? she wondered, as she began a circle of the room that would bring her to him. Normal like Cora, an old-fashioned girl. Was that who he wanted? She would try, she would, she must, she wanted to.

340

Love, love, where was it hiding? In the garlands of daisies and baby's breath hanging from the sconces, in the tall tapers' flickering flame? O please.

I Love You, Cora, Sam had written on the four-tiered wedding cake. *I love you, Patrick; I love you, Patrick,* Harriet murmured as she passed by.

O let it be true! Let Virginia's assurance that she wouldn't have married him if she hadn't loved him be true! Let it be revealed. O let her wake! If there was waking to be done she was willing. O please. Let *him* be the prince who would wake her with a kiss, banish her uncertainties, and release her from the nightmare in which she found herself suspended.

"What's her problem?" Patrick asked Alice. Surprised the question had popped out, he shoved his hands in his pockets. "Never mind," he added, but Alice took his arm and walked him out the paneled doors and onto the front steps of the church.

"Need a breath of air myself," she said, the bubbly making her see double. Exhaling on her glasses, she shook her head at him. "You two lovebirds. . . !" She didn't mind playing Cupid if it would help.

Patrick shrugged. Ashamed to reveal personal anxieties, he was as agitated as his wife. Today's affair, with its gaiety and good feeling, was too painfully ironic. And when he'd danced with Harriet, he felt he was in never-never land. She was ethereal, vanishable in the flick of an eye.

"Dreams and realities," he muttered. "I wish I weren't here," he added, tongue loose with champagne and the mysterious and heightened atmosphere of a wedding, where truths are bared that wouldn't be otherwise. Patrick stared out at the street. A boy with an inner tube walked by; it seemed an incongruous sight for November. Hard put to keep himself together these days, he shook his head. What had happened between Harriet and himself had stunned him. Compensating, he'd thrown himself into work, spent the afternoons trudging down job leads in Leveret, brain never ceasing to come up with some kind of scheme that would bring in money and save his paper. What time was left he spent outside the mill. His anger was a bright flame, the cause a just one, his sympathies respected and acknowledged, the issues clear. But with Harriet he was in quicksand.

"It must be me."

"No. I don't think so." Alice wanted to ease him, but didn't know how.

"It must be." Bitterness was ready to pounce. She was too high-strung for her own damn good! "I can't make hide nor hair of her. Hell's bells! I'm not such a bad fellow. I thought she—" He stopped himself, unable to say it.

"I think she does. Probably doesn't even know she does. You know how she is. She's . . . uneasy. Give her some time and—"

"I thought I knew, but—" Why should he be made the villain of the piece? What had he done? He felt like he was climbing an endless wall and the top would never be reached. "What the hell's her problem?" he blurted desperately. "It's him, isn't it? What else could it be? She still loves him, doesn't she!"

"Yoo-hoo! We're going to take photos before we cut the cake. Gather round. First I want Reverend Peabody and Mother and Father . . ." Making sure every nip, tuck and smile of her wedding was chronicled properly, Cora directed the photographers as well as the best man, who wielded Sam's camera.

"Now I want another. Just the family. . . ."

"Cora," they joshed after several more poses. "The cake'll get stale!"

"No, it won't. Sam baked it with magic flour."

Another photograph was snapped to be inserted in the scrapbook later, the first of many that would be filled, documenting the Hoskins' girls and their husbands and children in years to come. Familiar faces would grow older in the photographs; little dumplings in bassinets developing into nieces and nephews, the Winslowe jaw uniting them all. Letty's grandchildren and great, too, would find their past in the thousands of photographs taken over the years by those indefatigable chroniclers, Cora and Sam.

"All right . . . yoo-hoo . . . I want the bridal party . . ."

"Where is he?" Harriet whispered to Alice.

"I may have stepped out of line. . . ."

"Harriet . . . Alice . . . we're waiting."

"What do you mean?"

"He still thinks you're cuckoo for Elliot."

"Of course I'm not."

"Girls—they're waiting for you," urged Letty. The sisters joined the other bridesmaids. "Like a rainbow, isn't it, Letty?" Ada sighed as she gazed on the lovely sextet, each in a pastel of her own. Snap, wind, snap. And then again. Harriet smiled, then cocked a troubled and questioning gaze at Alice, the expression caught for posterity.

"Now I want married couples."

"Cora," they all moaned, pretending as people often do that the taking of their photographs is a chore, whereas in truth they were having a grand time.

"Out of line? What do you mean?"

"Iris and George . . . you get in the middle. Clara and Arthur and . . ."

"He's jealous of Elliot. And I told him he shouldn't be."

". . . and Mr. and Mrs. Cousins and Harriet and Patrick . . ."

"You did what?" Harriet nervously fingered the buttons on her elbow-length gloves and stared at her sister, who looked guiltily away.

"Told him. About Elliot. About what happened."

Hiding a gasp, Harriet brought hand to mouth. "You had no right to!" she whispered angrily.

"Harriet . . . where's Patrick? You're keeping us waiting again."

"I'll find him," she called to Cora. "We'll be in the next. How could you?" she went on in an urgent whisper.

"I was trying to help. Me and my big mouth. I'm dippy today and—"

"What did he say?"

"Nothing much. I'm sorry," she added as Harriet turned away, her heart slamming in her chest as she spotted Patrick, who stood poised across the room in the doorway. Fearful to approach him, she knew she had no choice.

"Cora wants a picture . . ."

He shook his head.

"Patrick—"

"Don't bother."

"Alice said—"

"I know I'm naive but—"

From behind his own wall, Patrick stared at her. Fury burned in his gut, and he had to get out.

Harriet missed the cutting of the cake, for she went looking for him. She knew she mustn't let him go off like this. At the same time she felt a strange relief that it was all out in the open. If she'd felt like she was carrying stones, now the weight seemed lifted. Perhaps it was better he knew. But what had she to offer him now? Agitatedly, she glanced into the empty church, then turned and hurried out the front doors. What explanation could possibly suffice?

But no matter her own anxiety, she sensed the next few moments were crucial. A delicate soul was in her hands, and her concern for him superseded anything as she searched. Relieved, she found him on the mossy, flagstone path down behind the church. Turned away, Patrick sensed her approach and turned further.

"Patrick . . ." she said after a silence, broken only by the painful aching of the tall elms, which swayed above their heads in a light breeze.

"I guess I don't have any illusions why you married me."

Harriet wanted to give him some, but didn't know how. "I'm . . . sorry," she murmured softly, hating herself for the paltriness of the words. "I—"

"I want to be by myself—"

She nodded and moved slightly away but couldn't leave. Apologies and a fervent desire to make it up to him careened in her, and she tried to find the words that would ease him. "I know," she began after another long

343

silence, "what you must be thinking. "I'm—" *Everything you think I am.* "I'm—" The words caught in her throat as Patrick turned and she was frightened of the violence in his eyes, which were red with weeping.

"I'm sorry," she pleaded again, weeping herself now, loathing herself for having caused his suffering. "Don't go," she added as Patrick quickly walked up the incline and disappeared around the front of the church. Harriet called after him, then followed, but he was gone. She went inside, looked again into the empty pews, and had to sit.

Finding her, Alice said, "I could cut my tongue out." Harriet shook her head and asked her sister if she'd seen him, but Alice hadn't. A moment later she returned to the reception hall; Uncle Harold swept her up for a fox trot, but she had little sense of it, and when it was over she looked about, dazed. She was startled when she found Patrick staring at her from the vestibule, and she went to him.

"Dance with me," she pleaded, but once again he turned from her and went into the pews, interrupting an intense confab between the flower girl and several friends, who giggled and hurried out.

"Talk about rebounds. I didn't know . . ."

"It wasn't . . . I didn't. . . . It wasn't on purpose or—"

". . . what I was talking about, did I! I *did* fall into the trap, didn't I!"

Brain maddened and insides roaring, he wanted Harriet to make it all better, but he wasn't able to reveal the longing. Nor allow it, either, even though she tried. He walked up the aisle to the altar, where the heavy odor of the flowers made him feel faint. Like her, he felt a vague relief that was mixed with the horrible rest—relief to know what the devil was and not be subjected to gnawing guesswork. Initially, he hadn't believed Alice, listened uncomprehendingly; but when she faltered, he insisted she go on. The revelation of Elliot's sickness had turned Patrick's stomach in primitive, unthinking abhorrence. The fact of Harriet's discovery of it on the night of her engagement might have ordinarily prompted a passionate sympathy and desire to care for her, but Patrick couldn't feel anything save overwhelming panic, hurt, and outrage at her use of him.

"I'm not going to be a baby," he said finally. "I want this settled."

Harriet came up behind him, hesitated, then put her arms around him, but he rebuffed her.

"You don't love me." The words echoed in the empty church, reverberating in his head until he thought he would cry again.

"I want to," she heard herself reply, the truth of it giving her hope for herself, but Patrick couldn't hear. It wasn't enough. If Alice had asked Harriet did she need a cupful of blood, Patrick needed more. A rebuttal of muscle and bone, assurances of steel. "Don't do me any favors."

"It wouldn't be a favor."

"Always pride yourself on your integrity, don't you?" he lashed sarcastically. "Were you honest with me?"

"No," she replied with a simple dignity that earned her nothing, for he cut her off curtly when she tried to continue.

"Go away. Get lost!"

"No."

"You heard me."

"If it suits you to paint me as a monster, go ahead. It couldn't be any worse than the way I feel about myself right now. Come back with me," she pleaded. "Dance with me."

He wanted to but couldn't. "Are you nuts?"

"I didn't mean to hurt you. It wasn't premeditated or—"

"*I told you I don't want to talk about it.*"

Harriet retreated halfway down the aisle. "You *are* a baby." A few steps more and she hesitated by the doors. "Patrick. . . ? Please?" she added and waited a moment longer. "I'll be waiting for you," she finally said and returned to the reception, where she caught Letty's eye. *Even at your sister's wedding?* Embarrassed, she pretended to examine the table piled with gifts, but all she could see was Patrick's face before her, and she was frightened and didn't know what to do. Keeping up a stream of conversation and the façade of a smile to the world, her eyes gave her away as they darted to the vestibule, but he wasn't there. She danced with George, Then, while she was dancing with Sam, Patrick cut in.

Grateful for what she knew was a costly effort on his part, she didn't dare say anything, and Patrick didn't either. The anger was buried, burning in the usual place. Harriet tried to catch his eye, those Irish eyes she'd always been taken with, but now they seemed not so much Irish as Russian, full of sadness and sudden silence.

But something subtle had shifted between them—infinitesimal cracks and rumblings beneath the surface of the earth.

"They're young, Father," murmured Letty, watching. She said a silent prayer for the troubled couple. "They'll bounce back," she added, and in truth they seemed to. Strangely closer than ever before, they danced again. Harriet felt lightheaded and warm and willing to let Patrick waltz her until she dropped into a pool of giddy exhaustion. And as for Patrick, he forgave her everything. *Martyr,* he argued with himself, *here we go again, the penitent relishing pain, a fool with no pride, you should be wary.* And he was, but she was in his arms, butterflies were in his stomach, and he was awed as always by her beauty. He had little to go on but faith, but the way she looked at him made him feel she really was seeing him, the usual distance seemed to have vanished, and he dared to hope.

Both of them wanting to fly, they shared a glass of champagne, and at one point Patrick whispered in her ear, "Do you love me . . . a little?"

"Of course," she replied quickly, her heart going out to him. She thought she would weep, but she didn't, and neither did he. Surprised at the sudden tingle that rose in her from seemingly out of nowhere, she flirted with him from behind her bouquet. "You're an awfully good dancer. What did you say your name was?"

"Patrick the Magnificent," he grinned in return, willing to play Let's Pretend and put it all behind him, willing to dance to any tunes she might invent.

"What's yours?" he asked as the merry throng trooped out onto the steps to watch Cora toss her bouquet.

"Can't tell you," Harriet murmured, wagging a finger at him, "I'm traveling incognito today."

Overhead the elms traced patterns on the gleaming white façade of the church.

"Are all you girls ready? Sam, do you have your camera?" Cora raised her bouquet of white rosebuds in the air and posed.

"I want you to catch it," Harriet reminded Alice and giggled. Relieved at Patrick and Harriet's togetherness, Alice positioned herself among the squealing bridesmaids—and did.

"You're next, Alice," cried Cora happily, clapping her hands and wishing she could be married all over again.

"Circe? Is that your name?" Patrick whispered, as Cora and Sam started down the steps in a hail of confetti. "Circe, who drove men blind?"

"I thought she turned them into piglets."

"Where's your mythology?"

"You're the scholar."

Down the path went the newlyweds, ducking and laughing as the confetti rained down. The honeymoon itinerary was worked out, the savings account started toward a house of their own, the china and silver patterns picked, the linens stacked, the thank-you notes for the wedding presents ready to be written. The marriage would proceed with the same loving care and attention to detail, calm and unruffled as the bride herself. But at the last moment, Cora turned to Letty and her large moon-calf eyes filled with sudden tears. *Mother.*

"There now . . ." Letty embraced her oldest and smiled over her shoulder at Sam, who was holding the car door. Sam was kind. Cora would be fine. A perfect match. But what would she ever do without her?

"Goodbye, goodbye," they all called as Cora, smiling again, got into the car and waved for a final photo.

"Deirdre of the Sorrows?"

"Not this kid." But Harriet did weep, wept joyous tears for her older sister as the flower-bedecked car started off in a final burst of waving and goodbyes, while Frankie gave a blast on his trumpet.

"Do you live nearby?"

"Can't tell." She smiled, wiping her eyes and gazing at the car that turned the corner and disappeared.

"Maybe I'll drop by."

"Weddings," murmured Harriet to herself, echoing an earlier thought that now was more substantial. Somehow they made everything seem . . . possible. Twinkle returned, she gazed up at Patrick. Linked to his arm, she felt connected to him by invisible threads. "It's you!" she exclaimed and backed away, turned quickly, and showered him with a handful of confetti. "Mulberry Street," she whispered as he caught her by the hand.

Harriet took a swig from the bottle of champagne that she and Patrick had brought home from church and broke out in such giggles that she had to bite her wrist to stop them from being heard. Lightheaded and very tipsy, she set the bottle back down on the bathroom floor and resumed the delicate maneuver.

Was there anything more hair-raising than lying on the floor, staring up at the entrails of the sink, legs propped on the toilet seat, trying to get the damned slippery thing in properly, while legions passed by in the hallway outside?

Finally she was ready, panties back on and slip pulled down. But a muddle presented itself. Swaying slightly, she debated whether she should get into her gown again or put on her bathrobe. And if the latter, what if any one of a houseful of relatives should spot her as she returned to the bedroom where an unsuspecting Patrick was waiting for her to change into a street dress or whatever else he might be thinking? Yes, what *would* he be thinking, the debate continued, if she appeared at four o'clock in the sunny afternoon in a bathrobe?

Involuntarily Harriet ran her hands over her breasts. Apprehension rose, but it was hazy, banished in a further eruption of giggles as she opted for the robe.

Taking a final peek at herself in the mirror, she tossed her hair, and confetti flew out. Pressing an ear to the door and excited by the delicious danger, she made a mad dash, champagne bottle in hand, and was caught by Harold as he reached the top of the front stairs.

"Oh, ho!" he laughed. Harriet turned crimson, popped inside the bedroom, shut the door behind her and leaned against it, gasping like a disheveled hoyden caught with the proverbial hand in the jar.

"Made it," she announced in a loud voice, then repeated it in a whisper and laughed at Patrick's nonplussed expression as he sat up from the bed on which he'd been daydreaming. Harriet took another swig, passed the bottle to him, jumped on her own bed and threw her pillow at him.

"I'm so sleepy," she sighed by way of explanation for her robe, but no explanations seemed necessary as Patrick got up and tussled with her and the room spun.

"Oooo," she cried. "What will my family think?" she added as Patrick, a sheet or two to the wind himself, discovered Harriet was ticklish and went at it, until they were gasping for breath and astonished at the fun of it all.

"Here's for your family!" He cornered and kissed her. "I'd like a large family," he whispered intensely.

"Me, too . . ." she whispered back, hearing him vaguely, for everything was fuzzy and accelerated at once as Patrick pulled her to him and tickled her again. She played limp in his arms and slid to the floor with a plop and a squeal.

On her way to the bathroom, Iris pretended she hadn't heard.

"With me chained to the stove?" Harriet asked, reconnecting with the thought and laughing at Patrick who looked comical, a sudden whirlwind, as he tore off clothes and got caught in his pants and tumbled on the bed.

"*Shhhh . . .*" She took another swallow and passed the champagne to Patrick who did likewise, kicking off his shoes at the same time, which only made her laugh the more.

"Nope, nope," she giggled, playing sack of flour as he tried to pull her up. Gripped with desire and purpose, Patrick scooped her in his arms and lay her on the bed. "Oh," she murmured, startled as he lay beside her and took her to him, covering her face with rapid kisses. There was a momentary lull and she was scared, and so was he because she was, but it vanished quickly. "Not right away," he whispered, nuzzling to banish her apprehension, knowing he must be gentle.

"Hmmm," she murmured, not sure what he meant, not particularly caring as he kissed her again. "Oh . . ." she nodded to herself, remembering. She smiled dreamily and felt immeasurably closer to him for his understanding. "Don't worry," she sighed, wanting to let him know that everything was fine. "I've prepared myself," she added intimately, while she gazed into his eyes that were so close she could see inside him. Tasting the champagne on his lips, she felt tiny and nice as his arms went around her and she fell into a reverie, then realized that he'd stopped kissing her. Surprised, her eyes fluttered open as what she'd said caught up with Patrick and he extracted an arm.

"What do you mean?"

Confused, Harriet shook her head and wondered what she'd done, tried to think and couldn't.

"It's a sin," he pleaded.

Her mouth opened, but she couldn't speak. The room spun again, and she willed herself to concentrate.

"*It's a sin!*"

Patrick reached out, lifted the floor lamp and smashed it to the floor.

20

The Spectator continues to call for negotiation and compliance with the law. *The Spectator* continues to wait for justice to be done. Eight hundred employees wait for their jobs to be returned.

Yet you have not responded, Mr. Phelps.

Jericho is still waiting.

Less than a month ago *The Spectator* repudiated Father Coughlin and the Union Party. Humbly we quote ourselves:

Sic Semper Tyrannis! Thus always to tyrants!

May they sink in their own darkness and be repudiated.

> Excerpt from an editorial in
> *The Jericho Spectator*,
> Nov. 17, 1936

The temper outside the mill escalated. "Jericho A Tinderbox" headlined the *Boston Herald*. "Jericho Paper Takes On Phelps; Situation Tense" echoed the *Globe*.

There were rumors on Main Street that Phelps had requested Governor Curley to put the National Guard on alert. Communist agitators had moved in, he told the Governor, inciting insurrection.

Patrick Flynn might have been one of those Phelps had in mind, for *The Spectator* had become a thorn in his side, its challenge unable to be overlooked. If Phelps had assumed that his employees would be begging to return to work within a day or two after he locked them out, *The Spectator* had galvanized a certain amount of resistance to such a move. But time was running out for both sides and Jericho, too.

The majority of the town had watched *The Spectator* with amusement in its Irish birth, responded with guarded concern at its liberal turn to Roosevelt, and taken a none-too-supportive stand since. But the two issues that dealt with the lockout caused everyone to sit up and take notice. The

349

workers had their champion, but the town wanted the whole thing settled, and *The Spectator* was caught in the cross fire. Argument and discussion raged on Main Street. If there were many who applauded the ethical rightness of Patrick's stand, there was as large a body of opinion that felt all he had done was stir an already volatile situation. Antagonizing Abraham Phelps, it was reasoned, would not lead to the negotiation Patrick called for, but the opposite—a further hardening of Phelps' position and no end in sight to the conflict. Patrick, it was thought, should lay off.

"Who'll speak up for their rights if I don't?" he replied to the latter argument, and when he arrived at the mill with this week's issue, he was greeted warmly as a comrade in arms. The crowd was larger than usual; it spilled from the guarded gates to the parking lot and around the edges of the millpond, a tense and nervous excitement gripping everyone as Patrick removed bundles of *The Spectator* from Jerry Finneran's truck. "Find me when you get your next pay envelope," he told those who tried to press nickels on him. As he had the previous week, he continued to refuse payment, and the gesture was appreciated. People knew he was as broke as they were, that he was struggling for survival, had sold his car. *The Spectator* had, like the rest of Main Street, been thrown a punch by the lockout. The sudden loss of the Phelps' payroll had put a dent in business; those merchants who'd advertised in *The Spectator* had been forced to cut back. That Patrick was giving his paper away for free at the gates of the mill garnered him a great deal of good will, and the evidence of it was here this morning, gratifying him and giving him hope.

Quickly passed by willing hands, the copies were as quickly read. "That's tellin' him, Pat," they nodded. " 'Bout time someone told him off!"

"DON'T BE FOOLED!" cried Meyer Shapiro from the union sound truck. He knew he had the fight of his life on his hands.

"What's he mean, Pa?" Patrick found Joe at the coffee wagon the union had set up. Cups were passed, and lunches were being prepared for the crowd. "Phelps let Marienetti and a few of the boys in," shouted Joe, trying to be heard above the strident cry of the loudspeakers. "He's making us an offer right now."

"A SMOKE SCREEN. . . !" Shapiro climbed out of his truck, bull-horn in hand. A small man, he wheezed with asthma as he perched on the running board and tried to get their attention. But Shapiro was still on trial. No matter that he purported to represent their interests, he was regarded with suspicion. He was a Jew, an outsider; if it hadn't been for him coming to Jericho in the first place, the old-timers agreed, none of the mess would've happened and they'd be inside where they belonged, instead of out here in the street with empty pockets. In the last two weeks, less than a hundred of Phelps' employees had paid their half dollar and carried a new union card in their pockets.

But if Shapiro and the union he represented hadn't yet gained the confidence of the crowd, it was unanimous in what it expected from Abraham Phelps. "Jericho's waiting!" someone cried, echoing Patrick's editorial. The cry was repeated by others, their faces turned to the mill, rising in volume, taken up by the ladies in mending and weaving, by wives and families who'd come to join their men, until five hundred of them had it on their tongues in a thunderous roar that penetrated into Phelps' office and suspended momentarily the ultimatum he was delivering to Paul Marienetti and his delegation.

A moment later they appeared and were let out the gates by the despised Pinkertons. "We're not fooled, Shapiro!" shouted the intense Italian as he climbed atop the coffee wagon to address the crowd. "He'll let us back . . ." began Marienetti, and his words produced a ripple of anticipation. He paused and consulted his notes. "Fifteen more minutes for lunch . . . a break in the afternoon. He guarantees no reprisals."

The anger in him obvious, Marienetti paused, then continued. "*No raise in pay! No vote! No union! Anyone joins the union can't go back. You accept his terms, you can. He's given us nothing!*"

"Who's surprised," Shapiro muttered to his lieutenants, but his old eyes dilated with energy. Quickly he seized the bullhorn and the initiative.

"WHAT HAVE WE BEEN SAYING?" he scolded them. "WHAT HAVE WE BEEN TELLING YOU?" he added sorrowfully, like a schoolmaster forced reluctantly to reprimand bad boys. "HE LOCKED YOU OUT, DIDN'T HE? NOW HE SAYS HE'LL TAKE YOU BACK? GIVE YOU A COOKIE OR TWO? JOIN US. JOIN THE UNION. WE CAN HELP YOU. YOU CAN'T DO IT YOURSELVES! JOIN US! TOGETHER, WE'LL WIN!"

A few cheers broke out, but there were just as many boos. In the first few days of the lockout, fueled in their determination by Phelps' betrayal, the majority had been unanimous in its determination not to return unless Phelps settled grievances and atoned for his outrageous action. But almost two weeks had taken its toll. Familes were hungry, debts piling up, mortgages and rents due. No matter the pride that would have to be sacrificed, there was plenty of sentiment to accept Phelps' offer and return to work.

"No!" shouted Marienetti, who had become the unofficial leader of the faction determined not to give in. "I'm for union," he continued. "I'm with Shapiro. Let's hand Phelps a strike, is what I'm sayin'! Let's make it official! Let's get together! Show him we mean business!"

Marienetti raised his fist and shook it at the mill to a chorus of agreement, matched by an equal measure of rebuttal.

"Any man joins the union, he's finished."

"We join, he'll never give in."

"Can he do that, Pat?"

Knots of discussion broke out in the crowd. "The law says he can't,"

Patrick replied, "but he's got the cards now. You need your jobs back, and he knows it."

"JOIN US," pleaded Shapiro. "WE'LL GET YOU YOUR WAGES. WE'LL GET YOUR INCREASE. BACK WAGES, TOO! DON'T LET HIM GET AWAY WITH THIS!"

Angry mutterings broke out, the crowd shifting this way and that, unsure which way to turn.

"What do you think, Pa? Would you go back?"

Like many, Joe was torn. Once again Shapiro got their attention. "IT'S UP TO YOU NOW. THE UNION CAN HELP YOU, BUT IT'S UP TO YOU TO GIVE ME THE WORD!"

"It doesn't seem like Phelps has addressed himself to what you want," Patrick said to the tight knot of men gathered around him. He knew there were no easy answers, yet he wished he had one or two that would allay the anxiety in their faces. Cries grew for him to speak up. "What's to prevent him shutting you out again tomorrow if he wants to?" he asked, cupping his hands to make himself heard. Pushed up onto the back of a truck, Patrick was momentarily embarrassed at the sudden silence around him as the crowd raised their faces. Hesitating, he glanced toward Marienetti, then to Shapiro, who was watching.

"It seems to me," he began slowly, "that Phelps thinks he has all of you. I guess he's been under . . . that impression for a long time. The real issue is that he locked you out. That's against the law, but he did it."

Stunned by the size of the crowd and the sudden reality of their listening, Patrick faltered, then got his bearings again.

"He'll give me my job back—that's good enough for me," a voice shouted at him. There was a round of agreement.

"But he can take it away tomorrow," Patrick replied. There were cries from the rear that he couldn't be heard, and he found a bullhorn thrust into his hands by one of Shapiro's men. "I said that he may give you your job back today . . . but he can take it away tomorrow if he wants to. . . ."

Startled by his voice, which echoed from the storefronts across the street to the mill and back again, Patrick paused, almost bemused. Yet, at the same time, an exhilaration rose in him that was like nothing he'd ever experienced. For a moment he was tongue-tied, then found his thought again. "I think Mr. Shapiro's right. If you stick together, you have a chance to win some protection. Can you take Phelps' word any longer? It seems . . . to me . . . that he's demonstrated what he thinks of you. Reprisals? Is there any one of you who doubts they'll start as soon as you go back?"

"Not against *us*," called out Harold Shaughnessey, an old-timer and the emerging spokesman for those who wanted to return. "We didn't sign Marienetti's petition. We got no quarrel with Mr. Phelps."

"You're a mouse, Shaughnessey!" cried Marienetti in disgust. "No quarrel? What'd we ask him for? A vote! He says no, so what do we do? Be good boys? Flynn's right," he added, moving through the crowd and jumping up to join Patrick. "How many years do we hafta look over our shoulder before we say what's on our mind? Are they gonna disappear?" he went on, shoving an angry finger at the force of twenty or so Pinkertons who stood by the gates with cold blank faces. "How many times," he bellowed to the crowd, muscular chest heaving, sturdy lungs needing no amplification, "do we take a cut in pay because he tells us he's broke? Flynn's said it"—Marienetti clapped a hand around Patrick's shoulder; mutual energy caused their eyes to meet, a friendship born—"we need to stick together! If any of you go back, we all lose! Don't be chumps!"

"What good's the union gonna do me if I don't have a job?"

"I HAVE A JUDGE WAITING IN BOSTON." Adroitly Shapiro revealed this nugget of information, and it caused a hush. "WE'LL GET AN INJUNCTION TO FORCE PHELPS TO RE-OPEN. WITH NO CONDITIONS. WITH THE UNION BEHIND YOU. BUT I NEED YOU WITH ME FIRST. JOIN US. YOU'VE GOT RIGHT ON YOUR SIDE. YOU'VE GOT A HUNDRED YEARS OF INJUSTICE THAT HAS TO BE ANSWERED TO."

"Takes his orders from Moscow, Mr. Phelps," muttered the head of the Pinkerton guards as the two men watched from the windows of the weaving room, a half acre of stilled looms behind them. On edge with the rebellion in the street, Phelps nodded. Then he zeroed in on Patrick. "Flynn," he murmured to his chief security officer whom he'd always trusted to take care of whatever dirty work was necessary. That Gert and Joe Flynn's son had turned against him so passionately seemed doubly traitorous to Phelps. With close to thirty-five years' wages between them, he considered he'd paid for their son's upbringing and education. Patrick's inflammatory editorials were bad enough; that he was now actively inciting Phelps' employees to hold out caused the latter's black marble eyes to dilate in fury. He found himself thinking of Harriet. The quick marriage hadn't surprised him. Dismissing the possibility of ethics and morality playing but the smallest of parts in the human character, including Harriet's, he wondered if she was inciting Patrick to get her revenge.

"Dad. . . ?" With an ashamed sheepishness that had characterized his relations with his father since his engagement had blown up, Elliot appeared behind the two men. "The lieutenant governor's on the phone. He—"

"I'll be there." Contemptuously dismissing his son, Phelps returned his eyes to Patrick, the stare echoed by Elliot, who felt an overwhelming envy.

Sensing his son still behind him, Phelps was filled with bitterness and defeat. "They'll come to their senses, Abe," Lawson, the Pinkerton chief, was saying. "You've made them a fair offer."

353

"I hope they all join the union," Elliot said and walked quickly away as Phelps shouted after him:

"You'd be married to her! Instead of him! You—"

Shaken, the epithet swallowed, Phelps turned back to the windows. He would starve them all until they crawled back on their bellies, begging his forgiveness.

"How do I feed my kids?" someone called as the debate continued in the street. "What do we eat? His promises?" added the speaker, pointing a finger at Shapiro.

"THE UNION WILL SERVE LUNCHES EVERY DAY TILL YOU'RE VICTORIOUS," was the reply. "BRING YOUR FAMILIES. YOU WON'T GO HUNGRY. HAVEN'T WE BEEN HERE EVERY DAY? GIVE US A CHANCE."

The discussion went back and forth for most of the morning until Patrick came up with a suggestion that Shapiro had considered a week ago, but he wasn't sure—and still wasn't—that he had the votes. But Phelps' contemptuous offer had produced a situation that might be now-or-never ripe.

"FLYNN'S GOT IT," bellowed Shapiro. "TAKE A VOTE YOURSELVES! THE LAW GIVES YOU THE RIGHT. WAGNER ACT. PASSED BY CONGRESS. IT'S THERE IN BLACK AND WHITE. COLLECTIVE BARGAINING. AS FLYNN'S BEEN SAYING—IT'S THE LAW. THAT'S WHAT WE ASKED HIM FOR. HE WON'T ALLOW IT? TAKE A VOTE AND DECIDE FOR YOURSELVES. NO SKIN OFF MY NOSE. YOU DON'T WANT THE UNION HERE, I'LL PACK MY BAGS. . . !"

That night there was a rally on Bartlett's Field, over two thousand in attendance, including representatives of ten New England dailies and a couple of New York papers with their photographers.

A vote was to be taken on whether to return to work or join behind the union and authorize a strike.

There were those who remembered a hot Fourth of July several years back on the very same field when Abraham Phelps had assured Jericho that each and every one of them was his family. He would never close, he told them that day, and when Paul Marienetti reminded the crowd of the promise, a swell of resentment shook the field, echoed by stomping feet on the hard-packed earth as people tried to keep warm.

Asked to speak, Patrick was next.

"Phelps told me this would all blow over," he told the crowd from the flatbed truck in the infield, as he reported on Phelps' visit to *The Spectator* office only hours before. "He told me he felt he'd been reasonable.

Reasonable to Mr. Phelps means a return to the status quo. Is that what we want here in Jericho?"

No, they responded, as his own "we" reverberated in him. This morning's incredible exhilaration had returned, tenfold increased. "Phelps reminded me," he continued, "that my father has worked for him for twenty years. The implication was that my father wouldn't have a job back if I continued to speak my mind. My father and I feel the same. . . ." Patrick found Joe in the front ranks, looking up at him. Joe nodded, and emotion welled in Patrick.

"We don't intend to let Phelps tell us what we can and can't do! *The Spectator* will continue to support you! Whatever you decide, *The Spectator* is behind you one hundred percent! Mr. Phelps suggested I tell you that if you don't return to work, you'll be digging your own graves. I say it's his own grave he's digging, not yours!"

Patrick's voice soared over them. He had no sense of himself, he was the voice, he was them, their energy his. He was Lindy. Words that had begun haltingly earlier in the day now surged. Fueled by Phelps' threats, the blush of this morning had turned to a fiery glow of indignation. "*The Spectator* won't be silenced," Patrick continued, and cheers broke out. "What have we asked for? Decency. What was Phelps' reply? Contempt. And if we don't all join together now, what chance do any of us have?"

The speeches, pro and con, continued, and Patrick had a moment to himself. He smiled as a thought struck him: he would have argued he was totally unfit for what had been thrust upon him today. Yet, undeniably, the man who had waked this morning was no longer the same man tonight. He was certainly not the soft-spoken seminarian whose only previous experience in public was the leading of prayers in a silent chapel. If a sense of displacement still lingered, the feeling that he was where he belonged grew stronger.

As the vote-taking began, Patrick's thoughts returned to his confrontation with Phelps this afternoon. Alone in the office, he wasn't surprised with the visit. The battle lines had been drawn instantly between the two men, their animosity fanned by opposing viewpoints that had no chance of reconciliation. Like Phelps, Patrick had wondered what part Harriet played in his new militancy. Was his condemnation of his father's employer dictated solely by the issues—or was it fueled in some small part by Phelps' underhanded treatment of his wife? It was hard to distinguish one from the other, for the man was the same, his lack of morality stunning in its nakedness. But even if he tried to avenge Harriet's honor, Patrick realized sadly that he'd get no credit from her. She would give him neither the opportunity nor the satisfaction. She seemed to want to give him nothing.

The tumult on the field was no larger than in Patrick's head. Brought back by the shouting as the vote was announced, he was engulfed in cheering. By the slightest majority, the decision had been made to support the union. *"Strike!"* rose from the field, and Patrick, Marienetti and Shapiro were surrounded as the crowd surged forward to embrace its newly formed triumvirate of leaders—the young Catholic intellectual, the Italian family man and Meyer Shapiro, who was as old as both of them combined. Shapiro couldn't have been happier. God had granted him the muscle and fervor of Marienetti, a man of the mill and one of the first with the courage to talk with him when he began his vigil in Jericho. And as for the other—Flynn of the violent eyes and a newspaper, to boot—he'd done Shapiro's job for him this morning, continued to do it tonight. *A firebrand in the making*, chuckled Shapiro. *Give me ten of Flynn and the textile industry will be a union shop in six months.*

Pulling his ever-present fedora down low on his forehead, Shapiro's suddenly cautious and experienced eyes swept the crowd. Yes, they were again galvanized, the pendulum had swung his way once more, but how long before necessity caused it to swing back? He'd been in too many a labor battle not to recognize that this one was a piss-cutter with a first-class son-of-a-bitch as his adversary.

Later at the Depot Tavern, the strike committee of fifteen charted plans and raised hopeful glasses. Patrick was filled with pride by his comrades' acceptance of him. Humbled by their courage, he prayed he was worthy. Here was the flock he'd been trained to serve. He was part of them, no longer isolated, had found his place in the sky.

Yet the bitter irony of his situation was inescapable. He had the trust and respect of these simple and honest men; he wondered what he had to do for his wife to give him the same?

What was she doing here?

Harriet's eyes wandered around the interior of St. Mary's.

What an ugly place—the design much too cluttered, the windows garish in their stained glass—no subtlety at all; the statues so fake and the general color scheme of pimento and gold enough to make anyone repent. Mother was right—Catholics had no taste.

The congregation rose as Father Gahaghan appeared from the sacristy and the bells tinkled. Glances swept from Harriet and Patrick (head bowed in escapeful prayer) to the Flynn family ensconced in their usual front row pew. Hearts beat quicker at the unexpected drama here at Mass this morning. The biddies nudged each other. To have a reprobate son like that! Broken her heart, he had. There were few who didn't know of the rift between mother and son. And here he was, larger than life, with the cause herself!

Rose's rump shifted, diverting some of the eyes. Oblivious to the expectant faces behind her, Gert's lips moved silently. There were those who'd said she'd aged mightily in the last two weeks. The Hibernians, to a woman, laid the change (when they weren't blaming Harriet) at Patrick's doorstep.

Harriet caught sight of Teresa, who slipped in late with Matt. Receiving Harriet's mental message, Teresa turned, grinned and winked, nudging Matt, who did likewise. Two friends, thought Harriet gratefully; two friends in a time of need. Her neck burned.

Teresa spotted Gert and prayed for reconciliation. Her efforts to bring Patrick, Harriet and Gert together had so far failed. There was to be no burying of hatchets as far as Gert was concerned—unless they be in Protestant flesh. Patrick was still persona non grata, and neither he nor his bride would be welcome on Essex Street.

Teresa had come up with the inspiration that Harriet should accompany Patrick to Sunday Mass. Her presence would be construed by Gert as an offer of peace (from both Harriet and Patrick), a reaching out that Gert wouldn't be able to reject.

"Don't worry, Mother, I won't put so much as a nickel in the basket for the Pope," Harriet had assured Letty this morning, her gaiety disguising her apprehension at the foray into enemy territory. Anxieties hadn't been alleviated by the intense scrutiny she'd received on the steps outside, nor was she calm now as she dared raise her eyes and found she had a momentarily clear view, through myriad heads and shoulders, of Gert. Quivers attacked her stomach. What an outlandish hat. Well, what would be would be. If harmony could be achieved with his mother, perhaps there'd be a lessening of tension all around. Harriet glanced sideways at Patrick, who was echoing Father Gahaghan, saying the Mass under his breath. She was losing him, she realized, losing him, and she wasn't even sure she wanted him. Did he appreciate her coming with him today? She didn't know.

The stalemate had continued and escalated. Whatever tenuous closeness they'd achieved at Cora's wedding last Saturday had been shattered like the globe of the lamp that Patrick had crashed to the floor. There had, needless to say, been no further attempts at lovemaking on Patrick's part, certainly not on Harriet's.

Head buzzing, she tried to concentrate on Father Gahaghan's sermon, which had to do with the strike. Violence was a sin. Even the temptation to violence. Inwardly she flinched at the memory of Patrick's fury. The glass in terrifying shards exploding. Like waking from a nightmare.

If she'd married him under false pretenses, hadn't she tried to make up for it? And what had she got for her effort? Patrick's behavior had astounded her. Worse was his refusal to even discuss it with her later. But Catholics don't believe in birth control, Alice had replied, when Harriet confided in her. *I'm* not a Catholic, she'd retorted, irritated that Alice always took Patrick's side. It seemed to Harriet that of all people, Alice should understand the necessity of precautions. Was she to take a chance on getting pregnant with a man she didn't love? Aside from that, Patrick had ruined a moment in which—for the first time—she'd felt herself relaxing. And had condemned her ever since. It was the old Patrick, she reflected, a Patrick she wanted no part of, the rigid and unenlightened Patrick whom she'd first encountered this fall, the Patrick encumbered by his background, who clung to rules and superstitions with a jaw-set tenacity.

Hoc est enim Corpus Meum. The bells tinkled and Father Gahaghan raised the Host.

Comforted in the safety of the Mass, Patrick felt Harriet glance at him. Eyes traveling to Gert up front, he couldn't care if peace were made or not. Let her suffer. Who gave a shit? One thing he knew for sure: he didn't want his mother to have an inkling of the estrangement between Harriet and himself. Yet a part of him was pleased Harriet had consented to come today. Was it a sign? He didn't know, was past trying to figure. Harriet was as much an enigma to Patrick as he was to her. Sin? Harriet was the sin as far as *he* was concerned. Her action was unpardonable, an insult to his authority, manhood and morality, further evidence of her unyielding resistance to him, concrete proof that she'd pulled the wool over his eyes and didn't love him. Even her saying she wanted to "try" was a mockery.

Heavenly Father, he prayed, *I need guidance. Thy will be done. But let me know. This can't continue . . .*

He was brave, Harriet couldn't help thinking. What a scandal he must have created when he returned from Washington. Yet had vindicated himself with his commitment to the strikers. A third of the parish worked for Phelps, and Patrick had been surrounded outside on the steps before Mass. She sighed inwardly. The bells tinkled and everyone stood like trees around her. She stayed in place to let them know she was only visiting. What was she going to do? Make a go of it, or leave him? For both their sakes. The former seemed impossible, the latter, too. Annulment? Unheard of. Divorce? The same. Through five generations, there had never been a divorce in her family. Marriage, no matter the discontent, was writ in concrete. Women were shackled and kept on smiling. She couldn't subject her parents to a divorce. Nor, she realized, could she do it to Patrick. Or herself. The failure wasn't allowable, nor the admittance that she'd perpetuated this whopper of a marriage.

Living between a rock and a hard place, her passivity appalled her.

The Mass ended with a flourishing exit of Father Gahaghan and the altar boys. Were they going to take a curtain call? wondered Harriet, her irreverence giving her a respite of pleasure.

What on earth was she going to say to Gert?

Good morning, Mrs. Flynn—remember me?
Good morning, Mrs. Flynn. I apologize for having married your son.
O Mrs. Flynn, I am heartily sorry for having offended thee.
Dear Mrs. Flynn, I don't want him, you can have him, he's too much for me.

"Look who's here!" Beefy Jack Flynn, Joe's irrepressible brother, called out a greeting. "Hallo there, kiddo!"

A dozen or so heads turned.

"We been wonderin'," guffawed Jack, "when you'd be over to visit us, Pat? Don't be such a stranger, lad. Where's Gertie?"

"Not out yet," replied his wife, Fay, looking pinched as she always did when Gert was mentioned.

"So here's the bride," continued Jack, loud enough for another dozen heads to swivel. "Ain't she a pretty thing! Does his uncle get to give ya a kiss of congratulations?"

"You certainly do," responded Harriet, raising her cheek, very conscious of his oafish gaze scrutinizing her carefully as he blarneyed on.

"Come ta see how the other half lives, have ya?" Jack laughed. "Ya gonna join the church?"

"I don't see why not," she bandied back. "It takes all kinds, doesn't it?"

Jack roared good-naturedly and gave Patrick a resounding slap on the back. "Oh ho, Pat, got yerself a live wire, I see. Good for you. Best wishes, lad. Never could see him as a man of the cloth," Jack continued, leering at Harriet once again. "Not at all holy, is he now? You'd know, I'm sure."

"Jack," remonstrated Fay weakly, "you're embarrassin' them."

"No, I'm not. It's a strike now is it, Pat? You've got your hands full, lad." Patrick and Harriet were surrounded, everyone talking of Father Gahaghan's sermon and wanting to know Patrick's reaction. Gahaghan had cautioned patience and conciliation and generally taken an arch-conservative position. But all such discussion played second fiddle as the Flynns emerged into the sunlight.

Dennis spotted them first. "Look, Ma. . . !"

"See who's here, Gert." Teresa nudged her sister, who froze.

"Look who's here, Gertie," echoed Joe, taking Harriet's hand in his warm paw, earning another goblet in heaven. Around the two camps, parishioners found whatever excuse was necessary to linger and overhear.

A feather quivered on Gert's hat as she turned ever so slowly, eyes meeting Patrick's, then Harriet's, whose heart did a sudden nervous jig.

"Good morning, Mrs. Flynn."

Gert's eyes fled, focusing on the Virgin Mary standing on the church lawn.

359

"Hello, Ma."

"What would you say, Father. . . ?" asked Gert of the priest who appeared at her side. "What would—?"

"Hello, Father Gahaghan," Harriet said, anxious to be acknowledged by somebody.

"Well now . . ." he replied lamely, his allegiance torn between his worthy right arm and her son with his new bride. So he'd brought her to Mass. Gahaghan cleared his throat and smiled quickly at Harriet. He *had* liked the article she'd done on him. "Welcome, dear," he said quickly, hoping Gert wouldn't take too much offense.

"Gert," prompted Teresa.

Jack grinned provocatively. "Say, Gertie, don't they make a handsome couple, the two of 'em!"

"She should at least say hello," Dennis whispered to Rose, who shrugged and turned to Timothy, who'd been invited for Sunday dinner. Timothy pursed his baby mouth, remembered Patrick's turncoat betrayal in the election, and wasn't at all unhappy at the public humiliation being inflicted.

"Welcome to St. Mary's, Harriet," offered a brave Dennis.

"You'd *think*," commented Rose rather loudly, "that *she* would go to her own church. She's not even Catholic."

"You noticed, did you, dear?" Teresa shot a look at Rose and turned back to her nonbudging sister. "Go on, Gert," she urged, wondering if she herself had been spared by not having children. Spared this awful grief caused at seeing a son and his bride, a grief that went beyond making any sense of it, beyond to a kind of derangement. "They want your blessing, Gert," she whispered, eyes pleading, but Gert seemed hypnotized. Uncharacteristically, she faltered, gaze transferred from the Virgin to her own stout feet as she struggled. Even if she longed to forgive Patrick and take him to her, she wasn't able.

"What would you say, Father, about a girl who rode one horse for all she was worth . . ."

"Now, Gertie . . ."

"Gert . . ."

"*Ma* . . ."

". . . and then when the ne'er-do-well threw her over . . ."

A buzz.

"Mrs. Flynn—" interjected Harriet.

". . . as we all knew Elliot Phelps would—she ups and helps herself to my son. What would ya think of such a girl, Father?"

Gahaghan blinked uncomfortably. "Now, Mrs. Flynn . . ."

A tremor shook Gert as her eyes met Patrick's again. "Are ya satisfied?" she demanded, unable to help herself. "I heard ya was lookin' for work. I hear the paper's foldin'."

"Ma—"

Gert cut him short, condemning eyes turning to Harriet. *"I wish to God you'd married Phelps and left us alone!"*

Rose nodded.

"Gert!" gasped Teresa, her shock echoed in the onlookers.

Patrick's jaw worked, but he couldn't speak.

"Lost her marbles," someone whispered.

Blinded momentarily, Harriet sought Patrick's hand—perhaps in solace, perhaps to keep from punching Gert, perhaps to get him to come to her aid. But he said nothing. As the surrounding faces returned somewhat to focus, it was Rose's supercilious expression that lit the fuse.

"Do you know what you are, Rose? A shrew. I pity Mr. O'Brien."

Gert's gasp drew added fire. "And you, Mrs. Flynn, are a first-class bitch!"

Harriet burst into tears, fled the gaping crowd and rushed home alone.

21 Letty knew holidays were always difficult for Franklin. He had only to remember those days at the orphanage, the terrible loneliness and forced gaiety of boys who knew they'd been abandoned and no one was coming to claim them.

On Thanksgiving morning he started early, taking nips from his rye bottle in the cellar as he stoked the furnace.

Upstairs, on edge with what Franklin and the day might bring, Letty snapped at Harriet: "Are you going to peel those potatoes—or memorize them?" Finding her daughter's lassitude irritating, Letty continued, "Shit or get off the pot—as your father would say, girl."

"What are you talking about?"

"I watch you and Patrick," Letty went on, shucking oysters for her stuffing, "and I can't help thinking how much you're alike. You're as self-absorbed as he is. Neither of you seems to realize you're a couple."

"Oh, dear," said Harriet, sighing, "giblet gravy and Thanksgiving homilies. Alike? We're nothing alike. Couple? Like Cora and Sam, I suppose? They're both going to get diabetes, they're so sweet."

Stymied momentarily by another of her daughter's smart remarks, Letty finished washing the oysters and commenced chopping. In no mood for mother-daughter chitchat, Harriet smiled and tried to present a picture of well-being. In truth she felt as raw as the oysters, but she didn't want Letty to know. Enough was enough; she was as sick of herself as she was sure the family was. "Now, how many of us are there? Eight—not including Albie." Harriet continued her peeling, and Albatross thumped a tail, looking from Letty to Harriet and back again in hope of a scrap that would do a dog's heart good.

"You'd never believe Sam was in here at the crack of dawn and made four pies. He's neat as a pin. Harriet, why are you upset with me?" Letty asked tartly, feeling it was high time she make a point or two. "I haven't badgered you. You ran off and got married and didn't care to ask for my advice nor have you cared to make any explanation for what was, you'll have to admit, an extraordinary situation. I don't give a fig about Elliot—or what happened between the two of you. If you want to know, I felt relieved."

"I'm not upset with you, Mother. Why should I be? My, *don't* those pies look wonderful."

Aware her daughter was avoiding her, Letty busied herself for a moment and collected her thoughts. She and Harriet hadn't talked in ages. Letty marveled at the ease that she and Cora continued to have with each other, a trust and delight she didn't have with Harriet, or Alice either. Letty sensed Alice was troubled, knew it had to do with her worry for her friend in Spain, but she'd been more than usually impossible to talk to. Her youngest daughters were two of a kind with burrs under their sweaters lately, and Letty was concerned.

"I'm not a busybody," she went on, "but snap out of it, girl, whatever it is. You and Patrick remind me of a couple of angry children. That's exactly who you remind me of. You're casting a pall over the house and—"

"Mother—you're exaggerating. Pall? I don't know what you mean. I really don't. Everything's fine." She was hard put to conceal her sarcasm. "It's just that we've been so busy."

Thank God, as far as Harriet was concerned. She'd thrown herself into work, just as Patrick had. Most of the last issue she'd written herself, tracking down this and that, interviewing wives of the strikers, setting up a free classified section for Phelps' employees. Plus, she'd found time to keep up her diary and start a short story. Salvation, as it always had, lay in work. "And we have a few minor problems," she went on, "such as no money . . . and we're living here with you all"—she laughed gaily—"in a goldfish bowl. *And* the paper's going under . . . but nothing serious, nothing serious. Tra-la-la . . ."

"Any young couple starting out today has the same—"

"Ain't it the truth!" From out of nowhere popped: "It's not my fault he's an ass!"

Harriet retreated from the pantry as Letty cocked an eyebrow at the outburst. "I understand the pressure you're under," she said, following her daughter into the kitchen where Harriet put the potatoes on the stove. "The paper may close. But your marriage is forever. The two of you act as if—"

"*Mother. Please.* Sorry," she added quickly, fleeing into the pantry once again and trying to get a hold on herself.

"Everything's fine?" Letty asked. "I'm glad to hear it. It doesn't look that way to me, but if it is, so be it. I trust we won't be subjected in future to the unpleasantness the two of you shared with us on Sunday."

Wielding her rolling pin, Letty crunched a paper bag full of dried bread for crumbs and shook her head. The yelling had been heard halfway

363

up the block when the Hoskins returned from church and found Harriet crying as Patrick fled out the back door.

"It *wasn't* my fault," insisted Harriet, hot under the collar all over again at the memory of what had happened after Mass. "Since you seem to imply that everything's *my* doing—"

"I said no such thing. I believe I said 'both.'"

"Always the woman's fault, isn't it?" insisted Harriet, who hadn't heard her mother, for she was hearing little today.

"Did she tell you she called Mrs. Flynn a bitch?" grinned Alice, coming into the kitchen as Harriet finished revealing her encounter with Gert.

"You didn't! Harriet!"

"'Fraid so. I'd do it again. What would you have done? Smiled and turned the other cheek? You're you, and I'm me."

Letty responded to the challenge with a brisk snapping shut of the oven door. The clash of the generations echoed in the cozy kitchen; mother and daughter took each other's measure, and Letty composed herself and tried to diffuse the tension by winking. "Bitch, hmmm? Good for you! She deserved it. I've a good mind to pay her a call myself and tell her what I think of her."

"Mother and Mrs. Flynn," Alice commented wryly, sitting at the kitchen table with the morning paper. "*That* would be fun."

Letty felt more than ready. "But I can see why Patrick was upset," she continued. "To call his mother—"

"Upset? It seems to be his middle name lately. He didn't even defend me! Who knows, he may have thought I deserved it! I'm sure he did!"

"Hoo-hoo," called Cora from the front hallway, interrupting things as she and Sam arrived pink-cheeked in the kitchen. Back from Niagara Falls, they were an inseparable duo.

"What a beautiful morning! Perfect Thanksgiving weather," she cried, arms full of bittersweet and dried goldenrod, which she and Sam had picked on their already traditional morning constitutional. "A nip in the air and Sam says we'll have rain later. Sam has a sixth sense about weather, don't you, hon? He's never wrong. Isn't that turkey in yet? You girls must've been gabbing. My, that coffee smells good. Harriet—where's your smile? It's Thanksgiving!"

Harriet tried to close her ears to Cora's babble. Having revealed way more of her turmoil than she wished (and with no desire to prolong the discussion), she nevertheless had a point to make, for it continued to stick in her craw. "Do you understand, Mother? I went to Mass with him as a gesture and look what I got for my troubles! Not only didn't he defend me, he was furious later. I got no credit at all. In a sense *I* was defending *him*—she gave it to him as well as me—but he didn't see it that way."

"Harriet, calm down. I said I understood. Obviously, Patrick didn't.

And I don't think he needs your help in defending himself. From his own mother?"

"Only from Harriet," quipped Alice, getting a quick glare from her sister.

"Where *is* Patrick?" asked Cora. "It seems he's disappeared."

"A strike meeting."

"On Thanksgiving morning? All right, Alice, if you'd let me have that space, I'll do my grapefruit sections."

"Hurry, girls. Time's awasting."

"Why aren't you with him?"

"I wasn't invited." Nor would she be, she knew that. He'd made it perfectly clear that distance from her was what he preferred. Patrick spent most of his time at the union's command post over the dry goods store, while Harriet stayed at the office. "I'm not on the strike committee," she continued. "I hardly get to see him anymore myself," she added, which was fine with her, but she made it seem the opposite. "Sometimes he just falls asleep right at his desk he's so tired," she sighed, trying to offer a believable rationale for the family's consumption as to why Patrick had missed dinner since Sunday and spent two out of three nights sleeping over at the office. Even if things had gone from bad to worse, it was an embarrassing situation.

"Sam, chip some ice, would you?" called Cora. "And check my cranberry mold. Don't Sam's pies look delicious, Mother? Sam and I took one of the mince meat to dear Mrs. Basset. She was so grateful and tickled."

Sam and I this and Sam and I that. Harriet felt like throttling Cora and Mulberry Street, too. Instead, she peeled a Hubbard squash with quick, agitated clips of the knife.

"I think Harriet feels Patrick's stolen her fire, that's what I think."

"What on earth are you talking about, Cora?"

"He *has* become a celebrity of sorts. And you always wanted to be, so—"

"Sew *buttons*! I never heard of anything so ridiculous. I'm proud of him."

"Jealous of her own husband," hummed Cora, winking at Sam, who sat by the woodbox and lit his pipe. "Land sakes!"

"Cora, if you know of a place where they give brain transfusions, why don't you get yourself an appointment!"

"Hee hee."

Furious, Harriet left the pantry and went to the dining room, where she set about putting an extra leaf in the table. "I don't need any of *your* helpful hints, either," she whispered to Alice, who joined her. Together they spread a white damask cloth over the mahogany. "I know you think he's God's gift to the hallowed masses all of a sudden, but—"

365

"Are you crazy? You used to call him an unbaked loaf of bread, and now that he's developed a nice crust—"

"Are *you* crazy? He's said three words to me all week!"

"Relax."

"Relax? When there's a conspiracy not to understand me? Relax? *You're* telling *me* to relax?"

"I have more reason to be a nerve end than you."

"Why? He's on his way."

"I haven't had another letter. I don't know where he is, and I won't breathe easy till I see him." A sudden cramp caused Alice's face to pinch.

"Are you OK?"

Alice nodded, stole a glance to the kitchen to make sure Letty hadn't noticed, and took a breath. "I'll tell you one thing," she went on. "I wish I never told Patrick about you-know-who."

"Water over the dam, I'm afraid. I may have led him down the garden path, but he's planted prickle bushes at the end, let me tell you."

Suspicion had been added to his arsenal. There was his "you've done me wrong" look; or the impatient, belligerent look; perhaps the "you're guilty" look, which fueled her own miserable sense of inadequacy. Then, his rigid and dogmatic look, or his meat and potatoes sulk look, and in the last few days—no looks at all. "He's getting even with me—that's what he's doing!"

"We'll use the cranberry goblets and Gramma's good plates, girls." Letty glanced from Harriet to Alice; there were secrets in the air, and she was the outsider.

Franklin's head appeared in the bay window as he climbed up a ladder to fill the bird feeder. Letty waved to him and gave a gay smile that concealed a kernel of anxiety for his flushed face.

"What do you think marriage is?" she asked Harriet. "It's hard work and compromise, that's what it is. And your responsibility." Letty helped set out the silverware and stole a glance at Franklin, praying he wouldn't lose his balance.

"Isn't it a man's responsibility as well as a woman's?" asked Harriet, who had no idea what marriage was supposed to be, but it surer than hell wasn't supposed to be the disaster she had with Patrick. "I guess you don't feel it is," she added sarcastically, glancing from Letty to Franklin, "since you've done most of the 'work' and *all* of the 'compromising.'"

"There you go again, Harriet. For such a bright girl, you have so little understanding. Women are smarter. Don't you know that yet?"

"Do you know what I think?" bubbled Cora, placing her centerpiece of magnolia pods and goldenrod on the table. "I think it's a man's world. It makes everything so much nicer."

"Really, Cora," groaned Alice, exchanging a despairing glance with

Harriet. "Doesn't she have a *modern* viewpoint!" commented the latter wryly. "Let's embalm her quickly."

"But it *is*," insisted Cora. "Isn't it, Sam?" she called into the kitchen. Getting used to nodding, Sam nodded.

"Don't upset your sisters, Cora." Letty laughed and winked. "You know who they are. Suffragettes."

"*Suffer*-gettes." Surprised at her wit, Cora pealed a laugh. Letty joined in, surveyed the table, and allowed herself to dream. "We'll have to get a bigger table soon. Where will we put you all when you bring your children to Thanksgiving?"

Awash in individual ironies, Harriet and Alice exchanged another glance, while Cora giggled and looked back into the kitchen at Sam. "I'll pass," commented Harriet, noticing that Alice had hidden behind the newspaper in Franklin's chair. Why didn't her sister just tell Letty and have done with it? wondered Harriet, admonishing herself for her nasty thought even as she had it: would Mother think women were "smarter" *then*?

"Pass? You sound like I used to. Your gramma used to say I was rebellious. Thank goodness I wasn't *too* rebellious. All of you would still be drifting in the ether, waiting to be claimed. Ladies," Letty went on, with a provocative smile, "should spend less time on rebellion and more on reconciliation."

"Ladies? You're sounding more like Gramma every day! You've become so respectable I hardly know you. Rebellious? If you'd been a little more rebellious, you might have been successful."

"Successful? Where do you get such ideas? I consider myself a great success. Do I sound like Gramma?" Letty added. "That would be odd, wouldn't it? I loved her, but I never liked her. Mothers and daughters," she went on, recalling her endless battles with Sarah over what ladies did and ladies didn't, "—do we have to be oil and water? Perhaps it's inevitable. Supposedly a mother has a son till he marries a wife, but a daughter for life. . . ."

"Spare me . . ." moaned Alice.

". . . but *you* two," continued Letty, "are giving me a run for my money. Why can't you both be like Cora?" she added, and they all burst out laughing at the well-worn plea from their childhood.

"*Cora never gives me any trouble,*" singsonged Harriet and Alice.

"Why should I?" Cora fussed at her flowers on the sideboard, rearranging the last of the tenacious roses and snaps that had weathered the frosty nights, dauntless in the face of the final kill. "I've always been happy."

"Speaking of *sons* marrying . . ." commented Harriet, as a groggy Frankie appeared in bathrobe and slippers and headed for the coffee. "What about Jeannie?" she called, hoping to get a rise out of Letty. "I think we need another marriage," she went on, grinning wickedly. "Jeannie's Catholic, isn't she?"

"Sure," he murmured, not sure what he was walking into.

"Your brother's not interested in her," Letty replied firmly. "Catholic or not."

"Is he or isn't he?" Harriet kissed Frankie good morning while simultaneously tickling him. Avoiding her, he retreated.

"Are you and Father going to the game?" Letty called after him. "I guess," he replied. "Why don't you ask him?" suggested Letty, as she glanced down into the garden to see if she could spot Franklin and told herself not to worry.

"Remember, Mother," remarked Alice, who'd been trying to ward off the anxiety that talk of children had produced, "the Catholics gave us Michelangelo and Titian."

"And the Spanish Inquisition," added Harriet. "Know locally as Gert Flynn."

"Don't be provocative. Girls—we're dawdling. See to your squash, Harriet," Letty added, returning to the kitchen.

"When are we going to meet that family?" asked Cora.

"At my funeral," replied Harriet, smiling tentatively as Franklin came up the cellar stairs and entered the kitchen.

"Cup of coffee, Father?" Letty tried to tell him with her calm gaze that everything was fine. She could see he was in his own world.

"I'll get it." Harriet went to the stove. "Game of cribbage, Mr. Hoskins?" asked Sam. To Letty's surprise and relief, Franklin nodded.

"Why don't I play the winner?" Harriet set the coffee down, her hand lingering on Franklin's shoulder to no response. "Did you feed the birds?" she asked, trying again. Franklin nodded, eyes on the board.

"My name is Harriet."

"I know what your name is," he replied curtly, irritated with her for breaking his train of thought.

Letty sent Harriet a look and gestured for her daughter to follow her into the parlor. "What is it?" asked Letty, pulling the sliding doors together. "What is what?" replied Harriet, trying to maintain a brave front.

"Why upset him like that? Or yourself?"

"Me? I don't think he *does* remember my name any more. Does he know yours? Or any of us? Mother, I really don't—"

"Want to talk. I know, I know. Indulge this old fuddy-duddy. You're flying around in so many pieces I'm surprised you don't collide with yourself. He's your father. What good does it do you to condemn him?"

"Didn't you smell it?"

"Harriet—"

"You just put up with it, don't you!"

368

"I'll fight my own battles, thank you. I know you think I'm suffering, but I'm not. Why don't you learn to accept Father as he is? And Patrick, too."

"Patrick?" Harriet bit her lip. Agitated, she sat in the window seat, then got up again, glanced at Letty, then quickly away. It seemed as if she blamed her mother for everything and didn't know why. But the antagonism was there and had much to do with the man playing cribbage in the kitchen.

"Harriet, what is it?" pleaded Letty, who felt keenly her daughter's distress and would do anything to break down the barriers and help, but Harriet shook her head. "Why didn't you leave him?" she demanded, for it was easier to heap coals on her mother than reveal her explosive feelings about Patrick.

"Ever since you returned from New York, you've had a bee in your bonnet about something or other. None of your business. I told you to let me fight my own battles. I don't need your help. I'm sorry to be blunt, but you're trying my patience."

"I don't believe you. Are you trying to tell me your life's rosy? I've seen—"

"Harriet," warned Letty, "you're behaving like a child. I don't blame your father. He's more than any of us can bear sometimes, but I remember how he used to be, and I look to the future. Don't *you* remember? You and he were so close. Now you're at each other."

"He's changed. You know that. I've *tried* to get through to him. And since I got married, it's worse. He hates Patrick and—"

"Of course he doesn't." But Letty wasn't able to marshall convincing proof. "He's much better," insisted Letty, who had to believe it and, out of necessity, did. But a moment later Franklin appeared out front, and she wondered why he wasn't playing cribbage. She hoped he would go to the football game; it might relax him. "*Much* better," she repeated, smoothing her apron. "You were gone for two years. You don't—"

"Remember?" interjected Harriet, looking after Franklin and filled with bitterness that seemed unfathomable. "Close?" she continued, turning on her mother again. "Who was the one who you sent to get him that day? I guess I remember all right. Do you think I'll ever forget?"

Letty turned guiltily away, and Harriet stared at the pattern in the rug. How many years had she blamed Letty for sending her to the Salem Hotel and stopping her heart?

"What has this to do with you and Patrick?"

"Who knows?" Harriet murmured belligerently, not wishing to get into any discussion of her marriage.

"Do you love him?"

"I don't know. No."

"Learn to."

"Is that what Gramma said to you? Shall we bind my feet and have done with it? You have no guts, Mother. Father—"

"Would you have thought better of me if I'd walked away from a man who needed me? A man who has had more personal hardship and struggle than you or I will ever know? I'm ashamed of you. I had no choice in the matter. Nor—"

"*I* do."

"Harriet—"

"I have my dreams," she blurted, but all of a sudden she couldn't remember what they were.

"Is Patrick keeping you from your dreams?" asked Letty, trying to pick her way through the labyrinth of her daughter's flailings. "I thought you and Patrick had a dream *together*. The paper. When you got married, I assumed it was a natural outgrowth—"

"Us? I married him to escape a blow to my pride, and he married me— I don't know why he married me. I'm obviously not his cup of tea."

"What happened between you and Elliot?"

"Nothing." How could she ever tell her? She couldn't. "Ancient history. I'm leaving Patrick," she added threateningly, as if it were somehow all Letty's fault.

"Don't talk rubbish."

"Accept him? I've tried. I hate him." What had she done that was so terrible?—except to marry him when she wasn't sure she loved him. Was she to punish herself and be punished for the rest of her life? By him and his mother? "Everything I do is wrong," she added, and stared desultorily out the window. "I *have* tried. You don't know him. I don't either. My mistake."

"What have you done that's wrong?"

"Married him," Harriet replied fliply.

"Of course you don't know him." Letty realized she didn't either. Patrick was a mystery, as guarded as Franklin, with the same temper. A hothead of an Irish mick. "How could either of you be expected to know each other after so short a period of time? You'll learn about each other," she added, hoping to leaven Harriet's depression with a touch of humor. "You'll wish you could get back to 'not knowing,' you'll know each other so well."

"Hah-hah."

"Why are you so angry? It seems you have a chip on your shoulder and—"

"*Me?* You would say that, wouldn't you? *I* didn't break the floor lamp. He did! I *am*. I'm leaving him. I'm not putting up with it any longer. I'm not you. I'm not going to settle. Who do you think taught me that? *You*. Till you turned into a mouse."

"If it helps you to attack—" Bristling, Letty got up, plucked a wilted blossom from an African violet, and composed herself. "I'm trying to understand. I know you don't think I am, but I am. You don't make it easy, my girl," she added, more determined than ever not to let her daughter reject her. "Don't I get a point or two for trying? Mouse? Why do you say I'm a mouse?" Harriet shrugged again. "Because I'm not 'success-ful'—as you put it? True, I haven't painted in years. I may get my paints down any day and surprise you. Do you think I regretted my decision? Yes, sometimes I did. When you were all little and Father was on the road so much, I wished I had my job back. There were days when I wanted to be back at my studio in school. Wanted to pack my bag and let Gramma have you all. Everyone has days like that. They pass. What I wanted from life changed . . ."

"Father kept you pregnant."

"No. I told you. *I* wanted children. Your father, I'm sure, would have been satisfied with two. No man 'keeps' his wife pregnant without her consent. It takes two, doesn't it?"

"Apparently not."

"Are you pregnant?" asked Letty, searching for clues.

"Hah." She couldn't help thinking of Alice, who *needed* to be asked that question.

"Is it sex?"

"*Mother. . . !*" Blushing and embarrassed, Harriet looked away. The eight-day clock chimed the half-hour in an awkward silence between mother and daughter. Harriet would have rather died than reveal to Letty that there'd been no lovemaking of any kind between Patrick and her since they'd been married. And the lack of it, she knew, was like a time bomb ticking. He didn't seem interested any more, maybe no longer wanted her, maybe she *had* lost him, was it all her doing? Despite her anger, the possibility that she was at fault only confused her more, and the reality of this almost three-week-old, loveless marriage made Harriet feel like a terrible failure, worse—some kind of freak. "God," she murmured, shak-ing her head to stem the obsessed rigamorole that ran there.

"I took precautions," she blurted.

"Oh?" Letty waited.

"He broke the lamp and screamed at me."

"Precautions?"

"Mother—are you that old-fashioned? A pessary."

"Oh." Caught off balance with the unconventional revelation, Letty was at the same time interested in—and appreciative of—her daughter's resourcefulness. "But Catholics—"

"Screw Catholics!"

"But how did—?"

"I told him." What would it take to claim her? Alice had asked.

Gentleness and understanding, not his dogmatic refusal to understand her motives. "We can't afford a child right now. Even if we could— It's my body, isn't it?"

"Don't tell him."

"No. I refuse to lie. Ever."

Letty had a glimmer that Harriet's vehemence and grievances were only the tip of the iceberg, but she was hard put to fathom what lay below and had no knowledge of her daughter's larger fears and ambivalence about the opposite sex.

"I'm sure it can all be worked out," she said, wishing she could be less vague and more helpful. Everything pertaining to the bed was difficult in the first year or so, but Letty naturally couldn't reveal to Harriet that her own pleasure in sex had come even later. "There's always a period of adjustment . . . but when two people love each other . . . they find . . . an accommodation. I didn't know that I loved your father . . . that way . . . for quite some time. It's always . . . difficult for a woman at the beginning."

Harriet sighed. The image of Franklin and Letty making love caused her to feel squeamish, but she felt relieved that she'd at least told her mother some of the truth. However, none of what Letty had to say seemed to help.

"I have to baste the turkey." Letty rose, looked out the window, then lay a tentative hand on Harriet's head. "I know it seems to you like the end of the world, but it isn't. You know how you are. But you're twenty! You and Patrick may have got off to a shaky start but . . . be patient. Rome wasn't built in a day."

"Oh Mother—"

"I know. More clichés. But how true it is." She sat on the window seat beside Harriet and put a gingerly arm around her shoulders, glad she wasn't rebuffed. She could feel the tension in Harriet—it ran like electricity. "Your whole life's ahead of you."

" 'Fraid so."

"And what a tiger you are! You can have what you want."

"Don't know what it is any more."

"You expect so much of yourself, you're your own worst enemy. Butt your head against life and all you get is headaches. Give in a little."

"Nope."

"I know what you think of me, but—"

"Sorry. I don't know what comes over—"

"I'm just as tough an old bird as you ever saw, Harriet. I'm not a hothouse flower. You may call me a mouse if you like, but I consider myself a fortunate woman. I've raised four children I'm intensely proud of. Look at me. Especially of you. There, there. Here, blow your nose. You're a trial, but you're a pilgrim in your own cranky way, and if I had a hand in that, I couldn't be happier. Yes, I taught you to be independent and develop your talents, but I didn't mean you should climb on the barricades like your sister. You don't have to. If I ever met anyone who could be successful in having her cake and eating it, too, it's you."

"You don't understand."

"Ayea. I'll keep trying."

Harriet wished she could lay her head against her mother's bosom and rest, but she couldn't seem to. Pausing by the doors, Letty had a final thought. "I'll wager you care very deeply for Patrick. Or you wouldn't be as angry at him as you obviously are."

"Who knows?"

Frustrated and wishing she'd been able to break through, Letty returned to the kitchen a moment later. "Where's Franklin?" she asked Sam, who was sitting by himself at the table. Sam replied that he'd gone to check the furnace, and Letty wondered what stage he was in now. From nostalgia to melancholy to anger and back again. Glad of Cora's warm and comforting chatter, she basted the bird, but her thoughts kept returning to the parlor where Harriet gazed at her parents' wedding portrait, feeling trapped and utterly alone.

"What's going to happen to *The Spectator*, Pat?" asked Sam, as the family gathered for sherry in the parlor before the feast.

"I'll print it on napkins if I have to."

"Of course we will. We're not going under. We can't. People *need* The Spectator." Harriet smiled brightly at Patrick. The same kaleidoscope of conflicting feelings battered her, but having no choice, she was determined to get on top of things. See this transformation taking place? her eyes asked. If it's up to me to end the stalemate between us, I'll do my damnedest! "Now, who wants to loan us a thousand bucks?"

"What's your collateral?" asked Frankie.

"A few dolls in the attic . . . one unfinished and discarded novel . . . and my undiminished abilities to make petunias grow from . . . manure." She had no intention of becoming the abject heroine of one of those pieces from the *Ladies' Home Journal*: "Doctor, Can This Marriage Be Saved?" *She* would save it; how, she didn't have the foggiest. At least he'd come for dinner. She could've imagined him pleading work as an excuse not to. Grateful for Patrick's presence, Harriet smiled across the parlor at him once again and sensed his distance.

"Maybe we should try and get Albatross into the movies," she went on, trying to catch his eye. "A dog who understands Latin? He's a gold mine." She tossed a nut to Albatross, who caught it with an agile gulp. "What do you think?"

Needing to keep up a façade for the family's sake, Patrick nodded. After three weeks of squalls, he wondered what they thought of him.

373

"Can I help, Mother?" called Harriet. Letty signaled her to stay where she was. She and Cora bustled back and forth between kitchen and dining room, occasionally popping in to visit for a second, then they were off again. A heavenly odor sneaked into the parlor, causing saliva to build and stomachs to growl in anticipation.

"Did we win, Father?" asked Harriet. Franklin nodded. Flush-faced, he was in a temporarily boisterous and jovial mood as he relived this afternoon's game for Sam, the victory of Jericho over its arch rival, giving him a transitory feeling of power. Three-quarters of a bottle since this morning fueled his exhilaration as he got up to demonstrate a play. Patrick pretended interest but knew Franklin wasn't including him. He had *that* continued hostility to contend with, too, and when Cora asked him if his family had a large gathering on Thanksgiving, Patrick wished he were there instead of here.

"Ma always throws a big bash. About fifteen or so. Her sisters come up from Jamaica Plain."

At least with his own family he knew the territory and the traps, whereas here he was the underdog.

"I told Mother I think we should all get together," Cora said. "Didn't I, Harriet? If it couldn't be Thanksgiving, perhaps at Christmas."

"What a good idea," responded Harriet, thinking the opposite, but what else could she say? Parched for approval and normal relations, Patrick nodded gamely and knew she was pretending, knew her well enough to know her bright line of chatter was her way of keeping the world—and him—at bay. What was the point in the two families getting together when he and Harriet hadn't? *What was he doing here?*

"Thanks," he said, thoughts interrupted as she replenished his sherry. Both wary, they exchanged guarded smiles. Filled with self doubt on the one hand, Patrick was adamant in his belief that the ball was now in his wife's court. Was he even up for the game any more? Once again he thought of Gert and what had happened at Saint Mary's. No, he decided, he had no desire to be on Essex Street today.

Anger caused his jaw to clench, but it wasn't directed solely at his mother. Even if her insults to Harriet were unconscionable and had horrified him, he damned sure wasn't going to allow Harriet to get away with insulting his mother and sister back! In front of a crowd of people whom he'd known all his life, who looked at him afterward with the sympathy reserved for the husbands of crazy women out of control. No matter the provocation, when added to everything else, when lumped with what Alice had told him and the rest of Harriet's mystifying, unreachable, unreasonable and inappropriate behavior, last Sunday was the final straw.

"I think it stinks. . . . Patrick?" Jolted back to the parlor, Patrick got up and joined the sisters. "Here the two of you've struggled to keep the paper going . . . oh . . . do you know each other? Patrick Flynn . . . Harriet Flynn?" Alice winked, Harriet and Patrick smiled, but he wasn't in a mood for games.

He nodded as Alice lamented that *The Spectator* had become a force in Jericho, and here they were fighting for survival. "Everyone is," he said, eyes meeting Harriet's, both of them knowing it wasn't only the paper. "The economy of the town's at a standstill," Patrick went on, smelling her perfume. But the effect wasn't the same as it used to be and he was plunged into despair at his lack of desire. The usual hard-on no longer responded to the curve of her shoulder, the sparkle in her eye, nor those legs that hitherto prompted unendurable fantasies of wrapping themselves around him. The strike, by default, was his only lover; his dream of perfection a fantasy, his heart broken. *Snap out of it, wallower,* he ordered himself and kept an oar in as the conversation continued about the town's suddenly shaky condition, while undercurrents and cautious glances continued between himself and Harriet.

"Who would've thought it would ever happen in Jericho?" asked Cora, coming into the parlor to exchange a kiss with Sam. "Thank goodness for all of us. We're fine now. But eight hundred families!" she added, clucking in sympathy. "We're ready in five minutes," she added, smoothing Franklin's collar. He nudged her and laughed a laugh that sounded queer to Alice.

"No pay envelopes in close to three weeks and no credit at the markets." Alice watched Franklin out of the corner of her eye and couldn't help her distaste. "It's as if the Depression finally caught up to Jericho."

Pausing in the doorway, Letty was glad to see them all together. Relieved that Franklin seemed robust, she debated carving the turkey in the kitchen or letting him do it at the table. The latter, she decided. It would keep him busy. "Sherry, Mother?" Letty shook her head and returned to the kitchen, admonishing herself not to worry. He was three sheets to the wind, but there was no sense in borrowing trouble.

"Hoo . . . hooo . . ." called Cora a few minutes later. "Start for the table everyone. Where's Father?"

"Went to check the furnace," replied Alice, exchanging a glance with Harriet. "Good for him, it's nippy out," replied Cora, who refused to acknowledge the euphemism of cellar for bottle. Like Letty, she believed in not turning over a rock unless one had to. And who knew?—there might be a violet, searching for the light.

Down in the cellar the coal glittered. Franklin lost himself in the darkness as he shut his eyes and felt the comforting burning spread through him. Above his head the boards creaked in a muffled sound of footsteps in the dining room. He set the bottle down; the furnace glowered and was warm, too. He knew he had to get back upstairs, but suddenly he didn't

375

want to. Staring at the coal, a memory stirred. A house in Haverhill downriver with a coal bin where he'd played and got himself filthy. But someone else had told him that he'd played there. A neighbor whom he'd met when he'd gone back to that same street and found the house where his mother had left him. *Left him.*

Franklin turned as sweat bathed his forehead, and he imagined her coming down the cellar stairs.

Patrick bowed his head and prayed for miracles. Cora finished grace and he crossed himself furtively, noting Franklin's stare. The belligerence obvious, he concentrated on his grapefruit cup while Franklin carved the turkey with trembling hands.

"Doesn't it look delicious!"

"Hmmm . . ."

"Dark for me, Father, if you please. And Sam wants a drumstick, don't you, hon?"

"Patrick . . . light or dark?" asked Letty as Franklin glared at her, and she tensed at the sudden change in him. Franklin got back to work. *Serve her right if he hadn't come to the table at all!* The knife sliced through the crinkly brown skin, the fork clattering to the platter as he lost his grip. "Stop fussing," he growled at Cora, who tried to help. Momentarily disoriented, he glanced down the table at his wife again, her face out of focus. Blood rushed to his head, and he muttered to himself and continued carving, while conversation bubbled up around the table, all of them suddenly walking on eggs. Finally, Franklin was finished, and the plates were passed to enthusiastic murmurs as the dollops of squash and mounds of whipped potatoes were added.

"Sam, these rolls are light as a feather."

"Scrumptious."

"Mother, the stuffing. Mmm!"

"Black olives, Patrick?"

Pass the gravy and didn't the turkey just melt in the mouth? Eating united them all. A cacophony of forks and sighs of contentment disguised the anxieties; the talk of food and compliments bestowed were strained in the face of the potential tornado at the head of the table. The presence of Sam and Patrick, two outsiders, caused the rest of the family to be even more on edge.

"What are they eating today?" Alice asked Patrick, a moment or two later.

"I think between Meyer and the churches, all the families got some food. Not as delicious as this, I'm sure, Mrs. Hoskins," he added. Letty smiled warmly. She had suggested he call her by her first name, but Patrick still wasn't able to, for he sensed her disapproval of him. She seemed nervous today, he noted vaguely, but was too caught up in his own thoughts to make anything of it. Like Franklin, only a part of him was here.

"Tell them about your barter plan," suggested Harriet, forcing him out of his ramblings.

"With so little money in circulation"—Patrick lost his train of thought, then found it again—"we tried to think of what people could use instead. A farmer might be able to exchange a dozen eggs or a barrel of potatoes for half a cord of firewood. The men out of work could exchange their labor for food. Like that. We're going to try and set up a market right outside the mill."

"Another dole," muttered Franklin, as Alice expressed her enthusiasm. "Hah," he added, chuckling to himself. "She works for the biggest dole in the history of the world. Goddamn WPA. Biggest dole in the—" Franklin stopped eating, then started again. "Turkey's dry. Free lunches for lintheads. Where's it going to end? Nobody ever gave me a free ride, tell you that."

"I think, Father, it's more a case of people trying to help each other."

"Did I ask you?" Franklin shot a glance at Harriet, whose comment inflamed him. Her lipstick was too red. Confused, he retreated, then darted another glance at her. Filled with hurt, he tried to put the pieces together but couldn't. "What's that?" he asked a moment later, overhearing a comment of Letty's that her heart went out to those unfortunate families. "I said," she answered carefully, while her fingers groped unconsciously at her wedding ring, "that we all have a great deal to be thankful for."

"Speak for yourself," mumbled Franklin petulantly, for he heard his wife's comment as a criticism. Embarrassed, Letty ignored his rudeness and changed the subject. Self-conscious chatter quickly arose to help her, and second helpings were accepted readily. Frankie took over the carving. Franklin didn't notice. He went back to his food, and everyone breathed again.

"We need more gravy."

"Let me, Mother . . ."

"I'm already up."

Stirring the gravy, Letty found herself redoing the kitchen. New wallpaper, perhaps a canary yellow for the woodwork and—once they got completely out of the hole—a downstairs john. Recalling Harriet's accusations, Letty wondered if she'd deteriorated into a decorator of rooms. Yet changing a room always helped her maintain her equilibrium, which was, at the moment, sorely pressed. He was bad today. Darting a look into the dining room, Letty was hard put to recall her assurances to her daughter that she didn't blame him. Chiding herself for her sudden anger, she replenished the gravy boat and returned to the dining room. She could see that Franklin was gone again and she couldn't help but wish that he'd remain wherever he was and let them get through the meal unscathed.

"An unlikely combination—Meyer Shapiro and the churches of Jericho getting together to distribute turkeys. . . ."

"Pass the butter, please. Because he's Jewish?" Cora asked.

Alice nodded. "And a labor organizer. Neither guaranteed to get him invited to too many parties. Right, Patrick?"

"Pardon?" Brought back from a place where he wouldn't be provoked into telling Franklin what he thought of him, Patrick agreed. "There's as many—more, in fact—who're suspicious of him than believe in what he stands for." Patrick had no sympathy for a drunk, felt disdain and anger for this man who held his family at his mercy and spoiled a dinner.

"What's going to happen, Pat?"

"The rumor is that Phelps is going to try and reopen," he replied to Sam. "It's a test. He knows there are men who'll return no matter what he offers. Several hundred didn't vote with the majority. They've stuck with us so far, but they want to go back."

"And he'll turn hoses on the rest of you," Alice said, "like his buddy, Henry Ford."

"Meyer said it could get ugly. I pray it won't. I don't think violence accomplishes anything." Patrick lowered his eyes and didn't dare look at Harriet. Perhaps she felt he didn't have a leg to stand on regarding that particular subject.

"He treated them fairly. Now they turn on him." Franklin raised his face and squinted down the table at Patrick as if he were suddenly surprised at his presence. Patrick didn't look up.

"But he locked them out, Father—"

"Goddamnit, don't argue with me. What's come over you today?"

"Stop picking on her." Frankie stopped eating.

"I'm not picking on her," muttered Franklin. Shame lapped at him, but it was feeble in the face of the chaos creeping up again. Harriet smiled to cover her hurt feelings and wished she'd kept her mouth shut. There was no reasoning with him, she knew that. Her eye met Patrick's, and she could tell he was angry. *I'm fine*, she smiled, *I'm used to him, don't worry.*

"I prophesied it for years," Alice was saying. She had little desire to spar with Franklin, who she knew had meanness in him, but on the other hand she was sick to death of having to censor every other word and thought. "He's gotten away with murder for years. Now it's caught up with him. Can you hold out?" she asked Patrick as Franklin interrupted: "Were you there?"

"Where?"

378

"Murder?"

"I wouldn't put it past—"

"No union'll ever get into Phelps."

"You may be right. They've tried. Up to now he's managed to keep them out. But—"

"Never." Angrily Franklin buttered a roll. Letty sent Alice a look to cease, but Alice had a point to make. "I agree with you, Father. He may very well win. As Patrick said—"

"Patrick?" Once again, Franklin turned flinty eyes on the stranger, then back to his plate.

"Look what happened in Leveret in nineteen-twelve," Alice continued. "The whole city went out, but they had to go back. They couldn't hold out. There were food riots, and the unions didn't gain a toehold. Mrs. Flynn must remember those days."

"Oh . . . yes." Once again, Patrick controlled himself. He felt the same contempt for Franklin as he did for Phelps, both cut from the same cloth. "Ma was at American Woolen that year. When they struck, she led the women of the mending room right out the front door."

"Your mother?" It didn't sound like the Gert *she* knew. "Well, I guess we have to hand it to her for that, don't we?" added Harriet, hoping Patrick realized she was bending over backward to offer a compliment. Patrick didn't know whether she was being sarcastic or not. "It's always the same," Alice commented, getting his ear again. "Yesterday's rebels become today's reactionaries."

"I guess so," he nodded, able to acknowledge the truth about his mother from Alice more readily than he could from Harriet.

"Don't try to pin that label on me, Alice," laughed Letty, hoping Franklin hadn't noticed his daughter's comment, but Franklin gave no sign. Gone again, he ate methodically, tasting nothing. Alice raised her water glass to Patrick. "To the man who's giving Phelps a few sleepless nights. Pass another roll to 'the conscience of Jericho,'" she went on, grinning. "Did you know Phelps called him that, Mother?"

"I don't think he meant it as a compliment." Patrick noticed Harriet retrieve Franklin's fallen napkin, saw Franklin ignore her as she returned it. What went on between those two? he wondered, trying to understand the complexities between his wife and her father. Why didn't she tell him off? Why didn't they all? Rise up and slay the son-of-a-bitch! Shocked at the degree of his fury, Patrick tried to concentrate on Alice, who was telling him something about Wayne.

"I wrote to him . . . about what you're doing."

"Oh," he replied, noticing Harriet's downcast eyes. "It's not me. It's Meyer. He's the inspiration."

"I'd say you were more than helping. I told Wayne he wouldn't recognize you as the same person who argued with him about Coughlin a few months ago."

"I'm a quick learner. And I had a good teacher," he added, looking at Harriet.

"Why, thank you," she replied, blushing. Cora giggled. Glances continued between the two of them—a connection as fragile as the tiny dried flowers of the centerpiece of goldenrod—cautious glances that might signal their need to end the emotional torture between them.

"William Wood . . . president . . . American Woolen. I'm proud to say he was a friend of mine. Abe Phelps' father, too. Know them all. Did you know that?" challenged Franklin.

"I didn't," replied Patrick carefully.

"Do you remember, Father?" asked Letty, "the party we went to at Mr. Wood's? He had an elevator in his house. I'll never forget it. Pass your father the potatoes, Cora."

Franklin shook his head. They'd left him to rot. Phelps and Wood, too. All looked the other way when he needed a job. And now he was selling sewing machines, which he loathed. At half his former salary of the old days. Bile rose in Franklin's throat and he felt hot with failure. Distantly he heard Letty telling Patrick that he'd sold to the mills for twenty years.

"And still could."

"How would you know?" Franklin glanced sharply at Harriet. "Father," she murmured sadly, and her bowed head was more than Franklin could bear as he ran the gamut from embarrassment to guilt, gripped in an irrational resentment that wouldn't allow her love.

"You're still a crackerjack," she managed to say, as a horrid sense of déjà vu hit her, and she was back with him in a hotel room on a snowy afternoon in Leveret, frightened of his vacant eyes and terrible pessimism. All day she'd been colliding with the memory of that afternoon when she'd gone to rescue him. "Knows the business backward and forward—don't you, Father dear?" she went on, trying to break through to him, more determined than ever. Unable to face her, Franklin stared out the window as an artery pounded in his temple which his daughter recognized. Once again, Harriet smiled and reached her hand to him as her grievances melted away, and she felt mean and petty for having been so angry with him. Yes, he had suffered. Who at this Thanksgiving table, aside from Letty, knew that better than she? Even if he dismissed her, she would never give up on him as Alice and Frankie had. She would mend him again, for she couldn't bear to lose him.

But the compliments and boosting, even his daughter's love, had the opposite effect. Alternately staring past her and down at his food, fury ate at Franklin. Lost chances and the wreck his life had become rushed helter-skelter as bits and pieces of conversations ran relentlessly in his head, and he saw his final consciousness before death and knew it was over and he hadn't even started.

Letty could see the madness rising. Fearful, she tried to steer the conversation away from the woolen business. For a time she was successful, reminding them all that Christmas was coming and did they have their lists ready? To Sam and Patrick she explained the tradition of exchanging Christmas lists after Thanksgiving dinner. Cora began to chatter, too, her voice taut with barely controlled tension, as she told Harriet of the three rooms she and Sam had seen and might rent. "Maybe we can walk over later. I'd love you to see—"

"What about you?" Franklin turned on Harriet again. "Are you going to live here forever?"

"What a question, Father," interjected Letty.

"Mr. Hoskins—" Patrick threw his napkin down, disgusted.

"No, Patrick—it's all right. He doesn't know—"

"You owe her an apology."

"No, Frankie, he doesn't—"

"She never listened to me . . . never asked my permission. Not about Elliot Phelps, either. . . ."

"*Father. . . !*"

Franklin saw Harriet's tear-streaked face from a distance. He wanted to say he was sorry, but the torrent raged and tossed him. Waves of disillusion and frustration swept him up; the faces of his children mocked him.

"Who was responsible?" he exploded, the edge in his voice causing Albatross to sit up, suddenly alert. "Who ruined it for me? Roosevelt . . . and Shapiro. Down to Bangor . . . twenty-eight. I saw him. Troublemaker. Two of a kind. Kikes! They always do. What are you trying to accomplish?" he added, voice rasping in the shocked silence at the table as Franklin turned furious eyes on Patrick, who'd usurped his place and stolen his daughter—the black-haired enemy whose youth and vigor were a terrible reminder of the loss of his own. "You a radical, too?"

"Father, please. Of course he's not."

"I want to hear what he has to say! *You!*"

"Franklin—"

"I'll ask what I like, woman! *Well?*"

Albatross barked a warning. Insides seething, Patrick shook his head, but Franklin's taunts continued. Hands clenched in his lap, Patrick refused to respond.

"Chicken-shit mick!"

"Father—"

"Mother, stop him."

"I don't like the word radical, either."

"Patrick, don't—"

381

"Speak up!"

"I don't think joining a union is radical." Patrick stood.

"Patrick, please—"

"I'm sick of this!"

"Alice, *no.*"

"Father, guess what? Sam's baked pies. Your favorites—" Terrified, Cora felt for Sam's hand under the table.

"Sam. . . ?" The rage deflected from Patrick momentarily, Franklin turned on his other son-in-law, then away quickly, his eyes raking the table, the irrational barrage splattering everyone. "You'll find out," he went on, zeroing in on Patrick again.

"Here it comes . . ." someone called, as a gust of wind sprayed raindrops against the window and everyone's attention was momentarily diverted. Franklin stood, eyes on the window where the rain plummeted him to a fearful place. *The matron bore down and he flinched as she raised the strap.* Stepping backward, he knocked his chair over and fought to keep from screaming as frightened eyes swept his family, who were frozen— some still in their seats, others halfway up as danger flickered around the table. Harriet called, but the terror was stronger. Harriet threw her arms around Franklin, but he pushed her off. Gasping now, a hand grasped at the table, clenching at the cloth and pulling it. Water glasses toppled and the whipped potatoes thudded to the floor as Franklin saw Harriet again. Somehow she'd lied and betrayed him, told him how wonderful it would be, but it wasn't, never had been, *never.* He raised his hand to strike at her as Cora screamed and Patrick caught Franklin's wrist and bent him swiftly to his knees.

Like Franklin, Patrick heard voices calling to him from a distance. His dog's furious barking echoed the relentless staccato beating of his heart as he stood over his father-in-law, blinded and burned by a rage that was more than a match for Franklin's. Trembling like the cowering figure beneath him, Patrick's fists clenched, ready to smash the white head, while his foot cried out to send a kick to the stomach that would fell Franklin to the floor and silence him forever. In an infinitesimal fraction of a second, all the possibilities for maiming and death were considered and rejected simultaneously as Patrick scooped arms under Franklin and pulled him up, propping him like a broken marionette in a chair.

Giving a rebellious jerk, Franklin tried to get up.

"Sit now," ordered Patrick, restraining him. "Sit," he said again as Franklin tried once more, then hung his head in terrible shame.

"You're fine now. Aren't you?" Patrick added gently, possessed of a sudden calm.

Franklin's shoulders shuddered, and his head bobbed with a weeping that produced no tears. "It's all right now," Patrick continued, accepting a glass of water from Harriet, which he brought to Franklin's mouth. "It's passed now, isn't it? Yes, it's passed now. It's all finished now. It's passed. Here . . ."

Once again, Patrick brought the glass to Franklin's lips and lay his hand on his bowed head, surprised to find the hair soft as a baby's.

"All right now. It's all right now." The words continued, almost whispers, as Patrick rubbed Franklin's neck. "I understand. It's gone now. It's OK. Isn't it?"

The barest nod from Franklin. Mesmerized by the continuing words, he stared at the potatoes on the carpet, blobs of white pillows that threatened to stifle him. Another fearful shudder passed through his body but was soothed again by the young man above, whose hand never left Franklin's neck, the hand radiating a calm through Franklin that was almost warm.

Somewhere there was weeping. Neither Franklin nor Patrick heard it. "All gone," the latter crooned. "Gone. Raise your head, Mr. Hoskins. Come on. Raise your head, Mr. Hoskins. Look at me."

Hesitantly Franklin's eyes left the potatoes and journeyed to the edge of the table and its soaked cloth. Higher they flickered over the remains of the meal, careened slightly in fright at the faces, darted back down, then started up again, the eyes seeking now, searching higher, until they found Patrick's and rested safely.

Usually the Hoskins played charades after Thanksgiving dinner. Christmas lists and charades; neither seemed possible nor appropriate tonight. With Franklin put to bed and the rest of them sitting in the parlor like stunned but grateful survivors, Patrick excused himself and went for a walk.

The rain was by turns light and heavy, but he didn't mind. The bleakness that had weighed him down earlier in the day had disappeared, replaced with exhilaration. His conduct had pleased him, he'd learned much about himself; he felt possessed of a lightness and purity that was incandescent as he strode briskly, arms swinging, while Albatross darted under wet bushes, sniffing at creatures of the night.

Much was on Patrick's mind as he walked the rain-slicked sidewalks, passing homes where families sat stuffed and sleepy by radios. Occasionally he witnessed a leavetaking, paused to watch the hurried good nights as mothers and fathers scurried down front-porch steps and the kids waved goodbye to Gramma. "Hurry now. It's raining . . ."

"I'm hungry . . ."

"You *can't* be hungry . . ."

"Night . . ."

"Call us tomorrow . . ."

If he felt momentarily homeless again, the sadness was temporary,

383

manageable. All happy families were alike, he reflected, recalling the opening lines of *Anna Karenina*, while each unhappy family was unhappy in its own particular way. He thought of Franklin, whose anger Patrick recognized as his own, the destructive impulses familiar, too, the torment belonging to each and every one of them. They were all souls who hovered, seeking God's grace, buffeted on this mysterious journey. If the routes were different, the destination was the same.

Mothers and fathers and children. The vast complexities between them had been reduced in Patrick's training to a series of formulas and rules that were so many dried twigs compared to the frightening realities. The power of love was as terrifying as healing. Patrick felt God had been in the Hoskins' dining room. Franklin would never have acknowledged it as such. Patrick had known Him. He had been His instrument, a conduit. The experience had left him with a clarity he'd never experienced before, in touch with that force he'd spent twelve years of his life seeking. Father Morelli had been right after all. God had not failed him. God had been with him today, visible, burned him inexorably, and Patrick was awed.

"Drive carefully . . ."

"It's pouring!"

"Drive carefully . . . the roads'll be slippery. . . ."

Car doors slammed and headlights blinked on as Patrick watched. Who lived in these houses? Protestants, Gert had sneered. Suggesting also, they were the enemy. In any event they were different. Patrick had always sensed that Gert had wanted something they had—a respectability and surety of belonging. Who were they? he'd wondered, those Protestant families. For years they had seemed so inviolable and safe behind their picket fences, white façades, porches and green lawns. They were unreachable to a Catholic boy growing up in Jericho, those mysterious bastions of calm and tradition. But now Patrick knew there was as much mayhem lurking in the hydrangea bushes as hidden behind the lace curtains of his mother's windows into which, on tiptoe, he found himself peering to see what he could see.

Having tackled Franklin, he could certainly handle Gert. Surprised to have found himself in front of his house, Patrick laughed. The sudden playful mood carried him impulsively up the steps where he rang the bell and was startled by his mother's ability to turn him momentarily to jelly, as she opened the door and filled it, spectacles glittering from the street lamp.

"Happy Thanksgiving, Ma." Patrick shifted from one foot to the other. Gert glanced past him as a gust of wind rattled the branches of the maples.

"I'm alone," he replied as she looked up the street, then down. "Just me and Albie."

"You're soaked. What are ya doin' out?" Gert added, suspicious.

"I came to see you."

"You sold the car?"

"You know I sold the car."

"I don't want muddy paws."

"I'll clean them."

She turned, leaving the door open. A moment later he followed down the dark hallway, past the unlit living and dining rooms, struck, more than ever, by the sepulchral oppression of the place.

"Your pa's gone to bed. . . ." Into the brightness of the kitchen where she was finishing a mountain of dishes. Patrick hesitated in the doorway. "God love'm," continued Gert, feeling ill at ease in her son's presence, "he gets up in the mornin'—same time as ever—and doesn't know what to do with himself. How long's it goin' to last? I don't like it. Have ya been eatin' properly? What'd they have today?"

"Meat loaf," he replied, covering his awkwardness with a grin.

"Meat loaf! Aww . . . pulling my leg, are ya? I don't see what you've got to be smilin' about. You're fightin' a losin' battle down there and ya can't pay your bills. Don't think I don't know."

"I'll manage." How he had no idea, but he hadn't come to discuss the strike or his failing newspaper. He wasn't sure *why* he'd come; he knew he was as angry at Gert as ever, but the anger didn't fit with the rest of him tonight and he didn't want loose ends.

"I don't like what's goin' on down there. Why'd ya get involved? I don't like the danger of it."

"I didn't have a choice," Patrick replied, accepting the cup of tea she handed him and sitting carefully at the table. The kitchen smelled of turkey and memories.

"I guess not. I guess I'm not surprised. Nothin' ya do lately surprises me." Agitated, Gert plunged her hands into the sink and scrubbed at the crust on a pot.

"Ma—"

"Your pa and me'll be OK," she said quickly, sensing something in her son that made her all the more nervous. Relieved that he'd come, she felt guilty for her part in their estrangement. Yet she couldn't say anything. "We're not starvin' by any means," she went on, "but I don't like what's happenin'. I'm not for stompin' in mud puddles no more. I'm tired."

"I was telling the Hoskins about you today."

"Oh?" Hackles rising at the name.

"About you at American Woolen. In nineteen-twelve."

"What for?"

"It came up. Who'd you have?" he asked, trying to make a more personal contact.

"The usual. The fat-ass was up from Brookline. Your sister and him's out for a drive. God knows where your brother is. He's becomin' secretive. Do ya want a sandwich?"

385

Patrick shook his head. Gert wiped her hands on her apron and left the kitchen, returning a moment later with a letter which she placed before him. "This come for ya."

Patrick's heart seemed to stop for an instant, for he knew what it was, understood the foreign stamps, the postmark: *Roma*. Fingers trembling, he broke the seal and read the brief paragraph written in Latin. "From the Superior General. The final release from my vows."

"Vows, is it? I figured as much." Gert went back to pots. The arrival of the letter had been as difficult for her as the day Patrick was supposed to have been ordained, as momentous as the day he was to have said his first Mass across the street.

"Finished . . ." murmured Patrick, more to himself than to his former partner on a journey that now officially had ended. Staring bemused at the letter, a plethora of complexities washed over him. The letter seemed more of a beginning than an ending, an acknowledgment of something that was already his, yet it was also a symbol of his past that carried tremors.

The reverberations were manageable, he told himself, as his power returned. But he didn't know exactly how to use it. If he'd emancipated himself from this woman who'd ruled his life, she was still his mother; she possessed enormous weight. The old fear had escalated upon his arrival but it was gone now, replaced with tenderness. He had no wish to harden his heart against her.

"Ma. . . ?" She seemed smaller as she sloshed the pans—as if her bones were shrinking before his eyes. Soon she'd step over into oldness and be gone. "I'm sorry if I hurt your feelings, Ma."

Flustered, Gert blushed. "When I think of what it took to get it started!"

"Ma, did you hear me?"

"I heard you. I'm not deaf. If you'd listened to me—"

"If I'd listened to you, I'd be a pebble in O'Brien's pocket—" Patrick stopped himself and realized he'd risen to the bait. "Ma—"

"Who gave ya the opportunity?"

"You did. But I had to do it my way. If I have to throw in the towel, at least I know the kind of paper it should be. I'll get it started again. I'm not giving up. Ma, that's not why I came by."

"Why'd ya come?"

"It's Thanksgiving. I missed you."

Gert turned, struck by the sudden innocence of him. What if he made himself a success? A strange fear mushroomed in her but she buried it quickly. "I've always wanted what was best for ya. I wanted all my children to be independent," she added hastily, torn between his attaining it and the loss of him. "For all of youse," she went on, sloshing water once again and beginning to talk of Rose, for it was easier. "After all I've done for her! I'm breakin' my back with the preparations for her weddin', and do I get a word of thanks? Nothin' but criticism. Don't think I don't know that when she's sittin' pretty on Chestnut Hill with the fat-ass, there'll be no place for me or Pa. We'll be left in the garbage, that's where we'll be! And your brother," she continued, shifting her gaze to Dennis, who was coming in from the back hall, "accuses me of not havin' his best interests at heart."

"Me? Hi, Pat. Say, Pat—guess what we found at the office? Some suspicious inkblots on the tax rolls. I'm going to conduct an investigation. I thought you should know."

"Small potatoes," sighed Gert, taking Dennis's hat off. "Where were ya?"

"Over at Billy's. Listening to music."

Gert made a face and glanced at Patrick, his calm making her anxious again. "You'll leave me, too," she said, turning once again to Dennis. "Well, you've got my permission." A lonely old woman, Teresa had warned. Hated by your own children. "All of ya," she added, having to turn away to compose herself.

"I—" Dennis shrugged. "I'm not going anywhere, Ma."

Patrick thought of Father Morelli's words of a few months back. *You have permission to live, Patrick.* Did he need permission from his mother, too? She would never give it willingly, no matter what she said. He'd had to seize it. And would make her understand that he loved her and needed the same.

"You'll look after your ma, won't ya, Denny?" asked Gert, the question making Patrick angry. "Let him live his life, Ma," he said, trying to be conciliatory. "Didn't you say you were tired? Don't you think you could give yourself a rest? Nothing's going to happen to us."

"Is that so?" Not hearing, Gert went on about some girl Dennis had brought to the house, an idiot without a thought in her head as far as Gert could see. Patrick shook his head in frustration as he watched his brother wince. Didn't Dennis know that no one, no female on the face of the planet, would ever pass muster?

". . . and if he didn't spend his time chasin' after tarts with Billy Meeghan, he'd recognize a proper young woman if she happened to pass by. And I'd be the first to give my blessin'."

Dennis backed out of the kitchen; was sleepy, he said, and going to bed. "Don't look at me like that," snapped Gert, after he left. "I know what's best for your brother."

"OK," Patrick replied, knowing it was useless. Whatever feeble flicker of resistance left in his brother's heart had been slowly, inexorably extinguished by the weight of his mother's need. Worse was that Denny had let it happen and needed her as much as she needed him. "Nothing's changed around here, I guess," he said sadly—and immediately chastised himself for having been diverted from his purpose.

"What did ya expect?" Gert settled heavily into a chair opposite her son.

"I love you, Ma. I want your blessing. I'm married, Ma."

Unable to hear, Gert reached for her handbag, got out her purse and extracted a bill. "Somethin' to tide ya over. . . ."

Patrick shook his head quickly. "I'll manage. Thanks, but—"

She pushed the bill across the table. Another symbol, thought Patrick, and shook his head again. "I'd like your blessing, Ma. I don't want this to go on the way it has. I'd like you to apologize to Harriet."

"Who's to apologize to me?"

"Let me go get her. Why don't I? Right now."

A tear slipped out. Gert's shoulders hunched, and Patrick was caught in the web and felt awful.

"And ya won't take nothin' from me. . . ."

"I'm married," Patrick pleaded. Fearful of her sobs, he reached his hand across the table and took Gert's.

"Is that my punishment? Ya won't take nothin' . . ."

"No," Patrick protested, wondering if there was a hidden truth. "I'd take your love, Ma. Don't you know I love you?"

Staring at him, her heart ached, and the words came painfully. "I'm sorry, Patty. If I've done wrong by ya."

"Let's put it behind us. Let me go get her."

Gert couldn't look at him, looked at his hand instead, the hand holding hers, seeing it tiny with Rosary beads clutched as he said his prayers to her when he was little.

"I can't, Patty. Not now. Some other time maybe. I can't, Patty. You'll hafta forgive me. I can't."

The rain was steadier as Albatross and Patrick hurried down the incline and ducked into *The Spectator* office. Patrick was nicely surprised to find Harriet waiting for him.

"How did you know I'd be coming? *I* didn't even know."

"I willed you to," she replied, smiling hesitantly. "I have the teakettle on. What a night!" Rain lashed the window, the wind sending stinging drops which made a sudden racket.

"More tea," he murmured. "I went by the house," he explained. "Cozy," he added, noting that only one of the fluorescent tubes was lit, making the office seem different and intimate.

"Am I still considered to be carrying the plague?"

"Maybe the flu. Oh, nice," he exclaimed, seeing the glow that came from the Franklin stove Gert had installed a month back. "I put some coal in," Harriet said as Albatross discovered the warm spot, shook off the droplets clinging, and lay down. Patrick warmed his hands and took the tea.

Feeling as vulnerable as a freshly hatched cuckoo bird, Harriet didn't know whether to sit, stand, talk, or smoke. There was silence between them but it didn't seem fraught. The patter of the rain against the window caught their attention and they sensed something new between them.

"Do you remember the day I hired you?" Full of sudden possibilities, yet as vulnerable as his wife, Patrick glanced nervously away as her yellow slicker stirred memories. "I served you tea."

"And it was raining then, too. You *were* a curmudgeon."

"You were pushy."

They smiled quickly, like strangers who didn't want to be, who wanted to catch up quickly. But they had to be careful, for every glance, pause, tone or inflection might carry danger and misinterpretation.

"Do you know I almost fired you that day? I wrote you a letter, but I never mailed it."

"What good sense you had."

The past was a temporary haven, able to be laughed at, so much easier than the reverberating present, where anything might go wrong in the space of a look, where they both knew a wealth of cracks lay hidden to trip them up, bits of straw embedded to catch a skate blade, real and imagined slippery places to be avoided at all costs.

"Where did you go?"

"Just wandered. Home."

"You always go for walks when you're mad at me . . . or troubled."

"I'm not," he protested quickly. "Either one. I guess I was," he admitted. "I know you're unhappy with me."

"No," she protested in turn. "If I am, I should be shot."

"I'd be awfully bereft." Patrick grinned. Nervous and ordering herself not to be, Harriet sat at her desk, sipped her tea, shifted aimlessly through copy and knew Patrick was watching her. But when he asked her what was wrong, she shook her head.

"What did your mother have to say?" She glanced up at him, suddenly confused at how different he looked. She tried to put her finger on what it was but couldn't.

"Nothing much."

"At least you went."

"I tried."

"But—?"

He shook his head. "She is who she is, I guess," he said, not really wanting to talk about Gert. He forgave her. She would have to come around in the end; he was sure of that. Wondering at his calm, Patrick smiled to himself.

389

"I'm sorry . . . what I called her. I guess it didn't help matters."

"You were provoked. She does that."

"I've noticed."

"But, thanks. I asked her to apologize to you," he added, wanting Harriet to know that his mother's hurtful action hadn't gone unnoticed. Wanting also to make up for his inability to rise to her defense last Sunday.

"You did?" The messages were received. She was grateful. "And?"

"She will. Someday. Maybe not the exact words, but you'll know." From the pocket of his topcoat, he removed a waxpaper-wrapped package of date bars that Gert had thrust at him on the way out the door. Then he felt for the letter in his breast pocket and handed it to Harriet. "I'm a free man."

Free of me? she wondered with a spasm of anxiety that surprised her.

"The final release from Rome. I've burned my bridges behind me."

"You've made a lovely blaze."

The banter rescued them from potential potholes. "Date bar?" he asked politely, slipping off the rubber band from the package and offering her one. "To go with the tea?" She shook her head. "How does it feel?" she asked, looking at the letter.

"Strange. Fine. I don't know. How's your father?"

"Still asleep I guess. What are we going to do?" she asked, glancing around the office.

"We'll find a way. We always have."

"Is she letting it go down the drain to spite me? She could bail us out, but because of me . . ."

Patrick shook his head. "I wouldn't accept it anyway. I decided that weeks ago. I took date bars instead." He bit into one. "Far fewer strings attached. It's odd. . . . Love goes into cooking, yet food seems to bring out the worst in people. The worst fights seem to occur at dinnertime—"

"*You were wonderful with him.*" Sudden tears flooded her. Quickly Patrick squatted and put his arms around her.

"I'm here . . ."

"You . . ." she whispered timidly in return, almost a question. "Patrick . . ." she murmured, as if his name were foreign and surprising. Once again, she had the sensation of seeing him differently as she dared raise her eyes to his and discovered not just the familiar blue, but something else she hadn't known or dared to acknowledge. "You . . ." she said again with a half gasp, struggling to express herself but had no words. Hiding against his chest, she wept afresh and gulped for breath, for the sudden wind change in her heart seemed more than she could bear. "What's wrong with me?" she muttered, taking a deep breath to calm herself as she got up and crossed to the fire, blew her nose.

"Nothing," he answered, recognizing the nervousness, knowing it

390

had to do with Franklin and with him as well. But he had all the time in the world for her.

"I watched what happened between them . . . since I came back. I wanted to believe . . . I prayed. . . . You don't know what he used to be like . . . with me. He was my father. The only other man I ever felt remotely as close to was Mr. Phelps . . . but Father was Father. Oh," she gasped again, hiding her face in her hands. "It's awful to hate him the way I do sometimes. I can't stand myself. Mother accuses me of being 'young' when I get angry at her for putting up with him . . . but I can't help it. I can't help it."

Once again, Patrick went to her, but Harriet was too nervous to be comforted, found herself rushing in her head like Chicken Little and the sky was falling. "I always prided myself on being the only one . . . who could . . . reach him. But it's all gone now. I'm sorry to be such a crybaby. . . ."

"I guess I understand what you said to me once." A part of Patrick was still back there with the men she'd been close to, aware of her omission of himself. If the latter hurt, he was more than ever determined to banish his fears and move forward. "About your feeling that marriage was a trap. But it doesn't have to be, does it?" he asked formally, causing her to smile. "What?" he asked.

"You look so solemn. And dear . . ." she added quickly, struck by the new word and the feeling behind it, which unaccountably only made her tense again. "God," she murmured brusquely, moving past him, past the counter to look out at the rain which drummed like the inside of her head.

"I don't want to trap you," he said, searching for clues as Letty had this morning.

Harriet shook her head, confusion welling. "Sometimes I stand outside myself and I look at myself, and I'm not sure who she is! What happened?" she blurted, turning back to him.

"I guess we got off to a bad start."

"That's putting it mildly." Elliot hovered and she felt angry. "I guess it's all my fault."

"I wasn't very understanding. Or forgiving."

"You've been . . . shutting me out."

"Self-defense."

"Really?" She paused. "I guess I did have my guard up."

He nodded. Harriet was willing to accept it if he said so, which was strange to her, that she should so readily.

"Alice said you don't trust me."

"I—"

"But I'm your husband."

"Isn't that . . . simplistic?"

391

"Maybe so. Anyway. It's all behind us. Isn't it?"

Over the littered and body-strewn field of their marriage, they regarded each other. The grievances and suspicions that had fired the blood, the accusations and violence between them seemed momentarily stilled. For a moment neither of them spoke; neither dared.

"Isn't it?" he repeated. Rushing again, Harriet nodded.

"Kiss me."

"What?"

"You heard me."

Letting out a tiny gasp of a nervous laugh, she went back behind the counter and did as she was told. A cautious kiss on both their parts, they smiled self-consciously and caught the other's eye, each wondering what the other was thinking and where do we go from here? Harriet broke away, knelt by the grate and stroked Albatross.

"Are you cold?" Patrick asked, following. Fighting a battle with his fear of her possible rejection, he lay his hand on her hair. "You're so lovely," he said, and she glanced quickly up at him. "No, I'm not . . . some women are . . . I never thought I was. Oh," she exclaimed softly as he took her hand and pulled her up, silencing her with a morsel of date bar which he brought to her mouth. Closing his eyes and trembling as his fingers touched her lips, he was surprised at the rush of desire that overtook him, for he'd been sure it would never return. Harriet accepted the sweet, her defenses beginning to fall like the crumbs from her lips.

"And—" She stopped herself and wondered what it was she wanted to say. "Your eyes are so blue. Do you know what Alice said to me? Something about marrying you like that and—" The words seemed to rush out.

"Like what?"

"Without loving you. But she said I did. That I'd married you by mistake but that you were the right man. The right man by mistake? Of course I thought *you* were the mistake." *Stop talking.*

"I guess I knew that."

"You were brave."

"I'm Irish."

She smiled. "I'm—"

Once again, Patrick stilled her nervousness as he took her hand and kissed it, inflamed when she sighed. His sense of power swept over him again, and he found he wasn't at all upset by what she'd just said. The scent of victory was in his nostrils as he gazed at her, unfazed as her eyes skittered away. How could he have ever blamed her for anything, this delicate creature he held in his arms? She'd filled his lungs with her vibrancy and exhilaration, breathed new life into him, and no matter the trouble she caused him, no matter that she was a mystery, no matter that she'd thought him a mistake and maybe still did, he loved her and would wait till she found out the truth.

392

"The honeymoon suite . . ." he began, unable to go on, for Harriet started laughing at his imitation of the night clerk in Atlantic City. "Wasn't he awful?" she groaned. ". . . is booked," he continued, "but there's this newspaper office that's very cheap, and we may not have it much longer so let's . . ." He trailed off, blushing, glancing at the cot to the rear.

"What an interesting idea. . . ." Relief and anxiety assaulted her simultaneously. Suppose she didn't please him? "Oh!" she gasped, startled, as Patrick wrapped his arms around her and pressed his mouth urgently on hers.

"Sorry," he mumbled, sensing he'd frightened her.

"No . . . I just . . ." She slipped away and into the bathroom. Outside, she could hear the wind thrashing branches against the steps that led up to the parish hall; the thrashing echoed her raggedly beating heart. Supposing he asked? That other girl had been at it again, had prepared herself in a daze only an hour ago, just in case. *Don't kid yourself, you knew what you were doing.* Don't tell him, Mother had suggested. The other girl had come to the office tonight, hoping Patrick would appear, determined and wanting to give him herself, yet she felt guilty at her decision to prepare herself, yet knew she'd had to, yet, yet, yet . . .

Toes curling on the cold linoleum, Harriet returned a moment later in her slip to find Patrick in undershirt and shorts, stoking the fire. "You look so funny . . . with your shoes on," she laughed, not recognizing her own voice. The office was dark, lit only by the glow from the grate, and the shades were drawn. One side of Patrick was bathed in rose from the coals. He hadn't not been able to wonder at the very thing Harriet had thought he might. *Forgive me for not asking her,* he prayed, not wanting to know. This maneuver of conscience took vast second place as he turned and gazed at her.

"Are you warm enough?" he asked, rising and approaching, putting his arms tenderly around her waist. Harriet nodded, tried to think of something amusing, found her head hot, brain like scrambled eggs.

They sat on the edge of the cot together and Patrick lay back and pulled her with him, and she was shivering all over. "I guess . . . it is . . . chilly," she murmured, ordering herself to stop, which only made it worse. Vaguely she heard him whisper gently and flinched in anticipation of his weight as he loomed above her and held her against him, supporting himself on his elbows and wrapping her in his arms, the full length of him on top of her. She felt him pressed hard against her belly while her heart beat frantically like a wren on the edge of the nest, anxious, but determined to fly.

And still she couldn't stop shaking and had to clench her teeth to keep him from hearing the chattering. *O please,* she murmured to herself, miserable that he was seeing her so agitated, *let it be fine.* She tried to remember all of Virginia's advice, thought of Harris and his wet kisses that

393

had never really moved her, of Elliot and Leonard Jacobs who had hurt her, and Patrick, who had hurt her, too.

"There now . . . there." Determined to stop her trembling, Patrick had no idea how. Her apprehension gripped both of them; the night at the icehouse hovered, the subsequent failures and misunderstandings ready to rise like demons and slay them. "It's me," he whispered. "I know," she whispered back, opening her eyes and smiling quickly to reassure him. Wanting to make him happy, she once again ordered herself to relax as Patrick kissed her and tugged at her slip, trying to pull it out from under. Giving up, he slipped her straps down but had no idea how to get her bra off, so Harriet did it, tensing once again at the sudden passion of him as he buried his face against her breasts. Feeling nothing much at all except upset that she was such a cold fish, she tried to respond, stroking his hair, determined not to spoil it, determined he wouldn't see she didn't like any of it. A terrible failure, she lay back.

It seemed over before it started, then again it seemed to go on forever. Harriet opened her eyes. Patrick had got barely in her and climaxed, crying her name. Now he lay beside her, holding her hand tightly, but neither of them could look at the other. Harriet remembered Elliot telling her she didn't know how to kiss and went into a tailspin of blaming herself. Beside her, Patrick was doing little better. Had he been too rough? Joyce had called him a bull in a china shop.

"I'm sorry," she murmured; "Excuse me," he said simultaneously, both of them too embarrassed and ill at ease to talk. She wanted to tell him it wasn't his fault. She could sense him distant from her and didn't, she told him in her head, blame him at all. Not that she'd ever expected anything would happen to her; Virginia's Roman candles and the like were obviously meant for other women. But she couldn't reveal any of this.

The rain splattered at the window and the wind moaned, making the silence between them obvious. Patrick wondered if he'd made love improperly, but he wouldn't have understood if Harriet told him she felt like a train had rushed by leaving her on the platform waving her ticket—and she wouldn't have had such a thought in the first place.

"Cold?" he asked as she shivered again. He was sure she wouldn't want him to take her in his arms. "Hmmm," she murmured, trying to make the best of it and banish her sadness. They both sat up; she covered herself decorously with her slip, gave him a quick kiss on the cheek, and fled to the bathroom, disliking herself intensely.

When she returned, dressed, she found him still in his shorts, squatting beside the stove and talking to Albatross. His naked back seemed fragile, yet strong and beautiful, like something she'd never seen before. They smiled bravely at each other and she felt she'd explode. "I'm not sexy . . ." she blurted, the words out of her unintentionally. "No," he protested, going to her. His own thoughts in as much of a whirl, he felt buffeted like the building, shaken by the wind that blew a gale in him.

"Are you . . . angry at me?" he asked. Devils lurked, ready and willing to provide answers to what had happened. The powerful calm he'd felt earlier was long gone; he'd obviously been the cause of her shivers and fright. *Because she doesn't love you,* whooshed the voices.

"No," she replied, her vehement denial helping and stalling the awful doubts. "I'm sure you are with me," she added shyly. He put his arm around her tenderly in rebuttal, relieved she didn't flinch.

Albatross sighed and shifted position. Harriet and Patrick didn't dare move. They held onto each other and were almost afraid to breathe, lest they disturb the sudden mysterious closeness that enveloped them. A moment later they dared a glance. "I love you," she whispered, wanting desperately for it to be true. Patrick prayed that it was and started to kiss her, and she closed her eyes and he asked her not to.

They didn't hear the car outside. A brick crashed through the front window, shattering the glass. The wind rushed in, causing the shade to flap madly as papers blew from the desks and Albatross began to bark. Too frightened to even shout or scream, Patrick and Harriet clutched each other, frozen.

"*No . . . Patrick . . . don't . . .*" she cried as he suddenly ran for the door and rushed outside in his undershorts, in time to see a car's taillights disappearing down the street in the pelting rain.

"Phelps," he muttered, upon returning. "One of his boys. . . ."

"Oh, my God," she whispered. "Patrick . . . I warned you . . . he's dangerous."

"*I'm* dangerous now," he replied, fury galvanizing him. "C'mon, help me. They won't be back tonight. It was a warning, that's all. Help me with this."

Glad to be told what to do, Harriet grabbed for the wildly careening shade, and the two of them tacked it to the windowsill and propped chairs against it to hold it in place against the wind. Albatross continued to pace in agitated circles, sniffing and barking. Harriet swept up the glass. "Shouldn't we call the chief? Patrick, what are we going to do . . . ? Patrick, I'm frightened. . . ."

"Don't be. I'll talk to McGee tomorrow. But what can I prove? What can he? Leave those," he ordered, taking her hand and stopping her from picking up the papers scattered over the office. He took her in his arms and kissed her.

"That bastard," she murmured. "That unmitigated bastard! What are we—?"

"Shhh," he whispered, trying to calm her as she darted glances toward the window. "Easy now. Where were we?" he grinned, leading her back to

395

the cot and sitting her down. He poured her another cup of tea and sat beside her.

"But—"

"No buts. There's nothing we can do tonight. Phelps may smash my window, but I don't intend to let him interrupt me making love to my wife."

Harriet glanced apprehensively to the front again.

Out of his shorts popped Patrick's erection, startling them both.

"Touch it," he whispered, his voice hoarse.

How warm it was. Harriet didn't know what to do with it, so she held on, then loosened her grip, then tightened it, which she discovered caused Patrick's breathing to become ragged. Like solemn children, who were anxious the task be done properly, they began to take her clothes off. A moment later, she was down to her slip again, and they were sitting, frightened but willing accomplices, on the edge of the cot. Harriet took him in her hand once more as his fingers caressed the inside of her thighs, moving up to touch delicately at her vagina.

"I've lost my immortal soul to you," crooned Patrick. Fingers probing between her legs, the surprise of a sudden slipperiness there inflamed his curiosity. Embarrassed at the intimacy, Harriet almost recoiled. Part of her remained logical; part of her was watching. Twenty years of fighting fiercely and a day-to-day cry that she was in charge of her destiny didn't allow for sudden thrashings into ecstasy, and she fought to retain a semblance of control over the situation. But her body had destinations in mind beyond her imagination; it arched helplessly of its own accord toward Patrick's willing fingers.

Far in the distance, a train hooted as it came around the bend alongside the river, its sound carrying Harriet to the depot. She held Franklin's hand for protection while she counted the cars and had the exact number as the caboose rolled by with its lantern flickering, coffee cups jiggling on the table as the crew looked out rain-lashed windows on Jericho.

The whistle was lost in the wind and her father, too. Harriet bundled his scarf around his neck and made sure his fedora was on straight and waved goodbye. She heard herself say "Patrick . . ."—the saying in a voice she was sure wasn't hers. But it was—the other girl was gone, disappeared. A last-ditch stand was taken, a final cry of independence before the rebels took the hill, but they didn't seem so terrible and Harriet gave in, felt herself falling and might have been scared but found she only had to look in her husband's eyes to be caught, saved, held, made safe, never to hit the ground and splatter. Legs that were hers seemed to float upward as she lay back on the cot and Patrick knelt over her. She saw his chest and nipples and lay a hand on his beautiful skin that was phosphorescent like his eyes, which had snared her long ago on a day of thunder and black cassocks.

"Yes," she said as Patrick entered her. She was astounded by the simplicity of the word. Part of her laughed; she didn't know why. She might have had thoughts. She wasn't thinking.

Patrick wanted to sing a High Mass, wolf down the world and blow like the wind, toppling all that stood in his way.

Wires above the street snapped and whipped. In the great houses at the lake, in the tenements of Jerusalem, on Mulberry Street and Essex, too, crackling static interrupted Jericho's radios tuned to "Kraft Music Hall" with Bing Crosby and Bob Burns, while Victor Bay held forth on NBC Red with "Essays in Music." Children sat up in their beds, and mothers looked out windows as families gathered together in a Thanksgiving lassitude, glad to be home and warm. At the mill the Pinkerton guards huddled over fires burning in gasoline drums and peered at the street. A quiet night, but there might be trouble. The one recently returned from his late-night raid sipped a coffee. Rain splattered the smashed *Spectator* window and the wind moaned, echoing Harriet, whose head tossed from side to side, sweet perspiration drenching her face as Patrick took her, carrying her away like the blowing leaves, stinging her like the rain on Jericho and the Merrimack Valley, the tumult transporting both of them to the country of the Infinitely Surprised.

22 In a gesture of gratitude toward his son-in-law, Franklin offered to raise the mortgage on Mulberry Street and loan him whatever he needed. Moved, Patrick had reluctantly refused. There was a certain amount of pride involved, as well as the knowledge that the Hoskins family, only lately out of the woods themselves, had no business supporting a newspaper that was on the shakiest financial legs, with no hope in sight that things were going to get any better.

Meyer Shapiro came to the rescue with a linotype machine. Thus, *The Spectator* changed from a slick, professional weekly to a strike sheet, whose coverage dealt exclusively with the events down on South Main.

Even if the paper had been reduced to a couple of small sheets stapled together, Patrick and Harriet were jubilant they'd been granted a reprise. From behind the boarded-up *Spectator* window, they ran off copies that, to shouts of encouragement, they distributed free to the crowd outside the mill.

The strikers were equally pleased that the paper had been given a new lease, for they'd come to think of it as theirs, and the violence against it was added insult to their injury. If there were those who wouldn't have minded throwing a few bricks through the windows of the mill in retaliation, Patrick pleaded for calm. In print as well as in the daily meetings of the strike committee, he warned against the temptation of violence, adding that aggressive action would only play into Phelps' hands. But over three weeks of pent-up anger and frustration finally came to a boil when Phelps attempted to reopen the mill.

Ads calling for experienced hands had been placed in the Leveret papers. Five hundred came running.

Braving a gauntlet of angry strikers, who were ordered aside by Ed McGee and his hard-pressed force of three, men from Leveret seeking employment arrived early in the morning and were greeted by a roar of oaths and cries of "dirty scabs!"

But the most scathing condemnation was directed at former fellow workers who felt they had to return. "Judas!" was the mildest of the epithets

398

slung through the chilly morning air. Patrick's plea that brother should not fight brother was ignored as the strikers tried to prevent their former friends and neighbors from passing through the gates. Fighting broke out, several of the hated Pinkerton guards were roughed up, and the Leveret police were called to help restore order. McGee ordered the gates closed to prevent further violence, and a cheer rose up from the strikers. But the confrontation provoked bitter resentment.

"HE WANTS TO DIVIDE US!" cried Meyer Shapiro from his sound truck. Appealing to Phelps' former employees who'd tried to return, Shapiro exhorted them to think twice. Clustered in angry knots across the street, separated from the main body of strikers in the parking lot and around the millpond, they booed him.

"EVERYBODY CALM DOWN! THIS ISN'T GOING TO GET US ANYWHERE!"

Missiles rained from one side to the other. The open-air market that the strike committee had set up was in disarray, carts overturned. Women hurried for cover as tomatoes flew through the air, answered with stones from the other side. Both groups' leaders pleading for it to stop, the flurry died down.

"DIVIDE AND CONQUER—THAT'S HIS OBJECTIVE! DON'T YOU KNOW THAT?" Shapiro pleaded to more boos. "STAY WITH US. WE'VE HELD OUT SO FAR! DON'T—"

"We have a right to work!" retorted Harold Shaughnessey, who was the leader of the group that had tried to go back. "Commies," cried several who were with him. "Are you gonna pay my rent? I'm evicted!"

"BULLSHIT!" bellowed Shapiro. "MY APOLOGIES TO THE LADIES," he added, climbing atop his truck, wheezing in anger. "THERE'RE NO COMMIES OVER HERE, AND YOU KNOW IT. DON'T PLAY HIS GAME. IS MARIENETTI A COMMIE? IS PAT FLYNN? OR HIS FATHER?"

"What have you done for us, Shapiro?" they demanded in return. "He won't even talk to you!"

"WE'RE IN THE JUDGE'S CHAMBERS NOW. IT TAKES TIME. HE CAN'T HOLD OUT FOREVER. AND IF HE TRIES TO REOPEN TOMORROW, WE'LL STOP HIM. JUST AS WE DID TODAY!"

A cheer from his partisans. The Leveret police who were guarding the main gates exchanged glances. So did Patrick and Harriet, who were standing with Marienetti. Patrick shook his head. "It's going to get worse." Troubled by the day's violence, which would undoubtedly be repeated tomorrow, his gaze swept over the strikers' heads to Shaughnessey, whom he knew would try to go in again in the morning. Looking up Main, he sensed the agitation in the gathered townspeople, who were as equally divided as Phelps' employees. And under everything, Patrick knew there ran a not so subtle prejudice. If Franklin had lumped Phelps' employees as "lintheads who never had it so good," he was part of a growing body of opinion in town that didn't hesitate to cast an angry glance at the micks, dagos and canucks who'd been given a chance to return to work and hadn't. Public sentiment, which had initially been sympathetic, was now apprehensive and growing hostile toward the strikers.

"STICK WITH US!" Shapiro continued to plead, and Patrick smiled to himself. Meyer had the stamina of three men half his age. "THAT'S HOW WE'LL WIN! HE'S WATCHING US ALL RIGHT NOW. LOOK AT HIM UP THERE."

The command was so urgent, both sides found themselves turning to the mill, as if Abraham Phelps were actually there—in a window or standing on the roof, taunting them.

"HE'S HAPPY AT WHAT HAPPENED THIS MORNING. CAN'T YOU SEE HIM SMILE? HE'S GLAD WE'RE DIVIDED! AS LONG AS WE'RE DIVIDED, WE ALL LOSE."

With no time to spend at windows, Phelps was in his office demanding assurance from the Leveret chief of police that the strikers would be repulsed and arrested if they tried to interfere with anyone returning to work or seeking employment.

Energized to a feverish pitch and more determined than ever to crush the rebellion, his next call went to Governor Curley, urging him once again to send the National Guard to keep order in a rapidly escalating situation, which, Phelps threatened, he would not take responsibility for. He vowed to open the gates again in the morning. Watching apprehensively from their offices across the river, Leveret's mill owners cheered him on. Each of them was relieved the union hadn't chosen *them* to make its stand.

A deadlock had developed on South Main. Now there were three factions, and Shapiro feared Phelps had the cards. Like Patrick, he sensed Jericho's mounting apprehension and escalating ill-will for his cause. From too many bodies pressed against it, a window in the hardware store across the street caved in that afternoon. Several other stores in the vicinity promptly closed, their owners boarding up windows. Phelps had warned Patrick that the business community would turn against the strikers. Teresa was in the minority, offering a free finger wave, strike special, to wives of Phelps' employees. However, old man Longbottom of the market spoke for the majority of Main Street merchants when he declared that Shapiro should get the hell out of Jericho and let everyone go back to work and much-needed normalcy.

That afternoon the *Leveret Eagle* contained the following story:

JERICHO MAN INJURED IN SPANISH CONFLICT

Jericho, Nov. 28— Wayne Thibeau, son of Mr. and Mrs. Floyd Thibeau of Jericho, was caught in a train bombed by rebel forces near Malaga, Spain, sometime last week. Mr. Thibeau suffered severe injuries, and his leg was amputated in a field hospital. Thibeau, a volunteer on the Loyalist side, arrived in Spain less than two months ago. He was reputed to be on his way back to the States when the incident occurred.

Letty was sitting in the rocker in the back bedroom that night, halfway through Frankie's Christmas sweater. Alone in the house, she relished the solitude.

How peaceful to sit knitting, losing herself in the rhythmic click of the needles—such a fragile sound to ward off the chaos all around. The mind wandered over hill and dale; pleasant subjects were seized on—such as Patrick and Harriet's transformation from cats and dogs to cooing doves. Harriet, Letty reflected, seemed an entirely new person. As for Patrick, Letty's reassessment of him approached nomination to sainthood. Franklin had been calmer since Thanksgiving.

Clickety, clickety and the mind stumbled over what couldn't be avoided, such as Jericho becoming a tinderbox, such as a world where young men were once again losing their lives and limbs as they had in the Great War so few years back. How easy it had been to agree with Franklin that the daily news from Spain wasn't our fight; they were foreigners after all, and let them stew in their own kettle. Except that Wayne Thibeau lived six blocks over on Morton Street, and Mrs. Thibeau made fine shirts and was pleasant to chat with at the market.

And earlier this evening when Alice had come home from work, where she'd received the news, Letty had never seen her so distraught. Like a coiled wire, barely able to hide it, her daughter's agony had not allowed Letty to comfort. In unfathomable pain, Alice left the house quickly, went to the Thibeaus for further details, then to *The Spectator* office to talk to Harriet and Patrick. She told the latter she was pregnant and intended to fall down a set of icy steps.

Letty heard the front door slam, heard voices. Patrick and Harriet removed their coats and sat in the parlor.

"*Mother!*"

Letty recognized the stridency of Alice's tone. The call came again

401

with an urgency that caused her to hurry out into the hallway as her daughter came up the back stairs, her eyes inflamed in the night light.

"They got another cable from the consul in Valencia. He's in a hospital. Still in shock. The bleeding's stopped. When he's OK to travel, they'll try and get him on a refugee ship."

Clipped and bleak, the words spilled out. "That's all I know," Alice replied curtly to Letty's questions. "How is one leg good news?" she retorted when Letty was hopeful. "Do you want to tell me one leg is better than none?"

Letty beckoned Alice to come in the bedroom with her. Sitting on her hands on the edge of her parents' bed, Alice stared at Letty and couldn't say it. *Go on!* Finally:

"I'm pregnant."

Time and the pleasantly creaking rocker both ceased.

"Wayne?" Letty found a piece of the puzzle. Why hadn't she guessed? What was wrong with her? "Alice . . ."

"Three and a half months. I'm in good shape." Belligerently, Alice continued to stare at Letty as if she could make her mother flinch or look away, but Letty didn't.

"I went to a doctor in Leveret."

"How many times?"

"Twice, so far. Shall I pack?"

And you knew a daughter would come to you one day with the joyful news, and you assumed it would be Cora, and what fun it would be!

Other people's daughters had this misfortune, didn't they? Other people's daughters in families down in Jerusalem, where they didn't know any better. Other people's daughters, whom you felt sorry for (and somewhat superior to); other women's daughters got that way without being married, didn't they? Other women's daughters, never yours.

"Alice, look at me."

"I don't want to."

Letty felt foolish and guilty. Why *hadn't* she guessed it? The signs were obvious—the shakier than usual temperament, the added roundness of breasts and hips. Where had she been? Getting ready for Cora's wedding, dealing with Franklin, upset over Harriet. And it was Alice who'd needed her.

"I want to get rid of it. Patrick tried to talk me out of it."

"Alice—why?"

"Because it's all different now. He's going to want to crawl into a hole and die, that's why! You don't know him. Do you think I want to saddle him with a wife and a child? Now? That's why he was coming back. I wrote to him. We were going to be married. I knew I was pregnant even before he left, but I decided not to tell him. But—"

"Why didn't you tell *me*?"

"I couldn't. Unmarried pregnant females aren't exactly welcome. Are they?" demanded Alice. "I didn't dare. I wanted to wait till he got back. Patrick and Harriet convinced me I should tell you. They walked me over. Saint Patrick, spreading his compassion. Anyway, do you want me to leave?"

"You're not going anywhere. Have we got ourselves so apart that you don't feel you can talk to me?" Letty got up and took Alice's hand. "We'll manage it."

"Manage it?"

"Ayea." Letty nodded and laid a hand on Alice's head. Alice tensed. "Ayea, we'll manage it." Once past the shock and the loss of breath came a numbness, then a return to a kind of reality where logistics had to be taken care of, logistics being the only way to deal with the tumult. "I want you to go to Dr. Alden in the morning. I'll come with you. He's taken care of you since you were a child. There's no point in having a strange doctor in Leveret whom we don't know."

Alice nodded, removed her glasses, put them back on, and sat back on her hands.

"You are going to need your strength," continued Letty. "I don't see that you've been taking proper care of yourself lately. You have more than yourself to think of now. I want you to stay fit."

"I don't want to bring a child into this kind of world. I don't want to burden him. If it hadn't been for me, he wouldn't have been on that train."

"You're not responsible for what happened to him." Letty remembered the night Wayne had provoked Franklin down in the garden, the night Harriet returned from New York. Letty hadn't liked him at all. "He was in a war. What happened could've happened—"

"That's what Patrick said. It's not true. I *am* responsible. I wish I'd never told him. I wish—"

"But he's coming back. Did he say he wanted to marry you, or didn't he?" She had three daughters, but Letty could never have believed she'd be having this kind of discussion with one of them.

"He wrote me he did, but who knows? He's a man of conscience. What else could he say? But *now*— Sure, he's coming back. One quarter gone. Below the knee? Above? Who knows? You don't know him. He was so active. He's a cripple."

Letty watched Alice fight back the tears. *"What a good child she is,"* Sarah used to say. *"She never makes a sound."* It wasn't natural, not at all.

"He'll need you, Alice. No, I don't know him, but I can't imagine—"

"I hate myself."

"Alice . . ." Letty tried to cradle her sitting daughter against her, but Alice got up.

"You blame me, don't you? I don't care what you think—"

403

"Alice, I don't blame you." Impossible to break through that barrier. "What's done is done. A child is a gift of God, no matter the circumstances."

"You sound like Patrick."

"I hope so. I don't understand how you could— I don't want to hear that kind of talk. I don't know whether you and Wayne will be married or not, but I won't have you making that kind of threat. You condemn the killing over there and yet you'd—" Letty couldn't finish the sentence. At a sudden loss, she sat on the bed and tried to collect her thoughts. "Am I understood?" she said finally.

Grateful for the firmness, Alice nodded. "What am I going to do?"

"I told you. We'll manage." It sounded so paltry.

"What am I going to do?"

"Do you love each other?"

Alice nodded.

"Then you'll trust in that. You've always taken the world's problems on your shoulders, Alice, but I don't see any compassion for yourself—"

"I don't feel guilty, Mother." She did. Oh, she did. And hated herself for that, too.

"I didn't say you should."

"Father will throw me out of the house."

"No, he won't." Letty dreaded his reaction. "I'll handle it."

"Did you enjoy Thanksgiving? That'll seem like a tea party."

"I'm going downstairs and get you a glass of port. I said I'd handle it." Once again, Letty went to Alice and tried to take her in her arms, but Alice wouldn't allow it.

Downstairs Harriet asked, "Were you shocked when she told you?"

Patrick nodded. "More so by—"

"She's angry. She's always been angry."

Patrick understood Alice's anger, but her threat to turn it on herself and her unborn child was incomprehensible. "A child is . . . a miracle."

"Passion leads to booties."

"If you're married, it's supposed to. Even so, she can't change anything now."

"She wants the baby. I know she does."

Patrick and Harriet exchanged a glance, as unresolved issues of their own rose suddenly between them. Neither wanted their new-found serenity upset with the potentially volatile subjects of contraception and children. Troubled, Harriet laid her head against his shoulder. Moved by his conviction with Alice, Harriet could now see that what she'd considered Patrick's dogmatic and rigid lack of understanding sprang from a deep reverence for life. But it didn't help her own dilemma. She could never abort a child—but contraception was another matter. Since Thanksgiving, she and Patrick had made love with a regularity that had forced her to see herself in a brand new (and yes, she had to admit, Oh, yes), delightful perspective. She had continued to use her diaphragm.

"I want children, don't you?" Patrick didn't dare ask her if she was still using it.

"Of course. But . . . right this minute?" Lovemaking, she discovered, brought them infinitely closer, yet it didn't necessarily resolve deep-seated differences. "Since you have," she added sexily, "taught me to enjoy the *modus operandi* . . ."

"It's Latin now, is it?" Patrick drew her to him.

". . . I might be able to accept the results with a . . . bit more equanimity."

"Hmmm . . ."

Keep it light was a mutal unspoken need as they held each other and kissed.

"Do you remember," Patrick asked, his throughts turning to Wayne, "the day we saw him off?"

"She said she'd never see him again."

"It's as if she still doesn't believe she will. She talked about him tonight . . . as if he were dead." Patrick held Harriet tighter. A rotten world, Alice had cried, but he wasn't willing to write it off. Her pessimism had fired him.

"How am I going to tell Franklin?" asked Letty, entering the parlor. "Patrick, how am—?" Needing to keep moving, she didn't wait for an answer.

Dissatisfied with herself, she returned upstairs and went to Frankie's room, where Alice lay awake in the dark. "We'll put Frankie in the back hall for now. You should have this room to yourself, then you can have Cora and Sam's when they leave." Letty sat on the edge of the bed and took her daughter's cold hand in hers. "Do the Thibeaus know?" Alice shook her head. "Would you like us to call on them together?" Alice nodded. "No matter what happens, Alice, I am on your side. Are you hearing me? You're a stubborn and foolish child, and you always have been. I can't make hide nor hair of you sometimes, but you're mine and I love you. I have always been on your side and you've never believed it. We'll manage this together. Are you listening?"

"I'm sorry, Mother. . . ." The tiniest of voices. *See how Father is irritated when Cora and Harriet cry? So I'll never cry and then I'll be the favorite.* Oh, how she longed to.

"To tell you the truth, I wondered what I'd do with myself after the holidays. Cora and Sam will be gone . . . Harriet and Patrick shortly thereafter, I'm sure. I'd thought to braid a rug for Cora, but instead I'll start a quilt for my first grandchild—"

"Mother . . ."

405

"Alice . . . dearest. There, there . . . that's right. . . ." Letty took Alice to her, enfolding her against her bosom, knocking that well-fastened chip from her daughter's shoulder as she rocked her. Alice's tears wet Letty's dress, and finally she fell asleep. Letty tucked her in and stayed with her. Then a stomping on the front steps announced Franklin's return and she went down to meet him.

"Father . . ." she began, but didn't dare finish.

"Got time for a cuppa coffee?"

Harriet recognized the voice, turned, and couldn't even say his name she was so stunned.

"I guess not." Heart in his mouth as well, Elliot smiled nervously as early Christmas shoppers on Leveret's main drag eddied around the twosome. There had been several occasions in the last weeks when he'd gone out of his way to put himself in a place where he knew Harriet would be. Needing to talk to her, he always lost his nerve at the last minute.

"Elliot . . ." she finally said as tinsel whipped and fluttered over her head, no more so than her heart, which did an agitated dance of its own.

"Does that mean 'hello'? Or 'Stay away, monster'? I can't tell." The quip hiding his anxiety, he looked guiltily away and wished he hadn't made the attempt. Harriet turned and left.

His urgent "Please, Harriet!" following her, she got halfway down the block, then had to glance back. Elliot was in the same spot. His downcast head caused her to feel ashamed, and she returned.

"It's the King," whispered the hostess of the Puritan Tea Room as the twosome entered a minute later. The restaurant was abuzz with excitement. At the cashier's booth, a radio blared, broken by bursts of static. "It's Edward! He's going to speak on the radio—all the way from London! I don't have a booth. Will that corner do?"

The irony of the game they'd used to play struck them both; neither mentioned it. Ill at ease, they settled themselves at a tiny table closely packed with others and ordered coffee. Anticipatory chatter rose around them, counterpointing and harmonizing with the delicate tinkling of cutlery from the crowded restaurant full of lady shoppers. Harriet stole a quick glance at Elliot and looked quickly away as their eyes met. A lifetime seemed to have passed since the night of her engagement. The memory caused her stomach to knot, and she was relieved when her attention was diverted by two ladies at the next table who were in heated argument.

"Why shouldn't he be allowed to marry Wallis? Isn't a king a human being?"

"Shirl, I'm surprised at you. He accepted a responsibility. Now he wants to welsh."

"Thanks . . . for seeing me." Elliot didn't want Harriet to know how agitated he was, but she sensed the turbulence in him as she returned his tentative smile with a guarded one of her own. Aware of her aloofness, his hand trembled as he dragged on his cigarette.

"Wallis is nothing but an upstart!" voiced their neighbor, as if she'd spoken with her on the party line this morning. It was a familiarity bred naturally of a year's worth of front page news; everyone thought they knew Wallis Simpson.

"Harriet—" Elliot began, then stopped himself. All that he'd rehearsed, he couldn't remember, everything he needed to say was gone. "I guess the whole world must be at their radios," he said instead, wishing she'd look at him, understanding why she couldn't.

"Yes." Battling with humiliating and painful memories, Harriet once again lost herself in the next table's conversation.

"Edward's only good for nightclub work! Did you see the bawling-out Westbrook Pegler gave him in his column?" Voice rising in anticipation at what was shortly to come on the radio, the woman continued: "He's no prince from what I hear. Had several women . . . married, mind you . . . on the string . . ."

"He's not the prince," reminded her companion. "He's the King now."

"Well, he was the prince . . ."

"No longer, I guess," whispered Elliot, leaning on his elbows, his eyes pleading, "as far as you're concerned."

"I—" Harriet didn't know what to say but was relieved of the obligation as a "*Shhhhh!*" echoed around the restaurant and the hostess turned the radio higher. A hush fell, and they heard above the crackle of the static the slow, measured words of Edward himself:

"*. . . At long last I am able to say a few words of my own. I never wanted to withhold anything, but until now it has not been constitutionally possible for me to speak. . . .*"

A storm somewhere out in the Atlantic caused the transmission to be interrupted with a burst of static. Exclamations of dismay rose from the crowd, some of whom left their tables to get closer to the radio as the hostess frantically, yet delicately, tried to tune the broadcast back. Service had long since been abandoned; the waitresses had left their stations.

"*I have found it impossible to carry the heavy burden of responsibility and to discharge my duties as King, as I should wish to do . . .*"

In a trance Harriet found herself rising, taking a few steps toward the radio, others with her.

"*. . . without the help and support of the woman I love. And now we all have a new king. I wish him and you, his people, happiness and prosperity with all my heart. God bless you all! God save the King!*"

Stunned silence followed as people looked at one another and purses were snapped open and hankies brought to eyes. Aware they'd all shared

407

something momentous, the hush continued as they returned to their tables. They might never cross paths again, but here they were—bonded together in the grip of a passion from across the sea, Edward's immortal passion for a mortal woman, an unimaginable sacrifice, which caused the men to feel romantic and strong, or humbled, perhaps jealous, while the women either imagined they were Wallis and, depending on the state of their relations with their husbands, were alternately hopeful or saddened.

Even the lady who'd expressed her dislike of both Wallis and the King was dabbing at her eyes. "A romance made in heaven," she whispered as Harriet, caught in the spell and head held high, returned to the table and Elliot.

"Well . . ." he murmured, moved, wishing he could love a woman and staring wistfully at her, as confused as ever by his feelings.

Harriet wondered if any man would ever love her, could ever want her, as the King loved Mrs. Simpson. In the asking came the answer: Patrick did. The thought made her feel suddenly strong, calmer, and much less nervous with Elliot.

"A romance made in heaven," she heard him say, echoing their neighbor, and she nodded. It was what she'd thought they'd had together. Yet her relationship with Elliot seemed spun of baby's breath and illusion compared to the bonfire between herself and her husband. Patrick loved her, and Elliot hadn't. She guessed, as far as the latter was concerned, it wasn't all that simple, for he was more than ever a mystery.

"I wanted it to be. I *did*," he insisted, then lapsed into silence. "I'm sorry, Harriet," he said a moment later. The simple dignity of his declaration moved her, but she couldn't pretend that none of it had happened.

"I guess it's not enough," he said.

"I—"

"I am, though. I've had so many conversations in my head with you—trying to explain, but—"

"You don't have to."

"I want to. If you'd listen. I don't see any reason why you should. Not after . . ." Once again he lapsed off and she recognized his expression— that of a frightened animal ready to bolt. *"Please,"* he said suddenly.

She had no wish to relive any of it with him, had no need of explaining, wanted no churning of her insides, but Elliot's urgency caused her to nod. "All right," she said, and stepped outside herself and watched the two of them in a corner of the Puritan.

He didn't know where to begin. "I guess you think I tried to put one over on you. I guess I did." Hopelessness attacked him, and he was silent. "Do you love him?"

"Yes."

"You look terrific. Marriage must be agreeing with you."

She realized it was important to her that she make it known to him.

408

"It is." Confused as to what he wanted from her, she waited, but he stared at his coffee cup.

"Are you happy? I never have been. Sometimes when I was drunk, but it was all an act. Are you happy?"

"Yes."

"I'm glad. Maybe I'm not. I'm sorry, I—" His eyes went to the mural around the four walls, and he hid among the black-hatted Pilgrims and Indians. "When I came back, I called you."

"Alice said you did."

"You wouldn't come to the phone."

"No. Where did you go?"

"Boston. Stayed at the Ritz. Even at my worst, I've got style." He wanted to tell her of what those four days had been like, four days of drunken horror, fantasies of killing himself, faceless bodies; needed to confess everything and receive her absolution and forgiveness. She would make it better. A part of him knew she couldn't—it was his responsibility to do that for himself, but the task seemed impossible.

"The next time I called, Alice told me you were in New York and had married Patrick. I'll never forget her voice. Cold as ice. Anyway, congratulations. No, it's the groom you congratulate, isn't it? But he's in town leading a rebellion. You didn't waste any time."

The deliberate provocation caused Harriet to collect her purse and get up. "*I'm sorry,*" Elliot pleaded, rising himself. "Please," he added, "don't go."

She hesitated, but his apology caused her to sit down. Wary again, she took a sip of coffee.

"I'm so nervous," Elliot whispered, taking a quick gasp of breath. "I can't seem to say what I— I *wanted* to make a go of it with you. I was scared. I didn't want to hurt you. You're the last person in the world I'd want to— You were my only friend." The sudden rush of words halted just as abruptly. The large, dark iris of her eyes and the shape of her mouth reminded him of Frankie, and he looked quickly away.

"The reason I called that morning was to ask you to give me another chance. Would you have?"

Harriet paused but knew she had no choice but to shake her head. A chatty waitress bustled by with coffee, diverting both of them. Fingers doing a staccato tapping on the table and eyes glistening with tears, Elliot turned away to the wall again.

"That night . . . I don't remember much of that night. I don't even know who he was—"

"Elliot—"

"I never know who any of them are. That night—I thought I was crazy. Dr. Moeller says I wanted you to catch me. I don't understand what he means. Maybe I do. He said that was my way of telling you."

409

"Dr. Moeller? Are you ill?"

"He says I am." A hint of Elliot's old irony leaked through the self-loathing. "Dr. Moeller is my psychoanalyst. All the best people have them. Very fashionable. Twice a week in Louisburg Square in Boston. Picturesque. You'd love it. I read about him in the paper and went to see him. I knew I had to do something. Get a grip, as you'd say. I almost drove the car off the bridge. I— Dad's paying for him. He doesn't like it. Cripples are supposed to be able to solve their own problems. Dr. Moeller wants to cure me. That's why I'm there. *You* were supposed to be the cure. I'm so sorry. . . ."

She felt his eyes on her and had to raise hers. No matter what she'd just heard, she couldn't help be moved. None of Elliot's quips and clowning seemed available; those defenses he always hid behind were down, and all she saw was naked misery.

"Elliot . . ." she began and didn't know what to say. His vulnerability had always loosened hers, but this was different. She'd never loved him, not really, she'd told herself in those terrible days after her engagement. To ease the pain, she'd insisted that Elliot was nothing but a gorgeous fantasy. Her relationship had more to do with his father than with the son. The latter might have truth in it, but Harriet found she couldn't deny the former. Surprising feeling, protective feeling and her old empathy for Elliot rose in her and she reached across the table and took his hand.

"Do you hate me?"

"No," she replied quickly, discovering it was gone. Had thought she always would, but the wound seemed healed. Had Patrick done it? "Of course I don't." The journey from numbness to betrayal and fury and on to forgiveness had been completed, its swiftness surprising her.

"Are you sure?"

"Cross my heart," she replied, smiling to reassure him. His fingers entwined with hers, gripping her hand tightly, and he took another breath and shut his eyes to try and prevent the tears from running down his cheeks.

"Elliot . . ." she murmured, feeling she'd weep herself.

"I haven't finished," he whispered, removing his hand and blowing his nose. "I haven't even started." He took a sip of coffee. As if asking her permission to continue, his eyes sought hers over the rim of the cup.

"There were so many times I . . . wanted to tell you. But I couldn't. How could I? I wanted to *try*. I wanted it to come true. It wasn't just his fault. He wanted what was best for me. I hate him, but I guess he did . . ."

If Harriet had forgiven Elliot, Phelps was another story. "He's an out-and-out bastard as far as I'm concerned. But I think what you say is true. Underneath, he cares for you."

"No. Respectability—that's what it means to him. But I wanted more than that. I wanted to love you. I still feel like I do. I don't exist for him any

410

more. He's so taken up with what's happening— But even if it weren't going on, he's written me off. He looks right through me. You know that look of his. You aren't even there."

"He was responsible for the window, wasn't he?"

"Sure. I guess so. He doesn't talk to me about it. He thinks Patrick has a vendetta against him. He's become obsessed with both of you. He looks out and sees them all waving *The Spectator* at him. He'll never negotiate. He has three weeks of back orders piled up and he heard this morning that the union has started to picket his Methuen plant. But he won't give in. He'll let it all go up in smoke first. I don't want to talk about that. Harriet, can I be cured?"

"I don't know. I—" Flustered, she didn't know how to respond. "What does Dr.—?"

"Moeller. He says I can. He says he can do it."

"What do you say to him?" she asked, hoping she didn't sound too naive. But she felt very naive.

"Everything. He just listens. Yesterday he told me I should try not to hurt my parents. My mother doesn't know I go. She doesn't know anything about me. Dad found out a couple of years ago. When he paid some blackmail. Are you shocked?"

"Knowing you, I think you'd like me to be," she replied, trying to get her balance.

"I don't know why . . . I'm the way I am."

Neither of them were aware of the restaurant emptying out, nor of the hour that passed as Elliot revealed the struggle that had caused his life to be such an unrelenting torment. The dull and disembodied voice in which he recounted his past, starting with Dobie and moving to the present, made the agony all the more telling for Harriet, who listened mesmerized and vowed never to complain of her lot again. Her own pain, the recent weeks of turmoil seemed infinitesimal, past disappointments paltry, in the face of what she was hearing.

Elliot had to move and they left the Puritan. Harriet knew she should get back to the office, but she couldn't leave him. He continued to talk, words pouring out as they walked through the crowds of shoppers and ended up on a bench on the Leveret Common.

"Sometimes . . . I thought I'd explode. Those were the times I went to Boston . . . hoping I'd get arrested . . . beaten up. . . . You used to ask me why I had no hope. Now you know. . . ."

The tour he took her on through an underworld she'd never dreamed existed was beyond her comprehension, but it was the lack of love that saddened her the most. Mute and humbled with Elliot's suffering, she felt helpless. All her instincts for pragmatic solutions and problem solving seemed impotent in the face of the reality of those years of loneliness, hiding and guilt. How confident she'd been that she could solve the

411

enigma that was Elliot; all that had been revealed was the tip of the iceberg, she realized, until today.

"So . . ." he said finally, "you were engaged to a fairy."

Exhausted, he wept in her arms while, nearby, workmen erected a crèche on the grass. The orderly pounding of their hammers and jovial byplay felt reassuring to Harriet, who was at a loss for words as she held her former lover and was struck by the power he continued to wield.

"I shouldn't have burdened you. I'm sorry. I seem to spend all my time telling you I'm sorry. You're well rid of me. . . ."

Yet a moment later, as they left the Common, he asked her if it was possible they could still be friends. Haunted by what he'd told her, she nodded quickly. "You'll be the only one," he said, and she thought of Frankie.

"He said you hadn't been by the Classic lately," she remarked casually, as a thought crept up on her that she tried to avoid.

"I haven't been much of anywhere," he replied, reading her mind. Salvaging whatever was left of his dignity, he knew he could never tell her about his painful love for her brother.

"You should call him," she said, unable to rid her mind of a nagging speculation.

"Maybe I will," he replied and set out to rid her of it. "I have an idea—why don't you fix me up with Frankie? Naw," he grinned quickly, "afraid he's not my type. Wish he were. He's a good kid."

The lie worked. Harriet was shocked at the suggestion but relieved with Elliot's denial. The scary moment passed for both of them.

"Ahhh, well," he said a moment later as they reached his car, "what did I offer you anyway—except a life of luxury you didn't really want."

"I wouldn't have minded it," she replied, amazed it was possible to banter again after the last hour. But she was more than willing.

"I would have been a lot of trouble. But I'm fascinating. You'll have to admit."

"I admit."

As he started the car, Elliot said, "Will you and Patrick invite me to your cottage on Middle-Class Lane?"

"Careful," she warned, but smiled.

"I'd like to come."

"You will."

"How's Patrick in the whoopee department?"

"I certainly don't intend to tell you," she replied, and laughed as Elliot rolled his eyes. She had an urgent longing to be in Patrick's arms.

"What are friends for? Does he know . . . what happened?" he added, his smile fading. Harriet nodded.

"He always loathed me. Now—"

She shook her head. "He's not like that."

"Tell him what I told you long ago—I'm harmless. A danger only to yours truly. Will you tell him?"

"Stop browbeating yourself. It's a bad habit."

"Thanks, Mrs. Flynn. Who would—as you would say—have thunk it? You're pensive," he added a moment later. Her own reality returning, Harriet nodded. "Everything. The business at the mill. The pressure we're under. I was trying to raise us some money over here today. We've lost all our advertisers. Even Gas and Electric. They were with us right from the start. Now they're threatening to turn out the lights."

"I have savings. I could help."

"I *wasn't* fishing."

"I know that. I mean it. I don't want you to go under. Don't you love the irony? The boss's son supporting the strike?"

"No."

"But I'm on your side."

"Tell your father. Convince him to negotiate. Don't think I'm not tempted, but I borrowed money from him once, remember? I think he thought I was a commodity."

"I'm not my father. *Let me*! I want to. For many reasons. Let's start with guilt."

"No."

"How about a belated wedding present? A christening gift in advance?"

"Aren't you funny. No, thanks. You don't owe me anything."

"Awww . . ."

"How would I explain it to Patrick?"

"But it's for a good cause. Don't tell him. Look!" he exclaimed, as they started the approach to the bridge over the falls. Below on the Boston and Maine Railroad tracks men on flatbed cars were tossing down bundles of Christmas trees. Elliot pulled over. "Look at that—there must be thousands."

"Elliot, please—I'm anxious to get back."

"So what are you going to do?" he asked as they pulled away.

"Sell my body to the highest bidder."

"Yes, you were always good at selling. Jam, wasn't it?" he added, grinning. *"Christmas trees! You can sell Christmas trees!"*

"You're insane," she replied as a light clicked on.

"I think the woman is common," Letty remarked, serving the scalloped potatoes, "and no amount of sentimental balderdash is going to

413

change my mind. Two husbands behind her—and still living—and now she's lassoed the King, the poor man. She has no morals."

Talk went round the Hoskins' table that evening, where everyone was seated to dinner.

Morals? Alice wondered if divorcées and unwed mothers got lumped in the same rowboat and set adrift. "Would you feel better if the husbands were dead?" she asked Letty, who paused slightly and knew she'd put her foot in her mouth. Quickly she sent a reassuring glance at Alice, glad it was returned. Sam smiled. He liked Alice's tongue, but from a distance. He nodded in agreement as Cora said, "Mother's right. Mrs. Simpson's upset a whole country and probably pulled the wool over the poor King's eyes. Is that moral?"

"Moral?" asked Harriet. "All this talk of morals is giving me indigestion." She and Alice exchanged a quick look, then Harriet glanced at Franklin who was hidden behind the paper. Letty had still not found a way, nor the courage to tell him about Alice.

"Harriet—you're the one told us she was offered a movie contract. Doesn't that just prove the kind of woman she is?"

"Really, 'Eleanor,' " retorted Harriet, "she was *offered* a contract, yes. But that's not her fault. I happen to admire her. There's the phone—it must be Patrick." She reached behind her from the table, but it was someone from church calling Letty.

"Where did you hear the broadcast?" Frankie asked.

"At the Puritan . . ." She had decided it would only complicate matters to tell them with whom; they wouldn't understand. There was no necessity of mentioning Elliot—or the money he'd loaned her. No one need know at the moment, including Patrick. At some future date he could be told that Elliot had been the one who'd come to the rescue.

"What is this 'big news' you have for us, Harriet?" asked Letty.

"I want to wait until Patrick gets here." Harriet grinned. "But," she added tantalizingly, "you're all going to be called upon. I'm going to need everyone's help."

Franklin cast an eye over the top of the paper that kept him insulated from the mealtime pandemonium.

"Everyone stopped work at the bakery," said Sam as the discussion of the King's speech continued. "At the Puritan, too," added Harriet. "We just sat there enthralled."

"Give us a hint of your news, Harriet." Cora was very curious. "And then we'll tell you ours, won't we, Sam?" Letty's eyes widened. Franklin looked over the paper again. Cora blushed and pealed an embarrassed laugh, realizing what everyone was thinking. "Oh, not— You tell them, Sam," she giggled. He was red-faced, too. "Mr. Fazzi's given me a raise," he began, and then Cora picked up the ball again. "Two whole dollars a week! So we're going to take those three dear rooms at Mrs. Drummond's.

It'll all have to be redone, Mother. Let's get out the wallpaper books this evening. Tiny patterns—because the rooms are small. . . ."

Sam nodded. Small or not, he couldn't wait to get away.

"Here he is!" Excited, Harriet waved as Patrick and Albatross arrived in the front hall, the former slipping quietly with muttered apologies into his place at the table, the latter wagging his tail in greeting.

"You go into the kitchen, Albatross." Letty pointed. "Your supper's in your dish."

"Now that you're here, Patrick, we get to hear Harriet's surprise."

"Let him get his breath, Cora." Harriet tried to catch Patrick's eye and couldn't. She passed him a plate of ham and scalloped potatoes, adding a dollop of Letty's mustard pickle.

"Delicious," he commented, taking a bite. He'd had a few beers with Paul and Meyer at the Depot Tavern; he hoped the family didn't see he had a buzz on. He glanced at Franklin and thought he understood why men became drunkards. Gert had called him to report that a friend had seen Harriet and Elliot in Leveret. Patrick had brushed off his mother's insinuations; but it was a call he'd rather not have received.

Sensing her husband's agitation, Harriet cocked her head, asking, *What?*

"Father Gahaghan wants us out. He's afraid of the violence spreading." Once again this morning, as it had for the last three days, fighting had broken out at the mill. The strikers had tried to prevent anyone from entering, and the Leveret police had restored order and closed the gates.

"His precious piece of real estate," Harriet muttered. "He wouldn't," she told the others, "let Patrick use the hall upstairs for meetings, either. He should be ashamed of himself. How long do we have?"

"Today would've been fine with him," replied Patrick, who felt thoroughly harassed.

"Is it true about Curley?" Alice asked. Patrick nodded. "He says he'll give Phelps an answer within twenty-four hours. If the National Guard comes in, we have no chance. They'll make sure the mill opens and it'll be back to business as usual."

"He's not going to send the Guard against a bunch of fellow Democrats," Alice commented.

"He will if he has to. It can't go on like this."

"I've come up with a plan!"

"Tell us," urged Cora.

"I'm going into business! The business of Christmas! I've bought five hundred Christmas trees, and they'll be delivered tomorrow. We'll sell them and make a profit of five hundred dollars between now and Christmas . . ."

"What?" cried Cora. Questions and chatter rose up, and Patrick blinked and tried to dislodge a piece of ham stuck in his throat. "Sounds

415

terrific," he gasped as Frankie slapped him on the back. "Terrific," he repeated, seeing Harriet's face alive with excitement and triumph. What the hell was she talking about? Christmas trees? Five hundred Christmas trees??? What the godammit to hell was she talking about?

". . . and if Father Gahaghan wants to evict us, we'll rent someplace else. *And* I'll pay off Smith and Houchins and get the paper printed properly again. Save *The Spectator*! We'll get some of our advertisers back . . . we'll be able to continue to support the strikers and—"

"Where did you get the money?" asked Letty, who could tell that Patrick was dumbfounded.

"I got them for a song . . . a mere hundred dollars. Twenty cents a tree and I'll be able to sell them for four or five times that. I got them on credit," Harriet continued, skating swiftly past thin ice. "I have two weeks to pay for them." It had been Elliot's idea that she say she got credit; a fib in a good cause and no one could get upset.

Patrick got the hiccups.

"Pour Patrick some more water," suggested Letty, glancing at Franklin, who found himself suddenly concerned for his son-in-law's welfare.

"Well? What do you think? Are you pleased?" Harriet sensed Patrick wasn't as caught up in her excitement as she wanted him to be.

"Sure," he mustered. "Just trying to get . . . it all clear."

"Here's the plan. The trees are coming tomorrow. The barn and the driveway will be our headquarters. I want to ask Teresa if we can use the parking lot behind her shop to sell. I want to make wreaths and swags, and we'll decorate them and sell them, too. There's no end to it!" The sap from the trees had risen in her; she felt *alive*. "Cora," she continued excitedly, "you'll be in charge of the wreaths. You're so talented that way. Alice, I'll need a few attractive signs painted with balls and holly. I'll need everyone's help *and* I intend to pay everyone. You'll all get . . . five cents for every tree you sell. How does that sound?"

"Excuse me . . ." said Patrick. Albatross had finished and wanted out. So did his master. Patrick and the dog headed for the back hall. "I know this is news to you," Alice called after him, "but maybe she'll pull it off."

"I think it's asinine," he called back and disappeared.

"Of course I will," insisted Harriet. "Patrick . . . !"

"She will," nodded Frankie. "I think it's a great idea. Did you hear about her gingerbread caper, Sam?"

"Gingerbread?"

"She made a batch of it and took it to a football game when she was ten . . ." Frankie began to laugh.

". . . in a basket with a red-checkered cloth," continued Cora.

"But she was too embarrassed to call out 'Get your hot gingerbread!' "

"So she ate it all herself."

"I did not," replied Harriet, looking after Patrick and worried. "I gave half of it to Rummy Johnny."

Franklin cleared his throat. "Was all this . . . news to Patrick?"

"Yes. I wanted to surprise him."

"I think you did," Letty commented. "Ayea, I think you did."

"Why do I have a sense I'm being given the third degree?" Harriet threw down her napkin and followed her mother into the pantry.

"Surely, Harriet, you understand about a person's pride—"

"I have mine, too. And if he wants to sulk—"

"But to go behind his back . . ."

"You did the same. Have you forgotten Uncle George and the money you borrowed?"

"And you condemned me for it," retorted Letty. "Have *you* forgotten?"

"I was young. I wouldn't now. If you had to do it again, would you?"

Stymied, Letty had to nod. "So would I," said Harriet firmly, "so I trust you understand." She returned to the dining room and wished Patrick would come back. Debating going after him, she was confused by his attitude. Asinine? It was a brilliant solution to their financial problems.

"You're in the *Eagle*," Franklin said to Alice, discovering her letter to the editor, as other sparks began to fly.

"What about?" asked Cora, clearing plates and looking over her father's shoulder.

"Nothing anybody's interested in," Alice replied.

"Oh," sighed Cora, "the war again." She gave Franklin a quick peck.

"The war again," mimicked Alice.

"*I'm* interested." Harriet shot a look at Cora. "If Sam had got hurt over there, you might be, too."

"But why should Sam—?"

"But why should Sam?" echoed Alice, seething.

"Stop being a martyr, Alice," cried Cora, very distressed. "You know how sorry I am about what happened to Wayne. You act as if it's our fault. I don't think that's fair."

"Skip it."

"I don't think Alice meant to imply that, Cora," began Letty but was interrupted by Franklin. "If you can explain to me," he asked, looking at Alice, "why we should"—he paused and read a part of her letter— " 'abandon our posture of neutrality and give aid to—' "

"Because they were German planes that bombed that train. Did you know that? Donated to Franco by Hitler. Nazi planes and Nazi bombs. Do you know how many congressmen, how many editorials are telling us we should remain friends with Hitler and not get involved? When are people going to wake up? And here we are . . . cozy in Jericho. Why do I bother?" she added, lashing out at him. "If you don't understand, you never will.

417

Let's talk about Cora's chintz. We can all agree on that. Men are dying and being mutilated. Let's pretend we don't know why. Pass the pudding."

"Alice," cautioned Letty. "That's disrespectful. We all feel terrible about Wayne. Including your father."

"Disrespect? He hasn't *earned* my respect."

"It's his own damn fault." Ignited himself, Franklin glared at Alice. "I told him that night," he went on, the memory of his battle with her fanatic of a boyfriend making him all the madder, "that he was misguided—"

"Father," interjected Harriet. "He's lost his leg."

"I know that. I can't bring it back, can I? I'm sorry he lost . . ."

Not wanting to hear any more or get sucked into another argument, Harriet got up quickly, squeezed Alice's shoulder and went to find Patrick.

". . . his leg," continued Franklin, angry at her for leaving. "If he'd stayed where he belonged, he—"

"That's obscene!" Alice rose up, trembling. Letty got up, too. Franklin sent her a "What did I do?" look as Letty tried to calm Alice, who turned on her father in fury.

"Your values stink. I think *you* stink. Morals? Is that what we were talking about earlier? You have none. You're not sorry for anything. I hate you. Do you hear me? I hate you." Alice began to sob and started from the dining room, then turned again on Franklin, and Letty knew what was coming.

"You son of a bitch!"

"Alice, don't . . ."

"Alice," cried Cora.

"Son of a bitch!"

Franklin went far away. His face was whiter than his napkin.

"You son of a bitch—I'm pregnant."

"Asinine!" Patrick repeated bluntly to Harriet, who found him in the barn in Alice's studio. "Christmas trees? A struggle is going on in town, and you buy Christmas trees? People can't afford to buy food and—"

"They always need a Christmas tree," Harriet rebutted, stung with his criticism. "Patrick, what's wrong?"

"Who says—Elliot?"

"What?"

"You heard me."

"Stop shouting at me."

"What were you doing with Elliot?"

"I ran into him in Leveret. There's nothing wrong with that, is there?"

"And spent an hour with him at the Puritan?"

"Were you following me?"

"My mother said—"

"I should have known. We always have your mother to contend with, don't we?"

"Don't try and change the subject."

"Why are you looking at me like I've boiled a baby? Have I committed another sin?"

They both stared at each other, hoping it wouldn't escalate.

"Patrick," she pleaded, "don't I have a right to have a cup of coffee with . . . with Elliot? Or anybody I choose—"

"No. I don't want to have anything to do with Elliot Phelps, and I don't want you to, either."

Harriet bit her lip and tried to be conciliatory. "I've come up with a wonderful idea that'll buy us some time. Aren't I allowed to help? I've always been good at selling. I'm not giddy. I can make a success of this. Shapiro isn't going to support us indefinitely. The phone's being disconnected and we don't have a dime. Don't you think I know you're at your wit's end? I did this for *us*."

"Do you want to be my wife—or don't you?"

"There you go again. What's that supposed to mean?" she retorted, hurt at his refusal to understand her motives. "You might as well know," she went on, inflamed, "since you're damning me to hell anyway. It was Elliot who loaned me the money."

Even as she said it, Harriet knew it was a mistake. Patrick flushed and walked out of the barn, almost colliding with Alice. "Elliot gave her the money," he said, and repeated it, dazed.

"It's a business deal!" Harriet called after him. "Alice, what is it?" she asked, attention diverted by her sister, who was trembling and holding onto herself.

"I told him."

"Told—?"

"Father. I got so angry, I told him."

"O my God, the house must be smoking. Patrick, did you hear?"

"What happened?" he asked, joining Harriet, their own quarrel momentarily suspended, and both concerned for Alice.

"I feel better than I ever did. I'm fine. He deserved it. I feel fine. I hope he rots in hell."

"Alice—"

"I suppose that's childish. I don't care. At least it's out now and everyone knows. He left the house. Cora's weeping. Mother's doing the dishes. What about you two? I could referee. I don't have anything else to do."

"There's no need. I'm sure Patrick will understand when he thinks about—"

419

"No, I won't . . . I don't . . ."

"Why don't you?" Harriet pleaded. She turned to Alice. "Elliot wanted to help and—"

"Elliot Phelps?" Alice was as flabbergasted as Patrick. "I'm getting a sense of déjà vu."

"Thanks, Alice," Harriet responded dryly.

"You lied to me," Patrick exploded. "You said you got credit." He turned to Alice. "Didn't she? Or am I crazy?"

"Yes, I lied. I knew you wouldn't understand. Your attitude proves—"

"I can't win, can I? You don't want me to. I never do with you."

"How can you say that?" Wounded, Harriet tried to explain to Alice. "I told him that I did it for *him*. For *us*."

"There is no us."

"Don't try to make me feel guilty."

"You are guilty. Guiltier than hell. Isn't she?"

"Listen, folks—" began Alice, caught in the cross fire.

"You Catholics and your precious guilt! Do you sprinkle it on your oatmeal?"

"How can you . . . ?" began Patrick, red-faced, "take money from that—" He stopped himself from saying the word.

"I assured Elliot you weren't small-minded. I can see I was wrong."

"You were wrong. After what he did? Where's your pride?"

"That's my business. How can you still be jealous of Elliot? He's frightened and he wants to be your friend. Don't you know he's envious of *you*? He wants to be in your shoes. Everything you've become, he'd like to be. Don't you know that? Plus you've got me—but you're losing me fast. Where's your compassion?"

"I hate everything he stands for. He never did a day's work in his life. He's a sap. Since when have you been so interested in strays? Or anyone else, for that matter. Besides yourself."

Patrick walked away again. Angrily he called Albatross and went down into the garden and struggled with himself. "Save *The Spectator*?" he called sarcastically a moment later as he returned to the sisters, who'd gone into the barn to get warm. "Are you nuts? Even if I were flat on my back, I wouldn't take money from Elliot Phelps. Can't you understand that? How do I explain it? Do I tell Meyer that Phelps is paying for the paper?"

"It's Elliot. It's not his father."

"Why didn't you ask me?" Patrick demanded. "Are you my wife or aren't you?"

"That's your favorite question. No. Not if it means a ring in my nose. I thought you knew that."

"Look—" interjected Alice, but neither Patrick nor Harriet paid any attention to her and didn't even notice when she left.

"It means you're Mrs. Patrick Flynn, that's what it means," he shouted, unhappy she had him on the defensive. "It's very simple."

"I'm Harriet Hoskins," she shot back. "And I don't intend to play second fiddle to anyone. Patrick," she pleaded, knowing they were both going way too far. He shook his head and felt betrayed. Nor was he alone. How could you do this to me? lingered at the heart of Harriet's anger, too. Both of them were consumed with an absolute amazement that the other could be so totally lacking in understanding. If you loved me, you'd understand, but since you don't, you obviously don't love me, and how can you *not* love me after the closeness we've shared, the intimacies exchanged, the vulnerable parts exposed?—and with variations, it was the same for each, but worse for Harriet, who felt she'd gone out on the most fragile of limbs for Patrick, only to find he'd chopped it down.

"Why are you so suspicious of me?" she pleaded. "I'm not your mother—"

"What's my mother—?"

"I've tried to help! Why can't you see that? After what I've done for you. . . . !"

"You think you're so hot," Patrick muttered, jolted with a mysterious desire to make love to her. "No," Harriet said, sensing it, and pushing him away when he tried to take her in his arms. "Absolutely not," she added. "I have something to say. You trumpet 'brotherly love' in the paper. You're all for decency and fighting for what's right and preaching equality in print, but with me you're still a reactionary."

"You're crazy."

"No, I'm not. You called Coughlin a tyrant and Phelps, too, but you have a lot of both of them in you, you conservative bastard!"

"Go to hell," he yelled. Shocked with his own curse, he left her, hurrying blindly back toward the house and leaping up the piazza steps, three at a time.

"I have liberty in my bones," shouted Harriet, running after him. "That's the tradition *I* come from. Patrick—come back here!" she called, entering into the back hallway, bursting out laughing at the ridiculousness of it all as she gasped for breath and leaned against the banister. "I want a kiss," she whispered up the stairs, exhilarated and needing him to come to his senses. But Patrick had disappeared into their room.

"That's better," commented Letty, overhearing as she entered the back hallway.

"Don't misunderstand, Mother. I still think he's an ass. Just think," Harriet added, "I almost swallowed hook, line and sinker your treacly philosophy of 'comfort in the past, look to the future.' Why, you've turned into Louisa May Alcott before my very eyes! Compromise? I don't intend to tiptoe around holding my breath"—she gave a startled Letty a quick hug—"as you have. Rule the roost and not let him know? No, thanks. Not

421

for me. You do it your way, and I'll do it mine. *That* was my mistake. I shouldn't have lied to him. My only mistake. *Patrick*," she hollered up the stairs.

"Harriet, stop shouting."

"Why? This house is used to it. Wouldn't be home without it. Is Father back? Don't worry—Alice is right. It's best that it's all out in the open. I'll try and talk to him." Once again, Harriet peered up the stairs. "*I don't intend to sacrifice myself on the altar of any man's pride,*" she yelled, cupping hands to mouth to make herself heard. Surely he'd appreciate it. Grinning and wanting him to make love to her, she blew Letty a kiss. "I have fences to mend," she said, a glint in her eye as she ran upstairs and found Patrick packing.

"*Patrick . . . what . . . ?*"

Methodically he placed each rolled-up pair of socks in his battered case as if his life depended on it. He wanted her to stop him.

"Cancel the trees."

"I will not," Harriet replied, the ultimatum infuriating her again.

"Cancel them."

"Stop giving orders."

"Sell them with Elliot then."

It was both their faults—even though Letty might have disagreed with the word—but the stakes were too high for each of them and couldn't be avoided, no matter how they both might have wanted to.

It ended badly. It ended with Patrick slapping her, and a part of him dying as he did. It ended so badly that Harriet told him she was leaving him, called Elliot and asked him to drive her into Boston, took the *Night Owl* to New York City and went to Virginia.

23 Harriet never forgot the eerie scene she returned to at a little after seven in the evening of the next day. Even the train seemed to anticipate trouble ahead. Slowing down in an unaccustomed place a mile out of Jericho, it inched in fits and starts along the river, blowing its whistle, while passengers pressed their noses to the windows, wondering what was happening.

Harriet noticed that Rummy Johnny wasn't in his usual place at the depot and the parking lot was filled with the gray-green trucks of the National Guard. The first one off the train, she almost lost her footing, for her eyes were drawn to the mill, its red-brick façade bathed in a search-light. Patrick was in there. Harriet had called Alice from New York this morning and was told that *The Spectator* had been broken into and ran-sacked and Patrick was in the mill. When Phelps had tried to reopen, fifty of them, with Patrick and Marienetti in the lead, had surprised the police, rushed inside and held it fortress.

"Harriet—here!" Alice had been waiting for her sister and broke away from friends to greet her. "Welcome to Jericho. *That* was a short trip. We're on the map, as you can see." Cheeks pink from the cold as well as exhilaration, Alice pointed to the Movietone News crew whose cameras were stilled for the moment. "You should have seen them earlier. It was a madhouse here. Reporters were lined up three deep in the tavern and also in the depot. Some of them had to run up to Noonan's."

"It was in the afternoon papers in New York."

"The battle? More of a skirmish, actually."

Momentarily stunned at the sight of the largest crowd she'd ever seen in Jericho, Harriet was speechless. The mass filled the intersection of River and South Main, held back by a line of uneasy guardsmen in uniform who ringed the mill, their breath issuing in tendrils of vapor as they stamped their feet on the pavement to keep warm.

Alice filled her in quickly. The Leveret police had been ordered to attack, and about twenty-five of them stormed the mill, firing buckshot. The men inside rained soda pop bottles and bobbins down on them, and a cheer went up as the police retreated. And the reporters had dashed to the

423

phones, and the story went out over the wire services, on the radio news, and would be on the newsreels in a couple of days.

"He's fine," Alice went on. "Don't worry. They're fine. A few stings of buckshot. Shortly after, Curley called in the Guard, and they've been here for about four hours. God, it's *exciting*," she cried, trying to be heard above the blare of the union sound truck and the buzz of the crowd. "Nothing like it's ever happened! They caught everyone completely by surprise this morning. You should put a little more pancake over that eye," she added. "Talk about plums!"

"How do you know he's—?"

"Relax. They're OK. There was so much confusion tonight, Shapiro managed to get food rushed into them. We were told they're in great spirits, playing cards and determined to hold out until Phelps negotiates with Shapiro. The rumor is the Guard's going to try and take the mill in the morning."

"Take it? You mean by force?"

"Any way they have to."

"Can I talk to him?" Harriet asked, her eyes riveted on the mill, which looked unreal in the garish light.

"Talk to him? I thought you left him."

"I did what I had to and I'd do it again," she replied stoutly, feeling alternately guilty and not guilty. "Don't be flip," she added quickly. "Why can't I talk—?"

"Because Phelps had the phones cut off. He wants to isolate them."

"Is Phelps here?"

"Are you kidding? Apparently he got out by the hair of his chinny-chin-chin this A.M., along with his supervisors and the Pinkertons."

The sisters pushed their way through the milling crowd until they reached the line of guardsmen, whose solid phalanx of backs prevented them from going further. An occasional vehicle patrolled up and down the street under the Christmas tinsel which sparkled ironically overhead.

"Teresa!"

"Harriet—where've you been?"

The two women embraced. Teresa caught sight of Harriet's eye and wished she hadn't. "She ran into a door," grinned Alice, "of the Irish variety. Just as you try and shut them, they swing back."

"I had . . . to go out of town," Harriet replied coolly, but there was no point in trying to outfox Teresa, and so she admitted she and Patrick had had a fight and she'd gone to New York. "But I'm back," she insisted, glancing apprehensively across the street to the mill, "and he doesn't even know I'm here. He must think I'm a monster. How will I let him know?"

"I'm wondering who the monster is," murmured Teresa, with another look at the eye.

"I probably deserved it. No," she corrected herself, "—I didn't. Women are always too ready to accept the guilt."

"What was it about, dear? If you don't mind my asking?"

"About?" Staring at the mill, Harriet couldn't remember. "Christmas trees . . ." It seemed ludicrous.

"Christmas trees?"

"By the way, they got delivered this morning," Alice said. "We're up to our proverbial ass in Christmas trees!"

Harriet ignored her sister's sarcasm. "I should've *been* here. Supposing he'd got hurt? Supposing—?"

"But he isn't," Teresa soothed. "And you *are* here."

"*Look!*" cried several people nearby. "You can see them at the windows!"

Heart pounding, Harriet peered across the street at the mill. Faces were vaguely visible, but it was impossible to tell who was who. She pulled her scarf off and began to wave it above her head. "He'll never be able to pick me out in this mob." Yet she continued to wave. Others did, too. "I'm sure," Teresa said, "that he knows you're here, dear. Senses it and—"

"That's not good enough." Ducking swiftly between two of the guardsmen, Harriet dashed across the street, calling Patrick's name.

"*I'm here*," she shouted, reaching the iron fence, only to be spun firmly but politely around by two soldiers, who escorted her back behind the lines. Several arms were waving from the windows, but she had no idea which might be Patrick's.

"My husband's in there," she protested. "That's his choice, ma'am," was the response. "Good try," grinned Alice. "I figured it wouldn't take you long to get yourself in the limelight."

"So's *my* husband, Mrs. Flynn."

Frustrated in her efforts, Harriet turned to the woman nearby, recognized her and several others. Families waiting; their faces worried. "They should have settled with Phelps," the woman said, her sentiments echoed by her neighbors. "Now look what's happened," another said angrily while she hoisted a crying child up and wiped its nose. "I blame your husband as much as anyone."

"Blame him?" retorted Harriet. "Did he *drag* your husband in there with him? Blame him? That's an odd thing to say. Who's been on your side right from the beginning?"

"Not my side," was the reply. "There's many wanted to go back, and they should've been allowed. Better than this should've happened."

Another woman nodded. "Shapiro's the one started it. We didn't need him here."

"Shapiro? It was Phelps who started it. You weren't doing any business, anyway," she retorted to several merchants who stood clustered together, their faces full of complaint at the upheaval. "If *you'd* supported the strike, Phelps might've listened!"

"I think they're brave" was on many lips. As Harriet and Alice moved through the crowd, the latter sentiment seemed most in evidence. Throughout the frantic day, people had been in turn bewildered, indignant, frightened and excited, but after the police action, an enthusiasm ripped through them. If there had been fighting these last days, with hostility and bitterness between the opposing factions, the bold action of the fifty who'd taken the mill had united almost everyone behind them. The sheer drama of it piqued the imagination; the daring caused hearts to beat quicker, warming bodies against the bitter cold.

"I want to see the office."

"You won't like it."

"Does Patrick know?"

Alice nodded. "It happened last night. He found it this morning."

"Alice—I'm scared."

"Me, too. I've been scared a lot lately."

Emily Marienetti was also. As Alice and Harriet started up Main, she introduced herself. "What's going to happen, Mrs. Flynn?" she asked, holding tight to her two youngest children. "He's a hothead, my husband."

"Mama—"

"Shhh. The police fired buckshot. They'll maybe do worse tomorrow. My husband has such respect for Mr. Flynn. There must be a way we can get them to come out. They can't win. Your husband must know they can't, don't you think? He's educated and— I'm worried, Mrs. Flynn. He'll listen to reason, won't he?"

But when Harriet saw the office a while later, she doubted Patrick was in any kind of a reasonable mood.

"No . . ." she murmured and could imagine his face when he turned the corner of the parish hall this morning and discovered the door to the office smashed, its glass in pieces, still glittering on the sidewalk now. The larger window, boarded up, had been battered anew. The devastation as he stepped past the broken chairs must have fueled his decision to abandon peaceful means of conciliation and resort to force.

Anger rose in her as she flipped on the lights. The office was unrecognizable—it looked like a typhoon had blown through. Reams of paper were scattered, the sheets littering the floor. Both typewriters lay in crumpled masses of metal near the mimeograph machine, which had had a baseball bat taken to it. Even the house plants in the windows had been dumped, the dirt thrown. She and Alice righted a desk, then gave up in frustration.

"Who're you calling?" asked Alice as Harriet picked up the receiver, only to discover the cord had been pulled from the wall.

"Phelps," she replied, his name a curse. The office had become much more than a place of work for Patrick and her; it was a warm refuge where they'd stumbled on their love. Now it had been destroyed and Harriet felt a chilling rage.

"Here's your landlord," warned Alice as Father Gahaghan came in the open door, followed closely by Gert and Joe, Teresa and Matt.

"I'm going to get this all fixed," Harriet assured the priest, who she could see was upset.

Teresa nodded. "When I see what's happened here, I wish I was in the mill with him myself." Joe agreed, wanting the same. "God love him," added Teresa, turning once again to Harriet and taking her hand. "We'll all help you, dear. Won't we now, Gert?"

"Brought it on themselves," muttered Gert, spotting Harriet's eye at the same time. "What happened to ya?"

Harriet blushed and couldn't think of a thing to say. "She fell in the bathroom," Alice replied quickly and Teresa nodded in support. Gert turned and said something to Gahaghan. Outside the mill ten minutes after Patrick and the men had rushed it, she'd spent the day on and off the street, alternately making calls to the Mansion, to Governor Curley, and to Monsignor O'Malley to try and get the situation handled peaceably. Harriet's absence had been noted, and several scenarios had occurred to Gert. "Where've ya been?" she asked bluntly.

Go stuff it, Mrs. Flynn, why don't you? was what Harriet wanted to say but controlled herself. The memory of their encounter on the steps of St. Mary's flickered in both pairs of eyes.

"Mrs. Flynn, I know how worried you must be." Harriet hugged herself for warmth and tried to find some common ground.

"Aren't we all?" offered Teresa soothingly. Matt nodded. Joe grinned. "He's a scrapper, he is, my Paddy. I always said he was a scrapper!"

"I'd rather he wasn't," snapped Gert, staring hard at Harriet. Added to her vast and well-thumbed catalog of grievances was the surety that today was all her daughter-in-law's fault. *She* was responsible for Patrick's having placed himself in jeopardy; *she* had pushed him down the radical path that led to the gates of the mill this morning.

"I'm going to get an issue out," announced Harriet, ignoring Gert. "Tomorrow," she added, the plan forming quickly, adrenaline surging. "Father, I know you're concerned about what's happened here. I know you don't want us to stay. Please, don't abandon us now. Don't abandon Patrick."

Uncomfortable, Gahaghan cleared his throat and clapped his gloved hands together. "An issue?" Gert scoffed. "That's not what we need. We need people comin' to their senses. We need to get 'em outta there!"

"The only way they're going to come out is if Phelps negotiates."

"He won't!" cried Gert. "Do ya want blood runnin' on Main Street? There's been enough fightin'! Don't ya see three hundred soldiers out there, girl?"

"It won't come to that."

"Are ya a seer? I want no more agitatin'! If—"

"*If* I know Patrick," Harriet interrupted, "he's not going to leave that mill until he gets what he wants. He usually does, you know," she added pointedly, "no matter how many obstacles get shoved in his way."

Flummoxed by the insinuation, Gert muttered something to Father Gahaghan. "That's why I want to get an issue out," Harriet insisted. "We have to rally the town. We have to support the men. We have to do what Patrick's been doing all along—keep pressure on Phelps. Patrick's doing it by being in there, and *I* intend to print an issue!"

"Good for you," murmured Alice, trying to walk, stepping over things, to keep herself warm.

"Father," added Harriet. "Please let us stay. Whether you like it or not, *The Spectator's* important now. It may not look like much, but the paper's become a symbol. Of justice. For what's right. I want to stay here! I'll find someplace else if I have to. But I don't think people will understand if you throw us out now."

"The Church doesn't condone violence . . ." he began evasively, looking to Gert for instructions. "Pat's broken the law and—"

"My God," cried Harriet, "whose side are you on? Aren't you proud of him? Mrs. Flynn—?" Pleading and angered simultaneously, Harriet turned to Gert.

"Don't be disrespectful to the Father," Gert shot back, raising an imperious hand to silence Harriet who, she could see, was ready to pounce. "*I'll* say something now, if ya don't mind." Deep down, unwillingly, very much so, Gert felt a flicker of admiration for the girl who stood before her with blazing eyes. "The Father's against violence and I am, too. I don't want my son hurt. I'm sure ya don't, either," she went on, a hint of the begrudging with the latter. "I don't know what's come over him lately . . . turned into a hot pepper, he has. And won't listen to anyone. But he's done what he done, God love him, and you're right. . . ."

"That's it, Gert," Teresa enthused urgently, offering support as Gert hesitated. "You and Harriet are thinking alike. What's this talk of sides? Harriet? We're all on the same, aren't we now? Gert? Isn't it time for the both of you—?"

Alice's ears pricked. Matt and Joe cocked ears themselves as they began to right the desks, but the essence of the struggle between Gert and Harriet was incomprehensible, evidence only of the ultimate perplexity and foolishness of women.

"Gert. . . ?" urged Teresa once again. "Don't you think it's time. . . ?"

Knowing what her sister wanted, Gert's hackles were up. Harriet wasn't at all sure she wanted to let bygones be bygones, either. *Rode one horse for all he was worth and then helped myself to your son???* she wanted to yell, wanted to remind Gert of any number of atrocities, public and private, wanted an apology and the recognition due her.

Sensing Harriet waiting, Gert cleared her throat and straightened her spectacles. On the defensive, her eyes bounced off the girl who'd usurped her place and continued to challenge her—by breathing, by her very existence, by her disheveled bangs and the tilt of her head.

"You'll stay," she snapped.

"Thank you," replied Harriet, very formal.

"Pa'll be down in the mornin' to help. You'll come in the mornin'," Gert called to Joe, took Teresa's arm and turned to leave.

"Mrs. Flynn?"

"What's that?"

"Thanks."

"Gert. . . ?" Once again Teresa nudged her sister, wanting something more, a step further, a gesture. But too much water had gone over the dam for Gert. She'd done what she could.

"Good night to ya," she said to Harriet, but didn't look back. "See to boardin' up those windows first, Pa," she added and left the office.

"I reached Elliot. His father and Governor Curley have been on the phone all afternoon. The Governor's trying to get Phelps to talk with Shapiro. Apparently, he told Phelps he *won't* order the Guard to attack." Harriet rejoined Alice, who was hunched over a cup of coffee at Noonan's counter. Overheard, the news rippled around the drugstore.

"That's a relief."

Harriet nodded. "It buys some time, that's all. But how long can they hold out? Violence," she muttered, thinking of Gert. "*She's* against violence? Don't make me laugh. I'll have a hot dog," she called to Tommy Noonan, who was busy at the grill. The drugstore had stayed open to accommodate the crowds, and it was buzzing. "She's the most violent woman I know," Harriet added, glancing over the heads at the tables to the street. People hurried home. Nothing else was going to happen tonight; it was time to get warm. "Look at them. They think it's a circus! Them, too," she added, nodding toward the out-of-towners, the city-slicker reporters from Boston and New York who sat together, a tight-knit fraternity, trading wisecracks while they waited to use the phone for a final call to their editors.

"They know they've got a good story here," she continued, "but I don't think they *care* a damn." The Christmas displays in the window caught her eye. "Three weeks till Christmas. It seems unreal. All those trees! What am I going to—? I have to get back to the mill."

"There's nothing you can do tonight. Come home. You look dead on your feet. I don't imagine you got any sleep last night on the train."

"Don't remind me. Cut your throat and smile at you a moment later," she muttered, thoughts returning to Gert. "It's an Irish trait, I guess. Violence? They have it in them, don't they." Gingerly she touched a finger to the bruise. "I wish I hadn't put any makeup on at all!"

"You're not still angry at him?"

"Of course I am. What happened today?" she added, not wishing to discuss it further. "How was Father?"

"Oh, he didn't look at me at breakfast. I'm a pariah. I've done him wrong. He left for Springfield. Didn't say a word to me. I'll live. Mother and I went to the Thibeaus after supper. Mrs. Thibeau's so upset and worried about Wayne, I don't know if it really registered at first that she's going to be a grandmother. Mr. Thibeau was . . . dumbfounded. I think he thought I was trying to trick him. But he calmed down. Mother was wonderful. She kept us all sane."

"Have they heard anything else?"

"Nothing else. He's still in the hospital. There doesn't seem to be any way to reach him. We just have to wait. You gulped that down fast enough."

A moment later, each in her own thoughts, the sisters started down the street. The remains of the crowd continued to stream past in the opposite direction as the clock on the town hall struck ten. "Which of the two families is more violent? I don't think it's an Irish trait. Look at us."

Harriet nodded. "I suppose. I'll bet she thinks she was quite magnanimous. God, it's cold! I hope it's warm in there."

The Guard still ringed the mill, but the crowd was down to a handful. "C'mon," urged Harriet, "stay with me. I just want to keep moving. Maybe he'll see me. Do you think he can see me? Maybe he doesn't want to see me."

"You have to give her some credit."

"Mrs. Flynn? For what? For being a halfway decent human being? For the first time in her life? Look at the family she's created. Dennis? Rose? Patrick barely escaped. She still has her hooks in him. Oh, don't get me wrong. She's well-meaning, isn't she? Only tried to run his life. Into the ground. What about Mr. Phelps? He's well-meaning, too. And look at the mess Elliot's in. Save me from the well-meaning ones of this world, if you please."

"My, my. I don't think you'd mind at all taking up the reins. Run his life? You'd love to. Fortunately he won't let you. He can't allow that to happen to him again."

"What are you talking about?"

"You and she are alike. Come on, you know that. Don't pretend. Why do you think he fell in love with you?"

430

"Alice, you are an ass! I've done nothing but nurture him. He married me for my energy and spunk. Doesn't he know that?"

"And gave him a hard time."

"Hard time? I don't give my heart that easily, if that's what you mean. And the way he was with me last night—was it only last night?—makes me leery all over again. I tried to help and I got slapped for my efforts."

And on the train, clacking through the night, she'd dozed and waked, remembering how Teresa had told her right after she and Patrick were married that he'd walk over coals for her. But she didn't need feats; she needed to be understood. A flight in fear, that's what yesterday was, a hurt more emotional than physical. That he would always be suspicious of her, try and keep her in her place, pull rank and not allow her to be who she had to be. And neither the coals he walked on, nor his worship, nor the lovemaking, nor the fact that she knew she loved him had been able to ease her.

None of it, she had to admit, seemed quite so frightening now as she walked with her sister up and down the sidewalk opposite the mill. No matter her vulnerability, no matter the issues between them unresolved, her only desire was to let Patrick know she was here and with him. Had he seen her run across the street? Maybe he had, but she had no way of knowing. Frustrated, she tried to think of a way to get a message to him. Alice left her shortly, and Harriet continued to pace behind the line of guardsmen.

Stopping to talk to Meyer Shapiro, she found him bundled up in blankets in the front seat of his sound truck. "Aren't you cold?" she asked him, but Shapiro burned from within. He'd been staying in the hotel in Leveret, but he couldn't leave his "boys," as he called them. Not tonight. Offering Harriet a sip of brandy, he was in excellent spirits.

"There are people saying that if you went away, it would all be over," she said, eyes never leaving the mill.

"Over? No. Of course not. Out of my hands now. There's a momentum. I'm not going anywhere," he added. "They've given me an opportunity. Your husband and the others. Brave boys. We'll win now. I feel it in these old bones," he went on, smiling, full of reminiscences of other battles, won, lost, but none so important as this one.

Harriet had to keep moving. Excusing herself, she got out of the truck and willed Patrick a message, willing him somehow to return it. The millpond's frozen surface glimmered in the light of a half-moon that had risen over Jericho. She ducked into the Depot Tavern, as busy as Noonan's, and had another brandy. Other reporters were at the bar, trading stories. Feeling exhausted, she hurried out, possessed of a sudden idea that she could talk to the commander of the Guard, get a word to Patrick somehow, but another idea hit her. Laughing out loud at the simplicity of it, she wondered why she hadn't thought of it sooner. Running now, she headed back to Meyer Shapiro and borrowed his bullhorn. A moment later, the troops were startled by the final message of the evening to the mill:

"PATRICK! PATRICK FLYNN! I'M HERE!"

The words echoed, startlingly clear on the now quiet street. Harriet repeated them, and Meyer Shapiro smiled to himself, thought of his wife and dozed off. Once again, Harriet could see an indistinguishable face or two at the windows, but there was no answering shout, nothing at all. Bumming a cigarette from one of the soldiers, she kept her eyes riveted on the mill. Perhaps he was so angry at her he didn't care to acknowledge her. The thought produced a spasm of anxiety, and she tried to make conversation with the guardsmen. Country boys and clerks who'd been called up suddenly, they had no desire to be out on a night like this. They were bivouacked on Bartlett's Field, they told Harriet, whose eyes scanned the windows of the mill as she hopped from one foot to the other to stay warm. She waited a few minutes more, then turned sadly away.

"Maybe he's asleep, miss."

"That must be it," she replied and started walking.

"Miss!" she heard behind her and turned back to find the soldier pointing toward the mill. From a third-story window issued a length of cloth, unmistakably green in the searchlight's glare. An Irish bolt unfurled, it fell twenty feet down and caught a breeze, its billowing message causing Harriet's heart to ache. Several of the soldiers clapped, grins on their faces. Harriet didn't know whether to laugh or cry; she was too cold to do either. "Patrick," she murmured, shivering, waving her scarf again furiously.

Phelps took the offensive in the morning. Enraged at Curley's refusal to order the Guard to retake the mill, he tried to flush out the invaders himself by turning off the heat. When the union tried to get food in once again, the Pinkertons stopped it. A coffee urn was overturned, sandwiches scattered, in a brief scuffle that the Guard ended quickly, Major Jenkins ordering Shapiro to desist in his efforts.

"PHELPS IS TRYING TO STARVE THEM. . . .!" Hoarse-voiced with fatigue, Shapiro was on the bullhorn immediately as the street filled up again on another bitterly cold day, with lowering skies promising snow. Most of the town's school children had played hooky; a few brought their skates, and their happy shouts as they glided across the millpond seemed inappropriate, almost callous, in the face of the fifty cold and hungry men inside.

True to her promise, Harriet had a *Spectator* in the hands of the thousand or so by five o'clock that afternoon.

Everyone had pitched in. As directed by Gert, Joe had reboarded up the windows before Harriet even got to the office. The stove was lit, a

432

temporary order restored. Alice, Cora and Sam arrived a few minutes later lugging a mimeograph machine and a typewriter from the WPA in Leveret. President Roosevelt, quipped Alice, wouldn't mind—he'd been responsible for the laws championing the workingman's rights in the first place, hadn't he? When Cora's arm ached with the turning, she was spelled by Dennis, then Frankie. Teresa brought lunch and a continuous line of merry chatter to keep spirits up. Gert herself put in an appearance in the middle of the afternoon, distributing Fig Newtons, taking a symbolic turn on the mimeo. To suggest that mellowing was occurring—in either of them—would be going too far, but common cause had brought her and her daughter-in-law together at least for the moment.

Finally completed and stapled, the two pages were distributed to the crowd, which had grown restless and peevish with waiting. Yesterday's excitement had died down. Everyone knew that Governor Curley had ordered the Guard not to take aggressive action and sentiment was building for an end to the stalemate. Phelps had made an offer earlier in the day: he would talk with Patrick and Marienetti and the members of the strike committee *after* they vacated his mill. Once again he adamantly refused to have anything to do with Shapiro. The offer was refused. There were many in the crowd who now felt the men inside were as intransigent as Phelps. If sympathy was with them and their action appreciated, a growing sense of futility had invaded the ranks. Abraham Phelps would win in the end; he always had, hadn't he? Shapiro's continued exhortations and pleas for support and unity had produced scattered boos as the day had worn on, the cold dampening spirits. Even the appearance of *The Spectator* was regarded warily in some quarters; people were tired of the whole damn thing and wanted it over.

But all that changed very quickly, and it was Harriet who was responsible.

One page of *The Spectator* contained an open letter to Phelps in which Harriet pleaded with him to end the crisis and negotiate with the union since the majority had voted for it. The second was full of personal messages from the wives, mothers, children and sweethearts to their men isolated within the mill.

Harriet's was simple: *I love you, Patrick Flynn.* She debated adding *I'm sorry* but would have had to explain she was sorry for running away (even though he *had* slapped her), not sorry for the purchase of the trees; no, nor the battle between them that, she'd have to remind him, she *had* tried to end, etc., so she settled for the *I love you* since that was the heart of the matter.

She made no attempt to request Major Jenkins that she be allowed to send copies into the mill. She had a bolder plan, which caused a ripple of expectation as she was helped to the hood of Shapiro's sound truck, from which, bullhorn in hand, she began to read *The Spectator* to the mill.

433

Photographers snapping, a hushed audience of a thousand spread out around her, Harriet's voice rang out, magnified over South Main, as she read the messages. The endearments echoed warmly in the icy stillness; the *I love you, Daddy*'s; the *stick to your guns, your pa and me are with you*'s; the *God bless ya*'s; and the dinners promised caused hearts to quicken and eyes to fill, regalvanizing the town as nothing else could. It was, Shapiro had to admit (wishing he'd thought of it himself) a brilliant propaganda stroke and he saluted Harriet with his battered fedora as she continued the messages, a lump in his own old throat when she got to hers, voice quivering slightly, a catch in her heart, a passionate *I love you, Patrick Flynn* that caused Teresa to weep and Gert to know that the girl on the top of the truck had won.

A train in the depot, long since unable to continue on, for its passengers had jumped down and were listening, too, gave a hoot as Harriet finished. Cheering erupted from the crowd; arms waved in response from the windows of the mill, and Patrick's cloth of green surged, shook by sturdy arms, the messages received. The cheering went on for ten minutes.

"JERICHO IS WAITING, MR. PHELPS," had been her final words, echoing Patrick's Thanksgiving editorial, "Jericho is waiting." The next morning, he sent for her.

Birds chirped angrily as Elliot's car entered the circular driveway and stopped under the portico. "Be careful," he warned. Harriet nodded and stared at the house. She'd never thought to return here again. "I'm not sure what he wants," continued Elliot. "I'll tell you this—he's got a court order. It orders them out by three o'clock this afternoon."

The organ room was dark, the drapes drawn. Phelps turned slowly, the sight of his son and Harriet standing together in the doorway causing him a momentary ache for what might have been.

"How pretty you look. . . ." An affable smile could not disguise the pressure. His eyes held a mixture of wariness, cunning—something imploring, too—as he stared at Harriet.

"Good morning . . . Abe," she replied coldly. The use of his first name had nothing of the personal, was a warning. Understanding, Phelps nodded to himself.

"Coffee?"

Harriet shook her head. Startling Phelps, the grandfather clock struck ten. The organ gleamed dully in the shadows as he walked to the fireplace and held out his hands, surprised that no fire burned. "Talk some sense into your husband," he said sharply, getting to business. "He can't win."

"Neither can you," she challenged in return, meeting his stare as their history passed in review for both of them in the space of a second that seemed longer. "You know you can't."

434

Phelps took a breath. "Your husband . . ." he began, glancing at Elliot, the word inflaming him, "and his band of ruffians have taken the law into their own hands . . . trespassed on private property"—the words were snapped in agitated bursts—"occupied my mill illegally. Broken the law!"

"So you intend to starve them?"

"Starve them? Don't be a fool. That's their choice. Not mine. I made them a reasonable offer."

"They didn't accept it."

"They'll have to." Eyes crafty, Phelps removed a document from his breast pocket, took it out carefully, an unmistakable air of satisfaction and triumph about him as he raised it toward Harriet. "I have here—"

"I know about your injunction," she said, cutting him off and spoiling his moment. "It won't matter," she added, revealing none of her concern about this new turn of events.

"I told her, Dad," admitted Elliot.

"Did you tell her what it means?" Phelps snapped at his son. She might have been his daughter-in-law, his ally, if only— Controlling himself, Phelps sat at the lacquered secretary.

"A court order," he barked, waving the document at Harriet. "Directs your husband and his gang to vacate my mill by three o'clock this afternoon! Otherwise, they'll be arrested and fined fifty thousand dollars! Can Shapiro raise it? Can he? Arrested! Do you want your husband thrown in jail? Three o'clock!" Eyes darted to the clock; he couldn't wait. "Take this to your husband. Tell him I mean business!"

"Why? Why do you want me to talk to Patrick?"

"Reason with him. I said I'd meet with them. I want this business finished. I'm giving them an opportunity to save themselves from—"

"So good-hearted, aren't you?" she retorted sarcastically. "No—that's not why you want me to go. You know you're going to lose. *That's* why. The Governor's against you. The town's against you. It's even spreading to your other mills. Isn't it! You can't hold out much longer and you know it. You want me to tell my husband to quit? The longer he stays where he is, the faster he brings you to your knees. Reason with him? The only thing I'll tell Patrick is to continue to do exactly what he's doing! You're going to lose. Negotiate!"

"Never. Shapiro will never set foot in my mill." Shaken by Harriet's vehemence, Phelps stood. "I won't tolerate others meddling. I didn't let Roosevelt . . . I won't let that goddamned Jew Shapiro, either!"

"You brought this on yourself," she retorted, disgusted. Years back, Phelps told Harriet he was a man besieged; it had been the unions then, too. The Labor Board, the NRA, an endless battle that he fought to keep control of his mills. "You started this long ago. You didn't count on them fighting back, did you? You had them under your thumb for so long, you

435

thought you owned them. You found out. You didn't count on Patrick, either. Did you think you could intimidate him with bricks through the window? You had his office destroyed. What did it get you? He's in your mill, that's what. It's his now. *His.* And I'll have a paper out on the street every day until I see you defeated."

"I don't know what you're talking about."

"Liar!" Harriet turned to Elliot. "Tell him. He can't hear me. Tell him. He *has* to negotiate. Tell him he's going to lose."

"Stay out of this," growled Phelps, picking up a delicate Japanese figurine and examining it, the exquisitely painted mouth and eyes mocking him in their sweet serenity.

"It's not worth it if people get hurt, Dad."

"What are you talking about?" Wounded by his lack of understanding, Phelps turned on Elliot. "I've kept them alive! For twenty-five years!"

Elliot gasped as the porcelain head was brutally snapped off, smashing on the parquet floor. Stunned, he rose, frightened glance meeting Harriet's. She stared at Phelps, whose black marble eyes had fleeting madness in them as he knelt to retrieve the pieces. "My wife will be unhappy," he murmured softly as he placed them on the secretary. Stiffly he pulled himself up by grasping the leg, faltering slightly, then rising to his full height.

"Dad, are you OK?" No matter how many times Elliot had wished to see his father powerless, the sight of him now filled him with dread. "Dad?"

"Get out."

"Dad, I'd like to stay."

"You heard me."

Left alone with him, Harriet was aware of her heart pounding as Phelps crossed to the window and pulled back the drapes. Outside, a few hesitant flakes had begun to fall. A minute of silence passed with only the ticking of the clock. When he turned back to Harriet, his face was calm; the terrifying moment had passed.

"Why do you treat him like that?" she asked simply, breathing returning to normal. "Don't you know he loves you?"

"Loves me?" A sudden gentleness coursed through him and was quickly banished. Once again he sat, slumping slightly in his chair, hands in and out of his suitcoat pockets.

"He does. He wants—"

"I didn't ask you here . . . to talk of my son. You know what it was I wanted . . . for my son. Harriet," Phelps added, with an almost pleading tone, as if he wished to rekindle their former intimacy, "I'm not your enemy. Even if you think I am. Didn't I help you? Haven't I always? I put money into the paper when you needed it."

Armoring himself against her coldness, he shook his head. Didn't she

436

understand that she'd made use of him as much as he'd exploited her? Harriet was thinking along similar lines. How could she explain to anyone, Alice or Patrick, the complexity of her relations with Abraham Phelps? Of what he'd meant to her, of the strengthening sense of herself—a validation of her special destiny, which no one else, including Franklin, had ever bestowed with quite such intensity. And of the subterfuges and hidden agendas—yes, those too—that each of them had employed right from the beginning when she approached him with jam in her briefcase and adolescent larceny in her heart.

"I thought we were friends," she said, wishing she hadn't, knowing she was still vulnerable to his betrayal. How many times had she composed speeches to him, lists of accusations? Today wasn't the time, but she was in the same room again; there was the table where she'd left the ring. The oak paneling seemed to suddenly close in on her. The same room where Elliot had slipped the ring on her finger, the same room in which his father had coldly left her that final, frightening night, left her to her own agonies, left her to fend alone, to put the puzzle together herself, left her.

"We *are* friends."

"No," she said, the memories intolerable. "No." She reached for her coat and purse. "I'm not going to advise Patrick to give up, if that's what you want. As I told you—I'm going to tell him to hold on."

"That's foolish. He'll be arrested. You're sensible. I think I know you pretty well after—"

"Know me?" Harriet blazed, an anger boiling in her that couldn't be stifled. "Did you think I could be bought with a world cruise? Even the advertising you gave us had strings, didn't it? The protestations of friendship, the lunches at the Red Tavern? All of it. Right from the beginning. You lied to me."

"That's not true," he protested.

"I've asked myself: how did I get into the mess in the first place? It would be too easy to claim I was naive and you bamboozled me. What's my Achilles' heel? I loved Elliot, that's what. But I was ambitious, too."

"You still are," Phelps retorted acidly. "Like your glory, don't you? You and your husband—what are you after? I'll wager you enjoyed yourself yesterday out there. Enough," he added, rising and trying to dismiss her, a familiar injured look on his face that made her all the angrier.

"Enough? Do you really think you can turn people on and off like faucets? Even Elliot—"

"Leave my son out of this."

"Do you know something? I almost dislike myself as much as I do you. I've always been intoxicated by you. By your power. Your money, too. Even though I've always vigorously protested the opposite, I see that it's true."

"You're being too hard on yourself."

437

"I'll decide that. It's my prerogative. Why didn't you tell me the truth?"

"How could I tell you something I didn't want to believe myself? Hate me if it pleases you. I wanted what was best. There were advantages for you, too. You admit you saw them. I'm sure you'll see them again when the time comes that you need something from me. Now I must—"

"I thought you respected me."

"I do."

"No. You tried to manipulate me. So understanding about my wanting to succeed, weren't you? I even imagined you considered me an equal. No man ever has, so I was a pushover, wasn't I? But you can't manipulate Patrick. Nor Jericho. You've tried. You'll fail."

"What are you after?" he snapped. "Revenge?"

"You would see it that way, wouldn't you? I feel sorry for you."

A part of Phelps, as it always had, responded to the fire in Harriet, but whatever guilt he felt counted for nothing, was of the past, had no power in the face of his current troubles. Even his admiration for her counted for shit as the memory of his father rose before him, his father bellowing defiance at those same gates in 1912 as a mob screamed for his death and got it. By God, *he* would never give in. *Never.*

Propelled by the terror of that long ago morning when a guilty joy had filled him as the hated tyrant clutched his chest and fell, Phelps rose swiftly and started for the doors. A patina of perspiration glinted on his forehead as he turned to Harriet.

"You're a bright girl." Black marble eyes were riveted on hers. "An ambitious girl. Yes. Why do you think I picked you? We both know why I picked you."

"I loved him!"

"I'm sure you did. There are people who would agree that he's lovable, certainly his mother. I'm sure you did. But the honey pot was there, too, wasn't it? Don't get me wrong. I admire your good sense. The worst memories of old age are rejected opportunities. I offered you one, and you took it. If only Elliot had played his part, you'd be in this family now. But it didn't work out the way I planned it. Don't waste your time feeling sorry for me. For anyone. You'll never get what you want. Take this to your husband." Phelps thrust the document at her. "Tell him to get out. If he doesn't, he'll be arrested at three." All pretense at gentility had vanished, the patrician tones had become the snarls of a man perilously close to the edge.

"If he resists, I'll see that he gets his head cracked. The law is the law. Our mick of a governor has personally assured me that he will carry out the orders of the court. Three o'clock. Is it clear? Tell him. He gets out or the Guard goes in after him. Their commander assures me they'll have no trouble at all. I have no intention of losing."

24 Leveret's mill owners sat tight in their offices as a tension crept over the city like the snow. A few got on the phone to Phelps with expressions of support, swearing with each other, powerful men who were fearful today and didn't want to admit it. What might or might not happen in Jericho affected them all. That it had come to this! they protested, injury and piety mixed in the pudding of their rage. The American way teetered on the edge of anarchy, they growled to each other, damning Roosevelt with fresh malice. A riot in Jericho might cause all of Leveret to walk. Aging dinosaurs, their control over their own fiefdoms in jeopardy, they clung to the hope that Phelps would stick, Curley would do his duty, the agitators would be thrown in jail, the law upheld, justice done, and the threat of the union banished. Agitated, they paced to their office windows and looked down on the black Merrimack, which flowed swiftly yet placidly until it reached the dam— then thundered over the falls.

Rushing now, the river roared like a hundred thousand voices seeking justice. Pounding at their red brick fortresses, it caused a quickening of pulse in clotted arteries. Frightened of the river's message, the scarred valves of their hearts opened and shut with an exploding frequency as they watched it rush past them and out of Leveret, swirling and spreading as it reached Jericho, crashing again over the falls at Haverhill, moving steadily now, triumphantly powerful, pulling them with it, inexorably pulling them no matter how they might struggle and swim against its mighty current, pulling them downstream, eleven miles to the coast, the river majestic and calm now, unstoppable and serene in its fitness, giving them a final chaotic thrashing as it burst through the jetties at Newburyport, where it met the tide and carried them to sea.

Elliot was envious, tried not to look, had to, couldn't take his eyes off Patrick and Harriet who embraced and held each other as if they couldn't let go.

Taking a cigarette out of his case, he glanced down the so familiar hallway outside his father's office, where fifty men who knew him only as

439

the boss's quirky son eyed him distrustfully or with barely concealed contempt.

"I wanted to cut my arm off," Patrick whispered, impassioned. "Smash my hand. I never hit anyone in my life and—" The still faintly bluish cast above Harriet's cheekbone filled him with terrible shame. "Can you forgive me? It's unforgivable."

"I have. I do."

"Oh, Harriet. I'm such a fool. I almost lost you, didn't I?"

"I'm here."

Neither of them could speak. Patrick held her to him again; his eyes sent messages that were acknowledged; the chemistry was electric in a moment of exquisite closeness, but there wasn't time for anything more. "Say, Pat!" called Marienetti from the end of the hallway. Speculating among themselves as to why Harriet and Elliot had been allowed in, the men were restless.

"Here—" Foraging in her purse, Harriet came up with candy bars. "I thought of making sandwiches . . . there wasn't time."

Patrick nodded and accepted the newspapers she'd brought as well. Glancing at the front-page stories of his siege of the mill, his hand reached unconsciously for hers.

"I told him I wasn't going to try and talk you into giving up. That's what he wanted. Patrick, I'm frightened."

"What's he doing here?" he asked, echoing the men's questions as he glanced at Elliot.

"He wants to help," Harriet replied, sensing Patrick's antagonism.

"Does he?" he replied vaguely, brain busy as he scanned the injunction.

"Mr. Phelps didn't want him to come with me, but he did."

Marienetti called to Patrick again. "OK," he said to Harriet, who wondered if Patrick was even seeing her. Burning with an inner current, he took her arm. "C'mon. We'll go tell the others."

"Patrick . . ." she reminded, nodding again to Elliot, who remained by himself in the doorway.

"Thanks for coming, Elliot," he called. Too much animosity had passed between them for anything else. Elliot shrugged and came closer.

"Is he going through with this?" Patrick asked. Elliot nodded.

Brusquely Patrick started down the hallway.

"Shall I wait here . . . or am I invited?" If there was a hint of the old insolence about Elliot's question, he hadn't meant it. Apprehensively he glanced down to the men. "What I mean is . . . I guess they're upset with me, too—"

"Why should they be?" Leaving Elliot and Harriet to follow in his wake, Patrick joined the others. "Into the office," he called, the urgency of him commanding immediate attention. Chins hunched down into muf-

440

flers, the men tipped their caps to Harriet and offered greetings. Her activity outside the mill had kept their spirits raised and they were glad to see her. Cold, they swung their arms and stomped in place, bellies growling with hunger as they shouted questions and trooped into Phelps' office. Some sat on the broad tables and unrolled bolts of cloth, wrapping the fabric around them to keep warm.

"Phelps sends us greetings," called Patrick, holding up the injunction. "He wants to know if we're cozy and comfortable."

Rowdy laughter greeted the words, and Harriet passed out the few bars of candy, which were eagerly broken in quarters and shared. Her few packs of cigarettes were as quickly depleted. Elliot hung by the door, uncertain, an outsider in this office that was no longer his father's. As Paul Marienetti sat in Phelps' chair, Elliot couldn't help his sudden intake of breath at the sight of a commoner usurping his father's throne.

"Why're ya here, Phelps?" asked the rough Italian, feet up on the desk, eyes challenging Elliot to do something about it.

Elliot wanted to put the wop in his place, but he didn't dare. He could feel Marienetti's scorn, knew the rest of them considered him a lightweight. Averting his glance he met his grandfather's eyes in the portrait. *Drive out the invaders.*

Sensing Elliot's difficulty, not to mention the tension that his presence caused among the men, Patrick spoke quickly. "Elliot's here because he's with us. Is that right, Elliot?"

Grateful, Elliot nodded. There were murmurs. "An eleventh hour conversion?" muttered one of the younger men. Marienetti nodded. "How do we know he's not a spy?" he asked, relishing keeping Elliot on the spot.

"I never spied," he protested. "Look, I didn't have to come." He glanced to Harriet for reassurance.

"Glad you're with us, lad," called Jack Tyler, an old-timer who'd known Elliot since he was an infant, remembering well how Phelps had used to bring his son and carry him through the mill, showing him off.

Elliot smiled fleetingly, the approval relaxing him a bit. There were a few others who expressed similar sentiments as Tyler, but most were still reticent and kept their distance.

"Phelps has a message for us," announced Patrick. He passed the injunction around. The legalese of it baffled them; Harriet made it simple and explained it. Respectfully they listened, muttering angrily when she repeated Phelps' ultimatum.

"He's bluffing," scoffed Marienetti.

Harriet shook her head. "He's got the Guard—"

"Curley won't do it. He hasn't done it so far—right, Pat?"

"Curley told him he would," continued Harriet. "Didn't he?"

Elliot nodded. "They talked again this morning. If you aren't out by three"—all eyes went to the clock—"Curley will order Major Jenkins to

441

carry out the order of the court. They'll come in and get you. My father said he'll meet with you. But you have to be out first."

"Old news. What about Shapiro? What about the union?"

"He hasn't changed his position. If anything, he's more determined than ever. He said . . ." Elliot paused, ashamed. "He says he'll destroy you."

The office erupted angrily. The viciousness of Phelps' threats chilling her all over again, Harriet glanced at Patrick, surprised to find him absorbed in a newspaper. But the seeming calm was deceptive, she realized, when he lowered the pages and she saw his face.

"Destroy me?" His eyes were almost distant, the familiar flash of them gone, replaced with a cool determination that was mesmerizing and frightening at the same time. "Destroy me?" he said again, almost casually, the strange hint of a smile about him.

"We're to bring him back your answer," Harriet said, trying to reach him, but he was staring into space.

"We *are* the union," shouted Marienetti, banging his hand on the desk, causing the nearby photographs to tremble. "He can't talk to us and not to Shapiro. We'd have won nothin'! He'd squeeze us again. No dice! Right, Pat?"

"How do you feel?" Patrick asked, turning to the others. The debate was on, quickly settled. Even if many of them would never have dreamed of finding themselves in this situation, they hadn't come this far to back off now.

"Answer?" Patrick looked at Harriet. Calmly he picked up the injunction. "Here's our answer." As a tense silence gripped the office, Patrick walked to the windows and opened one. At the guardhouse down the sidewalk, one of the soldiers saw him and called to Jenkins, who emerged and caught Patrick's eye. Tearing the injunction in half, Patrick threw it into the falling snow. Jenkins shook his head and returned inside to call Phelps.

"*Come and get us, you sons of bitches!*" bellowed Marienetti, replacing Patrick at the window. The Italian turned back with a grin that was echoed tentatively by the others, the momentousness of the possible consequences causing second thoughts.

"I think," Patrick said, "that anyone who wants to leave should have the chance. I don't think any of us would think less of you. Even if you left now, you'd have made your mark."

The sudden solemnness of him caused them to look at one another. Scattered eyes were on the clock again as consciences were examined, internal debates struggled with. No one made a move.

"OK," nodded Patrick. He knew that even if all of them had chosen to walk out the doors, he would stay.

"Let 'em try and arrest us!" Marienetti shouted. "We'll get our licks

442

in—right, boys? Ya remember Tuesday? We had the cops runnin' their tails off, didn't we? Bash a few heads *this* time—right?"

"Patrick . . ." Frightened, Harriet gripped Patrick's hand, but he seemed a million miles from her.

"Won't we, boys?" continued Marienetti, clapping backs, inciting them. Stirred by Marienetti's vigor, Harriet watched the office ignite. She couldn't help thinking they were unlikely revolutionaries. More like Robin Hood's merry band as they shouted and laughed, faces alive with excitement, voices tumbling over one another as they proclaimed their defiance. Men of little education, many had spent their adult lives in this mill. They washed the wool, ran the dryers, the looms and the carding machines, ears deafened by the daily racket, permanent coughs from the ever-present lint in the air. An ordinarily mild-mannered bunch, the hell they raised was once a year at the Elks banquet; now the older ones were young again, and the youngest could taste the sweet surety of power as they pummeled one another, the cold unfelt, their hunger forgotten, fear banished. Three days together had united them; they were soldiers ready to go over the top.

"C'mon, boys," bellowed Marienetti, "we've got a few hours. Let's smash every loom in the place. Phelps may drag us out fightin', but the son of a bitch won't have a mill left!"

There were shouts of approval. "No," cried Harriet, even before Patrick did. "No," she said again. "Wait. *Think*. If you destroy the equipment, you're cutting off your own noses."

Unused to women voicing opinions, let alone interrupting him, Marienetti tugged at his earmuffs and looked to Patrick, wondering what he made of it.

"My wife's right, Paul. He's vindictive enough to get his revenge. He'd close down permanently. You'd be the losers."

"Losers? He *tried*, the son of a bitch! I say we—"

"No."

"—teach him a lesson!"

"No. The lesson we want to teach isn't necessarily a lesson for Phelps. He won't learn until he's forced to. But them . . ." Patrick gestured to the crowd that could be seen milling across the street. "Those are the people we need. Public opinion. The reporters out there and their editors, too."

"He destroyed your office, Pat. Have you forgotten?"

"I haven't forgotten. That's partly why I'm here. But I don't want the equipment sabotaged. That's playing his game. I intend to play another. We kill our cause if we destroy his mill. We have most of them out there on our side. . . ." Patrick picked up the newspapers. "But we don't have the *Leveret Eagle* nor the *Boston Herald*. We're branded as lawbreakers. We are. We had to. They call us hoodlums. We aren't. The country is watching us. I want them to see who we are. What we stand for. It's not destruction."

443

Patrick turned to Harriet, his eyes on Elliot, too. He wondered what Elliot must be feeling to have heard his father vilified. "Tell Phelps we've made our decision. The only way we'll come out is if he negotiates with Shapiro."

"He won't," Elliot replied hoarsely.

"Then we'll fight."

"*Patrick*—you can't win," Harriet blurted.

"I know that," he replied evenly, ahead of her. "I know we can't win—"

"*Pat*," protested Marienetti.

"Wait. We can't win a fight. With bobbins and soda pop bottles? There're three hundred of them. Door hinges against rifles? But I want everyone out there to understand what we're saying. And if we have to be taken by force, we will. I want those movie cameras to see it. I want in the papers that fifty men fought for what they believed in. If a few heads get bloodied, that's worth the victory. That *is* the victory. The rest of the world will catch up to us. That's how we'll win."

"Wish we had you in 'twelve, Patrick," called Jack Tyler. The older ones nodded. "We had no chance. We went out for a day. Sort of a sympathy thing with the boys from Leveret. Not all of us. Maybe a hundred or so. We were young. And his grandfather"—Tyler nodded to Elliot, then to the portrait—"died right outside the front doors there. And we went back the next morning. I'll never forget it."

Only a handful in the office had been around then. Patrick nodded. "My father told me about it."

All of Leveret had walked out in the great strike of 1912, including Joe and Gert. In the third week, a mob from the city came over, demanding that Jericho walk, too. " 'Join us!' was what they hollered," continued Jack Tyler, stroking his brush mustache and recalling how he and the others had got fired up and gone out. Phelps, Sr., had rushed after them, screaming they were traitors and worse. Then he fell.

"We all returned the next day. Elliot's father took us back. Never let us forget it, either. Tightened the screws, he did. We had no chance after that. No choice at all."

It was collective guilt that had brought them back, Patrick realized. Phelps' death had hung over the mill for years, cowing its employees. The awesome power of guilt, which Patrick understood well. "It wasn't the time," he said. "You have no cause to blame yourself, Jack. The country wasn't ready. But it's changed now. History isn't going to repeat itself. The climate's changed. We're no longer a feudal society," he added. "Roosevelt's seen to that. It's all changed now. *We've* changed it . . . here in Jericho . . . these last few days. Phelps has done his part, too. He locked you out. Miscalculated. No, history isn't being repeated. For one thing—this time we're in here, and he's out there."

444

Patrick clapped his hands together and stepped in place. "That's the part we play. That's why what you've done is so important. You dared to take a stand. You dared to put your money where your mouth is and you're still here. It won't be easy. But we're all in this together and we'll fight if they force us. We'll probably be arrested. Some of us may get hurt. That's the price of progress sometimes. A few men dare. You're the men.

"Tell your father," he went on to Elliot, "that we're in his office. He can have it back if he meets with Shapiro across that desk. Otherwise, he'll have to drag us out. But we'll be the winners. Tell him that. Tell him he can throw us in jail. But we'll come back. And others after us. Tell him. Judged by the cold eye of eternity, we're the ultimate victors."

Marienetti had incited them with his animal force and the incendiary claim he made on their guts, but Harriet could see that Patrick had touched their souls. His cheeks were flushed with cold, he might be blushing, his chin was stubbled with beard, but a clarity reverberated from him, a powerful cleanliness that caused Harriet to shiver. She couldn't help thinking of how often he'd referred to his former life as a mistake and questioned his calling. But he had the power to move people. She didn't know if he'd discovered his morality and sense of justice in the Church; she doubted it sprang from Gert. It was deep in him.

"Amen . . ." murmured Marienetti and crossed himself, the gesture repeated by all the Catholics as bowed heads and a shared sense of rightness gripped the office in a sudden and peaceful hush that had God in it.

Moved himself by Patrick's eloquence (jealous, too), Elliot looked across the office at his grandfather again. He'd heard enough stories about the legendary tyrant; his mother had told him how his father had hated *his* father; *that* was history repeating itself. And he was next in line, groomed to succeed in a business he wanted no part of, raised to carry on a tradition that he loathed, a ruthlessness expected that wasn't his. He wanted to tell them it wasn't his doing, that he was sorry, that he wasn't his father's son. He wasn't even born in 1912, he wanted to remind them. The crimes weren't his. He'd never cared what went on in the mill and didn't now. Why should he? Their concerns weren't his, he certainly had nothing in common with them. If he didn't know where he belonged and never had, it certainly couldn't be with this bunch, yet Elliot felt a strange closeness. Surely it was a pose, he told himself, mocking the feeling as too foreign to be believed. He looked at Patrick and Harriet, who were deep in private conversation. That he wanted their approval was evident, easier for him to understand.

"I'll stay with you if you like," he said to Patrick, surprising himself. "Why don't I stay with you?" he asked the rest, almost eagerly.

Patrick glanced at the clock in the hallway as he walked Harriet to the door. "You'd better get back there now," he said, taking small steps as if he

445

could stretch their remaining time together. "Tell him what we've decided. Tell him Elliot's here. It just might work."

"That's what he thinks, too." Her arm around Patrick's waist, Harriet glanced back to Elliot, who was pacing, then sitting and up again. She recognized the manic exhilaration in him, but she doubted his presence in the mill would make any difference.

"He won't let Elliot get arrested," insisted Patrick.

"Patrick—I told you what he was like this morning. I hate to be negative. He *is* obsessed."

"He'll lose face if Elliot—"

"That's what I'm trying to tell you. He isn't reasonable. He's not thinking."

"It's worth a try. Would he take a chance on his own son getting hurt? If I know Elliot," he added, glancing back down the hallway, "he won't take a chance on that, either."

"Patrick, why can't you give him some credit?"

"I don't believe in instant transformations."

"I watched him while you were talking. You caught him in your net."

"If I didn't know you better, I'd say you had a touch of Irish in you."

"Oh?" she retorted, mock-feisty. Trembling, she clasped Patrick to her. "You wouldn't happen to have a roast beef dinner for fifty in your purse, would you?" he asked, trying to calm her. "Do you remember the miracle of the loaves and the fishes? We could use a miracle now. You're my miracle."

"Patrick, suppose the Guard comes in? They have rifles. You said yourself—"

"Buckshot. Or bullets? In either case, I have faith."

"Patrick—"

"There has to be some decency buried deep in Phelps. I'm also pragmatic enough to consider the possibility that there isn't. And if so—"

Once again Harriet saw the look in Patrick's eyes that was unrecognizable and distant, unreachable in its intensity. "Talk to Phelps," she pleaded suddenly. "He said he'd talk with you."

"But not to Shapiro. You heard Paul. That's what it's all about. I can't stop now. I can't abandon Meyer. I believe in him. Both Meyer and I know the value of this. Even a fight if it comes to that. I don't want to see anyone . . . get hurt. Neither does Meyer. Well," he added wryly, "Meyer wouldn't mind if a few heads got bashed. All for the cause, you see. It has to be."

"*Patrick.*"

Hers was so great, Patrick tried not to let his own anxiety show. "Don't worry. I'm not going to provoke anything. I'm no hero. It's up to Phelps now."

446

"But he said the same. He thinks you're his enemy. He—"

"I am. And I intend to win. I'm a pigheaded Irishman. He's pushed people around long enough. It's time he was stopped. I have to do it, don't you see? *I* have to. I told you—I'm a reluctant hero. Not so noble. I'm the man who hit you. Maybe I'm atoning for that. The public man expresses nobility of purpose and slugs his wife in private."

There was so much he wanted to say, but he wondered if now was the time. "No," he continued, shaking his head, "I'm no hero. Not to myself. Maybe a bit of a martyr. It's in the blood." He grinned for the first time since Harriet had arrived. "And right now, I'm cold and hungry and . . . scared. But I know why I'm here. How's Albie?" he asked quickly, changing the subject. "Have you seen my mother? How's Alice doing?"

"Albie misses you. And your mother actually helped us. Took a turn on the mimeo. Issued a few orders. I'll be going over later to say the Rosary with her. . . ." Harriet rolled her eyes heavenward and winked. It didn't seem possible they could laugh at such a time, but they had to. "She's out there in the crowd," Harriet continued. "Alice feels better. No more news of Wayne, though. She and Mother—"

Patrick held her to him suddenly. "Have you forgiven me?" There was so little time. "Yes," she replied, head against his chest. Through the windows of the front doors, they could see the snow, falling steadily now, swirling in sudden gusts. Desks could be piled against the doors, figured Patrick, thinking ahead.

"Go," he said again, but held tight to her hand. "A 'conservative bastard'? You really let me have it. What came over me? I worship you," he added, eyes filling. "Go on," he said brusquely, reaching for the knob and pulling open the door. Snowflakes whooshed in and he couldn't let her go.

"Last night I couldn't sleep. I walked through this place, trying to stay warm . . . trying to figure out what had happened. It was the principle of the thing, don't you see? It seemed to me you acted as if I didn't exist. Blanked me out. I let people do that to me for years. I couldn't let you get away with it. You're my wife."

"I am. I am. But I'm also—"

"You see, I never believed you really loved me. Not that I deserved—"

"No," Harriet protested. "I was impossible. For so long. You were right about that. Alice used to ask me what I was waiting for. When I look at you now, I can't believe what a fool I was. I guess I don't need to shoot my big mouth off all the time. Mother tells me I don't have to get up on the barricades and—"

"You were terrific yesterday. Up there on Meyer's truck. I felt awed. We all did. And I thought to myself how close I came to losing you." Patrick didn't understand the whole of his fear. Or why he should feel so threatened by Harriet, whose independent ways stimulated yet scared him. Hers was a freedom he'd never dared claim for himself, until recently. "What would I be without you? If it hadn't been for you, the paper would've folded. Ma'd be searching for something else for me; I'd be dating some nice Catholic girls and turning into Dennis."

"You could never—"

"I was close. But you changed all that. It's frightening to admit owing your life to someone. It scares the pants off me. You scare the pants off me. When I left C.U., I only vaguely knew why. But now I do. I left because . . . of you. I didn't even know you existed. And . . . here you are."

Letty had spoken of the healing power of love, and Patrick and Harriet were mending each other. Clinging to him, she stroked his whiskers and kissed away his tears.

"I'm not going," she said suddenly.

"Yes, you are."

"You know how I feel about being given orders."

"Harriet."

"It's settled. I'm safer than you. They won't hurt a woman. That's where our inequality has its benefits."

"Harriet—"

"I'm staying."

"Where is my son?"

"He and the girl are still in the mill, sir. It doesn't look like they're coming out."

Phelps swore under his breath, looked at his watch, and slammed down the receiver. Fifteen minutes later, he called Jenkins back and was told the situation hadn't changed. Desks, the commander informed Phelps, were now barricading the main doors. "Apparently they intend to resist, sir."

"Do your job. Drag them out."

"What about your son?" The "sir" was missing.

"I don't have a son," Phelps snapped, startled by a quick movement at the library doors where Nancy stood, overhearing, and raised her hand to her face as if warding off a blow. Phelps set the receiver back into its cradle, shriveling at the pure hatred that struck him from her eyes.

"How do you do, Mrs. Flynn?" Common as clay was Letty's immediate impression. Painted-up, tinted hair, the eyes behind the spectacles suspicious. "Hello, Mrs. Hoskins." A contest of wills, two pairs of eyes locked, neither giving ground. Two strong-willed women, they had nothing in common save for the anxiety each felt for her child today, save for the terrible waiting as the time ticked off.

Word of the three o'clock deadline had rushed through town like a fire in dry grass, and by two o'clock the largest crowd ever had gathered.

From surrounding towns they'd come as well, many having not returned to work after lunch, all of them drawn to the drama in Jericho. Some of Leveret's textile workers came, too—the braver ones, who risked instant dismissal by leaving their looms for the afternoon and taking the trolley to Jericho.

As the clock on the town hall struck quarter after two, the crowd took a collective breath. Twenty feet deep on the sidewalks and curbs, perched on cars on the side streets, hanging over building fronts, it watched the guardhouse and the mill while Letty and Gert, introduced by Alice, eyed each other.

"Do you know my Rose?" Snowflakes on the inky hair under her hat, Rose raised her head and offered a nod. The packaging, thought Letty, was impressive. She'd heard enough about the Flynn daughter to know the contents weren't. "Do you know my daughter, Cora? Mrs. Cousins." Gert had met Cora previously and assessed her as foolish. And how much alike they all looked, these Hoskinses, with their large Protestant mouths and coats out of style by a year or two. Gert nodded to Frankie. Dennis shook hands with Sam. "Well, here we all are," said Alice wryly, "the two camps met."

Both Gert and Letty ignored the comment, but Teresa, holding tightly to Matt's arm, nodded. It was danger to kin that had them all here, brought them within a stone's throw of each other as nothing else could. "God love her," murmured Teresa. "Inside there with him, sharing the risk of it. They're brave ones, they are."

"What do ya make of it, Mrs. Hoskins?" Gert asked, working her rosary beads inside her plaid coat pocket. Letty shook her head, glancing along with Gert to the mill, each new movement of the troops causing frowns. She wasn't surprised that Harriet had elected to stay with Patrick. Harriet would naturally be in the thick of things, and Letty was proud of her.

"Mr. Phelps won't allow anything to happen. Not with Elliot. . . ." Cora said. All of them nodded, wishing Cora were right. "Don't be naive," Alice retorted. "He'll sacrifice Elliot. He's out for blood." If only Wayne could be here today!

Letty wished Alice hadn't taken away the hope quite so forthrightly.

"You have to give Elliot some credit, I guess," Alice went on. Frankie nodded, wanting his former friend to be seen in a good light.

"Maybe they took him as a hostage," Dennis suggested. Envious of

449

his brother's boldness and rise to fame, his ulcer burned. "I heard the rumor."

"That doesn't sound like Patrick," Letty said, eyes meeting Gert's again. "We're all very fond of Patrick," she added. "He's a wonderful boy."

Moved, Gert nodded thanks. "Don't we all feel the same about Harriet!" exclaimed Teresa, glancing at her sister. Once again Gert nodded, a nod a long time in coming, a necessary nod. "She's a brave girl," she murmured. *Worthy for my Pat*, she might have added, but enough was enough.

"Curley's coming. The Governor's coming himself."

The rumor spread through the crowd—along with others: Leveret General Hospital had been placed on alert, Roosevelt was sending Harry Hopkins, Phelps was on his way, Phelps had been shot.

"Curley?" scoffed Alice. "He doesn't want to be anywhere near here today. It's too much of a hot potato."

Her feeling that there was no way out seemed affirmed as two trucks of additional guardsmen lumbered up the street, stopping at the command post. The soldiers hopped down; the snow couldn't absorb the sound of their boots, which smacked ominously on the pavement. The sight of their rifles shook the crowd into a sudden terrible tenseness as it pressed itself against the line of soldiers that held it back. Joe stared at the mill. Faces had been visible at the windows, but barely, obscured by the snow. Now they had disappeared. He wanted to be with his son, knew that if the time came he'd be joining the men who were gathering with barely concealed crowbars and baseball bats in the alleys, ready to go to the aid of their fellows inside. At Morin's Garage by the depot, Jerry Finneran had a tire iron within reach.

"Father . . . here!"

Franklin spotted Cora waving to him and moved through the crowd. Back from his three-day road trip, he was filled in by Letty and introduced to the Flynns.

"My daughter's in there," Franklin said a moment later to one of the soldiers. "I want to talk to who's in charge." The soldier walked across the street, returned, and escorted Franklin to the guardhouse. "My daughter's in there," he said tersely to Jenkins. "I want to talk to her."

"I have orders from Governor Curley, sir. No one is allowed in." Harassed and on edge, Jenkins eyed the crowd.

"I want to get her out! Let me talk to her. Don't you want to avoid this?"

"It's out of my hands, sir."

"He has forty-five minutes to make up his mind."

"Patrick, he's not going to change his—"

"I'm praying that he does."

Behind the two of them in the vastness of a room the size of half a football field, the men stood in quiet groups of two and three. Dwarfed by the huge machines he used to operate, the hanging lamps from the grid two stories above him dark, Marienetti paced through the stilled looms, a caged panther. Like a boy rattling a stick along a picket fence, he whacked a two-foot wooden bobbin against the machines, and the clatter echoed in the strange, hollow silence. Others had similar weapons; pockets revealed pipe wrenches.

"Patrick," Harriet pleaded, "don't let it happen. Don't fight. Get arrested but—"

"It's not enough. About those trees," he added, giving her an enigmatic smile, trying to calm her.

"Trees?" Harriet had to think for a moment. "Oh, the trees! I wish I'd never bought them."

"I have an idea. When this is over . . . we should develop a campaign for subscriptions. We always said we needed to mount one. What would you say to the idea of giving a free Christmas tree to everyone who buys a six-month subscription? Sort of an inducement."

"My trees? My Godforsaken Christmas trees that caused a civil war? Are those the trees you might be referring to? Not *those* trees."

"Those are the ones. *Our* trees."

"I love you," she said, hugging him to her.

Patrick had to keep moving, for the waiting was intolerable. Swinging his arms like an athlete primed for the game, he had an overwhelming urge to take Harriet by the hand, lead her to the far recesses of the plant and make love.

"Look," he exclaimed suddenly, nodding out the window. Across the street the Movietone crew was setting up its cameras on the roof of the hardware store. Huddled under a blanket, the operators hoped they wouldn't lose the light before the action started. Reporters hung out the doors of the depot, ready to spring for the phones. The presence of Harriet and Elliot in the mill gave the story an added fillip of appeal. Typewriters clacked at the impromptu desks set up on the benches in the waiting room. The boss's son and the wife of the editor who'd held the mill for three days! One of them, he was, they'd been telling each other since they got to Jericho. Flynn, a newspaperman who'd placed himself in jeopardy. And if they had filed stories that were sympathetic, they couldn't be responsible if their editors and owners expressed a different opinion on the editorial pages and in the board rooms of the great papers of the East. "RENEGADE EX-SEMINARIAN HOLDS MILL" wrote the sob sisters who had readers waiting for the latest happening. "RIGHT VERSUS MIGHT" cried the tabloids that were on Patrick's side. "COMMIE SYMPATHIZERS" scowled the others.

451

And from inside the mill Patrick continued to watch them, while the cold eye of eternity he'd spoken of was watching him. All his life seemed pointed to today. He had no doubt Phelps felt the same. History and destiny had brought them together. A rush of events had propelled them both. Patrick's confrontation with Michael O'Brien seemed small and unpretentious compared to the enormity of today. Aquinas was in his thoughts; the three necessary steps toward salvation were for a man to know what he ought to believe, to desire, and what he ought to do. Patrick felt he knew the answer as never before. "Because he's evil," he murmured with the simplicity of the fanatic as well as the saint. "I wasn't trained to embrace it."

And when Harriet asked him what he wanted, he replied simply, "Power. The power to right wrongs." He was quoting her, for she'd said the same to him a few months back.

But today seemed on the one hand to have everything to do with Harriet and nothing at all. It was his own salvation that Patrick wrestled with and the inevitable question that had to be answered: Would he give his life?

Once again, the light was in his eyes, that mysterious glow that set him apart, the question answerable and not. Once again he prayed it wouldn't come to that. He wanted none of his flock to be hurt; he knew he would still be alive when the day was over and nighttime fell. He had no doubt of that. For if he were to die, he would lose Harriet, and he had no intention of losing her. So yes, the answer had to be yes, yes he would do what he had to, but nothing would happen to him; he felt almost serene.

"It's Mrs. Phelps!" The shout undulated from upstreet as Nancy Phelps' roadster honked furiously, scattering the crowd. She reached the line of soldiers and was let through, past the town hall, whose clock now read two-thirty, the car stopping at the command post. "It's Mrs. Phelps," buzzed the crowd, her unexpected appearance raising hopes for some kind of a solution.

Without a glance at the mass of humanity, Nancy Phelps stepped resolutely out of her car. Black hat set low on her head, blond chignon glinting above the mink collar, she disappeared inside the guardhouse, conferred with Jenkins, then reappeared a moment later, causing a stir as the gates were pulled back and she started up the walk to the front doors.

"Elliot," she called, banging an elegantly gloved fist against the glass, the cry to her son ringing out, repeated, the urgency and fear causing a tightening in the chests of other mothers, in Letty and Gert, all of whom understood.

"Elliot!"

Inside, Elliot appeared in the hallway. He couldn't get close to his mother, could see only a part of her through the desks piled in the way. "Where is he?" he shouted, growing nervous at the hysteria he recognized in her eyes. "He's coming, isn't he? He's going to stop it?"

Urgently Nancy shook her head no, pleading with Elliot to join her. Elliot was tempted, wanted to push aside the desks and have his mother take him away. Feeling some of the men behind him watching, he flushed. "I'm staying," he shouted at her. Filled with a resentment he didn't understand, he added, "I'm going to fight! Tell him that!"

He had no idea why he said it; the satisfaction he felt at Nancy's expression caused him to be frightened and confused, and he turned away and found Harriet and Patrick. "He's going ahead with it!" Behind him he heard Nancy calling to him. "I always come when Mummy calls," he quipped. But he ran from her, down the hallway, and pushed through the swinging doors that led to the looms. As if he could still hear her, he placed his hands over his ears and dashed through the stilled machinery to the far side of the building where Harriet found him trembling.

"I need a drink. Harriet, I— You heard—he's going ahead with it. I don't want to be here. He wouldn't, would he? She always tries to save me. She—" Holding onto himself, Elliot jabbered. "I'm a coward."

"You're not!"

"I'm missing Dr. Moeller. I should be in Boston. Is she gone?" Elliot rushed to a window, rubbing it feverishly to clear away the encrusted lint. Past the loading dock, he saw another truckload of troops forming at the River Street gates. "My being here hasn't done any good! It hasn't done any good! Look! He's not going to stop it! He doesn't care. He—"

In the moment after Elliot had asked if he could stay with them, Tyler had clapped him on the back and suggested he sit in his father's chair. Elliot had—he even picked up the paperweight and shook it, the gesture causing the men to laugh. It was a moment of pride and exhilaration that he mocked now.

"My redemption? All a sham. What good has it done? Maybe I thought I was Rhett Butler. I'm reading *Gone With The Wind*, you know. Have you read it? No—Patrick's Rhett. I'm Ashley, and you're Scarlett, and the Yankees are coming. *I don't want to fight anyone.*"

Fearful for Elliot, Harriet asked Patrick to help. They found him sitting on the floor of the dye room among the thousand-pound bales of South American wool. Patrick wondered why he should expend any effort on Elliot Phelps, who continued, as far as he was concerned, to play too large a part in his life.

"I want to go. What do you think of me now?"

"Then go. Take Harriet with you."

453

"I'm not leaving, Patrick."

"We're going to barricade ourselves in Phelps' office. You and Elliot stay here."

Trembling, Elliot jumped up and paced through the bales and around the huge vats that towered over him. "You've never liked me—"

"You're right. I didn't."

"Why should you? I don't think much of you, either. Oh, shit!" The dye room was dark and frightening, closed in and airless with no windows to the outside. "What's wrong with me?" he mumbled, trying to calm himself. "Why didn't I just go?" Silence enveloped the threesome, but his mother's cries still rang in his head. "I wanted to do my part . . . what difference does it make? It hasn't made a damn bit of difference. It never has. He'd like to see me hurt. He wants to—"

"Why should he?"

"Because I'm queer! Were you happy when she told you? I'll bet you were!" He glared at Patrick and demanded an answer to his question again. "Were you? If it hadn't been for me, you'd never have got her. You should thank me. Why don't you?"

Unwilling to be provoked, Patrick understood Elliot's self-laceration, but the rest of him was as much a mystery as it had been to Harriet. He knew Elliot had spoken the truth. If not happy, there was a part of Patrick that felt vindicated his rival had proved to have feet of clay.

"I love her, you know. I'm *not* what you think. You probably don't believe me." Whatever part of Elliot was rational found his own incoherence as baffling as Patrick did. "I wanted to stay because . . . I thought I'd win a little respect . . . and here I am . . . running from my mother. OK. I wanted *you* to respect me. *You.*"

"I do."

"No—" Elliot took a swing at Patrick, which the latter deflected easily. "I don't want to get hurt," he cried. Ashamed, he turned away.

"Nobody's asking you to. Get a hold of yourself. Are you hearing me? Nobody expects you to fight."

"I'm trying," Elliot replied, biting his lip and struggling to regain some semblance of control. "I don't want to be like this."

"Don't you think I'm afraid, too? It isn't the mark of a coward. I want you to stay back here with Harriet."

"No," protested Elliot.

"I want you to look after Harriet."

The shaky side of the triangle stared at Patrick, then to Harriet. "Elliot," she pleaded, "listen to him!" She marveled at Patrick's patience.

"You took a courageous stand to come here," he insisted. "And to stay. I respect that. I don't require you to do any more. Who am I anyway? I'm not your judge and jury."

• • •   454

Deflated, the crowd watched as Nancy Phelps made a U-turn and drove slowly up the street. Once again, the guardsmen let her through and the crowd retreated. Accelerating, driving swiftly back toward North Parish, on Great Pond Road she saw her husband's Cadillac bearing down on her. Rushing like a black hearse through the snow, the car sped past the deserted fairways of the country club, sped past Nancy, racing for town. She turned and followed.

"*It's Mr. Phelps!*" A collective sigh gripped the northern edge of the crowd as Phelps' car approached and stopped. The sheer force of his energy scattering the bodies, they fell back mesmerized as he strode through them and appeared in the middle of the street.

Hatless, eyes burning, he started for the command post. Hands holding hammers tensed, bats were gripped and stones in fists fingered, but Phelps' sense of authority and defiance held them in check. "It's Mr. Phelps," went the cry, almost respectfully now, for his bravado intimidated them. Gert crossed herself as enormous relief flooded her.

"ELLIOT'S JOINED THEM!" challenged Shapiro, his voice seeming louder than ever. "WHAT ARE YOU GOING TO DO?" he added, the question causing frowns in those who didn't want Phelps provoked at such a delicate moment. Others expressed satisfaction at the public humiliation inflicted as Shapiro hammered it home again. "YOUR OWN SON, PHELPS! HAVE YOU GOT THE MESSAGE?"

If he did, Phelps didn't show it. The taunts continued as he approached the guardhouse and glanced at his mill with an almost yearning fondness. The vulnerability was short-lived; his Pinkerton guards, led by their chief, Lawson, met him in a hurried conference, and the armada continued until it reached Major Jenkins.

"Mr. Phelps—" Harried and uneasy at the potential violence that was brewing, Jenkins was as relieved as the rest of the crowd that Phelps had appeared. "I've been trying to reach the Governor," continued Jenkins, nodding to Phelps to enter the confines of the guardhouse. Phelps refused. "I'm sure some kind of compromise—"

"Why?" Phelps snapped. "The Governor's given you your orders."

"The situation is explosive—" Jenkins eyed the Pinkertons who stood around Phelps. Marauders in business suits, natty scarves at their necks, they fingered pistols in overcoat pockets.

"Do your job," demanded Phelps.

"I feel the Governor should be apprised of the situation."

"The Governor? You're in charge here. Aren't you?"

"The situation, as I say, isn't what it was." Jenkins nodded to the mill. "They don't intend to let us arrest them. *They* won't allow it, either," he went on, glancing worriedly at the crowd, knowing it was a coiled wire ready to snap at the slightest provocation.

455

"Won't allow it?" snarled Phelps sarcastically. "There're three hundred of you!"

"And over a thousand of them."

"Fire a few shots. That'll send them running. Do I have to tell you your business? Do your job! Give me my mill back! *I'll have your ass if you don't.*"

"Mr. Phelps—" Jenkins wasn't used to civilians giving him orders; neither was he prepared for this sudden clash with Phelps, whose maniacal intensity threatened to escalate an already dangerous situation.

"Abraham—"

Phelps, Jenkins, and the Pinkertons all turned as an enraged Nancy Phelps thrust herself among them. "Are you insane?" she cried. "Stop this. Get him out of there. You can't allow this to proceed. If he's hurt, I'll—"

"This isn't a safe place for you." Phelps nodded to his men. "Escort my wife—"

"If Elliot—"

"That's his choice."

Jenkins' stomach curdled; Nancy Phelps began to tremble. "Abraham," she pleaded, "don't do this. I'll divorce you," she snapped, her mind desperately grasping at threats. Armoring himself against the vengeance in his wife's eyes, Phelps turned away and once again directed the Pinkertons to remove her.

"Your *son* . . ." pleaded Nancy, who knew her husband was beyond hearing or seeing her. Maddened, she threw off Lawson's arm, stepped swiftly in front of Phelps and slapped his face. Phelps grasped her arm firmly. *"Your* son—" he spat bitterly, color rising in him that had nothing to do with embarrassment at dignity trampled or nastiness revealed.

"It's Dad!" cried Elliot, who returned to the office in response to the others' shouts that had echoed through the mill.

"I told you he'd come!" he cried, peering down to the guardhouse. Shocked at the sight of his mother being led off by the Pinkertons, he gripped Harriet's arm.

"Dad!" he yelled as if Phelps might hear him, but chaos had once again returned to the command post.

"Do your job," Phelps shouted as Jenkins tried to reach Curley on the phone. But the Governor was unavailable, and Jenkins knew why. The Governor was 'unavailable' because he didn't want the ultimate responsibility. Let Jenkins bear the burden and hang himself. The clock on the town hall struck three, while in Leveret—in defiance of their owners' wishes—mill whistles began hooting in sympathy.

Jenkins conferred with his lieutenants; the Pinkertons with Phelps. The latter turned on Jenkins. "You take care of this, or I will. But if I have to, I'll make sure I finish you. You won't have a command. You won't—"

456

Phelps' insinuations that he would demolish his career didn't bother Jenkins as much as what came next:

"My men will use their guns if they have to."

"The Governor has ordered no shooting," Jenkins replied quickly, but Phelps turned and began giving orders.

"Son of a bitch!" murmured Marienetti, "the bastard's going through with it." He and some others rushed from the office and up to the second-floor windows overlooking the scene below as a reluctant Jenkins ordered a contingent of soldiers up the sidewalk.

"*It's gas—they've got gas!*" Patrick took Harriet's arm. "Elliot," he ordered, "take her back to the dye room. *Now.*"

Stunned at his father's betrayal, Elliot couldn't move. Patrick grabbed him and spun him around, pushing both Elliot and Harriet out of the office.

"Patrick," pleaded Harriet. Forcibly, Patrick hurried the two of them down the hallway, pushing them through the doors to the weaving room. "*Move.* Go back there. I'll join you. *Go. Elliot—take her!*"

Harriet took Elliot's arm, and they began to run.

Hopes dashed, aghast that Phelps was allowing it to proceed, the crowd grew angry. It strained against the troops as the first contingent of guardsmen broke the glass of the front doors and lobbed canisters of tear gas into the hallway. Trampling the shrubbery, the soldiers retreated against the sides of the building, only to have pots of dye thrown down on them from the second story. Splattered with the dyes, the snow under their boots stained yellow and seeping umber, they scattered and the crowd cheered. A second contingent of twenty, wearing gas masks, started up the sidewalk. The creatures smashed through the remaining glass and forced the doors. Crashing through the desks, they entered the deserted gas-filled hallway, then proceeded cautiously. Phelps' office was empty. Slowly they continued and entered the weaving room. Suddenly the machines came to life as Patrick and his group turned them on, each man hiding at a loom, all of them weeping and coughing from the seeping gas.

Startled by the cacophony of the erupting looms, jumped from behind by Marienetti and the others, the soldiers panicked. Several were knocked unconscious, their rifles grabbed. As Marienetti and Patrick and the men fled the weaving room—smashing windows on their way to let out the gas—the soldiers withdrew, dragging their comrades with them. The sight of them retreating out the doors in obvious disarray brought the crowd to a frenzy.

In the pandemonium that was the command post, with milling troops grown nervous and angry at the sight of the wounded, Phelps spewed a torrent of abuse upon Jenkins, who was hard put to keep control of a situation that was rapidly escalating toward anarchy.

457

"I thought you told me you'd have no trouble—"

"Phelps, let me run this." The only comfort Jenkins had was his decision, made earlier in the day, to issue buckshot to his troops instead of ammunition. One civilian hit by a stray bullet and he had a riot on his hands. Appalled, he watched a section of the crowd, led by Jerry Finneran and some of the strikers, break through the troops on River Street. Their intention to enter the mill from a side entrance was thwarted by warning shots fired in the air.

"Do something!" shouted Phelps. Back at the second-story windows, Marienetti and his band jeered at the soldiers below, who were waiting orders from Jenkins.

"Toy soldier," Phelps spat contemptuously. "Go in after them! Go in the back. Cover the loading dock."

"I'm not going to send my men into a situation with which they're unfamiliar."

"*Cocksucker!* Flush them out!"

"I don't know where they are," barked Jenkins, containing his desire to knock Phelps to the ground. "They could be anywhere in there. I don't have enough men to—"

"There are only fifty of them," screamed Phelps as Jenkins walked away from him, shouting orders. He pulled more men away from the mill and sent them to keep order in the street. "I need every available man. Do you want a riot?"

Tormented by Phelps, Jenkins ordered him arrested, but the Pinkertons quickly surrounded Phelps and drew their pistols. "Try it, you son of a bitch," screamed Phelps as the whistle from his own mill began to blow in short staccato bursts, answering the whistles from Leveret. Now the mob was jeering him, too. Mocked on all sides, his own mill whistle the final insult, Phelps went berserk. There was none of the previous ranting, however. Something more deadly and terrifying struck his heart as he felt an intimation of his own death and saw his father. The mob was the same and the cycle completed, yet Phelps almost smiled as immortality rushed in him and he knew he could never be harmed, would live forever.

Snow dusted his baldness, flakes glittered on the velvet collar of his Chesterfield coat as some finely tuned wire snapped and he turned to his security chief, Lawson, then started quickly up the path. Automatically the pack followed their leader. Two of them picked up canisters of gas dropped by the soldiers. The sight of Phelps and his armada headed for the main doors caused the crowd to be suddenly quiet, but the whistle continued like hammers against Phelps' head. Disregarding Jenkins' cry that he could not be responsible for his safety, Phelps entered his mill.

"Those boys'll use 'em," whispered Marienetti from the window above as the Pinkertons disappeared into the building beneath him. As

458

Phelps and his bully boys moved quickly down the hallway, Marienetti and his group stalked him from the upper floor, keeping tabs down stairwells. Red-eyed from the lingering remains of the gas, several of the Pinkertons drew guns while others tensed, ready to throw fresh canisters. The sight of the unmanned looms clacking away as he entered the weaving room caused Phelps to become enraged. Rushing from one to the other of the ravenous machines, which years of feeding with mile upon mile of yarn had never satiated, Phelps shut them down one by one until a ghostly silence descended on the mill.

"Pa— How—?"

"Don't I know more ways in and out of this place than anyone?" Joe grinned and clapped Patrick on the back.

Holding an unaccustomed rifle in hand, which he'd wrested away from one of the earlier disabled guardsmen, Patrick took Joe back down the steps into the boiler room where he, Jack Tyler, and about fifteen others had reconnoitered.

"Himself's inside, Paddy."

"Phelps?"

Joe nodded. "Along with Lawson and his boys. Ten or so."

"The soldiers?"

Joe didn't know. "Lawson's more the danger, Paddy. He's a mean one." Patrick nodded. What was the plan? the others wanted to know. The younger ones were ready to fight; the possibility of taking on Phelps himself fired them anew, but Patrick was cautious. Signaling the others to hide, he started back up the narrow iron stairs.

"Ahhhh . . ." murmured Marienetti, adrenaline pumping at the game of cat and mouse. Leading his band stealthily above Phelps' head, crossing into the mending room, he could hear Phelps and the Pinkertons below. Out of touch with Patrick, he paused, listening. Other groups of three and four were scattered throughout the three acres of buildings, no one exactly sure where his friends were. Footsteps echoed as Marienetti continued to stalk Phelps, who passed out of weaving and into the deserted spinning room. The Pinkertons paused, ears cocked.

"If anyone resists—shoot." Lawson glanced at Phelps for a confirmation of his order. As if it were obvious, Phelps nodded curtly, and the armada continued.

"Boilers," ordered Phelps, and three of his men fanned out in that direction. Hearing Phelps' command, Patrick ducked inside. Marienetti, too, heard Phelps. Inching down from upstairs, rifle in hand, he tensed. Hearing the Pinkertons approach, he waited in a stairwell, saw them pass, then darted down the stairs and sprayed them with buckshot. Crying out, the Pinkertons turned and fired, but Marienetti had already dashed up the stairs, his laughter inflaming the Pinkertons, who gave chase. Rushing through a corridor filled with wicker baskets of raw wool which were sent careening, the Pinkertons shouted to one another.

In the dye room Harriet and Elliot heard the shots and the distant shouting. Back in the boiler room, Patrick heard them, too, and headed in their direction.

The Pinkertons regrouped. Two out of commission with wounds in their legs, the others wanted revenge. The blood lust in their eyes, they began moving, their purpose deadlier now as silence once again wrapped the mill.

From behind the bales, Harriet held her breath as the doors to the dye room swung open and Marienetti and several others entered. Unsure who it was, her hand tightened in Elliot's; then she recognized Marienetti's voice as he and the men started out again. "Paul?" she whispered.

"Shhh," she got in return as he hurried toward her. "Where's Patrick?" they asked each other simultaneously, both shaking their heads in answer. Marienetti's eyes glittered in the darkness as he turned to Elliot. "Your father's in here . . . with his friends."

"I'll—talk to him. Where? I'll—"

Marienetti shook his head. "It's too late. C'mon—we can't stay here." With no other way out from the huge room, Marienetti and the others, followed by Harriet and Elliot, quickly headed for the exit. Just short of the doors, Marienetti flattened himself against the wall and gestured for the others to retreat.

Approaching outside, the Pinkertons paused, listening. In the far distance there was a shout, then silence. Inside, Marienetti signaled his men to take position behind the enormous drying machines. Hiding behind those huge ovens fit only for giants, they waited. Crouched behind the bales again, Harriet and Elliot heard voices in the corridor.

Phelps nodded to the Pinkertons, who advanced cautiously. Their shadows loomed against the vats as the doors swung open, admitting what little light there was. Like trained dogs sniffing the quarry, they backed out again, nodding to their employer.

"Use the gas."

Elliot recognized his father's voice. He tried to cry out, but couldn't, thought he had—as one often does in a dream—only to wake and find that all the action and shouting has been unconscious. Harriet put her arms around him, but the gesture only increased his trembling. The first canister hit a few feet away; a slight hiss and the gas was released. Elliot called his father's name again, but there wasn't a sound. Harriet got up and tried to pull him with her, but he couldn't be budged. He lay down and hugged himself as the gas seeped around him.

Weeping, Harriet ran to escape the fumes, ran past the vats until she reached Marienetti. *"Go,"* he whispered urgently, covering his face with a handkerchief as the gas inexorably approached, poisoning the air. "Get out. . . . They won't hurt you. . . . Go . . ."

Gasping and disoriented in the dark, Harriet tried to find her way back to Elliot. Calling his name, then Patrick's, she lost her way and stumbled. *"Elliot's in here!"* she screamed as she collapsed, overwhelmed by the fumes.

Harriet's cry caused Phelps to freeze in surprise. "Get him," he barked to the Pinkertons who had taken position, pistols raised at the doorway. The order could not be carried out, for Patrick, Joe and the others appeared at the end of the hall, and the Pinkertons whirled their guns on them.

I am going to die. Hallucinating, Elliot heard shouts, but they came from a great distance. A coughing nightmare erupted around him as Marienetti and the others, crazed with the necessity to get out, rushed past. Crawling now, he started for the doors and found Harriet, who was semiconscious.

Bursting from the room, bellowing in fury, Marienetti fired, the buckshot peppering wildly as chaos broke out. Shot, Marienetti spun to the floor, holding his arm as Patrick and Joe rushed forward.

"No!" ordered Phelps, as other men crashed wildly out the doors. Stumbling over Marienetti as they tried to rush the Pinkertons, they fell, gasping.

"Stop," cried Phelps, but his dogs weren't obeying. Forces he'd unleashed now beyond his control, the Pinkertons continued to fire on their attackers as Patrick tried to get into the dye room and was stopped by Lawson, who aimed a pistol at him. Like a bull, Joe charged the Pinkerton chief, knocking him to the floor just as Elliot, carrying Harriet, staggered into the melee of flailing bodies.

"Stop it!" Elliot screamed, letting Harriet slide from his arms. Gasping for air, he found Phelps, who had retreated into the stairwell. "Stop it!" he screamed again, and with a rush of energy he started through the hand-to-hand fighting toward his father. There was a moment, he was never able to remember it clearly, when he saw Lawson raise his pistol and aim it at Joe Flynn's back. The deliberateness of the gesture seemed in slow motion. Later, Elliot was to say he stumbled. Phelps saw the instinctive movement; Patrick saw it, too, saw Elliot step between Joe Flynn and Lawson. The bullet entered Elliot with a soft thud, penetrating above his unsuspecting heart.

"Dad," he murmured, almost plaintively, as if it were a question. "Dad," he said again, then his knees gave way and everything suddenly stopped as Major Jenkins and a contingent of guardsmen arrived, full of the sudden importance of soldiers who had missed the battle.

Frozen in place, the combatants seemed momentarily stunned as

461

Jenkins took charge. "Call a doctor," someone yelled in the strange silence, broken only by the murmurs of the wounded. Seeping gas from the dye room had them all weeping as Harriet knelt beside Elliot and took him in her arms. Blood darkened his shirt as she pulled back his overcoat. Patrick and his men were surrounded and disarmed, the Pinkertons likewise, but the action seemed matter of fact and unimportant as Phelps approached Elliot, whose eyes were open in a shocked calm as he met his father's.

"Elliot . . ." Phelps reached a hand down. "Elliot," he repeated, the name softer. Almost falling, Phelps knelt and took his son from Harriet, cradling him gently against his chest.

25 🞖

UPRISING IN MASS. TEXTILE PLANT PUT DOWN;
   OWNER'S SON WOUNDED, FIFTY-THREE ARRESTED

Jericho, Mass. Dec. 4— Ordered by Governor James Curley, National Guard troops took back Phelps Mill after a battle in which eight were wounded by gunfire, including the son of the owner.

Three weeks' worth of unrest and a near riot culminated in the arrest of the fifty-three insurgents who had seized the mill on Tuesday. Arraignment in Leveret District Court is expected tomorrow.

Governor Curley ordered the Guard into Jericho on Tuesday to bring order to a rapidly escalating situation in this mill town of five thousand, twenty miles north of Boston.

NEWSPAPER EDITOR AND WIFE ARRESTED

Patrick Flynn, owner and editor of *The Jericho Spectator*, and his wife were among those in the mill at the time of the action. Flynn, according to Major Charles Jenkins, was one of the leaders of the uprising and had locked horns with Phelps in the three weeks since the latter closed the mill down to thwart representatives of the American Federation of Labor in their attempts to organize his operatives. "We've won a great moral victory for organized labor," Meyer Shapiro, union representative, was quoted as saying. Abraham Phelps was unavailable for comment. His refusal to negotiate with Shapiro was one of the causes of the strife that has rocked Jericho since the middle of November.

OPERATIVES SIT DOWN AT LOOMS

In an apparent sympathy gesture to their fellows in

463

Jericho, operatives at ten other mills in the Phelps chain are
reported to have sat down at their looms and refused to work.

excerpt reprinted from
The New York Times
Dec. 4, 1936

JERICHO STILL TENSE; BAIL DENIED LAWBREAKERS
PHELPS DENOUNCES ILLEGAL SIT-DOWNS,
CLAIMS RED INFLUENCE; PERKINS ENTERS PICTURE

Jericho, Mass. Dec. 5— Denouncing the unprecedented
sit-down that has continued in his plants at Dracut, Methuen,
and Providence, R.I., Abraham Phelps vowed to continue his
battle against the A.F. of L.

Meanwhile, Labor Secretary Frances Perkins has been
working, along with Mass. Governor James Curley, to bring
the two sides to the negotiating table.

Calling them "dangerous lawbreakers," Judge James
McCallister denied bail to the insurgents. Essex County prosecutor, Lyman Farnsworth, expressed satisfaction. Trial is set
for January.

All sides traded charges today. In Jericho, where the mill
remains closed and tension high, Phelps waved a court order at
assembled reporters and insisted his action in taking back his
mill had been legal. Phelps added that Judge McCallister's
decision to deny bail was a courageous one in the face of the
"mobocracy that threatens to take over our streets and business
under the guise of organized labor."

Phelps' son, meanwhile, remains in critical condition in
Leveret General Hospital. Phelps refused to answer questions
as to his son's possible involvement in the uprising. Seven
others remain in the hospital.

Phelps denounced Patrick Flynn, the ex-seminarian
turned newspaper editor, as "a radical who set out to fan the
flames of insurrection for personal gain." Flynn and his wife
remain in jail along with the rest of the insurgents.

Meyer Shapiro of the American Federation of Labor accused Phelps of "forty years of provocation. The Pinkertons,"
he was quoted as saying, "fired on unarmed men." Asked if the
rebels hadn't broken the law themselves in their seizure of the
textile mill, Shapiro quoted the Wagner Act, which gives labor
the right to organize. Denied that right by Phelps, Shapiro
continued, the strikers had no choice.

Denouncing Judge McCallister's decision to refuse bail, Shapiro implied the Essex County justice system was under the influence of the textile industry of Leveret. He accused Phelps and the "textile aristocracy" of a "ruthless determination to keep the working men and women under the heel of their boot."

LEVERET ANGRY

Sentiment in favor of the insurgents is high in the textile city of Leveret, Mass., where an uneasy peace prevails. Judge McCallister's decision has provoked a storm of protest among the rank and file of Leveret's twenty thousand operatives . . .

excerpt reprinted from
New York Daily Sun,
Dec. 5, 1936

RALLY IN JERICHO; STRIKERS STILL JAILED

Jericho, Mass. Dec. 6— Led by Harriet Flynn, who was released from the Leveret Jail yesterday, a rally in support of the forty-nine prisoners who remain incarcerated was held on the main street of Jericho last night.

One thousand marched in a candlelit vigil to demand that bail be granted to the remaining prisoners. Speakers included several state and county officials. Matthew Tobin, Massachusetts Attorney General, was quoted as saying that "release of those held would diffuse the lingering hostility that permeates not only Jericho, but Leveret and the other textile centers of Massachusetts as well."

Sources in the Governor's office confirm that Curley is working behind the scenes to force Judge McCallister to alter his decision to refuse bail.

Meyer Shapiro, who spoke at last night's rally, restated his demands that Abraham Phelps negotiate with the A.F. of L. Shapiro denounced the "unlawful holding of prisoners," and repeated his charges that "Judge McCallister takes his orders from the textile magnate, Phelps, and William Wood of American Woolen," who has strongly supported the action of Judge McCallister.

Shapiro said the union was ready to post bail in any amount necessary. He offered his continued support to the operatives in the rest of Phelps' empire, urged them not to waver, and applauded the unprecedented sit-down strikers as the "brave men and women who have vowed not to return to their looms until the prisoners are released."

HARRIET FLYNN SPEAKS

The wife of Patrick Flynn and co-owner of *The Jericho Spectator*, which led the battle against Abraham Phelps, said that she was released because she was a woman. Insisting she had been released against her will, Mrs. Flynn urged a continuing public outcry against Judge McCallister.

The insurgents were arrested three days ago.

excerpt from
The Boston Herald,
Dec. 6, 1936

44,000 AUTOWORKERS SIT DOWN IN MICHIGAN

Flint, Michigan, Dec. 6— Echoing last week's action at Phelps Textiles in Massachusetts, Flint's automobile workers, enraged at General Motors' refusal to negotiate with the United Automobile Workers, abruptly sat down on their assembly lines yesterday morning. Copying the action in Jericho, Mass. a week and a half ago that saw Phelps Mill invaded and held by a band of fifty strikers, the auto workers have held the plants fortress and vow to continue to hold them until General Motors' management negotiates with their union. Plants affected included the Fisher Body No. 1 and 2 at Flint and the Fleetwood and Cadillac plants in Detroit.

excerpt from
The New York Times,
Dec. 6, 1936

GOVERNOR CURLEY APPLIES PRESSURES
PHELPS FORCED TO BARGAINING TABLE

Boston, Dec. 9— Governor Curley announced this morning that Abraham Phelps and Meyer Shapiro of the A.F. of L. will meet tomorrow at the Parker House.

Forced to the table by the continued revolt throughout his empire of twelve mills, Phelps has agreed to negotiate. The threat of federal prosecution delivered to Phelps by representatives of the Department of Labor was called the determining factor.

excerpt from
The Boston Herald,
Dec. 9, 1936

INSURGENTS RELEASED FROM JAIL;
CURLEY DENIES OPPORTUNISM

Leveret, Dec. 10— Bail of fifty thousand dollars was posted by the A.F. of L. in Leveret today. Undisclosed sources disclosed Judge McCallister implied that Governor Curley had employed strong-armed tactics. The Governor denied the charges and revealed that the Justice Department in Washington had applied pressure.

Essex County prosecutor Farnsworth attacked the Governor's motives. "Curley's scared of alienating his constituency," Farnsworth was quoted as saying. "He's more interested in feathering his political nest than keeping a radical element off the streets." Farnsworth vowed to prosecute the offenders with all the muscle the law allows. Trial date is set for February 10 in Leveret District Court.

FLYNN AND OTHERS RELEASED

Patrick Flynn told a cheering crowd in Leveret yesterday that justice had been done. The ex-seminarian, who was arrested last week, held a reunion with his wife on the steps of the Leveret City Jail as an impromptu noontime rally brought thousands of this mill city's workers out into the streets.

Flynn told the crowd he intended to continue his fight. Reminding them of the negotiating sessions that continue in Boston between Abraham Phelps and Meyer Shapiro, he urged the crowd to make itself heard. "The fate of justice and fair play in the textile industry," he told the crowd, "will be decided this week in Boston."

Asked his plans, Flynn said he intended to go home and get a newspaper out . . .

excerpt from
The Boston Herald,
Dec. 10, 1936

Fitful, Elliot lay asleep. Under Gert's watchful eye, the nurse patted the perspiration on his forehead, then checked his bandaged chest. A

467

moment later she left the room and made no attempt to remind the solid woman in the corner that visiting hours were over. They'd got that settled the day after Elliot came out of surgery. No matter rules and regulations, Gert had made it clear that on her daily evening visits, if Elliot were asleep, she intended to be at his side when he waked.

Dissatisfied with the job the nurse had done, Gert removed a bottle of witch hazel from her bag, took a fresh washcloth from the commode, and tenderly applied the dampened cloth to Elliot's forehead.

Sitting again, she let her eyes close. Snatches of prayers for Elliot's welfare rose in her heart, followed by thoughts of Joe, who'd looked in earlier and was down in the lobby waiting. A smile played on Gert's face for the husband she'd taken for granted for so long he'd become invisible. But no longer. Joe had been spared, and Gert saw him now with a fresh eye. How could she have ever got along without him? was only one of the revelations she'd experienced. Joe's survival was a sign, yet it produced none of the usual ego-ridden substantiation of Gert's special pact with the Virgin, but something deeper. An awed serenity lay in her heart, an uncharacteristic humbleness, a desire to reach out. And on a long list of those who needed her, the troubled boy in the bed, who'd revealed that he didn't care if he lived or died, was uppermost.

Sheer and overwhelming gratitude had impelled her to the hospital the first day, waiting along with Phelps and Nancy until the bullet was removed and Elliot placed on the critical list.

Returning, Gert found Elliot on an intravenous tube, and for the forty-eight hours that life ran into his arm, she stared watchfully at the fragile connection and said her beads in tandem as the clear fluid flowed.

In the week since, an instinctive understanding had taken hold: Elliot was the most undernourished boy Gert had ever laid eyes on. The broth she made for him daily might put color in his pale cheeks, the tales she spun of her girlhood in Ireland might bring a smile, but Gert knew that all the broth in China would make only a small start toward getting Elliot Phelps in the world again and whole in his soul. He needed a mountain of mothering; she felt a powerful desire to see that he got it.

"There now . . ." she murmured as Elliot's hand rose in a spasm, then fell back. His ragged sleep continued. The blue veins on his wrists reminded Gert of his mother, who as far as Gert was concerned was no mother at all, with her brittle smile and air of distraction. No one that thin could be a proper mother; the thinness, for Gert, was symbolic of a larger deficiency, and she had arranged her visits so that she and Nancy Phelps didn't run into each other.

Nancy came in the mornings (sometimes again in the late afternoon), Phelps at odd times, and Gert in the evening, after she'd done her duty at the rectory. Her eagle eye had noted that Phelps and his wife came separately. On the rare occasions she saw them together, the estrangement and tension between the Phelps provided her with the clue as to why Elliot was the disembodied spirit he was. Gert understood post-surgical depression; the shock to the body would take mending time, but her instinct told her that Elliot's deprivation had to be laid on the step of a loveless marriage between a father who had other concerns and a mother who chattered of her activities and asked her son how she looked. He was a pawn between them, Gert decided. Neither of his parents gave Elliot what he needed most—a place to rest. His pouring out of his heart to her only confirmed it.

"How is he, Mrs. Flynn?"

Surprised to see Phelps at this late hour, Gert stepped back as he approached the bed. She nodded. Phelps recognized the curtness and looked at his son.

"Did he have supper?"

"A lamb chop. It was overdone, if ya ask me, but he ate it all."

Gert had worked hard to temper the contempt she felt for Phelps. Sorrow for his meanness had replaced her fury, and she tried to include him in her prayers as a way of atonement for the hatred she felt. If she'd once been impressed with her former employer, had assumed they had a friendship, that had all changed. Everything had changed the day she stood outside the mill and saw Phelps send the soldiers in against Patrick.

"Late meeting," he muttered, explaining his presence at this hour. He sensed Gert behind him and was uncomfortable. Gert knew the negotiations were going on, noted the drained tautness of Phelps, who grasped the back of a chair and sat heavily, staring at his sleeping son with haunted eyes. Gert and Phelps hadn't discussed his daily confrontations in Boston, nor whether the mill would reopen, nor anything since she'd accosted him in the corridor outside Elliot's room a couple of days after the battle. With Patrick and Joe not yet released from jail, and Phelps' public insistence that they belonged there, Gert had been unable not to speak her mind. "I'm ashamed of ya, I thought ya was a decent man," had been the least of her condemnation. "How much ill-will can any man carry to his judgment day without payin' a terrible price?" she'd demanded, frustrated with his coldness and lack of response.

A day later on her evening vigil, she found him sitting by Elliot's bed in undisguised misery, and Gert knew that somewhere, buried, Phelps' guilt gnawed. His suffering softened her slightly—not enough to blot out that snowy Thursday when she'd vowed vengeance on him; no, never enough softening to make up for the sight of the wounded carried out on stretchers, with her not knowing who; never enough to make her forget Patrick with his hands up and a rifle in his back, nor Joe behind him, nor the hush of the crowd, nor what might have been, as someone shouted that Elliot was one of those shot.

The irony had been inescapable to that stunned crowd—and for Gert, too—until later at the police station in Leveret when someone in the mob of relatives and reporters told her that Elliot Phelps had a hole in his chest because he'd deliberately stepped into a bullet meant for Joe Flynn. Irony had been replaced with astonishment and a necessary reassessment of a boy she'd considered a spoiled loser.

"He looks better," Phelps whispered hoarsely. "He is, and he isn't," Gert replied, all too familiar with Elliot's bitterness, which she'd tried to combat on her daily visits. "The body is mendin'," she continued. "It's not what I'm talkin' about. It may be none of my business"—the words were mere formality, for Gert intended to speak her mind—"but he's a boy in his prime with no hope. His heart's shriveled, Mr. Phelps. Shriveled in loneliness."

Did he hear? Did he have it in him to respond? A man who sent his goons against his own son? Who hadn't even said he was sorry? Outrage filled her again.

"I've tried—"

"Try harder."

In the moments when Elliot had been in surgery, Phelps had prayed. The latter activity was unusual for a man who had no belief in God, who in his secret soul believed he *was* one. Forced to accept that he would be responsible if his son were to die, Phelps had known anguish. Nancy had made sure her husband heard that terrifying condemnation, but Phelps hadn't needed his wife to remind him of his pain or his impotence as he waited for the doctors. Other hands held Elliot's life or death in their control. Phelps had vowed that if Elliot recovered he would be a better father, but the vow had no specifics and Phelps didn't know how. The impotence was doubled in the days since, as he watched his son's eyes open, lucid, then not, but a message unmistakable from Elliot, who regarded his father's appearances from an impenetrable distance, as if a stranger had entered the room. Phelps knew he wasn't wanted.

But he came every day. Sometimes twice, when he could break away. Compartmentalized, his grief and guilt were not allowed to affect his behavior in the outside world. If there were those, Gert included, who expected that his son's near death would mellow Phelps to a conciliatory position, they were mistaken. Humbled on all sides, Phelps continued to fight with undiminished ferocity, even as he was dragged to the negotiating table by the very forces he'd given life and power to with his intransigence.

Elliot murmured. Her concern radiating in the white room, Gert took his hand, for she knew he often woke with demons.

"I appreciate . . ." murmured Phelps, and found it hard to find the words. "I know ya do," Gert replied sternly. He looked shriveled himself.

"That day—" Once again Phelps paused, as the madness of it returned. "I tried to . . . put a stop to it."

"That day is past. I'm for forgettin' it myself. I won't forget what *he* did," she whispered, looking down at Elliot, whose head gave a start, then rested again. "A brave lad. Who won't even take credit for it," she added, wondering if Phelps knew that Elliot had mocked his instinctive action, wouldn't accept her nurturing praise, and told her that he'd done it on purpose, not to save Joe's life, but to end his own.

"Have ya told him what he means to ya? How many of us go through life forgettin' to say it? Have ya? Have ya told him ya love him?"

Phelps took a breath, lids drooping as he stared at Elliot, whose arm thrashed as he muttered something neither Gert nor Phelps could make out.

He was safe! He made it to shore and pulled himself out, looking over his shoulder at the sinking house with his parents in it. The windows disappeared under the water, except for an attic one. He watched in horror as his mother, then his father, emerged and began to swim toward him.

He ran through a strange city, cutting down alleys and up streets as they gained on him. Terrified, he darted this way and that, knowing they were closer. Suddenly his father caught him. Arms gripped him forcibly, holding him in place for Nancy, who raised the gun and shot him.

"It's over . . . there now," crooned Gert as Elliot tried to get up. Terrified eyes went from her to Phelps. Elliot cried out, then went limp. "Oh . . ." he murmured, holding tight to Gert's hand, "not a . . . good one. Not a good one. . . ."

"Just a nightmare. Over and done with." Gert bathed his forehead until Elliot's fearful eyes calmed. "My angel of mercy . . ." he whispered. "In a sea of fools," he added, giving Gert a relieved grin.

"I'll let you and your pa have a visit," she said, noting Elliot's eyes cloud. Seeing the same, Phelps flinched inwardly but gave no sign. "I'll be back to say good night to ya," Gert assured, feeling sorrow for the both of them, this father and son who glanced nervously at each other across a bed that was endless.

"How are you?"

"Fine."

"Is it still itching you under the bandage?"

Elliot nodded and focused on the chair in the corner where Gert usually sat. Suspicious of his father's concern and shaken by the nightmare, he ran a tongue over his lips and refused to look at Phelps.

"Are you thirsty?"

"No." *Do you know what he said? "I don't have a son." That's what he said.*

Nancy's words sliced through Elliot's head, and perspiration shone on his temples.

471

"We haven't had a chance to talk," began Phelps haltingly. "Now that you're feeling better . . ."

The words trailed off. Barricaded behind a necessary indifference, Elliot suppressed an angry retort. Talk? One of those famous "talks," whose result was always to make him feel inadequate?

"Who came to see you today?"

"Mummy. Patrick and Harriet." Elliot imagined his father's eyes dilating at the hated names, but he didn't look. He wished Gert hadn't shut the door, wished she'd return. He inhaled as he felt his father's hand take his; he pretended to cough as an excuse to remove it.

"Try and understand," Phelps began after an uncomfortable silence. He needed Elliot's forgiveness, but the latter's refusal to acknowledge him made it impossible to ask.

"Why should I?" On guard, Elliot shut his eyes. What good is this hatred? Gert had asked him. Someone has to bend. Nobody wins in a standoff of hardened hearts.

"I never meant . . . it to go as far as it did."

Wouldn't you rather I were dead? Unable to be reminded of the horror of that day, Elliot shook his head, heard Phelps sigh, and there was silence again. Win? He'd never had a chance.

Hearing his father clear his throat, he opened his eyes and glanced quickly at him, but Phelps' bowed head and hunched shoulders provoked suspicion again. "How's it going in Boston?" he asked, as the old scenario of baiting was replayed. "Patrick filled me in on what's happening," he added, eyes focused relentlessly on the slats of the venetian blinds. Surprised the provocation produced no reply, he stole another furtive glance at his father, whose air of submission might have brought Elliot joy but evoked something else as a dry heave shuddered through Phelps. Quickly Elliot looked away, then had to look back, drawn into the inner wasteland of those dark marble eyes.

"You're going to lose," he heard himself say, armoring himself against a strange and unsettling tenderness that might be used against him.

"I know."

The whispered, unexpected response caused Elliot to catch his breath. "You know? That's news."

"Son . . ."

The unusual word frightened them both. Elliot shut his eyes.

"Elliot . . ."

"Don't bother."

"Son . . ."

"No."

472

CURLEY ANNOUNCES SETTLEMENT
UNION VICTORIOUS; CHARGES DROPPED

Boston, Dec. 14— After a week of negotiations, Governor Curley was able to announce a settlement between Abraham Phelps and the A.F. of L.

A jubilant Meyer Shapiro held a news conference in which he revealed the union will become the exclusive bargaining agent for the nine thousand operatives of Phelps Textiles in twelve plants throughout New England. Official elections will be conducted in all plants under the union's auspices, with the Federal Labor Board monitoring the results. Results of those elections will enable the union to renegotiate contracts if the operatives vote it in. In view of the unprecedented work stoppage that spread through the Phelps chain in support of the Jericho fifty, the consensus is that all will do so.

GOVERNOR ANNOUNCES CHARGES DROPPED

A smiling Governor Curley told reporters that he saw no reason why the fifty insurgents who held Phelps Mill for three days should stand trial.

Sources close to the negotiations said that Abraham Phelps, threatened with a federal lawsuit for having broken the Wagner Act, had agreed not to press charges. A grim-faced Phelps shook hands with Meyer Shapiro and left the Parker House with a brusque "no comment" to reporters' questions.

INROADS IN TEXTILE INDUSTRY

Meyer Shapiro was quoted as saying that the settlement with Phelps would lead to ultimate victory in an industry that has been "impregnable until now. Phelps is the first step," he told a crowd of supporters. "A giant step has been made on the road toward equity and justice for American labor."

Shapiro reminded his supporters that the road would not be an easy one. He called attention to the stalemate in Michigan where over forty thousand auto workers continue to hold the plants in defiance of General Motors.

Meanwhile, in Jericho, Phelps Textiles is expected to reopen tomorrow.

excerpt from
The Boston Herald,
Dec. 14, 1936

CHRISTMAS TREES!

Spectator Announces Subscription Drive! FREE Christmas Tree (large selection) Given Away With Each Six-Month Subscription. Only One Dollar For Twenty-four Issues! Subscribe Now and Pick Out Your FREE Christmas Tree!

advertisement from
The Jericho Spectator,
Dec. 16, 1936

26   Would Christmas ever come? There were those who doubted it.

Two nights before, a freezing rain fell, forming icicles that hung from eaves and telephone wires, too, coating limbs and branches of trees, the husks in the fields. Jericho looked out its windows, hearts quickening as the sun came out, creating prisms of crystal, an opulence of rainbows. Even blades of grass shimmered and sparkled, and the town knew that Christmas was upon it. What was past was past.

Christmas Eve found a sparkling clear night over the Merrimack Valley, the sky lit with a million stars, and carols echoing over the hills. Parties, large and small, seemed a necessity—parties of victory, celebration and relief that it was all over and peace restored, parties of hope.

Her own peace tenuously reestablished with her husband, Mrs. Abraham Phelps entertained fifty at a buffet supper at the Mansion, while down at the depot Rummy Johnny had a celebration of his own, a sprig of holly in his tattered lapel as he raised his brandy bottle to the passing freights.

Abraham Phelps raised his bourbon to George Appleton of Pacific Worsteds and toasted survival. "We *must* survive," he added, and told Appleton he was considering following in Nate Woodbridge's footsteps and relocating his main plant in the unionless South. See what Jericho would do without him!

And on Mulberry Street the Hoskins' family and friends gathered for the traditional Christmas Eve open house, mingling gaily, their faces reflecting the warm glow of the candles. "Merry Christmas," they cried with a fervent gladness, for if there were ever a year to keep company and share their gratitude and joy, this was it. "Merry Christmas, Merry Christmas!" exchanging handshakes and kisses, the comings and goings constant as neighbors departed, on to other family gatherings, while friends arrived stomping snow from boots, cheeks flushed and spirits high. For it was Christmas, and each of them was an innocent child, the magic alive again.

"This is nice," whispered the president of the Young Socialist Club of Leveret to Alice, who was taking him around and introducing him. Like a hungry child outside a bakery, Steve Bobeck gazed at the angels and the

475

holly, the cones and balls on the mantel. He inhaled the fragrant greens and joined the neighbor's children in the parlor where they were stringing cranberries and popcorn on Harriet's finest, a ten-foot spruce.

"Nice," whispered Steve again. "I come from a small family. We never had anything like this."

"Not too bourgeois? Too middle class and comfortable to be true?"

"The warmth—it's contagious."

"'Tis the season to be jolly'? Hah! For me, it's the season of waiting. I seem to have spent the last months doing nothing but. I won't rest until I see his face. When I was at the hospital visiting Elliot—" Alice stopped herself and smiled. "Visiting Elliot. Me! That shows you what a crazy Christmas this is. Anyway, I talked to a surgeon. They have all kinds of new devices these days. Plastic legs. Called a prothesis. The fact his knee is still good means it'll be that much easier."

"Your father's giving us the once-over again."

"If he knew who you were, he'd do more than that."

"*Alice*," exclaimed Teresa as she and Matt arrived. The black strip of cloth pinned around Alice's upper arm caused Teresa to quickly cross herself. "—not Wayne Thibeau!"

"No, Wayne's on a boat. This is for the ultimate death of the Spanish Republic. Unless we help. My way of making sure people are reminded."

"On Christmas?" Teresa exchanged a look with Matt. "I was worried there for a minute, dear," she added, giving Alice a kiss. "Why, his letter that Pat printed in the paper . . . it was moving, it was. But you say he's on his way back? Isn't that grand news. Isn't it a grand night!"

Full of her usual zest, Teresa cried out prettily as Matt planted a fast kiss on her lips and she laughed as he pointed to the mistletoe above her head. "You don't think it's too bold, do you, dear?" she asked, turning back to Alice as Matt removed her coat, revealing a bright red sweater. "The color?"

"Perfect. Blood red."

"Blood—?" Not sure if Alice was pulling her leg, Teresa smiled warily. "Come down to the shop after the holidays, Alice. I'll give you the works. Do you a world of good. Why, you've the Thibeaus!" she exclaimed, calling out greetings to those she knew. "Sure they must be needing a bit of Christmas cheer, what with what happened to Wayne. And don't we all, come to think of it? Why, Mrs. Hoskins! God love ya, don't you look a picture? So becoming with your hair swept up like that."

"Merry Christmas, Mrs. Burke. We're delighted to have you."

"Mr. Burke and I are tickled ourselves. And your house—coming up the street—a candle in every window! Clear up to the attic Mrs. Hoskins!"

"'Letty,' please. Won't you? We're all in the same family now. Teresa," she added, "—may I?"

476

Teresa nodded and beamed as Letty took her arm and led her to Sam, who was spooning eggnog at the sideboard which was spread with Letty's Christmas cloth of hand-painted cones and berries.

"And here's my handsome nephew! Where's your darling wife?"

"Still dressing. We only got back an hour ago. Jerry loaned me his truck and we gave out the last of the trees down in Jerusalem."

"God love you, Patty. If there's many still calling you a hothead, you're a saint to me. When I think—" Shuddering inwardly, Teresa caught sight of Paul Marienetti, whose arm was still in a sling. And Alice's armband prompted her to shake her head again. "There could've been many of us wearing black tonight. Almost three weeks it's been, but there isn't a day goes by when I don't think of what might have happened. To you. Or Joe. It *was* a miracle—just as you wrote in the paper—that nobody was hurt worse. I'm on my knees in thanks every evening, Patty. I'm sure your ma is, too. It makes us realize how fast it's all going. How important it is for us to love one another while there's still time. It's changed us all, Patty. Listen to me!" she laughed, eyes misting. "I'll be bawlin' in another minute. You're dear to me, darlin'—dearer than ever, which doesn't seem possible, but it's true."

Sitting in her slip, Harriet's hand trembled as she tried to write an entry in her diary, but she only got as far as the date. From far away she heard the party downstairs, and her eye glanced at previous entries, finding one that announced her arrival back in Jericho. The pages seemed to fall open of their own accord, and she discovered another entry: *Today at the Red Tavern, Mr. Phelps, to all extents and purposes, proposed to me for Elliot.* A few pages later, she found: *Love blinds and maims those eager souls who dare enter his kingdom,* which she'd written in the terrifying days after her engagement; then a more recent one the day after the battle at the mill, from a cell in the Leveret Police Station:

Events have plummeted us all to a place none of us would have ever dreamed. I know I love him. I know I am married. And when the river rises and you have to get across, you find it in you and dive in, and when you're on the other side—you're there. And you didn't worry about the lack of boats, the fast current, or the hidden rocks. You're just there.

Once again Harriet put pen to page, but once again she couldn't write. Taking a quick drag on her cigarette, then a quicker sip of sherry, she stared at herself in the mirror. But nothing had changed, she still looked the same.

"No, no, no, *no*." Denials surged. Get a hold of yourself, cried a voice to a girl already lost in the desert. It *could* be the excitement of the last few weeks; often she was late, had been from the start; had always been irregular, but no rationalization, no reasons mustered could explain—

477

Had the pessary slipped? Questions and a frantic accounting of the last seven weeks raced as Harriet gasped and sat on the bed, and that was how Patrick found her.

"You're not ready."

"I'm not ready." The phrase reverberated with sudden new meaning. "Not ready," she echoed as the truth rushed at her with an even greater intensity than it had a moment ago when she'd found something in her eyes, an unconscious realization, her *knowing* knowing it was true, the knowing dazzling in its power—as if she'd been hit by a falling star and shattered into a million pieces.

"I can . . . hear you all down there. Sounds so festive . . ." She darted a glance at Patrick as if she were surprised to find him in the room. "Let's see . . . let's see . . ." she murmured, trying to remember what she had to do next. Dress, earrings, shoes, muddled brain. "Don't muss me," she cautioned, as he took her in his arms. "I've done my face."

"Your face . . ." Patrick began, holding her at arm's length, examining her lovingly. " 'Is this the face that like the sun did make beholders weep? Is this the face that faced so many follies and was at last outfaced by' "—he paused, grinning—"Patrick."

"That's beautiful. Shakespeare? How many eggnogs have you had? I see a flush beneath your Irish pallor."

"Only two. But I warn you—I'm in a fierce and celebrating mood. What?" he asked, following her glance to the mirror where they saw themselves reflected. "What is it?" he asked again, trying to read her dazed expression.

"Nothing . . . um . . . open that," she added, breaking away and pointing to a special delivery package from Virginia, which had instructions to open *before* Christmas. "What?" she asked as he tore off the wrappings and burst out laughing.

"*Bed Manners—How to Bring Sunshine into Your Nights.* She takes it seriously, doesn't she?" he added, scanning the pages of the small volume. "You're not smiling."

"Oh. Yes. It is amusing." A diversionary rifling through dresses in the closet and her head was burning.

"Listen to this. Chapter Two is called 'Getting Undressed.' Then there's 'Bed Manners On A Friend's Yacht' and—" Patrick put the book down and slipped his arms around Harriet's waist. "We don't need this book, do we?" he whispered, lips brushing her ear. Hoping he wouldn't see how agitated she was, she shook her head, smiled quickly and slipped away again. "What shall I wear . . . what shall I. . . ?"

"Guess what just arrived downstairs? A case of scotch from the Governor."

"From? Oh. He's wooing you."

Patrick nodded. "What do you think?"

"What do I think?"

"His special assistant—that's how he put it the other day. His trouble-shooter. Learn the ropes. Then run for McGinty's seat next year. It's a safe one. I'd be in Congress. What is it?" he added, for Harriet seemed hypnotized in place.

"It's exciting, I—"

"Aren't you feeling well?" he asked, lowering his voice as if she'd cast a spell over both of them.

"Fine . . . fine. I . . . tell me more. You said . . . you weren't really interested. Didn't you? The other day you said—"

"I think I'm changing my mind. There's a lot to consider. The paper. But he really wants me. It's ironic. Ma always dreamed that Denny would run for McGinty's seat and now— What *is* it?" he insisted gently as her eyes filled.

"Patrick, I'm . . ." *Pregnant. Oh shit. Oh no.*

"What?"

"Nothing. Overexcited, I guess. It *is* exciting. I'm just . . . keyed up," she added as she took a tentative step toward him, searched his eyes, then stumbled into his arms.

"Patrick. . . ?" Alice called from the hallway.

"Be right there."

"Your family's arriving."

"OK. *Tell* me," he added urgently as he held his trembling wife, who hid against his shoulder and clung to him.

"It's Christmas . . . that's all. Go . . . your mother . . ."

"She can wait."

"I'm fine . . . I am. Go—or I'll never get done. Go. I love you," she whispered urgently. *I hate you.*

Like a diva about to greet adoring fans, Gert swept through the front hallway. Dressed to kill in her favorite green twill with a conch shell of a hat and a squirrel around the neck, she entered the dining room with a brio that cloaked her nervousness at this first-time foray into Hoskins' and Protestant territory. Small (and large) boats bobbed behind her: Rose (in muskrat) on the arm of Timothy O'Brien, Joe (blinking) and Dennis.

"Good evenin' and Merry Christmas. I'm Gert Flynn," she announced to the world at large. "Alice!" she exclaimed, heart skipping at the black armband. "Has there been a death?"

"Spain."

"Spain?" Gert's eyes narrowed. "What's wrong with Spain? It's still there, isn't it?" she added with a cackle. Yet the black symbol on the Hoskins' loony daughter produced the same vibrations of potential loss that Teresa had felt, and Gert linked an arm with Joe in a sudden need to be close.

479

"There ya are! Mrs. Hoskins—Merry Christmas to ya!" With a loudness that caused heads to turn, Gert led her entourage toward Letty, who was momentarily transfixed, caught with a serving platter of sliced cold ham in hand.

"Merry Christmas to all of youse now." Brogue thicker than usual, Gert held her hand out as the two families gathered.

"The same to you, Mrs. Flynn," replied Letty, recovering her aplomb, serenely transferring the platter to Cora's hand and taking Gert's as the guests smiled warmly on this inaugural social coming-together of the Hoskins and Flynn families.

"Don't your house look cheery, Mrs. Hoskins?" Gert bestowed compliments as hands were shook and greetings exchanged. Timothy, already eyeing the buffet, was introduced, eggnog was ladled, Cora kissed Rose, the two fathers-in-law tried to think of something to say to each other, and Letty and Gert's eyes met, each simultaneously feeling the need for something more. For they'd stood outside the mill together in shared anxiety. Gingerly they touched cheeks in the common bond of a bad dream lifted.

"This togetherness is sure to give us all indigestion," quipped Alice, as Letty and Gert, surprised at their emotion, backed off. "A Christmas truce," she added to Steve. "The Capulets and the Montagues. Watch it. The eggnog's poisoned."

"Where's—?" The question answered by a sudden buzz, Gert turned from Patrick, eyes widening as Harriet made her entrance. Frankie improvised a trill on the keys as she paused under the mistletoe and received a quick squeeze of the hand from her friend Marcia, who whispered an awestruck, "Harriet!" then turned to Allan. *Look at the dress!*

Gert blinked, then focused sternly on the bare-shouldered, provocative and clinging, turquoise (splashed with silver poppies) gown.

"Where'd ya get that dress?" was all she could say. *Whatever happened to the idea of hidin' your charms? This one seemed to be advertisin'!* "Merry Christmas," she added, finding tongue again, her once-over concluding at the vulnerable spot between Harriet's breasts, the whole shebang of glittering poppies sustained by the thinnest of straps.

"New York," Harriet heard herself say. The mischievous tilt of her head camouflaged a continuing state of dazed wonder and potential turmoil. She might have enjoyed Gert's fluster but was seeing her—seeing them all—as if through the wrong end of an opera glass. "Klein's. Only twelve ninety-five," she added, gratefully grasping Patrick's hand which sought hers. Afraid to meet his eyes, she felt ashamed and confused by the rush of violent anger toward him only moments ago.

"Twelve ninety-five?" sniffed Rose, not at all pleased that male perusal had now shifted to Harriet.

"Well, don't ya look—" *A dress like that? She'd catch her death.*

"—stunnin'." Wondering what Patrick made of this femme fatale of a wife, Gert's eyes shot him a look and discovered he'd long lost custody of his.

"Thank you, Gert."

Gert? Pulling herself up at her rival's brassy first-time use of her first name, Gert deflected the challenge with a plastered smile that threatened cracks.

Flesh pressing, the two women took the obligatory measure of each other. *I don't intend to kiss her,* decided Harriet. *Should I kiss her?* wondered Gert.

They kissed.

"What's that silly grin on your puss, boyo?" Gert caught Harriet's eye. *Don't misinterpret this, dearie . . . I don't like ya any more than I ever did . . . I'm here for him.*

Chastising herself, she heaved a compensatory sigh and raised her cup. "To the both of ya . . ." O the difficult linkage. "To my son . . . and his wife." O the tremor of the very word, the public acknowledgment.

Harriet mustered her courage and smiled shyly at Patrick. What kind of deranged women was she to feel anything but love for this gentle man who had conquered her heart, body and soul? Yet his adoring gaze made her unaccountably nervous, hammering nails into the coffin of her fast-fading independence. Sudden panic flushed her and she wanted to run, but held tighter to his hand instead.

"The great powers have initialed the treaty," Alice whispered to Steve. "Don't think the battle for the territory won't continue," she added as Patrick bowed to his wife, then to his mother, linked an arm with each as Frankie lit into an upbeat "Hark, The Herald Angels Sing," and the party was on.

"Are you with us?" Alice asked Harriet, whom she sensed floating.

"With you. Oh, am I with you, Alice."

"You're sure you're OK?" Patrick asked, her mysterious smile intriguing him. Yet he felt a distance in her.

"Wonderful!"

"I'm lonely," said Alice matter-of-factly. "I wish Wayne were here."

Harriet stared at her sister and saw herself reflected. A poignant sadness welled at their mutual predicament: two singular women, who'd fought for what they believed, done what they could—and ended up classically vulnerable. Stop it, she ordered herself, grappling with a host of fears. *I've joined the club. Me! Who'd of thunk it?* She could imagine Alice's ironic laughter. If a part of her wanted to share the bond that united them, she knew she wasn't ready to reveal the astonishing tap on her soul. Nor to Patrick. Not yet. As if she weren't able to give her discovery credence, she tried to imagine how she'd tell him and couldn't.

481

No, it was hers for now, this alternately troubling yet mesmerizing secret was hers, her ambivalence to be wrestled with herself, until the appropriate moment when she would whisper exquisitely in his ear, could join him unabashedly in what she knew would be his unalloyed joy, a candle in each ear and up on the roof, broadcasting to the planets that a special child was on the way, a dazzling child who—

Carried away, Harriet shook her head to clear it and tried to concentrate on Alice: ". . . the nearer he gets, the more scared I am. I try and guess what that first moment will be like . . ."

"It'll be fine."

". . what he'll say . . . what I'll say. A normal reunion—but it can't be. Everything's changed."

"Nothing's changed." Harriet sipped her eggnog, trembling fingers grasped the cup. "It'll be fine. You'll see."

"You have nothing to worry about," added Patrick, and Harriet willed it for herself. "You love each other," she heard him say, "and that's what counts. Everything else will fall into place."

She nodded. If only it were so simple. Let me be calm, she prayed, and when Patrick whispered, "Are you happy?" she murmured yes, which was so true and not at all true. Oh, why did she have to be so complicated? Guilt for what she was sure were inappropriately angry feelings washed over her again. "Happy," she repeated, wanting to conquer her anxieties for Patrick's sake. Guests interrupted, chatter intruded. Harriet was in turn vivacious, then pensive, and when Patrick left her to replenish their cups and she lost his anchoring arm, she grasped Alice's in replacement.

"You're brave, Alice." With sudden urgency, she pulled her sister into the privacy of the back hallway. "You look so pretty. I guess what they say is true. Alice—"

"What is it?" Alice replied, curious as to the agitation, but Harriet shook her head and laughed an amazed gasp.

"Can you feel him yet?"

Involuntarily Alice inhaled, as if to make herself thinner. The loose-fitting dress she'd chosen disguised her growing plumpness, yet she was angry she had to hide. "Dr. Alden says I should feel a kick or two within the next few weeks."

"Dr. Alden. . . ?" *Hello, Dr. Alden; Hop up on the table, Harriet; Soft cervix, breasts firming; Congratulations, Harriet; Bring me a urine sample—just a formality; Dead rabbit, poor little rabbit; Do you want a boy or a girl?*

"Should I take this off?" Alice asked, fingering her armband. "Mother said I'd made my point."

"No. Do what you have to. Never stop doing it. No matter what!"

Alice cocked an eyebrow at Harriet's vehemence, but her sister revealed nothing. The roller coaster she was riding swooped and plummeted her, and she tried to lose herself in the gaiety of the party.

"I better see to Steve," Alice said. "He looks lonesome, too. For a revolutionary, he's very sentimental."

"Most men are, I've discovered. Much more than we are. Don't go yet. He's thinking seriously about Curley's offer," she added, eyes finding Patrick in the crowded dining room. And what would happen to her?

"I think it's great. He's on his way."

"He doesn't want anyone to know. Not till he makes up his mind."

"What about the paper?"

"He says we can do both for now." Would he feel the same when he found out? Would motherhood be a barrier to her own ambition? Did she have a chance at all?

The self-inflicted questioning continued, and she shook her head when Alice asked what was wrong. "Too many 'what ifs,'" she murmured, apprehension getting the better of her again, no matter how joyous she wanted to feel. "Tell me . . . are you scared? To have a child. . . . It must be awesome. Do you . . . are you . . . frightened that you might be a bad mother? That you'll fail him somehow? I mean—you're differerent than. . . . We both are. Aren't you afraid you may lose your own life?"

"Are you gathering data for a story? I don't intend to lose anything. Yes," Alice admitted, "sometimes I think I'll probably be the world's lousiest mother. Too selfish and— You're pregnant! Harriet—*you're pregnant!*"

Her blush gave her away and she fell into Alice's arms, the laughter she'd foreseen cascading as Alice held her, both of them whooping now.

"I haven't . . . told him yet. I just . . . discovered it. Maybe I'm not. No, I am. Oh, Alice!" Relief to be able to share it coursed through her.

"No wonder you're a disembodied spirit tonight. That dress!" exclaimed Alice with a glint. "Of course! A 'not quite proper for a mother-to-be' dress, right? I get the picture. What a character you are!"

"Do you still believe a man's the head of the household and the woman's the heart?" Harriet bantered a moment or two later. "Answer me," she insisted as Patrick grinned at her. "Who am I to you?" Who was she to herself? was more like it as she looked for answers in his eyes.

"You're my darling, my wife—"

"Put me on a pedestal, I'll scream."

"Why do I have the sense I'm being given a test?" he bandied. "What's with you tonight? A bee in your bonnet—as your mother would say."

"My mother?" Harriet gasped inwardly, glance seeking Letty. No

483

matter how she struggled, she was ending up like her mother, the excitement over.

"I refuse to play bridge," she announced after Marcia and Allan had joined them in superficial chatter. "All the sweet young marrieds," she added, her sarcasm masking the horror of becoming like everyone else. "Cora and Sam and Jerry and Deedee and Rose and Tim— No, not those two. Sweet is hardly the word for your darling sister."

"I ask myself—were you always a royal pain in the ass?"

"I take that as a compliment."

"So it is, my angel. Then I remember the day you stomped into Jerry's back yard six years ago, and I answer my own question. Yes, you were."

"Stomped?"

"I even remember how you looked."

"I doubt it."

"You had nice legs. I remember nice legs. You were wearing shorts."

Harriet found herself in the past, saw him in his black cassock, which she'd fliply called a dress to be provocative. She was a mere baby. "My sunsuit. I must have been wearing my sunsuit."

"See? I remember everything. My destiny was always with you, darlin'."

"Destiny? That's *my* word. Having absconded with my heart, you want to steal my manifesto, too? And what is with this sudden 'darlin'' business? You're even developing a bit of a brogue tonight. You're sounding like *her*. I'll divorce you if you keep it up."

"In touch with my roots, darlin'—the generations to come, those behind. . . . Ahhh, the sainted bogs of the ancestors!"

"You're delirious."

"Irish. What's that?" he demanded, responding to the saucy rolling of her eyes, "Don't you know the Irish are poets and Gods, makers of myth and the bearers of the world's sorrow?"

"Spare me," she laughed and found herself watching the neighbor's children, who darted in and out among the grownups. The awesome responsibility floored her again. Giggles masked her apprehension as Patrick whispered in her ear: "You've watered my soul. I'm home free." The latter words reverberated. "Don't red-apple me, buster," she winked, and wondered: Would he be as frightened as she? Feel the same terrifying sense of inadequacy?

". . . and that dress gives me definite ideas."

"And you a man of the cloth! I'm truly shocked. But then again—you always did have an admirable mixture of the sacred and the profane about you."

Wit masked the turbulence. Yes, he was on his way—and she'd had more than a hand in his success. What was left to *her*? Once again she felt guilty for her petty concerns. Once again she conjectured as to his possible response, endowing her with some kind of romantic ideal of pregnancy and motherhood, expecting her to fulfill his *own* myths—but they weren't necessarily *hers*.

"Don't be such strangers youse," called Gert, beckoning them to join her at the buffet.

But Harriet couldn't possibly eat. It would all change, her life would change, had already. Alice might call it the ultimate adventure, but Harriet—full of real and imagined jeopardy—continued to feel as vulnerable as the tinsel on the tree. How lucky she was, Alice had remarked. At least Harriet could *tell* everyone she was pregnant, but the latter had no desire to make an announcement in the midst of a party.

"Let's run away," she whispered to Patrick, the jollity of the festive gathering jarring. "Away?" he whispered in return as Gert interrupted, "I want ya both to Christmas dinner tomorrow. You've had them long enough, Mrs. Hoskins. What's this?" she added, eyeing an intimidating casserole.

"Hot scalloped oysters," Letty replied. "A recipe of my grandmother's that we traditionally have on Christmas Eve."

"Elegant," admitted Gert, taking a tiny bite as her expert eye calculated the cost of the spread. They must be better off than they had been, these Hoskins. If only the food tasted bad.

"Try this, Pa. Tasty."

Joe cocked an ear. "Deaf as a post, God love him," Gert explained to those nearby. "Go find yourself a seat in the parlor, darlin'," she hollered. "I'll fix a plate and bring it to ya."

Overhearing, Harriet smiled wryly at her mother-in-law's newfound mellowness. What would Gert's reaction be? she wondered. Hah, she had something for him his mother couldn't give him.

Her laughter a momentary respite, she let Patrick tempt her with a nibble of ham from his fork. "I hear you're a cook yourself," Gert was saying to Sam.

"A baker."

"What's yours here?"

"The rolls and the—"

"Sponge cake," chirped Cora. "You know, Mrs. Flynn, the best chefs are men."

"Call me Gert." *Since everyone else is.* Gert and Harriet exchanged a guarded smile. "Men? Is that so. Never met one myself—but I'm not above learnin' somethin' new. Light as a feather," she added, taking a nip of a roll, beaming on Sam. "How many subscriptions as of this afternoon, boyo? What's the total?"

"Over eight hundred."

"Our goal's double that," Gert explained to Letty, who nodded, noticed Harriet's faraway look, and wondered that she gave no sign of rising

485

to the bait of her mother-in-law's barely concealed message that she intended to stay very much involved with *The Spectator*.

"Have ya all signed up?" demanded Gert, buttonholing those nearby. "I told Patty the town would rally behind him and the paper. Why shouldn't they? He's a hero, that's what he is. Wouldn't ya agree, Mrs. Hoskins?"

"Emphatically." Letty linked her arm with Franklin, whose eyes filled with unguarded tenderness as he raised his cup to Patrick in a silent toast that had no need of words.

"And we're all here together tonight. . . ." Filled with a rush of the spirit, Gert toasted her son. "And I'll say we owe a great deal of that to him. God blesses us all—that's what he wrote in his editorial. I'll say the same. I'm blessed to be his ma."

Overcome with her own blarney, Gert's eyes misted, her sentiment echoed in Teresa, while Marienetti and some of the others raised their cups to a flushed Patrick and Harriet cocked an eyebrow. This orgy of sentimental bull threatened to suffocate her, and Patrick seemed infested with it, too. "To my wife—which is the least of her," he toasted. Was he looking at her differently? Or was it her imagination?

"To *The Spectator*! I may have started the dear thing, but it was my son put it on the map—"

"No, Ma," interjected Patrick.

"I haven't finished, boyo. And to Harriet," Gert continued, "who made the paper what it is and who's about the bravest lass I ever laid eyes on. And that's what I'm sayin'!"

"Next I expect to see Tiny Tim wobbling in on crutches," quipped Alice, drawing a laugh from Harriet, but large Timothy was peevish. "What's that about?" he demanded, pointing to Alice's armband.

"Death," Alice replied, inflamed by the fat face, cheeks puffed with cake.

"Jesus, Mary and Joseph!"

"The battle may be over in Jericho, but it continues in Spain."

"Here we go again," sighed Cora. "Why don't we sing some more carols?"

"Wayne is Jericho's first wounded in *that* battle, and that's why I'm wearing this."

"We don't want to hear about that stuff," muttered Gert, wondering why Letty didn't silence Alice.

"Spain?" grumbled Timothy, turning on Patrick. "Ya printed a letter from that fella in the paper, didn't ya! Don't ya know it's Franco whose defendin' the faith over there? Not Wayne what'sisname. Ya tryin' to turn *The Spectator* into a Red sheet?"

Gert bristled and sent a warning look to the fat-ass. What would the Hoskins be thinkin'?

486

"A buffoon shall lead them," murmured Patrick as Alice lit into Timothy. "Franco? Let me tell you something about your pal Franco—"

"*Wait* a minute," he interrupted. "I'm not interested in your propaganda. Nobody is. I'm *proud* to be an isolationist."

"Why do you call it propaganda?" asked Patrick. "The Church *shouldn't* be supporting Franco."

"And ya call yourself a Catholic!"

"I'm a lover, Timothy."

"And what would you be calling him, Timothy darlin'?" Gert's smile was sweet, but her hackles were up. "I'll thank Timothy to remember that my son prints what his conscience tells him, that's what I'll be remindin' him!"

"Suppose ya think you're a coupla celebrities," muttered Timothy to Patrick and Harriet. "Just 'cause ya got your picture in the papers."

"And in the newsreels," laughed Patrick, dismissing Timothy. But Alice was fired. "Who'll join me? We have a petition here. We want to put pressure on Roosevelt to dump the Neutrality Act."

"I admire your courage," whispered Steve. As for himself, he'd rather let the revolution keep for tonight. "In front of family . . . and friends . . ."

"Most of whom don't give a damn. Propaganda?" she demanded, thrusting an issue of *Life* magazine into Timothy's unwilling hands. "Look at this!" "Hitler's Armada" blared the headline above an artist's rendering of Britain, surrounded by German warships, German planes overhead.

"What does Hitler have to do with Jericho?" scoffed Rose, trying to steer Timothy away from the radicals. The others nodded. Not tonight, the women's eyes pleaded; it wasn't the time for it. But Alice had no choice.

"Hitler's living at Phelps' Mansion. The leopard hasn't changed his spots. He was forced to. Because some of you took action. Why can't you understand it's the same in Europe? Tyranny is tyranny! Look what almost happened at the mill. You almost lost," she added, pointing at Jack Tyler and Marienetti. "Don't you know how close you came? Men were almost killed."

Angered, Gert suppressed a retort, her intake of breath echoed in others who didn't want to be reminded of what might have been, who couldn't take life for granted any longer and saw their possibilities diminishing.

"Let's celebrate *life!*" insisted Gert, raising her cup to a chorus of agreement, her toast echoed by Reverend Peabody, who wished for a peaceful New Year that would prove Alice's warnings unfounded. "Amen," they cried, for this gathering on Mulberry Street, and in other homes, too, needed a chance to catch its breath. Coming together and counting their blessings was what was wanted—not a reminder of escalating violence in a foreign land, nor of Wayne Thibeau.

487

"Wayne's not a foreigner! He lives on Morton Street. You all know him. He worked at the Arlington with you," Alice reminded one of them. "Played ball with you," she said to another.

They nodded, realized Wayne wouldn't be running the bases again, and were uncomfortable. Even the presence of the Thibeaus was a painful reminder of a war that no one wanted to acknowledge.

"Look, Alice," interjected Gert. "We've lived through a perilous time. But a grand victory's been won. That's what we're celebratin'. And that's that," she added, determined to end the discussion. Cora nodded. "When's your date, Rose?" she asked, getting the subject changed.

"February fourteenth," she replied, putting on her society voice to impress the Protestants.

"How romantic. A Valentine wedding."

"Picked the date herself," offered Gert. "Oh, Mutha . . ." replied Rose, weary of her. It was mutual.

Timothy sweated as the conversation went on to the house he'd bought for Rose. "Chestnut Hill," she preened, "right at the top. It has eleven rooms."

"Not the size that's important," announced Gert for the benefit of the Hoskins. Timothy's ears pricked up. Size? It was the battle-ax who'd egged Rose on to the biggest and most expensive of the lot. And Rose had her eye on every appliance on the market. She'd better come across like a whiz-bang! Bemoaning his fate, he gobbled another piece of cake, whose whipped cream, lemony topping provided a momentary respite.

"That's not including the servants' quarters," Rose went on rhapsodically, ignoring Gert's stop-putting-on-airs look. Linked to Timothy's arm like a glittering barnacle, she told of the parties she'd be throwing for Archbishop Cushing.

"Can they hear themselves?" Alice muttered to Harriet. "I have to calm down. I have to."

Overhearing, Franklin nodded. "Tell her to let it alone," he asided to Letty, who prayed there wouldn't be a repeat of the Thanksgiving fireworks. Franklin watched Alice, saw the frustration build, saw her unable to control it. "Victory?" she demanded, interrupting Gert. "Wrapped up in a Christmas package and toasted? You can't be shocked by what happened at the mill and pretend everything else is rosy. We can't just let life return to normal."

"Why not?" demanded Gert, throwing an exasperated look, echoed by others.

"Because Jericho was almost in flames. And Europe *will* be—unless we get off the dime . . ."

Franklin shook his head, tried to shut his ears to the familiar litany.

"I know your heart's in the right place, dearie. But it's not gonna

488

happen again." Gert's statement produced fervent nods from the older ones—those who'd fought in the Great War or lost kin. They exchanged worried glances and turned away from Alice, who cried out in frustration:

"What kind of a world are we giving to our children?"

"Why does she have to?" muttered Franklin to Letty. "Has life in her and talks of death."

Jolted herself, Harriet found herself taking Patrick's arm as Alice's question hit home.

"Because she's thinking of her child," replied Letty, aware that Franklin had, for the first time, acknowledged Alice's pregnancy. "Talk to her, Father. She needs you to."

"She doesn't need me."

"What kind of a legacy are we going to leave? A world of orphans?"

Startled, Franklin met Alice's eyes. *Don't you* understand? *You* of all people, they demanded, those challenging eyes that contained a vulnerability that might be his. He wanted to go to the cellar but couldn't move. Mayhem lurked beneath his Christmas. No, he didn't want orphans. Wouldn't wish it on anyone.

"You can't pretend I'm invisible," she cried, to him and the others, too. "I won't let you. *You can't pretend!*"

There was a hush in the dining room now, and Franklin watched them turn from her, saw them whisper. Thoughts careened as he stared at Alice, whose isolation he recognized as his own, her estrangement his. He saw the suspicious looks darting, read the "she's crazy's," felt her anguish like a guilty jolt to his spine.

"Towns are being bombed. Right this minute. Children caught in air raids. You all make me sick!"

An empathetic shriek of his own coursed through Franklin as the unnerved gathering broke up and Cora called out that carolers had arrived out front and didn't they all want to hear them? His feet moved of their own accord toward his daughter, who wept in frustration. "I'm sorry . . . Mother. I didn't mean . . . to spoil things."

"No," murmured Joe, who'd lingered. Impulsively, he reached out and touched the shoulder of the sobbing young woman whose passion had stirred him.

"Dearest . . . there now." Harriet took Alice in her arms, saw her flinch as Franklin cleared his throat. Ready for the tongue-lashing, Alice hid her face.

"Alice," he whispered hoarsely, "I'm . . . proud of you."

Were those his words, the painful words he'd searched for? With the saying came a release, a firm nod that infiltrated Alice's wary posture. *Because she never believed you loved her as you did the others*, Letty had told him. Was it his fault? It didn't matter at the moment. "Did you hear me?" he asked, the gruffness disguising his emotion as he looked into his thorny daughter's eyes and saw her pain, which was his pain, and took her hand, which tightened in his.

"Father . . ." murmured Harriet and wept herself, wept for all of them.

"I'm leaving Jericho. The day after Christmas."

Harriet had no time to question him, for Gert interrupted, embracing Elliot with such gusto that the sharp points of her holly corsage threatened to wound him all over again. "Are ya still stiff, darlin'?" Pleased with the air of revived spirit about him, she sat Elliot beside her and the party rekindled, bubbled up as if after a storm, the participants more than ever determined to immerse themselves in Christmas.

Surrounded by well-wishers as Gert retold the story of his bravery, Elliot found Harriet regarding him inquisitively. *Tell me*, her eyes asked. Marienetti and Jack Tyler clapped him on the back, the veterans reliving their exploits, trading anecdotes and memories, and she watched Elliot join in, more at ease than she'd ever seen him. "Harriet," they called, wanting her to join them, for wasn't she one of them as well? But she hung back, an awed stillness in her now, the inner struggle less severe as, phoenixlike, she rose slowly from the pit of her ambivalence.

The smallest things had enormous repercussions, such as the unexpected touch of Letty's finger on her arm, something transferred, unspoken yet communicated. And Harriet had been able to rest her head against her mother's shoulder and murmur "I've been glib"; had wanted to apologize for the condemnation that had slipped so easily from her these last months. A sudden empathy had taken hold, her ache of loneliness relieved, a lessening of the fear that it was all too much for her. And Franklin's gesture toward Alice opened undreamed of possibilities and hope; that moment of unity in the dining room possessing answers for all parents and children, for those mothers-to-be and fathers, too, a healing that had moved Harriet inexorably.

And if questions might continue to pile up in her head and doubts could be overwhelming, she found all she had to do was find Patrick's eyes. Patrick, as she discovered long ago, was always there.

She found him at her side; he whispered, "Do you need to get away for a while?" and she smiled gratefully at his sensitivity and was filled with pleasurable anticipation. "Let's go to the office," she murmured, for what more appropriate place could there possibly be to share with him her news? "In a bit," she added, for she wanted amplification of Elliot's startling announcement. He seemed intriguingly different as he exchanged horror stories of hospital food and nurses, an eager participant with these men whom he had little in common with save that day of madness which had united them all.

"You're enjoying yourself, aren't you?" she said to him a moment later, getting him to herself. If it was a surprisingly simple question, she found a simplicity about Elliot tonight she couldn't put her finger on. "I guess it's time," he replied, nodding to guests, full of compliments to the ladies—but even the latter had a ring of outwardness and sincerity, as if Elliot were truly extending himself.

"That's a damn swell-elegant outfit, m'dear."

"Mother remarked that it might be in *Vogue*—not, however, in Jericho."

"Mothers. What do they know? You look sensational. You were always a hundred years ahead of this burg."

"Thanks," she replied, needing to hear it. "Well—are you going to play cat with the canary?"

"New York, here I come," he whispered, face flushed with excitement. "Farewell to Jericho. Time for that, too. I'm going. No real idea what I'm going to do. First things first. Want to come with me?" he teased, lowering his voice conspiratorially. "Goodbye to Dr. Moeller, too. Can we get alone for a minute? There's more—" He broke off as Patrick joined them. "So many people came to visit me in the hospital," he replied to Patrick's compliment that he was looking well, "that I finally had to ask myself: they can't be all wrong, can they? I decided you all weren't. Must have something going for me. If I keep repeating that—I'll find it."

"You sound like you've got religion. Did she convert you?"

Elliot laughed at Harriet's comment and glanced at Gert. "My guardian angel. I should get shot more often. She's terrific," he added to Patrick. "I admit I was feeling pretty glum there for a while. Your mother has a way about her when she gets her mind set."

His smile faded momentarily as he heard Frankie's burst of laughter from across the dining room and felt him get closer. Elliot cloaked his vulnerability with a hearty, "Merry Christmas," shook his hand, kissed Jeannie, and wondered if he would ever be able to look upon Frankie Hoskins with equanimity.

"Buddy Berrigan's coming to Lowell. You gonna catch him?"

"Like to," Elliot replied, then remembered. "Guess not. I'll have to catch him in the big city." Somewhere deep was an only barely conscious feeling of hurt—a *lost your chance, Frankie*; perhaps even a fantasy that if only Frankie had possessed a sixth sense, or made a move, then it would all have been different.

Shaking his head to clear it, Elliot raised his cup. "See you at Roseland, kiddo. . . ."

"Roseland. I'm envious," Harriet interjected and found herself back on a warm, late summer evening when the two of them were down in the garden, her brother teaching Elliot to blow trumpet. He was so beautiful. Like an exposed nerve ever since. But not tonight.

491

". . . You'll be there soon, Frankie," Elliot added. "I'll beat the drums for you. Pat, tell me about the paper," he went on, as he tried to end the painful chapter of his life called Frankie. "Are you out of the red yet?"

"Gettting there. Thanks to you and a few Christmas trees. You're going to New York?"

"Day after tomorrow. Cutting the cord."

"Tell him *your* news, Patrick." She wondered what Elliot's reaction would be to *hers.* Any number of possibilities came to mind. Perhaps hurt, or jealousy, a sense of loss at what might have been—she didn't know. But he would understand her fears, maybe even more so than Patrick. She would have to write him, she told herself, and with the thought came the reality of his going. The candles lit his hair like the dream they'd weaved about each other, and she felt sad.

"I haven't decided yet," she heard Patrick caution as he told Elliot of the momentous possible escalation in his life. "He's cogitating," she added, "but he's really excited. Aren't you?"

"Yes and no," he admitted, as Gert sailed toward the trio of husband, wife and ex-fiancé with a possessive nod as if she'd brought them all together and found it fitting.

"I guess I'll be saying goodbye, Mrs. Flynn."

"New York?" asked Gert, feeling a pang at *any*body's leaving *any* time. "Good for you," she decided, straightening Elliot's tie. "There's a moment when a young man has to leave the nest and make his mark. You'll be in my prayers." Fondly she grinned on him, then at Patrick, who wondered if Denny had overheard Gert's suddenly magnanimous view on nest leaving. "Now what I wanta know from *you*," she said, nudging him, "is when can I expect my first grandchild?"

"I think she thinks she's a contender for first prize as life of the party," murmured a nonplussed Harriet, who'd managed to return Gert's parting wink, but barely.

"She's neat." Elliot laughed. Patrick nodded, and realized he had deliberately revealed none of this past week's excitement to his mother, nothing about his meeting with Curley, and wondered why.

"Well, here we are."

"Here we are."

"The three musketeers," added Elliot as the threesome raised their cups and Harriet wondered, who would have believed any of it? A while later, Elliot asked her if he could speak to her privately, and she took him out to the barn.

"There's something about you tonight. You're . . . incandescent."

"I could say the same for you," she replied.

"I feel . . . dandy." He laughed. "So, I'm going to bunk with a couple of people I knew at Princeton. I'll stay with them till I get my bearings."

"But what are you going . . . to do?"

"Do? Find out who I am. Does it sound too awful to be true?"

Harriet sensed him wrestling with something. "I told my mother," he said.

"Your mother?" She shook her head, not understanding.

"About myself."

"About. . . ? Oh."

He nodded. "She's giving me the money to go. *He* wouldn't. He—" Grim-faced, Elliot broke off. "I don't care. I don't care what he thinks any more. Anyway, she always talked me out of running, but now she understands. Besides—this isn't running. Seeking is more like it."

She saw the urgency. "Dr. Moeller," he continued, "told me I have to forgive him. Said I'm never going to be peaceful till I do. Maybe so. I'm not ready—that's all I know. Do you remember I asked you if I could be cured? I don't want to be."

Elliot waited for her reaction, saw the questions in her eyes; he wanted her support and she sensed it.

"Perhaps . . . it's not an illness."

His face lit with hope. "That's what Larry said."

"Larry?"

"He's like I am," he replied, and she was aware that something was missing, the self-loathing gone, replaced with perhaps the hint of a declaration in his simple admittance. Moved, she listened as he spoke of a new friendship with the intern he'd met in the hospital. "I told him everything. It just seemed to pop out one night, I don't even know why. . . ."

Elliot paused, remembering the words of understanding from the fellow who'd kissed him afterwards, a kiss that had the power to obliterate the nastiness and degradation of all previous sexual encounters. And Larry's counsel, and the alternatives he painted, had been linked with another's long ago, a stranger on a train who, if he caused Elliot to fear he was marked, had left him with other possibilities as well—the promise of a place, others like himself, a haven offered that now seemed to Elliot a vision of some kind that he needed to believe and had to find.

"I'm scared," he admitted and Harriet held him against her. "No," she whispered, "don't be scared."

And Patrick and Harriet knew they had to be alone together, so they left the confines of the party, walked out of the house and under that astonishing sky.

"I used to go for walks with Father. Now with you. There's something primitively correct about that. The air!" she exclaimed, taking a deep breath, gazing upward to the millions of brilliant pinpricks. "What a night!"

The events of this watershed evening ran in her, and something new—an escalating infiltration of a mystical power. Her awareness re-

493

quired none of her earlier effort of will, for its pull was stronger than her anxieties of entrapment, and she felt a oneness with the universe and the stars she walked under.

Albatross bounded ahead, and they caught up with the carolers and joined ranks outside a couple of houses, voices raised in the crystalline pureness, then continued their stately walk on Jericho.

Silent, then talking, they strolled arm in arm or holding hands. Yet separate, too—Patrick's thoughts causing him to increase the pace, moving ahead of her while she lingered, pensive, staring into lit windows of other parties. Then he would wait or come back to her, or she would catch up to him; always, in the end, together.

Crystal stalactites formed by last night's rain hung glowing from porches, the ice shimmering orange or red from candles in windows, and sometimes an eerie blue.

Down Main Street, shut up tight and quiet, feet crunching on the hard-packed snow, which was slippery in spots with a coating of ice. When they reached *The Spectator*, she murmured, "I won't give it up," the declaration more to herself than to Patrick, the words having nothing of the vehement about them.

"Who says you have to?" he asked, mystified with her shifting moods and caught up now in a kind of peace that emanated from her as she shook her head enigmatically, then giggled. *Be like the Chinese. Tend to your rice paddy, climb up on the banking when your time comes, produce, pat it on its ass, and get back to business.*

She took his arm and they continued on, for she'd changed her mind about telling him at the office, didn't want to be shut in now, needed space and the largeness of the night, would know the moment when it came. She was vastly untroubled.

"What are your doubts?" she asked him a moment later. "You told Elliot you were excited but . . ."

"Can I speak my mind freely in a larger arena? I've gotten used to it, but who knows? I don't want to be Curley's man—any more so than O'Brien's." Or the Church's, he might have added, but didn't think of it.

"You don't have to worry. Not you."

"The United States Congress? It's not Jericho. It's not writing editorials in *The Spectator*. It's . . . huge. And Curley doesn't want me because of my charm. I guess I've made a name for myself lately. And he wants to use it. McGinty may be in Washington, but he's never been much more than a cog in Curley's machine."

He was frightened, she realized. As frightened as she had been. Once again, she set out to reassure him. "You're right," he replied. "I shouldn't borrow trouble. I did enough of it already to last a lifetime."

"Elliot's changing," she said as they approached the mill whose chimneys were etched in black against the sky. She wanted him happy, wanted

494

his nightmares gone. "Am I still an iconoclast?" she'd asked him, needing reassurance on her own journey. "You're an artist," he'd replied. Yes, she knew that was true; her work was her identity: there might be others—she was ready—but the work was deep in her. She wouldn't let it go.

"You're going to miss him. . . ."

She nodded, felt the loss of that kindred soul already. "Did you feel what I did? A new confidence about him?" No longer keeping the world at arm's length. Less in fragments, and with an acceptance of himself as the young man who, in that final chaos of the mill, had behaved valiantly.

Did she believe in God? he'd asked her. Gert had insisted that he'd been protected, his life saved by a power that would continue to watch over him. Not necessarily a God of Sundays, he'd said, but some kind of spirit, perhaps. Did Harriet think there was such a thing? She didn't know. Certainly in a world seemingly bent on self-destruction there had to be something they could turn to, some necessary spiritual resource.

"An unlikely combination." She smiled. "Elliot and your mother. Wouldn't you say?"

"Other people's mothers . . ."

". . . are always greener."

Patrick nodded, reflecting that Gert had given freely to Elliot what she couldn't to himself, Dennis or Rose without enormous strings.

Harriet wondered how Elliot's mother had felt when he had told her the truth about his life. How would she feel herself? She hesitated sharing these questions with Patrick, for even though she knew he'd undergone the same reassessment of Elliot that many in town had, he and Elliot were on entirely different wavelengths. Even toward the man who had saved his father's life—and no matter how he might try to understand—she knew Patrick had trouble accepting what he'd once termed "unnatural," a deadly sin. But how could it be? she wondered. For weren't there larger and more important bonds that united people—a common goodness, a sharing of love and the unexpected surprise of courage in strange places—that had to be far more telling than who one gave one's heart to, even one's own kind?

"What's he going to do in New York?" Patrick paused at the gates of the mill, now liberated like himself.

"He said find out who he is." Which was each of their tasks, she reflected. Hers, Elliot's and Patrick's, too. Each of them fighting that lonely battle of individuality.

"What's his father have to say about that?"

"It's still a stalemate between them. But he's going—that's the important thing at this point. He's earned the right to live his life," she added, and knew she was saying something to herself as well.

They were all setting out on destinations. They might spend their lives trying to escape the houses provided by their parents. Stifled by the conventional wallpaper, stymied by the doors, dashing through to free-

495

dom—only to find other doors. Forced in the end to make painful accommodations with the furniture and settle down, redoing the den, pretending it's not the same house, doing what we can, putting in a new bath, opening up the attic. Did the essential dwelling remain little changed—no matter how we decorate and fuss, no matter how far and fast we run?

She had no ready answer. She wondered if Patrick did.

Patrick was wondering if he'd be enough for her in the years ahead.

His thoughts running parallel to hers, they led him to fearful questions of his own, unconscious spasms of a dead Patrick, the Patrick who knew he was unworthy, the Patrick who didn't deserve the success that would be thrust upon him.

Arm in arm they continued, past the mill and up the hill in the vicinity of the Red Tavern, where they could see the western tip of the lake. And were silent again, gripped in an almost solemn communion, as Harriet found herself drifting in joyous imaginings of their child and Patrick wondered what she expected of him. But as he gazed on Jericho and the world of men in which he'd seized his place, he knew he would conquer. He might have to spend the rest of his life working at it; Harriet demanded a continuing reappraisal of all the rules he'd ever lived by, but they were myths and valueless lint compared to the grace she'd bestowed upon him, more than he ever dared claim or dream was possible.

On Mulberry Street where the party was winding down, Frankie fetched his trumpet and went outside. Standing under the street lamp he played a startling solo that was partly "Joy To The World," partly improvisation. The cadenzas could be heard all over town, their echo rising to Harriet and Patrick.

And at the Mansion, on a walk with the dogs, Elliot heard them, too, knew it was Frankie and smiled, memories stirred by the boy who would never know the passion he provoked. "C'mon," he called and turned away, then back again, his eyes seeking the horizon.

A while later, Father Gahaghan's deacon gripped the rope and the bells tolled, echoing over the valley, and Patrick and Harriet knew they'd have to start back. Midnight Mass with the Flynns was the agenda, but they couldn't seem to move, wanted to stay here together, wanted nothing to intrude.

Even if she had totally accepted and succumbed to her love for him, she was Harriet Hoskins and had to be.

Even if he had allayed so many of her fears, did he know—could he accept—that she wanted more? She could taste her saliva, was more than ready for the fray. That insatiable hunger was still there. Never more so than tonight when she found herself in a miasma of change, stepped over an invisible line.

Patrick saw something overtake her, saw her flounder and held her to him gently and watched it pass.

She smiled and felt her power rush in her again, an omnipotence carrying her over Jericho, the earlier fragility replaced with a commanding surety. And if her valiant cry that she was in charge of her destiny was more than ever in question, she knew it was inexorably linked with the man who held her now. 'Go it alone if she had to' must have been the ranting of an idiot, for Patrick had taught her she didn't have to and she couldn't imagine her life without him.

Her eyes drifted to the lake, to the icehouse hidden by the water's edge. That had been the night. A child conceived in tumult. An irreverent irony possessed her, causing a ripple of pleasure: when she hadn't needed her pessary (Elliot) she had it; when she'd needed it (Patrick) she hadn't.

"I'm on a rising tide," she whispered as a shiver coursed through her that had nothing to do with the cold. "Patrick . . ." she began, eyes merry with secrets, a magic between them now as she turned to him and he saw a light on her face and would always insist forevermore that in that moment he knew what she was about to tell him.

"Patrick . . ." she murmured. She could hear those triumphant notes of Frankie. "Guess what?" she added and filled her lungs with an ecstatic gulp.

ACKNOWLEDGMENTS AND GRATEFUL TRIBUTES

Frances Spanier kept me honest, gave me courage, ideas and the stimulant of her creative energy. Ellis St. Joseph guided me with humor and patience as I produced my first fearful scratches. Sara Kinder has always been there, a rock of unceasing support. Her husband, Mel, was astute. I cherish Paul Mantee's enthusiasm and love. Anne Mantee was gracious with her comments. Bernadette O'Brien read my book early on and gave me hope (and a loan when I needed it).

Marc Jaffe endured my panic and stuck by me. Ursula Brennan was indomitable and pointed me well. Johanna Demetrakas gave me the benefit of her sharp eye. Toni Bernay listened and counseled. Cathy Camhy's excitement buoyed me. Alan Rinzler has been an ally; Arnold Stiefel, fervent; Alan Howard, loving; Ruth and Frank Thompson, willing reminiscers.

To all of you, I am in debt.

ABOUT THE AUTHOR

Anthony Costello was born in Andover, Massachusetts, educated at Phillips Academy, The Academy of Fine Arts in Florence, Italy, and the Rhode Island School of Design.

An actor as well as a painter, Mr. Costello has appeared On and Off Broadway, in regional theatre, on film and television.

Mr. Costello lives in Los Angeles and the California desert. *Jericho* is his first novel.